The
WERE
CHRONICLES

To Lisa —
Best wishes
Alma Alexander

ALMA ALEXANDER

KOS BOOKS

The
WERE
CHRONICLES

Random

Wolf

Shifter

ALMA ALEXANDER

Published by Book View Café Publishing Cooperative/Kos Books
www.BookViewCafe.com

ISBN: 978-1-61138-893-0

Cover design: Alma Alexander and Maya Kaathryn Bohnhoff

DEDICATIONS

RANDOM

This is the first book of mine that my father didn't live to see published. In his memory, then, Thank you, Dad, for a lifetime of love and support. I hope this one does you proud.

WOLF

To all of you out there who know what it means to be lost, and to be found.

SHIFTER

There is no one person out there to whom a book like this can be dedicated. But we all carry a bit of my "shifter" in us – and it is to that fragment, broken, and damaged, and heroic, and glorious, forever young in some ways and wise beyond our years in others, that this novel is offered. In acknowledgment, and with thanks.

TABLE OF CONTENTS

FOREWORD

Alma and I go back a long way. We have both had our long journeys to where we are now, me splitting my time between Taiwan and Portugal and Alma living in the Pacific Northwest in the USA. But it all started decades ago, at the University of Cape Town Microbiology Department, where she became my postgraduate student. When I met her, she was already writing – in fact, her first published fantasy novel ("Changer of Days", which became the "Hidden Queen"/"Changer of Days" duology) was partly created at her desk in the corner of my research lab. She was a good research scientist, but writing was her passion, and that won out in the end. I am glad it did, as her books have given me great pleasure over the years. (Her research was great, but it took 30 years and a whole genome sequence to find out why we were having such problems with the genetics of *Streptomyces cattleya* – it has two chromosomes, unlike almost all other bacteria.) The Were Chronicles trilogy reflects that background to some extent. All that laboratory work means that when you read these books, you need to know that it was written with a hand that has used the molecular biology outlined in the books.

Why should her old Professor write this foreword to the trilogy? One simple answer is that there are sixty years of SF sitting in my library. Notwithstanding my overcrowded bookshelves, it's because I want to emphasize that this trilogy is a rare SF treat. There two very rare types of SF. One is murder mystery SF (works like Asimov's "The Caves of Steel" and Randall Garrett's Lord Darcy series). The other is Hard Fantasy, which is the category this trilogy falls into.

John Clute and John Grant, in *The Encyclopedia of Fantasy,* defined Hard Fantasy as a genre where "magic is regarded as an almost scientific force of nature and subject to the same sort of rules and principles". This definition, and some of the examples that are suggested as Hard Fantasy, can be problematic (such as Tolkien's Middle Earth books). But there is an Arthur C. Clarke quote that is highly relevant to both Alma's trilogy, and to Hard Fantasy as a whole: "Magic is just science that we don't understand yet". So I would change Hard Fantasy's definition to a genre where "magic is a scientific force of nature and subject to the same sort of rules and principles as all other science".

Alma's were-creatures are a classic fantasy trope but we begin, in this trilogy, to understand how and why they exist, as well as how this works in terms of basic genetics, the latter forming an integral part of the story. They do not just jump out of the urban jungle fully formed, which is the classic approach to vampires, were-creatures, fairies, gods, etc., in modern urban fantasy. These books are a well-written, and a rare treat; there are few of this genre around.

Random, Wolf and *Shifter* are all "coming of age" stories. The first book tells us little about why were-creatures exist, but it explores more deeply the themes of displacement and bullying. Read this first book and sympathize with all the displaced children in the world who are "different". In this it has some similarity to <u>*Buffy the Vampire* Slayer</u>, but it is darker, more realistic. Alma was born in a country that no longer exists, has lived in multiple countries on three continents before settling in Washington State with her husband. Most importantly, she went to various English medium schools in Africa before reaching my lab at the University of Cape Town. She may speak and write perfect primary-language English of the native speaker, but it remains her "second" language, which she had to learn and use rather like the protagonists in *Random*. What you get are insights that I think come from the heart.

Random is not overly Hard Fantasy but the premise is there if you look for it and Alma sets the stage for it in the second book of the trilogy. *Wolf* moves us from the more static world of Jazz and Celia to the more dynamic world of Mal. If you look closely, you can see Alma's time in the laboratory reflected in this book and, as all researchers have always known, the back-and-forth and the frustrations of sheer repetition, the if-at-first-you-don't-succeed dogged pursuit of elusive solutions, and the shock and disappointment of failures. We gain insights into why were-creatures exist as the story moves on. Finally, we take a small step back again and in *Shifter* look at the bigger picture in the story of Chalky, a true shape shifter and a hybrid. I might have reservations about the physiology of shape-shifting in general (how do you input the information from the target to be copied to the cells to be changed! But then, that's where the magic comes in...), but I think the genetics is as good as you can get.

If you have never read Alma's work before, these books are a good place to start, but do try the rest, they will always surprise you. Alma tends to write stories that play with the boundaries. *The Secrets of Jin-shei, Embers of Heaven,* and *Empress* push the edges of Historical Fiction/Fantasy, just like this trilogy does for Hard Fantasy. I particularly love *Empress* because I have a soft spot for Justinian. He was a "good" Emperor who had a major outbreak of plague during his reign and was never able to reach his full potential, partly because of the plague. *Empress* is a great story about how people react to real power, and it is – in the manner that Alma has made a trademark – based on fact. In these present "plague years", there should be a particular level of sympathy for these two men and their particular trials; I look forward to seeing Alma tackle other stories that hold up mirrors to our realities, our past and present, our myths and our science.

Professor Ralph Kirby MA PhD LLB LLM
Professor Emeritus, National Yang Ming University, Taiwan.

THE
W E R E
CHRONICLES

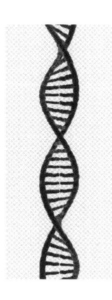

BOOK 1: RANDOM

Prologue:
The Boy in the
Basement

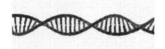

Vivian Ingram, the family caretaker and my babysitter, arrived just before the ascent of the full Moon, as usual – locking everybody except me (including poor Mal yet again) into their Turning Rooms in the basement and making sure everything was secure.

Charlie was with her.

The first time she'd brought him, he had been thirteen and I was only eleven. You'd think that a newly-teenaged boy would have disdained the company of a kid like me, but we somehow bucked the odds – we missed out on the standard boy-from-girl-from-boy recoil in response to unnamed cooties, and we had become buddies instead. Of course, he was going on sixteen now, and he'd Turned – at his proper new-Moon trigger, only a few months before – into a vampire bat, like the rest of his family.

My older brother Mal had glowered at Charlie as he was escorted into his Turning room in the hope that this time would finally prove the charm. Mal, almost eighteen, still un-Turned, visibly chafing at having to be marched off into yet another attempt at becoming an official adult in the Were community, being watched by a boy two years his junior who had already passed him on that road.

Charlie knew better than to offer any commentary while Mal was still in hearing range – but once my brother and his temper were safely locked away behind secured doors, he gave me one of his crooked smiles, half sympathy, half mischief.

"Still no joy for him?"

"Nope. And he's kind of running out of time. They're not sure what they're going to do if he passes his eighteenth birthday and is still... like this. Is it even possible for someone to un-Were?"

"What is he trying for this time?"

"Still a weasel. It's been quite a come-down, really. He started out all gung-ho, with the wolverine, but after my folks had to keep hiring the wolverine for months it got...a little expensive. So he's had to bring his sights down some. He wanted something with teeth, though, so – well – weasel."

"And if that doesn't work, what, a rat?" Charlie asked.

"Don't be mean," I said sanctimoniously.

"Shall we stay and see how he and the weasel are getting on? The Moon ought to be up by now – or is about to be, anyway. It should be fun."

I smacked him on the shoulder. "You know how he hated seeing us peering in the last time."

"We'll be careful," Charlie said. "Come on."

Vivian was busy – one of her other sons fortuitously picked a perfect moment to call her on the phone, and while she was talking to him she had momentarily lost track of Charlie and me. We hadn't really bothered to check on the Moon's status in the sky – it was close enough for our purposes. We stood jostling outside the door of Mal's room, and I stood on tiptoe to peer inside through the glass window set into the door.

"What's he doing?" Charlie asked, crowding in beside me, careful to keep to the edges so he could duck away if Mal showed signs of looking up and seeing us there.

"Nothing," I said. "As usual."

Mal was in fact sitting in the middle of the room, cross-legged and wrapped in his Turning cloak, staring with smoldering eyes at the weasel which stood with its back to the wall staring back at him. Other than the staring contest, which was a sadly familiar outcome of locking Mal into the Turning Room at the advent of full Moon, there was nothing of any interest going on inside – and it looked like Vivian would soon have to let him out, as she had done every Turn so far since he was fifteen, and he'd still be... Mal. The full Moon was up in the sky; if he hadn't Turned by now, he probably wasn't going to.

I had already lost interest, but for Charlie, this was a train wreck he couldn't stay away from. He was still staring into the room by the time I had turned away – from Mal and his continued failure, from the annoyed weasel in the corner – and I was actually looking at Charlie's fascinated face when something began to impinge itself on my consciousness.

There was nothing going on inside the room. But out here in the corridor, outside... I was starting to feel distinctly strange. Ill, even. There was something deep in the back of my throat, an odd sort of nausea, but it didn't feel as though I wanted to throw up – it was just... there... as though I had tried to swallow something, either too big or too disgusting, that I shouldn't have even considered putting into my mouth, and now it was stuck halfway down my gullet and was making breathing difficult. My skin felt prickly and itchy and hot, like I was about to spike a fever or suddenly sprout an exotic rash; my eyes were watering and there was a tickle behind my nose not unlike those times when you desperately want to sneeze but the sneeze just won't come. My bones felt... oddly liquid. It isn't an easy sensation to describe but the closest I can come is feeling like I was about to *change phase*, like my solid flesh wanted to melt into a puddle, or evaporate into a gas; in a fanciful moment I imagined my hair going up in literal smoke, dissolving strand by strand into a strange fog which was swirling around me. It felt... well, the synonyms didn't get any more helpful in clarifying matters, It felt odd. Weird. Strange. I had never felt anything like it before.

I realized that I had started almost panting, trying to get air into my lungs through my mouth, gasping mouthfuls of it – that my hands had closed convulsively into fists against the door – that my knees were feeling decidedly weak, and that if I did not sit down, right now, I would collapse into an undignified heap or, perhaps, dissolve into that puddle that I had already considered becoming. And just as I realized it, so did Charlie. He turned sharply towards me, dismissing Mal's situation and sizing up my own instantly and completely.

"Oh, no," he said unsteadily. "Oh, no, no, no, no, no! Not now. Hang on. Don't move." He backed away from the door, from me, until he was at the foot of the basement stairs and then, without letting his eyes leave my face for one moment, angled his head just enough to yell urgently up the stairs for his mother.

I pushed myself off the door, turning around, blinking rapidly at him, trying to figure it out.

"What's going on...?"

"Did *nobody* tell you about this?" Charlie said desperately. "There's a *full Moon in the sky* – you're Were-kind – work it out!"

He glanced up the still-empty stairs, but there was no sign of Vivian. "There's an empty room back there, isn't there? Can you get there? Quickly? Mom! *MOM!* Now!"

It was starting to percolate through to my fogged brain. "Are you telling me... I'm *Turning*?"

"Dammit – get into that room – I can't handle – where *is* my mother? Go on, back away – into the room – at least I can close the door and then we can deal..."

There was, in fact, a room behind me, a room that had been set aside specifically for this moment, for me – but it had not been prepared. Not yet. And it seemed as though it was too late for any of that. *Way* too late for that. That liquid sensation that I felt building up in my bones suddenly turned into an exquisitely sharp agony, as though I were pulling my own body apart and trying to reknit it back into a shape in which it didn't belong – which, come to think of it, was precisely what was going on. I tried to obey Charlie's instructions, I *did* – I took a precarious step in that direction, and my feet failed me completely. I crumpled bonelessly on the basement floor, feeling the cold stab into my legs and my butt from the bare concrete below the thin layer of linoleum that had been laid down over it, and then I couldn't seem to move at all anymore.

"But it's... I'm... my fifteenth is still..." I was finding it very difficult to speak, to form words with my lips, with my tongue.

I was Turning. I was *Turning*, and I was still two months shy of my fifteenth birthday, the traditional age at which the Were first Turned. And nothing had been prepared.

I whimpered and closed my eyes at last, allowing myself to fold into a little heap of misery on the floor.

I was a Random. The primary form of Adult Randoms was the animal they had become at their first Turning, if no outside stimulus had been presented to change that, such as another warm-blooded creature waiting to steal their form.

But I hadn't Turned yet so I *had* no primary form. Nothing to fall back on. In fact... whatever I Turned into right now, at this instant, that would remain my primary form forever. I had thought about this, had planned to present myself with an animal of my choice come my fifteenth birthday, to *control* this Random thing as best I could – but there was nothing, nothing – unless someone simply assumed that Mal was not going to Turn again and barged into his room and stole his weasel – but I didn't *want* to be a weasel – and anyway what if he needed the thing – and did it count that I had actually been watching the weasel through the glass insert in the door just before this started happening? But was the weasel the *last* thing that I had seen? What if some mouse had scuttled right in front of me as I had turned away from the door – we were punctilious about pest control in this house, for obvious reasons, but it wouldn't be beyond the realm of possibility that the occasional mouse did find its way down here, it was a basement after all – would I really be stuck with being a *mouse* – but no, I hadn't seen, hadn't recognized, hadn't registered – did that count...?

And then the pain became so incandescent that I actually screamed – and then it was all gone, as though it had never been. Wiped away. Wiped clean.

I sat there, my hands over my eyes, panting....

...wait...

...my hands over my eyes...

...so I hadn't Turned after all?

What was going on here?

I took my hands away from my face and then several things suddenly began to clamor for my attention.

One, the hands that my eyes lighted on as they came away from my face *were not my hands*. I should know, okay? I'd been living with my hands for nearly fifteen years and had been observing them on a daily basis, and these weren't it. They were Somebody Else's Hands.

Two, Charlie's face wore an expression that was a cross between open-mouthed astonishment and a rapt, wide-eyed fascination.

Three, more or less the same expression graced the face of his mother – Vivian had come racing down the basement stairs in response to the urgency in her son's voice, but she had obviously been too late to prevent...

Something had happened. Something. Something was different.

"What..." I began, and then shut my mouth abruptly. The voice was not my own, either. It was a voice that had a high note, but which then broke into a lower register halfway through that single word I had tried to utter, like a teenaged boy whose voice was in the middle of breaking.

"Oh, my giddy aunt," Charlie said, his own voice very faint. "*Jazz*?"

I examined my hand. It was more... robust than I was used to. Slightly bigger. The fingers were longer, flatter, the nails almost spatulate. The hand emerged from a wrist that seemed to be far too angular to belong to me, as if the very bones were knit differently.

I lifted that hand, and touched my face.

I did not recognize anything that my new fingertips trailed across. The nose was the wrong shape. My lower lip was fuller than I remembered it. My *teeth* felt different under my tongue. My hair...

It was shorter. Much shorter. And not curly any more, like mine. Short, and it felt straight.

More like Charlie's hair than my own.

"There will," Vivian said, her voice shaking ever so slightly, "be hell to pay over this. Charlie, what were you thinking?"

"It wasn't *my* fault!" Charlie said sharply. "How was I to know that..."

I tried not to think the wrongness of my voice – and chose to whisper, instead, thinking that whispering at least would sound a little more like I thought I should sound. "What's going on?"

Vivian gave a helpless shrug. "Honey... you Turned. But it isn't..."

I put out a hand, tried to struggle to my feet – which hurt, as if they had been stuffed into shoes two sizes too small. My clothes felt strange on me, tight in all the wrong places, constraining... and then, finally, something clicked.

The funny voice. The bigger-boned hands. My hair. The sense of a different breadth of shoulder and of hip. The... oddness about my body.

I looked down at my crotch, and gave an inelegant yelp.

I had Turned, all right. But not into an animal. The weasel in Mal's room had not been the last thing I saw at the crucial moment. Neither had that mythical mouse I had been briefly worried about.

The last warm-blooded creature I had set eyes on as I started to Turn... had been...

Had been Charlie.

I had Turned... into a boy.

Halfway up into a crouch, the thing was finally borne in on me in its full enormity, and I sat back down again, heavily. Something of the panic and disbelief that swept through me must have shown in my face, in my eyes, because Vivian suddenly took a deep breath and began to assert at least a minimum of control over the situation at last.

"Right," she said. "I would be willing to guess at a couple of things. You've changed into a form which still more or less fits your clothing, so you didn't embarrass yourself by having it all shred off of you – but you must be less than comfortable right now. Can we borrow something from Mal's closet for you to wear for now?"

"I guess," I said, unwillingly, using as few words as I could manage, hating the sound of my unfamiliar voice. My head was aching, and I felt dizzy and disoriented. How on earth did they manage, the others, if they felt like this when they Turned? How did any Were-kind survive their first transformation, out in the wild, if they felt weak as newborn kittens in the instant after they Turned? Wasn't there supposed to be a built-in way of adapting to the change instantly and becoming what you had changed into...?

Or perhaps they did, and it was just my own weird switch into a differently gendered body that confused me so?

"Get your shoes off," Vivian said. "Charlie, help her up."

"*Her*?" said Charlie incredulously, and I felt myself blush like... like a *girl*.

"I'm still *me*," I said crossly, but my voice broke on the last word, slid into a squeak, and I felt the blush deepen. Trying to cover it up, I scowled, and bent to work on the laces of the really uncomfortably tight sneakers I wore on my feet. But I had been counting on hair to fall forward and hide my shame. My Jazz hair. A girl's hair. That wasn't there; no concealing curtain came to my aid. And the knots on the laces were defeating my unfamiliar fingers.

After a moment I felt Charlie thump to his knees beside me.

"Here," he said, "let me do it. They're not your hands yet."

It was a *very* odd remark, and yet it made so much perfect sense that I simply did as he said, without hesitation. We didn't look directly at each other, we couldn't quite manage that, it was just too difficult to reconcile the fact that less than two minutes before this I was Jazz Marsh and I was a girl and none of this impossible stuff had ever happened with the inescapable fact that it *did* happen and that I was no longer Jazz Marsh and no longer a girl... or was I...?

My feet were foreign to me, too, when they were yanked out of the suddenly too-small sneakers which they had been stuffed into. One of the socks came off as the shoe was being pulled off, and I stared at my bare foot. I had never liked my toes, I thought they were small and stubby and ridiculous, but my new toes were preposterous by comparison – they were long and they had distinct joints and by the looks of them I could make them prehensile without too much trouble if I cared to try.

"I've got weird feet," I said, wiggling those toes.

Charlie cleared his throat in an embarrassed kind of way.

"Come on," Vivian said. "Let's go upstairs and think about this for a second."

"What are we going to do, Mom?" Charlie asked, lifting his head to look up at her, my sneakers hanging by their laces from his left hand as he came to his feet.

Vivian gave him a long helpless look. "Honestly? I have no idea yet. It isn't as though I have any precedent to go on. This is the first time, that I know of, in living memory at least, that somebody Turned into... into..." She shook her head. "Let's go upstairs. I need some time to think. I need coffee. To be perfectly honest, I need a shot of brandy, but let's not complicate matters. Come on, Jazz."

"Don't call her that," Charlie said quickly, impulsively.

My head jerked up and for the first time since I had changed he did manage to look me in the eye.

"Sorry," he said, apologetic but unrepentant. "You just aren't. Any more. Not like this. Jazz is a girl, and you are not. You're gonna have to pick a different name."

"She just needs to come out of the basement, right now," Vivian said. "Come on. Are you steady? Do you need a hand?"

I had come to my feet but I was still woozy, as if I'd just come off a rollercoaster. But I shook off everyone's offered hands and after a moment took a deep breath and then a step forward.

Yup, I still remembered how to walk.

"I'll be fine," I snapped.

Vivian climbed the fifteen steps ahead of me, turning around to glance back every few seconds to make sure I was still upright; I followed, clinging a little tighter to the banister than I usually did but otherwise steadier than I thought I would be; Charlie brought up the rear, still dangling my sneakers from his hand and looking shellshocked. When we got up to the living room Vivian made me sit down in one of the armchairs and sent Charlie into the kitchen to make me a sandwich.

"I'm not hungry," I protested.

"Oh yes you are. Or you will be as soon as you stop to think about it, or smell food. Trust me, I've been Turning for a good long time and you're always ravenous just after you do it – it takes a lot of energy. And at the very least we have people food in the kitchen which at least is a little bit of a blessing – I can feed you, properly, in the wake of this."

"Do I look that bad?" I said, when she was done, because all this time she was kind of looking everywhere around me but not *at* me, and she blinked, and finally focused on me, managing a crooked smile.

"Honey," she said, "I'd have more trouble *feeding* you if you had suddenly Turned into a saber-toothed tiger, but I could *look* at you far more easily than I can look at you right now. You do realize that you've just done something... that I don't think many people – if any – have ever done before? And all the people I could ask what to do about this are currently cats or dogs or bears or ravens, and until the full Moon wanes and everyone gets back to being human again I have absolutely no idea about what to do with this thing that you've just dumped into my lap...?"

"Here," Charlie said, coming back from the kitchen with an untidy sandwich dripping bits of chicken and cheese and dribbles of mayo on a paper plate with birthday balloons on it, "eat something."

Vivian was right about that, at least, because the moment I set eyes on that sandwich I realized that I was in fact ready to devour half a buffalo if one had been set before me. I took the sandwich, mumbling a belated thanks to Charlie through a mouthful of chicken-and-mayo mush, and concentrated on trying to remember if I still knew how to chew my food what with the new jaw that I had to master. But after I was done with the sandwich, and feeling less hungry if not sated – I could have polished off at least three of these sandwiches if Charlie was willing to keep them coming – I finally pushed myself out of the armchair and stood up. I was surprised that I was almost taller than Vivian in this form.

"Where are you going?" she asked.

"The bathroom," I said.

"Mom," Charlie said urgently, but Vivian was way ahead of him.

"You want to know what you look like," she said. "Fair enough. Let's go find a mirror."

I stared at myself for a few long minutes in the vanity mirror in the bathroom, clutching the edges of the sink with both hands. I had almost come to terms with the fact that I had turned into a boy – but for a while there I was afraid that I hadn't turned into just *any* boy, that I had in fact turned into a copy of Charlie and that this was why he was so disconcerted

13

by the whole thing. But no, I had turned into something different. Something else. Some*one* else. Into the boy I might have been if I had been born male.

I was taller than I had been as Jazz. My eyes were closer-set, and darker. My hair was an odd rich shade of chocolate brown, and yes, I did have that much fuller lower lip than I had had as a girl. I also had an Adam's apple, which I'd never had before. I had good teeth, though. I bared them at myself in the mirror, trying a smile. It didn't quite come off.

"Really," Charlie said, watching me explore my new self, doing it with me, almost, "you have to pick a name. A different name. A guy's name. I can't call you Jazz, not when you look like this, it's completely ridiculous."

I had been thinking about this. I had been named Jessica. Back when I was much younger, they had tried calling me Jessie, and then Jess, and then I mangled that into Jazz, and then I liked the sound of that, and it stuck. But now I could go back to that old original name and change almost nothing at all.

"Jesse," I said. "Just call me Jesse."

That actually brought a smile to Vivian's face, the first I'd seen since all of this had exploded around us. "Well, *Jesse*," she said, lightly emphasizing the new name, "if you're, if you will forgive the expression, starting to feel a little more *human* again, there will be a great many questions once everybody gets wind of this, and some of them you can only answer right now – so how do you feel about getting a few things down on paper so we'll have something to show them later?"

"Sure," I said. "Although I don't know what I can tell you. I really have no clue what hit me."

"I've a notebook in my purse," Vivian said. "Charlie – take her... take... take Jesse back into the living room – you want another sandwich?"

"I could eat," I said.

"I'll go make it," Charlie said. "You're almost out of mayo. But I'll improvise."

I made my slow careful way back to the living room and the armchair where Vivian had first parked me – I was still moving very gingerly, I felt as I had only minimal control over this new and strange body, and if I flung out an arm or a leg too fast it would fly out at the wrong angle and start breaking things. And I was starting to be seriously cheesed off by my voice. If I'd had to Turn into a male of my species, why couldn't I have kind of skipped this particular embarrassing stage of development? How long did I have to deal with talking like I'd been at helium balloons?

I tried to answer Vivian's questions as best I could, through another large sandwich, but all I could provide were the basic visceral details of what things had *felt* like at the time of the change, of what they felt like now. I could offer no real insight as to why any of it had happened, or why it had happened at least two months prematurely, before anybody had even thought to secure me for a possible Turn.

My clothes were increasingly uncomfortable, and it was some ten minutes into this gentle interrogation that Vivian remembered her original idea to go raid Mal's wardrobe in order to get me some more appropriate apparel.

It was right about the time that Mal's name got mentioned again that we all became aware of a steady thumping sound from down in the basement, and Vivian suddenly threw down her notepad and her pen and pressed both palms to her cheeks.

"Mal!" she said. "I'd forgotten all about him – I was going to go check on him – but then all of this – "

"He had still not Turned by the time we were looking into the room," I said.

"And Jazz... *Jesse*... did," Charlie said. "Which means that the Moon is up, and if he's hammering on the door, he's probably still Mal, and he's probably had time to work up a good head of steam..."

"You'd better let him out," I said, "but very carefully."

I was just starting to think the rest of this through. My *still* apparently un-Turned seventeen-year-old brother was about to be released back into a world which he was probably ready to cordially loathe and despise right about now, as usual – at least that had been the pattern for months now, for *years*. His mood was usually pretty grim when Vivian released him from that room, for very good reasons. And that was before – before he emerged to find a situation like this flung at him.

I counted it up, the insults that would be poured like salt into the wounds of the not-Turned-again injury – not only would he have had, in any event, to deal with the presence of fifteen-year-old Charlie whose very existence and properly Turned status were provocation enough, but now, suddenly, he would have to cope with the added pile-on – that his younger sister had Turned ahead of him -- and had Turned into... something... impossible...

"How on earth are we going to tell him?" I whispered, appalled that I was actually afraid of my brother but aware that I very definitely was. All of a sudden, I would not have been caught dead pilfering his wardrobe for more comfortable clothes, and was profoundly grateful that such a thing had not been accomplished already. "He's going to kill me..."

"Of course he isn't," Vivian said, but she didn't sound entirely convinced, or perhaps I was just unable to hear conviction in anybody's voice right now on this particular subject. "I'd better go let him out. Wait here."

Charlie skittered after his mother and lurked at the top of the stairs, peering down the stairwell. The pounding stopped, and then Charlie, who had been eavesdropping earnestly with his head tilted to one side, loped back to the side of my armchair.

"Uh oh," he said. "Mal's not happy."

"We knew..."

"He asked what was for dinner. Mom just blurted she completely forgot about dinner. And then she started to explain..."

That was all he had time for.

I could hear Mal's heavy tread on the stairs, Vivian's lighter running footsteps following; I shrank back into the armchair, wishing I had Turned into something small, really small. That mouse I had been so afraid of becoming was starting to sound really appealing right now – I could simply burrow into the back of the cushions and Mal need never see me, never know I was there...

I was expecting the fury that was on his face as he erupted into the living room. I had braced myself for that, could perhaps have handled that. What undid me was an added layer which I perhaps should have expected but which still managed to catch me by surprise. Betrayal. A bleak, horrible, bitter betrayal. There was something in the twist of his mouth that ripped into me like a dagger.

We had talked about Turning, he and I. His tardiness to step up to the grown-up table. What he would do, when the time came. What *I* would do, when the time came. In none of those conversations had we remotely touched on this, on what was happening right now, on what he was served up and had to deal with. It was irrational, I know, but I could not help a stab of pure and undiluted guilt. If I could have undone the events of the previous hour – well – I would have given worlds to have been able to do that right now.

"What?" he said, coming to a halt a few paces away from me, standing with his feet planted solidly on the carpet, his hands fisted at his sides. "*What? WHAT!?*"

Charlie shrank into a crouch behind the far armrest of the chair, trying to efface himself.

I cleared my throat, but Mal swiftly raised a hand to forestall anything I might have been about to say.

"Let me get this straight," he said. The words were strained through clenched teeth, as if he was unable to unlock his jaw, as though he had been the one to have woken up to a new face, not me. "You... *you...* are Jazz."

My voice cut down into silence, I nodded.

"You Turned."

I nodded again.

"Into this. Into a... into.... my sister is now my *brother?* What? This can't happen. This has never happened.... It's impossible! What are you... who are you really? And Jazz – "

I finally spoke. I had to. And my stupid, stupid voice broke again, right at the top it all.

"I *am* Jazz!" I said.

"I don't believe it," he said, flatly.

My hands clenched on the armrests. "How am I supposed to prove it? You don't ask Dad to prove to you that he was a cat for three days."

"I know he is a cat. I've seen him Turn. I've seen my entire family..." He stopped, swallowed hard. "You... you aren't even of age yet. It's all – it's all so – "

His eyes suddenly slid away from me, as though he couldn't bear to look at me any longer.

16

"Have you called anybody?" he flung tersely over his shoulder at Vivian.

"Who?" she said, throwing her hands into the air in a gesture of pure helplessness. "Absolutely nobody of any importance in the Were Administration or hierarchy is actually available right now – the only Weres who are walking around in human form right now are the New-Moon kindred like me and Charlie, and you well know we have no authority to do anything. And we have no special wisdom to bring to bear, either. I have never heard of this happening before. Ever. To any Were-kind. Not Random; certainly not the Clans. It's a whole new..."

"But there she is. The only Were walking human," Mal said. "There's *her.*"

"Yes. She is the problem, though, not a source of counsel."

"There's me," Mal said, and his voice was suddenly very quiet.

"You least of..." Vivian began, and then clenched her teeth on her words even as I roused from my chair, trying to prevent her from going on. But Mal had already heard her. Too late.

He turned from me to rake Vivian with hot eyes. "Me least of all? I know. I'm the problem, too. Well, then. How about the human authorities?"

Vivian actually did a double take. "The human authorities? The government agencies? What on earth would they know about any of this?"

"Know *about* it – perhaps nothing. I'm betting they'd like to *know* about it."

"Mal, no," Vivian said, and at the same moment Charlie found his voice, surging from behind the armchair.

"They'd come get her," Charlie said. "They would. That's what they would absolutely have to do, by the book. We're all supposed to be locked away when we're changed – and it's easy enough to lock away someone like your parents, or like me – cats and bats – it's obvious, right? There they are, the animals, there's the cage. But her – Jazz – Jesse – they couldn't know, unless they *knew*. There's nothing on her right now that marks her as Were. She could walk the street and nobody would turn a hair. They'd come get her, and *we would never see her again.*"

"It would solve the problem wouldn't it?" Mal said. "Quite neatly."

I felt as if the breath had been driven from my body, suddenly. As though he had kicked me right there, underneath the ribs, where the diaphragm was, and every last molecule of oxygen had been driven from my blood. I literally felt my head spin with sudden vertigo. Mal could be snide, and occasionally his practical jokes or commentary on things I did or said could be downright malicious – but this, this was not him. This angry, wounded animal, turning on me for no other reason than that something that I had done – something way beyond my control, which he *knew*, dammit – had ripped a hole in his soul.

But if I had been rendered speechless, others had not – and everyone had heard the same wild edge to Mal's words.

"Solve... the *problem...?*" Vivian sputtered, finding an edge of outrage, standing back and crossing her arms defiantly. She was a head shorter than Mal, but in that moment she looked as though she was looking down at him from a great height. "Oh, *fine*. Then you go to the Were Council, in a couple of days when they're ready to listen to you, and you tell them how you took one of our own and handed her out of our jurisdiction, to the people who are determined to own and control us all. *You* do that. *You* tell your parents that this is what happened, when they come out of the Turn in two days' time. You tell them that *you* took your little sister and handed her over to the government. *You* tell them. They've already lost one daughter to the outsiders, to the others, to the humans."

And just like that, I suddenly understood a great deal more about this whole thing than I had done until now.

Vivian had invoked Celia.

The oldest of us. The one who had died. The one with all the secrets; the secrets at the heart of this family.

Celia was at once an open wound, and an old scar; either way, it hurt my parents to pick at it, and they had long abandoned me to it, they had turned away from my need to know, from any questions that I might have had about my own family's past.

Celia's diary. This had all started when I found Celia's diary, and started to learn the truth about... about everything.

There was a good chance that this was what had stressed me into Turning prematurely.

Mal and I had never really talked about this. I had tried to, once or twice, but he had slid away from the subject, would never go there with me. Not even when I asked directly and specifically, at least once, about what he remembered about Celia. Perhaps *especially* not then.

Well. We'd all have to talk about it now.

I began to get up, out of the chair, and Mal actually took a step back, recoiled from me, and then turned away, gathering his Turning Cloak around him and stalking away from the living room into the corridor which led to his own room.

"Where are you going?" Vivian called after him.

"To get dressed," he said, throwing the words over his shoulder like shards of broken glass. "And then out. To find something to eat. To pick a fight in an alley. I don't know." He paused, very briefly, just long enough to turn his head to look back at us, his face twisted in what was almost a snarl. "Don't worry. I won't go snitching. Not until my parents know. But I don't... Jazz, whoever you are, right now, I can't *look* at you. I don't want to be under the same roof as... I don't..." He set his teeth, and a small pulse beat in his cheek as he clenched his jaws together. "You'd better call the animal guy," he said to Vivian, in a low, blackly bitter voice. "Tell him he can come pick up his weasel. Any time he wants."

And then he was gone, vanished down the corridor, and in a moment the door of his room slammed shut behind him.

Vivian buried her face into her hands.

"Oh, God. This is a mess," she said into her curled fingers.

Over at the armchair, Charlie's hand crept forward and gave mine a quick, reassuring squeeze, and then it withdrew again, helpless.

In the silence, I knew that there really was only one thing to do. I had to try and live through the next two days, and try and figure out how to adjust to this new identity that I had been presented with. I had to figure out what – and how much – needed to be explained to the Were-kind in positions of authority, who would have to be told about this when the full Moon began to wane and they all came back to their human forms. One way or another, when this full Moon was done, we would all be living in a world that was different to the one that had existed before the Moon was full.

All because I lived, and was changed. And because Celia had tried to change, and had failed. And had died.

Part 1:
The Girl at the Party

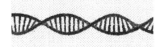

Thereは...

There had been a time when I had lived in a certain kind of ignorance and innocence. I knew the history and the lore of the Were-kind in far more detail than I ever knew the history and the lore of my own family.

Oh yes, I knew the broad strokes, I was still living their consequences, but that was kind of limited to the obvious. I knew that my family originated from Elsewhere and not This Place – and that inevitably we had brought over more baggage than it was considered appropriate to load a child with (which I was still very much considered to be).

I knew that there had been a changing of the guard – the family had started out with two children (Celia and Mal) who had existed when my parents immigrated here, and then there had been three children (Celia, Mal and me) for a little while, and then there had been two again, Mal and me, with a Celia-shaped hole in the middle of the family after she had died. But the details of all of that – well, if the matter was discussed with me at all, it was more or less a constant refrain of my being told that I would find out more when I was "older".

But then I found the hidden diary that Celia had left behind, and I had begun to see all sorts of things far more clearly than I had, perhaps, ever wanted. And then came the blog. And then...well...

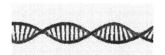

I don't exactly remember where all of it began. Perhaps it was simply finding that diary. But if I had not started to blog about it and think about it, I wouldn't have been in the right place at the right time to rattle the world of the Were in the manner that I did. And if it hadn't been for -clockwork-crow-, I would never have started that secret blog. I would have stayed Jazz and never become Echo, and if I had never become Echo I might never have become Jesse.

So maybe it all circles back to the Baudoin Solstice Party three months ago. And the night I *really* met Nell Baudoin for the first time.

The Annual Baudoin Solstice Party that year – a Ball in all but name – was remarkable only in that it was the first one I had been obliged to attend.

That had been Mal's fault. Well, things usually were, that isn't anything new, but this time it really did turn out that way. It was the usual drama – he was well past his seventeenth birthday and still a Turn virgin – and people knew it. He had gone to a couple of these parties over the course of the last handful of years, but he had been fifteen then, and sixteen, and only just barely past his Turn date... and then the months and years piled on, and here he was, once more. He loathed the idea of going to the party, yet again, as the one who would get giggled at, pointed at, discussed in lowered voices behind concealing hands, more pointedly than ever before. He was almost eighteen years old. He was from a were family of decent repute – a Random family, to be sure, lower on the social scale than some but by no means at the bottom of the ladder – and he had not Turned yet. He was *almost eighteen*. He would be the lightning rod for every titter and snark and stray piece of gossip that would be flying around that party – left alone lest his Turnlessness was catching, abandoned in a corner but scrutinized as an object of interest if not fascination, treated with a mixture of recoil and curiosity that probably made him want to rip someone's throat out.

Well, I could at least understand that.

He was not given to smiling – he was the classic moody and misunderstood teen, or at least that was the face he showed the outside world – but at the merest mention of the Baudoin party any shred of good humor fled and he dropped right down into "foul", to the point that he actually refused to entertain the idea of attending the party at all.

"You're not taking *her*," he said, nodding darkly at me.

"She's not fifteen yet," Mom said, trying for patience, but the words coming out rather sharper than she might have intended. "She hasn't even Turned..."

"Neither have I," Mal said savagely.

"I'm not *supposed* to have Turned yet," I managed to squawk.

"And I *am* supposed to have Turned. I know," Mal snapped. "Thank you *so* much for pointing that out."

"Malcolm..." My father never used the short version of Mal's name. My brother had been allowed to choose it himself, when the family had arrived here from the Old Country, a new name for a new world, something to help him fit in better – but to his parents, our parents, the name was foreign and artificial, not the name *they* had given their son, and there was a kind of formality that Mal's choice had introduced between them which never quite went away. "Malcolm, the invitation is from the Baudoin family, to ours. To the whole of ours."

"But I don't have to go yet," I said, a little desperately. Heaven knew I had no real social life to speak of – but this was certainly not the sort of social life I'd had in mind when I had contemplated ever having one. I could think of nothing more stultifyingly boring than being forced to spend the evening at the Baudoin Solstice Ball. "I'm too young."

But Mom had scented a compromise.

"You do have that nice velvet dress," she said.

I knew that tone. The wheedling note in it. I had dug in before, in the face of it, and I prepared to do so again.

"The one you bought me when I was *twelve*?" I said. "No way."

"It still fits you," Mom said reasonably.

Sure it did. I was small-boned and delicately built, and I hadn't put on much in the way of height or width in the previous couple of years; what used to be the relatively loose-fitting top was maybe a little tighter than it once was across the bosom but I was far from busty and it wasn't like I looked as if I were wearing a younger sister's hand-me down. The thing still fit, that was hardly the issue, it wasn't that the dress would be too tight, or embarrassingly short. It was just... that it was a child's party dress, and I would be wearing it at a grown-up party, and I would get nothing but pats on the head and offers of candy like I was three years old and oh, it would be mortifying.

But Mal had found something to smile about. "If she goes in *that* dress I'll go," he said.

It was becoming one of his little practical jokes, now, but by this stage my parents had taken the whole thing and were running with it. There was, short of throwing a tantrum fit for that three-year-old I desperately didn't want to be treated like, no dignified way of getting out of this.

"I'll *get* you," I managed to snarl at Mal as I was herded out of the room to see if the dress needed any modifications before the party.

He actually grinned at me, a pure victory smile. "Let's see you try."

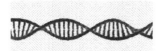

So we all went to the party, and we were barely speaking to each other by the time that we did. Mom and Dad appeared to be distracted by things quite other than the party they were dragging Mal and me to; Mal was not quite in the foul mood he'd been in when this had started but was still lost in a definite blue funk; and I was stiff and uncomfortable in a dress of black velvet which crushed horribly the moment you sat down in it, which was unavoidable, getting to the party, and which in turn meant that I was going to make an entrance looking like something had chewed me up and spat me out, a messy kid tossed into the grown-up and immaculately turned out crowd like a Solstice Sacrifice.

We arrived at the huge and brightly lit Baudoin house and then the party split us neatly up. My father quickly gravitated, drink in hand and a bright smile on his face, to a knot of his colleagues and superiors, people who worked at Baudoin's Bank. Mom parked me in a corner near the punch bowl and told me to behave, and was then swept away by some woman I didn't know and never got introduced to – the only feature of hers I managed to register with any degree of certainty was hair of such an improbable red that the odds were good it had come straight out of a bottle, probably an hour before the party started.

This looked like it was going to be it, the whole night, skulking by myself in corners, owning up to my name if anyone asked, but pretty much passing the rest of the party wrapped in silence and solitude. As far as I could tell I was the only person my age there.

I had made a desperate stab at a congenial companion – I'd asked Dad if I could bring Charlie Ingram with me, as a sort of, um, date – but my mother had vetoed that idea saying I was way too young to be dating and in any event Charlie was not included in the invitation.

I'd already run the idea past him – and he was hardly overjoyed at the prospect but he hadn't said no, not in so many words. I'd had to sort of uninvite him, after my parents nixed the idea, and it was hard not to feel just a little put out at the genuine relief that had been obvious just before he offered me his condolences.

I never saw Mal again once we came through the front door, of course – he had managed to make himself scarce in that way he had about him – he had a genuine talent at making himself disappear, and it was something that I found myself envying deeply as I stood in my corner, pretending to keep my eyes cast down but observing everything through a screen of lowered eyelashes, and kicking at the paneling behind me as savagely as I could while pretending I was doing no such thing.

And I was concentrating so hard on this that I completely failed to notice that somebody had stopped beside me until she tapped me on the shoulder. I was actually startled by it, and turned rather abruptly, and with a face less-schooled than I might have wanted to show. But the expression on it seemed to amuse my new companion, because she suddenly grinned at me.

"We haven't met properly yet," she said, sticking out a hand and obviously expecting me to shake it. "I'm Ellenor Baudoin. You can call me Nell."

"I'm..." I began, but she forestalled the rest.

"You're Jessica Marsh."

"Jazz," I said automatically. And then shook my head. "How did you know...?"

"You're the youngest here, except for me and for Bella, and I heard my mother talking earlier and your name came up," Nell said. "You want to split? We can go up to my room if you like. Nothing down here except boring gasbags and fish eggs."

"Fish eggs?" I gaped at her.

She waved a regal and dismissive hand in the general direction of the far side of the room where tables groaned under platters of food.

"Caviar," she said. "My father thinks he is obliged to like it because he has the money to buy it. It's still fish eggs. Come on, I've got better upstairs."

We didn't really *socialize* with the Baudoins on a regular basis – well, not at all, to be honest, outside these annual parties – but of course I knew her. Or at least of her. Ellenor Baudoin was one of the reigning princesses of the Corvid clan, the youngest Baudoin child. I knew of her by reputation, from Dad's stories about his employer, from her presence on the Net; I think we'd met *briefly* at some children's function or other at a Company do, but nothing more than a glimpse across a room, maybe a word or two exchanged over our heads by our mothers, no more than that.

She had celebrated her milestone fifteenth birthday a few months before but she had Turned just before her fifteenth birthday, into her clan's iconic raven. She was pretty, a true Were, and a major heiress. She was, according to Dad, already starting to be considered marriageable by families who might have an interest in gaining a foothold for themselves in the rich Baudoin legacy by virtue of finding a way to marry into it. I remember thinking – when my father first mentioned Ellenor and I began to understand her position – that I might have been worse off than I was, being born into a new-immigrant Random family of no reputation or fortune. At least I had a hope of having some say in my own destiny, eventually, at least after I grew up sufficiently to be independent of parental fiat like this party had been. Ellenor Baudoin would be bestowed somewhere appropriate by her father, probably, when the time came for her to leave the Baudoin fold. And that family would be very selective about whom they'd allow into the inner circle; Ellenor herself may or may not have been considered of sufficient influence to actually be consulted about it.

For a mad moment I contemplated throwing a wrench in those works, and asking the biggest Corvid heiress of her generation if she'd met my brother.

But for all her reputation and renown, this particular Corvid princess seemed to be reasonably nice, if inevitably snooty, but that came with the job description, I guess. At any rate, she offered an escape from the suffocating hall where the adults stood sipping cocktails and talking about nothing. Nell drifted across the room, effortlessly dodging the party-goers – she had obviously had practice at this – and I followed in her wake until we gained the sweeping stair that led up to the second story.

Nell paused for a moment, turning to look at the panorama spread out below her – women in bright silks, the glitter of jewels at ears and throat and wrist, and men in dark suits... they looked like a flock of...

I thought it, but Nell said it.

"A murder of crows," she said. "They look like our aviary out back looks during the Turn. Full of squawking black birds."

"You have an aviary out back?"

She looked at me oddly. "The law," she said. "All Weres confined safely during the Turn, you know? And our house is big enough for... well, let's just say it isn't *an* aviary, but rather that half the yard has been netted over – we always have a hundred cousins and friends or more coming here to spend their three raven or crow or magpie or whatever days out in the aviary. Every year we get somebody new – my father would never send any Corvid who comes knocking at his door to a Turning House."

She was still looking at me as we started to climb the stairs again, and she saw me wince at her words. "What did I say?"

I tried a small disarming smile. "Say...?"

"You looked like I just tried to peck your eyes out," she said. Corvid. She would go there.

But she asked, so I gave it to her.

"To you it's just a horror story," I said. "They probably used the Turning Houses as threats when you weren't doing what the grown-ups wanted. But when my family came out here..."

We had reached a landing, and then turned into a wide carpeted corridor with wall light sconces that spilled a warm creamy light – completely at odds with the darkness of the Turning House stories, somehow skewering them, making them oddly unreal, almost irrelevant. I was taking her to task for believing in them only as fairy tales – but what else could she do, from this corridor, from this protected circle of golden light?

"In here," she said, pushing open a door. "There's stuff to eat over there on the chest. Help yourself."

I paused in the doorway for a moment, taking in the room. It was twice the size of my own, furnished with a certain style; her bed was a miniature four-poster, its head draped with artistic folds of black velvet and lace. There was a portrait on the wall, a young woman with a pale, pale face framed with loose raven-black hair spilling across her shoulders and two huge dark eyes outlined with dark liner skewering any visitor to this room as they stepped over the threshold– it took me a couple of seconds to realize that this was Nell herself, in full Goth get-up. It kind of suited her. Scarily. On her, black velvet looked entirely natural, as though she had been born to wear it, and of course it would *never* wrinkle or crease. On me, it looked like a badly crushed twelve-year-old girl's Three-Year-Old-Party-Best. Life just wasn't fair.

"Hi!" said a bright voice from the window, breaking my focus, and I realized there was another girl in here, a fair-haired sprite who was smiling at me from across the room. "I'm Bella."

"Cybella Marley, Jazz Marsh," Nell said. Good, she had been paying attention. "Bella's Dad is one of the VPs of the bank."

Another Corvid aristocrat. Great. Granted, at a lower level – but still. Here she was, lollygagging around with the resident princess. I fought the urge to back out the door and run – I was hopelessly outmatched. Out*classed*.

"Jazz was just telling me about Turning Houses," Nell said, and met and held my gaze. Challenged.

Oh, fine. I would give it to her, both barrels. To them both. It would do them the world of good.

"No such thing back in the Old Country," I said, glancing over the food offerings on the chest. But my tastes ran more to savory and Nell appeared to have a distressing sweet tooth – nothing really appealed to me, and besides, it would somehow have been an affront to be munching on a frosted cupcake when telling a Turning House story. "The way my parents tell it, the Were-kind lived more or less in peace – so long as nobody knew what they were. As long as their true identity was kept secret, they lived with the normals as part of the society, in the closet, yes, but otherwise perfectly okay. Yeah, they were terrified of being found out most of the time – but no more so than other isolated and different folks..."

"So what happened if people found out?"

I shrugged. "The worst that could happen? If the normals found out that you turned into a cat – or a crow – every month when the Moon turned full – well – they'd hunt you down and kill you."

That had happened, in my own extended family. Close family, in fact. An aunt, my mother's younger sister. That was a big part of the reason that my mother and my father were here in the New World at all. But there was a time and a place, and I didn't think I needed to go there – not right now, not here, not with these two.

But apparently I had already said quite enough because Bella turned a whiter shade of pale and gasped, "Oh, *God*. Are you *serious*?"

"What?" I said, ignoring the waking of the quiet pain of my own past, needled into a kind of defensive nonchalance by Bella's obvious horror. "It's a perfectly straightforward exchange. You knew where you stood."

"We have laws against that sort of thing," Nell said. "Have done for a long time. Things are *civilized* here. You were born here, weren't you? Why do you call it the New World?"

"Because it is – to my family and me– it will always be. I might have been born here but I came from somewhere else – in *here* – " I tapped my temples with my forefingers. "To you it's history, if anything. Ancient history, at that. But to me – it's my family's own story. It could have happened to me, if I had been born just a very short while earlier. It's... fresh."

"But they knew," Nell said, quietly insistent. "Your parents – didn't they know there are laws here – different laws?"

"Of course," I said. "But they were out of choices – and anyway you never hear the whole story, when you relocate like this – you always learn a few things the hard way when you land in your new country, things you never quite expected and have no idea how to deal with. With them, it was the Turning Houses. They were expecting..."

"What?" Bella said.

"Well, they had to get *away*. Far away. And they had heard the stories that over here Were-kind were not hunted down," I said. "They knew that; they believed it... sort of. They hoped they could get jobs alongside normals, send their children to school alongside normals, have a completely open relationship – no longer having to hide what you are, who you are..."

"But all that is true," Nell said.

"Oh, really?"

She started to contradict me but then paused, chewing her lip.

Bella appeared to be unable to prevent any thought that crossed her featherbrain from escaping out of her mouth.

"But we have laws," she said, repeating what Nell said a moment before.

"Yeah," I said. "Laws. And however generous they might sound... they were put on the books by powerful people who didn't have the well-being of Were-kind on their mind when they did so. The laws were made to raise a wall, and to make sure we all stayed safely behind it."

"But it's absolutely fine to be Were-kind out in the normal world," Bella insisted. "So long as you..."

"So long as you carry your little ID card with the little paw print, right? And have to produce it if you're asked? It's okay to be Were as long as everyone is aware of that small fact and can behave accordingly..."

It was a subject I would get quite heated about, actually. We had been studying history, my mother and I – she homeschooled me, after all, and she had a certain amount of wiggle room as to what to include on the curriculum. So I knew far more about all of this than any average young Were might, taught as they were the sanitized versions in the schools which they went to (some, to be sure, with normals – others in special segregated schools for Were-kind only. Where the kids from the better-off Were-families went, anyway, and the irony of that had not escaped me – everyone was so proud of being considered an equal to a normal but given half a chance they all fled back to their ghettos...)

Nell actually managed a short bark of a laugh. "Well, when I went down to get you, I didn't expect a political lecture," she said.

I had the grace to regret my little outburst. There was a time, and a place, and like Nell, I hadn't been expecting the political undercurrents when I had arrived at the party-of-the-year.

"I'm sorry," I said, feeling that the very least I owed her was an apology. But she wasn't looking for one, after all.

"It's OK," Nell said, waving my 'sorry' aside. "You still haven't told me anything about the Turning Houses, though. Other than they are evil."

Me. Not *us.* She was leaving Bella out of this – somehow it had shaken down to something shared between a Corvid Princess and a Random waif-and-stray she'd brought in from the cold. An odd warmth spread into my cheeks. Was this what 'making a friend' felt like? I found myself vaguely astonished by the sensation – as well as by the stray thought that it was somehow rather pathetic that I should be discovering it at this late stage in my life, that the only real friendship I had in my life which I could really call such was an accidental relationship with a boy who happened to be my babysitter's son.

I had not realized how lonely my world had been. Until this moment.

But I had to ride it, now, because there were other things at stake here. Nell had laid the challenge down, and I cast my mind back over my parents' stories. There was a law on the books when they had arrived here, a law you broke at your peril, that a Were-creature had to be locked away while in its non-human shape – for "public safety". If no secure place could be established at the person's residence, and "secure place" was something that was at the sole discretion of the authorities, then Were-folk were obliged to report to Turning Houses, government facilities where a lockdown could go into effect once the change took over and the resulting menagerie of squawking, grunting, roaring, chirping, snarling, whining cawing fauna into which Were-kind turned could be kept safely under lock and key.

In theory it might have sounded like a workable solution, but in practice the conditions were appalling. It was hard to cater to all the possibilities, so the containment rooms were as near generic as they could be, for Were-sparrow and Were-tiger alike, and there were... accidents...where predator and prey were inadvertently housed too close together.

In the beginning, my parents rented and had no permanent home which was considered to be safe enough for a lockdown when they Turned – so they were obliged to report to the nearest Turning House, a few hours' drive away, during their times of the month. The fact that they had two – and, soon, three, counting me – young children who had not yet Turned was not the Government's problem. My mother had to make arrangements for her children's care and then abandon those children for three days while she endured her change – arrangements which had to pass muster with the very government which had made them necessary or else that government had the right to take care of such offspring themselves.

When they finally managed to find a house they could afford to buy, the first thing my father did was set up a suite of secure rooms in the basement, so that none of us would ever be flung to the mercies of a Turning House again. None of us kids had seen the inside of one; my parents told us enough about them that none of us ever wanted to be anywhere near anything like it as long as we lived.

We had a caretaker – Vivian Ingram came every month, while my parents were out of it, to take care of the kids who had not Turned yet. For a long time I had thought she was a normal, although that did seem rather strange – but I had found out in due time that she was something lower on the social scale than even us Random Weres. She wasn't a Full-Moon Were, she was one of the New-Moon Were, the kind who Turned at the dark of the Moon rather than the full that triggered the rest of us. I had not known of those before we had come to the New World, and Vivian hadn't talked about it much – but there we were, anyway, flung at each other's mercy during the Turns, because my mother had done the same thing for Vivian when she had still had young and unTurned children in her house. Now they were all fledged, her three boys – a nice, neat family of vampire bats.

"What's it like, being Random? Is it true that you can literally Turn into anything?" Bella, of course. She couldn't help it, poor dear.

"What, you've never met one of us before?" It came out snarkier than I had intended it. "So what are you, then? I assume Corvid – crow?"

"Magpie," she said brightly. "I'm online as -Shiny!- actually."

I almost groaned. She *would* be.

"What are you?" Nell asked.

"I haven't Turned yet," I pointed out. "But when we do, Random Were can choose our primary form... if we're lucky."

"What do you mean, if you're lucky?" Nell asked.

"Accidents... happen," I said carefully. "That's why we have Rules."

They heard the capital R. "Rules? What kind of Rules?" Nell asked.

Oh well. Spilling family secrets. As though anybody would care.

"Some of them are family Rules. No pets in the house, not ever."

Bella actually giggled. "I can understand *that*," she chirped. "You could Turn into *anything*, and that could get awfully inconvenient..."

"Yes, well," I said. "Anything warm-blooded. I once asked Vivian – our babysitter – in a state of complete panic, if I could murder somebody by swatting a fly, and she told me that nothing cold-blooded and nothing chitinous will trigger a Turn..."

"So you could have had pets," Nell pointed out. "So long as you had a snake or a frog or an ant farm, or even a goldfish..."

"It might not have been triggery but it might have been tragic," I said. "And my parents figured that it was best to spare the family the potential of *that*."

"Tragic?" Bella said, frowning.

I gave her a long look, keeping my face without expression. "My father... is a *cat*."

It took her a moment. I could see the thought working its way to the back of her brain. And then, as she sat back with her hands over her mouth, envisaging the carnage wreaked amongst family pets (or family members who might have Turned into creatures like family pets) by a Pater Familias Turned carnivorous predator, Nell asked the other obvious question.

"And your mother?"

I hesitated. This was something my mother would have really had little to no control over, and perhaps she would not have wanted anybody to know, but I was already waist deep and wading deeper, so whatever.

"That was... one of the accidents," I murmured. "She and her sister were both inconveniently close to a farmyard when they first Turned. Her sister's primary form... was a rabbit."

"Well, a rabbit isn't that bad," Bella chirruped brightly. "What about your mom, then?"

"My mother..."

I hesitated again, and Bella leaned in closer.

"Yes?" she said

"My mother is a chicken," I said lugubriously.

The tone I had used was tragic, but for some reason those words... just came out funny. Hilarious, in fact. My mood was strange, volatile, and that fatal image of a bewildered clucking pullet in the farmyard blossomed into my mind and obliterated everything else – and after that, all I could do was laugh.

We all giggled. We made the mistake of catching one another's eye, and the image of that chicken took over – we simply cracked up. It took a few moments for us to collect ourselves, and even then it came in stages because one or the other would invariably start again just as we all calmed down and set the others off. But eventually we sat up, wiping at our streaming eyes.

"Oh, you'd be a riot at school," Bella gasped at last, pushing her hair back behind her ears. "How come you don't go to our school?"

My mood had shifted again. Damn, but she was good, this Bella. She was a pointed stick, poking at everything inside of me – and this particular jab brought me back to the politically passionate arena.

"Not many of us do," I said.

"Who's 'us'?" Nell asked carefully, aware of the shift.

"The Random Were. Most that I know of – those that my parents have met – are not exactly flush with the kind of money it would take to send one kid, let alone several, to a school like yours. Mal goes to a far rougher place – a school full of normals, perhaps a scattering of Were – he's had to fend for himself – "

"Where do you go?"

"I've never gone to school," I said. "Not like you. My mom homeschools me. I haven't Turned yet – everything is dangerous..."

I had *never* gone to a real school. I was never within smelling distance of a real school; I was watched and supervised and hovered over pretty near almost every moment of every day. That pang of acute loneliness I had felt a little earlier came back with a vengeance, all the more intense for having been buried, for the moment, in a pile of other stuff. But the truth was, I didn't have any friends to speak of outside of a few so-called ones I had met online. I had no life, in fact – I didn't go anywhere, didn't do anything. This would not be a concept these Corvid social butterflies could hope to comprehend.

Mal, at least, either had permission to go out and hang out somewhere outside the house, or didn't care and went anyway; my outings were always carefully planned, more often than not with one of my parents or some other supervisory presence. I had never in my life had a birthday party – I wouldn't have had anyone to ask; neither (to my knowledge) had Mal, for that matter, but he seemed to like it that way. It didn't seem to do much for him, as far as that went, or improve his disposition any – and he came home with bloodied knuckles or a black eye often enough for anyone to suppose that he can't have had all that many friends out there. Those were the times he would pull further into himself and I would lose him, sometimes for days; when he did not feel like talking he had a very effective way of preventing any advances of unwanted communication. By anybody. I knew the signals he sent out when he wanted to be alone, and I respected them. The weird thing to me, at least back when I was younger, is that *he* seemed to resent *me* – and I could not for the life of me understand why. He was the one with the freedom; I was the one locked away in an ivory tower.

And it all circled back to Celia, really. Celia, my oldest sibling, had died less than a year after she had first Turned. She had been only barely fifteen, having Turned precociously, well ahead of the appointed time. I was seven back then, the youngest in the family, the only one born here on the soil of our new country. I was old enough to remember the big picture – the tragedy of it all – but I had been too young to remember, or to have been told, all the details. I didn't know what questions to ask to get clarification on the things I never understood, and even if I had found the right words for those they would never have been answered to my satisfaction. My parents kept Celia's memory alive by their very silence on the matter, and my brother, reluctant to speak to me of her, used the same means to bury it. I was on the outside, looking in through dirty windows, seeing only shapes and shadows...

But this was not something that I could begin telling these two girls, whom I was suddenly aware that I had barely met. Funny, I could betray my mother's fowl nature – I could hint at the darkness of the Turning Houses – I could begin what Nell had started to call a political lecture – but I couldn't talk about Celia. I changed the subject, turning it around to the two of them – who knew I'd be so interested in things Corvid? Bella seemed to buy into my bright and interested fascination and burbled on happily enough about life as a magpie. Nell... was quieter, and under the shrewd and level gaze of her dark eyes I could see that she knew exactly what I was doing. But she let Bella be the buffer, and things went tolerably well, if not swimmingly.

I can't say I was not at least partly relieved when the summons came from downstairs that my presence was required because my family was about to take their leave, my parents first having to extract Mal from a game of cards in the back of the house that looked rather less innocent than he protested it to be. He affected a sulky and wounded mien, but he threw me a wink in the car when he was sure neither of my parents were looking, with the beginnings of a very small and very smug grin playing about the corners of his mouth.

I knew better than to ask out loud, so I asked by gesture – *What happened?*

His response was to rub thumb and forefinger together. They'd been playing for money, apparently. I had no idea where he would have gotten enough to buy into a game like that, but apparently he had, and he had done well enough at it to be quite pleased by his efforts that night.

But he wasn't about to admit that to Mom and Dad, and, well, neither was I. At least outwardly, the journey home from the Baudoin party was every bit as sullen and silent as the outward journey had been, except for the fact that I had stopped caring about what my dress would look like when I came out of the car.

It was less than a week after that evening that I found Celia's diary.

Part 2:
The Ghost in the Diary

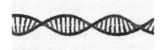

I had never – *quite* – had my own room when I was growing up. As a baby, and a small toddler, I had been tucked away into a corner of my parents' bedroom; when I turned five, there began to be talk of redoing the tiny alcove off the living room, which we liked to call our dining room but which was barely large enough to contain a table, into another bedroom for me. While that option was being discussed, I had been moved into Celia's room.

I was too young to be consulted on any of this, simply moved around to make life easier for everybody in the short term, and I remember only disconnected fragments, but looking back it all makes perfect sense *now*. The fact was that my older sister was less than pleased to have to share. I can hardly blame her, at this point in my life when I'm roughly the same age she was back then; having a five-year-old foisted into her personal space is hardly something she would have welcomed. She made the best of a bad situation, managing never to be unkind to this small intruder who was always underfoot, because it was always being seen as a temporary solution and she was holding out for a return to privacy when she Turned because then she would be officially an adult...except, of course, that this never really happened according to plan.

Everything changed when she died.

In the aftermath of that, I kind of simply expanded into and inherited her room as if by right. It had been gutted and refurnished at some point but in an oddly similar style, as though my parents could not bear to look at any of the stuff that had been hers but at the same time couldn't bear the idea of her choices and personality having vanished from their house altogether. This was why it was painted a color I would never have picked myself, and had furnishings that seemed to belong to a different and far more "girly" girl than I actually was. But I made do – adjusted what I could, lived with the rest – and I made it as much my own personal bolt-hole and sanctuary as I could.

But apparently they had not been as thorough in the gut-and-redecorate push as they thought they had been because there was a gap between the skirting boards and the floor in the back of the closet, usually buried by assorted junk and thus was practically invisible. Why I had never really poked around the area before I have no clue – but in the aftermath of the Baudoin party my closet became something of an immediate concern to me, partly because I wanted to make absolutely certain that the black velvet dress (and while I was about it, other items that might resemble it) was evicted from it as soon as possible, certainly before another outing could be manufactured where such outfits could be trotted out as appropriate attire. The junk at the bottom of the closet came out as well, at this point, to be sorted and dealt with, and became curious about that skirting-board gap.

I poked at it and much to my astonishment it popped right out, as though it had never been fastened at all. Behind it was a hidey-hole, a dark and cobwebby space, just wide enough to stick a hand into. And inside... was a cache of three hard-cover notebooks. Notebooks that looked like they were a diary of sorts.

I left them there in the safe space, all but one, the *first* one, from the bottom of the stack, which I took out and carefully hid away underneath my mattress to take a closer look at later. I don't know why I didn't say anything to anybody about my find when I first came across this stuff, but it was a strange instinct that commanded my silence – it was as though my sister had reached out to me, and to me alone, and finally shared a secret with me. And the secret was between her and me – cross my heart and hope to die – at the very least until I could find out more.

It was a secret to the point that I could not bring myself to read it during the daylight hours when everybody else was about the house. I began reading it in the best tradition of flashlight-under-the-covers after I was supposed to be safely asleep and long after everybody else actually *was*.

The first of the notebooks, the one I began with, had been started back before the family had left the Old Country – and it was scrawled in unformed childish handwriting, and written in a language I had never been taught to read; all I could really figure out was the date at the top of every diary entry. I flipped forward through the book, but it seemed to be filled with more of the same, the handwriting that of a child, the contents, although I could understand none of it, therefore less than promising by definition. Why would I want to read my sister's childish babblings...? And why on earth did she think this was valuable enough to keep – to *hide*?

The early entries had been fairly sporadic, with days, sometimes weeks, passing between entries whose dates I could decipher. But the last entry in the book... was different. It bore a date that placed it as nearly three and a half months after the last entry before it had been made, and it was written in a different, shakier, apparently much 'younger' handwriting – but the reason for this was obvious. The entry was written in an alphabet that was new and strange and unfamiliar to her, in a language she had barely begun to know. The contents of the entry was decidedly odd, until I realized that she had not, in fact, written it – she was copying something out, from a magazine, perhaps, obviously just to practice the language skills she was acquiring, and the date placed her already here, already living in her new world. She would have been seven years old, approaching eight, by the date of this last entry.

I actually contemplated getting out of bed and prying loose that board and hauling out the next notebook in the sequence – but I wasn't remotely sure that I could do it quietly enough not to wake up the entire house. It would have to wait until daylight. And anyway... if the rest of it was just more copying exercises... it might not be worth it.

But I could not believe that a girl who had filled a notebook with diary entries before she was nine years old would have stayed content with simply copying out pages from magazines, and if she had, there would certainly have been no need to tuck these things away in a secret hidey hole like Celia had done. She had managed to get my attention, and now I wanted to know more.

I switched the notebooks as soon as I could the next morning, and fretted my way until lights-out that night, so that I could go back to my treasure. The rewards were almost immediate. My sister had been intelligent and articulate; after only two or three more uninteresting copying exercises she had hit on the idea of practicing both languages that were now in her head – the one she was perforce losing, the old language of the old country, and the one she needed to conquer in the new place – by translating a selection of the earlier entries which she had made in the first notebook. This in itself began to open windows into my past which I had not known were closed – it seemed my parents' stories had been selective, and edited to fit what they believed to be a child's sensibilities before they had passed any of them down to me. But very quickly Celia had begun to intersperse her translations with entries which shone a new a light on the early days of the family's life in the new place.

She wrote about the family – about a brother whom I barely recognized as Mal, about a set of parents whom she called Mama and Papa (I called them Mom and Dad), and they too were different people from the ones I had come to know.

She would eventually come to write about me, the little sister who arrived when they were already here, in this place which must have seemed so foreign and strange to her and which I took so much for granted. I suppose this shouldn't have startled me, but it did. It felt like my dead sister had reached out and touched me with a cold little hand.

She wrote about this new world she was living in, about having to learn so many new things and to adapt to so many new rules.

And she began, with hesitations, as though she was too wary to commit her thoughts to even these secret pages, to write about school, and the things that were going on there. The way she always wore the wrong clothes, somehow. Used the wrong words, spoke with the wrong accent. She wrote about the small cruelties, the laughter, the curled lips of sneering contempt. She wrote:

> *They called me a peasant. I know that they did not*
> *mean it as anything good. I hated it when either*
> *Mama or Papa spoke in front of any of these kids. I*
> *hated it when I had to speak in front of them. My*
> *words sounded thick, wrong. Every word I said out*
> *loud told them that I did not belong. Mama told me*
> *that I was losing my accent – but maybe she was just*
> *hearing me speak in a different way than she was*
> *used to. The people in my class always asked me to*
> *repeat what I said, sometimes more than once, as if*

> *they really could not understand me. I only spoke,*
> *after that, when I had to.*

She must have been about ten, then. Writing in a new and foreign language, still practicing, even though she had apparently been coerced into not uttering out loud these new words she was learning because they would laugh at her. I didn't remember an accent – certainly not one that pronounced – but I had been a baby, back then. Such a baby.

"Do I have an accent?" I asked my mother, a few days after I'd read that part of Celia's journal, while we were packing up at the end of our school-day.

She turned to stare at me, her eyebrows halfway up her forehead.

"An *accent*?" she repeated, in a tone that reflected astonishment. "Where did that come from?"

"I was watching something on the Net," I lied, without breaking a sweat. Well, it was true, in a sense, I had seen something on the Net – but the reasons that I had gone looking were deeply buried underneath the eventual 'discovery'. "Something about how people on TV have a kind of middle-of-the-road accent and everyone can understand them – or is supposed to – but real people from different places talk very differently in real life."

"That is true enough," Mom said. Well, now that I was listening, she actually said, *Dyat iss true enyoff,* her vowels much softer than they were supposed to be. Perhaps not as exaggerated, but now that I was listening for it I could *hear* it, every syllable of it – and she was trying to bury it. I was suddenly and uncomfortably hearing what someone else, an outsider, might have been hearing. And taking it back into context. Into the school. Into the classroom. Back to Celia.

"So if even people from the same country have an accent if they come from different parts of it – so then – do I have an accent? I mean, I'm not *from* here – "

"Yes, you are," Mom interrupted. "You were born here. I have your birth certificate to prove it."

"That's a *technicality*," I said. I had discovered that word not too long before and I loved it to bits. It was such a wonderful way of countering almost every objection that could be raised to *anything*. And in this conversation, it was even literally correct. "I learned how to talk in this family, not out on the street. Or in school."

She winced a little, at that. I saw it.

"You went to kindergarten, with a lot of other kids," she said carefully. "And there was Vivian, who speaks with that TV accent that you just mentioned. And you are always watching things and listening to things, television and the Net. You might have learned how to talk in this house, but we tried to make sure you belonged out in the world beyond it."

"You do have an accent," I said. "And so does Dad."

"Of course we do," she said, sounding a little exasperated. "We learned the language when we were all grown up, and our patterns had already set..."

"Mal does," I interjected. "And he was practically a baby..."

"He does not," Mom, said, with a touch of heat. "He has picked up the way they talk in that school. I would maybe like to see him be using a different language."

Sometimes their grammar did strange things, both of them, Mom and Dad, but they had always insisted that English be the spoken language inside the house. It was as though they were closing the door on everything that had gone before. When this family had stepped off the boat and onto new soil, they shook off everything old. There was only one book I knew of in our house which was not in English – that book, and Celia's original journal...

"He does, when he gets upset," I said. "But do I...?"

"No," she said, closing a book with rather more force than necessary and looking away from me. "You don't."

I had wanted to go on and ask about Celia – but I was never given a chance to. The conversation, at least for now, was closed.

I tried it with Dad, but ran into a similar wall. And then I actually asked Mal, and to give him his due he did try to discuss it – at least where he and I were concerned – but he would clam up when I tried to circle around to Celia. That was a tough subject to broach in our house. But Mal had *been* there, at the same time as Celia – they had grown up together far more closely than he had ever done with me, shared the whole immigration experience, which I had never had to face – and some of the things she was saying in the diary were making me feel... queasy. I wanted him to tell me that she was making it up, making it worse than it was, making drama out of nothing at all.

"I wouldn't worry about an accent if I were you," Mal said in the end, and that was a conversation stopper, for that particular conversation, for that particular time. "It's not as though there's anyone but Mom and Dad to notice – and I doubt if they would. Or care."

Well, but he didn't have to tell me that I practically did not exist outside of this house, that I would change the fabric of reality if I tried to go out into the average workaday streets and try to pretend I belonged there. It wouldn't be a matter of accent so much as not knowing what on earth people my age talked about, or what the new hot thing was. I was on the outside, outside, outside. But if I didn't have an accent – the way Celia did, and apparently paid for – then what was stopping me from trying? Just Mom and her paranoid protectiveness?

It was a sudden frustration with my entire existence that propelled me past Mal's usual stop signals, into territory where I would not have ventured under ordinary circumstances.

"You do," I said, flinging caution to the wind.

He had considered the conversation over, and was on the point of beginning to ignore me – but that got his attention. "What's that?"

"Have an accent. Especially when you get riled. Like right now."

"*Watch* it," he snapped at me, obviously irritated. "You wouldn't know a proper accent if it bit the nose off your face. And why do you care, anyway?"

"Did anyone ever rag you about it? In school... ?" I swallowed, and decided to brave the name. "You, or Celia...?"

He stared at me in silence for a long moment, and then his forehead slowly knit into a deeper frown. "*Celia*? Where's this coming from?"

"I just meant – I wanted to find out – "

"It won't happen to you, you know. Not ever. Mom will make sure of that."

"What won't happen?" I said, every antenna suddenly snapping to high alert. "I never asked for – " The expression that crept onto Mal's face as I began to speak frightened me, and I stopped, the words getting stuck in my throat. And then, with the remnants of the same lunatic courage that had brought me here in the first place, made a final try. "So did they ever – with her – did you ever...?"

Mal flexed his hands and then rolled them into fists.

"Anyone try it with me," he growled, "they'd soon regret it. And anyway..."

But then he suddenly looked as if he had realized that he had said too much, spilled some guilty secret – and that was what I was getting from him, guilt. It was guilt that was making him angry, not the things that I was saying. He clamped his lips together in a tight line, and pushed his shoulders up about his ears, ramming both hands into the pockets of his jeans.

"When you're older," he said, "maybe they will talk about Celia..."

But even that wasn't to be given to me. He dropped his eyes and we shared a moment of doomful silence before he left me without another word.

That exhausted all my prospects except Vivian, and she wasn't due in for another two weeks, at least, according to the Almanac sheet held to the fridge by a magnet.

My dead sister was speaking to me through her journals. And I could not talk about it, or her, with any of the still-living family who had known and loved her. My parents could not seem to bring themselves to discuss the one lost daughter with the one still in their lives. My brother – for whatever reasons – had decided to simply build a wall between the living sister and the one who had died. He was the bridge – the only living bridge – my generation, Celia's, someone who could have understood, could perhaps have explained. But he was hoarding that knowledge, those memories, as if he could not bear to share them lest they shattered under the strain. I came to an inevitable conclusion that something truly terrible must have happened, and I resented being shut out of my family because of that tragedy. It almost felt, irrationally enough, as though everyone blamed *me*.

At some point in the aftermath of these attempts at shedding some light on the mysteries of my past, sitting and staring at my computer screen in a moment of blank and frozen inaction, I noticed that -EllenorBaudoin- was online. I had investigated Nell Baudoin's presence on the Net after the party; she was still, and would always be, a Corvid Princess *first* but honestly I couldn't hold that against her, and she had been interesting enough, from our brief acquaintance, to warrant it – and besides, there had been that moment of a potential budding friendship there, back at the party. I remembered the sensation clearly. I didn't want to let that potential go that easily. So I'd ended up friending her on a social network page. I had only added another name to the couple of hundred which were already there; I didn't think she'd notice, or care.

But she did – notice, and apparently care, and certainly remember.

Because –feeling alone and I typed in *Hey!* in the chat window, and hit send.

And the response came back, almost instantly.

<Hey. Jazz? That you?

I hesitated, and nearly broke the connection. What did I do a thing like this for? But she was there, and she was somebody to talk to...

<Hey, yeah, Jazz.

<I saw you'd friended me. What's up?

<I hate my family sometimes.

Whoa. Where did *that* come from?

But the cursor was blinking, and back came the response.

<Who doesn't. What's the matter?

<don't listen. won't talk.

<Oh, THAT.

<yeah, THAT. You make it sound as though it's normal.

<It IS. You should do what I do.

<Which is?

<Write angry poetry.

I actually laughed out loud at that. My fingers flew back over the keys

<I don't write poetry, I typed.

<Doesn't have to rhyme, or anything, Oh, just blog about it. Keep a journal. Write it out. Whatever it is you can't get them to talk to you about. Sooner or later you wind up answering all your own questions anyway.

<They READ my blog. At least I think my mother does.

<My mother reads MY blog, too, silly. The PUBLIC one. She doesn't know about the other one.

<You have another one?

<Of course I do. Doesn't everybody? It's in deep friends-lock, and I've only got maybe seven people who read it and even then only every so often. But it's just wonderful for when you think you're just screaming into the ether and nobody is listening.

<So what do you write about?

There was a pause, long enough to make me wonder if she'd decided that I was asking far too many questions. But the cursor blinked again, presently, and back came the unexpected response.

<I'm -clockwork_crow- at Blogword. If you want to, you can send in a

friend request. I'll approve you. Pick a screen name; we all have one. Just let me know what it is so that I know it's you.

It didn't take me long, in the end. I'd been thinking far too intensely about me and Celia, about my Mom's attitudes to me and Celia, about what she represented, about what I had inherited.

<*I will be Echo*, I typed in.

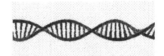

I had to create my own profile before I could claim a screen name, so I did that, without really thinking about whether or not I would actually start a 'secret' blog – I confess to a certain amount of basic curiosity, in the beginning, as to what the secrets of someone like Nell would be like. Her life was so different from mine that even the most ordinary of things in her sphere would probably baffle me, and my life would make no sense to her at all – but there had been that unexpected connection between us, that night at the party, and now I was interested. What's more, I had been *invited*. It would be rude not to go.

The Echo identity fell around me naturally enough, as though it was something that I was curiously familiar with, both an admittance to myself of certain motives I could see more and more clearly in my mother's relationship with me and my own rebellion against my parents, an avatar that both understood and shrugged off someone else's ideas of what it should be or do. I could see writing about *that* in my new secret blog, which I named 'Is there an Echo in here?" But first, I poked around until I found -clockwork crow- and sent in my friends request.

Nell approved me practically instantly, as though she'd been sitting there staring at her screen waiting for me to hurry up and arrive already, and I found myself in a cyber-Goth-palace, decked out in black and dark blue and dark green. The type was white on dark blue, and for some reason that was hard on my eyes – and a lot of it seemed to be poetry. It wasn't *bad* poetry, as far as I could tell, but I as I had told her I was not really bitten by that bug so my opinions were moot; there seemed to be rather a lot of it, however, and it was something I found myself rather impatiently wading through to get to the heart of it all. Assuming it wasn't the heart of it all. But, ah, there it was – the occasional snippet of prose where Nell thought she could communicate something without the added layer of poetic drama.

The whole thing was carefully constructed – this was a persona, and she was obviously taking care to cultivate it. The ideas behind it somehow mattered. But when I burrowed beneath the skin of it all – the alienness of the darkness that she presented as her outward face, and the intrinsic aristocracy that came from her social position – she seemed almost as lonely as I was. The secret blog, encrypted and password-protected and friends-only, had only seven names, or eight counting me, in the Friends list. The girl who had everything had only seven friends...?

I wasn't going to suddenly turn into a poet, not even here, in my little secret Echo chamber, but all of a sudden it felt as though I had been given an odd gift – I remembered a story my mother had told me, a long time ago when she was still telling me stories, of a boy who had seen something he shouldn't have seen about the Emperor of the land. He buckled under the weight of the secret he could never tell, until he was advised to dig a deep hole in the ground and whisper his secret into it, and then bury it there. He did this, and felt a deep sense of release from his burden.

It was a little like that – I chose not to draw the parallel to the rest of that old tale, which then told of a plant which grew on the spot where the boy had buried his secret, and in time that plant's hollow twigs proved to be wonderful for making little flutes for shepherd boys to play while minding their flocks... except that the only 'tune' these flutes would play was the secret that had once been buried at the root of the plant: "The Emperor has the ears of a donkey!"

Here was my hole in the ground. I could tell it my secrets. I just had to hope that no betraying flute-plants would take root here in the cyberworld.

I tinkered forever with the set-up and the skin of my new blog. I found a picture of a rustic flute, and used it as wallpaper. You might say I was throwing a flute-shaped gauntlet down to fate – but that was only amusing for so long, and then the reason behind my having created the thing in the first place came back to remind me of its existence.

It happened to be the first of January. The first day of a new year.

It was as good a day as any to start on a new project.

So I wrote my first blog entry.

1 January

It's all messed up.

> *I'm not entirely sure what I'm doing here, and if I wind up worse off than before it's all your fault, -clockwork_crow-.*
> *I'm finding out secrets. Secrets are out to get me. Nothing my parents ever said to me seems to be quite true. I can't trust my own memories.*
> *I found my sister's hidden diary. My dead sister's diary. Celia's diary. A proper diary, handwritten in an actual notebook, not tapped onto a screen, like this, like me. Celia was old-world. She knew how things were supposed to be done. I seem to be out of step with all the rules, old-world and new alike, these days.*
> *You might say I probably shouldn't have read that stuff. I probably should have given it to my mother. She'd have taken it and then, when I couldn't see her do it, cried over it and then put it away*

*somewhere in a shrine which I've never seen but which I know exists,
a small mound of things that once belonged to Celia which my
mother cannot bear to throw out, never will. If we ever move from
this house, she'll take all that stuff with her, the discarded
possessions of Celia's ghost. To her, in a weird way, Celia is still
living in this house – in the room that's now supposed to be mine –
sometimes I get the creepy feeling that I am somehow supposed to
become Celia, take over, exist in what was supposed to be her place.*

*I am an echo of my lost sister. I am an Echo. Instant
cybername. There you go.*

*But I am not her replacement. I am me. I don't want to become
Celia 2.0; I have no clue how I would even supposed to even try. But
whatever. That's the least of the things that is messed up, Celia's
dying like that.*

*The stuff in the diary – I didn't know most of the stuff in the
diary. Or I knew it in some watered-down form which was
considered appropriate for me – maybe they thought I was way too
young for it, or that I wouldn't understand – but it turns out there
was always a good REASON behind my being homeschooled and
never sent out into a proper classroom after a short dabble in
kindergarten and I never did really know why... before now. I never
really bothered to ask, I didn't care that much. But now I know.*

*It was the classroom that killed Celia, or at least that's the way
my parents saw it. The way my mother did. I... am supposed to be
Celia, but I am also to be prevented, at all costs, from becoming
Celia, lest I should wind up the same way.*

*I don't know if Mal ever had to cope with any of this. He never
really talked to me about it, anyway – but then, he's 17. He's
practically grown. Less than a year and the Law will allow him to
get out of this house, if he wants to. He'll have options. If you ask me
I think he's chomping at the bit to go. I asked him once if he wanted
to leave, but I picked one of his 'moods,, and I got an answer all of
two words long, but it was two words that haunted me – "Wouldn't
you?" he said. For whatever reason he won't tell me about, he feels
trapped here. I don't think he has the first idea what to do or where
to go, so long as it isn't what he's doing right now, and so long as he
isn't doing it here.*

It's crazy how badly botched this family really is. We're fragile.

*Sometimes I think that Mal seems happiest, most relaxed, most
himself, when he's away from the rest of us – and really, there are
times I understand this perfectly.*

*My father is always anxious about everything at all, and in my
worst moments I despise him as weak, as an eager toady who would
never say no to anybody because he's afraid that Bad Things Will
Happen. I never took it far enough to really understand that it was
the consequences to us, his family, that he was afraid of, and that*

46

would perhaps have made it better – but I stopped where I stopped, and it left him looking bad.

My mother and I... have a strange relationship. I know she loves me, maybe obsessively, but all I really know of her is that she wears an outer skin that's efficient, and detached, and cold – sometimes when she looks at me sideways I think I may possibly see a glint of affection escaping her eyes but at other times it's as though she can barely stand to look at me, let alone hug me or kiss me goodnight. And yet it was she more than anybody who had pushed me into my cage and locked the door behind me and protected me fiercely, it seemed, against everyone and anyone else.

Maybe it was that my family is an immigrant family, and maybe it was because they had fled their own world under a shadow and not from choice – I don't know – but whatever solace they had hoped to find over here in the New World has eluded them somehow. Their shadows have followed them here after all. And the strict rules in this new place they have found are a mystery to them half the time. I think perhaps my father's attitude to those he worked for pretty much came from the conviction that he and therefore his entire family are here on sufferance, and that if he – or any of us – breaks the tiniest regulation somewhere, anywhere, we'll all be herded right back to where we had come from – and that isn't something he could even think about.

Back into their past.

From which they had fled.

Which – and I get this even though they hardly ever really spoke of any of it to me – they missed. It was not really by choice that they had left their world behind, after all.

My parents brought Celia and Mal out of something – some darkness – fleeing from something far worse than what they found here – and tried to throw themselves into the society – and failed really badly – and then Celia died, and Mal turned into... Mal... and then they had me after they got to the New World as though I was supposed to be the thing that healed everything.

I can see a balancing act between this poisonous nostalgia which they felt weirdly insane to be indulging in, after all that the Old Country had done to them, and the blind terror that they would be sent back there after all. It must all have weighed on them in ways I have no hope of ever really understanding – and I probably didn't know the half of it – and the rest of it, the stuff I'm finding out from Celia's diary, can't have helped matters.

There's Mal, almost three years overdue to Turn, perhaps the oldest not-yet-Turned child of his generation. There's me, getting far too close to my own fifteenth birthday, the age at which most of us Turn for the first time – and the closer my birthday comes, the tighter my parents hold on to me.

Anyway. Got to go. I think somebody hollered for dinner.

Is there an Echo in here?

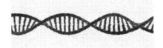

I don't know that I was *waiting* for a response, at this point. The blog was friends-locked, and -clockwork_crow- was the only friend to whom I had granted reading privileges. I had half-convinced myself that she'd just requested the friending as a reciprocal thing, because she'd accepted me on her own list, and probably had better things to do than sit there reading me blathering on about things that could not possibly have been that interesting to her, about my family's equivalent of the Emperor's donkey ears. (Actually, we were more likely than most to *have* them, being Were-kind and all. I could see some sort of weird accident leaving behind the ears of an ass on some poor unfortunate who had just Turned back into human shape...) But about an hour after I had posted that first blog, I kind of meandered past the page again... and was rather astonished to find a comment by -clockwork_crow-.

<Wow. Intense. What was going on in that school?

And then another friend request came in, one I recognized – Bella from the party – Nell must have said something to her, they seemed to be buddies and were certainly fellow Corvids, and there was a moment that I actually felt rather annoyed about that. If it was supposed to be a *private* blog and Nell only knew about it by default she really shouldn't have gone blabbing about it to other friends. Particularly not Bubblehead Bella. But on reflection – and with a streak of pure Mal-ishness which made me actually think that there was something to this genetics lark and Mal really was related to me after all – I accepted her. She probably needed to be rattled out of her complacent little-rich-girl cocoon, and damn, Celia was going to do it. Bella might come out on the other side being the better off for it.

Intense, Nell had said. And it was. Those diaries sucked me in like a whirlpool; I drank in the poison of Celia's life in great gulps, and I could feel it changing me as I did that. I was a different person at the end of every single diary entry than I had been when I had begun it.

For a few days, I just read what she had written, trying to get it straight in my own head.

I had thought that I'd use the Echo blog to talk myself through this, to answer, as Nell had suggested, some of my own questions. But the thing had quickly changed from under me. Celia changed it. Celia's own words were powerful, so powerful that I could not bring myself to just sit there at the computer yapping *about* them. I needed to share what she herself had written, had realized, had felt, had learned.

Not all of it, ah, not all of it. Some passages I read by torchlight under the covers reduced me to tears – and there were parts of those I would never allow out into the world other than paraphrased by me because they were so deeply personal that they felt like they had been written down for me alone, a cry from my sister from wherever it was that she had gone after she had left this life. If it was selfish to gather those up and tuck them away from any harm that outside eyes might have brought on them just by virtue of falling upon them, then I was selfish. So there. Afterwards, when I read that first *real* entry, I realized I had sounded awfully defensive about it, to begin with. But I was feeling my way, and it was difficult to make those decisions at first, what was to be talked *about* and what was to be given just as Celia had written it. Because some things would be, I would transcribe them from the notebooks word for word, because her voice was so beautiful and so full of pain that I could not hope to do any better than she had done... beginning with stuff that she'd written when she was so much younger than I was now.

I had been too young to fully realize what I had lost, when she had died. I had mourned a sister. Now... now I mourned the loss of all that she could have been, the loss of a beautiful soul.

I cracked open the blog again almost two weeks after I'd poured out that first overwrought entry. I actually considered wiping it and starting again from scratch, it sounded so much like any random Jane J. Teen whining about her (admittedly somewhat shattered) life – but okay, it had a comment on it. Just one, but it sort of made it legit. So I let it stand. But from here on... I was going to have to do better than that. I was going to have to be a much better Echo than that.

12 January

> I'm not going to sit here and transcribe the whole of my sister's diary. Quite frankly, some if it isn't anybody's business but hers. But some of it... ah, some of it.
>
> She talks about coming to this country. She was seven when my family moved. That's about as old as I was when she died – but she seems to have had a far superior memory than mine. That, or nostalgia makes things stick better, or tragedy makes them flee faster; all I can tell you is that she remembers the sort of detail about the place where she was born that... makes my eyes water... and no, I am NOT crying... But all of that, it's in the distant past now. A different world.
>
> It's when she gets here and begins again, reinvents herself to suit her new place in the Universe, that things start to get incredible, and painful. It's like... stepping into a weird kind of a dark fairy tale, all set in the everyday world, you'd think there wasn't a thimbleful of real magic out there but she found it, and not the good kind, either. She stepped through a mirror and found herself in a land where she

49

did not belong. And she tried and she tried and she tried, right until she could not try any longer.

It turns out I never really knew my sister. I never really knew how much she had to give up to fit in and then never really achieved it at all because of the fear and the prejudice of others.

She began by giving up her name. Here's what she had to say about that:

> "We didn't have the time to plan it all out, not after my aunt was killed. The way I heard the story, once the other people in the village found out she was Were, they'd been waiting when she Turned into her rabbit form one moonlit night... and she didn't survive to see the next morning. Once she had died, and died like this, revealed for Were, then the whole family was tainted and in danger; my grandparents were too old, but they told their remaining children – my mother, her younger brother – to run. We could have just moved to the next village, or the next town, or across the nearest border into the next country – but in some ways that would have been so completely pointless that it was hardly worth the pain of uprooting the family and doing it. They both chose to flee to the New World, my uncle and my mother with her family, with all its promise and its shiny new dreams.

> When we left my grandparents' house it was with one suitcase apiece – for the grown-ups, that is. I was 7, and what I could carry was not all that significant, and of course Goran, my younger brother, was only four and a half and he could hardly be expected to carry anything larger than a small parcel and even that taxed his strength. We took very little with us – just what we could carry, and the burden of tears.

> But two of us did not cry.

> My grandmother, Babushka, because she was frozen in place and could do nothing except just squeeze our hands, squeeze them hard, not even looking us in the eye; she was not saying goodbye, she was taking her last leave of us, ever, because we would never see one another again. She knew that; she knew that by staying she and Dedushka were choosing to die, because the ones who feared their kind would find them now, and come for them, sooner or later. They would probably not even be buried properly; certainly there would never be a grave with a carved stone

50

bearing their dates of birth and death. Nobody would be there to raise such a thing, or to care for such a grave. Their bones would be thrown out somewhere, or buried deep in a nameless marker-less hole, to be forgotten and never more brought to mind.

And I, because somehow I knew these things, and I realized that they were giving their lives to us, to take away, to make what we could out of those lives, because we had reached the end of the road in the place where we had all been born, and would shortly be denied the right to continue existing there. I did not cry. I could not. I was seven years old and I was dry-eyed as a statue.

On the train out, my father began to talk to us all about what he thought should be done.

"They speak a different language Over There," he told us. Well, maybe not in so many words – he probably would have called it by name. But I had begun thinking of the new place as Over There, certainly not Here, not ever again...

"Our names would land strangely on their ear. I've 'translated' our surname, so that we can stay us, stay who we are, just in a different language. Our new surname will be Marsh. It isn't a precise translation, but it's close enough, and it's a name that they will accept, that will let us blend in."

"What about our given names?" I asked.

"I will just change the way I write and pronounce my own," Papa said. "Instead of Tomas, I'll be Thomas, Over There. Your mother's the same – she's Silvia, and she'll just change the way it looks to them so that it would be easier - into Sylvia."

He wrote them out for us and showed us, the old names and the new. He said them. I could hear the difference – barely – and written down they looked strange to me, and they tasted strange in my mouth, those familiar names, in their new clothes. Thomas Marsh, Sylvia Marsh, the names were just familiar enough to now be very hard to recognize in this new mask that they had put on.

"Your brother and you... it's different, for you," Papa said. "We never named you thinking that we would ever live in a place where the names we gave you would be a burden. And there is no easy way to change your names and let them stay familiar, like with your mother and me. You'll have to choose new names for the new world. Become new people, when we get there."

In some way I could understand this – our names were very much tied to the place which we were leaving behind, and so we would have to leave those names behind, too. I could no longer be Svetlana, or even Svetya, which was Babushka's pet name for me. My brother could not be Goran. Those people were gone.

I asked what kind of names we were supposed to pick. My mother knew a few, and told me, but I liked none of them, and neither did Goran – but we were supposed to pick before we got to Over There. With my brother – he was still a baby! – it eventually turned out that my father would ask the name of every one of the attendants on the ship we took to Over There (we had no money for an airplane...) and one of the young men working in the cafeteria was named Malcolm. Goran kind of liked the sound of that, so he became Malcolm Marsh on his new papers. With me... it was more difficult. It had to mean something. In the end I chose Celia because although it wasn't quite a translation of Svetlana they both kind of mean 'light' – and I wanted to keep that, because that was who I was, I was named Light when I was born and I didn't want to give that up, not for anything, particularly not in the face of the darkness raised around us by the world that feared us. So I arrived Over There as Celia Marsh. A new beginning, you might say, in an old light."

So she came out here, and she clung to the idea that her name was Light...it sounds prophetic now, as if she knew that she was sailing into darkness, and that holding on to that name might be the only flickering candle she would have to hold it back from her.

Is there an Echo in here?

I thought I'd have another hiatus after that, just reading, but stuff was now coming down in a flood, and the blog reflected that. I did several entries in quick succession over the rest of January, and through February.

14 January

    I followed Celia – still obstinately clinging to Svetlana, still Svetya, right until they sighted the shore of their new land from the deck of their ship and until the moment that she took up new papers with a new name on them – across the sea. She wrote about the life she had left behind, and she made it all come alive for me – but it was so different from my own life was, from what hers changed into when they first got here, that I might as well have been reading pure fiction even if she WAS writing about my own parents and about Mal, people I'd grown up with, people I lived under the same roof with every day of my life. It was very like reading fiction about people who were almost but not quite the people I thought of as "us", my immediate family. But also, maybe it was a combination of the fact that she had written down a lot of this when she was very young, that she was inevitably in some ways re-writing it now that she was older and might have even been adding or rephrasing the stuff she now found too simplistic and inevitably informed with new insights, and the fact that she was actually TRANSLATING all that stuff she had written when she was very young into a language with which she was still coming to terms, this part of her diary might be something I can pick up and tell to someone else as a story. But I wouldn't transcribe it here.

    But then she wrote about their first days, and weeks, and months, out here in what my entire family then called (and still refers to as) the New World. And things began to come into real focus for me, as truth, as a true account, not as a story told by a child-storyteller.

    Here's a bit about that time – it's not a single coherent entry, because it was culled from several of hers. She painted pictures with words, but that was her thing – and there's other stuff I need to get to, so instead of providing a single and complete work of art set into this blog like a ruby into a ring setting I'll just do a Celia collage, and give an idea of the background against which her short and tragic life in the New World played itself out...

    ...It took a long time to cross an ocean. Mama said we had better start to learn our new language. A nice old lady who was also a passenger took care of Goran and me while Mama and Papa were in their Turn; she also began to teach us our new letters, and new words. Goran was still very young and I am not sure how much of any of this really helped – as for me, I knew the names for all kinds of things you could find on a ship by the time we first saw land on the horizon,

and that was interesting, but I did not see how that would help me once we got off the ship unless we were going to be living on a boat somewhere. My father talked for a long time with some men wearing uniforms, when the ship tied up to the dock, and the men did not seem very happy with him but in the end we said goodbye to the old lady who knew the names of ship things and we got off.

Mama had one hand around the handle of the big heavy suitcase, which she was almost dragging on the ground, and the other held on tight to Goran. Papa had his own suitcase in one hand and our papers in the other. I was left to follow by myself, carrying the single small bag that they had given me. They had tried to make it light enough for me but I still had to carry it with both hands in front of me, bumping it forward with my knees as I walked.

I thought that we knew nobody here, but Papa saw a man waiting, and called to him – and the man came over to us and spoke to us in our own language. I was happy to see that somebody out here actually spoke it – I had become secretly afraid that I would spend the rest of my life trying to find ship parts out there on dry land, so I could have something to talk about to people I met. Papa's friend looked at us – my brother and me – with eyes that were very bright, and I thought he might want to cry. I did not know why.

...we stayed in a single room, all four of us, in a lodging house in a narrow winding street. The houses were different from the ones I was used to, and the place smelled different than the street I had lived in before. Sometimes you could walk down the street at dinner time and you could smell the things that other people were cooking, and it smelled different than the food I was used to. Some of the houses just had a sort of cobbled front yard – but some of them had tiny gardens, and the flowers sometimes reminded me of Babushka's window boxes because here too there were red geraniums. I wanted to tell the women who sometimes swept their front porches that I liked their flowers, but they did not seem to be either willing or patient enough to wait while I tried – and I was still learning the names of all the new flowers. They had

*not been part of my shipboard-learned vocabulary –
there had been no geraniums on board the ship.*

*It would only be for a little while, my parents said,
until we got settled, until Papa's friend could find him
work. I asked my mother about the new place – it
scared me, it was so big, and so noisy, and so full of
people who spoke a language I still did not
understand. But soon, Mama said to me, I would start
school, and I would learn things quickly then – and
she said that I would be telling her about everything
then because I would know so much more than she
did. I asked if this was the biggest city ever and she
said one of them, but we might not stay here, and then
said that there were other cities in the New World, as
big as this one, and we might go to one of those
instead, it depended on where Papa could find a job.*

*Papa's friend got him a job, not a real one but just so
as he could start getting paid in New World money; it
was working for someone from the Old Country, to
begin with, and he did not have to learn how to speak
a new language well enough to work in it
immediately. We all got our new papers – Papa's
friend arranged it – they told me to call him Uncle
Perry. Mama showed me mine, in my new name, and
I liked it that they had a little drawing of a pawprint
on them. Mama did not like that part. I thought she
thought it was childish, and I didn't understand why
she did not like it, but I thought she was only being a
grown-up and all serious about it and this was fun,
put there just for me.*

*...Papa looked for a place to rent, but that took a long
time – and we did not even know if we were going to
stay in this city after all or go to those other ones
Mama had been telling me about.*

*We were still living in that little room in the lodging
house (and I was starting to learn the names of things
in here, now, not just things on board a ship) when the
first full Moon in the New World came."*

*I could just see her, a little girl with fair hair in braided pigtails
and carefully tied off with ribbons, carting a small bag still too big
for her, trotting after the rest of the family on the docks of the New
World with no words to describe anything she was seeing to anyone
other than the people who had come all this way with her – finding*

*out that there were Others Like Her here – find out that there were
many more who were not like her at all. My heart went out to that
little lost girl. But she had not yet really figured out what that cute
little paw print on her brand-new papers meant.*

*She was about to. That first full Moon in the New World...
would be the beginning of her real education.*

*My parents had spoken, a little, about Turning Houses. But they
were stories, to me. They were very real to Celia. She was still too
young to go to one – too young to Turn – but Mama and Papa, my
Mom and Dad, were not. And when that first full Moon came they
had no choice but to report to their nearest one. And the children
now known as Celia and Malcolm Marsh... they'd learn about the
Turning Houses, and what they meant, the hard way.*

Is there an Echo in here?

19 January

    *The girl who had become Celia Marsh was not yet eight and the boy
who had become Malcolm Marsh was not yet five when the Moon turned
full for the first time in the New World, and her account of that,
translated and then later rewritten by her... actually deserves its own
entry.*

> Uncle Perry came round with a car on the morning of
> the full moon, and the three of them, Mama, Papa, and
> Uncle Perry, all shut themselves into the parlor of the
> boarding house and they stayed there a very long
> time. When they came out I could see that Mama had
> been crying, and that Papa's mouth was pressed very
> tightly together, like it sometimes was when he was
> angry. Uncle Perry had his hands folded in front of
> him and was tapping his thumbs together and looked
> cross. Mama looked at him, like I looked at her when I
> wanted something I knew I could not have. But he
> shook his head and said that she HAD to.
>
> So Mama grabbed me and held me very tightly.
>
> "You have to be a very brave girl today," she told me.
> "And look after your little brother."
>
> And then she took Goran and held him so tight and so
> long that he began to cry – and then Uncle Perry
> tapped her on the shoulder and said they had to go,
> and Mrs. Lorne, the woman who owned the boarding
> house and was kind but stern, actually came out

*drying her hands on her apron and pried a crying
Malcolm away from Mama. They had to physically
remove every clutching finger from her skirts, and he
fought and screamed and kept on trying to grab
another handful of Mama's clothes as soon as one
handful was taken from him. It was as though he
knew something that I did not, and I felt the panic
rising, but I was frozen, frozen and still, not helping
either my brother or the people who were tearing him
from Mama's arms. Mrs. Lorne told Mama that she
would keep an eye on us – and it only then dawned on
me that Mama was GOING somewhere, that she and
Papa were both GOING somewhere, and that they
were leaving us behind – and I began to cry, too,
because I was suddenly afraid. But Mrs. Lorne took
my hand and pulled me away into the kitchen, me and
Goran – I suppose I have to get used to calling him
Malcolm now – and gave us cookies and milk and
kept us there so that we would not have to watch
Mama and Papa driving away with Uncle Perry in the
car. Malcolm would not be comforted and cried into
his milk and held onto his cookie until it grew soggy in
his hand. I tried to put my arms around him but he
pushed me away and just cried like his heart was
breaking and so was mine and I did not know why.*

*It was full Moon – I could see it through the window,
from my bed at night. I knew very well what it meant,
I knew who I was, I knew it had something to do with
Mama and Papa having to leave us, but I was afraid
that somehow in the New World it meant that they
had to leave us behind and never come back, that they
would have to live somewhere apart from my brother
and from me and that I would have to take care of him
as best I could – because I already knew that Mrs.
Lorne and her milk and cookies would not be
something that would go on forever.*

*They were gone for three days, for the three days that
they were Were-form. Mama was very pale and quiet
when they finally came back – and a great burden fell
from my heart when Uncle Perry drove them up to the
house and let them out of the car. He did not stay, just
dropped them off. It looked to me as though everybody
was unhappy with one another. But Mama just took
me in her arms and held me and held me, and I made
no protest – and even Malcolm was very quiet about*

it. *Eventually, days later, I asked where they had been and Mama said, "To a place called a Turning House." And I asked what that was, and where it was, and she explained, a little – how it was a big house where a lot of people like us had to go when the Moon was full, so that they could be kept safe there. I did not understand this part, not completely, and she did not try and make me, not then, not yet. But I overheard her talking to Papa about it late at night. I was crouching just outside the door of the parlor where they had gone to talk so that they would not disturb us children (but I had been awake and I followed them down).*

"It's the law," Papa said.

"It is a stupid law," Mama said, and I could hear her voice was full of tears. "Next time, we'd better make better plans."

And I was suddenly terrified, because they were talking about a "next time" which meant that they would leave us again to go to these places they called Turning Houses. And I hated this place, then, and I hated the law, and I missed Babushka and the soft wordless songs that she sang when I was being rocked to sleep back when I was very young. We had not heard from Babushka and Dedushka since we had left their house, on our way to come to the New World – and I wondered if they had gone to a Turning House, too, and how come they never let us know that they were all right, that they had come home.

And if they had not come home... and if Mama and Papa went away again... would they never come back for us? Just like Babushka and Dedushka had never come again?"

Not two months into their New World lives, and all Celia had to hold on to was fear. She writes, in the next entry or two, about watching the Moon fade from full to last quarter to new – and then writes about watching it waxing again, growing ever closer to full, bracing herself for being torn away from Mama again as she and Mal were left behind while the parents were driven off to a strange and scary destination where the two children could not follow, a place called a Turning House, which grew in the shadow of that dread and I could see it crouching there at the edge of Celia's world like a monster out of a fairy tale, dark and brooding, just waiting for some child just like her to go wandering by to uncurl into a great *living creature with fangs and with claws, ready to devour that unwary prey if it came a step too close.*

She wasn't wrong, of course. The second full Moon came, and they went, Mom and Dad, again leaving the two of them behind. This time Celia and Mal had not been left to Mrs. Lorne's tender mercies – Mama had engaged a young woman to take care of the two of them while she was gone. It was the first time that Celia had heard of a New-Moon Were, and she was distracted enough by asking lots of questions of this young babysitter (who WAS one, the very first of her kind whom Celia had ever set eyes on) for this second separation to pass in a manner considerably less traumatic than the first. Mal, of course, was still too young to care about things that might distract him from his hopeless and helpless grief and terror as he saw his parents being herded away from him

and into a car which took them away somewhere where he couldn't follow. Celia wrote about how she sometimes cried into her pillow at night – but Mal didn't cry, he woke screaming in the middle of the night as the nightmares sank their claws into him, and then she and the young New-Moon Were girl would spend up to two hours comforting him and rocking him back to sleep with the tear tracks still wet on his cheeks.

And then several things changed, all at once... and more about that, next time...

Is there an Echo in here?

<Wow, Nell wrote in the comments to this blog when I first posted it. <No wonder you were so intense about the Turning Houses, back when we met at the party.

<She was still too young to be told the details, back then, I wrote in response. <Still just a fairy tale.

<Yeah, they sound like it. They sound like something that was made up, to scare small children with... but they were small children, really, so your mother found someone to stay with them for a few days while she was locked away. What on earth did women do with their newborns? What did your mother do with you when you were just a baby? I mean, yeah, it's only three days, but a baby that young, torn from its mother...?

<Funny you should ask, I replied.

Because that was the very next entry. The one where I kind of enter the whole story.

22 January

"And then there were three...

Uncle Perry brought us a letter, the day after Mama and Papa came home from the second trip to the Turning House. Papa smiled when he read it, and Mama cried, and then they told us that Papa had got a good job – in a different city – and we would be moving there, at once. We packed our things again, not that there was that much to pack, and then Uncle Perry took us to the train, and we were gone. I looked out of the train window as the train pulled out of the station, and I thought about the red geraniums in the window boxes back in the street where our boarding house was, and I wondered if they would grow where we were going.

We got to the new city, and Papa started a new job, and Mama started to look around for a place where we could live. She took Papa along to look at a house, one day, and they came home very unhappy because it was a nice house and it would have suited us very well, but it cost too much. But Mama kept looking. And I watched the Moon, and was afraid all over again – would they still have to go to the Turning House, here? And who would take care of Malcolm and me?

But when the Moon turned full this time, Papa went away to the Turning House... and Mama stayed with us. She told us that she was going to have a baby, a baby brother or sister for Mal and me. Back home, back in the Old Country, that was always what happened – a woman who was expecting a baby could not Turn, and had to live always in her human shape until the baby was born – it was something that we were told that we would find out more about when we needed to and I had never thought about it much but there was always SOMEBODY, and the Were-children who had not yet Turned always had some woman - an aunt, or a cousin, or a neighbor – who was still around, big-bellied with the baby, and could take care of us all for three days while our own mothers and fathers were in their Were bodies. But when we came out here, there was nobody – and that's why Mama had to leave us alone or with strangers – but now she was the one who would have the baby and at least until it came we would never be alone again.

Mama kept looking for the house that would be ours, but it was almost five months later that she finally found something. Papa said that even that would be hard, but Mama said that there were the children to think of. I asked her, then, more about the Turning House, and she told me a little – about the rooms that they would all get locked into, alone, when it was time to Turn, or the cages (if they Turned into birds), or the big padlocked stalls (if you Turned into a horse, or a donkey) – and about the people who took care of them there, who did not seem to know or care what an animal needed when the people who went there Turned into their Were forms, and she even began to tell me about how often they forgot to feed the ones locked into their rooms, or forget to give them water, and certainly the stalls and the cages and the rooms were not cleaned while they had somebody in them, so things smelled bad and the Were inside the locked place was always hungry and thirsty and dirty and everyone hated everyone else and the place above all – but it was the law, and they had to go, unless they could show that they had somewhere ELSE to go.

That is why she wanted the house, her own house, so very badly – none of her children were ready to Turn yet, but it was coming, and I could see her face change when she looked at me and thought of me in a Turning House.

The bank where Papa had a job now bought the house, and Papa had to pay them back every month from his pay. Mama cleaned and painted, until her belly got too big and got in the way, and Mal and I helped; and Papa, every chance he could, was down in the basement building us all our own special Turning rooms – one for him, one for Mama, one for Mal, one for me, and even one for the baby that was coming. It took a long time and he went back to the Turning House twice while he was building them, but then he was finished, and a big stern man from the Government came to do an inspection. Papa waited while the government man paced things out and tested the deadbolts and the extra padlocks on the doors and the way that the rooms were built and the strength of the walls – and he asked a lot of questions – and finally he said it was all right and gave Papa a piece of paper in a big envelope (they showed it to me,

*afterwards – it was a letter saying that we did not
need to go to the Turning House anymore because we
could stay at home, in our new rooms in the basement,
for the three Turned days.*

*Mama found another New-Moon Were and they made
a deal – she would stay in our house and take care of
our family while we were Turned, and Mama would
do the same for hers, when her own time came. Her
name was Vivian Ingram. I liked her.*

*....Back in the Old Country , babies were often born at
home – but that was when you had a lot of people
there to help. Here, Mama said, you had to go to a
hospital to have the baby, and she went there, finally,
in May, when the spring was about to turn into
summer, and she came back a few days later with my
sister. They had decided to call her Jessica because
Mama liked the name. She was very small, with these
tiny perfect hands, and she looked at me and curled
her entire hand around one of my fingers. Mal said
that she was as ugly as a frog, but he was very young,
and he was a BOY, and so we forgave him and then
we ignored him. I told Mama that I would always
take care of my little sister, and Mama said that she
was glad to hear that, and that she was happy that the
baby had a big sister who loved her and would help
her when she was growing up.*

*She slept a lot, and ate a lot, and cried all the time and
kept us all awake at night – and she was only a few
weeks old when Mama left her with me and with
Vivian while she went down to the basement room
and was locked up for the three Turning days – but
this time, it was all going to be all right, because Mal
and I both knew that she was right here, right in the
house with us, and it was not nearly as scary as
before.*

*And I had my little sister to take care of. So I had to
learn to be brave, and not to be afraid anymore."*

I cried a lot, and ate a lot, and I was the precious bundle that
Celia decided to focus on to push all of her own fears away. In some
ways this was really hard for me to read – because she was so
completely determined to "take care of me"- and yet, here we were,
years later, and she was gone. And I was missing the big sister that I
never got to have, not really, not so that I would remember it...

But this – all this – was still Before My Time.
From here on, it gets REALLY hard – because Celia was writing about a life that I was now a part of, and I was seeing that life through her eyes, and it didn't quite seem to be the same one that I remembered.
I started growing up, and Celia... started Real School.
This is where the secrets began.

Is there an Echo in here?

Celia had always had a love for reading and she had started to read things in her new language as soon as she could string enough of it together to understand what she was seeing on the page. Some of her books were too young for her age but she read them anyway, because the language in them was at the level that she needed it to be. She had a gift for picking things up fast, though, and quickly went on to other stuff, more interesting to her in terms of content – and even beyond that, into things that most of the rest of the kids in her school would have found *way* beyond them (and I know what they were, because she wrote about them in the diary, and I know that even I, bookworm as I am, would probably have skipped them). So that was great – except for one thing – her vocabulary quickly outstripped that of her friends... but many of the words she had learned were dead letters on the page.

In the language she had learned in her cradle, the way things were written down and the way they were said out loud were identical – the language was completely phonetic. Her new language, the language she shared with her friends and her teachers in the classroom... was not. And when she tried to shape out loud the syllables she knew from the written page, she got it wrong – because often things that looked alike when written down were pronounced very differently and things that looked different sometimes came out indistinguishable when spoken. She did not know – could not know. And when she got it wrong, she was mocked and teased for it. One or two of her peers started laughing with her. Then they started to swirl together with others, and they reached a sort of critical mass, and then they started laughing *at* her.

The diary from this period in Celia's life reads like she was gritting her teeth and soldiering through it. She talks of girls with whom she started school – Cindy Moynihan, Karen Engler, Mary Williams, Chrysoulla (or Soulla, as Celia knew her) Ioannou – and of her first days in the school, of being the "new" girl, of being one of the few foreigners there. And then the lists begin – the dogged little lists of words and phrases. things she had somehow flubbed or stumbled on at the first try. She wrote them down phonetically as best she could, while still clinging doggedly to the new language that she was learning.

Things like this:

AWRY is "awe-RYE", not "AW-ree". AWRY is not like ENVY.

"HOW NOW BROWN COW HOW YOU'VE GROWN" – au, au, au, au, au, but ou. Similar words: COW, BROWN, HOW, TOWN, DOWN, FROWN – but not GROW, LOW, KNOW, BLOW

Doubles – SOW can be like COW when a female pig but like LOW when you're planting seed; ROW can be like COW when you're having a fight but like LOW when you're in a boat; BOW can be like COW when you're on stage, like LOW when you're using it to shoot an ARROW (which is also like LOW)

THROUGH and TROUGH are not the same

WIND ("i" like in SIT) blows but you WIND ("i" like in LIKE) something when you wrap it around something else

WAR is like OR; FAR is like STAR

TEAR like in SHARE when you rip something; TEAR like FEAR when you cry.

It tangles its way through everything – it seemed that every time she made some kind of mistake – and she was goaded into them by a particular clique who found first her errors and then Celia herself vastly amusing. She had allies in the beginning, because there were other foreigners and new immigrants in her class – but some of those other kids didn't care as much, maybe. And there were some who took weapons where they could, and used them as they had to. At least one of them, the Soulla who appeared early on in the diary as, originally, a friend, had been described as "pretty" in the diaries, and she used the shine of the pretty to deflect the torment, even turning on Celia if everyone else had found something to laugh at, effectively crossing the aisle and leaving Celia abandoned and alone on the far side.

My sister learned – oh, she learned. She tended to make a mistake once, and only once – because she'd note it down, and remember it, and never make it again. There was also the fact that our parents had decided, when I was born, that we would henceforward speak amongst ourselves, at home, in the language of our adopted country and not the one from the land we had left behind. They figured, I suppose, that I would then not grow up confused between two tongues (it would also mean that I was never to be bilingual, the way Celia and Mal both were, but I don't know if that was collateral damage or the ultimate goal of the experiment). It was also a way of saying that here we were and here we would stay and we would never go back to where we had come from. I was the final break with the Old Country.

My parents, of course, could never quite shed those clotted accents that they had brought with them, because their mouths could not help but shape syllables the same way even if they were no longer the same syllables. But us kids – and particularly me – were growing up with the new language and were doing much better than that. None of us, perhaps, would ever have a perfect native "accent" – but Celia and Mal would grow up with only a slight overlay of "foreign", as slight as my parents knew how to make it. And I, despite the fears I had expressed to my mother, never really had an accent at all.

Celia and Mal, of course, never really forgot the language of their earliest childhood – and they spoke it between themselves, sometimes, when our parents weren't listening. I was never taught it. I picked up a smattering here and there, but I was certainly never taught to read and write it, witness my being defeated by the original notebook of Celia's diaries, written in an unfamiliar alphabet in words which would have been difficult for me to completely understand even if I could have properly read them.

Celia learned, and began to blend into the new background, take on what she thought would be the camouflage that would protect her against further snickers. Perhaps she believed that once she learned to talk like everyone else around her talked, she would finally be accepted as one of the crowd. But neither of them, Mal or Celia, would ever be that.

Mal had always responded in the way that he would continue to respond as he grew older when he felt threatened – I had never known him to back away from a fight, and he brought back souvenirs in the shape of black eyes and bruises and, once, a broken arm, from some of those schoolyard scuffles.

But Celia was different. Gentler. More easily got at, more easily hurt, certainly far less able to defend herself physically and although I knew – who better than the kid sister? – that she was certainly no meek-and-mild wimp at home, she simply could not seem to find her footing in the classroom and give back as good as she got.

She never got past being immigrant, being foreign – or at the very least being seen as that.

But that was only the first strike.

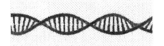

The second... well, she was growing up. The girls around her seemed to be growing up... faster, and somehow better. She referred to herself several times in the diary as "the ugly duckling".

I found, to my horrified chagrin, that I could not clearly remember Celia at all, her face and form – and what I did remember didn't match up to what was coming out from her diary.

I also realized about this time that my mother had carefully tucked away out of sight any photographs of Celia that might have been about the house. I suppose I could have asked her – but she would have wanted to know why, and I could not really tell her that I wanted to see if Celia was as ugly as she said she was.

I actually tried sneaking into the boxes at the back of my mother's closet during the Turn, once – hoping, I guess, to find some hidden cache of Celia in there. But Vivian caught me with my backside hanging out of the closet and demanded sharply to know what I thought I was doing ransacking my mother's "private stuff".

"I wanted to find a picture of Celia," I said truthfully enough.

"Why?" Vivian asked, her hands on her hips.

"Because... I don't remember her," I said, truthfully enough. This was Vivian, not my mother; her, I could cheerfully lie to if I had to, she was only my babysitter, and my mother was currently a chicken in the basement and beyond an immediate appeal to parental censure.

"And you can't ask your mother to just show you what she's got?"

"Vivian, she won't even talk about Celia." That, at least, was no word of a lie.

Vivian's arms came down reflexively, in a gesture that was comprehension, and sympathy. I saw an advantage, and followed it up, sitting back on my heels.

"You remember her, don't you?"

"Of course I do," Vivian said, her voice choked with emotion she was struggling to keep down. "She was... very special, your sister."

"What did she look like?"

"You really don't remember?"

"I remember that she had dark hair, and that it was long, and that there was a fight about her not wanting to wear it in braids to school any more. She told Mom that they all wanted to know if she would bring in her cow to milk the next day."

"I remember that," Vivian said. "Children are cruel. And growing girls are vicious." She glanced down at me. "You wouldn't know," she added, a shade defensively. "You've been spared the worst of it, in this house, Nobody ever offered you a cruel word."

"Vivian – do *you* have any pictures?"

"I think so," Vivian said. "I have one photograph of the family when Celia was starting high school."

"Can I see it?" I asked, and then, thinking about what she had caught me at, said quickly, "And you don't have to tell Mom. It would only..."

I left it unfinished, but I didn't need to finish it. Vivian was aware of the silence in this house where Celia was concerned, of the Celia-shaped hole at the heart of this family.

"I'll bring it, when I come next time," she said.

And she did as she promised, she brought back a handful of photographs – she even let me keep one, when I begged for it. And later, by myself, with only Celia's words from her diary as company, I stared at the photograph and tried to reconcile what she said with what she was.

It is not a close-up – the photo shows her full height, and in it she is half-turned towards the photographer, as though she had just responded to having her name called. She is standing outside, somewhere, and there is a breeze – her hair is long and loose and lifted by that breeze so that a strand is flung back across her face. That means that her features are somewhat obscured, but I could see enough there – the stubborn chin, the square line of her jaw, the strong nose which would never be pert and perky, the large eyes framed by a set of arched eyebrows and set, perhaps, just a little too close together. She was not, in point of fact, pretty – but I looked on my sister and I found her beautiful and no, it was nothing to do with the pull of blood between us. But the photo had been taken when she was almost exactly my age, and I could see an awkwardness in her that I could not find in myself. I was built differently – I was shorter than Celia, softer and more rounded, more child-like at this age maybe than she had been. Celia seemed to have been constructed from a set of mismatched components – her legs were too long for her torso, her arms were impossibly thin and slender and I could see the prominent bones in the wrist of the hand she had raised in the photo to draw the strand of windblown hair from her face. Her body bore no girlish form, as yet. In this photo, taken on the cusp of puberty, Celia had no hips, no waist – barely a hint of breasts. She was long and lanky and unformed and intense and clumsy – oh, how this picture brought back little snapshots of memory I had not even been aware I possessed! – she seemed to own a pair of feet that were too big for her and which she was always tripping over. Her long shins and thighs might have, one day, if she had been allowed to grow up, been head-turning legs – but right then they seemed rather more stork-like than anything belonging to a human girl-child.

This was the creature who had stepped into the zoo that was a high school. Some of the clique who had made her life a misery in her previous school year, came up with her and therefore all of her reputation came into the high school with her. The difference was that now, here, other layers were added in.

RANDOM

But it isn't for me to say; I was going to let her tell her own tale. I went back to Celia's diary, and the blog.

3 February

> "Soulla actually came to sit with me for lunch – but
> then Kitty Lawrence walked in, with her cronies, and
> Soulla kind of cringed. There was no way that she
> could get up and leave fast enough – not without
> being seen – and she was seen. I saw her just drop her
> eyes and flush as though they had caught her in doing
> something wrong and dirty. I saw Kitty's mouth curl,
> into a knowing little smile. I knew (and I knew that
> she knew) that Soulla would go crawling back to them
> as soon as she got a chance, and that she would be
> tormented for this, and that she would take it without
> a complaint and endure it as long as she needed to
> until they took her back again. She liked being one of
> the Beautiful People – because she could be, with that
> hair of hers and the gorgeous eyes. We both knew that
> they did not want me and never would, But she'd
> made her choice – and in some way this hurt, far
> worse than Kitty and that crowd being mean. For
> them, it was just the way things were. But Soulla – she
> and I had understood one another, once. Had been in
> the same boat together, once. Rowing in the same
> direction and hoping to get to the same place.
>
> I suppose it just hurts because she abandoned that
> boat, first chance she got, because the other boats had
> prettier paint on them. And I suppose they at least
> thought they were going to a different place than
> Soulla and I believed at first that we were going to.
>
> This morning one of Kitty's crowd tripped me in the
> corridor. I didn't see which one it was – they had one
> of those 'let's all wear the same shoes' days and it
> could have been anyone's foot – but they all laughed
> when I stumbled. I managed to stay on my feet, but
> my backpack, full of books, slid forward and pulled
> my shoulder with it and it <u>hurt.</u> My shoulder ached for
> the whole day afterwards, and I had to carry the
> backpack back home on my other shoulder. I thought
> about that morning all day and then later on too when
> I got into bed and I couldn't get comfortable because
> my shoulder still hurt. I doubt any of them stopped to
> remember it, after they had stopped laughing. Not

even to plan what they would do tomorrow morning. Time enough for that when they see me creeping in and hoping to avoid them all.

Even Soulla. Especially her.

They hunt in packs, the bullies – there's never just <u>one</u> of them hanging out somewhere. And there's never a corridor that's empty of them. It's like they have guards waiting at corners and they somehow let the others know, the ones who lie in wait, that someone they can get their teeth into is coming. But they're ruthless with their own, too – the packs aren't even real packs, they know nothing about the rules of a real pack, not like any Were-kind would do. There's a hierarchy and there's always an alpha but if one of them gets hurt – even if it is the alpha – especially if it is the alpha – they will turn on each other. They don't feed on the prey so much, they feed on the hunt, on the chase. I've never been in one of those girls' bedrooms, I never will – perhaps Soulla has seen them, I don't know – but I imagine they wear their triumphs on their walls like trophies. They gather up the tears and the misery and the humiliation and they hang them on pegs above their beds and somehow when they look on them it makes them stronger.

I am not afraid of them. But they do <u>scare</u> me. Because I cannot understand why they do it. Because I can understand them all too well. Because I know them better than they will ever dare to know themselves. Poor Soulla."

That was Celia. She looked on her friend's defection, and she saw the long-term future of it – and she was already bracing herself for Soulla's eventual potential ejection from the clique that she valued so much, because she was still, when all was said and done, a foreigner in their midst and once they were done with her they would probably find that they had little enough in common with her.

I could see another lunch, still coming, when Soulla would have come back to Celia's table for lunch. And Celia would have probably smiled, and asked her where she'd been so long.

And on <u>that</u> day, just like on the day that she had Soulla sitting in sudden and unwilling guilt across the table from her, Celia would have come home from school and when Mom asked her how it was like she always did Celia would have said, "fine". Because she had always said that. I know, because I know that when some of this stuff eventually came out (not all of it – some would go to the grave

69

with Celia, other than what remained behind in her secret diary) my parents were surprised by it. I don't know why she never said a word about it – was she too humiliated to tell us that she always ate lunch alone, that she was tripped up in corridors by people who thought it was funny, that she hurt when she went to bed at night? We shared a room for a little while, she and I. I don't remember seeing her cry, if I had I was young enough to ask why without any of the privacy filters which might have happened later – and I never did. She chose to carry it alone. I'll <u>never</u> know why she did that. I don't know if any of us could have helped, but it might have made it easier to bear. But she didn't want to get Mom and Dad involved.

And I know why. She wrote about that, a little bit.

Next time.

Is there an Echo in here?

That one got me another comment from -clockwork_crow- after about an hour or so of it being up.

<*Bullies ALWAYS run in packs. It isn't much different in my school.*

<*But your bullies know better? I shot back.*

<*Bullies are bullies.*

It sounded awfully wounded. I actually wondered if she'd ever been the butt of anybody's jokes – but then I blinked and shook my head. Nell Baudoin? The pretty? The rich? She belonged in Kitty Lawrence's crowd, not Celia's – if anything, Nell ought by rights to have a fawning circle of her own even it was composed entirely of sycophants.

Maybe she did, and knew it.

Maybe she knew all about this thing that Celia had been going through. From the other side.

For a moment I considered hating her.

But then another comment came through.

<*She was wrong in thinking that knowing how a pack functions makes it any less awful. She should have known better, thinking that a Were retains a memory of the beast*-mind.

<*She hadn't Turned yet, herself. Anything of that sort would have been second-hand stuff,* I pointed out.

<*Oh,* Nell typed in after a pause.

<*So what's it like, in YOUR school?* I asked, daringly.

<*Dog eat dog,* Nell responded.

Given that some of the people in the school *were* dogs for at least three days every month, that actually made me wince.

<*A murder of crows...?* I typed in after the cursor had been blinking at me for a moment or two.

<*HAH,* Nell said. <*Funny.*

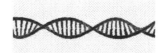

I'd told Charlie Ingram about the Echo blog, in the meantime, and he too had been added to my friends list. He used his initials as his moniker, which had him on my list as -CGI- . This was something he held against his mother. Deeply. Apparently Vivian had failed to take into account the disaster that her boys' names would one day become – her method of naming them, according to Charlie, had been that they got one "royal" name and one family name per boy; that left Charles Gregory Ingram as CGI, and his youngest brother, Henry Elliot Ingram, with HEI, which frequently meant that his older brothers would simply call him "HEI you". The oldest brother rejoiced in Edward Colin Ingram. Charlie resented the lack of obvious acronyms there and retaliated by coming up with a myriad version of what the initials could have stood for. Extremely Cranky Idiot was one of the kinder things he came up with.

<I liked your sister. I was pretty young, but I do know we met at least twice when Mom brought me over to your place, Charlie wrote in comments. <I had no idea of ANY of this. I'm at the same school she went to – but I don't remember ever seeing any of this. Maybe I never looked. Come to think of it, our class has our own victim – might have been me if I'd made the mistake of letting anyone know what my middle name was. But instead it's some poor nerd by the name of Martin Hammel. He wears glasses, and he always speaks very slowly – I think he has a stutter and tries very hard not to let anyone see it. I don't think I ever poked at him, myself, but I never stopped anyone else from doing it either, I guess.

<Were-kind? I asked.

Pause, and then, <I honestly don't know, Charlie said. <He actually disappeared from school, not too long ago, very suddenly. It might be that he did Turn – and into something inconvenient – and got taken out of that environment. Probably better off for it.

But Celia had not Turned yet. She was still just the clumsy foreigner, nothing more. Not yet.

10 February

I could see the Diary becoming a place where Celia could go to lance her boils. Her way of coping with things was simply to write it all down – every humiliation, every put-down, every shove and trip and tease and mockery and indignity visited on her.

She wrote about the time that her tormentors somehow managed to wedge the door to her bathroom stall closed so that she was finally reduced to wriggling out through the gap underneath,

*crawling on her belly on the floor with all kinds of who knows what
unspeakable stuff on it, in order to get back to class.*

*She wrote about the time that she was approached by a boy and
asked whether she had plans for an upcoming school dance. Perhaps
she should have known better, but hope springs eternal, even for
clumsy foreign immigrant girls, and she said she didn't. That was a
shame, he said, because he did, and he was taking a pretty girl. Celia
heard them laughing when he walked away from her to go back to
his cronies. She wrote about that, too. There was a part of me that
hated my parents for not knowing any of this, for not standing up
for her, for not going in there swinging and slapping those horrible
monsters silly. But even if they had known – and they might have
suspected, for all I knew – I kind of got it that Celia would not have
thanked them for it, and that when they left the arena she would
have been left even more alone afterwards. My parents weren't there
to see it happen, and the other kids, who did, kind of detoured
around it. If they didn't, they might put themselves into the frame
and they didn't want the kind of attention that Celia had managed to
focus on herself simply by trying to be as invisible as possible.*

*Maybe the teachers should have known. Should have seen.
Should have said something, or done something. But Celia didn't
write about anything that actually took place in a classroom where
it might have been actively obvious to the teacher in charge – and
Celia herself had set herself the task of being doggedly stubborn
about not letting any of this affect her grades. At least as far as that
was up to her.*

*She might have told the teachers. At least once she wrote about
some assignment or a piece of homework meeting some sort of
sabotage or a sticky end – with people "accidentally" setting fire to
something on her bench in the chemistry lab, or spilling soda on a
book she was reading for a report, or stuff going missing from her
backpack – but she chose to take responsibility for those. Maybe she
thought if she stayed silent on the bullies' role in any kind of disaster
visited on her she might have won some sort of respect from the
bullies – but that wasn't the way it worked. They saw her silence as
weakness, not strength. And they just went right on the way they
had been going.*

*Oh, I'm not going to go into all the gory details here. I thought
that was what I wanted to do, write it all out like she had done, put it
all up here on the blog, but it isn't going to help her, not now...*

Is there an Echo in here?

The comments came quickly.

<*It might help somebody else,* -clockwork_crow- said. <*All the gory
details, I mean.*

<*Everyone else isn't reading this blog,* I responded.

<Well, maybe they should be.

But I wasn't ready to open it all to the world. Celia had hidden it from her *family*, and I was keeping her truth from the family, too – and unless and until something changed there, first, I couldn't bring myself to throw it all out there for others to point and laugh at it. Or even sympathize. Of all things, I didn't think I could cope with sympathy. Not now – not when it was way too late for it to be anything but a Band-Aid applied to a large and a very festering wound. On a dead girl.

And then, of course, it got worse – and I found myself typing in Celia's words again, simply because I couldn't find any of my own that I could trust.

She Turned.

And it all happened in the worst possible way that it possibly could.

23 February

> *Things Get Worse Under Pressure. And pressure was about to get almost unbearable. There is no way I can tell this, except in Celia's way.*

>> *"I don't even know how to write about all of this because parts of it... I don't even remember. They told me that it's okay, that I wasn't expected to remember, that nobody ever really remembers – but still. It feels as though I ought to remember. It was one of the most important moments in my life – I was Were-kind, and this was coming – but it wasn't supposed to happen this way, it wasn't supposed to happen then.*

>> *What I do remember is what must have triggered it for me. I could see them all gathered around something, and laughing – and it was the sort of laughter I recognized, or thought I did. It was the sort of laughter that was usually aimed at me. But they were looking down to their feet into a locker at the end of the locker wall – the one that never did close properly and was never allocated to anybody – and something in me boiled over, I could see some other kid, just like me, whom they had maybe stuffed in there and now stood around laughing at their victim and not letting him, or her, out of there. And suddenly I was just angry, and terrified, and I don't even know what gave me strength to scream so loudly but I did and they all turned to look – and that's when the cat shot out from underneath everyone's feet, carrying one weakly mewling bundle.*

Cat. Kittens. It wasn't another kid. But something weak and defenseless was being ganged up on, anyway, and I just reached out for the cat. It was pure instinct, I didn't even pause, I saw it and I dropped into a crouch, I had a hand out which was supposed to tell the cat that it was okay, that I wasn't one of them, that it was all going to be safe with me.

And I don't remember much, after that.

This is what I was told, afterwards. That it must have been the strong emotions that kicked in. That it happened, right then, right there, right when they were all standing there and watching – and they all saw me begin to Turn.

I was Random, and the last thing I saw, FOCUSED on, was that cat – and that it was a cat that I began to change into. I remember that it hurt – oh, it hurt! – but it is not the kind of pain that I can describe, the way that your bones flow into other bones and your blood is pumped through a different form, and your senses begin to warp into the senses of some other creature.

Mama told me later that it ALWAYS hurts really bad the first time, that it's the shock of the body adjusting to being something that it didn't yet know how to be, that it gets better. And over and above that – there was the Turn in broad daylight. The full Moon was in the sky, somewhere, to be sure – but not over me, not yet, not quite, and somehow... it had not mattered. I Turned. Right there. Right then. In the middle of the school corridor, in broad daylight, in front of WITNESSES.

I seem to remember Miss Grant swooping down on me – but that might have come from the things I was told later because I know that Miss Grant was at least kind enough to gather me up – a hissing and spitting little brindle cat (somebody took pictures – I saw what I looked like, later) who didn't want to be carried – and took me off to the nurse's station, at least out of sight of the open-mouthed and riveted contingent that had been witness to this. The nurse knew that it was That Time of the Month and that she couldn't call my parents – but she called my house, and Vivian answered, and came to get me, and took me home.

74

I came back to myself three days later. I didn't remember what it felt like to be a cat, even though I tried to. All I know is, it hurts. I had asked Mama and Papa about it, before, about what they felt, what they remembered. They had always been vague about it, and now I understood why – they couldn't tell me what I wanted to know. There was very little there to tell. We don't get to keep a human mind and a human memory when we were Turned, it seems.

They kept me back from school for a few days, afterwards. They said, because of the shock of it all. I think I heard Mama tell Papa that it was disgusting that the school had actually complained about this – as though any of it had been my fault, or my choice, or my doing. It was just that maybe I would have Turned that night at home in far better circumstances, if that was what the full Moon was telling me to do, but instead I had done so in broad daylight and in full sight of everybody. And the school was suddenly... concerned... about the traumatic effect it could have had on the other kids. Honestly, I didn't know Mama knew language like that. They talked about pulling me out of school altogether, but Papa thought it would just make things worse, all things considered, and at least I should go back for the time being."

Is there an Echo in here?

At some point during the blogging process, which my handful of 'friends' on the blog seemed to follow with the kind of fascination usually reserved for watching an anaconda eating a live baby rabbit, it dawned on me that the story of my sister's life (and death) had gained me some real-life friends along the way.

Mom had blinked a little the first time Nell phoned me and invited me over. Socializing with the Baudoins, outside the Annual Ball, was something our family had done only rarely. But the invitation was genuine, and Nell even went so far as to get her family's driver (yes, they had a driver – for a very hoity-toity car indeed) to drop me home afterwards, even though I'd caught the bus over to her house.

"What on Earth," Mom said to me, mystified, after the second such visit, "do you two find to talk about?"

I shrugged, and shamelessly spilled my nickname for Nell. "Oh, she's quite the Corvid Princess. But she has some good ideas."

Mom shook her head. "Well, if it makes you happy."

She wasn't entirely oblivious to my isolation inside our own house, wrapped in silence and secrets, the place which Celia's absence had turned into her shrine. Or at least her mausoleum.

I had not realized how grateful I was for the escape until Nell provided me with one.

I was not really supposed to go anywhere *but* to Nell's, not without written permission in triplicate and properly supervised by a full first-response team equipped with (at the very least) a complete range of animal control measures in order to deal with every potential disaster that could happen to a Random Were at large (my Mom being the lovely paranoid soul that she became after she lost Celia) but once I was safely in Nell's house, and checked in with Mom that I had arrived without incident, Nell basically shrugged and said that what people didn't know wouldn't hurt them. Yes, it was true that I hadn't Turned yet, and yes, it was true that if I showed signs of it at the wrong place or the wrong time things might get out of hand fast – but Nell had read the account of Celia's Turning, and really, it could hardly be worse than that. And Celia had survived the Turning part just fine.

So Nell and I actually hung out in the real world, a little bit. I can't honestly say I found much of interest to me in a shopping mall – even had I not been under practically house arrest since I was in my cradle I doubt if I'd ever have turned into a mall rat – but the occasional visit to shops that sold things like *books* wasn't altogether unwelcome, and the two of us even dropped in on a movie a few times. Nell could not believe it when I told her that I'd never really been to a cinema before. I don't know what Mom was afraid of, inside a darkened theater – perhaps somebody would sneak in a ferret when nobody was looking or something – but I think she just found it easier to crack down on everything rather than graduate social outings into acceptable or non-such. Nell tended to pick the movies, and I didn't really care, although there were moments that I found her choices... rather strange. But then she was a rather strange person, period, and one I was starting to like rather a lot.

Nell called round a few days after I had posted the "things get worse under pressure" blog, and took me out for a pizza in some new and trendy place which of course she would know about. The attitude was appalling (the place had bought a little too hard into the Genuine! Traditional! Italian! experience, and it shouldn't matter but there's just something about being greeted in badly-accented Italian at the door from the lips of a Viking-blonde hostess who'd obviously never been within smelling distance of Italy in her life) but the pizzas were actually not half bad, so I suspect that the people in the back, where it mattered, had the right credentials after all.

We talked, of course, about Celia.

"It freaked you out," Nell said, "I can tell. This business about her Turning in the school corridor."

"At our house, all my life, it's been getting on for dusk, just as the Moon rises..."

"Jazz," Nell said, "have you NEVER seen the moon up in the daytime sky before?"

"Uh. Sometimes. It happens."

"Most of us – those with a few Turns under our belts – we can manage to tune it out, that Moon, until it becomes too obvious to ignore and darkness falls and we get to safely Turn while nobody's watching. But with Celia – she had no experience to fall back on, it hit her like a ton of bricks, she was emotionally overwrought and her defenses were zero – and you get a situation where she's in a crowded school corridor and bang! It's time, and there's nothing she can do about it, or knows how to do about it."

I flexed my hand. "You really mean that any time – even just out in a pizza place, like right now – if it was full Moon – I could just – "

Nell laughed. "In theory," she said. "In practice, it very rarely happens. There are ways of actually hanging on, for at least long enough to get out of the public eye. It's like when you are suddenly absolutely certain that you're going to throw up but you *can't* right at that specific moment, so you kind of keep swallowing until you can get to a place where you can do it with some dignity, and not into someone else's lap."

"Yuck, *gross*," I said, biting into my pizza.

"Yeah, but you know what I mean."

"Um. Yeah. Think so. It's just that every time I think I know something about how this whole thing works somebody throws a wrench in the works and I have to start figuring it out all over again."

"That's *always* the way it works," Nell said. "Anyway, don't worry about it, stuff like this happens. Being a Were is often more of an art than a science. You have to understand just enough to make it look good on the surface, and the rest you just suffer through until it's done and then you dust yourself off and pick up your life from where you dropped it when the Turn caught you."

"Open the book at the bookmark and carry on reading from where you were," I said, grinning.

"Speaking of bookmarks," Nell said brightly, "I wanted to ask you if you wanted to come with me to a book club."

"What, one of your hoity-toity parties?" I said "I'd probably be the only non-Corvid who..."

But she was shaking her head. "No. A *real* one. A place where they actually read real books. You know, the books that normal people read. Not just the stuff my parents think might be appropriate. I mean, I read a lot of contraband anyway, they don't exactly search my room every night, but still – there is the stuff that I should or should not be reading. And their approved reading list can be... well – don't your own parents vet stuff all the time?"

"Oh, yeah," I agreed emphatically. She didn't know the *half* of it.

"Well, then. There's a book club at the library, Teen Night or something like that, I've looked at some of the stuff they've been reading over the past few months, and it looks kind of interesting. And really, it's in a *library*, and it's supervised, but if your mother wants to think you're at my place, that's fine, too. Except that I would have to come up with something different – "

That felt like a little bit of ice water poured down the back of my shirt. I kind of pulled back a little, staring at her. "Because your parents don't *really* approve of your slumming it with a Random?" I asked.

"*Exactly*," she said, and then blinked, startled, and sat up, responding to the expression that must have crossed my face at those words. "No – wait – I don't mean it like *that*. You know I don't. I'm sorry." She reached out a hand and wrapped it around my wrist, her grip surprisingly strong, her eyes earnest, and painfully sincere. "I'm sorry. I kind of... don't get out much. Sometimes I forget how to talk to normal people."

I blinked at her. "*You* don't get out much?" I said, astonished. "What can you say about me? At least you get to talk to other kids at school – I have Mom, Dad, Mal, and occasionally Vivian Ingram and Charlie or one of his brothers when Vivian comes to babysit us all over the Turns. I don't think I've talked to so much as the postman in a while, as far as non-family is concerned. This... you... *eating pizza in a restaurant without my parents hovering over me...* it's the most freedom I've had for... well... since I can remember, really. I've been locked inside my cage for years..."

"Well," Nell said, releasing my arm but not taking her hand too far away from mine (and it was a gesture that flooded me with warmth again – this was a friend getting ready to hold my hand, if that was necessary or called for by whatever it was that I said next). "You know why. At least you know better, now. Now that you've read the diaries. Celia's life was not exactly calculated to bring *you* any kind of rewards."

"But I am not Celia!" I burst out, and hated the fact that my eyes suddenly filled with tears.

Nell took my hand for a moment, in that gesture that she had hinted at, and then let go. Her expression was wry. "We are both so trapped," she said. "Each in our own cage. You're starved in yours, I'm suffocated in mine, but it's the same thing, really."

I sniffed, and rubbed at my brimming eye with the back of my hand. "The book club sounds nice," I said, the flame of rebellion lit.

That got a smile.

"I'll fix it up," she said, and there was real enthusiasm in her voice. "If you don't want to tell your mother and you don't exactly want to lie directly to her yourself, do you want *me* to tell her you're coming to my place?"

"I'll handle Mom," I said. Brave words. I had no idea how. But I wasn't going to let Nell do the dirty work.

I was not Celia. It was about time I stepped outside the arbitrary boundaries my parents had set because of what had happened to somebody else entirely – about time I stopped paying the debts left behind by the older sister who was gone, who had been gone for years. I could take care of myself. And even if that wasn't true, I would be with a friend. And I didn't think anybody would willingly mess with Nell Baudoin – her father could exact too much retribution against those that tried, and I'd be right there hiding in her shadow.

I was not Celia.

But even here, even now, her shadow was a long one – or perhaps Nell was simply telepathic, and picked the name off the surface of my mind, from the glitter in my eyes.

"So, then," she said, apparently (but not quite) changing the subject. "When are you going to post the next blog? I want to know what happened to Celia after all the drama."

So I posted another installment, when I got home from the pizzeria.

27 February

> She went back to school, maybe a week after the events in the corridor. I'm going to let her pick up where she left off.

> "So I went back. Two days after I Turned back into me. I was braced for it, having to face them all again. As me.

> Not braced enough.

> I don't even remember who started it – but once the first one did, it became a contest – who could come up with something better. I was "Pussycat", I was "Furface", I was "Little Miss Purrfect". People would beckon me from doorways with "Heeeeere, kitty kitty kitty". Somebody left a dead mouse on my desk... twice... in two different classes. Somebody else followed that particular course with a decomposing fish in my backpack. There was a saucer that followed me around the school into which I stepped at least twice because it was left at my feet during class and I stood straight into it when I got up from my desk – it got refilled with milk constantly but not often enough to keep it fresh – and I had to go into the girls bathroom to get the souring milk off my shoes. And when I did go to the bathroom somebody thrust one of those disposable cardboard litter pans under the door – "in case you need it," came the whisper that accompanied it, I couldn't tell whose voice it was but it didn't matter, I could hear others smothering giggles in the background. I stayed in the stall, with the litter box at my feet, until I could hear that they had all left, and cried, and was late for the next class myself.

> One of the boys wanted to know if I did tricks for a treat (he even had a bag of cat treats on him, to shake at me. They came prepared for this.) One of Kitty's gang (and wasn't it ironic that SHE was Kitty and they were all dumping on me...) followed me around all day throwing dried catnip at me any chance she

got – not that I minded THAT so much, I didn't mind the smell of it, and it could have been far worse stuff that she was throwing, but it got OLD after the fourth time I had to pick the stuff out of my hair. And when I finally told one of them to just LEAVE ME ALONE of course seven of them overheard.

"Oh look, the cat has claws after all!"

"Oooh, are you having a hissy fit?"

That was all I heard, endlessly, afterwards. If I tried to fight back, that is. If I tried just keeping quiet and letting it wash over me and pretend that it wasn't happening, it would change to
"Oh dear, what's the matter, cat got your tongue?"

They didn't know the details about the Random Were, but somehow somebody got hold of the fact that I was one, and they had the basics right – and after that I started to get really scared, because they were discussing – openly, out where I could hear it – what kind of animal they were going to bring in for "next time". I could see myself turning into a lab rat, and then being turned loose in the school (in defiance of the actual law, I might add, but that didn't matter, not to them) and because I would be just a rat with no human intelligence I could just as easily get myself caught in a trap, or eat rat poison, or stuff like that.

I did tell Miss Grant, and she at least was reasonably kind.

"They would never let that happen," she said. But then added, "Perhaps your parents could just keep you out of school from a day before you were due to Turn…"

Just in case. The school, itself, couldn't really take the responsibility.

If they ever "ratted" me I would be on my own, I guess.

It wasn't that I was the only Were-child in that school. Enough of us existed scattered throughout the student body for the three-day absence of some students to be an accepted fact. But none of the others really came forward to talk to me, or to tell me anything that I might need to know, or to warn me about anything in particular. I guess it was partly a question of payback – nobody had done it for them either, so they didn't feel like they had to do it in turn. But partly it was just that, well, every new Were had to fend for themselves. There were no Were-kind cliques or groups or societies in the school – we were already outcast enough not to want to glory in it by banding together and showing off to the rest of the normals. So in effect we isolated each other – hoping, I suppose, that without a critical mass of us we would not be singled out.

It didn't work that way. I quickly found out that it didn't work that way."

I knew – we all knew, even those of us who pretend that we don't – that the normals might kind of sort of accept us, but that they neither like us nor trust us. If they did there would never have been a Turning House. But instead of being human beings who were Another Thing for three days out of every month of their lives, we were, to them, that Other Thing which happened to be human – and false, somehow fake, somehow pretending to be normal – for all but those three days of our lives during which we could not help but show our true shape. But in polite society it's all kept under careful wraps. It was Celia who laid it all out for me, dissected it with a precise scalpel, made me understand. Made me think about who, or what, I myself was.

Is there an Echo in here?

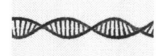

I was with Mom at the Ingrams' place when that month's New Moon began to wax again and the bat family Turned back to the humans. Mom and Vivian sat down for a chat over a slice of the lemon meringue pie Mom had brought over to feed the Ingrams, and Charlie's brothers went off to do their own thing. Hank, the younger, gave me a shy little smile like a small vole before scuttling off somewhere in pursuit of his own concerns and Edward, the older, offered his own version of a smile which was more like a leer – but I'd heard enough about him from Charlie not to fall for that kind of come-hither (apparently it seemed to work well on other girls, I certainly don't

81

know why) and besides he was an older brother and I'd had plenty of practice in my own house when it came to ignoring those. So eventually he gave up and went away in something of a wounded huff, which left Charlie and me on our own. Which was the way we liked it.

"Anything new on the Celia front? Did you post while I was out of it?" Charlie said. He, too, had been caught up in the Celia-into-Cat Turn in the school corridor, and was following the unravelling of the story with a sort of self-conscious fascination.

"Haven't posted the next bit yet," I said. "I was thinking about the whole thing over these last few days, actually. You know, for the first time in my life, posting that particular segment, I think I was actually *grateful* to my poor fearful mother for, you know, keeping me at home and homeschooling me, away from... all of that stuff that Celia was going through."

Charlie scorned lemon meringue pie, so I'd brought along blueberry muffins for him, and he'd already gone through half the box. He reached out for his fourth one now, and munched on it thoughtfully, looking at me with his head tilted at an angle and his eyes narrowed a little.

"One way or another, you know, you *are* in the middle of all of it now," he said. "And honestly – for all that it was actually happening to Celia herself at the time and not to you directly – what makes you think you aren't experiencing it all yourself, right now?"

"Yes, but Celia...."

"Mmmhm?" he said encouragingly, through a mouthful of muffin.

"Celia was articulate enough to think about it all, and to analyze it, and to write it all down like she did, and perhaps that's how she drew the poison... Mal tends to solve his own problems by simply wading in with fists flying, at least that's what he seems to have resorted to for as long as I've been paying attention... and me... I don't know that I could do either, really. I'd just... bottle it all up... blow it into a big balloon one evil little thing after another... and then just explode one day, when it all got too much for the balloon to hold..."

Charlie swallowed the last of the muffin and looked at me, very seriously.

"Jazz," he said, "not only are you handling it on your own right now but you're handling Celia's part of it, too. Whatever makes you think your particular balloon isn't strong enough for all this? And besides..."

That 'besides' seemed to have been an afterthought, and he hesitated over it. But I sat up and stared back at him.

"And besides, what?"

"Celia didn't seem to have made many friends that she could talk to about any of this," Charlie said, almost unwillingly, as though he were saying something bad about Celia and he really, really didn't want to, not to me, anyway. "If anyone was about to blow up with it all, she had nothing *except* that diary. You... you've got a little more than that."

"Yeah?"

"You *have* friends."

"I do?"

He flushed. "Well, there's me..."

That warm flush I'd felt when Nell had offered the hand in friendship spread through me again. It was... it was... an offering.

I felt a strong urge to hug him, so I reached out and did.

"I know," I said. "I'm lucky I've got you. You, and Nell." I lowered my voice, looking around for our mothers – but they were too far away to overhear and apparently deep in a conversation of their own. "She and I – we've kind of snapped the tether, just a bit."

Charlie sat up with a worried expression on his face. "What. Did. You. Do."

The warm-and-fuzzies of a moment ago were still with me, and it was rather endearing to watch his concern about what kind of muddy waters I had waded into. I almost hated to disappoint him.

"We joined a book club," I said, knowing exactly how tame and completely un-tether-snapping an activity that sounded like. There we were, a couple of leggy young teenage girls, and our way of rebelling was to go and join a *book club*?

But Charlie took it seriously. "What club? Where?"

"There's a teen reading club at the library," I said. "It meets every second Tuesday. We've been only once, so far. Relax, Charlie. It's completely harmless. It's all out in public, and nobody can do anything at all to us..."

"But your people don't know you are there," Charlie said. "Jazz, you're Were. Anything can happen..."

I waved it away. "Like what? We won't go, the week of the full moon. We just won't, we know better than *that*. But the rest of the time – it isn't as though we all morph into animalcules at the drop of a hat."

He glanced towards Vivian, and I sat up sharply. "If you tell anyone, I'll never tell you anything again!"

"All right, all right!" he said defensively, swallowing the last of the muffin and wiping his mouth with the back of his hand. "I wouldn't snitch on you. You *know* I wouldn't do that. I don't have to like it, though."

"You're a *boy*," I said. "You wouldn't know anything about it. You can do what you like and go where you like. You have no idea, the freedom you have – you, and Mal, the likes of you all – and there's the sisters, like Nell, like me, who are supposed to sit at home and embroider samplers like it was the Middle Ages."

"It isn't that simple," he retorted.

"Of course not," I said. "If it were simple, we'd all be equals. *Real* equals."

"Oh, you *are*," he muttered, now annoyed.

"Nuh-uh," I said, shaking my head. "You just think about it for a little while. Look at your brothers, just now. They wanted to go, and they went. Do you see me just drifting out of the front door of my own house, like that?"

"But that's different," he said. "There's the context. There's Celia.

83

There's – you haven't Turned yet – "

"Mal hasn't either," I pointed out, a little maliciously.

He had no answer to that one.

"Just... you know... be careful," he said lamely.

And that, somehow, restored my good mood. "Nothing to worry about," I said, waving his concern aside – and then, when he still looked vaguely anxious and bothered, I relented. "I will," I said. "Of course, I will. We both will. We aren't stupid, just because we're girls."

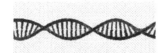

But the book club – however much fun it was proving to be, both in the planning of the unsanctioned outings and the content of them – was just a diversion. In the meantime, back home, I continued to read Celia's diaries, think about them, plan the next post in the blog.

Until, in early March, *everything* came to a head.

I was well into the third notebook at this point, and I could see it all unraveling around Celia, and I was half appalled that it had been allowed to get this far (although of course she *never said anything at home about any of it* and as far as my parents knew, at the time it was happening, everything was just fine...) and half astonished that she retained enough rationality in the face of all of it to actually write it all down in these books, for me to read. The very short and very simple version of Celia's story that had been passed on to me through my parents was that she died, and that it had all been a terrible accident.

But Celia... told me that it had not been.

3 March

> *Celia is a describer. If she'd been allowed to grow up and explore the kind of thing that she might have wanted to do as an adult – well – I wouldn't have been able to tell you then but now, after reading this diary, I am perfectly convinced that Celia would probably have written books, and would have made a name for herself at it.*
>
> *In an earlier entry, when she first started at the new school, we met a Creature Teacher, the kind that gets stuck in novels about boarding schools as the villain of the piece. This guy:*
>
> > *"History: Mr. Barbican Bain – I heard other teachers call him 'Bic' which if it were me I would have found very annoying but he doesn't seem to mind and*

anyway with a given name like Barbican what can you do? It sounded like a word, not a name, and so I looked it up – and it IS a word, and the dictionary says that it basically means "an outer defensive work; especially a tower at a gate or bridge". So he's a fortification. It's weird, but all the other teachers just seem to have name-names – like Miss Grant is Evangeline and Mr. Burton is Joseph and Mrs. Denver is Cynthia, and like that – and of all of them, out of all of them, before I really truly met him I kind of felt drawn to this teacher whose name MEANT something, like mine did. If I was "light", and he was "tower", we had something in common, and it felt important, it felt as though I should really connect with him.

But that wasn't to be. I don't know what made me shiver when I first saw him, because he was smiling, but there was something, just something. Perhaps the dark hair, slicked back with hair oil against his small skull, and the thin-lipped small mouth that to me spoke of malice, or the tiny perfect teeth that barely showed when he smiled. He wasn't tall, if anything he was on the short side, barely taller than some of the kids in his class – but somehow he filled a room, and it wasn't in a good way. He projected an outer glow of serenity and calm and tranquility. If he lifted his hand it felt as though it would be in blessing, as though he was a priest.

But there was something... something... underneath it all. His light was dark. He glowed, yes, but it was a glow that made me afraid – even before he introduced himself to us all in a soft and steady voice which invited confidences and trust. But as he did that he looked out over his class, met and held the eyes of every one of the students in the room, and I could see that it had a different effect on different people. Some relaxed, and smiled back, and it was an almost visible bond between the two of them, teacher and student, a bond that said 'you are one of us'. The eyes that met mine, however, were not filled with that welcome. They were hard and glittering, even though he was still smiling that same smile that he had smiled at the student beside me who was not Were The smile that turned into something else, something dangerous, a promise of OPPOSITION.

*He knew what I was. Me, and a handful of others in
that room. You could see that, also, if you were
watching closely – when Mr. Bain's eyes met those of
a child who was Were-kind, that child did not smile
and lean forward into the teacher's fond and
benevolent affection. The Were-kind, myself included
although I was yet unTurned when I first crossed
paths with him, found ourselves flinching, drawing
back, as far back as the desk would allow us. I could
see that he was well named – there was a fortification
in his mind and in his soul and it was turned against
us, the Were-kind, even as he smiled upon us in
exactly the same way he smiled at those who were not
us, We were marked in that classroom right from that
first moment. We all knew who the 'enemy' was – and
we, the Were, knew immediately and very well that
the enemy was us."*

This was Barbican Bain, the History teacher. He would pop up in the
diary again. The first time he did, it was when he gave a pop-quiz to his
class on the first day of the full Moon... when none of his Were-kind
students were there to take it. The marks obtained on that test were then
factored into the year-end mark – and that meant of course that
everybody who was not there had to re-take it at another time. But he
didn't stop teaching new material in the meantime and he scheduled the
make-up test for almost three weeks after the rest of the class had taken
theirs which meant that the Were-kind kids were buried under a dual
layer of work they had to keep up with. Some of them did far less well on
the test than they probably would have done had they just taken it when
the stuff that was on the test was taught in the first place. Or maybe Bic
Bain just marked them down anyway, because he wanted to – because it
quickly became apparent that this was not the last time that something
like this would happen in his classroom.

Is there an Echo in here?

And there was more about this Mr. Bain, as the diaries got more and
more intense and more and more clear, and more and more painful. Mr.
Bain would loom large over Celia's days. I had to take a breather between
entries concerning him, because the idea of him was starting to choke me
like a poisonous gas.

6 March

*More of Mr.Bain - when Celia started out in Mr Bain's class she
had still not Turned and was thus in a position to observe his actions
and attitudes. She wrote of him, later:*

"I suppose the first class test that he gave during the three days of the full moon, when Were-kind kids were not in school, might really have been an accident of timing (although I don't really believe that he simply failed to notice that some of his students were missing). All of the students who had missed the test had to do a supplementary exam, which meant staying behind after school for a week (as he organized it). So they did, and they took the test, and they whined and complained where they could that Mr. Bain was 'out to get them' – but we didn't really believe it, any of us, not even the unTurned ones at the time, not REALLY, because it wasn't fair and it was supposed to be against the law to do something like this. Until Mr. Bain did it again. And again. And apologized for it very nicely every time he did it, but carried on doing it. Because he could. Because we were the thing that he hated and distrusted, because we were not like him, because he would get us any way he could. I was astonished at how much new material he always managed to cover during the days that the Were-kind were absent.

Before I Turned and was still there in his classes while the others were not it quickly became obvious to me that the class was looking forward to these days – Mr. Bain would find movies to show to illustrate some point that he wanted to get across, or he would recommend extra books (which he would never mention again when Were-kind students returned to their desks). He was somehow more pleasant, more animated, more THERE, on the days that he knew his class would be free of Were-kind.

When they came back, he turned down the light – and the subject he taught became heavy and stodgy and boring and kids would squirm and whisper and pass notes and throw spitballs. It wasn't lost on the rest of them that things were different when the Were-kind were not there. On the days leading up to a full Moon, there was a sense of eager anticipation in the classroom as if the normals could not wait for the Weres to be gone so that the REAL Mr. Bain would have a chance to return once again and enthrall them.

He was never directly unkind or harsh to a single Were student in his class – but he managed to make them a target for resentment and frustration and impatient fury, and their welcome in Mr. Bain's classroom was quickly withdrawn, if it had ever existed. And even though other teachers did not do this kind of thing, the attitude from Mr. Bain's class was catching. The normals in our class, if they could, would have banned the Were-kind from the classroom completely – because it seemed obvious to everybody just how much BETTER things were when Were-kind were... not there.

There was more to history than Mr. Bain taught in his class, though. And it was only here that I found myself missing the old country, where at least it was honest fear and hatred that showed Were-kind where they stood. I know that Mama and Papa had expected it to be different here – and it was not, not really. The only difference was – and it was a word I had only learned after I had come here – a certain kind of HYPOCRISY. And that meant that here at least some of the people only PRETENDED to think that Were-kind were really a part of their society, and smiled fake smiles and spoke with fake sincerity, but underneath it all we were still The Beast, and they would keep us out from their homes and their hearts with nice lies if they didn't have anything else to turn against us."

Mr. Bain was teaching history, all right. By example. Those who graduated from his classes would apparently "know" all kinds of things that were not completely true. It didn't take Celia long to understand him, and the kind of man that he was. I never met Mr. Bain – and it did not take ME very long, either, to decide that I never wanted to. That, or Turn into a bear, and EAT him. Proving his point, I suppose.

But he was one teacher. He could have been merely an annoyance.

He was not. He was to become something far worse than that.

Is there an Echo in here?

And, on the heels of that, another.

7 March

And so the battle lines seemed drawn, and increasingly entrenched. Mr. Bain manned the ramparts (well named after all, it appeared) and made himself into a wall between those he considered Us and those he considered Them.

Celia and he did seem to establish a certain sort of a special relationship. But not the good kind.

"Mr. Bain teaches lies. I actually went and researched some of the stuff that he says is true and it is NOT – but he gets to rewrite the history because he is the teacher, and he's got a bunch of them in the class who are his Warrior Angels and they'll do whatever it takes to protect him. When he wants us to look at something the way he sees it he'll hand out a Special Bulletin – which is more or less something he's written up and slanted the way he wants it to be seen.

He doesn't often touch on the history of the Other within the history of his own people – and Were-kind, although our story has always been entwined with the normals, don't get much mention at all.

Except that one time, when he actually made a Special Bulletin about civil rights – and he included mention of a number of different kinds of minorities who were protected by law here. They included people who professed faiths different to his own, people who were a different color and race than he was, people who chose life partners of their own gender, and of course us, the Were-kind. I was still learning about the struggles of the others, but our story I knew rather well – not, perhaps, exactly what had been going on in the New World in living memory and the exact reason behind the laws such those that gave rise to the Turning Houses, but I was fairly certain that the examples he gave in the Special Bulletin were at best exaggerated. So I looked it all up, and I scribbled notes all over his Special Bulletin where he had got it skewed, and – I don't know how I even dared, but I was remembering my aunt, maybe, who was killed for being Were and for all I knew the grandparents whom I had loved who might have ended the same way – I stuck up my hand in class to question the Bulletin.

"I don't think this is right, sir," I said, and he smiled at me. Smiled. And folded his arms across his chest as he crossed the classroom to stand before my desk. He might have been a short man, but I was sitting down, *and he was holding the high ground anyway, and he suddenly looked like he was looming over me.*

"And what is it that I have got wrong, Miss Marsh?" he said silkily in that steady quiet voice of his.

My timing might have been better. I was suddenly and uncomfortably aware that I was alone. It was Full-Moon days and the other Weres in the class had all Turned – and none of them were there. Except me. I had not Turned, and I was the last of us in the class who had not done so yet, and I if I had thought about it I would have realized just how isolated I was – and what Mr. Bain's reasons were for handing out this particular Special Bulletin at this particular time.

Maybe I should have backed down. But my heart was already beating fast enough to come leaping into my throat, and I'd already cast my lot. So I opened his Bulletin to the first place I had marked.

"There was no slavery," I said, and if my voice trembled a little it wasn't because I was unsure of my facts. I had discussed this point with Vivian, who was in a better position to know than Mr. Bain would ever be. "The new-Moon Were-kind were not chattels to the full-Moon kindred. Not ever. They seem to be a New-World phenomenon – the first I heard of them was when my family moved here."

Oh, I was doing so well. Underlining everything that made me 'special' – my foreignness, my nature. If anyone in this class had actually had any doubts about any of it, I had just removed them all with one stroke.

"Miss Marsh, you are a recent immigrant to this country?"

I nodded.

"What makes you believe that you are a greater expert in its history than someone like myself...?"

"I know people who have lived this," I said, bravely, and a little desperately. "There is a woman who comes to take care of us kids in my family while my parents are... not there. She is new-Moon. So was her

husband. He was full-blooded Native American and she herself is half – her father was white, but her mother was full Native American also. They have known about their nature for generations – and their ancestors have interacted with the full-Moon Were-kind for a long time. Never have they ever been enslaved or owned by the full-Moon kindred. They were never a possession or a chattel like the black slaves were in the plantations of the south."

Mr. Bain's eyebrow was up. "Anything else...?"

I probably should have stopped, right there. But something had a hold of me in that moment, and I spoke up, and asked questions, and then I realized that nobody wanted to hear the answers to them and that I was sitting in a pool of silence and stares from narrowed eyes.

I finally folded back the Bulletin and dropped my eyes.

"Well," said Mr. Bain, looking up from me and smiling at the rest of the students. "Moving on..."

After class, a couple of the bigger Warrior Angels cornered me against my locker.

"You don't get to talk back to Mr. Bain," one of them said. He actually had his hand in my hair, it was wrapped around his fingers, and he was pulling hard enough so that I had to tilt my head back and expose my throat or risk having my hair pulled out by the roots.

"You don't know nothing about what he's trying to teach us," the other said. His hand brushed my throat, just brushed it, but it stopped my breath all the same. It was a brush with fingers which itched to make it a blow, and his skin told my skin that, his fingers tingled against my neck.

"Boys," said a quiet voice from behind the two of them. I did not need to see who had spoken – I knew that voice, quiet, gentle, serene, but unyielding in its convictions. "This is not necessary. In the name of grace and charity, let it be."

And they did, at his command. They looked at their leader for guidance, received a nod which was a dismissal, and melted away, leaving just the two of us alone there by the locker. Just Mr. Bain, and me. And he stood there smiling at me, and I was suddenly frozen by stark terror, like a rabbit might be at the sight of a weaving cobra.

"You see, I CAN stop them," he said. Only that, but the words he left unsaid fell between us like stones. I can stop them, he was telling me, but someday I may not choose to."

The message had been heard, and understood – and it was not something that she could handle on her own. And it was not the kind of threat she could take anywhere else. Mr. Bain had done nothing – except, perhaps, to "defend" her against thuggery in the school corridor. But she was far more thoroughly afraid of his soft-spoken non-threats than she had been even of those fingers against her throat. This was somebody in a position of power over her, and willing to use that position in whatever way he saw fit or necessary. He would teach civil rights and the protections they gave the minorities and the disenfranchised, he would do it because it was in the curriculum and he had to do it, but he would do so by apportioning blame and justification of "defense" against the encroaching Other that threatened his own world view.

And then, of course, Celia Turned, the way she did, and her fate with Mr. Bain was sealed. Not only was she Were-kind, but she had sinned egregiously and in public – she did not even have the grace to go and do her filthy Turning thing somewhere private so that good decent people didn't have to witness it. No, she did it in the corridor, right in front of everybody. And she was marked, from then on. The Were of all Weres, stuck out in prominence, the lightning rod, the figurehead on the prow of the ship on whom the ocean broke. And Mr. Bain seemed quite happy to have somebody identified as such – somebody to whom he could, on the outside, show all the "grace" and "serenity" and "compassion" dictated by his professed faith and the laws of the land in which he lived, but someone under his control, nonetheless, on whom he could exercise his vengeance for all of the things that he had to do to preserve a public image.

But Celia knew her enemy, all too well.

Is there an Echo in here?

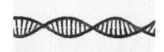

"Charlie thinks I'm probably doing nobody any favors," I said to Nell at one point, during the March barrage of blog entries. We were back at her house, lounging about in her room, listening to the current odd music that she liked (and she always liked odd music).

"Why?" Nell said, biting into an apple and unconsciously beating time of the song she was listening to on her knee with her free hand.

"Well, three of you are reading this stuff. It might as well be still buried in the back of the closet, really – I'm hardly making it public."

"Why, were you supposed to?" Nell said. "It isn't a matter of who's reading you, it's a matter of who you're writing for. And if you are writing it all out to reconcile yourself with what really happened, that's fine. You don't have to be aiming for an exposé or the bestseller lists."

"I feel like I ought to at least tell the family," I said guiltily.

"Then do," she said.

"I can't. Celia never did..."

"You're overthinking," Nell said. "Just write it, for now. It's perfectly safe, tucked into its own little cocoon there. You don't have to decide what to do with the whole thing until you're actually *done* with the whole thing." She gave me a long look through narrowed eyes. "I know what's eating you," she said, tossing the apple core into a wastepaper basket with an elegant flick of her hand.

"Oh?" I said. "What?"

"How much of it is left?"

She got it in one.

There was a sense of doom and dark destiny that was building in Celia's diaries as I got deeper into them, knowing as I did how the story ended. There were times it was almost impossible to keep reading, because I found myself holding my breath; I had to put the notebook down and just close my eyes and feel the prickling of hot tears on the back of my eyelids and wish desperately that I had been old enough to know, back then – old enough to help.

It would not have mattered, of course – if I had been old enough I would have probably been in a similar situation myself (my parents would not have known any different, they would not have had Celia's death to shape my life with). And besides... besides... there were others who were plenty old enough to have helped her, and she had not trusted any of them to do it. Not Mal (well, all right, I could understand *that*). Not her own mother. She would probably never have confided in me anyway.

Not then.

But she was now, through the diaries, over that black gulf of life and death. Now, when it was too late for me to do anything other than grieve.

"Not too much," I said carefully. "Just the worst part."

"That's what you're bracing yourself for," Nell said. "She died years ago, Jazz. And none of it was anything to do with you."

"Well, not back *then*," I said. "But now... I feel as though I'm colluding with her on a secret that will kill her. If I tell – and yes I know how crazy this sounds – I might stop it, this time around. You know. If I tell her secrets she would not have been alone with them. Would not have died alone with them."

"There might well come a time that you are going to give this to your family," Nell said. "But I don't think that's here yet."

"She lied, and now I am," I said.

"Lied?"

"Well, sins of omission," I said. "She said nothing to Mom and Dad, or any of us – actually, I still have no real idea if Mal knew any of it – at least not the details of it. And now here I am, doing the same thing, repeating the family history. Staying silent."

"But you are *not*," Nell said gently. "That's just it. You're reading this, what she wrote, and you're adding your own voice to it, and by the time you're through with her story you'll have made it yours, too – and maybe you'll both be stronger for it, her memory and your life. The silence... erases it. If you had simply read the diary, and then reburied it – if you'd given it to your mother, and let her bury it – it would have made Celia's own life and her leaving of it just a meaningless jumble of cold facts. But you're here now, and neither of you are alone any more. And yes, it's been hard to read, even for me, and I am just a stranger's pair of eyes. I can only imagine what it must be for you. But I'm glad you're doing it. No matter *who* you think you're doing this for, really, or who you will end up showing it to."

"I probably can't make it public, not ever," I said, finding that my eyes had filled with tears at this, and trying to deflect the truth that was aimed squarely at myself.

"Possibly not, but why do you say that?"

"Because I figure that Mr. Bain would probably sue me."

"Truth is the best defense against that," Nell said.

"Yes but it would be his living truth against a dead girl's diary," I countered, "and I have a feeling from Celia's description of him that he'd have any jury convinced the sky was puce with lemon yellow polka dots if it was just him out there giving witness."

"Yeah?" Nell said, grinning in a dangerous way that made my heart swell with a sudden gratitude. "But the dead girl has eloquent defenders, methinks. By the way, we still on for next Tuesday? The club is starting on something new..."

I was grateful to have Nell, to have somebody to talk to, to have somebody to talk to about both stuff concerning Celia and about other things, things that had nothing to do with my dead sister, things that freed me from the clutches of her loving ghost– and Nell was right. I was approaching Celia's endgame, the end of the notebook, and there were still things in there that I was bracing myself for. She was right, also, that I had to own the secret – all of the secret – before I could make a decision on handing it over to somebody else, somebody like Mom who might decide to bury everything because it was too painful to face.

But that meant keeping my silence at home about the diary, about the blog. And I allowed it all to build and build inside of me. Some of my own grief and empathy and understanding and, yes, incomprehension and rage – some of it spilled over into the blog, into the comments I was adding to Celia's diary entries – but not all. Not all, not by a long way. And enough remained tucked away inside of me, a secret not my own but one which I instinctively kept, perhaps because *she* had chosen to keep it when it was still hers to share and I could not bring myself to break that confidence even now when it was far too late to do anything at all about it.

I had been too young to know much about my sister's death at the time that she had died, and I had certainly been way too young to understand any of it. But I was not too young now, and I was learning all about the things that I never knew, and I understood everything far too well (even if my parents had taken pains that I should never experience any of it at first hand). And as I read to the end of what Celia had written, what Celia had left behind, the story that now screamed at me from the pages in her voice and her pain, I became obsessed with it – when I wasn't doing anything that was absolutely required, like schoolwork stuff that I absolutely had to give to Mom or face penalties or be present at a family meal or anything like that, I was in my room, poring over Celia's pages, or typing stuff furiously into the blog...

She might have been afraid of this Barbican Bain person, of all the things that he could, in his position, do to her – but she was also a passionate person who found it impossible to stifle her own convictions and beliefs – and it inevitably flung her at Mr. Bain again...

10 March

> *Celia's battle with Mr. Bain was not over. Not yet. They crossed swords directly at least twice more. Celia wrote that she was more and more afraid of him – not that it stopped her – but it was the second of these accounts which riveted me, because Celia had thought so much more deeply on her identity and her culture than I had ever even begun to, or would have done even now if I hadn't read the things she wrote in her diary. If I had ever really been expected to become her, another version of her, another incarnation of her, an echo of her, I had failed miserably – I looked at what she was, at who she was, and I seemed to fall so much short of all that. I looked at her and I saw an ocean; I looked at myself in the mirror and I saw a suburban fishpond with a couple of tired koi swimming around in circles. But I was deepening, yes, I was deepening – her*

life, given to me in these diaries, had made certain of that much. My koi were slowly growing, and somewhere far away they could hear whale song.

Why do I say this? Well, let Celia explain.

"I didn't MEAN for Mr.Bain to overhear any of it but he had a way of coming up to you on his tiptoes and then waiting just behind you until you said something incriminating. He had done that to plenty of people, and handed out detention for it afterwards, serene as a passing cloud. But I had learned already that he believed what he believed and that I was not going to be the one who changed those things – and I hadn't meant to try. But I wasn't talking to him. I wasn't thinking about him. I was talking to my friend, in the library, in practically whispers, during a free period while we were supposed to be doing free study.

It was only coincidence that I happened to be talking about a subject on which, once again, I had found myself disagreeing with Mr. Bain on during his presentation in class. I had said nothing to him then, not again, I wouldn't put myself out there anymore – but I still had opinions, even if they weren't welcome. And he was none the less wrong for my not having stood up in class to challenge him on it.

I was whispering to Karen Lowery, who was a Corvid Were and a crow in her other form, about a book that I'd found out about on the Net – out of print now, and I had a hard time getting our library to track down a copy of it – but they did eventually find a tatty old one somewhere and got it to me on Interlibrary Loan. I read it from cover to cover, twice; it used to belong to somebody who studied it carefully because it had notes scribbled in pencil in the margins, and I read those too, all of them. It said that even things considered as holy scriptures, from not one but several religions, recognize that animals have souls. Just like a human being. Quotations about it, attributed to GOD – and surely God knows whether or not he gave souls to animals better than anybody who takes it on themselves to interpret his words.

And after that, I looked for other things on the subject. I found another book, only just over ten years old, called 'The Souls of Animals'. It says animals can communicate, play with one another, grieve. They can

96

have a sense of right and wrong, according to their own lights, just as humans do; some of them mate for life, so they can have fidelity, just as humans do; they are quite capable of self-sacrifice, if it's called for.

I had it with me; I had it open, was showing Karen things, underlining passages with my fingers. She muttered something about being on my side. I suppose that could have meant that I was supposed to shut up about it, already.

But I couldn't stop. It was after one of Mr. Bain's classes, and he had already tossed it out, just casually, over the space of several days though so that it stuck, that the 'lower animals' – by which he meant anything other than himself, I suppose, and certainly the Were-kind would fall under that definition for him – did not, had never had, a soul. He'd done it the day before – that's why I had brought the book, perhaps I'd even meant to show him, but of course I never did – and now I was hammering poor Karen with it.

When her eyes got wider and she looked somewhere behind me at first I was too swept up in my rant to notice. But eventually I did, and stopped talking, and turned slowly around – and of course he was there, Mr. Bain, standing in the aisle between two shelves, quite nicely within hearing range even for a whispered conversation, and smiling that narrow-lipped little smile of his.

Karen suddenly realized she had somewhere else to be, and swept up her stuff into her bag, and slunk out of his sight – but I, of course, was nailed there, because it was on me that his focus was, those glittering eyes.

"And yet again, Miss Marsh, you appear to have taken it upon yourself to point out the error of my ways," he oozed at me.

At least there weren't witnesses this time. I closed the book I had been sharing with Karen and lifted it in my hand, showing it to him. "Not just me. Others have said so."

"So a dog has a soul."

"Yes," I gulped.

"A cow."

"Yes." A little quieter, perhaps.

"A chicken."

*My mother was a chicken, when she wasn't a woman.
"Yes!" I said, louder now, with more conviction.
Because this, I knew – not from a book – from my life.
If my mother had no soul then she had no soul (and
some of the books I had read argued about women,
not just animals, having no souls – only human MEN
were apparently worthy of eternal life and existence.
What a boring heaven they were all going to.) But she
was HUMAN and she was a Were whose other form
was, yes, a CHICKEN – so if animals had no soul, then
what happened to my mother when she Turned? If she
died when she was human was she damned because
she was a chicken for three days out of every month?
If she died when she was the chicken was she just
damned anyway because she was soulless for those
three days?*

*"A chicken," Mr. Bain said. "Really. You think the
chicken is the equal of a man. What about a domestic
turkey?"*

*"A brain is not the same as the soul, Mr. Bain," I said.
"And the Were..."*

*"Ah, yes, the Were. Your sort. You of course have a
vested interest in seeking out those who believe in
animal souls..."*

*"And if we Turn?" I said, desperately. "It is not choice,
it is something inside of us, that we cannot control. We
are what we are, and we have souls – and if you insist
on separating the animal from the other then we
carry not one soul but two inside of us – if the animal
soul is different from the human then we carry them
both, and if the animal carries the human soul of the
Were when that Were is in their human form then the
animal has that soul. Or is it easier to believe that we
have no soul at all, even though you are talking to a
human being right now?"*

"Are you really?" he said quietly. "Are ANY of you?"

I wanted to ask him if HE was, that he should think such a thought. But I said nothing, just dropped my eyes.

He was carrying a manila folder in his hand and he glanced at it, with the same curious glitter in his eyes when he looked back up at me, his smile a little wider, more smug.

"I've just taken over the Literature Club," he remarked conversationally, as though we had talked of nothing at all of consequence before this moment. "I see you're a member. Interesting."

My heart sank into my heels. I'd been a member of the club for only about a month; we met every week, discussing books and writers, talking about our own writing. I had been planning to show them some of my own stuff – but I probably never would, now. I might never say anything at the club meetings any more. Not if he was there, Mr. Bain, presiding over everything with that cool self-satisfied sense of complete superiority over everybody in his sight. Everybody. But especially me..."

Someday, I think I'd like to meet this Mr. Bain, and stand in front of him, somewhere public and crowded, and accuse him of at the very least a conspiracy to cause as much harm as humanly (and I use the word advisedly) possible. But I read Celia's accounts of their encounters, and I wonder if he would even hear my words, or whether he would just hear the same thing that he apparently heard whenever a Were-kind stood before him – just the snapping and hissing and snarling of animals, put there to be lorded over by the likes of himself...

Is there an Echo in here?

Nell phoned me after I posted that entry.

"He doesn't work there any more, you know," she said, without preamble.

"Who doesn't? Work where?" It took me a moment, but then I found the thread of her conversation, and sat up. "Oh?" I said, with sharpened interest. "How do you know?"

"I phoned that school, to find out," Nell said.

My eyebrows rose another notch. "What for?"

"I just got to wondering whether he was still there working his black magic, after I read about him and Celia," Nell said. "Well, the good news is that he apparently doesn't work there anymore."

"Small mercies," I said. "I'm sure that whoever replaced him probably has an agenda of their own. Still, I do wonder what became of him, if he left the school. And *why* he left the school, exactly."

"With a name like that it's easier to trace him than most," Nell said. "Apparently he resigned from the school right after your sister died. And then he started some sort of consultant business."

"Doing what?"

"I'm not sure, exactly. He seems to be... and I hate to even think this, but I found a website, and I *think* it's linked to him, but if it is then it's worse than ever – he isn't a teacher any more, not in a school, but he seems to have set up as a sort of counselor person, guiding troubled teens..."

I actually gasped. "I sure hope none of them turned out to be Were kids."

"Yeah," Nell said grimly. "There is that. But in theory he isn't supposed to discriminate so if any *did* show for his particular brand of counseling, he'd have to take them and try and help them, by law."

"Just like he 'helped' Celia," I said.

"I wish I knew how to get at him," Nell said. "If he is still out there, doing his damage..."

"Actually," I said, "I've got the next Bain bit ready to go on the blog. Celia had her own ideas about that."

"Post it," Nell said. "Let me see."

It took me a couple of days. But that next blog set the stage for the end and I kind of lingered over it, tasting Celia's words, enjoying the privilege of still being inside her living mind, before things got out of hand, before she let the world slip from her fingers.

12 March

From Celia, more drama on Bic Bain, and a few questions:

"Maybe I'm just imagining things, but it's been worse than ever in Mr. Bain's class of late. He's even become a lot more open about pointing a finger at the Were-kind – for anything. For everything. It's as if he has to find something he can blame us for or else his own existence becomes somehow less important. But he is the Teacher, and we are all underneath him, and yes, one of the Were kids actually took it all the way to the Vice Principal once (not me, learned my lesson...) and got absolutely nothing in return except a reprimand in her own record. Mr. Bain emerged washed clean in the Blood of the Lamb.

Perhaps I should not be surprised that he thinks the way he does. The faith he professes once rested on animal sacrifice. The idea that animals are – were – could have been – people, well, it might make him think twice about admitting that they have anything at all to do with the Real People, the People-With-Souls, people like him.

But it's more than that, I think.

I don't know him well. I don't know him at all. He doesn't want to be understood by the likes of me, I get that. But I am not blind, and I can read between SOME lines at least – and part of his hatred is raw fear.

Mr. Bain is AFRAID of us.

That is why he uses his position to try to keep us down. It's all he's got that is standing between him and what he thinks will be complete chaos. Perhaps I can even say that it isn't even his fault, that it's just the way he has been taught that life is. Enough of the normals have been taught, over the ages that we and they have existed together, that we are dangerous to life (both this, here, and the one everlasting, I guess) that Mr. Bain is hardly alone in what he believes.

But I don't understand any of it. They are afraid of us when we are animals, for three days out of every month, as if it is those three days absolutely define us and not the other twenty-seven or so that every month gives us as human. Except... that we don't share the memories of the two forms. I found that out when I Turned myself. I kind of recall the moment of Turn, as a human being; after I become that other thing that I am, I am THAT, and not human any more, not for the three days that I live in that body and that mind. And then I Turn back, and I don't remember the things that happened to me while I was Cat, or dwell on them. We are two separate souls being carried in the same spirit, the Cat and Celia. We share nothing except that spirit that binds us together – when we exist, we exist separately, in two different bodies, in two different minds. What are they afraid that the Cat part might want or do that the Girl part can't or won't...?

I tried to ask my mother about it.

101

"It's complicated," she said. Well, I knew that, but even if explanations weren't simple there had to be something – so I persisted.

"We are the same, or we are not the same," I said. "The human form and the Were form. That much isn't complicated – are we, or aren't we?"

"That's precisely what IS complicated," Mama said. "We can hardly be said to share the same body, after all."

"So we're different."

"But we change from one from to the other. Constantly, consistently."

"So we're the same."

Mama heaved one of her exasperated sighs. "All of your life, you have asked the questions to which the only answers lie in a study of theology, metaphysics, genetics, and physiology combined," she said. "I can't ANSWER that in a sentence."

"Is there anyone ELSE I could ask?"

She stared at me as though she were trying to read me, to see the things that were going on in my mind, behind the wide-open eyes that I had turned on her.

"Uncle Perry knows some," she said at last. "But he's in a different city – and I don't think you can phone – "

"Can I write to him?"

She sighed again. "I'll give you his address. But don't be surprised if you don't get the answers you're hoping for. And what brought this on right now, anyway?"

I suppose I could have told her. But that would have meant telling her everything – and Mr. Bain was not something she could do anything about. If I could get some information, I could maybe use it as a shield in school – for all of us – against his poisoned arrows. So I'll write to Uncle Perry, and ask my questions – even though it seems that either nobody else has ever been

102

interested in any of this before, or else there ARE no answers to be had. We'll see."

Why is it that the first (and sometimes the only) answer to a question asked by a kid is always "It's complicated", especially when it IS, and that's the reason that the kid asked in the first place? You'd think you learn a few things, growing up...

Is there an Echo in here?

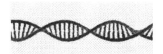

I t was while Charlie and I were out on a walk (my mother, in the ignorance-is-bliss state of affairs that left her sublimely unaware of where I was spending every second Tuesday evening of my life, had mellowed enough to permit me to walk in the park with a friend, seeing as nothing dramatic had happened the first time I tried) that this latest blog entry came up in conversation.

"Did you really think that grown-ups knew everything, by definition?" Charlie said, kicking at a root trying to push up through a concrete path as we came upon the crack.

I actually opened my mouth to answer that one, and then shut it again. It wasn't an answerable question. Instead, I lobbed him a question in return.

"And what makes you think they don't?"

"Jazz, my father left when my younger brother was two," Charlie said morosely. "No amount of asking my mother about it has given me any idea why. Maybe he hated my mother. Maybe he hated me...or hated all of us. Maybe he just left to get a better job and forgot to let us know where to follow him. Maybe he stayed a bat and just forgot about us altogether."

"Can you do that?" I asked, diverted. "Turn, and then never Turn back?"

Charlie shrugged. "I made that one up. I guess not. I don't know anyone who ever has, anyway. But it gives my Dad a reason, anyway. Did your Uncle Perry ever reply to Celia?"

"If he did, it wasn't with anything she wanted to hear, or write about," I said. "But I've been dreaming about the whole thing. The two souls. The separate memories. I mean, I have a hard time getting my head around it all sometimes, never mind idiots like that Mr. Bain of hers. It's like somebody stuffed him in a barrel full of moonshine-proof cluelessness and then left him there to get *pickled* in it while it fermented into malice."

Charlie glanced at me with a twisted little grin. "You're turning into

Celia."

I actually faltered in my step. "No I'm not!" I said sharply, tucking my head down between my shoulders as I quickened my pace and left him scrambling to catch up.

For some reason that ordinary little sentence suddenly terrified me.

I knew why he had said it. I had used a fanciful turn of phrase, the kind that sometimes peppered Celia's diary entries – I had left everything in there exactly as she wrote it, and she definitely had a way with words. In one sense Charlie had just given me a compliment. But on the other hand – there was everything else. Everything that she did, and didn't do, and became – and Charlie hadn't read that part yet. The hard part. The most difficult part.

I didn't want to be Celia.

"I'm sorry," Charlie said, finally falling back into step beside me. "Don't run off, if I go home without you, your mother will have me made into bat soup."

That got the desired effect, at least – a smothered giggle.

"Do you remember – anything – any of it at all? Being a bat?" I asked, slowing down obediently.

He shook his head. "Ed thinks he does but I think he's full of it, actually."

That sounded interesting. "How do you mean?"

"I mean he flaunts the actual law, sometimes. Deliberately. Ask your mother about it, she's lost him a couple of times – he likes to Turn early, so that he's already a bat at twilight, and his bright idea is that he should be turned loose to flit and sparkle out amongst the streetlights as they come on and tease the girls..."

"One look at a bat and the girls will run screaming," I muttered. "We've all been fed the story about how if a bat gets into long hair you have to cut the hair off to get the bat out, there's no other way – and I'd rather not have to take a pair of scissors to my hair, thank you very much, even if a sparkling vampire bat *is* tangled in it... Besides..."

The 'besides' was an afterthought. The human Edward Colin Ingram might have been thinking about impressing human girls (and being silly about it) – but the bat Edward Colin Ingram might have been trying to impress a different species of female altogether.

If a female Were got pregnant, in either form, she had to live out the term of the pregnancy in that form – like the baby locked it in, or something. I didn't suppose a sane bat-girl would be out there batting (sorry – just couldn't help myself...) her eyelashes at Ed, but still, there might be. And the idea of leaving her out there stuck with being a pregnant bat for however long bats took to produce their young – ew. Things could get really nasty. Especially if she got caught.

Which led to the next question. "Was he ever caught?" I asked.

"Ed? No. He's the luckiest idiot in creation. Once he nearly was – Turning back into naked boy right there in plain sight but in a back alley, wouldn't you know, in a place where he had a chance to duck under a tarp until somebody went and looked for him. And once he was damn near killed, Turning back somewhere up in the rafters of downtown, and he only just managed to scramble onto a flat roof and then scuttle home and hope nobody was watching."

"Naked?" I said, diverted by the mental image of brother Ed scuttling home at dawn in his birthday suit.

Charlie's grin answered that one. It must have been a morning to remember.

"And you?" I asked him.

"Me what?"

"Ever been tempted to try?"

Charlie gave me a disbelieving look. "To do what? Sparkle? Not at all. Besides, Mom knows by now that we all ought to be locked up in the attic, our own Turning room if you like, by the time the sun starts going down on the nights of the New Moon. And your mother knows all about enforcing that, these days. It's different when you share the responsibility."

"Well, if it makes you feel any better, your mother had to chase down my Dad a couple of times," I said, grinning. "Bats, cats, same thing. He was quite eager to go padding about the back alleys, my Dad was, before your mother basically grabbed him by the tail and then unceremoniously dumped him into his room. She has the scratches to show for it. She learned her lessons, too – my family all get locked into Turning rooms well before nightfall. *While* they're all still safely human..."

"Even your brother?"

I sighed. "Especially him. He's the most unstable of everybody right now. At least Mom and Dad *know* that they are going to Turn. Mal... just hopes for the best."

Charlie stuffed his hands deeper into his pocket and kicked another inoffensive tree root. "I suppose I can understand it," he said. "*Them* being afraid of *us*. Afraid of talking to a girl on a date, and then having to fight off a leopard – or paying for groceries in a store when the guy at the cash register suddenly turns into a bear or something..."

"But it doesn't *happen* that way," I said, interrupting him.

"That doesn't matter," Charlie said morosely. "They just have to *think* that it does, and it's game over. Facing down a bear with a human mind can be disconcerting to imagine."

I thought back on Celia's diary, on my own thoughts. "But it doesn't happen that way," I said again, more slowly, piecing it together. "The bear... is just a bear. It will act with bear instinct. It is simply not going to go lumbering off the street to find the neighbor who owes it money or something – it doesn't remember being human, it doesn't remember having money, or a neighbor who borrowed any. It's just going to be a bear. And you can trap it pretty easily if you use bear sense to do it. When a Were is an animal it's *just* an animal, and probably less dangerous by far than when it's got its full human intelligence. And there's nothing more dangerous than a human being."

"They keep an eye on you when you're that, too," Charlie said.

"Pawprint on the ID, remember? All anyone has to do is take a look at that – and I've read up on it, I know – and if it's anywhere *near* a time of Turning they can lock you up. Just for carrying it."

"Lock you up where? In jail?"

"You'd probably be better off there," Charlie said. "No, the nearest Turning House. And then, often, they forget. And the ones who are in charge of keeping your body and soul together there... may not always remember that you're present, or that you need *human* food – or any specific kind of food – I've heard that people have starved there when they were in Were form because their caretakers threw down raw steak for them when they were a Were-wren and then wandered off and forgot about it."

I'd heard the same stories. Turning Houses had always been a horror fairy tale for me.

They had certainly been for Celia.

"But they don't lock up humans in there," I murmured, in response to Charlie's remark about human food.

He gave me another strange intense look. "Oh yes, they have been," he said quietly. "If you take Adaptadyne at the wrong time..."

"I want to go home now," I said, rather more abruptly than I had intended.

He had not read Celia's diary. Not all of it. He could not have known what came next.

What I had to go home to transcribe, and to relive, and to watch my sister die again, returning to the ghost that she had been all these years, before I had found her notebooks and she had sprung to life before me. Losing her now... would be like losing her all over again. And this time I was plenty old enough to understand, and to grieve, and to mourn.

But before I could do *that*, the book club scheme unraveled on me. In the worst possible way. The *worst*.

I had said in the blog, only a few days before, that I would have liked to have met Celia's Mr. Bain, that I would have liked to confront him in a public place, and accuse him – accuse him of being my sister's murderer, maybe. Even if he did not put a hand on her himself, his actions had goaded hers, and those had led to her death in the end – he was just as responsible as if he had put down a poisoned bowl of milk for the cat that she was when she was in her Were form.

I had not known, when I wrote that, that I had the power of making wishes come true.

Perhaps, in some ways, this was my fancy coming home to haunt me – I had shouted secrets into a hole in the ground, and lo, a plant had grown on the place where I had buried those secrets, a plant whose fruit was a flute which threatened to play my secrets out loud to the listening world.

That was the Tuesday night of my last book club meeting. That was the night that Mr. Bain, whom some of us might have thought to be safely buried in the past, in the pages of Celia's diaries, rose up to haunt our living reality.

106

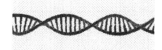

I t wasn't anyone's *fault*, exactly. Certainly not Nell's; she had no way of knowing that this Tuesday would be any different from any of the other Tuesdays that we had snuck out of her home to be here at the library with the other kids – with Joey, and Lucy, and Tessa, and Mark, and Wendy, and Smitty, and Bob, and Julie. And as far as any of *them* were concerned, there was nothing at all out of the ordinary happening – other than the fact that our group leader, a plump and pleasant middle-aged librarian by the name of Mrs. Gowan (oh, but she was a classic – round wire-rimmed spectacles perched on the end of her nose and bunned-up hair aging gracelessly from faded blonde to dusty ash-grey) was a little late that night. All right, quite a lot late; we were sitting there chattering away at an increasing level of noise and rambunctiousness – in fact, I think at least one of the boys had reached the stage of throwing paper airplanes – when a quiet throat clearing from the door of the room we were all in got our attention and we all turned to look... and I froze, just like my sister had once described that she did, a rabbit under a cobra's gaze.

There could not have been two men in this world who matched the description of the one who now stood in that doorway.

And who confirmed his identity with almost the very first words that came out of his mouth, through smiling lips that revealed those perfect teeth that Celia had once written about in her diary.

"Good evening to you all," this apparition said. "My name is Mr. Barbican Bain. Mrs. Gowan has been unavoidably detained, and she has asked me to lead the group tonight, in her place. Perhaps we might start by you all telling me your names...?"

I realized that Nell was holding my hand in a grip so tight to be almost painful. *He knew all our names.* Mrs. Gowan would have told him. There was no reason that he might recognize Nell's name as being Were – although he might, if he was paying attention and knew about her father's bank and who ran it. But even if had no clue that Celia Marsh had ever had a younger sister, the name Marsh would be a trigger. And there was no way out of this.

Luckily, one of the others started the introductions, and offered only a first name, no surname. Mr. Bain smiled and nodded, and did not ask for further information, at least not out loud. When he came to Nell she gave him her name, and then it was my turn.

"Jazz," I said faintly.

"Interesting name," he said. He had not commented on anyone else's. I swallowed hard, but said nothing.

And he seemed to have decided not to force the issue – if indeed he knew anything was out of the ordinary here –if he knew anything at all – but there was something in his face, in his eyes, that told me that he was watching me.

"Well, then," he said, settling back in a chair and flipping open the book he had come in holding in his hand at a bookmark which had been neatly tucked away inside it, "let's start with..."

There was a rushing sound in my ears and I felt dizzy; I lost the rest of what he said. His voice disappeared into white noise – I could hear, far more clearly than his words, the ticking of the clock that hung above the doorway. Tick, tick, tick. The slowest seconds of my life.

Nell's hand was still over mine. For some reason I suddenly became terrified that he would notice, that he would see, that he would ask why us two girls were clutching at each other, and I pulled my hand out from underneath hers – and then realized that it felt cold, exposed, somehow incriminating in an even worse way. My voice had curdled in my throat and I could barely breathe.

I glanced at Nell, and she looked back at me through lowered eyelashes, her own alabaster skin even whiter than usual.

We were sending one another a message, a terrified, hopeful, wish-fulfilling message – *it's going to be all right.*

Actually... it might have been, in the end. We kind of ignored everybody at the end of our little session, busying ourselves with our bags and our books, and one of the others had gone up to talk to Mr. Bain and his attention was elsewhere – but the two of them walked out of that room just in time for Mr. Bain to glance up, still smiling that small quiet smile of his, and look across the library's hallway... and meet the cold and bitter eyes of my brother.

"What's *he* doing here?" Nell hissed into my ear, for the first time since I had known her looking like she was close to panic.

I'll give Mr. Bain this, what ran in his veins was not blood but ice water. All he did was lift an eyebrow that signaled a brief acknowledgment, a recognition. He may have glanced back in my direction – or I may have just imagined it, in my own panic – but he did no more than that. He folded his hands around the book that he still held, cradled it against his chest, and walked away from Mal.

Who, then, turned those frightening eyes... on me.

I had never been afraid of my brother before. Until now.

"Mom knows... I'm with Nell," I said faintly, as he crossed the hallway in three long strides and came to our side.

"*Here?*" was all he said in reply.

"I'd better get home," Nell said, her own voice sounding fragile and on the edge of disintegration.

Mal turned to her, all cold courtesy. "We'll make sure you get there safely. And then I'd better take Jazz back."

"Okay," Nell said meekly. She was more cowed than I had ever seen her.

We took a cab to the Baudoin house. Mal got out of the car with her, told the cab driver to wait and nailed me to my seat with one withering silent look, and waited until Nell was at her front door, until it was opening for her, before he climbed back into the car and tersely gave the driver our own address.

"I'm... I'm sorry..." I began to babble, but he cut me off, his voice like a steel edge.

"*What were you thinking*?" he demanded.

"I didn't know that he... he isn't the one who usually... this was all just a huge..." I took a deep breath. "He didn't ask for my full name – he doesn't even know – "

"That's Barbican Bain. He knows. He *always* knows. And he has his agendas."

"Did you *know*?" I gasped. "About everything? About Celia?"

He gave me a sharp look. "The question is... *you* know?" he asked. "And don't act the innocent with me, Jazz, I know you too well. You were too scared to breathe out in that corridor and there was no earthly reason for you to be – I mean, I know Bain is scary enough to be in your nightmares, but that's irrelevant, he can be pleasant enough, and he had no reason not to be pleasant tonight. So you were afraid for a reason. How much do you know?"

"I know he made her life a misery," I said.

Mal gave a small humorless bark of a laugh. "And ain't that the understatement of the year. Given what he... given that he..."

"He killed her," I said.

I saw the cab driver's eyes lift briefly to the rearview mirror. So did Mal. "Later," he said. Only that. And then left me to stew in my silence.

He stopped the cab driver a full block from our house and unloaded us at the intersection corner. "We'll walk the rest of the way," he said.

We did, in silence at first, crossing from pool to pool of streetlight circles on the pavement. And then he spoke, quietly, with an almost preternatural calm which terrified me all over again.

"Did it ever occur to you to question any of the circumstances of your life?" he asked, walking beside me with both hands stuffed into his pockets and staring straight ahead. "Did you think about just why you were so carefully protected, inside the house? Did you ever wonder just how come you ended up there instead of the school where Celia..." He broke off abruptly, and hunched his shoulders a little, as though he was trying to force down an unpleasant thought or memory.

"I know – that Mom wanted to – to make sure – "

"Jazz, she pulled you out of that school the day after Celia's funeral. You would never be left to your own devices like she had been. Mom was panicked, obsessive, crazy. If she weirds you out now, you should have seen her back then. You don't remember this, do you? The decision to home school you, here, in the house, safe and sound and away from those like *him*, like Bain, with the power to hurt you?"

"She can't lock me up forever," I said, a little desperately. "I wanted to – I needed – I had to have *air* – "

"Yeah. Air. And out there in that... *air*... you let him in again."

"I didn't! He doesn't know – did he even know that Celia had a sister?"

"He does now," Mal said grimly. "And if it didn't occur to you before, think about this for a moment. Mom did not do this with official sanction. There was no time for that. No time at all. You had to be safe, safe, safe, right now, right away, there where she could watch you, watch your every breath, make sure that if anything threatened you she was there to stand between you and that danger like she had never done... never done for..." He stopped, shook his head. "Jazz, if he made the connection, if he joined the dots, if he got the right idea, he could call in the authorities," he continued, his voice even softer, even more dangerous. "He can call the wrath of the Government on us – we are just Were, and there are plenty of laws – Mom can lose you, we can all lose you, they can take you and put you in foster care somewhere so that they could ensure that you had a proper education – and you don't even realize what that could mean."

I didn't, but I was properly scared out of my wits now. "What?" I whispered, just as we turned a corner and I could see the lights on our house, on the house I had thought was such a prison, that now looked like a castle that would shelter me from all the storms in the world.

He turned his head, just a little, to look at me for the first time. "Foster care... was not designed for the likes of us," he said. "There might not be a convenient Turning Room waiting for you in a basement when your first Turning Moon comes upon you."

He didn't finish the thought. He didn't have to. The wraith of the Turning Houses rose up dark and malevolent before me, solid and brooding and reaching for me.

My feet stopped moving. I stood there, rooted to the pavement and staring at the sanctuary of my home only a few more steps away (but it might as well have been a world away), and burst into tears.

Mal sighed, and turned to wrap his arms around me in a comforting grip. "Don't worry," he whispered into my ear, his lips so close that his breath stirred the stray hairs that fell about my temple. "I'll take care of it. I promise you that."

I didn't know what he meant. I didn't dare ask.

He released me, and we went into the house in silence, going our separate ways into our rooms. I heard him stop by the living room and a murmur of voices as he spoke to my parents – but facing them was more than I could have done right at that moment. I went scurrying into my room and closed the door... and then, as though I needed Celia's tragedy – old and fragile like pressed flower petals falling from between the pages of a book – to drive away the knife-edge of potential tragedy, brand new and honed sharper than I knew, that I might have brought down on my family's heads, I gathered up the diaries.

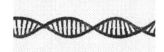

I posted the next entry two full days later. It took me that long to learn how to breathe again, to stop listening for the knock on the front door, for the heavy tread of the feet of some official person sent to take me away, for Barbican Bain's unctuous voice in my own living room, where I myself seemed to have invited him in.

I'd had to find my way back into Celia's story, to crawl back into the understanding that I had thought I had of it all. Because everything suddenly seemed different, all over again, now.

15 March

I knew about Adaptadyne. Of course I did. I am Were-kind, so is my family, and I recognized the little blue envelopes from the Administration which came every month with a prescription for it – one prescription a month, for three pills, no refills, expires at the re-Turning of the named prescription holder to human form. One pill delays Turning for six hours – it was a last-ditch emergency measure which was only supposed to be used when no alternatives were available. You could get the Government prescription scrip by going to the Administration offices and filling out a form.

You're supposed to toss any pills that you have left at the end of every Turn. Mom might have given up hoarding hers, but Dad couldn't afford to do that – he worked, he might find himself in a position where he needed the help of a pill to delay a Turn for a couple of hours if some emergency came up. It was the same for other working Were-kind. I knew there was a stash of the stuff in the house.

Celia must have known it, too.

You were supposed to have parental consent for the scrip for the period in between your first Turn (usually at fifteen, Mal notwithstanding) and when you became of legal age (which was 18... for normal humans. But it was actually 21 for Were kids. It was laid down by a special law, and easily enough enforced... through the ID cards with the paw print on them.) But in any event, as with everything, it turns out there are many ways around that. Laws were made to be broken and people did it constantly.

In my time, what pills remain in the house are in hiding as well as under lock and key. Apparently, in Celia's time, only a few short years ago really, things were much more innocent than that. Or at

least in this family they were. But it had not occurred to Celia that
Adaptadyne was useful in her own situation at the school. Not until
her "friend", Karen Lowery, took her by the hand and led her
straight down into the maw of it all.

But it's Celia's story.

Damn it all, it is Celia's story.

It's so easy for me to sit here so many years later and play the
games of what-if and if-only with everything that happened. I
wasn't there. I was not the one who made the choices.

And I'll let her write about them. Painful as it is for me to read.

"I suppose I should have seen it all – it seems so
obvious now – it seems like something that I would
have been blind or stupid not to have noticed. Perhaps
I was. The thing about the drug, it might have been
something that everybody else in the school knew all
about anyway, something that every kid in this
country grew up with – it had to be, everyone knew it
as Stay, for obvious reasons, even though that was not
its real name – but for me – for me everything was a
revelation. I had always been taught to play by the
rules, and this was bending the rules so far that they
felt as though they were broken, no matter what
Karen said.

And she had plenty to say, once I suddenly realized
that she had a mid-term exam result which she
couldn't possibly have had.

Because she was a CROW at the time.

"Stay," she told me when I asked, and looked
astonished that I DID ask. "Adaptadyne. What, did
your parents never tell you about this?"

"It's the Turn-delay drug," I said. "I know what
Adaptadyne is."

"Well, don't your parents get the Government supply
of it?"

I had seen them arriving, the little blue packets. They
came quarterly, with a small orange plastic tube of
pills inside, twelve at a time. They disappeared to
wherever my parents kept them, and I had not given
them another thought – I knew what they were
supposed to do, and I knew (at least in theory) that
every Were who could prove having Turned was

112

entitled to a supply. But I kind of thought you had to fill out forms and that kids younger than 21 need not bother without a parental waiver. Apparently I was wrong.

"I sneak a couple of pills from my Mom's stash every so often," Karen said. "She doesn't sit there and COUNT them, you know. She'll never miss them. And I get to push back my Turn just a couple of hours, and sit Bain's stupid exam, and get my grades up."

"But don't they realize that you aren't – I mean, aren't you supposed to be locked up while you're – don't they count heads?"

"Course they count heads. But my family goes to a communal secure rookery for the Turns, and there's plenty of crows to go around – and they all look alike, anyway. Nobody misses me if I just make sure I slip out during the muster. It's easy enough, it's complete chaos, half the folk are Turning already and half are not so there's crows and ravens and magpies and jackdaws and all such flitting around the place and there's a dozen people trying to Turn there on the ground, and one less crow..."

"But how do you get back in there, after?" I asked.

She gave me a strange look. "When I take the Stay, I'm out," she said. "For that Turn, I'm out, and on my own."

"Out – out like in the wild?" I gasped. "What if they catch you?"

"One crow looks much like another," she said, shrugging her shoulders. "How would they know?"

"But what when you Turn back?"

"I've had some close scrapes," she said, grinning. "But it's okay. You learn to figure it out on the hop. And it's worth it. Look at this – Bain might not like it but I turned in the test and he had to grade it and I did okay. And now I don't have to do make-up work, like you do. You should try it, really. I have an extra pill or two, next time, if you want them."

I turned my back on it.

Then.

But when the finals came and one whole quarter of the marks was bundled into a test which fell on the second day of that month's full moon, I took a handful of pills from Karen.

I lied to Vivian. I told her that in the Random Were families it wasn't unusual for a very young Were to sometimes be erratic in their Turns. She didn't quite buy it, but by the time everyone else had already well and truly Turned I had obviously not done, and she let me out of the Turning Room after I pointed out that since I was still me I might as well go in and have a proper breakfast. That was Day One. She insisted that I sleep in the Turning Room, and I did, but I was still very much Celia and not Cat the next morning too and I suggested a proper breakfast again. While she was still fussing about it I snuck out of the house behind her back and went to school.

It was almost worth it all, just for the look on Bain's face when I slipped into the desk in the classroom. I even managed a smile for him.

I wrote the exam, but I already knew that I wouldn't have done well on it. To be able to make the thing, I had to take a minimum of four pills, and I'd taken five, just to be certain – and it was tricky, trickier than Karen told me, or I was doing it wrong – I was timing it so that I took another pill just in time to prevent the Turn, so every six hours. Precisely. If I messed up the timing I would never be able to calculate precisely just how long it would last – or I'd miss the point of no return and become Cat anyway and after that I was stuck with it for the duration. So I timed those six hour intervals very, very tightly, and by the time I took the fifth pill my heart was beating at four times its normal speed and I was feeling like I wanted to throw up a month's worth of lunches all at once, with a constant taste of bitter bile at the back of my throat that had me gagging practically at every breath.

I got back home after the test, Vivian blew a gasket, I knew there would be a reckoning with Mama and Papa, but by this point I had accomplished my goal and as for the rest of it I was too sick to care. I let Cat take over when the last six hours were done, and it was almost a relief.

"Those pills are not a plaything, and they are not for children!" Mama screamed at me once we had all Turned back into ourselves. "Where did you GET them?"

"You can buy them at the school," Mal volunteered.

Mama stared at him, utterly horrified. "At YOUR school? But you're BABIES – and   Celia – "

"You can buy them at my school too, I am sure, although I've never done it," I said. "A friend gave it to me."

"And where did your friend...?" Mama was all but incoherent with rage and fear. "I'm taking you to the doctor, right now, to have him take a look at you. Heaven knows what damage you might have caused. How many did you take, Celia?

"Only five – but I got my final exam done – Mama, don't fuss. It was just scheduled for the wrong time, and a bunch of us took pills so we could make it. EVERYBODY does it sometimes, for an important test."

"Only FIVE?" Mama asked, appalled. "Have you done it before? How did we not know about it?"

"No, I've never done it before. But Karen – "

"And you'll never do it again" Mama said. "If they schedule a stupid test for a time that you can't be there, then you re-take it. Come to think of it, you've done a number of those."

"Yes," I said carefully, "a few of the teachers..."

"I'll talk to the school," Mama said, a look coming into her eyes that I did not like. She would wade in, and she would only make it worse..."

Suffice it to say, she apparently did... Actually, I remember <u>this</u> little incident fairly clearly – not so much the initial pill-taking and sneaking around, but the confrontation. It was hard to miss it, *really, because there was so much shouting going on and everybody was just so CROSS and I was still a BABY, practically, and I do remember thinking that somehow somewhere it was all my fault (even though nobody yelled at me, directly...) But the fallout, I remember that. I remember that Mal went around for quite some time with a face like a thunderstorm because he was handed sanctions which were a direct result of his sister's troubles and which he sincerely felt he did not deserve at all – and there was no going anywhere near him without being treated to either a display of towering temper or sullen silence.*

Celia... got her marks, but also got both Mom and Dad at once mad at her and scared for her. Mama did go to see the principal. I seem to recall that she was rather deflated when she returned from that particular visit and as for Celia, well, it's only now that I'm reading the diaries that I realize the reasons behind her sudden moodiness at that time.

Mr. Bain might have been given a talking to by the Principal's office. He might not. Not much, apparently, changed, in either case, according to a further entry or two (post this event) in Celia's diary. But need I say that Celia was now yet again painted with a target, and that Mr. Bain was just biding his time until he could take his best revenge on her...?

Is there an Echo in here?

I was down to the last handful of entries now. Celia's days were sand in an hourglass, and the sand was running out.

I found it hard to get to sleep nights, after reading these final entries, retyping them into the blog, posting them, watching them come up on the screen. I could not seem to remember at all why I had started this project, and why I had stuck with the whole thing, when it hurt to *look* at what I had just written down. And who would care, in the end, anyway?

But it was like holding a candle in my hand. And the superstitions in my family ran to the idea that you never blew out a candle if you could help it, because any time you did that somebody died. It made no difference at all that Celia was already dead – I was holding the last guttering candle end of her life and I could not stop doing this now, blow the candle out. So long as I held on, the flame burned. Somewhere. Inside of me.

There were things I wanted to say, needed to say, but sooner or later all of it was just getting in her way. So I just let a few sentences of my own stray commentary wander by occasionally when a scaffolding was necessary (if I skipped an entry or so, for instance, and needed to bridge the gap from the last one I had posted). Other than that, I stood back. And let Celia speak. And cry out. And make all of her choices all over again.

Who was I, to tell her if they had been right, or so bitterly, finally, wrong...?

17 March

Turns out... my sister DID want to be a writer. Maybe. Kind of. Sort of. Some day. That was part of the reason she joined the literature club at the school. It was the dogged reason she stayed, even when the club fell under Mr. Bain's malign influence.

The club boasted maybe twenty members, all told – it wasn't like it carried social cachet or anything like that. The number of Were-kind involved, counting Celia, two. Herself and another girl, Sophie Somebody, I don't think I ever saw Celia write down her full name. Sophie was a mousy little thing and self-effacing to the point of invisibility, particularly after Mr. Bain came on board – she was of absolutely no help at all to Celia, particularly when Mr. Bain tried to change the day and time of the club's meeting to the middle of the full-Moon days, thus effectively cutting out the two Were-kind members completely. Sophie shrivelled and said nothing; Celia tried a last hurrah and said something about how unfair it was to her English teacher, who agreed, and tried to intervene; but the only reason that the meetings were not changed according to Mr. Bain's fiat was because at least three of the other ("normal") members could not make the new date and thus Bain was forced to let things stay the way they were. But it was yet ANOTHER black mark in the ledger for Celia.

And it turned out that he had the perfect weapon to retaliate with.

But, again, it's her story. Let her tell it. Let her tell it all, to the end.

"Emily Winterthorn is AWESOME. Utterly and completely awesome. I picked up one of her books by absolute accident, because I had never heard of her before in my life, but three pages into it I already knew that I would finish this one and then go out and look up everything the woman had ever written down – it didn't matter if it was fiction, or blogs, or her grocery list. She had effortlessly leapfrogged an entire pantheon of other writers whom I had thought I would never find the equal of, and now sat at the absolute top of my list, with about half a dozen empty spaces below her before the next name on it. THAT's how awesome she is.

She wrote about ME. About people like me. Not all of her books had Were-kind in them, but some did, enough did, and they were amongst the few that did. So far as I could tell she was not one of us – but she had taken us into her world, more completely and *with more understanding that I had ever seen a normal have before, and I was hungry for that. All the Were-kind kids were.*

When Mr. Bain announced that she was coming to visit the school, it was the best day and the worst day of my life. The best because I would finally get to see her, to meet her, perhaps to talk to her (although I didn't know just exactly how coherent I would be if I tried). The worst... because he also announced on WHAT day she would be coming to the school.

In about three months' time.

On the last day of the three-day Full-Moon Turn cycle. At perhaps the only time that anyone of Were blood could not possibly be there. She wrote the books that spoke to us... and not one of us could be there to hear her talk about them, or about the new one that we of all people would be waiting for with so much impatience.

I knew EXACTLY why Mr. Bain had invited her, and invited her for that time. It wasn't because he was particularly taken with her books, it couldn't be, I had learned enough about him to know that much. It was payback. To all of us. Particularly to me.

Emily Winterthorn was coming to the school, she'd talk to several classes and then perhaps specially to the literature club... and I would be a cat, locked away in a Turning Room in my house.

The cat would not care much. The cat would not have any idea about what was going on out there. The cat would be perfectly happy if it had a full water dish, a pile of kibble in a bowl, and a warm place to curl up and sleep.

But I, the real me, the human me, the one with the hopes and the dreams and the wishes, I would care – and there was nothing, apparently, I could do about that.

I even took my life in my hands and went crawling to Mr. Bain.

"Could she not come one day later...?" I asked, my hands tightly clenched together.

He smiled at me. SMILED. "She's in the middle of writing her next book," he said, all earnest and polite. "She said she'd tell us more about that when she came out. But she doesn't really have the time to spare so that she can plan her visit to YOUR convenience." And then he ruffled his papers, which I knew was a pretext to give him time to think, and then, having apparently thought of something new, he looked up at me again with his head tilted at a sympathetic angle. "We could cancel it," he murmured, "although the others would of course be disappointed ..."

It was a guilt trip and it worked – but still, there was that last little selfish whimper deep inside. "But I won't be able to..." I began, desperate, and his smile widened. Just a notch, but I saw it.

"I am so sorry to hear that," he murmured." But you do appear to be the only one affected, and my priorities have to be with accommodating the rest of the interested students who WILL be able to attend at the time scheduled. It's all been arranged – I WISH there was something I could do..."

I looked up her schedule, online – she had a website and it had a section on it that listed her commitments. If she WAS writing another book, I was all for that, and I would be the last person to want to stand in the way of it – I would be the first in line to buy it when it came out, after all, and I couldn't wait to read it – but there was no mention of that on the site (well, there probably wouldn't be...). But her schedule did seem to be relatively open. Our visit was listed there. There were a couple of other school visits on the roster, too, both of them in counties close to our own. For the week AFTER the full-Moon Turn.

So she would be coming out here again. Or maybe staying out here for the duration. Either way, she was not desperately tied down to her desk writing away like Mr. Bain had implied (not that I believed him. But still.)

I contemplated begging somebody to be able to join those other schools somehow when she was there, so

*that I'd have the opportunity to at least glimpse her –
but that would mean skipping a day of my OWN
school, and I didn't think I could get a note of absence
approved just because I wanted to go listen to a
favorite writer talk.*

*There was one other option... but it was not something
that could be done easily, not again, or lightly.*

*I had promised Mama that I would not do the pills
again. The Stay. And besides, taking them for this
would mean not just postponing the Turn but
completely skipping one. Was that even possible? And
if it was – and it worked the same way as before -
then I would need to take... I did the math... twelve
pills altogether if I wanted to stay Celia throughout
the Turn cycle. TWELVE. I didn't know that Karen
would give so many to me. If anybody would. If
anyone would even sell them to me. I suppose
technically I could go into the Administration offices
and fill out the form and see if they'd give the ones that
I was entitled to as a Turned Were-kind to me even if I
was still under twenty one. But the odds are that they
would not. They'd want to know why, at the very
least, and I somehow don't think that my situation
would really count as anything like an emergency for
them.*

*I might have to consider buying them from Mal. He
knows more about it than I do, and he's barely
TWELVE."*

*I know less than Mal, it seems. I know that they exist, I know
that my parents receive regular prescriptions from the Government,
but for only a handful at a time, not nearly enough for Celia to have
access to as many as she would have needed. I have no idea how or
why they work, really. I've been asking myself if I'd take them, if
there was any reason at all that I would consider THIS important –
and I can't say. Not yet. I've never had to choose.*

*But I might have to find the information about Stay somewhere.
A part of me really doesn't want to know about it, about the gory
details of just exactly how my sister died. Another part of me
demands to know. Because if she did, have others? How many are
there? Why is this drug out there?*

*What does it mean to have to choose between what you can't
help being and what you want or desperately need to be in the hour
that you cannot? Why are people like Mr. Bain allowed to always
put people who have the luxury of choice before those who do not...?*

120

Is there an Echo in here?

The response from Nell to this particular entry was almost immediate, the first time she had contacted me since the fateful book club night:

<About Stay...

<What?

<Can you come over tomorrow?

Mal had apparently told my parents nothing about the events of that Tuesday night. This scared me stupid at some incoherent level, particularly when I remembered his parting words to me that night – and if he had 'taken care of it' he hadn't told me about it, and I wasn't at all sure, truth be told, that I wanted to know. But his silence on the matter meant that for my mother Nell was still a cast-iron good risk outing – and she seemed... to have... information.

We carefully did not mention our last meeting at all.

"Did you look it all up already?" Nell asked when I turned up at her house the next day.

"About the drug? Some," I said.

"When it first came out, they sent it out to everyone in batches. A tube of pills, every month. They sent out a long screed with it, but no real instructions – and there *were* people who took too many, back then, for whatever reason, and then there was the whole re-sale value thing when people built up huge stashes and then the normals found out what it could do for them – do you know what they call it, the normals?"

"Why would normals want to take a drug that delayed a Turn?" I asked.

Nell clicked her tongue. "That's not *all* it does. *They* call it SGD. The 'Seeing God Drug'. Apparently for them it does no more than takes them on a trip to fairyland. And there's always people willing to pay plenty for that. It wasn't just the Were-kind who were in the market to buy the pills illegally, at schools or wherever. They were in demand by *everybody*. Here," she said, handing me a much-folded piece of paper with a lot of fine print on it. "That was one of the original inserts. Ever seen one before?"

"Where did you get this one?" I asked, unfolding it.

"They're around. And so are some of the stashes, still. They're totally illegal now, you're supposed to destroy any unused pills at the end of every Turn period, or else return them to the Administration. Yes, I know, it's a complete nightmare, but it was a bigger problem than that, before. That was why they changed the law."

"I know," I said. "They changed it the year after Celia died."

Nell tightened her lips. "That might not have mattered that much – or changed things."

"Just where did this come from in the first place? There was nothing like it, back in the old country. You just had to deal with things, as best you could... none of this... I stopped and stared at the paper in my hand. *Goats?* Really?"

The Adaptadyne scrip in front of me literally began, *Adaptadyne was originally developed from a species of mushroom found only in the mountain pastures of the Balkans. Initial calming effects noticed by mountain goatherds after observing goats which had ingested the mushroom and its active ingredient. Research found the refined drug to be effective in calming other large mammals, followed by further developments connected with Lunar Transsubstantiation Syndrome (LTS).*

"Is that what we've got?" I said, lifting my head. "A disease? We all suffer from LTS? Who *developed* this thing?"

"Keep going," Nell said.

I read further: *Mechanism of Action: Unknown, Believed to cause a massive release of epinephrine and nor-epinephrine in neural synapses around the hypothalamus at the same time yielding an increase in metabolism due to increases in Monoamine Oxidase of the catecholamines. There seems to be no false-transmitter effect similar to other non-catecholamines. Effect: amongst LTS sufferers, a short-term but possibly cumulative delay in the transformation process. Not effective as long-term control as the drug's effects degenerate rapidly after a six-hour period.*

The thing rambled on about something called "pharmacokinetics" – that the drug was readily absorbed orally, that effects became measurable fifteen to twenty minutes after ingestion, five minutes if administered by IV...

"IV?" I said, lifting my eyes from the paper, hoping I wasn't looking as horrified and appalled as I felt. "They can actually just stick this directly into your vein? Whatever for?"

"Jazz... it was a *control drug*," Nell said carefully. "There were some aspects of it that were useful in context, to Were-kind, and initially they were issued freely, but that was before it began to be misused, and before it became so valuable out on the streets. But initially the Administration sent it out because they thought they could keep on top of the Turns – it was another aspect of the Turning Houses, if you want to look at it that way. They could, if they wanted to, if they thought it necessary, control the Turns. *Everybody's* Turns. If there was a Were whom they wanted on a job during his Turn phase, there the pills were. Nobody really figured on the recreational angle of it all and maybe they should have but at the very least they aren't admitting it."

"I don't understand half of this stuff," I muttered.

Nell snorted. "That's the idea," she said.

"Look at this," I said, pointing. "*Readily crosses the blood brain barrier. Adaptadyne and its active metabolite, 3,5,methoxy-adaptadyne, are metabolised in the liver and excreted in the kidneys....*" I stumbled over the words. I read further down the page, and my finger stopped at the very next section. "*Common side effects: hypertension, hypotension, tachycardia, bradycardia, nausea and vomiting, diarrhea or severe constipation (in different patients), dry mouth, hallucinations, catatonia, possible death if extreme adverse reaction.* Did Celia *read* this stuff?"

"The first time she took it? Not hardly. She got the pills off that friend of hers, remember, according to her journal entry? I seriously doubt that the leaflet would have been handed over when she got the pills."

"But later?" I whispered. "The second time? She took this again, knowing all of this? Everything that happened next, after that last entry I posted..."

"What happened next?" Nell asked gently.

But I was dragging my finger down the rest of the page. Things were leaping out at me: *Potential for abuse: High. Known as Stay (by Were-kind) and the street name of SGD (Seeing God Drug) among non-Were users. Often abused on the streets and on the club scene. Precautions: The drug should be used with caution in populations with cardiovascular problems, and is contraindicated in the case of pregnant or lactating female patients. Drug should ideally be used under a physician's care. Because of potentially dangerous and even fatal side effects multiple doses should rarely be used, or required. Toxicity: due to Adaptadyne's narrow therapeutic index and long term use tolerance (the more often it is used the higher the dose needed to get the same effect) it is difficult to place an upper range on human populations. Lethal dose fifty on rats: 20mg/kg.*

"It just gets worse and worse. If she didn't know this about the cumulative stuff she might have been way off in thinking she only needed twelve pills. Maybe she needed more. A lot more."

"How many did she take?"

"I don't know," I said. "I don't know if anyone knows." I was looking down towards the end of the page of fine print. "Look at this," I said. "Available in 50mg tablets, an 200mg extended release tabs, or an injectable dose – and it says that you should start with an in-office injectable loading dose so that the doctor can 'monitor for unwanted initial side effects' – like hallucinations or catatonia, I suppose."

"I've seen the tablets, and the long-release tabs," Nell said carefully. "If you weren't familiar with this stuff, it isn't *that* easy to tell the difference. If she took the tabs thinking they were the short-term pills... what did they say, when she died? You said before that they thought it might have been suicide."

"I don't know any more," I whispered. "I don't know if she wanted to die, or wanted to live so badly that she was willing to risk dying..."

"Jazz... where did she get that second batch...?"

I crumpled the paper in my hand. "I have to go home," I said. "Nell, the next entry or so... it's hard. I've got to go home. I have to finish this, I have to finish it now, or I'll never finish it. I'll leave it hanging, and it'll be a poison I'll carry the rest of my life. Now that I've started it, I've got to end it..."

"Do you want me to come with you?" Nell asked carefully. "Do you need somebody there with you?"

"I'll be fine," I said. "Maybe later – in the next few days – if I need somebody to talk to..."

"It's Full Moon, day after tomorrow," Nell said.

It took me a moment to figure out what she was saying. "You'll be somewhere in your aviary," I said.

"Maybe you should hold off, on that last one," Nell said. "Until you can have us there for support if you need it."

"I'll have Charlie," I said, after a beat. "He's New-Moon, he's going to be around. But I do wish that you were there..."

"I could..." Nell began, and my hand clenched harder around the Adaptadyne leaflet.

"Don't...even...think it." I said.

The Corvid Princess reached out and actually hugged me.

"I think you're very brave," she said. "I think she was, too, your sister. And whatever they told you, I don't think she *wanted* to die. Just keep thinking about that."

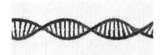

19 March

> And so, it ends.
> I won't get in Celia's way. Not here, not now.
>
> "I have been thinking about promises. You make them.
> Sometimes you mean them. Sometimes you make
> them because they make somebody else feel better. I
> seem to remember Babushka once making me promise
> her that I would always be happy. She must have
> known that I couldn't possibly keep my word – but it
> made her happy, then, to think about me being happy
> forever after, and I was a child, and it made me happy
> to make my grandmother happy, so I gave away the
> promise lightly and without thinking too hard about
> it.
>
> I don't think I ever PROMISED Mama I would never
> touch Stay again. She couldn't have held me to it
> anyway, not once I became a legal adult. But the
> trouble was that I was still some years shy of that and
> if I hadn't promised, exactly, it had certainly been
> taken as read.
>
> And if it hadn't been for Emily Winterthorn perhaps I
> could have endured the last few years of school, and
> Mr. Bain, and everything tangled in that, but there it

was. Emily Winterthorn embodied the future I wanted. If I didn't find a way of being there, to touch that future, to hear it speak, it would NEVER HAPPEN. And I could not bear that thought.

Karen gave me three Stay pills. She said she could not spare more.

It was not enough. Not nearly enough.

Help came, unbelievably enough, from Mal.

"You could take what you need from Mama's stash," he said to me, two days before the Turn was due. He was innocence itself, standing there before me, all little boy with tousled hair and that big full lower lip of childhood that everybody seems to have and everybody loses when they grow up.*

"Mama is watching me," I said. And then it occurred to me that this was my first thought – THAT I WOULD NEVER GET AWAY WITH IT – not that I should not do it or that it was wrong or that there was any ambiguity at all about the fact that it should be done, that I wanted to do it.

"I can get it for you," Mal said calmly. "I know where she keeps the stuff, I know where she keeps the key to the box she's locked it in, I know how to get it. Tell me how many you want."

I stared at my brother, the twelve-year-old criminal mastermind cat burglar. I opened my mouth to say no. My mind said no, loudly.

My traitor tongue said, "Do it."

"How many?"

"At least twelve."

"I'll get a handful," he said. "You can start a stash of your own if there's any left over."

And so I let my little brother steal the key to the cabinet where my mother kept the pills which would allow me to put myself in the path of my future. I don't know how he did it, or when he did it, but the morning after we'd had that conversation he came into my room, looked around to make sure I was alone, and dug into his grubby pocket, pulling out a double handful of pills. Some were round, some lozenge-shaped; so far all the ones that Karen had given me had been round but maybe they'd changed things around when I wasn't looking.

I stared at the pile of pills on my bed.

"You probably shouldn't have done this," I said.

"How are you going to get past Vivian?" was all that Mal asked.

I had already thought up and discarded half a dozen plans, on that account. She'd got into trouble with Mama the last time, and it wasn't likely that she would let me out of her sight – not even if I managed the pills, and stayed myself and didn't Turn at all, if I allowed myself to be locked into the Turning Room I would probably stay there whether I was Celia or Cat, Vivian couldn't take a chance. The only thing I can think of is that I should take them all at once, at least those twelve pills I think I'll need, maybe one or two more, just in case. And then just tell Vivian I did it. She couldn't make me un-take them, it would be done, and if she tried to stop me from going to Emily Winterthorn's talk, well, I would have to deal with that then. But I'm going. I'm going. I WILL go.

Yes, I read up on Stay, after the last time, after Mama's reaction, after feeling as awful as I did – and yes, I know, there isn't a single thing that I have done or am doing that I can defend on any grounds whatsoever. It isn't safe, and it is certainly not honest.

This is my life, and I will live it in the way I choose to live it, or it isn't worth living at all. I will not let Bain win. I can't."

That was the last entry in Celia's diary. Nice and neat and tidy, and that last full stop she put in there is violent, full of fury, indented into the page as though she had almost pushed the tip of her pen through the paper when she had ground it in. It was more than just the end of a sentence, it was the beginning of a life lived at her own terms.
Or so she thought.

I can only piece together the rest, from the bits and pieces I remember, from the half-truths I have been told, from the silences that have been left to fester for so long in this family. I can begin to understand the reasons, but there is still so much here that I do not know – and now that I have truly met and got to know a sister who had been taken from me when I was far too young to know the real loss. I want to know it all.

Because there have always been inconsistencies in the accounts that have survived. There have been hints that Celia's death might have been suicide – which, now that I've read her diary, now that I've had a chance to read the diary she so carefully hid away against future need, I don't believe. But neither do I believe that this was just pure accident, a senseless tragedy. There was a conscious act, in here somewhere. A choice.

'I will not let Bain win,' she said. If by life or death she could conquer him, she would.

I love my sister. I love her courage and her magnificence. I love her vulnerability. I love how strong, and how fragile she was.

I hate Barbican Bain with an unreasoning hate, because he took her from me. And I don't mind admitting that he utterly terrifies me, because there is just that much more damage that he can do.

I wonder if Emily Winterthorn came to the school. If she ever knew of Celia. If she ever knew how much Celia had risked – and lost – for a chance to speak with her.

I wonder if the world remembers that there was once a girl who bore two names both of which meant 'light', and whose own light burned for so short a time.

I never wanted to become her, or a substitute for her, but I will carry her inside me, If nobody else will, I will remember her.

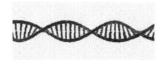

And I *do* remember some of the rest of it. I was young, but not that young; some things do stay with you.

Vivian had kept me away from Celia – I never saw what the pills did to her. But I remember clearly the chaos and noise and lights when the ambulance came, and I know I saw them wheeling my sister out on a gurney, a bunch of emergency response paramedics in dark jackets, one of them leaning over to adjust a plastic mask over Celia's face, others talking quickly and quietly to each other over her. I remember seeing Celia's hand, lying palm-up on the gurney beside her hip, twitching uncontrollably while they wheeled the gurney out – I remember because the twitches looked almost as though she was desperately trying to signal something to anybody who might be paying attention.

We'd followed the ambulance in Vivian's car, Vivian driving, me, Charlie, and a strangely subdued Mal in the back seat. She might have wanted to leave us behind but we were too young to abandon on our own and things apparently unraveled too fast for her to find an alternative babysitter for us. As it was, she was abandoning my parents down in the basement to their own devices, even if only for a little while.

The more I thought about it the more appalled I was at the realization that Celia had died *alone* – without a single member of her family beside her – Mal and I were children to be kept away from the tragedy, and my parents were out of it entirely. It was only Vivian who was there. Vivian, who had been our babysitter and caretaker for some years, but who was still a stranger we only saw for three days a month when she was in charge of the house in our parents' Turn absence.

Vivian, who had been silent on all of this all of these years – who must have been thinking about it and remembering it every time she set foot into our house – who probably felt bitterly and brutally responsible for it all because it happened on her watch – who was a grown woman and who must have recalled the whole drama in deep-etched detail. A girl had *died*. A girl who had been her responsibility.

I remembered Mal's question: *How are you going to get past Vivian?*

I considered asking him about it. But he was preparing for yet another Turn which he might or might not come out of as a full-fledged Were – and he kept to himself in his den where I knew better than to beard him.

And when Vivian arrived for that month's Turn duty, she brought Charlie with her.

I wanted very much to corner Vivian somewhere and talk about all of this with her – but Dad had picked that Turn to be difficult again – he had Turned a smidge earlier than anticipated and Mama and Charlie and I literally had to herd the cat down into the basement and the Turning Room while it hissed and spat and tried to claw our faces. Then Mama told us to lock her up, fast, and even while I was fastening the door with her inside her Turning Room Vivian came down escorting Mal, dressed in his Turning Cloak, scowling. His pattern-animal, the weasel, was already in his Turning Room, waiting; Vivian began to wish Mal good luck, thought better of it, ushered him into the room with the weasel, closed the door.

"Come on, you two," she began, turning to Charlie and me, and then the phone rang upstairs and she bounded up the basement stairs to answer it.

And Charlie and I were left alone in the basement with my Random Were family locked away in their animal shapes (or not, in Mal's case) in their rooms for the next three days, the full Moon was rising in the sky outside.

And all of it came crashing down on top of me – the moment, the heartbeats surrounding me and the one which was so painfully not there and would not ever be there again – Mom, Dad, Mal, Vivian, Charlie, Celia... *Celia...*

It affected me – the whole exercise of the diary and the blog could not

have failed to affect me – but I had no real idea about just how much...
until the full Moon of March 19 rose above the horizon, and it all boiled
over in a thoroughly unexpected way... and I Turned into an impossible
thing two months before I should have Turned at all.

Part 3:
The Boy in the
Basement
(Take Two)

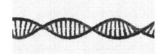

Mal had done exactly as he had threatened to do – he had vanished into his room, had emerged shortly afterwards wearing black jeans and a black hoodie, and had stomped out of the house without looking back at any of us. I knew that he and I would have to talk about this, soon, but what there was to be said was between us – and he was perfectly right to keep it that way. In the meantime, with him out of the picture, Vivian, Charlie and I were left there in the living room, awkward, waiting for something to happen, for someone to break the silence – and it was a doozy, as silences go. Waiting for everything to shake itself off like a wet dog and change back to being 'normal'.

But it didn't.

I had to talk to Vivian. About Celia, about things utterly unrelated to the current state of affairs. But right now her head wasn't in that space – she was still trying to figure out what she would do with Jesse-the-boy who was supposed to be Jazz-the-girl until my parents reverted and began to be able to take up the slack of making that decision.

In the end, I saw that I had to give them both a little bit of space – for Vivian's thoughts to stop circling about like a disturbed flock of crows and for Charlie to stop looking so bewildered, and anxious, and awkward. With a sigh, I heaved myself up from the armchair where I had been sitting.

"Where are you going?" Vivian asked immediately, her head snapping up like a hunting dog's.

"I'm going to go take a shower," I said, "and then I'm going to dig out a pair of sweatpants and maybe one of my dad's sweaters. Eventually, I figure I'll probably need some new clothes."

Vivian latched onto that. "Okay. Maybe we can go grab you a few things, later."

For some reason the very idea of going clothes shopping with Vivian in tow – *as Jesse* – gave me the willies. But it was a small constructive thing that she could focus on doing and it made her feel better just to be thinking about it. So I simply nodded, and made my way to the bathroom via a small detour to my – to Jazz's – bedroom.

It's hard to describe this without starting to sound a little crazy, but stepping into that room felt... strange. Everything in it was *recognizable*, in the sense that I knew what items were, whether or not they were in the place they were accustomed to being, and that there was connection between them and the life of the girl who had grown up surrounded by them. None of it was *familiar*, in the sense that it felt like it belonged to me, to the person I now was, to Jesse. There was a hairbrush on the bedside table – I picked it up, experimentally, and folded my fingers around it. They didn't fit. The brush was awkward in my hand. And yet there was a clear memory in my mind of holding it, of using it, of having used it constantly and continuously for years. It all felt as though somebody had done a very thorough and competent job of creating a detailed and elaborate stage set for a play. But which one of me – Jazz, or Jesse – was the actor, and which the character?

I rooted around in the closet with an unnerving sense that I was rifling through clothes that did not belong to me although I knew every individual piece extremely well. There was a limited amount of useful stuff in there, under the circumstances, but I unearthed a pair of black sweatpants I had almost permanently retired because they were a shade too big and baggy for me and belatedly remembered that I had begged Mom for what was technically a boy's sweater not long ago (but it was really cool and I liked the look of it and anyway I wasn't going to pair it up with a frilly skirt and pink ballet slippers anyway so who'd know or care that it was meant for a boy?) Who knew that it would come in handy now...? I opened up the drawer that held my – Jazz's – underwear, and found myself blushing furiously as my boy's hands rummaged around all these dainty female undies. I was... Jazz was... still almost flat-chested enough to be able to go braless and so there were only one or two of those amongst the camisoles that I – Jazz – habitually wore under things. But putting on one of those right now would feel like I was violating both bodies. I couldn't bear the idea of wearing any of the girls' panties, either. This really *was* going to be something I would have to address in short order – I couldn't really go around with everything dangling for three days a month – but under the circumstances I resolutely shut the underwear drawer, resolving to go commando for now. The idea stirred at once both a weird guilt and a huge sense of relief; clearly, there were issues looming for Jesse that I had not even begun to consider in detail.

But first things first.

I took the sweatpants and the oversized sweater I'd picked out into the bathroom with me, and piled them untidily on top of the toilet lid – and then paused for an instant to stare at them there, perfectly certain that it was *Jesse* who had dropped them there in that heap, and that *Jazz* would have at the very least folded them up into a neat little pyramid of clothes to be at hand for when I – *she* – God, I had to stop doing this, it would drive me crazy in short order – stepped out of the shower.

I caught another unfamiliar glimpse of myself in the mirror as I finally shucked the clothes I had been wearing as Jazz, and paused to take stock. My hands ran over my new skin, feeling out the shape and the contours of me. My shoulders were bonier, broader; where Jazz curved, Jesse provided flat planes (no trace of the breasts becoming visible under Jazz's tight T-shirts, no incipient curve of waist and hip) and there was the new confusing and embarrassing external plumbing to take into account.

There were logistics to this new body that I had not even begun to work out – and quite aside from the obvious stuff – how on earth did one do the simplest thing like going to the bathroom with this new set of below-the-waist equipment? – I had to sort out the implications that were only now coming home to me as I stared into the mine-but-not-mine eyes in the mirror.

Memories.

Celia had written about this – when we Turned, we Turned, and became Something Else, with its own instincts and memories and none of the other form. Cat did not remember being Celia (well, as far as Celia knew, anyway); Celia did not remember what it felt like to be Cat. It was two separate things, two separate beings, two separate souls, and the body that carried them had rearranged and adapted in order to accommodate them.

If things had been running according to that set of rules, I ought to have by rights found myself sitting there in my basement *with no memory of who or what I was*. Jesse – the creature I was now – had never existed before that moment. He had no instincts to fall back on, like a cat's – he was a boy, a functioning, normal HUMAN boy. But humans did not exist on instinct alone. Humans needed a context. The only human context that the Turned creature knew was... Jazz.

It was only now beginning to dawn on me how extraordinary all of this truly was – that I may have accidentally turned into the only Were to carry a full set of memories, memories that belonged at once to both minds resident inside. I could not even be sure, I thought to myself with a pang, that it would last – perhaps some intrinsic physiological trigger would suddenly remember to switch back off and I'd be left staring at the faces of my family and my friends and having no idea who they were, or who I was, or having forgotten the concept of language completely and simply standing there opening and closing my mouth like a goldfish with nothing coming out at all.

I stepped under the shower and stood there with my face turned up to the spray and my eyes screwed shut, as though the water could wash all the problems off this new skin that I was in. It was only after Vivian banged on the bathroom door and demanded to know if I was all right and I had better answer her or she was coming in, ready or not, that I finally realized that I had comprehensively lost track of time. I had no idea how long I'd been standing under this water spray.

"I'm fine," I called out, running my unfamiliar hands back through my wet unfamiliar hair, dropping my gaze down to my unfamiliar feet and trying to get them to function in a manner that would not leave me sprawled on the bathroom floor.

For all the foreignness and the discomfort and the unintentional indignities that my change had forced upon me, I was sort of starting to come to terms with my new self. Slowly. Like a newborn centipede figuring out that it didn't need to count every step of every leg in order to perform forward movement – and that in fact keeping every leg in mind all of the time only served to leave it tangled up in a puzzled knot and going nowhere fast. I would still have to figure this out one leg at a time, eventually, but right now it was enough just to know that I still knew how to walk. The shower had made me feel a whole lot better, and the sweatpants were a lot more comfortable around my new nether parts than my jeans had been, and I found myself starting to be more curious than afraid.

And still hungry, apparently, which Vivian appeared to have anticipated because her first words to me, after asking yet again if I was sure I was all right, were that she had phoned for a pizza and that one would be delivered to the house in another twenty minutes or so. But it was obvious that she had spent those precious moments of alone-time that I had snatched for myself in doing some thinking of her own. And coming to some very similar conclusions.

It was Charlie who alerted me, sidling up to me after Vivian had gone back into the kitchen to busy herself with what looked like make-work to me.

"Mom's scared," he whispered, perching on the arm of my chair. "She doesn't know what to do next."

"Neither do I," I said quietly, trying to marshal my uncooperative voice into a softer tone. "Charlie... I shouldn't know who you are. Or who she is. I ought never to have recognized Mal. I told him I *was* Jazz when he came into the room, earlier, but I'm not, am I? I can't be. But if I'm not then who am I? It's easy enough to give myself a name but it's like calling blue the new green – that doesn't change either the blue or the green, really..."

I was *calm* about this. Almost dispassionate. As if it was happening to someone else entirely and I (for whatever value of I you might chose to plug in at this time) was simply standing on the sidelines, looking on. It was all about logic, not emotion.

"If Mal comes back from wherever it is that he's gone and has two burly policemen in tow, Mom's probably going to let them take you," Charlie said.

"He *won't*," I said. "Even Jesse knows that he won't, and Jesse only met him, what, an hour ago...? Jazz is perfectly certain, however."

"How do you know that? How can you?"

"I don't know. But I know that I know." I gave him a helpless shrug. "Look, I understand him perfectly. Right now probably really *is* ready to cheerfully murder somebody, and I honestly wouldn't want to get in his way out there in the next little while. But it's all *him* – it's all to do with him – he'll never throw Jazz to the wolves."

"That might all be perfectly accurate, but Mom's had time to think. And she's panicking. I can tell, I know, I see it in her face when she does that. She did it when Hank went missing once – my youngest brother – went out playing in the neighborhood and didn't come back for hours and wasn't where he said he'd be and his friends said they hadn't seen him and it was the day before New Moon and she had that look on her face then, that little bit of white around her mouth. She's *this* close to losing it."

"How come you aren't?" I said.

"Me?" Charlie said, taken aback.

I spread my arms. "I'm *not* Jazz," I said, "am I?"

"Well, no, but..."

"Then how come I remember being her?" I asked immediately,

pouncing on the question, on the issue, desperate for another opinion. And fighting my own panic, thank you very much. "Charlie... you think your Mom's scared? What do you suppose I am?"

Well. Fear was an emotion, I suppose. But this was *thinking* about fear. Analyzing the reasons I should be afraid. It was not visceral terror.

The doorbell rang, and Vivian looked up from her work on the kitchen counter.

"Charlie, there's a twenty in my pocketbook. That'll be the pizza. Go get it."

Charlie gave me a long warning look, and went to obey her.

The pizza turned out to be a large one with everything on it – and ordinarily I didn't like these kitchen-sink pizzas (and I had to stop to think about that again – for what value of 'I' was that true? Jazz? Jesse?) but I really was hungry enough to eat rusty nails. I was nibbling the crusts of my fourth full slice before I saw Charlie grinning at me and became embarrassingly aware that I'd single-handedly devoured almost half the pizza myself.

"Feeling better?" Vivian asked, managing a smile.

"No," I said honestly. "Well, yes. Not hungry. Not as hungry as before, anyway. But..."

There it was. It was a big 'but', and it hung there between us, twisting slowly.

She drew her breath to speak, but I suddenly realized that this was probably the only chance I would ever get of having the story of what had happened to Celia out of the only adult person I knew who had been present in the last hours of her life. And so I used her fears, my own fears, to wrestle the topic of conversation in a direction she did not expect.

"I don't know what happened, Vivian," I said. "But I think I know why."

Her head jerked up at that, her jaw muscles tightening. "Maybe I should be writing this down."

"No, wait," I said, reaching out to stop her before she slipped out from behind the kitchen table where we were all sitting around the devastation of the pizza box. "Before you start scribbling things down... *before you make a record of anything yet* – you have to tell me... about Celia."

I saw her recoil – I saw her entire body whip away from me, as though I had thrown a tarantula at her face.

"*Celia*?" she repeated, her eyes wide. I could see her pupils dilating in shock. "Celia's been gone for years!" I saw the memory of that hit her, physically, her entire body shuddering convulsively from the shoulders all the way down. In a way this was a dreadful repetition of what had happened once before – she had been the one to handle Celia's overdose during the absence of our parents; now she was here again, being asked to handle yet another emergency, alone. Celia had died and I was still here but that was a technicality – she had to all intents and purposes lost Jazz, another child she had been entrusted with taking care of, just as she had once lost Celia. She had been presented in my case with what might have looked like a viable substitute – at least there wouldn't be a dead body to present to my parents again at the end of the Turn (or at least hopefully there wouldn't be – I was just starting to realize that I had absolutely no guarantees of that) when Vivian added, her voice thin and strange, "What has Celia got to do with any of this?"

Charlie gave me an odd look. He'd been following the blog, of course – but it was only recently that his mother had become tangled up in the story. In any event, up until now it had all been safely contained inside the friends-locked blog. It was about to come spilling out. All of it.

So I gave it up, the secret. I probably should have talked about it all to my parents, first, but there is only so much intelligent conversation you can have with a cat and a chicken – and until I could have my parents back and in command of their human faculties, Vivian was all I had. Vivian, who had been the one who had been there on the spot, after all. Who was a huge part of the puzzle.

"I found Celia's diaries," I said. "She wrote her last entry just before she took those pills."

"Celia's... diaries?" Vivian whispered, her voice thick with tears. "She wrote a diary? About what happened? Until when...? When did she...? Damn it. *Damn* it. She confronted me with what she'd done when it was already too late. I came to her room – to get her – your parents were waiting until they could see her safely stowed in her Turning Room – but when I got there – "

"They hadn't Turned yet?"

"Not by the time I went to get Celia. But they had gone to the basement – and it was close – they thought she was already down there, and your mother couldn't take the risk of running back up and arguing with her, the Turn might come at any moment, so they held on as best they could and they sent me to just go and *get* her – and by the time I got to her room *you* were the only one in there – I found Celia in the bathroom, she was sitting very calmly on the edge of the bathtub and told me that there was no point... and I had to go back, and take care of your parents – if they Turned, without me, loose, a cat and a chicken – "

Yes, I remembered there was a certain amount of chaos. I remembered the racing up and down the stairs. I had been in my room, in the room that Celia and I shared; the younger kids, me and Mal, the yet-unTurned, had been told peremptorily to stay out of the way as much as we could while Vivian dealt with the rest of the family during the Turn. And that was hardly unusual – those were the orders we were always given at this hour, when Vivian fulfilled her caretaking duties for the Turned Were members of this family.

But this time it had been different, it was frantic, and I remember that I came up to the door and cracked it open, peering outside – that Vivian was disappearing into the kitchen and down the basement stairs as I looked out, with a phone clamped to her ear.

That stopped me, all over again.

I remembered.

I should not have had these memories. They were Jazz's memories.

They did not belong to this boy who was sitting here right now in the self-same kitchen, the door to the basement stairs ajar in front of me. Jesse had never seen this kitchen, this table, these stairs. He had never seen VIVIAN before. He had never had a sister named Celia. He had NEVER EXISTED before today. How was it possible that he knew all this about a past that was not his own?

"Who were you calling?" I said. "You had a phone..."

Vivian shot me a startled look. The fact that I could not possibly have known any of this stuff, not personally, was starting to come together for her, too. But she didn't ask me, not then, not yet. "An ambulance," she said, instead, choosing to simply answer the question. "I was screaming for an ambulance, for her. I went racing down to the basement again, and we had to waste precious moments chasing your father around the basement before I cornered him and flung him into *his* Room, and then I managed to shut the door on your mother just before she started to Turn, I'll never forget the look in her eyes – she knew something was wrong, something was badly wrong, but it was just too late for her to do anything except know it. And then I just bellowed out the address and told them to get here in a hurry and then... And by the time I went back to the bathroom – it was – she was..."

I made myself let go of the edge of the table, which I had folded my fingers around with a frightening strength, and allowed my hands to fall back into my lap. "What?"

"I have no idea what she took, how much she took. All she told me was that she had taken 'enough' to make it all stop."

"Twelve," I said. "She worked it out. She said she would need twelve. She said that she would do that, take it all at once if she needed to, she had no idea if it would work but it would be because she needed to make *you* let her go to this thing, this visit to the school by her favorite writer..."

Vivian closed her eyes, screwing her eyelids tightly shut for a moment, and I stopped talking, watching her expression.

"*That's* why?" she whispered. "I never knew why she really did it. I didn't even know what I would tell the paramedics when they got here, other than I believed she had overdosed on Stay. I was counting on her telling them, on her being able to tell them, that they would be able to bring her back from the brink and she'd be herself again and would be able to answer questions. But by the time the ambulance arrived she was unconscious, and seizing. I did what I could but I had no training – they told me later that I had done as well as any ignorant bystander could have done, that there was nothing that I could have done to stop it. I left the front door open and I went to the bathroom and I tried to keep her airways open..." She swallowed, hard. "It was an act of defiance, and right when your parents could not possibly do a thing to get in the way of it. It seemed to me she chose her moment because of that, not because she wanted... to go and see... a visiting *writer*..." Vivian covered her face in her hands and sobbed.

"It wasn't your fault," I said quietly.

"Your mother always took the blame," Vivian said.

"Why? She wasn't even – "

"Her pills. Her stash. That's where Celia got them from."

"No," I said gently. "Celia did not take them. Mal did."

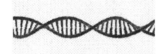

"**M**al did what?"

It stood to reason that everything that could go wrong that day probably would. In a piece of spectacularly bad timing Mal had returned to the house – for whatever reason – and had arrived back just in time to hear me say his name. Who knew – he might have returned for good reasons, with a plan, something, anything – but here was this creature who was clearly no longer quite his sister talking about Mal himself behind his back, apparently blaming him for something.

Charlie literally jumped, scraping his chair back across the floor with his recoil. Vivian lifted a tear-streaked face with an expression of pure consternation.

I turned, slowly, to see my brother leaning one shoulder against the doorjamb, his arms crossed over his chest.

"What *exactly* do you know about what I did, or did not do?" he said.

"Celia told me," I said.

He straightened, his arms unfolding to drop down to his sides with both hands balled into fists.

"Celia is *dead*," he said, in a tight voice. "And *you* were a baby."

The Jesse part of me perked up at this. Mal has said 'you'. To Jesse. When he had clearly meant Jazz. Whatever he said, whatever his reactions might seem on the face of it, he was accepting this, somehow. Had accepted it. Might not have been happy with it, but he was ready to face it.

Maybe *that* was why he had come back.

Either way, I wasn't going to jinx it, letting him know that I had noticed. I simply took his words at face value when I responded.

"Not *that* young," I said, "And Celia... she wrote it all down. Everything. In a diary. I found it. When she decided to take the pills – you knew that she had decided – you knew she needed them – you told her you could get her what she wanted, from Mom's stash. She said twelve pills. You said you could get her more."

Mal's eyes glittered with a film of tears. "Who the hell *are* you and where did you come from?" he managed, through clenched teeth. It seemed a step back from his earlier words, but I understood what he was saying. He was asking the same question I was asking. What had conspired to make a thing like me possible at all?

I turned back to Vivian. "Celia spoke of two kinds of pills – round and lozenge-shaped. I read up on it, just the other day – the leaflet says that the thing was available in two dosages, and one was 50 mg, and the other something they called an extended release tab, 200mg."

"I didn't know," Mal said, his voice barely above a whisper. "I didn't know anything about that."

"Vivian… she didn't mean to do it. She didn't! But she must have taken one or more of the bigger-dosage tabs. All at once. That's what hit her – she might have been sick as a dog but still fine if she had just taken the 50mg pills. But she must have had enough in her system by the time everything kicked in for it to completely overwhelm her…"

Mal subsided onto the nearest chair, burying his face in his hands. "They were all in there, jumbled together," he said. "I just… took a handful. I gave her what she wanted, and a few more. I hung on to the rest."

"The *rest*?" Charlie blurted, unable to help himself. "How much of the stuff did you get your hands on?"

"Enough," Mal said. "They were valuable, I knew that much."

"You were twelve," Vivian said. "You were *twelve*."

Mal's head came up sharply. "Some of us," he said, "aren't allowed to be twelve for long."

"Your mother still blames herself for this," Vivian said, glancing down towards the basement. "You think she knew it was you?"

A small strange grimace twisted the corner of Mal's mouth. "As you say," he murmured. "I was twelve years old. That was way too young to be involved. I said nothing. I said nothing, and I let her think – I let her believe that it must have been Celia who pilfered her stash – Mom threw them all out, after that, did you know? Every last pill. I watched her do it, after Celia was gone. I watched, and I was maybe going to confess – but she didn't have time for me then, or for anything that I might have done, or wanted, or needed. And so I waited, and I was going to tell her later, and then later still, and then… never. There came a point after which telling her anything at all would have been… just unkind. Even to this day, the scrips that come every month, she never opens the envelope, you know. She just destroys them. She *kills* them, violently, like she is taking revenge. I've watched her do it. She hasn't seen Stay since Celia… died."

I had been running our previous conversations over in my head – I could not believe that I had never, in so many words, actually mentioned the diaries to him before. He knew – he had to know, given my reaction to Mr.Bain – that I had recognized him, that I knew at the very least who he was, and something about what he had done. But he had not asked me, that night, walking down the empty street underneath the streetlights, *how* I had known, or how much. We had been locked into our own little bubbles, he and I – he far too concerned with consequences to coherently question the immediate circumstances and me far too terrified by what I knew – and thought I knew – and all the things that Mal was throwing out at me as Things That Could Yet Be – to actually offer up any explanations which might have been required. Mal might have thought about that, after, might have picked up the conversation, might even have asked the right questions – but then, the Turn came... and this. This situation, where I was sitting here staring at him through what he could not see as anything but a stranger's eyes. In some ways, he had been willing to let certain questions slide, to assume that as a member of this family I had simply been aware of more things than he had realized or had thought of me as being in a position to be.

But now, now that he was not looking at Jazz who was his little sister but at Jesse whom (even if he accepted at some deeper level that Jazz lurked deep inside the stranger boy's skin) he had no reason to trust, now that he knew exactly how I knew, he wanted those answers. All of them.

"I want to know exactly what Celia said about it," he said. "I want to see those diaries."

"I'll give you the blog URL," I said.

He actually did a double take. "The *blog*?" he echoed. "You blogged your dead sister's private diaries?"

"It's friends-locked," Charlie said defensively. "It isn't like she threw it all out for everyone to drool over. And it's a story that needed to be told."

"What, and *you* were one of the friends?" Mal said. "Mom and Dad don't know any of this, I take it? You tossed something like this out onto the Net without telling your own *family* about it first? The consequences..."

The specter of Barbican Bain stood between us, as solid as if he himself had been present in the room right then. Mal had said that he would 'take care of it', but that was before... before all this. Everything had changed, yet again. Mal stared at me across the room, I stared back at him, and the unspoken hung there – he didn't have to do anything at all, potentially, so long as he stepped back from dealing with the Bain threat. But now – now it was no longer a question of merely neutralizing Barbican Bain so that he was unable to wreak physical havoc with our family. Now he had been pushed into a position of needing to do something far more direct. There were secrets to protect. My ignorance. His actions, and his guilt over what he might have inadvertently done. Our mother's wasted years of grief and yearning.

"I wasn't the first to keep secrets. That was mutual," I said. "I knew nothing real about Celia before I read what she wrote."

"And did it occur to you that there might have been a good reason for that?" Mal said, and his voice had a tone of almost comic disbelief in it. "For God's sake! She wrote it down in a *diary*! A personal and private journal, not for public consumption! And the first thing you do...It's out there, now, you know. In the wild. In practice, everything's crackable. You might have a wider readership than you know."

I shook my head in fervent denial, but he wasn't done yet.

"And now," Mal said slowly, "there's *you*. Celia's dead and gone, but you're very much here, alive and kicking. If we were to obey the law of the land to the letter, you really ought to be locked up in that room downstairs, right now."

I stared at him. "If somebody took me away and gave me every test in the book – well – I don't know for certain, of course, but I can take a pretty good guess that I would test absolutely normal. As a human."

"There are genetic markers for the Were," Mal said.

"So I would be a Were in human form," I shrugged. "Still not lockable."

"It's Full Moon," Mal said, savage and thoughtless. "If you tested as a real Were, one who has on the evidence and witness of others Turned, you *should* be in your animal form right now..." He stopped abruptly, his eyes flickering to Vivian and Charlie.

"Or she could be a New-Moon Were," Charlie said. "In which case, she's still legal."

"She can't have it both ways," Mal said faintly, burrowing his hands into his hair into his temples and allowing his hands to fold over his face.

He'd done it again. That 'she'. He knew. He understood. He accepted. He *had* to.

It didn't mean he had to like it, or to be easy with the creature which I had just become.

I had never really analyzed it before. It just... *was*. This was my family: the distant but smotheringly protective parents, the vanished sister, the brother with whom my relationship had always been just that little bit rocky. What little I had tried to put together into some coherent explanation of it all had usually centered around me – that it was a lack in me, or too much of something in me, that made the living respond to me as they did...and I had never really extrapolated my relationship to Celia because it had never really had the chance to fully develop from my own side – I had simply been too young. But now – after the diaries – after finding out a whole lot of stuff I had never known – the central figure of it all wasn't me. It was Celia. It was the *lack* of Celia. My parents were not protecting me so much as protecting another child from Celia's path and Celia's fate.

My brother... whatever he and Celia had shared together, I still did not know, but there was a big part of it that was simply the fact that I was not, could not be, the sister he wanted, the sister he knew, the sister with whom he had grown up and shared the upheaval of the world. That sister was gone, and he had to live with the knowledge that he himself had a hand in that – and he had maybe been as cool towards me as he had been known to be because he simply didn't want to love another sister as much as he might have loved Celia. Because if he did not put his heart out there, it could not be broken.

But for all his darkness and his prickliness and his air of 'do-not-touch-me', there was always something about Mal that I had... I don't know... been in awe of. I might not have liked him much at times, but he was the only older brother I had – and I... kind of... loved him.

He had called me names. He had on occasion threatened dark retributions (which never came) to some small sin of mine he'd taken exception to. He had ignored me. But he had never had to cope with an instinctive rejection of me, of this person who sat in his house pretending to be me... until now.

But he couldn't stretch that far. Everything sane told him that what his eyes insisted was before them was violently wrong. And yet...He looked at Jesse, and somehow he could see past Jesse, through into the Jazz who was still underneath.

Could see it. Had trouble getting through all the impossibilities that stood in the way. He was struggling with this, just as hard as I was. I could see how it could have been layered over for him with all kinds of other stuff, too – the pattern-weasel, after all, was still safely locked up in the Turning room in the basement and Mal... was yet again just Mal.

In the end it was I who could not cope with any more of this, not yet, not just then. Jesse had a hard time with emotions, and we had crossed the line from pure fact into raw emotion some time ago.

I just ran. Stumbled to my feet, flailed for balance in the unfamiliar new body, staggered forward and through the door, and into that strange, only half-familiar place that was Jazz's bedroom and did not belong to Jesse at all but which was now the only sanctuary.

I thought I might cry. Jazz probably would have. Jesse... just sat there, in silence, in solitude, willing away those who came to knock diffidently on the other side of the bedroom door asking if everything was all right.

It wasn't.

It might have been Jazz who first woke to the secrets which drifted like ghosts through the family. But it was Jesse who was coming to terms with the fact that this change, this Turn, would either break the family wide open... or would add another layer of secrets, secrets so strong and so deep that we would never surface from underneath them again.

Mom and Dad would never meet Jesse, not under any sort of normal circumstances. But they would have to be told about the Were-thing I had become – and then they would have to decide what to do about it all.

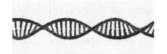

Mal and I were both aware that the two of us had to square off at some point – but it was a kind of mutual decision that neither of us could really handle that while I was still Jesse. It would have to wait, all of it, after I Turned back... if I Turned back... into Jazz. He kind of kept out of my way for the rest of the Turn– it was as though we didn't live in the same house, he ghosted through the place so much, avoiding me whenever he could, I don't know when he ate, probably by himself in the kitchen at two in the morning when he could be absolutely certain that he would not cross my path.

Charlie clearly struggled to adjust to the new state of affairs but at least he tried gamely to be there for me, as much as I wanted him to. It was

Charlie who suggested that the two of us go out by ourselves to the nearest mall that sold clothes – because Jesse desperately needed something appropriate and of a correct size to wear. Vivian wanted to go with us, but Charlie glared at her when she suggested it.

"Mom. It's embarrassing enough for *me* when you insist on coming with me and choosing my clothes," he said. "Just how unbearable would it be for someone like Jesse?"

"But you need somebody there, just in case things – "

"We'll stay out of trouble," Charlie said "I promise."

But that was easier said than done, really. Going into a clothes store was a dizzying shift in perspective and Charlie had to keep a constant eye on me – I might have Turned into a boy, and my body might have been male, but the residual memory of this place was Jazz's and she knew where the *girls* went. The male section of the store was suddenly a complete mystery to me. The sizes made no sense because I had no idea whatsoever what sort of size I was after.

Vivian had given us the necessary cash for the required purchases, but just buying a packet of boys' underwear was a mortifying chore in itself. It was a necessity, to be sure, given the fiasco with Jazz's drawer of underthings, but I was acutely self-conscious all over again and for much the same reasons, standing there, sifting through packets of underpants. The topic of underwear left both the Jazz and the Jesse parts of me vaguely squeamish, with a sense of rooting around in stuff we were not supposed to be into. Just trying to figure out which ones were supposed to fit me now was... interesting. I had drawn the line at having Charlie in on this aspect of things. It was bad enough having to march up to the cashier with said underwear in my hand and offer money for them to the pretty young cashier, my face on fire and unable to meet her eyes, and my new equipment responding in unexpected and acutely embarrassing ways which necessitated carrying my purchases in a strategic manner in front of my crotch for at least until I could figure out a way of getting everything down there back to manageable parameters. I wasn't having *Charlie* offer his best judgment on the size of said equipment.

But it was Charlie who picked out a pair of jeans he thought looked right when I flaked out on that, standing there looking bewildered.

"Go on, try those on," he said, pushing me towards the men's changing rooms. "At least it'll give us an idea. The important thing is to find out what's actually comfortable when you've got it on. They've got to let you *sit down.*"

"Of course I need to sit down..." I began, and Charlie gave me an extra shove between the shoulder blades, just to shut me up.

"Trust me," he said," try sitting down in them. You'll see what I mean."

I found myself irrationally embarrassed at the whole idea of going into the men's changing rooms at the mall. I did not particularly want to catch glimpses of any other men in a state of undress and I most emphatically did not wish any other males to catch sight of me in the same condition. It was an evil moment of struggling with the maleness of my new body with an appalled part of my mind which was still locked into Jazz's sensibilities; I would have been just as happy if I could have tried on the jeans with my eyes closed and never having to look at myself in a mirror at all. In fact, I was aiming as close to that as I could get away with. Luckily Charlie's initial judgment proved reasonably sound and I was spared the mortification of having to trek back and forth between the racks and the changing rooms with armfuls of clothing at a time, like some cheerleader queen bee on a shopping spree.

Even without Vivian there, even without a mother there to fuss and supervise, it was an exquisitely embarrassing afternoon – but at least at the end of it I had a serviceable Jesse wardrobe that I could make do with in future Turns without being too ashamed to be seen in public.

"You want to go home?" Charlie asked, diffidently enough, at the close of the expedition.

"Feels like everybody's staring at me," I muttered, clutching the shopping bag with my loot. "Like I've got a sign on my back that says *freak*."

"They wouldn't know you from any other kid in a line-up," Charlie said.

"*You* can't look at me."

"That's because I know what I should be seeing. Nobody else does. And anyway, I'm getting better."

"That woman just turned to look at me. Tell me she didn't."

"She *so* did not. Come on, stop spazzing out. Don't you get it? You're free – like none of us have ever been free. Whatever anybody thinks they know about you isn't true – you can make it all up, be whoever you want to be..."

"I'm not sure I know how to be... *this*," I muttered, half-lifting my hands in an expansive gesture that took in all of Jesse.

"If 'this' is what you are going to be whenever you aren't... her... you'd better get used to it," Charlie said practically.

"Do you think it's... too weird?"

"Yeah," he muttered, "but that doesn't help anybody. I can live with it, I guess. If I don't think about it too closely. I mean, I *saw* you..." He broke off, his gaze dropping to the fake-marble floor at our feet, and then, after a moment, he recovered. "Hey, you want to stop off for an ice cream?"

"That sounds good," I said, and then stopped at the note of enthusiasm in my voice. Jesse was genuinely looking forward to the explosion of icy sweetness in his mouth. Jazz had *never* really liked ice cream, particularly the too-sweet commercial concoctions.

We were already diverging, and it wasn't just a matter of what kind or what size a pair of jeans either of us would feel comfortable wearing.

I thought the three Jesse days would last forever... but in the end, they seemed to rush past, in a physical and emotional overload of things that I had to learn or re-learn how to do in order to exist in my new avatar, my new body, my new life.

Not counting the occasional time-out with Charlie, which kept me sane, I spent most of the rest of my Jesse-days rejecting any sort of human company at all. (If I could avoid the hovering presence of Vivian, it wasn't too difficult, in fact, seeing as Mal and I had apparently established this unspoken pact of avoiding each other for the moment.) It was a time that I dearly wished that my family *did* have pets, that we had a cat, an ordinary cat, something that would simply curl up next to me and purr and be happy to be with me and not judge me for who I was, or was not, or could never be. I even came close to wanting to go down to the basement and see if the cat thing would work with Dad – but the idea of Jazz-as-Jesse seeking comfort from Dad-as-Cat while sitting on the beanbag in his Turning room somehow gave me the creeps. It just wouldn't be the same thing.

And as it happened, I Turned back first. Maybe because I was anxious and shivery and frightened at the prospect, remembering what it had felt like to turn from Jazz into Jesse in the first place and not relishing enduring a reverse process; maybe because I knew that I was living in whatever calm there was before the storm – before *all* the Were-kind came back to being human, and decisions would have to be made concerning this thing that had happened to me, and frankly the waiting was *killing me*. I just wanted it over with.

Vivian was particularly clucky that last day, more of a mother hen than my own mother (who was a *real* chicken down in the basement at that moment in time) – waiting for the Turn-back, wanting to be there when it happened for me, to be there with me, for me, even though there was nothing for her to do and no role for her to play in the process. There was a part of me that might have welcomed having my hand held, even just figuratively, but as it turned out I was actually alone when it happened. In the shower, actually.

At first I wasn't even aware that anything out of the ordinary was going on – for values of 'ordinary', that is, that applied to these last three days. We had funky plumbing in this house and it was a regular occurrence for one of the family to be in the shower, screaming threats of dire things to come, while somebody else innocently turned on some other faucet in the house and inadvertently doused the showerer in cold water. In a way that was exactly what it felt like when the Turn-back began – and I yelped as icy water trickled down my spine, cursing Vivian for turning on the water in the kitchen while I was in here. But then the pain came, the bones turning into lava and then back into stone, my body re-setting itself to its usual parameters. I bent over, gasping for breath, and strands of long wet hair fell forward over my bare wet shoulder. Jazz's hair. It was a moment before I could gather enough ability for coherent movement to make my hands obey me but then I ran them over my body, blindly. Jazz's breasts. Jazz's waist and flat stomach, the curve of Jazz's hip, the familiar smooth and protuberance-free mound between my legs and then sliding down into a slim *feminine* leg...

I must have lost myself for a moment, a minute, ten minutes, half an hour, I had no way of knowing – because the next thing I was aware of was that I was on my knees in the middle of the tub, curled up with my head turned sideways and my cheek against my knees, my arms wrapped around me with my hands curled around my heels, with the water sluicing from the shower head over my back.

By the time I dragged myself upright and turned off the shower, I could hear things outside the bathroom. I heard the basement door open. I heard footsteps, hurried and almost running, panicked. I heard voices. I heard my mother cry out. Then I heard the footsteps come padding right up to the bathroom door, and my mother flung it open with little regard for proprieties or privacy, her face a mask of fear and disbelief, her eyes wild.

"Jazz? Jazz...?"

I had the big bath towel wrapped around me by this stage, and was using a smaller towel to dry my hair; when she opened the bathroom door I turned to face her, wet towel in my hands, damp tendrils of hair clinging to my shoulders and bare upper arms.

"Yes. It's me."

Mom came inside, slowly, almost unwillingly, reaching out with her right hand and then drawing back just before she touched me. I could see her hand was shaking. Badly.

I had both of mine hidden under the convenient camouflage of the hair-drying towel. So that she couldn't see that mine were shaking too.

"Vivian said... Vivian said..."

"It's true."

Her eyes got a little wilder. "But how...?"

"Mom," I said, "I'd better get dressed. I'll be out in a minute."

I took a chance, freed one hand from underneath the towel, gently turned her around by the upper arm, guiding her out of the bathroom. She went, docile, with no more apparent self-awareness than a porcelain doll, her eyes glassy and unfocused.

I closed the bathroom door behind her and fought down nausea.

If I was going to feel this sick every time I Turned, the rest of my life was going to be a *carnival*. Just my luck. But perhaps it got better, with time. Mom can't have Turned back too long before she came charging up to the bathroom to find her changeling child – and she can't have been wanting to throw up as she raced all the way up the basement stairs.

I should have probably had The Talk with them before now – asking what I should expect, what kind of thing was waiting for me – but they never broached the subject and I just coasted along assuming everything would happen on its own schedule. Perhaps, given the problem of Mal, I should have known better than to assume anything at all about Were-kind in general – and this family, in particular.

But I couldn't hide out in the bathroom forever and this talk would have to be had, sooner or later. I gave my wet hair a final decisive pat and then cracked the door open a sliver and peered out to see if the coast was clear between the bathroom and my bedroom (where all the Jazz clothes were. I had gone into the bathroom as Jesse. I didn't think Mom was ready for anything as in-your-face as seeing me in the boy-clothes I had bought for the 'son' she never knew she had.) I wouldn't have put it past Mom to have waited just outside the bathroom door, but the corridor was empty, and I padded on swift and silent bare feet to my room. Picking Jazz's clothes off the rack in the closet was weirder than it had any right to be – it wasn't as though I had been Jesse for weeks, or months. It had been three days. *Three days.* That was all. And yet I was struggling to get it together – perhaps because I hadn't been given the chance to ease into any of this at all. When I had Turned into Jesse it had been witnessed, by Charlie, and then everything snowballed after that; this time round, I'd at least been alone for the duration of the change, but only barely, and now I had interrogators waiting for me in the living room who would want the story, the full story, all the details. Who would demand to know things that I could very well not have the answers to at all.

But I was Jazz. I was also Jesse. I was *both* of us, I carried both of us inside of me now. What answers there were, they were within me.

Of course, it was only going to *start* with me. It would circle, sooner rather than later, to the one subject that my parents had always been reluctant to talk about.

Celia.

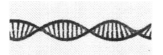

B y the time I emerged from the safe cocoon of my room, they were all waiting for me – Mom, Dad, Mal. Vivian. I would have welcomed Charlie's presence, the only one there whom I would have been absolutely certain about being on my side (in anything at all – although it was instructive, in itself, to make my entrance knowing that I had a 'side' and that I might be alone on my side any line that might potentially be drawn). There were decisions waiting to be made here, and the weight of them was making the very air in that room stuffy, heavy with brooding and portent. This was the sort of moment that defined a Before and After – Before, we had been one thing, one sort of family; After, we were likely to be something else entirely, and the change was already beyond our control.

"Hi, Mom. Hi, Dad." I had to say something, say something *first*, because the silence that met me was unbearable. "I'm fine."

Mal actually had to stifle a laugh at that.

Less than helpful, I thought indignantly, as I walked steadily enough into the room and settled into a chair.

"Vivian has told us some of what happened," Dad said, after clearing his throat twice in order to release his voice. "I find it... almost impossible to believe..."

I glanced at the coffee table. Charlie had taken some photos, with his little point-and-shoot digital camera, and Vivian had made prints of them

– and there they were, spilled across the coffee table, pictures of a boy looking trapped and confused, and then a close-up of him attempting a smile, and then a full-length shot of him standing there awkwardly, his hands in the pockets of his new jeans, looking at once ill-at-ease and oddly (and newly) comfortable with the body he was still getting accustomed to. They had obviously asked Mal to corroborate Vivian's story, and those pictures were a mugshot gallery of the changeling in their midst – Mal would have been the one to confirm the identity of the strange boy in the photos.

Mal's eyes were glittering entirely too strangely when he looked my way. I couldn't meet them for long. I was usually able to tell what he was thinking, where he was going to jump next – but right now, he was just closed off, wary, waiting to see what happened next and what his own actions needed to be to try and either shore up a crumbling edifice to the best of his ability or figure out how to start clean-up.

"I told them what I know," Vivian said gently. "What I've seen."

"Did they talk to Charlie...?"

"Charlie?" Mom said sharply, turning to Vivian, who flushed.

"No," Vivian said.

"Why Charlie?"

"Charlie was there. He saw it happen. He was standing right next to me when I Turned."

"Maybe we should talk to him," Mom murmured.

Vivian sat up sharply. "Yes, he was there, but I was there almost immediately after and he might have seen it beginning but I was there to see it happening, and to see it end. There's nothing that Charlie could add to this discussion."

"All right, all right," Dad said, lifting both his hands, palms down, in a gesture of calming the waters. "Jazz... perhaps we'd better hear the whole story."

"But Vivian told you..."

"From *you*."

Oh well. That was inevitable, I guessed. I took a deep breath and began from the beginning, stammering a little over how we had gone downstairs to watch Mal... well... not Turn. I couldn't even look at my brother during that part of it, the whole tale seemed to be nothing more than pouring the salt of insult into what had always been a deep (and deepening with every passing month of Mal's life) cut of an injury. I had Turned before my time, while gawking at him while he failed yet again to Turn well past his own. In the telling, the action felt... crass. Gloating, even. Like the entire chain of events had been somehow set off just to mock him.

And then the moment of the Turn. I told them of the surprise of it. Of the unexpectedness, when it swirled around me; of the pain. Of what it had felt like.

I could feel them drinking all of that in. My parents and Vivian, veterans, who had never really had this yardstick of changing into one fully conscious and sapient creature from the shell of another, who were hearing this story as though it was the first time they had *ever* heard of a Turn or what a Turn felt like. Mal, listening with what felt like a potent cocktail of anger, and fear, and, yes, envy. He was last, now, in the family. He would *always* be the last one to have Turned.

I told them of the confusion, and muddle of memories, and the way it had felt to be a *different* human being from the one I had grown up as. This was a little more queasy in the telling because not one of them could have anything to contribute to this – it was all my word, and my word alone. They could believe me, or they could try and pick me apart, or they could simply shy away.

No. Not that last. Not one of them could do that. This needed to be solved, settled, the cause of it found, the way forward from here discussed. It was uncharted territory. Beyond the tale I was telling them now, there was nothing – no path ahead had been mapped. We would have to discover things and learn things and stumble over things and out-and-out make stuff up from here on because there were simply no precedents at all.

I told them what I could, of the events themselves, and I could see my parents were trying to put the pieces together – and I *was* going to bring it up myself, I was, but Mal finally roused and sat up, and they looked over at him.

"I have no idea how it all happened," he said. "But he – whatever it was that Jazz became – seemed to think he knew why it had happened when it happened. It seems it was all... Celia's fault."

The name ran through my parents like a shock wave. I actually saw my mother's entire body tremble at it, flung so baldly between us, down there on the coffee table amongst the photos of Jesse.

I shot him Mal a look that was at once frightened and exasperated. I should have been the one to have broken the silence on this one. In any event, I had to take control of it, now, before it got twisted it into something else entirely, or my mother finally gave way to the vapors.

I simply switched tacks and told them a different story. The other story. The underlying story. I told them about the diaries, and the blog...and about the real reasons behind Celia's overdosing on the Stay. Just in case they never really knew it.

"She wanted to live!" Mom sobbed into the hands she had buried her face into, at the end of it. "All this time it broke me up that my baby girl wanted to die – that's what they told us at the hospital, before it all went haywire. And that was bad enough. But she wanted to *live* – and that's worse..."

"They told you at the hospital? They told you what at the hospital? They talked to her? How could they know...?"

"They took her," Vivian said, her voice flat. Of course, it had been her who had been there in the beginning – her, and Mal and me, two kids who could do nothing at all to either help or understand. Vivian's responsibility, all of us, and Celia – Celia had just done something irrevocable. "They took her, and they raced off in the ambulance with her, and I just – I just grabbed you, Mal and Charlie - I could hardly leave you here on your own -

and I followed as best I could. By the time I got to the hospital they'd already taken her someplace behind closed doors, for intensive care of some sort, and I just – I never saw her again. I couldn't get hold of a doctor who would speak to me, and the nurses kept telling me I had to wait outside, and so I sat there in the waiting room with te three of you until all of you curled up on the chairs and went to sleep. And the nurses just filed past, every so often, and told me they were doing all that they could and there would be some news soon... right until one of them came out shaking her head, just as all of you were stirring and starting to wake up and said that she was sorry, so sorry, but Celia's heart had stopped and there was nothing else they could do – I asked how long ago and she said oh maybe a quarter of an hour or half an hour before – we had been sitting there for some time with her *gone* on the other side of that wall..."

I saw my mother's hand reach out blindly and grope for Dad's, and his fingers curl around hers. Hard.

Vivian seemed to be on autopilot.

"They wouldn't let me in to see her. To see the body. They just kept telling me that her parents needed to come – that they needed to see the parents as soon as possible..."

"But you still had two days," I whispered, looking back at my parents. "You were still two days from the end of the Turn."

Dad nodded, the motion abrupt and jerky, mechanical, like a puppet whose string had just been pulled.

"Two days we lived in blissful ignorance... and then came back to catastrophe," Dad said.

"Much like now," Mal said. "Except Jazz is still kind of with us."

It was crass, and it was cruel, and I knew where it had come from – and I could also see that Mal tightened his lips, after, as though he would have given anything to snatch the words back out of the air and swallow them away before they could hurt people he loved. Because they did exactly that – I saw my mother flinch as though she had been stung by them, and Vivian's hands clench in her lap.

"You might have been too young to know better back then, but you are *certainly* old enough to do so now," Dad suddenly said. I had been watching the women, and not *him*, but now I sat up straight at the tone of his voice and turned my full attention to him. There was something in there I had never really heard before. Something vivid, and elemental, and dark. Dangerous. For the first time I could see the source from which Mal's own temper might have come.

But Dad apparently exercised an iron control over his own. I think it might have been the first time I'd ever seen my father truly angry.

It might have been one of the few times that Mal had, too. His expression was one of astonishment, and of consternation.

"I only meant – I didn't mean – "

"You never 'only' mean," Dad said. "You say, and you do, and you wound, and you run – and you take no prisoners, nor care what you leave behind."

"I loved Celia," Mal said, caught flat footed, thrown on the defensive – coming up with the strongest defense that he could think of. Possibly the *only* one.

"Yes," said Dad, dismissing it effortlessly, relentlessly. "So did your mother. Probably considerably more than you. And I was there with her when we got to the hospital, after we Turned back, and they told us that there had been a mistake."

"A mistake? What happened?" I stammered.

Dad turned around to face me and his eyes glittered like a raptor's.

"I was there, with your mother, at the hospital. I held both her hands between my own because I could not bear to see them shaking like they were. I remember the fear and the hope and the loss in your mother's eyes. I remember them taking us back into the ward, to see Celia, and the nurse drawing back the curtain around Celia's bed... and seeing a girl lying there in the bed, eyes closed, a machine breathing for her, machines marking the beat of her heart, those green lines against the glossy black background, I can see it all today, as though I am staring at it right now. That's what my eyes had gone to, those lines, the lines that meant the difference between Celia's being dead, or alive. But your mother never even saw the machines. She looked at the patient. At the girl. And she simply said, 'That's not my daughter,' and fainted dead away in my arms."

Mal had not heard the full story before, either, because he was sitting up and gripping the arms of his chair, staring at Dad with wide eyes.

"Who was it?" I asked at last, into the silence.

"It took me three days to get to the bottom of it, because nobody would admit to having made any mistakes," Dad said, his voice soft, but I was past mistaking that softness for weakness. There was an edge to it which cut me, made me bleed. I was beginning to have a glimmering about what sort of demons he had been keeping on a tight leash all of these years, keeping us all safe in as protected a cocoon as he knew how to make... and then being faced with this, with Celia, with things wildly out of his control. With events that had happened because he had been too intent on keeping the entire *family* safe to concentrate on individuals within it, and had, perhaps, trusted to my mother to deal with the smaller troubles on every individual child's level. And somehow Celia had fallen through the cracks of that ignorance, that obliviousness. If my mother felt guilty because it had been her pills Celia had taken my father shouldered the worse guilt by far – the guilt that she had been forced into having to make the decision of taking those pills at all, that *she* had taken things into her own hands, that he had not known enough of her life to protect her from the things that scared or humiliated her... or from herself.

But it was Mom, surprisingly, who took up the story now.

"There had been two girls admitted into the hospital that night, within a half-hour of each other. One of them was Celia, and by this stage she was obviously unable to give them any answers – it was Vivian who had given them her identity and the basic facts, she was considered a caretaker who was the responsible adult in her case but was certainly not empowered, at least as far as the medical staff were concerned, to make any major medical decisions on Celia's behalf. The other patient was a normal, not Were-kind – and in her case it was an overdose from a party drug of some sorts – also brought in, unconscious, by somebody other than a family member who, again, could provide answers to basic questions of identity and address and such but could not legally make the decisions that were needed for her medical care."

"But she was a normal," I said. "And her parents could be contacted faster."

"Yes," Mom said. "They were at the hospital within a couple of hours. They saw their daughter, and then they were taken away to wait while the doctors did their thing. And sometime in those two days while they waited there and we were locked up downstairs... one of the girls died."

Mal rocked back. "One of the girls?"

"They were told it was their daughter," Mom said. "An only child, from what I understood later. Totally distraught, they gave instructions for the body to be cremated immediately. This was done; the hospital had a crematorium on call, apparently. They took away the urn with the ashes. By the time we came rushing to the hospital, your father and I, it was already... way too late."

It had been Celia who died. Celia whose ashes those other parents took away, believing them to be those of their own child.

"What happened to the other girl?" I asked.

"I don't know," Mom whispered. "All I wanted was Celia... back. To bring Celia home. I don't really remember much for a while. And then I woke up from the bad dream, and I knew that I had one child left to protect – you, Jazz. Mal was already too old for me to do what I needed to do, had already been exposed to the same noxious influences that had taken Celia..."

"You knew," I whispered. "At least some of it. You knew. It was in the diaries..."

She turned a look on me, a look that ripped me apart, a completely open and vulnerable look that handed me my mother's heart and folded my hands around it while it was still beating.

"Can I have them? The diaries?"

"No." The word had escaped almost without my realizing I had spoken – it was purest instinct, and it flew in the face of that vulnerability that had so touched me. But I knew that if I gave her Celia's notebooks they would disappear forever into whatever that shrine was where she was keeping Celia's memory, and I would never see them again. And I knew, instinctively enough for that refusal to come unbidden, that I could not bear to let them go. "But you can read it. On the blog."

The whole idea of the 'secret' blog had been to keep my parents from it. But I was tired of secrets. It was time to let go.

"You *blogged* this?" Mom sounded at once appalled and utterly astonished.

This, too, I could have handled better. I bit my lip.

"It's passworded," I offered, in a lame attempt at an excuse. "I'll give you the password."

"Celia's fault," Dad said, glancing from Mal to me. "Malcolm said this – what happened to you – was *Celia's* fault. What did he mean?"

"The diaries. I found the diaries." To my chagrin I felt my eyes begin to fill with tears and there was nothing at all I could do to stop it. "Dad, the diaries. If you read them, you will understand. I *met Celia for the first time in those pages*. I don't really remember her from when she was still here, she had her own life, her own concerns, her own problems – and it's only with the diaries that I really found out what they truly were – and I was way too young for her to share any of it with me so she was always this ideal Big Sister, an idea, somebody I might be one day when I grew up. And then she vanished, and I heard very little about it, and the stories and the secrets started piling up, and – Mom – you took *everything* away when you gave me that room, everything in it that had been hers. Even this writer she loved – this Emily Winterthorn – I never really heard of her, not until Celia mentioned her name in the diaries, until she chose to risk sickness and even death for a chance to meet this person in real life and tell her about her own dreams. But I knew nothing of any of that. And I found out I had this wonderful, talented, strong older sister whom I had never known – I read the diaries, and I never even knew that I missed her until I started to miss her so badly that I cried myself to sleep over her words some nights – and it started me thinking about things – and yes – it's Celia's fault... without those diaries, without the things she made me face, I would have still been a baby waiting for the years to roll by until the Moon said I was ready to Turn."

"But... a *boy*?" Mom whispered, freeing her hand from Dad's and reaching out to me – across the coffee table, where Jesse's pictures were. Halfway through the gesture her eyes dropped onto the table, and the pictures, and her hand fell towards them, her fingers curled around one, she lifted it up and stared at it. "A boy. How could that happen?"

That I had no answer to, so I sat silent. So did Mal. it was Vivian, in the end, who spoke up, who said the words that we were all, in some way, thinking.

"Somebody will have to be told," she said faintly. "And I had... no idea. I'm sorry, I left it all undone again, and waiting for you – because I had no idea where to take this. Somebody will have to be told."

Dad squeezed Mom's fingers once, hard, and then let go of her hand, getting to his feet.

"Somebody will be," he said. "Leave it to me, now. Vivian, thank you – and it is I who should offer my apologies to you – yet again you were on the front lines in a family crisis. We owe you. Sylvia – it will be all right. Mal – are you sure *you* didn't go blabbing about this to people who had no business knowing about it?" Mal shook his head without a word, and Dad nodded in satisfaction. "See that you don't. Jazz..." He turned to me and this was a different father than I had known, a stronger man than I had expected, somebody who saw a great load and had unhesitatingly accepted the weight and the responsibility of it on his own shoulders. All of my life I had thought him a weakling, a wimp, maybe even a crawling sycophant when it came to things like the Baudoin parties. But he was not – these were sometimes parts that he had to play to make absolutely certain that his family was in a safe and protected place which it was his responsibility to provide as best he knew how. And that was what he was going to do now. He knew somebody – he knew what to do – and all at once Dad was not the groveling and spineless worm at the feet of his 'betters' but a tower of strength into whose keeping I handed my problems over with a sigh of relief.

"Jazz," he said to me, "I promise you this. I will do whatever it takes to make sure that what happened here does not destroy your future." That was the second time that I had had that promise from a member of my family. Before Dad, Mal had promised me much the same thing. All of a sudden I felt like I had been ungracious and ungrateful all of my life – that somehow I had manufactured a story for myself in which my family didn't care, didn't understand... and yet, here they all were, standing shoulder to shoulder between me and the world, with promises that they would protect me. Promises all of them meant. "There will be questions and they will have to be answered somehow – but I will be here for you," Dad said. "Always. And now, if you'll all excuse me, I have some phone calls to make."

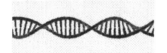

I t was just a hint of how bad things could have been, if they had all decided to close their eyes and push me into the maw of the 'normal' non-Were government research institutions – all of whom would probably have happily have cut me open while alive and conscious (and screaming) and then waited until the Full Moon rose again and they could watch to see how it was that I managed the trick from turning from Human into Human.

If the normals' authorities could harness that, they would have the absolutely ultimate weapon in their hands – they would, for at least three days out of every month, have access to a Brand New Person of an identity not on record with any enemy power, who could move freely within enemy territories, and spy, and sabotage, and do whatever the parent government wanted or needed. And then vanish, three days later, in a figurative puff of smoke. It was inevitably Mal who came up with this, he had the conspiracy frame of mind. They would *never* find the culprit of whatever deed had been done, he said, not even if that person had been seen and described by dozens or hundreds of witnesses. Especially not then.

We had finally snatched a moment alone together – without Mom hovering at my elbow, watching my every move – and I got a chance to ask him about the Barbican Bain situation.

"Actually, I think that's been taken care of," he said. "Chalky said you helped."

"Who's Chalky? And do I want to know?" I asked carefully. "And how on earth did I... help?"

"I can't tell you," Mal said, and sounded genuinely regretful about that. "Honestly, I would if I could. Let's just say that he is a kind of person who would be right at your heels if they ever took you in for vivisection – if he hadn't gone into the labs before you. He is a freaky individual, and he can do things that I would not have believed possible before I met him, but I can't spill his secrets."

"You spilled mine, didn't you?" I said. "You said I 'helped' – you told this guy about me, about the Turn... Dad *asked* if you'd blabbed about this to people who had no business knowing about it, and you said you didn't, but you did, didn't you? You went straight out and..."

"Jazz." Mal had his hand out, and it was heavy on my shoulder. A sort of iron calm flowed through it, relaxing the knotted muscles of my neck and upper back. "I did not 'blab'. I said no more than necessary, to someone who *did* have... a sort of business knowing about some of it. Trust me. Dad does things his way. I will do them in my own. One way or another, we won't let anything bad happen to you. To this family."

They did not hand me over to the horrors of an investigation that would have left me at worst dead, at best terminally trammeled and enslaved to a controlling power. But I inevitably became a Person of Interest to at least a few discreet and very carefully selected individuals high in the hierarchy of the Were authorities if not the general government which in theory ruled over us all.

Two people did come in to examine and to question me – and if they weren't exactly sticking wires into me and attempting vivisection, they did everything but that.

One of them was a large and balding man with round glasses, somebody whose head flowed into his shoulders via a succession of chins rather than an actual neck, and whom I never saw smile, not once. There were lines which seemed to have been etched into his forehead with acid – or at least they were present the entire time that he was in a room with me. I wasn't ever told exactly who he was, but I was informed that I could call him Dr. Torrance, if I ever felt the need to address him directly at all. Which I didn't. If ever there was somebody who gave an impression of wishing you not to speak until you were spoken to, it was Dr. Torrance. Whenever he was near, I tried to erase myself, blend into the wallpaper, pretend I wasn't there – an impossible task, given that I was his sole and complete focus.

He didn't seem to relish communicating with me. He was as monosyllabic as he could get away with, asking specific and precise questions and expecting the same by way of replies. He was a medical doctor of some sort because he gave me a physical examination the likes of which I will probably never have again in my entire life. I was utterly grateful and relieved when he was done with me – he had reduced me to tears several times, tears of frustration, of rage, of fear, of embarrassment.

Some of the more, er, *intimate* examinations had been relegated to a female doctor in the presence of my mother, but that didn't change the fact that I could hardly bear to glance into the mirror after these exams because I was too mortified to look myself in the eye. Mom actually turned into another tower of strength through all this, particularly after I happened to overhear an exchange between the woman doctor and Dr. Torrance (who was a machine, I swear, without a shred of human decency or empathy – he might as well have been a piece of computer software created to check out the state of my bodily plumbing. On this particular occasion, I overheard something about my ability to have children, along the line, and Dr. Torrance's clinical dismissal of the idea – his words had actually been, *under the circumstances, I see no likelihood of it ever being possible.*

That freaked me out. I have no idea why it freaked me out as much as it did – I might have cried myself to sleep on a couple of post-examination nights out of fear or shame or whatever, but this was the first time that I was outright hysterical – to the point that Mom intervened, and actually banned Dr. Torrance from anything further to do with me. She brought the other doctor in instead, a slender Asian woman with large dark eyes who looked at me with actual compassion.

"You know how pregnancy works in the Were, don't you?" she said gently.

"If you're pregnant, you don't Turn," I said, trying not to let my voice shake too much. "You just stay in the form that's carrying the baby, until it is born."

"Yes – and now think about that for a moment. The way that works is that the body now has a hormonal response to the pregnancy, and the fetus being carried is of a certain... kind. It is flatly impossible for a creature of one species to be pregnant with a fetus of another species – think of how many species there *are* – you can't have a cat being pregnant with a human baby, or a human woman with kittens, some of us Turn into birds who lay *eggs*, for instance – nature took care of that. The Turn from species to species is inhibited by pregnancy hormones – and so the pregnant female is anchored, by that, until she gives birth to the young of the species which she has conceived."

"Yes, I *know*," I said, rousing. "That's all Were biology 101 – but – "

"Now let's take your situation," the doctor said. "In your case... there is no trigger. No species-changing trigger. You have Turned from a human being to another human being."

"But that means that the pregnancy..."

"Jazz," she said gently, "in this case, it isn't the *species* that is the problem."

I figured it out, all of a sudden. No, it wasn't a species problem. It was a gender problem.

A male could not be pregnant.

"...Oh," I said.

The doctor was nodding. "Yes. Exactly. The thing is, anything before the second trimester of a human pregnancy is just... vulnerable. In your case the brain would simply assume that it had made an error, and quit ordering the production of the relevant and necessary hormones. If you could get to, say, the middle of the second trimester of pregnancy, then the triggers might yet kick in, and the body would resist the Turn into something that would not support the pregnancy. But..."

I was suddenly oddly calm about it all. "But I could never get to the second trimester," I said, quietly, "could I? The Turn would come and even if I'd got pregnant straight after the previous one it would still be only four weeks – and it would be too early to count. So I'd Turn, into a man, and the pregnancy would simply disappear?"

"Something like that," the doctor agreed. "In the best-case scenario, it might just be... erased. Reabsorbed. In the worst case scenario, I can think of... but hey, let's not go to the worst case scenario just yet. I'm sorry, sweetheart. This was... an unexpected side effect. And unfortunate. But I don't think that it's likely that you will ever have children."

Unless I fathered them, I thought, always assuming that I could... and I almost giggled at the incongruity of that – but that would have edged me back into hysteria again. So I asked other questions – I'd started my periods not too long before this, and it hadn't even occurred to me to wonder about any of that, until now. But this, too, would be affected by the timing of the Turns – and if I thought about it all too hard it made my head hurt. I could see the potential for real damage, if this were allowed to run its natural course. My body would shred itself trying to be both male and female at once. There would probably be medical issues down the line, reproductively speaking, one way or another.

"We'll figure it out," Mom said, sitting on the side of my bed, holding my hand very tightly. "We'll figure it all out."

The other man who came to examine me, the man who had selected and sent in the obnoxious Dr. Torrance (I didn't suppose the man's bedside manner entered into it, he must have just been the most qualified person to do it) to perform the preliminary and obvious medical examinations, I had met before. Sort of. At the very least, by proxy.

He was the Uncle Perry of Celia's diaries, a man whose full name turned out to be Peregrine Walker, and somebody who turned out to be rather more deeply involved in the Were ruling hierarchy and Were-politics than even Dad had ever been aware of. He, at least, was kind – he said I could call him Uncle Perry, too, but I just couldn't bring myself to do it. I told him that I had heard of him before. And from whom. And that I could not... *could not*... call him the same thing she had.

He just gave me a sad sort of smile, and said, "I understand. You can call me Peregrine."

He teased out from me far more details than Dr. Torrance had ever managed to do – stuff I barely realized that I knew. I told him exactly how it had felt, to change, the weirdness of it, and the pain, and the way I felt

159

straight after, and he took copious notes, encouraging me, telling me that this was literally the first time that any Were had been able to give such an account.

"It's like being able to remember your birth," he told me.

"That's not even possible."

"Some claim to be able to. But I would tend to agree with you there. However, here, you were already sentient – you were already *sapient* – you do understand the difference between those two words, don't you?"

"Sort of," I muttered. I didn't, exactly, but I wasn't going to admit it.

"Sentient merely means aware. Sapient means that you understand your environment at a deeper level, are able to think about it, draw conclusions from it. A sentient being would know it was in pain. A sapient being would be able to understand why."

"Okay," I said. "I get it."

I told him about my ability to retain the memories of Jazz while I was Jesse – another thing that was not possible, in the world as we knew it, and he was very interested in that, to the point that he asked so many questions that I became a little confused on the subject myself.

"So you think what Jazz thinks, when you're Jesse," he said. "Is that right? Are you telling me that the only thing that really changes is your outer carapace?"

"N-no. I kind of... remember what Jazz remembers. But what Jesse thinks about it is sometimes quite different."

I remembered my insight from when I first talked to Vivian about Celia, when I was newly Jesse.

"It's like... asking a question... Jazz relies on heart, and instinct, and clues pieced together from things she doesn't completely and for sure know. Jesse tackles it with the mind, and relies on actual data and not on clues. With Jesse, it's what he *knows*, not what he feels or what he thinks. But it's the same questions they're asking. They're just dealing with them differently."

"I see," he said, writing something down in his notebook. But the frown on his face told me another story. He was adrift in uncharted waters, just like me. Worse – all I had to do was cope with it, live it, and so far that had not proved to be the problem. What *he* had to do was make sense of it all.

Something of Celia rose in me then, and the questions which she had written about in her diary. Her pondering on her human form and her Were form, Girl and Cat, and her asking Mom about it. *Are we the same, or are we different...? We do not share a body – do we share a soul...?*

And my mother's response. *Ask Uncle Perry.*

Well, here he was. I did not know if she had ever written to him to ask him – but she was gone, and she would never get the answers she wanted, not ever again. But I could. At the very least, since I had Uncle Perry right there in front of me, I could take a turn at asking the questions.

"Celia wrote in her diary that she would write to you and ask you something," I said to Peregrine, as he sat scribbling into his notebook. "Did she? Ever?"

He paused in his writing, glancing up at me. "Not that I recall. Write to me? Why me?"

"All she could get out of Mom when she asked *her* was 'It's complicated'," I said. "And then Mom said she could maybe ask you."

His eyebrow lifted a fraction. "And what makes me such an expert on the complicated matter?"

I shrugged. "Maybe you're not. Maybe Mom just wanted to wriggle out from under the subject."

Peregrine laid down his pen, and actually laughed out loud. "All right," he said, "hit me. What is it your sister wanted to know?"

Mom was right, as it turned out. It *was* complicated. I had to think about how to frame the question. "She wanted to know if... if... well, when we are Human and we are our Were form, are we different? Are we the same? Do we share a spirit... or a soul?"

He sat back in his chair and gave me a long look. "Well," he said, after a pause, "looks like I came to ask hard questions but I'm in the hot seat for answering one instead. The answer to that one... is long, and detailed, and incomplete. People have been digging into the matter for too many years to count – the question has been something of a bedrock for the entire history and philosophy and the very existence of Were-kind. And in fact you, yourself, this thing that has happened to you, might influence the accepted truth of it all as it stands, as we think we know it, today."

"Okay," I said, "but what was the accepted truth before this thing happened to me?"

"There are variants of it," he said, "and I suspect that it would very much depend on who was talking to you about it, on what kind of mood that person was in when they began to do so, on what they had eaten for breakfast on that day, or on the phase of the Moon..." He actually stopped himself with those words, and then chuckled, and added wryly, "Well, of course, given that we are speaking of Were-kind, that *would* matter, wouldn't it."

"If you could ask a Were-cat or a Were-sparrow or a Were-raccoon, you think you'd get a different answer?" I asked.

"Those creatures, I suspect, would have no answer at all. There are people out there who will tell you animals have no souls in the first place and thus don't count at all when it comes to the Were-kind and their own hold on their soul – that Were-kind, in fact, own souls *in spite* of being Were-kind and not remotely *because* of it. There are other people who will argue passionately that any Were-kind who does not possess an animal part of their soul – the spirit in their animal avatar, as it were – has no soul at all. There are those who will tell you that each individual part of a Were-person's composition – human and beat – has a separate soul and that those two souls have nothing at all to do with each other."

"Mom was right. It's complicated."

"Very," he agreed. "There are tomes and tomes on physiology and theology and new-age metaphysics all of which insist that they explain the matter, but they might contradict one another twenty times before you're on page 50 of any given book. And of course there is always the more fundamentalist kind of mind, the people who insist that they know better without any book at all because they hear the voices of gods who tell them nothing less than the holy truth."

"Maybe it's just as well," I said, "that you didn't write all that to Celia."

Peregrine gave me a crooked little smile. "At least she thought to ask," he said. "Many people never bother to..."

He seemed to catch himself, mid-sentence, before he said something that he couldn't take back. Perhaps I should have left it, then. But I was Celia's sister and she was gone and her questions had remained unanswered – and besides, now *I* wanted to know, because it was very clear that for all his talk of 'people' who thought or believed this, that or the other thing – Peregrine himself had an opinion of his own.

'But... what do *you* think?" I asked.

He pressed his lips together and just looked at me again, for a long moment. "You're way too young for all of this," he said at last, abruptly. He closed his notebook with a snap, and started putting his paraphernalia away.

Something made me reach out a hesitant hand and touch his wrist, my fingers light as a butterfly's wing.

"I don't know why," I said, "but it matters. Somehow, it matters. You were going to tell me something. *Tell* me."

And so he told me.

Told me the *real* horror stories of the Turning Houses.

And of the Half-Souled.

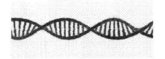

I needed to write it all out to get it straight in my head, and so I went back to the blog. And did a Celia. Wrote it down as it had happened. As... as a *story*.

5 April

I remember telling tales about Turning Houses to Nell and Bella up in Nell's room at the Baudoin party. I remember, further back, the tales I culled those from, the stories that were either told to me directly or the ones that I had figured out or extrapolated by myself. But it turns out that I had not gone nearly far enough, and that there are more secrets in the Were-kind world than just those which nest and brood in my own family circle.

Turns out, in fact, that the story of the Turning Houses has quite a lot to do with Celia's questions about what kind of a soul the Were-

kind have... because it seems to me that everything she wanted to know is answered quite comprehensively by the situation at the Turning Houses.

Turns out that it is possible for one of us, one of the Were-kind, to somehow lose our... other half, our animal avatar, the thing that we Turn into every month. I didn't think that could happen – I had always though that a Were was born a Were and then it was a question of waiting to Turn when your time came. Granted, I seem to have had the exception to that rule in front of me all my life – watching Mal struggling with his non-Turning and all that it implied – but that felt... different. You could not 'lose' something you never had, and he'd NEVER had the Turning experience. It was just a lack, not a loss. It made a huge difference in the way that I had seen it. Of course, Mal was a moody and annoying and frequently downright dangerous kind of guy, but I always figured that was just Mal, not any syndrome involving loss of soul.

(Turns out I was right about that.)

Turns out that the Turning Houses are so much more than the places where the normals send the Were-kind to be locked up for the duration of their Turn. They're also the prison for those unlucky enough to have somehow become severed from their second selves.

I said it sounded like the worst kind of insane asylum I could imagine.

"Not... exactly," the man my sister Celia once knew as Uncle Perry told me. "It gets complicated. Yes, by several different criteria they are very much insane – but they're missing half of themselves, after all, and it isn't entirely unexpected."

"So they're just cared for there, because they..."

"Uh. Well, if you're thinking of a hospital it isn't quite the same thing. They are there because that's a good place to keep them all together and in one place and controlled. They are not permitted to come and go as they please; if one of us is ever unfortunate enough to be in this situation, that person is assigned to a Turning House as the place where they will spend the rest of their lives. They are chipped, there's a tracking chip implanted in their legs, just above the ankle – it emits a specific signature signal, and there are readers posted on the perimeter of the grounds. Nobody who bears one of these chips is permitted to pass that perimeter from the inside."

"I read about invisible fences," I said. "They use them for dogs. I didn't think they used them for people. Don't they resent this? Doesn't anyone ever try to escape?"

"There have been escapes," he said, "but probably the less you know about those right now the better. They tend to be violent, and messy. But for the most part they don't have a reason to go anywhere else other than where they have been put. Most of them are depressed, some of them are close to catatonic, they are certainly incapable of independent existence in the outside world."

"They just lock them up – lock them away – and forget about them?"

"They work. They are the custodians of the true-Were who are sent there to Turn every month. They are responsible for taking care of them, for feeding them, for keeping an eye on the doors that lock THEM in."

"The inmates are in charge of the asylum," I said. It was a phrase that I'd heard Dad use sometimes – and it had never been as appropriate as when I used it right then.

"It's... not ideal," 'Uncle Perry' said. "But there are too many of them to simply institutionalize them and at least they are leading SOME kind of productive existence...."

"How many are there?" I asked, suddenly subdued, because I had begun to do the math in my head. There were a LOT of Turning Houses. A lot of Were-kind went to them. If the Half-Souled were the only 'staff' on the premises, there had to be a lot of them, too. A great many. More than I wanted to think about.

I wasn't given a number. Only an equation. "Every Turning House has to have a minimum complement of at least forty of them, to run it. But that's the minimum. I don't think you'll find many that function... on the minimum alone."

"How many can there be at a Turning House?"

"Some of the bigger ones... there are several hundred."

I struggled with the magnitude of this. "Several hundred...? But how do several hundred of us end up severed from our Turn-self? What happened to these people? Can it happen... to anybody?"

"A lot of different things happened," Uncle Perry told me. "And keep happening. It's an on-going thing – there are new ones coming in, all the time. They tend... not to live too long, the Half-Souled, once this happens to them. But somehow their numbers never really go down."

He didn't say all that much more. He didn't need to. At the end of that conversation I was more terrified of it all than I had ever been of anything in my life.

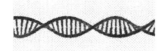

The day after I posted that entry to the blog, both Nell and Charlie both came to see me. There we were, the three of us, the Corvid Princess and the Lowly Vampire Bat and the Monster Random Were-Human all sitting there in my room – this had cut across everything that was extraneous and 'social', all the silly matters of class and our perceived positions in society. This cut us all to the bone of what we all, in the end, were at the bottom of all the accrued layers. We three, Were-kind. And it did not surprise me in the least that the two of them had reacted much the same way as me.

"So, then, what?" Charlie asked. We do have a single soul?"

I stammered a little over my response. I hadn't had time to figure it all out and present it in some sort of coherent form. "I guess," I said slowly, feeling my way through the morass, still testing each step before I put my full weight on it, "the only way I can make sense of it now is that I now believe that we have a soul that is... I don't know... somehow split between the Human and the Were within us. Part of our spirit belongs to one and part to the other."

"So I am Raven, but I am me – all at once, except that the bit of me that I am not at any given moment is kind of pushed into the background while the other bit is dominant?" Nell asked. "I can't...get my head around that..."

"The Raven part of you would tell you so, probably, if the Human was capable of communicating with it. They just don't speak the same language. It's as if you and some Japanese kid were left alone in a room and you didn't speak Japanese and he spoke only Japanese. You'd have no common ground at all."

"But Jazz, and Jesse...?" Charlie said.

"I can share those memories, because when it came to me it was Human to Human – that's the only way it works – although I saw things in a different way – how could I not? – I was still thinking like a human would think. I spoke the same language as... as myself. It was there for me to access. I would guess it's almost impossible to do that on the same level with a Were-creature which is fully itself."

"The animal part is more instinct and the human part more focused... ideas, thought, coherent issues? Is it just a matter of actually just having language?" Nell said.

"Ravens can learn to speak," I said.

She waved a hand in dismissal. "Yes, of course they can. But you don't have a philosophical discussion with a raven. You and I can talk about this now but Jesse would have a difficult time speaking about the same subject with me in my raven form during the Turn. Even if I was a raven who could actually talk. They learn to mimic, you know. They don't actually start spouting their own epic poetry."

"But it is still... one soul," Charlie said. "Raven and you. Together. Two parts that make a single whole."

"I didn't even know it was possible for a Were-kind creature to just, you know, stop being Were-kind," I said. "I thought you just couldn't help being what you were born. You couldn't just wake up one morning and not be Were-kind – anymore than it's possible for that Japanese kid to whom you were trying to talk, earlier, could wake up one morning and not be Japanese. Or a woman could wake up and not be a woman anymore."

"You did," Charlie pointed out with a grin. "Well, not go to bed one and wake the other – but you did turn into Jesse..."

"But never before, anybody else, that anyone can now recall," Nell said. "It's hardly a yardstick. You... you were... an accident."

"Thanks," I said wryly.

She grinned at me. "I just want to meet this Jesse," she said, "and we both know that's unlikely. So excuse me for being snarky."

"You'd like Jesse," Charlie said, smirking.

I smacked him on the shoulder, hard. He was still grinning as he shied away from me, but lost the smile as he took a longer look at me.

"Hey," he said, sounding genuinely contrite, "I didn't mean to say anything that..."

"What would it feel like?" I murmured, only half paying attention.

"What?"

"What would it feel like? Losing it? Losing that other half of you? I cannot even begin to conceive of it. When I even think about it, the whole idea feels... devastating... as though someone would have ripped out my heart."

"Well, your soul," Nell said softly. "It seems to me that Were-kind who lose the Were part of themselves don't just become... human. Not just an ordinary human. They...we...fall deeper and harder than that, become something different, something lesser."

"It's as though things get crossed," Charlie said, hugging his shoulders as if he were suddenly cold. "That – what would you call it – the human-thought part of us gets snatched away with the animal-soul and the animal-thought, the instinct, gets left behind, attached to the shell of the human body which remains. And it isn't living any more. The Half-Souled don't live, they... they exist. Their instincts, the animal instincts, tell them to eat, and sleep, and breathe – but it sounds to me like they lost everything else that there was to lose, that they're left without any higher thought, or idea, or dream, or aspiration."

"That's why they generally don't try to escape, then," I said.

"Eh?" Charlie said, looking like I had just woken him up from some sort of living nightmare.

"They don't run," I said. "They don't try to escape what's really a prison... because they don't have anywhere else to go. They probably don't even need those chips in their legs. They are in the only place that exists, for them, already..."

"Zombies," Nell said. "They're zombies."

"Were-zombies," Charlie said.

"Oh, don't," Nell said, and shivered. "That's just too horrible. They never change back."

"You know what freaks me out?" I said. "I keep thinking back to Celia's early diary entries – when my family first came here – my mother and my father went to these Turning Houses, in the beginning. They had to. They weren't given a choice. They would have met these Half-Souled people, half jailors to the two of them and half inmates themselves. They would have seen them. Known them. Perhaps tried to talk to them. They came into a Turning House to obey a law, but they were then allowed to leave – and they left all these drifting, empty husks behind. Always left behind. They never talked about that when they spoke to us kids about the Turning Houses. I wonder... what they were thinking, back then. Really thinking. How much they knew. Or... or if they ever wondered... why."

"What do you mean?" Charlie said, sitting up. "Why what?"

"When Peregrine was telling me about them, he never really told me how such a thing as this happens. Why it happens. Why it happens to this person and not to that one. I got the impression... that it's... well... random." A dry little laugh bubbled out at that word. Random. Like me. "There's no reason to it, nothing that marks you. For all I know, my mother or my father could simply... fail to Turn one day. Fail the month after that. No reason given, no reason needed. If it's deemed to be permanent... they could be packed up and taken away to a Turning House, and have a chip put into their leg, and be left there to fend for themselves and to take care as best they could of those luckier others who still Turned on their schedules and were thrust upon the Turning Houses for three days of every month." I glanced at Charlie. "Or six, I guess, if you counted the new-Moon Were-kind. The new-moon folk have to go, too, don't they?"

"Were is Were," Charlie said. "The Moon makes no difference. If you Turn you have to be safely behind lock and key. Yes, we have to go too – we don't get a free pass on anything."

I counted on my fingers. "No warning. No reason. No provocation. No appeal. It could happen... to anybody. At any time. It could happen to anybody in our family. It can happen to any of us – to you, or to you, or to me."

"You're scaring me," Nell and Charlie said, almost in unison.

"I'm scaring you?" I said. "Then three's company. I'm scaring myself senseless."

10 April

All right. They had my attention. I am afraid.

For the first time in my life, that thing that I am – something that I cannot change, and apparently if I could would destroy me if I tried – was not the bedrock of my existence, the definition of my being, of myself. It was shifting ground, slippery clay on which I scrambled to find purchase and stay upright, and even that ground was not solid under my feet but trembled as though shaken by a powerful earthquake.

There had been... some kind... of future. Something that was ahead of me, nebulous and full of drifting fog through which it was difficult to see, but there, nonetheless, the undiscovered country which was waiting for me. I would grow older, have a family of my own, grow old with them... now everything I thought was true and real was just dreams and fantasies. I had been told in fairly no uncertain terms that there would be no classic little family for me. That alone changed things, changed the future, changed...

everything. I was not so sure of anything, now. The fog had thickened into a wall, and I could no longer see further than a short hesitant step forward. If that. It was difficult to plan for a potential problem when you had no idea what the cause of it was, or from which direction it would strike, or when. From here on it would be a day at a time, and it would be turning often to watch my back as the nameless shadows stalked me from the darkness.

Celia had died for a future she could see in front of her, wanted so badly that she could touch it, that she was willing to risk everything for it. Me... all that I can do is cling to the wind. And hope it takes me as far as a new day tomorrow. Beyond that, I can't see, I can't even think about it right now. Maybe, some day, when the first rush of fear passes. Right now I can barely believe that I am alive and whole IN THIS MOMENT, let alone planning to be that way when I wake up tomorrow morning.

I think 'Uncle Perry' saw some of this in my face, just before he left that time we talked of all this. I think he might have regretted answering the questions he had been asked quite as frankly and honestly as he did.

A part of me... is grateful for the knowledge. It makes my mind a bigger place to know what I know. But that doesn't mean that I am not going to have Half-Souled nightmares from now on when I try to close my eyes and go to sleep. I had never been the kind of kid who was afraid of monsters under the bed – and I knew why, now. It was because in some way I had ALWAYS known that the monsters were real... and out there, waiting. With half their soul torn away and shredded and crying with a small voice, lost in the wilderness and knowing it could never come home again.

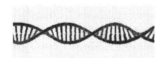

D r. Torrance had submitted his medical report – which showed absolutely nothing out of the ordinary or anything that they hadn't expected to see, but I remembered my earlier thoughts on the physiology of it all and thought grimly to myself, oh, sure, it's all fine SO FAR – but that was not the end of it. Peregrine said he wanted to run a few more tests, which would naturally take a few more Turn cycles where he could make direct empirical observations when it came to my particular talents.

"She did it once," he told my parents, when he came back to speak to them about the matter. (No, I wasn't invited to the conference, for all that it directly concerned me; but since it did pertain to what would happen to me next, I took the liberty of eavesdropping at the door.) "I would like to see if the event is reproducible. I'll be attending the next Turn in this house in person, in order to keep an eye on matters and prove a few things to my satisfaction."

"But it's – I mean, won't you yourself be in a position where you're Turning..."

"I would be taking advantage of one of your Turning rooms, when the time comes, if that's all right," Peregrine said. "But in the beginning, if I want to be an observer of things as they happen to Jazz, it would be a matter of taking a dose of Stay to delay my own turn by a few hours, in order to stay in a form in which it is possible for me to investigate this particular situation. Don't worry, Sylvia," he added, to what must have been a spectacular (and wholly understandable) response from my mother, "I will bring my own supply, and only enough for the purpose at hand. There will be no loose pills or an easy way for anybody to have access to them."

He was bringing Stay into this house – into the house where it had swept Celia away on a tsunami. It was going to be an interesting Turn the following month – I could see my mother's nerves going to pieces over this. Poor Vivian – she'd be the one left holding the bag yet again. Celia, and now this whole drama that I was part of – Vivian had certainly gone above and beyond the call of duty to my family. I would have to ask Charlie how we could make it up to her, or at least what to do to make sure she came out of all of this sane.

By the time the May Turn came around, we were a house of nervous wrecks. My father had taken to pacing the floors, my mother to biting her nails and looking in turns frightened, and so furiously determined that it scared me to speculate on what precisely she might be thinking or planning. But whatever it was she didn't talk to me about it – and all any of us could do was wait.

When the full Moon of the Turn rose, for once my entire family went to the Turning rooms with the docility of angels – no chasing my father around the house, no alternately cajoling and scolding Mal into retiring into his room with his customary weasel to await (probably) the inevitable. In the end the only ones left outside in the basement corridor were Vivian, Peregrine, and myself.

To avoid any possible embarrassing episodes, I had already cocooned myself in a Turning cloak which we all wore – a sort of wraparound blanket that fastened around the sides with velcro and covered any possible mishaps with outer clothing, protecting propriety and modesty, allowing a re-Turning Were to have something to tuck around themselves when they came back to being human at the end of the three days until they could get access to a bath and a change of clothing.

But Peregrine wanted the whole thing done by the book this time round.

"Indulge me," he said to me, "and let's use a Turning room for this. I would like a controlled environment. One of these is yours, is it not? Prepared for you for just this time?"

He must have taken Stay already because otherwise he would probably have been about to Turn or already Turning himself – and I found myself watching him closely for any signs that might have equaled Celia's dramatic experience. But he was calm, quiet, very businesslike and matter-of-fact, and at the same time sympathetic and kind. In some ways he was almost treating me as if I was much younger than I was – but somehow I found that less difficult to accept than I might ordinarily have done. He had a manner about him that defined that attitude as protective rather than patronizing.

I could see the sense in his request, so I stepped into the room that had been made for this moment, for me, so many years ago by my father. I'd seen these rooms before, of course, my entire life – my family had retired to them month after month for all my childhood. They were familiar places, and I could have described them to a stranger who had never seen them in the sort of detail that would have built the place in their minds not so much in a vision as in Sensurround. I knew the dimensions of this room, the materials of which it was made... everything, in fact, except what it felt like to enter one as a Were about to Turn.

Everything in the room, improbably, looked new and strange to me. As though I had never seen the place before in my life.

"It's okay," Peregrine said, seeing the sudden hesitation in my step. "It's safe. Everything is safe. We're all here to see to that."

I felt the itching begin, a tingling in my fingers, a twitch at the corner of my eyelids.

"It's starting, I think," I said, curling my hands into fists and then relaxing them again, bracing myself for the pain to come.

"Excellent," Peregrine said quietly. "Look over here a moment...?"

I had been staring at the floor, at my feet, waiting for the Turn to begin claiming me, but his voice drew my eyes back up, trying to follow his voice.

I have no idea what I expected. It was not what I saw. Right then, right there, in the throes of beginning to Turn, I met the curious but rather indifferent gaze of a mouse held on Peregrine's open palm.

And then the Turn broke open, and I cried out, and I... don't remember any more, not until I was sitting up and blinking owlishly inside the familiar-yet-unfamiliar Turning room with its door closed and my mother's anxious face at the glass window set into it.

I thrust my aching and uncooperative limbs into the sleeves of the Turning cloak, and fastened it around me with numb fingers; by the time I had finished with that the door had burst open and my mother had tumbled inside the room, practically sobbing, and had wrapped both me and the recalcitrant cloak into a tight hug.

It caught me by surprise. My mother was not a hugger. I could not remember the last time she had done that, or the reason for it.

"What happened?" I muttered, my mouth squashed sideways into her shoulder.

"You're all right," she said, and then kept repeating it, as if it was the only thing that she could bring herself to utter out loud. "You're all right.

You're all right."

"I'm fine," I said, irritated, starting to struggle out of her arms. "What happened? It was different, this time – it was – last time I remembered – is Turn over? Did I not Turn into Jesse this time? Where's Peregrine?"

"Right here," Peregrine said, from outside the room. "Are you decent?"

I pushed my mother away far enough in order to check the fastenings of my cloak. "Yeah. I'm fine." And then, for the third time, "What happened?"

Peregrine stepped into the room and around my mother, bearing a plate with a sandwich on it.

"Here," he said, offering it to me, "Vivian made it for you. She said the last time you ate an entire pizza by yourself."

"Did not," I muttered, but took the sandwich anyway. This much at least I remembered – there was a Turn, and I was hungry.

"Finish that, and take the time you need to get changed and feel a little more... human..." Peregrine had an infectious grin when he wanted one, and he flashed me one now. "I'll be waiting up in your living room when you're done. A few things we need to discuss."

I had a little trouble shaking Mom long enough to step into the shower by myself and get properly dressed. I was feeling considerably less shaky than the last time this had happened, although I did make a detour through the kitchen before I went to the living room as instructed, in order to raid the cookie jar.

I was starting to wonder how all Were-kind weren't overweight blimps, if we all came out of Turns as hungry as I felt right then.

Maybe it petered off with time, once a new Were got used to the experience.

They were all waiting for me in the living room, the entire family, much like the last time. Mal's expression warned me not to ask him if he had managed the Turn this time round. UnTurned, yet again. He looked... he no longer looked angry. He just looked... diminished. As though he had given up. Surrendered. It was worse than ever, now – having to watch me go through it and be the focus of this much attention, knowing that with every Turn I made I moved further and further away... leaving him further and further behind.

"Everything all right?" Peregrine said, as I came in

"I'm fine," I said, yet again, flopping into one of the armchairs and curling my legs underneath me. I wished everybody would stop asking me. I was starting, even to myself, to sound like a recording.

"Well," Peregrine said, leaning forward, his elbows on his knees and his chin resting on his interlaced fingers, "here's the thing I wanted to try and establish – whether what had happened to Jazz the last time was something that could be... derailed... by the proper circumstances. This is a Random family and by rights, according to all we know about that, it's a peculiarly accident-prone type of Were-kind, liable to being tripped up by circumstances beyond their control. So I used a wild card... in the shape of a mouse. Right as Jazz was beginning her Turn."

"Yes," I said, sitting up, "I remember that – you had one in your hand –

and then I don't remember any more after that."

"That's because you followed your family's type perfectly," Peregrine said with his lazy grin. "You traditionally Turn into the last living warm-blooded thing you see right as you are hit with the beginning of the process – well, the last living thing I made you see was that mouse. You spent the last three days in that Turning room as a very pretty little mouse, Jazz. You are, in fact, in every respect, a perfectly normal Were of your kind – you are a classic Random, in fact. You can send that in when you register, and you would not be telling one word of a lie – you are a Random Were, and that's where it ends, and you can put down your default form as mouse, and there isn't a single person in this house who would not sign off on that." Mal made an inarticulate noise at the back of his throat somewhere, and Peregrine bent a raised-eyebrow glance at him – but Mal found that he had nothing to say, after all, and had the grace to look away with a scowl. "As for – the other matter," Peregrine continued, turning back to bestow another of his disarming grins on me before glancing up at my father, "with your permission, I would like to attend one more Turn in this house, this time leaving things untweaked, just to make absolutely certain of what is happening."

"Of course," Dad said. "Thank you, Perry."

"I have a couple of requests," Peregrine said. "Should you Turn into Jesse again, Jazz, there is a doctor – a New-Moon Were – to whom I would like you to report for another full physical, in the Jesse form. This is a non-negotiable – I absolutely require a baseline medical for the Jesse persona, in a way that your mouse-form simply does not demand. Since I cannot myself be around to police any of it, I will have to simply ask for your word that you will do as I ask."

I didn't particularly relish another medical go-round, particularly when I was in that other, unfamiliar, and even more deeply embarrassing body than the one I was sitting there in right at that moment – and even more particularly given that it could give me even more unpleasant answers to questions I had not even thought to ask yet – but I could see his point. I nodded, once, sharply.

"Good. I will leave his name and address with you, and I will alert him that... a young man is going to come to see him for a physical. There is, I think, no need for any further information to leave this house."

"You're just going to leave her like that? As Jesse?" Mal said. "People keep saying it's never happened before, and it's just – not important – that she's turned into a male?"

"As to the importance of the whole thing I said nothing about it being unimportant," Peregrine said, very calmly. "When I have both medical reports, I will compare them very carefully and see what there is to be gained from them. If there are things that require further study or explanation, I will return, with questions. But you're absolutely right in that it's unique, as an event. And I wouldn't at all be surprised if there were those out there who could think of dozens of ways to exploit the matter. But unless you want your sister to be something that is a cross between a circus exhibit and a genetic goldmine, I think the best thing to do under the circumstances is to control the situation in-house. For now, at least."

"The government," Mal began, but Peregrine shook his head, silencing him.

"I am, of course, not the government," he said, lacing his fingers together. "But I have the ear of people who need to know, have to know… and should not under any circumstances know. It isn't as though she Turned into something with a Clan or a Guild of its own – as if she suddenly became a cardinal Corvid and owed allegiance to the Corvid Primary, for instance. Random Were just don't have that kind of fixed infrastructure. By definition. We have wiggle room here, and for Jazz's sake I intend to take as much of it as I am able." He paused, and turned his full attention to Mal again. "I very much hope that I never hear about this from quarters where I do not expect to hear about it, Malcolm Marsh. Only a few of us know the truth of the matter, and if I hear it leaked… there are only a few sources from which it could have come out. I will be able to find out with a reasonable degree of certainty from whom the information came. And trust me, I am enough… government… to be able to take a proper course of action about that. Are we clear on this, between you and me?"

"You make it sound as though I'd really go out and sell her," Mal said at last.

"There were things said," Peregrine said slowly.

"Yeah. I know." Mal's shoulders slumped. "I didn't mean any of it. You don't have to worry about me."

"You said you had several requests," I said to Peregrine, trying to change the subject, to get the attention off Mal. He was strangely vulnerable, looked as though he could be pushed right off the edge by somebody who just happened to say the wrong word, and for a moment there I was actually afraid for him. About his future, and not my own.

"Actually, yes," Peregrine said. "Obviously one of them is to continue to be in the loop of it all – and if anything should change, I need to know about it, first, and fastest. The fact that I don't want you to be a lab rat, Jazz – not in any form, either physical or mental, as it happens – doesn't mean that I don't think that what has happened to you isn't a remarkable thing, and I don't want to just forget about it either. You may, if you like, consider me to be the 'government' who will be keeping an eye on you. I would like you, in fact, to begin to keep a journal of your Turning experience, if you have not done so already…"

"She's already got a blog," Mal said, his voice oddly flat.

But I'd already told Peregrine as much, really, when I had brought up Celia with him. "You can read it, if you want to," I said, resigned.

"Thank you," Peregrine said, "But first I'd like to make your blog as safe from hackers as possible, for obvious reasons." He smiled in an obvious attempt to shift our attention from the dire consequences if that happened.

"I will read it with great interest. It sounds like there's things in there that I really need to know about. But what I meant was something rather more empirical and, um, as clinical as you can manage. I want a record of Turning, first-person, of a kind we've never really had before. Oh, we've had tales of it – fairy-tales – stories from the dawn of time, now myths, legends, cloaked in so much flim-flam that it is impossible to get any real facts out of any of it at all. You – you have a front row seat, direct experience. Absolute fact. That, if you like, will be your contribution to your people. Your experiences might answer any number of questions that have been hanging in the balance for generations. Perhaps since the beginning of our awareness of being Were-kind."

He didn't say it, not out loud, not here where it would only derail the discussion, but he was looking into my eyes as he said this and I could see it there, the words he was leaving unsaid. The answers to the question of a Were soul, its existence and its nature, might lie in your hands...

It was Celia's question. Peregrine had tried to give me some answers. I owed him.

Besides, it might prove to be an interesting thing to chronicle, anyway. Having had the experience of Turning into Jesse and Turning into the mouse, I could now see how different it was for the vast majority of Were-kind – who was I kidding, for everybody else except me, apparently.

I nodded mutely, and Peregrine clapped his hands together, getting to his feet.

"Then it's settled," he said, getting to his feet. "I'll return next month."

He shook my father's hand, gave a slow sympathetic nod to Mom (who couldn't seem to summon up the energy to get up off the couch), and departed, announcing that he would let himself out. Vivian left shortly after.

Mal and I passed in the corridor, after.

"Are you all right?" I was moved to ask, out of the blue, in tone that was half genuine and anxious inquiry and half a weird and inarticulate apology I had no clue how to formulate in any other way.

He made a small chopping motion against his Adam's apple with the edge of his hand; above it, his face broke into a slightly manic grin.

"Never better," he said brightly, "thanks for asking."

"Mal... seriously..."

"Seriously, little sister? Seriously, I've kind of had it. Had it with waiting. When it comes to patience, forbearance, I'm riding on fumes here. I've got nothing left. And frankly, the waiting is the part that is killing me. If I knew that it was just not going to happen, I might be able to live with it. Somehow. Although..." He swallowed, his eyes slid off mine for a moment, and then came back again, his soul raw in his eyes. "Jazz, it would probably break that bit of my heart that isn't already broken. But at least it would be over."

He turned away and slipped into his room. The sound of the door closing was final, and a clear un-invitation. There were things he needed to deal with without me meddling in it – and I knew, who better, that some of those things unequivocally had to do with my own circumstances, and in how he now saw himself as fitting into the family picture.

Dad was alone in the kitchen, drying off plates with a tea towel, when I wandered back into the living room.

"Hey," he said softly, glancing over the breakfast bar as he saw me wend my way past the couch. "You okay? You still hungry?"

"I have to quit eating sometime," I said, a little impatiently. "Daddy... can I talk to you for a sec?"

A few days ago, even, this conversation might have been impossible for me – back when I maybe believed that it was meaningless, that I would just be talking at a man who could not and would not do anything at all to address the concerns I might be bringing to him because he might have been afraid of the consequences. But now – it was different, he was a different man, I was a different girl, and Mal was at the end of his rope.

Dad put the tea towel down. "Sounds serious," he said. "What is it?"

"It's... it's Mal, Dad," I said. It felt strange, talking to my father about Mal behind his back, but I kept on seeing that bright, brittle grin that had wreathed his face just now in the corridor – a smile painted on the face of a mannequin, or to disguise the drawn-back teeth in what was really a snarl of frustration and impotent fury. "I feel as though I kind of... I took his turn... Dad, he hates it, you know. He hates it. The whole lock-me-up-with-a-weasel thing. It's killing him slowly, little bit by little bit."

"Did you guys talk about this?" Dad said, putting an arm around my shoulders.

"No – well, yes, not really, but you know, a little," I said.

"None of this is your fault, Jazz," Dad said. "You didn't choose any of this, the timing, the context, the consequences."

"Yes – but – what happens, when Mal is eighteen?" I said, suddenly aware of a potential yawning gap which I had not even considered before. "He's just going to go, the moment that he can, under the law – anything, to escape that room... and I don't want to lose him, too."

"Oh, honey. You won't."

"You don't know," I said, squirming free of his arm, all earnestness now. "Dad, how long does he have to keep at this? To have to keep enduring this? It's humiliating, and worse now that I'm... that he isn't... how do you know? If it isn't going to happen at all? Can a Were be, you know, un-Were?"

"He'll Turn," Dad said. "Eventually. Everyone of Were blood does."

"What's the oldest age that anyone ever did? And what happened to that person?"

"I'd have to look it up," Dad said. Too carefully.

"It's bad news, isn't it?" I asked.

He almost refused. Almost. I could see the secret – another secret – beginning to bloom behind his eyes. And then he made a decision – I was a grown-up now. Officially. By every Were law there was.

"To the best of my knowledge," he said, unwillingly, but at least for once he was telling me the truth when I asked him for it point-blank, "twenty-two years old. There are rumors of older, but I am not sure how far they can be trusted."

"And what happened...?"

"It was a young man," Dad said. "He didn't live to see his twenty fifth birthday."

"Why?" I breathed, appalled.

Dad shrugged. "There were... various explanations offered for it," he said.

He wasn't going to go further than this. He'd given me enough to go on, if I really wanted to find out more, but from the tone of his voice, the expression on his face, I figured that I was really better off not knowing the details. I circled back to our own problem. Mal.

"Dad – can't you just – let him go? Let him decide? If it hasn't happened by now..."

"But it will happen," Dad insisted, gently, but firmly. "And if it isn't to be the room downstairs, he knows that the alternative is worse."

I shuddered. "The Turning Houses."

"Yes," Dad said, after a short pause. "Those... were something that your mother and I never wanted for any of our children."

"But Dad... I don't know how much more of this he can take. Really. Or if I can bear to watch it. And as things stand, even Turned, I will have to watch it, all of it. And he'll have to come out of that room, if it doesn't happen the next time, or the next, and he'll have Jesse to stare at for three days. It would drive me crazy, and I know it will make him want to do murder, and I wouldn't blame him..."

"But what would you want me to do?" Dad said, his voice very soft. "You don't just... stop being Were-kind. I can't just say 'let's stop it' and let it go at that. We live by the law here, and the sufferance of the law. And the law says that a young Were cannot leave home before age 18, and even then certainly not without provisions being made for Turning..."

"But he hasn't Turned!" I interrupted.

"Not yet," Dad said. Implacable.

"What if he just isn't meant to be a weasel?"

"As opposed to... what? Like you were meant to be a boy? Or that mouse that Peregrine lobbed at you just before you Turned into it? Jazz, if he were meant to be something else – something that was not Random – he would have certainly done that by now. And if not even the Turn-prompt animal will trigger it as a Random Were, what makes you think that he is ready to Turn into anything else at all?"

"But what if he doesn't? Can you keep him locked up and in a Turning Room every time the phase of the Moon changes, for the rest of his life? That's prison..."

"I don't know, Jazz. I don't know what the answer is. All I can tell you is that I hope, every time I walk into my own Turning Room, that I'll walk out again and be able to slap Malcolm on the back and congratulate him on finally crossing that bridge. And there is nobody more disappointed than me when it does not happen."

"Yes, there is," I whispered. "Mal."

"Perhaps we can talk to Peregrine, at the next Turn," Dad said, a concession. "This time, it was all about you – next time, we can draw Malcolm into the discussion. Perhaps Peregrine will know."

"Why can't you just let him be?" I asked. "I mean, now you know the worst that would happen – could happen – he might just do the same thing I did, in reverse, and Turn into a girl...?"

"Same thing as before," Dad said. "He's out there, amongst other humans – he goes to that school – he is in contact with other people all the time. But he didn't Turn into one of them, did he? Not even at the cusp of the Full Moons. If he were ready to Turn, he would have Turned – and we would have had to deal with this situation with him long before you came along. You... only fell into this because nobody even expected you to be near Turning yet, and it all just happened, without anybody being prepared for it. But the point is, you were ready – and the Turn took you. We could do the very same for Malcolm but with him – well – you know how well prepared we have been, for him, for years – and nothing ever happened at all... weasel or human, it doesn't matter. He isn't ready. He hasn't found his shape, be it Random, or human, or some other actual Were Clan that he had a phantom attachment to that we did not know about. The Moon hasn't called his name yet."

"I wish you could make it stop," I said, my voice breaking slightly.

"So do I, sweetie. For all our sakes. So do I."

I sighed, and after a moment of shared silence it was clear that the conversation was over. I sidled out of the kitchen and went back to my room.

I thought I saw Mal's door closing softly as I turned into the corridor, almost deja-vu – hadn't he gone into his room with a certain sense of finality before I had had this little talk with Dad?... But even as I paused, listening, I could only hear silence.

I left it at that. For now. I had done what I could do.

I had to figure out my own path, from here. My life was only just supposed to be beginning. I was a full Were now, and considered adult in all the things that mattered. I had a million things to learn, in order to stay on the straight and narrow, to stay safe, to stay myself, to stay out of trouble.

To figure out who I was, and where I wanted to go from here.

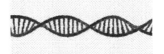

We had all been flayed by this. My parents because of a stark reminder of the great tragedy of their lives, and a new awareness of Celia's life before she was gone from this family; Mal for obvious reasons, but even that was complex – it was partly that he could nurse a grudge until it turned into a yeti-sized monster, and he certainly had good grounds for one, and partly because of that odd and heartbreaking surrender of his spirit that he had perhaps inadvertently allowed me to glimpse). As for me, well, because of any number of things – it was a motley soup, which had begun by stirring up Celia's bones and had then got seasoned with my unexpected Turning and the nature of it, and the whole Half-Souled debate. At least some of the festering secrets had been brought into the open, but they appeared to have hatched out of eggs, and now we were all kind of walking on eggshells around one another. The silences were different, but there were still silences, and things that we had to re-learn to talk to each other about.

One unexpected result of the storm was that one day I found a pile of six books on my bed – a couple of hardcovers and a handful of tattered, well-loved, broken-spined paperbacks.

All of them by a writer called Emily Winterthorn.

All of them once owned and read and loved by Celia.

The books... which might have been, if you chose to look at them that way, the reason that she was dead.

I started at the earliest one, published almost twenty years before, one of the hardcovers, and before I was fifty pages into it I knew what Celia had found in these books because I could see it shining through. I read them all, in chronological order – devoured them one after the other, more like, barely putting down one before picking up the next. The last one had been published the year before Celia's death – and that, of course, was where this particular collection had quit cold turkey, a snapshot of a life stamped out while still unfinished.

I went straight from the last book to the Net, reading up on Emily Winterthorn, and discovered that there had been (of course) other books in between that final one I had read and the present moment. Ones I hadn't even known existed, hadn't (of course) read. Ones that came... after Celia was gone.

Emily Winterthorn was not Were-kind. I scanned her online bio for clues, and they were not there. She was normal, she was one of *them*, not one of us, and yet the Were-kind characters who moved through her stories felt real, acted and spoke and feared and loved with a genuine and sincere *rightness* to every motion and every word.

I ran to Nell with all of it, of course. It did not entirely surprise me that she knew Emily Winterthorn's name.

"Yeah, she's cool," Nell said. "I have a lot of her stuff."

"Celia had everything," I said. "Everything this woman ever wrote, she collected her books right until the day she died. Have you got any of the new ones?"

"Two or three," Nell said. "You're welcome to borrow them if you want."

"Thanks. I will. But mostly I want to go out and just get them all, and have them all, *all* of them, I feel the same urge to gather them and brood over them that Celia obviously had. It's like you're blind, you've been blind all your life, and then you read a book or hear a story about a blind person just like you, and everything's right and perfect and true – and you know, you just *know*, that this story was written or told by someone who must themselves be blind else they could not possibly know so much or feel so much – and then you find out that they can see, and this rightness in the story comes from a rightness in the heart and not some stupid shared disability – and it's *bigger*, somehow. Because, even unable to know from the inside how it all feels, this person, this storyteller, somehow knows anyway. And it's amazing, it's just amazing to me that it's even possible."

"You sound like an evangelist for a new religion," Nell said, laughing, while she was rooting out four Winterthorn books from her shelf for me. "There, that's all I've got of the ones you won't have read – but I know that there's at least one more in *that* series, came out last year..."

"Last year? And you don't *have* it?"

"I'll get it," Nell said, grinning. "I promise. By the time you're done with those I'll have that last one for you to borrow."

So I read Nell's books, after Celia's. And fell deeper in love.

There was an email address on Emily Winterthorn's website, and sometime in the middle of this reading spree I wrote her an impulsive email.

> **To: Emily Winterthorn < _emily@winterthorn.com_>**
> **From: Jazz Marsh < _jmarsh@globenet.com_>**
> **Subject: You were my sister's favorite writer**
>
> *Dear Ms Winterthorn,*
>
> *My sister Celia was one of your greatest fans. She owned all of your books and she very much wanted to have a chance to meet you and talk to you because maybe one day she thought she might have wanted to continue to do for the Were-kind what she believed she saw you doing in your books – writing about kids who were like us, like the Were-kind that we were, understanding us so perfectly, writing about people we could recognize and accept as being one of us, one of our own.*
>
> *I only came to your books late, and I think I have now read or am in the middle of reading every book, every word, that you've ever had published, and I can only tell you that I think my sister was right, and that now it's me who is one of your biggest fans.*
>
> *Seven years ago you were supposed to come and visit Celia's school, and talk to the literary club that she was a member of. Her teacher scheduled that visit for the only time that Celia could not possibly be there herself – on the third day of the full Moon, when she, a Were who had already Turned, would have been locked away behind closed doors being the cat that she was in her alternate form. You write of us, of our kind, and yet not one of us could have come to see you talk at the school visit because every single one would have been somewhere else, and someTHING else,*

at the time – and the teacher who fixed your timetable knew all about it and scheduled your visit when he did because he meant for the Were-kind kids to be excluded. My sister was the only one (as far as I know) who asked if it was possible for the day of the visit to be rescheduled, and was told that it could not. But she was determined to be there, and so she took Stay – you write about the Were, you'll know what Stay is – on the night that she was meant to have started her Turn, to push it back, delay it or deny it, so that she could make it to your presentation.

She took too much. She died that night.

When I read your books I think of all the kids who are like me, but most of all I think about my sister, and I wish that she could have had that chance to meet you. I found her diaries, a long time after she was gone, and it was in them that I first heard your name, and also that my sister might have wanted to become a writer herself one day and that you were her inspiration and her guide – I think she could have done that, and been a good writer, maybe a great one, except for the prejudice and malice of a single teacher who stood in her way because he could and because of what she was.

I have only just discovered your books, and many of the later ones I borrowed from friends rather than own them, but in time I'll have them all, to put together with those other older ones which my sister loved and which are now mine. Please keep on writing, and believing in us, and making other readers believe that we are all real, and we all exist. Thank you for your stories.

Jazz Marsh

I read it over only once, and it sounded terrible, stilted and awkward and weird, but hey, it was the first fan letter that I'd ever written, it wasn't as though I had practice at it, and anyway it wasn't what I was writing it for. It just felt... somehow... *important*... that she know about Celia, about one single reader amongst many. It was a drop in an ocean, she probably got a gajillion of these fan mails a year, she probably never even saw them all herself, maybe she had an assistant who fired off little replies along the lines of "Thank you for writing, it's always great to hear from fans". I certainly wasn't expecting a response. It was simply me writing to her, building a bridge (from my end) to something that now connected so solidly with Celia in my mind.

I went back to reading the rest of Emily Winterthorn's books, and wallowing in them, and making a list of the post-Celia ones which I was going to submit to my parents as source material for every birthday and Christmas and gift-giving opportunity that arose between now and the end of time so long as there were new Winterthorn books in the world for me to covet.

My mother said nothing of the books when we resumed our school work together (all of the other stuff – well – it had happened, and it was done, but that didn't mean that I could simply quit my education because of any of it – a week or so after that last Turn I just found a new school assignment on my computer, with a due date, and no chance to argue). Mom seemed different, somehow – a sort of softer, gentler person – as though some sort of hard carapace had been cracked by the events of the last couple of months, permanently, and she could not quite close it up around her again. But she was also more wary, more careful, more thoughtful in what she said and how she said it. I think that for better or for worse I broke the Celia mold for her and she could no longer see me as any kind of Celia substitute. So there was that, at least. And the silences weren't so bad, when we had the schoolwork to fill them with.

I saw little of Dad for a little while, as pressure of work apparently swallowed him (or so we were all told). Mal... was just an absence, for now, a brooding shape in the shadows. Waiting for yet another Turn... that might not ever come.

And so the month unfurled, and that next Full Moon approached, the one we were all somehow waiting for, and Peregrine arrived on schedule to oversee the last of my Turns that he would be observing.

Part 4:
The Boy Who Cried
Lycan

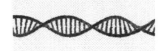

I'd been reading in my room when Vivian popped her head around my door.

"Time," she said. "The rest of them are on their way."

"Coming," I said, scanning frantically down to the end of the page of the book in my hand. The last of Nell's Winterthorn books. It was really *too* inconvenient of the Moon to rush into being full with this unseemly haste; I had about two chapters left to go, and now I'd have to abandon them – and if Peregrine pulled some other trick and turned me into a monkey this time those chapters would have to wait for three days until I got back to being me. They might have to wait anyway, even if Peregrine did nothing at all and I Turned into Jesse on schedule – I had no idea, really, if Jesse would be into reading these books the way I was or if I would *truly* remember anything that he had read, or that I would trust his response to what he had read...

I headed out the door, grabbing the Turning cloak off the back of a chair on my way. Mom (already wrapped in her own Turning Cloak) and Vivian were already waiting down in the basement. There was no sign of Dad, or of Mal.

"Where *are* those men," Mom said nervously, "it's almost time..."

"On their way," I said. Well, I didn't know that, not for sure, but I was hoping they were, anyway. "They were right behind me, I think. "I'll just pop into my room and change..."

Anything, *anything* not to be present when they brought Mal down and shoved him in yet again to sit vigil with his weasel. I didn't think I could bear to see it. Not now, not this time – and I could understand him perfectly, for once, understand just how bitter and trapped he must feel and just how much, even while still loving me as the little sister he had promised to protect, he must be resenting me right now, right in this moment. And he had a *right* to, dammit. He had a perfect right. He'd been screwed by his genetics and his kind and his circumstances and a law that made no provision for somebody like him – much like it had made no real provisions for somebody like me. The difference was that it might well look to Mal like I was being handed a free pass of sorts while he was doomed to a life sentence of something that was driving him quietly crazy.

I heard the door of Mom's room open and close, and lock. I heard Dad's voice, and stayed shivering inside my own room until I heard another door close. And then the third. Mal. Oh, my God, Mal. I suddenly felt close to tears, knowing that he would hate me for crying for him, hate me for the pity.

There was a knock on my own door.

"Are you decent?"

"Yes," I said, and turned back to the door which had been left ajar to face Peregrine. "What's supposed to happen now?"

"Now we just wait," he said equably, crossing his arms across his chest. "I want to see what happens if I don't produce a mouse from inside my sleeve. And I would like to meet Jesse, if he makes an appearance."

A part of me wanted very badly to broach the subject of Mal and his troubles – Dad did say that he and Mom would talk to Peregrine about it – but I had no idea how to broach the subject, and anyway I quailed at doing it by myself, alone out here with Peregrine. Dad was suddenly somebody I very much wanted at my back for this conversation.

Besides... besides...

That damn Moon was up. The bones in my body were liquefying again. The numbness in my hands and my feet, the feeling of being stretched like Silly Putty and then squashed back together into a different form as though by a careless child. The way my consciousness dissolved briefly into fireworks and white light, and my ears blocked, and face hurt, and my eyes watered, and a sneeze sat trapped just on the far side of my sinuses waiting to explode.

I reached out one arm for support, blindly, folding the other across my middle as I doubled over, retching dryly, the nausea I had already come to expect (and dread) rising at the back of my throat.

The hand that groped for support actually closed around a human arm, and I felt a hand come up to cover mine, and then reach out to steady me, guiding me gently down so that I was kneeling on the floor. I'd screwed my eyes shut, tightly, and was taking quick and shallow panting breaths, trying to get my rebellious body under control, but the first thing I saw when I opened them again was my hand splayed out on the floor next to my knees which were still wrapped in the Turning cloak.

No, not my hand.

Jesse's.

"Fascinating," Peregrine's voice came from somewhere to the side of me, quite close to my ear. "Jesse, I presume?"

I cleared my throat. "Jesse, *I* presume," I said. "On schedule."

I looked up and met his eyes, and they were sparkling, rapt. "Yes, I heard it all told," he said, "but a part of me still couldn't quite believe that it had happened, or that it could ever happen again. Come on upstairs, I had Vivian order in a pizza, just in case, and we can talk."

I couldn't help grinning at the pizza thing. That one, I – or at the very least Jesse – would never quite live down.

"Help me up," I said. "I never feel... quite steady... after these things. It's like I have to learn to walk all over again on a different set of legs."

"That, yes," Peregrine said. "Exactly that. I want every detail that you can possibly think of, no matter how small or unimportant you might think it is. Let's just say that *whatever* you come up with has probably never been said, or thought, or experienced before, not in this kind of personally experienced anecdote. Or at the very least not recorded." He helped set me squarely back on my feet again, and steadied me with a hand on the shoulder. "Everything in working order...?"

"I think so," I said, and took an experimental step forwards. I didn't fall over so that was already a good thing. "After you."

"Actually, you'd better go up first," Peregrine said. "I'll be right behind you. Just in case. It *is* a basement staircase."

We were out of the room now, passing by my father's Turning room, my mother's... coming up on Mal's. It was at this point that Peregrine, a step behind me as he said he would be, chuckled in indulgent amusement.

"Growing boys," he remarked. "Was that your stomach growling?"

I might have retorted some smart-ass remark to that, but I had glanced into Mal's room, despite vowing that I would not, as I passed – and what I saw in there had made me stop dead in my tracks and turn, staring openly, at what presented itself to my astonished gaze.

Peregrine had picked up on the tensing of my shoulders, moments before he stepped up to the door himself.

"What is it?" he said, alerted that something out of the ordinary was going on.

And then he was beside me, looking into the room, and he, too, had gone quite still.

"Oh," he murmured, very softly. "Oh, my."

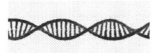

G iven the circumstances, it might be construed as strange – but perhaps it was just that what I was seeing was not really registering yet and so I picked on the second most obvious thing that I was seeing to comment on. Or not seeing, as it were. Because the words I heard coming out of my mouth were,

"Where's the *weasel*?"

"I think that might be it," Peregrine said, pointing with his chin into a corner of the room distinguished by nothing so much as a wet, bloody smear and what looked like it might have been the remains of a weasel tail. "Or at least what's left of it."

The only other thing inside that room... was not my brother.

Or at least not the brother I was accustomed to seeing in there, sitting morosely on the floor wrapped in a Turning cloak, engaged in a staring contest with the weasel.

I could see the Turning cloak, discarded and crumpled in the far corner; it looked like it had been through the wars, bloodied and ripped – no, shredded – and lying where it had been left when... when Mal...

Well. I took a firm grip on the matter, thorns and all, with both hands.

When Mal had Turned... into a *wolf*.

Because that was the only other thing in that room. A young, leggy, pale-gray wolf, with glowing golden eyes and a bloody muzzle which left little further mystery as to what had happened to the weasel that was supposed to be his pattern-animal. Not only had Mal not done the decent Random thing and Turned into the last warm-blooded living thing his human eyes saw just before the Turn began, he had gone and *eaten* that thing.

The wolf was aware of us, because those eyes were fastened on the window in the Turning room door, and his lips were drawn back from some fairly serious teeth. The doors of the Turning Rooms were sturdy and muffling but they were not wholly sound-proof; the growling which Peregrine had been so arch about had probably not been coming from my belly.

"Oh, oh," Peregrine said again, and I tore my eyes from wolf-Mal and lifted them to Peregrine's face. The expression on it made my heart lurch in a funny way – there was fascination there, and vivid interest, neither of which were unexpected under the circumstances, but there was also something else. A deep and visceral regret.

He realized I was staring at him and turned his head to glance down at me.

"You," he said softly, "are an anomaly, and right now you are numbered amongst the most unique Were-kind that had ever lived, simply because I can talk to you instead of looking at you through a glass window as we are looking at Mal right now. But like I told you before, you're a perfect Random – in that much, you are not so different from somebody like, say, your parents at all. You showed me, you *proved* to me, that I could make you turn into a different thing, simply by offering it to you at precisely the right moment. But what happened in *that* room..." He looked up again, away from me, back at the wolf who was steadily staring right back at him. "You, I can make a case for simply monitoring, and registering you as a Random Were – because there is no hierarchy, no Clan, no Guild, the Random cannot organize in that way by very virtue of what they are."

"But Mal is a Random, the family is Random," I said, but it sounded desperate and, well, *wrong* – even to me.

Peregrine was shaking his head. "No. Oh, no, he is not. If he were, there would be two weasels in that room right now – either at a respectful standoff or at one another's throats, that happens sometimes with Randoms and their pattern animals , but Mal did *not* Turn into the last warm-blooded creature he saw before he Turned. No, there was such a creature before him, for that very reason, and yet he Turned into something else altogether. Something... that is very rare these days."

"What? A Were-wolf?"

"Indeed. Two things have just happened here – your brother has Turned into a form that is apparently fixed for him, not Random at all, and he has turned into a form that once used to dominate our kind but has become very, very rare in modern times. You, I have the luxury of fudging – there is nobody to whom I am supposed to, or even required to, report directly at all. But there *is* an authority where Mal is concerned, and I am obliged to report the nascence of a new and wholly unexpected lycan to the Lycan Pack. I have to..." He shivered, and his hands spasmed on the door. "Jazz... "he said quietly, and then corrected himself. "Jesse... I had hoped to have more time with you – to talk as Jesse – but this – I think this has triggered – I think you'd better lock me into my Turning Room. Right now. We will have a lot to talk about, when I come back in three days' time. Oh, and don't forget to alert Vivian. She will need to procure the proper food for that wolf; I don't suppose you have anything suitable lying around the house. This was never expected or planned for. Hurry, now. I can feel the Turn beginning..."

He hustled himself into the empty room that was to have been Celia's, and I closed the door behind him. I didn't wait to watch him Turn; I went back to Mal's door and stood there staring, transfixed, unable to take my eyes off this thing that was my brother.

In some ways it was entirely right and proper – he had *always* been a kind of a wolfish type, even as a human. But there was just something unnerving in the fact that he had Turned into a wolf now, right at the point that he was about to give up, to surrender, ready to basically curl up and die rather than go through that weasel ritual one more time.

Well, he got that wish. He was hardly likely to be offered a weasel again, unless it was as his dinner.

"Is everything all right down there?"

Vivian's voice came floating from the kitchen doorway, and then I heard her step on the basement stairs.

I tore myself away from Mal's door to intercept her as she stepped down onto the basement floor.

"Hi," I said. "It's Jesse. I'm kind of... back. But I'm... not quite the problem anymore. At least not the only one."

Vivian's face began to assume a hunted expression that screamed, *Oh no, not again!*

"What?" she said carefully. "What now? And where's Peregrine?"

"He had to retire more quickly than he hoped," I said. "Don't worry, he's safe – he's in the Turning Room and the door is locked. You see, there's an advantage of sorts to having Jesse around at these times. An extra pair of hands."

The levity was kind of forced, and she wasn't buying it. "What's happened?" she said.

"I... um... you'd better come and see," I said lamely. "Do you know what wolves eat...?"

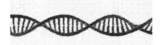

I t was hard to wait out these three days of the Full Moon, harder perhaps than it had been to do it than back when I had first Turned into Jesse myself. This time, it was *everything* that was up in the air, absolutely *everything* that had changed. I couldn't seem to tear myself away from the basement and from the window through which I could look into a room where a young wolf paced out his confinement. I watched Mal-the-wolf tear into bloody meat, watched those impressive teeth crunch bones without any effort at all, watched Vivian agonizing about what to do about the hygiene of the whole thing – but we didn't know enough to deal with it ourselves and didn't feel right about doping the wolf long enough to go in and clean up the mess in the Turning room. I kind of got the impression that this was some sort of Big Deal from what little that Peregrine had said before he too had gone under into the Turn, and so I didn't want to squawk out to somebody I didn't know was entitled to hear about this – and so Vivian and I just cringed and waited.

I called Charlie over – it was while watching the non-Turning Mal through this self-same window that he had stood beside me and saw *me* Turn into Jesse, and now there he was, standing next to Jesse, staring at the wolf.

"*Wicked*," Charlie breathed. "He is awesome. Some people have *all* the luck. All we've ever had in our family are stupid bats – you have all the excitement."

"I have a feeling there's more to it than that," I said. "Peregrine sounded very serious."

"What's this Lycan Pack?" Charlie asked.

"I've no idea," I said. "I plugged 'Lycan' as a search term into the Net and I got all kind of weirdness thrown back at me – and I don't know if any of it is really relevant. Peregrine is right, in any event, in that it used to be far more common once than it is now. There was a site I found where somebody had charted the frequency of different Were forms in contemporary populations – but I don't know what criteria were used or how accurate it is, and I have no idea how *old* it is."

"But what did it say?"

"The dominant form – at least when that chart was being compiled – was actually Corvid," I said. "Nell will be pleased."

"Eh. Or not. Just one of the crowd," Charlie said with a grin. "Where did bats rank?"

I laughed. "To be honest, I didn't look," I said. "I'll send you the link, you can investigate yourself if you want."

"Did you find any lycans?"

"They were mentioned," I said. "According to this site, they're one percent or less of the Were population these days, or so that chart says, whatever *that* means. A *Were-beagle* is more common than a Were-wolf."

"Corvids have their own web page," Charlie said.

"Yes, and?"

"Well, do the Lycans?"

"Not that I can find. Nothing obvious, anyway. Nothing that they seem to have put out there themselves for general consumption. Not only do they seem to be rare, they seem to be all secretive and stuff. It's like a whole little secret society. Half the stuff that's on the Net about them is password protected, or else I get a flat 'Not Authorized To Access Site' warning without any fussing about passwords at all, or the site seems to have gone bye-bye – and what *is* available is quite often so cryptic that it might as well be written in code, or so over the top that even I can tell that it's been written by either someone who hasn't a clue or someone who does, but doesn't want anyone else to, and is very good at confusing the issue."

"Oh, wow. Mal is going to register as a Lycan? So he gets the secret passwords? He gets to play?"

"I rather think that Mal kind of *has* to register as a Lycan now, from what I can gather from what Peregrine said, and I have no clue what they will expect from him. My poor parents. I think all they ever wanted was an ordinary life. And now look what's happened."

Charlie tapped on the glass with his fingernail. "Here, gorgeous, look this way..."

We both jumped back a foot as the wolf threw himself at the door, snarling his disdain and his outrage, his paws scrabbling for purchase on the inner smooth surface.

"Er, I think you made him mad," I said. "Just remember what happened to the weasel..."

Charlie made himself scarce long before the three days of the Turn were over. I didn't blame him, not wanting to be around when Mal came out of it. I was contemplating hiding under my bed, myself – but this was family, whatever happened to him affected me, and, well, perhaps Turning into even something as wild and violent as a wolf might have an end result of finally making Mal more... *human*... in the long-term.

So I was there – as Jazz – when they opened his door and led him out of that Turning room, wrapped in a clean blanket, looking blank and woozy, his hair matted and hanging in front of his face which still had smears of dried blood around his mouth, his hands visibly shaking where he was holding the blanket closed around himself as he stumbled and staggered up the stairs from the basement. The Turning room stank of blood and crap and urine, to the point that I gagged and almost threw up just catching a whiff of it. I didn't envy whoever would get the job of cleaning that place up – and it was obvious that it was hardly an ideal solution for a Were of Mal's ilk. It was fine keeping a cat or a chicken locked away in these rooms for a handful of days – but a large and dangerous carnivore was quite another matter, and even if there *were* no mysterious Lycans lurking in the wings there would probably have to be other arrangements made for Mal in the future. I had absolutely no idea how this could be done in any practical way. For once it was just good to be the youngest and the least important, knowing that I would not be the one on whose lap this problem would be left.

Mal took a long time in his shower – I could appreciate that, it had been a good place for me, too, that first Turn, and I hadn't been devouring bloody carcasses while out of it – but while we were all waiting for him to come out Peregrine dealt with the other problem, me.

"I don't suppose you went to see that doctor I wanted to look you over as Jesse," Peregrine said, his tone resigned.

I blinked. "I completely forgot about it," I said. "I'm sorry, I meant to – but then Mal – "

"It's understandable," Peregrine said. "But I do want your solemn promise that you will go the next time."

"I will," I said. "I will, I promise."

"All right. Here's what I suspect, from what I've managed to figure out so far – you are literally Were-human. Which means that in Jesse-form you will not test as Were, genetically. That's basically what I want this medical exam to establish. You'll need a set of personal stuff – ID card, that sort of thing – for when you are Jesse, and I'll undertake to provide documentation reflecting that – but if I am right it'll be an ID card which won't have a Were-mark on it. Which may be something that is greatly valuable – arguably it's only for three days out of every month but for those three days it might give you access to places where Jazz, with the Were-mark, might not be able to go. I am reasonably certain that I can trust you not to abuse this, Jazz, but let me also tell you that I will probably find out if you ever do, and the consequences of that might be rather severe."

"Uh. Okay."

"Right. Look out for a package of all that stuff soon, then. I'll use the photos that Vivian took of you, that first Turn, they can be made to do for the necessary mugshots, and if I need anything further, I will be in touch about it. It really is kind of *constraining* because I am so emphatically not available when Jesse is, um, here – but I may need to send you out to get a decent set of ID photos, eventually, and other things that will make themselves known in their own time. In the meantime – keep me informed, and let me know if anything changes, and remember you promised to keep that journal...?"

"I will," I said earnestly. "Promise."

He grinned at me, a little crookedly. "Well, then. Welcome to the grown-up Were world, Jessica Marsh."

It felt like a graduation of sorts – I felt oddly proud of myself, as though it had been a personal accomplishment that I just been offered congratulations for.

But that was my moment, all of it, and then it was over as Mal –

wearing black jeans and a tight heavy-metal black t-shirt and somehow looking more wolfish in his human form than he had ever done as the beast – slouched into the living room and collapsed into one of the armchairs in a boneless heap, his head tucked between his shoulders in an odd mixture of submission and defiance.

"All right," he said, his voice hoarse. "Here I am. Hit me."

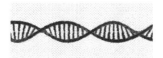

P eregrine gave us all a little bit of history that wasn't on the Net, or at least not anywhere I had known to look.

Were-kind were once known as werewolves – it was that simple, really. Once upon a time (I'd never known I was living in a fairy tale, but there you go) all known Were-kind were wolves. Werewolves. The very word defined them. Defined *us*. Everything we all knew about our race we had learned at the werewolf's side, or perhaps more accurately from inside a werewolf's skin; this was the way things were, the only way they could be.

But then something happened – a handful of centuries ago, at least. Things changed. Were-kind who Turned into different beasts began to appear. The manner and nature of creatures into which they Turned – so long as they remained warm-blooded – proliferated, and the more of that occurred the less able the original revered werewolf line seemed able to hold their pre-eminence in the race. The numbers of the true werewolves – or Lycans as they became known as the Were-clans branched out and reinvented themselves by giving their branch of the race a name, a guild, a hierarchy – dwindled; the wolves bred true, but sometimes they didn't breed at all, and they simply... withdrew into the shadows. Still the origin of the race, still venerated, still not a little feared, but getting more and more mysterious and enigmatic as the years and centuries wore on, and apparently more than content to allow new-fangled clans like the Corvids to assume the mantle of leadership for the Were-kind.

"There are to my certain knowledge maybe six Lycan Packs on this continent right now, certainly no more than ten that we know of," Peregrine said. "If you assume a pack to consist of a minimum of six to ten Lycans, you are still talking no more than a sum total of less than a thousand known full Lycans. You are *rare*, Mal. Rare as rare can be. And I have to let the Lycan Alpha know you are here. Trust me, if I do not he will find out even without my assistance. There simply isn't a way of hiding a wolf, not even in a Random family like this. Special arrangements would have had to be made anyway – as I think you found out already, to your cost, down in that Turning room this time round."

Mal wrinkled his nose. "I'll say," he muttered. "What special arrangements?"

"The Lycans will have a say in that, I suspect," Peregrine said.

"What will they want with him?" Mom said, clasping her hands in her lap, looking very white and drawn.

"Until I speak to the Alpha of the Packs, I don't know," Peregrine said. "I can tell you, though, that now that this has actually happened it all fits the pattern as we currently know it, for Lycans. They would not have declined so dramatically if they hadn't already been showing all the symptoms, if you like, that Mal might have been exhibiting, without anybody recognizing them for what they were, for years now. They don't advertise this or even allow it to be widely known but Lycans have been reputed to Turn much later than any other Were-kind did, and when they do Turn it's violent – I'm betting your insides are feeling a little raw right now, Mal?"

Mal grimaced. "Somewhat," he muttered giving away as little as he could. Already, he was learning to be a proper Lycan.

I, apparently, was not blessed with the same kind of self-control.

"But that wouldn't mean..." I began impulsively, and then clamped my mouth shut when both Mal and Peregrine turned to me.

"Yes?" Peregrine said, tilting his head a little questioningly in my direction.

"Well, if they only Turned *late*, that would simply mean that they Turned late, not that there would be a precipitous fall in numbers," I said, flushing deeply. I was spouting off about things I had no real idea about. "They wouldn't have turned from a dominant form to an endangered species. There would have to be... some other reason. Like they can't have children, or don't have many, or that some of the children don't Turn at all, not even late..."

"And right, on all counts, almost," Peregrine said. "They do have many of those problems. Perhaps there's something in the contemporary world which has increased in frequency from the days of their primacy as Were, something that interferes with their birth rates and Turn rates – I don't know, and they aren't telling. But the numbers tell their own story."

"Do they still pass it on if they bite somebody?" I asked. Mal narrowed his eyes at me and curled his lip above what was now a perfectly normal human canine tooth but which suddenly reminded me of the *last* time I'd seen it, dripping with blood from the poor weasel and then from the raw bloody meat with which we'd emergency-fed him. It might have been meant as a joke of sorts, but all the same I decided that silence was the better part of valor at this point, and simply shut up.

"I do suggest one thing – for the next Turn cycle, make an arrangement for Mal to be cared for at one of the specialized facilities – there are ways that large predators can be cared for during a Turn, and I can give you some contacts, but you'll probably agree that you don't want him Turning inside that cramped little room any more often than you can help it," Peregrine said, turning smoothly back to my parents and wresting the conversation back to relatively safer channels – if there were any such left, in this family. "Those rooms are perfectly adequate for the rest of you, but I don't believe they were ever built with a wolf in mind."

"Mom, stop it" Mal said sharply. Mom's eyes had filled with tears and threatened to overflow; we had all been uncomfortably aware of it, but Mal suddenly couldn't take it anymore. "Just stop it. It's finally happened, okay? I've finally Turned, I've crossed the damned river and I'm on the other side, so there's nothing more to weep and wail about now."

"But what are we to..." Mom began, her fingers twisting around one another in her lap like a nest of stubby serpents.

"I'll be fine," Mal said.

Peregrine got to his feet. "Well, I've done what I can, for now – I'll be in touch what with various things that need to be set in motion. Mal, Jazz, you kids take care. You're both of you... special."

Vivian had left already; Mom and Dad both rose with Peregrine and the adults moved off, for a moment, in a knot of lowered voices and quiet farewells... leaving us two 'special' kids behind in our chairs.

There was something... *something*... an awkwardness of sorts. A silence born of helplessness. There simply didn't seem to be anything safe left to say, not in that particular moment.

"Are you really all right?" I finally asked, in a low voice. It was sincere enough, one recently Turned sibling to another – I knew how it had affected me, I could have no real idea what it had felt like for him, but if it was like mine or worse he must have been feeling pretty grotty right then.

He rubbed his temples with the tips of his fingers. "I had not realized," he said softly, "that it would be so..."

"So... what?" I said after a moment, after he let the sentence trail off into silence.

He started, a little guiltily, as if he had been caught in betraying some confidence. "Nothing," he said. "Nothing. Look, if you don't mind, I think I need to think..."

I could think of nothing to say to keep him, and he pushed himself off the arms of the chair he'd been sitting in and loped back to his room. I was left in possession of the field, as it were, until my Dad came back into the living room to see me sitting where Mal had left me, frozen in my chair, alone.

"Your mother isn't feeling too well, she's gone to lie down," Dad said. "Where's Malcolm?"

"I guess he went to lie down too," I said. "That, or chew on something."

"It's frustrating for him," Dad said gently.

"He wanted to quit," I said. "Before he... before this Lycan thing. Dad, how could that happen? How could one kind of Were suddenly switch to something else?"

"There are whole volumes on Were genetics," Dad said. "I have to admit I never understood any of it, or paid that much attention."

"But you think it's *possible*?"

"It's possible," Dad said, shrugging his shoulders. "We saw it happen."

"*I* saw it happen," I murmured.

"Touché," Dad said. "Are *you* all right?"

That question was starting to feel distinctly repetitive, around here. You'd think that no Were kid had *ever* Turned before, the kind of attention Mal and I were getting.

Then again... the situation did warrant it.

"Dad... what's going to happen to him?" I asked abruptly, my eyes flicking back to the corridor where Mal had disappeared, and then, when the silence that followed that question had grown a little too long, back to my father's face.

My father looked resigned, worried, somehow older than I had ever seen him look before. I didn't remember the deep line that had been cut into his forehead. But he caught my eye, and tried to smile.

His answer to my question, though, was less than reassuring.

"I don't know," he said, and I could hear something breaking in his voice. "I know next to nothing at all about the Lycans, or at the very least the Lycans as they are covered by the laws of this country – or what this will mean to our family, or how on Earth it happened at all. We'll just have to wait and see what this Lycan leader is going to have to say."

Celia. Now Mal. Not to mention my own freakish anomalous status, which would have been more than enough to strain and unravel the fabric of any family.

No wonder my mother was not feeling well. She was losing us all – every one of her children. One way or another we had all managed to go off the rails. She and Dad had left everything behind when they came to this new place, and this family had been all that they had, all that they had treasured – and now the family was shattered into smithereens, and the future looked uncertain for all of us.

Dad must have seen some of this written on my own face, because he leaned over and touched my hair gently, like he used to do when I was just a young child.

"It'll be okay, Jazz. It will. It'll all work out. Now, Vivian said that you always come out of these things hungry. There's still a fair lot of that pizza left, I think – or can I make you a sandwich...?"

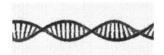

Whatever the Lycan mojo was, it really didn't take long for the wolves to come out of the woodwork. Less than two weeks after Mal's Turning, there was a knock on our door – and it was the kind of knock that made it obvious that it wasn't the postman. This was the Knock of Destiny – an authoritative rap, once, twice, three times, demanding entry.

As it happened, I was the one closest to the door when the knocking occurred, and it was I who stepped up to answer it.

The man who stood on our doorstep as I opened the door was *freakishly* tall; my head appeared to be on a level with his navel. His eyes were an odd amber-gold light brown, and fringed with the sort of eyelashes that would have made Helen of Troy weep with envy, but the luscious lashes did not disguise the fact that this was no damsel in any kind of distress. This was no Red Riding Hood. This was, well, the Wolf.

Yes, I know we were expecting one to call. I wasn't really prepared for somebody who so comprehensively looked the part.

"Hello...?" I managed. "Can I help you?"

"I am Yuri Volkov," he said, and there was just a trace of the accent there, just enough to underline that aura of danger that he broadcast. "I am Lycan Pack Alpha. I am here to see Malcolm Marsh."

I had no idea where Mal was, if he was even home. But this was not the kind of man you left standing on the doorstep. I stepped back, opening the way for him to come inside.

"Come in," I said. "I'll go and see if Mal is here."

"Thank you," he said, courteously enough, and stepped inside, looking around the house with an appraising eye.

I showed him into the living room, and Mom, who was in the kitchen washing breakfast dishes, turned at our entrance. She had the presence of mind to put down a plate she was holding before she dropped it, but I could see the color drain from her face – she knew who this was, even without the necessary introductions.

Which I provided anyway.

"Mom, this is Mr. Volkov. From the... the Lycans."

I heard Yuri Volkov say something acknowledging, like "Ma'am" or some such thing, but I was already out of that room. The conversation (or the silence) that would follow was not something I wanted to be present for.

Mal's door was closed, as always, and usually I'd give it a wide berth – but with the Volkov incentive I overcame that instinct, and knocked.

A growl answered me, which kind of sounded rather like "Go away!" but since that was no option, I took my courage in both hands and opened the door just a crack.

"Mal," I said. "The Lycans are here for you. The wolf is at the door."

The door was flung open from the inside, with such speed and force that I staggered forward and almost fell into the room. Mal stuck out a hand and half-steadied me and half-shoved me back out into the corridor.

"He's in the living room," I managed, before I was swept to one side and Mal stalked past me out of his room.

I know, eavesdropping is my sin. I might not have turned into the cat which my family seems to have favored – Dad and Celia, both – but the proverbial curiosity was still apparently something that was passed down the line. I scuttled carefully back down the corridor in Mal's wake, flattening myself just this side of the archway into the living room.

"You are Malcolm Marsh?" Volkov's almost-but-not-quite-unnoticeable accent gave the familiar name an exotic lilt which seemed only fitting, seeing as I was perceiving my brother in a whole new light anyway.

"I go by Mal," Mal said.

"Yuri Volkov. Lycan Pack Alpha. Are you ready?"

"Ready for what?"

"By your revealed nature, you are part of the Pack," Yuri said. "We are your family now. I am here to take you home."

"Mr. Volkov..." my mother's voice was high and thin, a wire almost stretched to breaking point. "What is going to happen to my son?"

"Ma'am, you can be assured that he has a future with us. As a registered Lycan he has a comfortable place to live and a safe place to Turn, a fully subsidized education, and a guaranteed job – we are scientists, and there is a place waiting for him to join one of our research teams when he is ready."

"But science has never really been his... What if he wants to become a..."

"Mrs. Marsh," Volkov said, and his voice hadn't changed at all, outwardly, but I heard a certain hardening in it, like it had just turned into a diamond knife, "this is not really an invitation. I am here for him, and he is leaving with me. There are no options or choices here."

Mom found some mettle, because I could hear her voice steady, sharpen – I knew how much that had cost her, but she did it anyway, because she was a mother, and she was trying to protect her young.

"That's practically kidnapping," she said. "You can't simply walk into a house and pluck a child from his family, just like that."

"Yes, I can. It is hardly kidnapping; he Turned into a wolf. That changes everything for him – it changes his family – and the law says that he now belongs to the Pack." The diamond edge again, slicing into a single word: "Ma'am."

He must have turned from Mom to Mal because his next words were, "You may pack a bag, if you wish. It is not necessary; all you will require from here on is going to be provided for you, the Lycan Pack looks after its own, but if you wish to bring a few personal things, we have no objection. No computers, no cell phones. You have five minutes, to decide what you want to take with you, to say your goodbyes."

"Half an hour," Mal said.

"Fifteen minutes," Volkov said, in a tone of voice that gave Mal a concession but indicated that the bargaining was over. "I'll be waiting outside."

I pushed myself off the wall and managed to skid into the bathroom just as Volkov came out of the living room, heading for the front door. If he was aware that I had been there at all I was insignificant enough to ignore completely; he did not even blink in my direction. No pausing to check out his surroundings, like he had done when he'd entered; he'd seen enough, he'd said what needed to be said, and he was done.

"Mal...!" Mom's voice, from the living room, was brittle, broken.

Mal's, when the response came, was unrecognizable. Almost... gentle.

"Mom. Mom, I'm going to be fine. It's what I am. I... I have to go."

I opened the bathroom door a little wider as Mal rounded the corner of the archway and stepped into the corridor. Our eyes met and held for a moment, and then he jerked his chin towards his bedroom door.

"Don't have much time," he said, in a low voice. "Come with me."

I followed him into his room, where I rarely been invited before. He had a gym bag already open on the bed as I stepped inside, and was stuffing what looked like random stuff into it, almost as though his mind was elsewhere and he was beyond paying attention to what he was actually doing. He paused as I came in, turned to glance at me, and then dropped the bag and the current half-packed item he had been holding and stepped towards an untidy desk which boasted a battered laptop with what looked like a screensaver consisting of a bloody skull and crossbones on its screen, and a wash of loose papers lapping at its back and sides. A rummage amongst the papers produced a pen, and Mal scribbled something on the nearest piece of paper that came to hand and thrust the page at me.

"Do this one thing for me," he said. "They said leave the laptop, leave the phone; you can't live in the world today without them so I guess I'll get new ones from the Lycans when they get around to it, but in the meantime it looks like I'm going to be incommunicado – and who knows how much they'll interfere in things later. Looks like they're going to insist on controlling stuff, their way. I'll try and find a way to get in touch – but in the meantime – this is my friend Saladin's email. He'll know who you are. Write him a note, just tell him I'm gone. And tell him why."

"Mal..."

"I don't have time for this," he said, grabbing hold of my hand and crumpling the paper into it before he closed my fingers around it. "Just do it."

"We don't even know where you're going..."

He turned back to the bag, finished stuffing inside the last item that had been hanging half in and half out of it, and zipped the bag closed with a finality that made my heart stop.

"I'll be somewhere," he said. "It's a life. It's mine. I'll deal." He hesitated, and then said, more abruptly than perhaps he had intended, without meeting my eyes again. "Mom's back in the kitchen crying her eyes out. Go make sure she's all right."

"But..."

"Good bye," he said.

Flinging the bag over his shoulder, he walked out of the room. He never looked around. He never looked back. He left his world – his family – his life – without a backward glance. One moment he was there, the next he was not, and I heard the front door open and then close – very gently, very quietly, without the usual slam which was almost Mal's trademark.

I realized as I stood there like a stupid speechless thing that I knew absolutely nothing about my brother – nothing that mattered – nothing that could have prepared me for this moment. All that I knew even now was an email address and a name I had heard for the first time only a few moments ago – a name of someone Mal called friend.

RANDOM

Celia. Mal.
Out of a house that was once the home of a family... there was now only me.

Part 5:
The Boy Who Bites

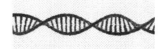

I wrote a note to this Saladin of Mal's, as he had asked – just a few lines, terse and to the point, no more than the bare facts of it all – but in this case the bare facts were kind of off-the-charts enough for a reply to come back to me by more or less return of mail, a single sentence: *Can we talk?*

"No way," Charlie, who was with me when the email came through, said. "You don't even know this dude. He could be anybody."

"He's Mal's friend," I pointed out.

"Exactly," Charlie said." He could be *anybody*. Besides, what kind of a name is Saladin anyway?"

"Saracen king," I said. "You know, the Crusades? Richard the Lion Heart? All that?"

Charlie aimed a kick at my ankle. "Yeah, yeah, smartass. *That* Saladin's been dust and ashes for a thousand years."

I looked back to the screen. "Well, this one isn't. And he wants to talk. Let's put it this way – I never knew Mal *had* anybody he'd have called a friend. You want to know something crazy? He was weird, every now and then I was actually kind of scared of him while he was here, but now that he's gone and we don't know where or what has become of him, I kind of miss him. It's like my shadow's disappeared."

"At least let me come with you," Charlie said, staring at Saladin's email on my screen.

"What are you going to do, challenge him to a joust if he misbehaves?" I said, laughing. "Don't worry, I can take care of myself."

"You could fix it for the fifteenth," Charlie said.

"That's the Full Moon."

"Right. And that means you could go as Jesse."

"Um, I don't think Mom could handle any more drama right now. If anything went wrong and I was next on the roster for abruptly leaving home. But I got my new ID, Jessie's ID." I said, turning to rummage on my desk for the envelope that had arrived from Peregrine only the day before. "Look at this."

Peregrine had been thorough about this, as he seemed to be about everything – there was a full set of papers included in the batch he sent, enough to establish "Jesse" Marsh's credentials to every possible scrutiny. How he did it I'd never know. He kept my name, but that was where the connection between Jazz Marsh and Jesse Marsh ended. Everything else was a careful fabrication, up to and including a new birth certificate for Jesse. The parents' names were not Thomas and Sylvia. There was nothing here to connect a boy named Jesse Marsh to a Random Were family who coincidentally bore the same surname.

There was a beginning of a whole another life. One I'd have to familiarize myself with.

"Why is he doing all this?" Charlie asked, sifting through the package of papers.

"A good question," I said. I turned over my new (and non-Were-marked) ID in my hands. "If all of this, my own Turn drama, had happened after Mal unexpectedly morphed into his wolf, I might have figured that Peregrine was doing all this because he was my folks' friend, somebody with influence and connections whom they'd brought in to save their third and youngest child from being removed from the family fold and dissected and studied like a rare butterfly. But instead..."

"Exactly the other way round," Charlie murmured. "*You* might have triggered *Mal*."

"You know, the way everybody's been so upset and astonished at this Jazz-into-Jesse Turning – I'd been told dozens of times that it had never happened before, and that I was doing something totally new and that I was sailing off into uncharted waters – honestly, I wouldn't have been a bit surprised if the men in white coats *had* descended on me and carried me off screaming to my new life as a lab rat. And instead, it's Mal who gets to do that."

"A lab wolf," Charlie said.

"Not funny," I said. "Well, but, anyway – Peregrine defused what happened with me by using that mouse – and then declaring me just a natural Random Were who... happened to have Turned into something unexpected by accident. After all, it's a documented occupational hazard with us – I'd lived with it all my life, so have all of us. Just remember what happened to Celia. And yet... and yet... there's the whole business of Turning from Human to Human, never been done before, all that. I can't figure it out, I just don't see how Peregrine could manage to use that 'no more than a perfectly ordinary Random Were' gambit to outweigh *that*, if it's as special as everyone thinks it is."

"Maybe he's playing a bigger game," Charlie said.

"I don't know what," I muttered. "He does want me to write it all down for him in detail..."

"Are you going to write down that you're going to wander off by yourself to meet this Saracen King...?"

'I haven't even decided that I *will*, yet," I snapped, a little annoyed.

Charlie stacked up the ID paperwork and handed it back to me. "I gotta go," he said, "Mom's expecting me home for dinner. At least promise me you'll keep me posted – if you go, where you go – somebody should know, this is a friend of *Mal*'s after all and Mal, well, he's a werewolf. Anything can happen."

"I *could* take Nell with me."

"Oh fine, blow me off but take another *girl* with you..." Charlie began, in a fit of high dudgeon.

I couldn't help but giggle. After a moment, he responded with a crooked little grin.

"Well, call me if you need me," he said.

"I will," I said, relenting. "*If* I go... I'll give you all the skinny."

"Be careful."

He really did just want to hang around and leap to protect me against my brother's more questionable acquaintances... if this Saladin proved to be one such. I liked that. I also liked it that he only pushed it as far as he thought he could, and then stepped back and accepted that if I said I was okay then I was okay. It was entirely possible that Charlie and I could have lived our entire lives without ever having met each other, except for the pure fluke which had made his mother our family's caretaker – but I was glad that the fluke had occurred and had made him my friend.

After Charlie left, I emailed Saladin back and asked what it was that we had to talk about.

The response to my message came so quickly that I had a feeling he must have been waiting at the other end for me to respond to him. It wasn't so much an answer to my question as a question of his own – a terse one, wanting (no, *demanding*) to know if Mal had taken his laptop with him when he left.

Mystified, I replied that it was still sitting on his desk.

The reply was even more terse.

Bring it.

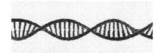

I actually did debate whether to take anybody with me – Charlie, or Nell – but in the end I trusted my instincts and my instincts told me to go it alone this time. We had agreed on a date and a time – lunchtime on a weekend, at a busy food court at a mall – and it didn't sound to me like I could put myself in any real danger in front of all these hundreds of other people who would be milling around. And, quite honestly, by now I was seriously intrigued.

When I arrived at the appointed place at the appointed time, Mal's laptop in a battered satchel over my shoulder, I actually had a sinking feeling of utter hopelessness – how could I have been such a complete idiot as to imagine I could meet with someone I didn't know, somebody I had no hope of recognizing, in the midst of this throng of chattering humanity? Yes, there was a certain safety in numbers, but that kind of cut both ways; I'd be *perfectly* safe if I never made contact with Saladin at all.

But somehow... it was easy.

I had no idea how long he had been sitting there, if nothing else just to hog the table, but I knew him as soon as I saw him, for no particular reason that I could give. He was just a scruffy boy with straight dark hair which he wore long enough to brush his shoulders, his skin a warm dusky shade that spoke of at least a touch of Middle Eastern ancestry, an earring made out of some dull pale metal in one ear. The first time I laid eyes on him I thought that he was a little too young to be a friend of Mal's – but then he looked up, as if aware of scrutiny, and met my eyes, and I realized that he was older than he looked.

At closer quarters, as I approached, those eyes revealed themselves as being a shade I had never seen before – dark green, luminous, like moss under clear water. And freakishly intense. Yeah, I could see this guy being friends with my brother. They kind of fit.

"Have you got it?" Honestly, that was the first thing he said, as soon as I was close enough for him to be able to speak to me in a voice low enough not to call attention to itself.

"Hi," I said sarcastically as I slipped into the bench seat opposite him. "I'm Mal's sister. Nice to meet you too."

He actually rolled his eyes. "Oh, social niceties. I see. Fine." He stuck out a hand across the somewhat unsavory surface of the food court table and said, in a voice which was suddenly dripping with a thick upper-class British accent, "My dear, let me introduce myself. Saladin van Schalkwyk, at your service."

I'd instinctively reached out to shake his hand, but the name caught me by surprise and I actually giggled. "Saladin van Schalkwyk? *Really*?" And then I tightened my fingers on his hand, instinctively, as something suddenly crystallized in my brain. "Chalky. You're *Chalky*."

"You could say," Saladin said equably, shaking himself loose from my grip. "Mal would call me that, sometimes. I very much wish you wouldn't."

"But you're the one – you are – "

"If you're thinking about a certain ex-teacher, yeah, Mal talked to me about fixing that problem for you," Saladin said.

"Mal said... I'd given you an idea," I said faintly.

Saladin shrugged. "So you did, in a sense. It helped."

"What...?"

"What did I do? I dealt with it. I don't think you need fear that ghost any more."

"Is he... Did you..."

"Oh, my, I must look ever so much more dangerous than I really am," Saladin said. "He's alive and well, no, really, I don't kill people. Promise. Cross my heart and hope to die." He lifted an eyebrow in the direction of the satchel. "That his laptop?"

"Yes, but hold everything," I said, still trying to get my equanimity back, waiting for my heart to stop beating against my ribs like it wanted out. "What's going on here?"

"His research, probably. Whatever he was able to save."

"Research on *what*?"

Saladin stared at me. "You two really didn't talk much, did you."

"None of my doing," I said, exasperated. "He didn't seem to find the time for heart-to-heart chats with me, if that's what you mean. Who are you, exactly, and what's going on?"

Saladin sighed and sat back, crossing his arms. "This business with Turning, he wasn't having much luck with it, your brother," he said.

"Tell me something I don't know," I muttered. "I always thought that was part of the reason he could be such an ill-tempered brute."

"Mal? Ill-tempered? Brute?"

"Are we talking about the same guy?"

"I suppose he was a little twisted about stuff," Saladin admitted, almost unwillingly. "Things got worse after you... Turned. He was spending his life waiting for it to happen. It was such a *waste*. Him sitting there with the animal-of-choice hoping that the Turning Gods would suddenly smile and he'd become something, anything, and then he'd be free."

"That's not how it works," I interrupted. "Are you Were?"

"Of sorts," he said cryptically. "The point is that Mal had absolutely no choice – and he was even stuck with an animal – "

"He picked the weasel," I said.

"Yes, but only after a wolverine became too expensive to rent in vain, and besides, why should he have to rely on any of that? Fixed Were simply Turn. Mal, he was forced to choose, and then dial down his choices, and everything was closing in on him – and he was *this* close to breaking."

"I know," I said. "But you don't just stop being a Were – he didn't exactly have a choice."

"Well, yes, about that," Saladin said. "He kind of did. He did choose. I don't know, all I can tell you is that he was ready to do murder by now. For pity's sake, just about anyone in your your entire precious Were society could name him if anybody asked them who the oldest unTurned Were kid was – Mal was a poster boy for mockery and finger pointing. It's nice being famous, but only if it's the right kind of fame, not this, not being famous for failing."

"Wasn't anything he could do about it," I said.

"Was, kind of. But it was a little desperate. Once he found his purpose, and figured out the Lycans."

I sat up sharply. "Mal was researching the *Lycans*?"

"And, um, I was helping. I have hacking talents he lacks. I could get him into sites from which ordinary looky-loos are comprehensively excluded." Saladin offered a grin that was almost but not completely apologetic. "Oh yeah," he said. "And I read your blog."

I didn't know whether I wanted to pick up Mal's laptop and wallop him with it or just walk out right now. There was a feeling of violation that was almost unbearable, sitting across the table from this nonchalant *twit* who had just announced that he'd swept my passwords aside like a word salad and read stuff that I had password-protected *for a reason*. If I had wanted the whole entire *world* to read all about Celia...

But then, I had given out the password myself. To people it was originally meant to protect against. I hardly had a leg to stand on, getting all outraged.

And besides, there was this other mystery now. The greater mystery. Mal and the Lycans. The thought crossed my mind that it sounded like some dweeby teenage garage band singing bad covers of popular songs, and it actually made me smile, which robbed my outrage of its edge anyway.

Saladin was looking at me with his head tilted a little sideways, like a puzzled puppy. "That was *never* your blog you were thinking about right now," he said.

"You're right," I said abruptly, wiping the smile off my face, "but that's not important anyway. Tell me the rest of it."

"Give me the laptop."

I laid a protective hand on the computer. "Oh no. Not before I get the full story."

"That's where the story *is*," he barked.

I hesitated for another moment, and then pushed the bag across the table to him in silence. For a moment he busied himself with setting up the machine – I got a growled, "You couldn't have brought it *charged*, could you? We've got maybe half an hour of battery on this thing..." – and then lapsed into silence as his fingers beat a swift tattoo on the keyboard, his magnificent eyes flickering back and forth as things appeared on the screen.

And then, still typing, still staring at the screen, began a sort of running commentary aimed in my general direction.

"What Mal is good at," he murmured as he worked, "is putting ideas together. He's not *original*, but he's the ultimate creative – he's never going to be somebody who sits there with the lightbulb going on over his head and chirping *Eureka*, but if someone gives him six disparate ideas from four corners of the world before breakfast he'll have a theory uniting them all by supper time. He never quite knows where to begin looking but he knows how to look, and what's more, how to find."

"*You* are the ideas man," I said.

He flashed me a grin over the top of the laptop. "Well, when I'm inspired," he said.

"What inspired you this time?"

"Mal. Himself. His own troubles and frustrations. When it came to the point where he looked like he was ready to jump off the nearest bridge or do murder, whatever it took, I did a collection of those disparate ideas. And when he brought up something you'd said – well - it was me who brought up the Lycans."

"Something that *I* said?" I repeated, mystified. "I don't remember ever even uttering the name – and what do *you* know about the Lycans, anyway?"

"You had a long chat with your Dad at one point, apparently," Saladin said. "About Mal. About him Turning."

"Yeah. I remember." I thought about the door I had seen closing. Again. Mal had been listening in the corridor – it was usually my trick, but then, he was my brother. He'd have the same arsenal that I did.

"Something you said, anyway. And then he put it together, as he does, and came up with a theory and a plan – and I figured the rest of it out. The

Lycans – they're scientists, they're rare, they used to be the Last Big Thing before their decline, they were possibly useful."

"Useful for *what*?"

"For giving your brother a purpose. Here."

He half-turned the laptop to me; it had half a dozen windows open, to various sites. Some of them I kind of recognized, from the research that I myself had done on the Net before. Others were new to me. I stared at them, clicking from one to the next, trying to get the connection.

Saladin poked a hand into my field of vision and began to point at things on the screen.

"*Here*, it gives a bit of history and *here* you have old wives' tales, and you can make a connection about how one arose from the other. Silver doesn't kill a werewolf – shame about all those silver bullets, what a waste – but it does poison them, slowly, and they probably eventually die from it anyway. None of the Were can handle silver well, really."

"Your earring...?"

"Steel," he said.

"So you *are* a Were."

"Like I said, not exactly." He tapped the computer. "Pay attention. Here, it talks about a theory of werewolf procreation, and the creation of new werewolves."

"I *asked* him if they still did it by biting," I said. "He seemed a little put out by the question."

"That's because you're right. There's two ways to make a new werewolf. One is for two werewolves to have a child – it *is* carried genetically, and they *do* breed true, and what's more some of the more classified sites even tell you what the genetics actually are, if you want to go that far."

"You've been to classified sites?"

Saladin gave me a strange look. "Of course. How else would I know the important stuff? You think they just leave that kind of information – something that might be essential for the survival of your species – just lying around for anyone to pick up?"

"You said two ways."

"Well, yes. The other – you're perfectly right, it can be passed by a bite. But here's where it gets interesting. It isn't just a question of a single werewolf chomping down on any off-the-street generic human. It's more complicated than that." He began to count on his fingers. "One, the hunt for a new victim – er, the new pack member – has to be done by the whole pack. In theory. That's partly because, item two, it's not just one bite that's required to change the victim to a wolf, it's *two* bites– from the alpha pair of the pack, the male and the female. Three, that victim already has to have a predisposition to Were-kindness, has to have a basic genetic bent to being Turned."

"But when the new laws came in, the Lycans were locked away while they were wolves, just like everybody else was," I said. "So, no pack hunting. Not ever."

"Right."

"And even if one of them or even the needed two of them, the pair, managed to escape confinement, they still had to find the right prey."

"Right."

"And they can't breed them fast enough to replace or maintain pack numbers."

"Right again."

"But what's all this got to do with..."

Saladin tapped the computer again. "Pay attention. Here – I told you they were scientists. Much of the research they do, if not most of it, relates to biochemistry and genetics and molecular manipulation at the DNA level. They've been dealt a bum hand, and they're figuring out a way from under it."

"But what has any of this to do with Mal?"

"Mal... was stuck in his place," Saladin said, sitting back a little and looking at me a little strangely as though he were perplexed that I still did not understand. "Almost eighteen, of genuine registered Were-stock, but still unTurned. Some of the symptoms of his troubles were actually Lycan – they always traditionally Turned much later than the rest of the Were-kind that followed – he could even lay claim to having the genetic baseline for it, but nothing was happening. Like I said, he was ready to start eating people by this stage; he was certainly being eaten alive himself by knowing he was the laughing stock of anyone who spoke his name amongst his own people. He was at the end of his rope, waiting for something to happen... so he decided to *make* something happen. And then... there was the other thing."

"What other thing?"

"Lycans are scientists."

"You already said that."

"But you didn't hear me. Or maybe I wasn't clear. One of their particular fields of interest is genetics and pharmaceuticals."

"Yes, and...?"

"Jazz... the Lycans invented Stay."

Things began to fall together now. It was partly pure frustration. It was partly... payback. This was for Mal, but it was also for Celia – Celia, who was still so much a part of our family and the choices we all made, despite being gone from us for so many years.

"Are you telling me... Mal *deliberately* went after trying to become Lycan?" I whispered.

"Well, bingo," Saladin said.

"But he – he *wasn't* – he was just a Random – like the rest of us – " I couldn't seem to put a coherent sentence together. Saladin's mouth curled into a smirk, and that finally galvanized me. "So if he wasn't born Lycan – and if they're as rare as they are – and if Mal was as stuck behind locked doors, in theory, as the packs were in any event during the Turns... *who bit him?*"

"As to that," Saladin said, uncrossing his arms and for the first time looking like he might be a little uncomfortable, "well, *me.*"

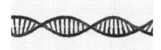

All of my life I had grown up in a world where there were two kinds of people: the Were, who Turned into some animal or another over three days during the correct phase of the moon, and the normal humans, who did not.

And now Saladin was telling me an entirely different story, building a whole new world for me, up from the foundations.

Across that food court table was a third kind, one that I had never thought about before, never met before, never believed possible outside of fairy tales. He was suddenly so unique in my eyes that I could not believe that the crowds in that mall could not see him shining out like an eye-splitting halogen light beacon.

Saladin van Schalkwyk was not a human without any gift of change at all, nor was he a Were constrained by the Moon to change into a single creature throughout their lives (if you except the Random Were and their ability to swing different ways given their context at Turn). He was something extraordinary, a shapeshifter able to morph his form into *anything at all*, and *whenever he chose*.

Or so he claimed.

I sat there and stared at him, aware that I had my mouth open like a beached guppy.

"That's not possible," I said at last, after a long silence, after he had told me the circumstances under which my brother Mal had become a werewolf. "It just... isn't."

"Like it's impossible that you should Turn into a boy?" Saladin said. "And by the way, that's happened before, whatever they told you – except that it might have happened too long ago for anybody to have really studied it or documented it, and nobody remembers it any more, not directly. So you're a throwback, if you like. To a more distant past than even the werewolf. Or maybe you're just more closely related to somebody like me."

"And what is somebody like you?"

"It's back to genetics," Saladin said. "As best I understand it, I'm a genetic freak on several levels – not the least being that I lack the switch-off trigger that ordinary Were-kind have, the one that switches off the change when the Moon stops being the correct phase and returns you to being, well, *you*. Or maybe I have it but it's under my control, and not the Moon's. The thing is, I have always been this way, and the truth is that I simply *do not know*. My parents were perfectly run-of-the-mill Were-kind, both of them – my mother a Were-serval, that's a kind of cat, and my father a Were-dassie."

"A Were-*what*?"

"A dassie. A little rock rabbit kind of creature, a hyrax, which is actually closely related to an elephant. Yea-big." He indicated something the size of a large dinner plate between his hands. "Little and furry."

"But related. To an elephant." I stared at him, trying to figure out if he was just pulling my leg.

He dropped his hands, shrugged. "Things are what they are. Maybe that's what had something to do with it all. When you've got that kind of confused and twisted genetic heritage, something's bound to give sooner or later."

"You're a gene pool of human, and sand cat, and elephant...?"

"When you put it like *that*," he said, grinning at me. The grin was infectious. After a moment I grinned back.

"So you just... you change into whatever... whenever you want to... but how do you *control* it...?"

"By choosing," Saladin said.

"So... can *you*... Turn into..."

He smiled again, but this time the smile wasn't entirely pleasant. "Into a different human? Yes, in point of fact. I can. *That*, young Jazz, was the inspiration you gave me, actually. Because I only found that out recently – I had simply never tried to do it before, because, well, as you yourself have had occasion to find out, it was simply an accepted fact that it could not be done. So I didn't bother doing it. But it worked quite well when it came to cowing your Mr. Bain into silence."

"What did you *do*?" I asked, halfway to appalled once again.

"Nothing fatal," Saladin said, baring those perfect white teeth at me again. "But trust me. I have put the fear of God into that scared, horrible little man. He won't get in your way again in a hurry."

"Do they know about it?"

"Does who know?"

"Well, *anybody*."

He threw back his head and laughed. "Oh dear. Well, I guess they know that somebody like me is out there. But I've taken care not to fall into anyone's clutches, if that's what you mean."

"Peregrine let *me* go," I said.

"Yeah. Well, you take care of it your way and I'll do it mine," he snapped.

"But your parents..."

"I haven't seen either of them since I was ten years old," Saladin said. "By then my father had gone back to South Africa, leaving me with my mother and with that preposterous surname – and my mother... well, she wasn't the most stable personality out there. I figured out what I could do by the time I was eight years old, and something told me even then that I should probably not let on to Mama."

"Eight? But Weres don't Turn until they're fifteen..."

Saladin shrugged. "Or thirteen. Or seventeen. Whatever."

"Eight is... awfully young."

"It was. But eh, what can I tell you. I knew. As I was saying, I figured that telling Mama would be the worst thing I could do about it – she'd be of no help whatsoever, and she could have easily got it into her mind to..." He sniffed, rubbed his jaw with his hand, thought better of going any more deeply into the matter. "I didn't. I kept quiet about it for two years, and in those two years I watched her slide – deeper and deeper – and the more I saw the more I realized I could never trust her with my real secret identity. At ten I simply... left home."

"And did what? And went where?"

"I made do," Saladin said. "I had a smart mouth and I was a quick learner; I found ways to make a go of it. By the time I was twelve I knew my way around computers pretty well – self-taught – and then I got picked up by a hacker group who knew a good thing when they saw it and figured I was young enough to be useful without having to be, you know, paid much. Well, that suited me at the time. I stayed with them for three years, picked their brains clean of everything they knew, and then I split. Created a dozen fake identities online. Hacked into everything from super-secret muffin recipes for a top hoity-toity bakery to classified government files, and it pays well. I kind of live off the grid, have done for years, and only a few people know my true name."

"But you told me," I said, after a pause.

"You're Mal's sister," he said. "And part of the reason behind this Lycan thing – well – they have the kind of resources that others can only dream about. They may be few but those that are around wield considerable power. There are limits to what they'll document anywhere where I can get at it, and I can't exactly infiltrate them. But Mal can. Mal wanted to. Mal, who can put the ideas together. He did it for his own reasons – but I have my own agenda. And he can give me the answers that I couldn't get before."

"But I thought it took two bites," I said. "The alpha pair. How come only you...?"

"Mal might have been halfway there already," Saladin said. "Or I managed to Turn into both the male and the female, and bit him twice as required. Something like that, anyway. I never said I had all the answers. But it worked, didn't it? Maybe that is one of those ideas he needs to put together while he's in there."

"What's he supposed to be looking for?"

"Anything," Saladin said. "Secrets. Looks like they have plenty of secrets to go around, the Lycans, and secrets sell, whatever they are; there's always someone willing to buy knowledge, especially if it's knowledge that is otherwise hard to come by. That's my part of it. Mal's is to simply get inside the keep when they lift the drawbridge again, and absorb information like a sponge. What he does with *his* part of it... that's his business."

"This whole thing is completely crazy," I said. "You could not possibly be certain that it would work."

"But it did."

"Or that he would be picked up."

"But he was."

"Or that he could communicate with you at all."

"That remains to be solved – but in the meantime, here *you* are, with the computer on which a lot of information already exists." He reached out and closed the laptop with a decisive snick, picking it up with one hand and starting to stuff it back into its bag. "Once I've had a chance to go through it all…"

"Wait, you can't *have* it."

"Why?"

It was a perfectly sincere question. He had simply assumed that I had brought the computer so that I would hand it to him.

"Because my parents might want to know…"

"So far as they are concerned, he took it with him."

"But this Alpha character who came for Mal, he specifically said no computers."

"And so Mal didn't listen," Saladin said, grinning. "It isn't like *that* would come as a surprise to anybody."

"Still," I said defiantly. "It's Mal's and I think I ought to tell Peregrine…"

Saladin laid his hand across mine – it felt like a light gesture, but I could feel his fingers digging into my skin.

"Say anything about this to anybody and you might kill him," he said, and he was absolutely serious. "So long as they believe it's a fluke – and yes, flukes happen, to everybody, everywhere, that's how things always begin – the Lycans will accept him, they'll train him, they'll teach him, they'll give him the answers. If they suspect that he's an outside agent who's somehow infiltrated the Lycan fold in order to spy on them – well, Jazz, they're *wolves*. Think about it. Crazy or not, it's done – and if it works, it'll be spectacular. But the only way it can have any chance at all is if none of us go blabbing about it to people who don't have to know."

"That makes me an accomplice," I said.

The grin that Saladin turned on me was positively wolfish, and I could suddenly *see* him Turning into the beast that had bitten my brother into the Lycan fold.

"Now you're getting it," he said. "If he gets in touch with you, let me know, would you? That email Mal gave you will always work."

"And if I don't?" I said, and I heard my voice tremble, just a little.

"I'll find out, Jazz," he said, and sounded eminently reasonable, as though he were talking to a recalcitrant four-year-old. "I'll find out anyway. But you're his sister, and he loves you – it would be nice if you'd help…"

"*Loves* me?" I burst out, interrupting him. "When he was still here, he spent half his time ignoring me and the other half sniping at me – yeah, we had a few conversations that we…" I stopped, biting my lip, ready to cry. Yes, he probably loved me. I for sure loved him. And right now I missed him more than I could ever have believed possible.

And he had done this crazy insane thing and put himself into possibly mortal danger.

"And yet he does," Saladin countered, quietly but firmly. "Maybe it turns out that I knew him better than you did – wouldn't be the first time a friend knew someone better than his family ever did. He never quite got around to forgiving himself about Celia – but he was too young to understand, really, back then. And then when he thought he did understand better, he never quite got around to forgiving anybody else about Celia. And as for you – "

"Yes," I said. "I know. I was an echo."

"He told me stuff about their escape, and their journey here, long before I read about it on your blog, in Celia's diary. About the things that happened on the way, and after they got here. It was him and Celia against everything and everybody – your parents took away their very identities and shoehorned them into quite different people and they had to reinvent themselves completely. He was just better at it than Celia quite managed to be, or maybe – well – I read the diaries – she was quite somebody, your sister. She had great courage."

"Stop it."

"But she did," Saladin said. "It takes courage to admit you're afraid. And Mal never quite did, to anybody – he just ploughed on ahead like a little pit bull puppy, life between his teeth, hoping for the best, relying on physical responses, on fisticuffs, to keep the rest of it away. At least Celia had both her hands in the dough, and was trying to shape a life into something she knew she wanted. Mal would have gone through it all just... reacting to stuff. Never making the choices himself. And then there's you."

"What about me?" I said, tears sparkling in my eyes despite my best efforts. I hated him *so much* in that moment, and yet I could not believe that a complete stranger could know my family this well.

"Well," he said, with that crooked grin of his, "you're no Echo. You're the hybrid of the two of them, the best of them, the child of this land who was born knowing the way. You're Jazz." He slid out from the table in one fluid motion, the laptop tucked under his arm. "Mal thought you were amazing, by the way," he added. "I think he was actually... jealous. Well. If he calls, let me know. Nice to finally meet you, Jazz Marsh."

Before I could muster a sufficiently blazing response, he was gone, vanished into the crowds

I was feeling... blank.

As though my entire world had been wiped clean, and rewritten in an entirely different language, and I couldn't quite get my head around the new story. There was just too much that had been flung at me of late. I felt as though the solid granite rock I thought I had been walking on all this time had kind of cheated on me and now that I knew what to pay attention to I could feel my feet sinking into the stone like it was viscous mud and sucking me down with every step.

I wanted to talk to somebody – to a friend like Nell, or Charlie; to a figure of authority, like my parents, like Peregrine – and yet those words of Saladin's muzzled me, comprehensively. *If they find out he's an outside agent infiltrating the Lycan fold... well... they're wolves.*

I needed to sleep on it.

I wished, suddenly and furiously, that I still had Celia.

Celia would understand. Celia was the only one who could possibly have understood.

Part 6:
The Girl Who Lived

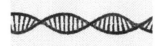

I n the rush of events, I had practically forgotten about my email to Emily Winterthorn.

It was not something I had been waiting for a response to – an expectation of a reply was not the reason I had written that note in the first place. Some part of me had wanted her to know, that was all.

When the response did come, almost four months later, it blindsided me completely, and I almost missed it in my inbox. And when I did find it, and read it, I had to read it several times because it was obviously *not* from a robot or from a secretary.

Emily, herself, had written the reply.

The ghost of Celia was strong beside me as I read it, and stronger still by the time I was finished reading. Celia's death would never *not* be a tragedy, the reasons behind would never *not* be indefensible (starting from the bullying and the ignorance from the other kids and culminating in Mr. Bain and his vindictive pious petty malice), but somehow – somehow – my sister's passion and her strength and her intelligence would not have been spent in vain. The fact that she had lived, and way she had died, would have if not justification then at least a glimpse of meaning.

Emily had obviously been devastated at the contents of my own note.

To: Jazz Marsh < jmarsh@globenet.com>
From: Emily Winterthorn < *emily@winterthorn.com*>
Subject: I have no words...

Dear Jazz,

Thank you for your letter.

The loss of a life, any life, at your sister's age is an unspeakable tragedy – and when such a loss is avoidable it is many times as heartbreaking. To read that I may have had a hand – however oblivious I might have been to that at the time – in your sister's death was a physical blow, and it is something that is going to haunt me. I have no suitable words at hand, even now, because to offer apologies or even condolences seems to be such a petty and inadequate thing to do. I offer both, anyway, for what they are worth – and I weep for all the things that your Celia wanted to be, could have been. She sounds like she was the kind of reader that it is one of the great privileges of my life to meet, young people who love my work, and who understand with an instinct that humbles me just what it is that I was trying to achieve with it.

I cannot ever bring her back to you, but with your permission there is something that I can and will do.

I am writing a new book, right now – and as of this moment its heroine, a young girl whom I am very proud of, is going to bear your sister's name. In addition to this, I am going to add a very special dedication to this particular book:

> *To the real Celia,*
> *Who offered her life as a sacrifice to Word and to*
> *Story*
> *Because she loved them so much*
> *And to Jazz, younger sister,*
> *Who ensured that the sacrifice would not be forgotten*

If you will let me have your mailing address, I will have my publisher send you the first copy of the new book when it comes out.

Beyond this, I can promise you one thing – I will do whatever is in my power to make sure that such a thing as this is never given the chance to happen again, and I will neither forget your sister's name nor ever quite forgive myself for whatever part I may have played in the circumstances that led to her life being so tragically cut short.

With my best wishes for your own bright future – and with all those unspoken words I cannot even begin to speak to you about your Celia –

Emily Winterthorn

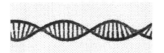

I actually sat there for a very long time and stared at this before I picked up the phone and called Nell.

"Emily Winterthorn just wrote to me," I told her. "Emily. Winterthorn. She says she's going to dedicate her next book... to Celia."

"What?"

I read her the email. She was making little inarticulate noises halfway through it, and when I finished she let out a small sound that was midway between a sigh and a sob.

"Oh. My. That is just... How do you feel about that?"

"I don't know," I said, sounding oddly strangled even to myself, which was not surprising since my heart seemed to have climbed into my throat and was making it difficult to breathe, somehow. "In a way it's just bringing the whole thing bitterly *alive* for me all over again. And then again, I read that, and I think about Celia, and I think... oh, how she would have loved this. If there was to be a memorial for her I think this would be the kind she'd have picked over anything else. And I feel... almost happy."

"Oh, *Jazz*," Nell said. "I'll tell everybody. I'll put in a pre-order at the bookstore right now. I just think it's – she's amazing. I'm glad you wrote to her and told her about it."

"It just feels like Celia got her wish, after all," I said. "You know. Meeting Emily Winterthorn. I have this really weird feeling like I can't really tell the difference between being awake, and being asleep and dreaming. I don't know which is the dream. You know – as though somehow the door is going to open and she'll walk right into the room, and she'll never have been gone..."

"She'll never be gone," Nell said. "She can't be, so long as she is remembered. And now, she'll be remembered. In a way she *did* just walk back into this world..."

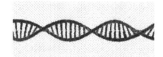

In a way. In a way, Nell was right. In time Emily Winterthorn's other readers might start to feel the same presence, once they got this latest story into their hands, but at least for a little while Celia's loving ghost walked by my side everywhere I went, I could see her sitting at the empty place at our breakfast table, I could hear her laughing in the room that used to be hers. I didn't know whether it was a good thing or a bad thing to have her summoned like this, to cling to the memory I didn't even rightfully have – I even 'aged' her a little, giving her those extra years she had never lived, imagining what she might look like if she were still here right now... if she had never died.

But none of this prepared me for the morning of October 12, two days before the Full Moon was due to rise and the family went into another Turn, when somebody began insistently knocking on our front door. Banging on it, even, as if whoever it was out there was hammering the door with a fist; there was a sense of danger, and urgency.

I was alone in the house. Dad was at work, Mom was out, Vivian was due to arrive the next day to supervise the Turn – but in the meantime, it was just me, rattling around in the empty rooms echoing with the persistent loud knocking at the door.

I almost didn't answer it at all – my first instinct was to simply go into my room and pretend that I had never heard anything at all. But something over-rode that, and I walked over to the door, slowly, reluctantly, and turned back the double-bolt. My hand closed around the door handle. It turned. I began to open the door, just a crack, and then, gasping, threw it wide.

He looked ten years older than when I had last seen him, like he hadn't slept or eaten or changed his clothes for a week, like he hadn't shaved in almost as long. His eyes were bloodshot and wild. The hand that dropped down to his side, the hand which had been balled into a fist moments before, the fist which had been pounding our door, was visibly trembling.

For somebody who had left for a better life with the Lycans, this creature at the door looked absolutely terrible – but it was, without a doubt, my brother Malcolm.

"Jazz? You on your own?"

His voice was hoarse, broken, but earnest and compelling.

"What are you doing here?" I gasped. "What's the matter? Are you all right?"

He started to take a step towards me, into the house, but staggered with weariness and obvious distress and reached out with his free hand to grab something for support. I instinctively flung out an arm, and his hand closed around my wrist, hard enough to hurt. But by this stage I was beyond caring about that – it was obvious that something far greater was at stake than a bruise from a careless grip.

"Jazz," Mal said. "Jazz... I found her. I found her. She isn't gone. She..."

"What are you talking about?" I said, really frightened now.

Mal crumpled to his knees before me, on our doorstep.

"Celia," he whispered hoarsely. "I found Celia. *She is alive.*"

THE
W E R E
CHRONICLES

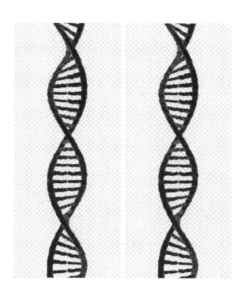

BOOK 2: WOLF

The First Mask:
A Boy By Any Other Name

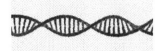

C all me Mal.

It's not who I am. Not really. Oh, I learned to wear the name – they tell me I picked it, after all, which counts for something, I suppose, but then again things are never that simple.

People don't know just how much of a visual, even photographic, memory I have but even so I was about four and a half years old when I stepped onto that ship that would take me away from the only home I'd ever known and towards something else, something new, something that would involve that choice. I trust the memory I have because I have always trusted my memories. But from the inside, it's always different.

I have a notebook, which I never show anyone, and a pencil which goes with it, which is always kept sharp. I draw my memories. And the things I draw come alive for me. It's like magic – it's always been like magic – I can look at a sketch and the reality of the scene unfolds around me like a holographic projection. It was years before I found out that it was only me for whom this was true. That's when I started hiding the notebook, and telling everyone else I couldn't draw a stick figure to save my life. But one of the first things I drew in that secret book, the one that nobody knew about... was that ship. That day. The day I took up the mask.

A brown-haired boy, standing on the rolling deck of a ship under way, steadied at the shoulder by his mother's hand. A man walks by, stops, smiles – he is dressed in a uniform, he is ship's crew, but his hair is white and his hands are not young any more. He wears a name tag, and it says "Malcolm" – it's shiny, engraved on a brassy background. Shiny enough to draw a child's attention. Shiny enough to stick in a child's memory.

He is kind. He always wears that smile, and it is sincere. This is his last voyage on the ship – that shiny pin with his name on it, he gives that to the boy at the end of the voyage. He no longer needs it, after all. And before the end of the voyage, sometime in between the moment of the boy standing at the side of the deck looking through the railings at the sea and the moment of the ship coming in to the dock in a strange new place, there was something else, there was the reason for the gift of that pin.

"We all have to do it," the boy's father's tries to explain. "It is a new world, and a new place, and we will have new names in it. You can choose one you like. Is there a name you like?"

But the boy is too young, and he does not know many names. He thinks about it and first offers the familiar ones, the ones that like the one he already bears, the ones that now have to be left behind. He is corrected, lovingly, and told that no, it needs to be a new name. A really new name. Something that will fit with the life that was about to start, which had nothing to do with the life he had turned his back on. And when he finally understands. the name that comes to mind is engraved on a shiny name tag worn by a man who is kind.

"Mal-colm," the boy says, breaking his tongue over the foreign syllables a little.

He sees his parents exchange looks over his head, and knows that they do not understand – but now he is stubborn, as only a four-year-old can be stubborn, and he insists. It is a name that has attached itself to him, and now ripping it away would leave scars.

So they leave it. He is Malcolm now. They say they will begin calling him that immediately so that he can get used to it, to the new name, so that he will answer to it when they get to their new home. They also tell him that his sister has a new name too. That she is no longer Svetlana, no longer Svetya, the sister whose name was a part of who she was in her little brother's mind. She is now different too. She is Celia.

Everything is different. It is all going to be different. Nothing will ever be the same again. The little boy has no name for what he feels, for the thing that flutters inside of him like dark wings. He does not understand it. It feels like anticipation; it feels like fear; it feels like nothing he has ever felt before.

But he is Malcolm now. A new person. Not at all who he was before.

It is only right that he should feel new things.

But I was still Malcolm, then. I couldn't even say it myself, not properly. The sister who was formerly known as Svetlana but must now be addressed as Celia told me that, later – we still talked between ourselves in the language we spoke from the cradle, sometimes, although our parents who wanted us to assimilate into our new lives as fast as possible frowned on it.

"You kept saying "Macom'," Celia said. "That middle L. It just wouldn't fit in your mouth."

"But it got shortened," I said.

"Eventually. But not for Papa. I think it was his penance, that he had to say the full name every time he used it. He felt responsible for making you give up your first name, your real name, and then this – when you chose it – he just took the name you actually chose and it became a sacred duty for him to call you by it. And besides..."

The besides was that I went as 'Macom', and then as full Malcolm, for quite some time. It was Chalky who turned me into Mal. Years after.

I must have been all of ten years old when Chalky and I first crossed paths.

By that age, I was starting to grow out of being the scrawny little boy of my early childhood and into the first adolescent promise of my adult shape. I had already developed a reputation for being "trouble" and knew every crack and stain in the corridor outside the Principal's office, where I was all too frequently sent to cool my heels after infractions, after my usual scuffles and fights.

In the beginning, those fights were responses – instinctive responses, in the only way I knew how, the physical, to the taunts and slights and teasing of the early days of my career in the public schools of our new world as a known Were boy. As yet unturned, to be sure, but I was "one of them", and I was foreign, and I was small, and this world was merciless to me and to those like me right from the start.

When I first hit out at a bully, it was with predictable results – and those results repeated themselves all too often in the fights that followed. Black eyes. Bruises. Scrapes and scratches. Bloody noses. Even, once, a broken arm. I gave as good as I got. I wasn't a punching bag. I was a miniature warrior, standing up for... for things I myself was probably too young at that age to fully formulate in my own mind. All I knew was that it was necessary. That words would only be laughed at the harder.

Celia had that option – and I knew something of her own troubles, and her loneliness, but she was a girl and she dealt with things in her own way, quietly, on the inside. It would only have made it worse if I had tried to do the same.

So I fought. I lost the fights at first, but I learned from every one of those losses. Until the day that I actually found myself left in possession of the field one day, breathing hard, knowing full well that a magnificent bruise was already starting to flower on my cheekbone, but still standing, and with no other combatants in sight.

For the first time... ever... I had actually *won*.

There had been two of them, that time, that I had taken on single-handed. And I knew that if I relied on physical strength alone it would have been a wash – but they had picked the fight, and I was always ready to finish one, no matter what the odds, and for once I fought quietly, coldly, using guile and strategy rather than simply strength, and somehow I was still standing after they had had enough and had slunk away.

I became aware of my audience only slowly, an awareness of a presence, and for a moment I braced myself, expecting a renewal of assault from a fresh adversary, knowing I had spent myself already and if this was the case I was simply going to have to curl up and take the blows as they came.

But it wasn't a third enemy. It was a boy whose age I found hard to guess, thin to the point of being almost scrawny but with a sense that he was made of steel and whipcord underneath the clothes which hung awkwardly on his wiry frame, his dark hair chopped by an obviously amateur hand so that it just brushed his shoulders, his face all hollows and cheekbones and in it were set eyes of an odd dark green shade which I'd never seen on another human being before. He gave me a half salute once he realized that I had registered his presence.

And brought into focus another thing.

There had been *three* of them who had jumped me. I had dealt with two. But there had been a third. A shadow somewhere behind me. A shadow which I had known was there, but was absolutely resigned to its doing whatever it needed to do because I had my hands full with the two opponents I was actually facing. I had no clear memory of what had happened, after, but that third shadow... it had just...

I thought I could hear a grunt, now that I filtered my blurred memories of the fight to focus on what I had not had the time to pay close attention to in the thick of battle. I thought I could remember a glimpse of *falling*. But it hadn't been my doing. None of it.

The boy watching me could probably see all of this unraveling in the expression on my face – the realization of what must have happened, and a blossoming resentment that my accomplishment, my winning this tussle, was not my own accomplishment. He grinned at me, revealing a mouthful of teeth which looked like they ought to be sharper than they appeared. His build and his looks might have hinted at vulnerability, but it was camouflage, and that grin was pure predator.

"I saw them jump you," he said. "I hung around to see if you might need help."

"Do I know you?" I asked, spitting the words out through uneven breaths I was still struggling to get under control. He was a total stranger; I didn't know every face of every kid in our school, to be sure, but I was pretty certain that I'd have remembered *this* face if it had been hanging around the halls. And I didn't know him. And there he was, offering unsolicited commentary, and apparently unsolicited help.

I was still out of breath, but I figured I could take him, In a moment or two. When I had recovered just a little.

But he didn't seem inclined to pick a fight. In fact, he looked about ready to leave me to it, shoving himself off the wall he had been leaning against and stuffing both hands into the pockets of his scruffy jeans.

"Just happened to be passing."

"What did you do?" I demanded, furious, as he turned his back on me and began to amble away.

"Not all that much. Didn't stop him from doing anything he wanted to do. He just happened to walk into something on his way there."

"Walk into what?" I said, still not mollified.

"My foot," he threw over his shoulder, together with a last flash of a grin.

"He'll just come back to finish it!" I yelled after him as he walked away, presenting me with a view of a thin back and a pair of long gangly legs clad in clean but obviously well-worn jeans.

"You'll get him next time," he said, as a parting shot, and vanished around a corner.

I was right, as it happened. They did come back again, the bullies who wanted to exact their revenge for the lost round of fisticuffs... but somehow it was easier that next time. I knew I'd done it once before. I took a beating, but I didn't go down. The next time they returned, there were more of them, and my guardian angel turned up again – doing nothing more than just being present, being a witness, and again occasionally introducing a foot into someone's path – I don't know how he didn't get his own dose of flying fists but it seemed that he was practically invisible to the ones who came for a piece of me – other than when they ran into him, literally, they didn't seem to notice him at all.

It was only then, the third time – or maybe even the fourth – that we learned more about one another and actually exchanged names. I gave him my "new" name, the full version, the only one I knew to answer to – Malcolm Marsh. He offered his rather fabulous one to which I returned what must have been an all too familiar double-take to him.

"Saladin van Schalkwyk?" I repeated. It was a mouthful. "What kind of a name is that?"

He shrugged. "Happens, when you have parents like mine."

I tried to get a handle on the name, but couldn't until he spelled his surname for me – and when I got the letters in the correct order and got over the pronunciation, I simply gave up and took the easy way out, calling him something that resembled that outlandish surname without having to twist my tongue around it. And he became Chalky. In return, it was he who first called me 'Mal'.

It had not ever occurred to me or to anyone in my family that my new portentous full name had the potential of being shortened. Not that diminutives were exactly strange to me, our entire lives we had known that there were pet names by which family members called one another. And when we spoke amongst ourselves in the old language, which was discouraged by our parents, but they couldn't supervise us all the time, I still called my sister by her childhood nickname of Svetya, and she still called me by my baby name, the first twisted syllable that I had uttered when I had tried to say my own original given name as a baby barely learning to talk, Gog.

But outside our house, to strangers, she was Celia and I was Malcolm – the full formal names – no nicknames or diminutives were permitted past the door. Perhaps it was this insistence by the ten-year-old me that my name was *Malcolm*, and nothing other than that, which might have fueled some of the early battles. They must have thought I was full of myself, and needed taking down a peg or two.

But when the boy I quickly came to know as Chalky took his leave of me by a cheery wave and a breezy, "See you, Mal!" – things began to fall into a better place. Because that I could somehow accept, could wear, far more comfortably than that 'Malcolm' which I had picked almost by accident because it was the only name I knew. I could be Mal. I could make myself into a Mal. A Mal would be leaner and meaner and more dangerous than a Malcolm could ever be. I could use that. It was protection. It was the first mask willingly taken.

If things had fallen out differently, then, I might have taken a different road. After I began to get something of a reputation for never backing out of a fight I began to realize that there were other boys, my own age or a little younger, who were starting to hang around in the back, the nucleus of a gang of my own, if I had wanted one, if I had felt the urge to swagger or to take on a more public leadership role. But somehow instead of making me cocky and self-assured and ready to step out in front of a gaggle of others ready to follow me, I turned inward instead. I kept to myself. I had been given to understand, all too bluntly, that I didn't belong, that I would never belong, and I ended up not wanting to belong – I was a solitary, out on the edges, happy with enough of a rep to be respected by those who needed to and to teach respect to those who didn't think it was due. And somehow it was Chalky, another outsider, another solitary, with whom I found a way to connect. If I had a best friend or a brother, he became that.

He never gave up all of his secrets, or at least he doled them out sparingly, a little at a time. I discovered that he was the closest thing I had ever known to a wild thing, that he did not in fact go to my school (or to school at all, by the stage I met him), that he was born Were, just like me, of two perfectly straight Were-folk parents, but that he himself was... something... else... something different, something strange. He hadn't bothered to give it a label –it was something he did, something he was, and he didn't think about it in terms of defining it. But when he finally opened up enough to tell me the truth, I found myself naming it at once.

"You're telling me you Turned at eight?" I asked him, astonished, when he told me that he was already capable of doing something that I myself would need *years* to graduate to. In fact, I squawked about it, feeling the sting of it. "But Were don't turn until they're fifteen..."

He shrugged. "Or thirteen. Or seventeen. Whatever."

"Still," I said stubbornly. "Eight is... awfully young. What did your mother do about it?"

His mother because one of the tidbits that he had already volunteered was that his father had abandoned the family when he was quite young. He had left his son with few memories and little more than that preposterous name, so it would have been Chalky's mother who would have had to deal with his precocious gifts. Alone.

He shrugged off the age. "What can I tell you. I was eight... and as far as my mother was concerned, I knew that I couldn't tell her. I knew even back then that she couldn't possibly deal with it. Mother... didn't exactly want to deal with a kid. Not really."

"You never told your *mother* that you *Turned* – how could you – I mean, aren't there laws about...?"

I already knew about the Turning Houses, where hapless Were-kind with no place deemed secure enough by the authorities had to report to endure their three days of the Turn. Were folk were not exactly permitted to roam the streets while in their secondary form. Even adults. And here was Chalky, telling me that he had been eight years old when he first Turned... and that nobody knew about it.

He looked at me sideways, in a way that he had which said a whole lot without him saying a word. And then he shrugged it off again, as if it was utterly immaterial. "I figured that telling Mama would be the absolute worst thing I could do about it. She'd be of no help whatsoever, and she could have easily got it into her mind to..." He sniffed, rubbed his jaw with his hand, thought better of going any more deeply into the matter.

"To what?" I asked. "She would have done what?"

"I don't know. But I didn't really want to find out. I just kept it quiet for a couple of years."

"But how could you...?"

"Well *she* was Were," Chalky pointed out. "She was Were-sandcat. Quite a pretty one, I saw her change, I saw her other form."

"She didn't go into the Turning House?"

"Not while I was around. I took care of her."

"But you were just a kid..."

"And as far as that went, I was still me during the Turn. As far as she knew, anyway. She couldn't ask because she had no clue that I had already found out. I had a secret life she never knew about. I couldn't trust her with it. She probably couldn't have handled it anyway."

"But if you had Turned yourself..."

He gave me a strange look. "You aren't listening. I didn't Turn. Not like you will Turn. Not at the full moon for three days regular as clockwork, you and your creature changing places."

"My creature isn't exactly regular," I said. "I am Random, I can probably change into anything, if I see it at the right time."

"But you get to pick your primary."

We had had that conversation, my father and I, about what I wanted my primary to be. This was a new world with new rules and it turned out I could choose – there were people who would let you hire an animal which you could have in front of you when you Turned, so you could Turn into an image of that beast, a palimpsest, and that would be a primary form that a Random like me would fall back on at any time if no other creature presented itself to his gaze at the wrong moment to derail his Turn. And I had already picked my beast – I wanted a wolverine. It was not an animal I had even heard of before we had moved to this place. They did not exist in the land where I was born, but I had read about them and the beast appealed strongly to me as my alter ego. My father had demurred at what would be an expensive animal to rent by the hour until such time as I Turned and it became unnecessary, but he hadn't said no, not firmly, and I thought I had a good chance of getting what I wanted in the end.

"And you...?" I asked, still not quite understanding.

"I don't *have* a primary," he said patiently. "I don't, really, have a Turn. I can tell myself to change, and I do. That's all."

"Into what?"

"Into anything I want."

"Anything?"

"Well, I guess the usual applies," Chalky said. "The kind of creatures that would be open to you. I don't think snakes and cockroaches are an option. On second thought, I don't know that I've ever really tried."

"And so when the full moon comes you just..."

He was shaking his head. "No. Not just then."

"When, then?"

"Anytime. Whenever I say so."

"Prove it," I challenged, with all the pugnacity of a ten-year-old who had been given something that was simply too hard to accept.

And then took it back, hastily, when I remembered the realities of shifting – that whatever he changed into would entail him losing the clothes that his human body was wearing, and changing back into a naked boy. I assured him I believed him, that I absolutely believed that what he said was true. I knew that it was impossible, of course, from my own point of view, from what I myself was – I, who was waiting for my fifteenth birthday on which I would come of age as a Were and Turn into my own alternate form, and face the reality of doing this, of being this, for three days out of every month for the rest of my life.

I wasn't certain at this point whether I felt happy about this, about the stability of this, or if I was just envious of the freedom that Chalky's own transformations gave him. He lived by no rules that I knew, in any respect – but I was already an outlier, an outsider, a loner. How much more of one was he, by definition...? Because he wasn't a Were, not really, not the way I knew the term. He was... he was...

"You're a shifter," I told him, defining him.

He didn't argue the point.

This was another picture in my sketch book, the transformation I asked him to produce in order for me to believe him.

A boy, crouching on the ground. He might be folded in a frozen position of what could be a bracing for something, or even actual pain – which would not be too far from the truth, probably, seeing as he is only shaped like a boy at the first cursory glance. If you take a closer look, one of his sneakers is dangling off a foot that is changing into a dog's paw, the other foot has claws which are tearing through its own shoe; the right hand, folded into a fist, with which he is leaning on the ground with his weight on his knuckles, in the process of turning into a hoof; the left arm bent back at the shoulder and lifted at an awkward angle above and behind him, its fingertips outstretched and beginning to turn into feathers; his hair beginning to fall into a mane about his neck and shoulders; his nose starting to elongate into a beak.

He was not a Were – not a classic one, tied to a single form – not even a Random, which could be shoved into any form by the right trigger – he literally was a true shifter, a shape-shifting thing which had somehow miraculously arisen unlooked-for out of the union of two apparently perfectly boring and ordinary Were creatures who were minding their own business with their secondary forms.

I asked him how he found out, the first time – and he said the first time he changed, back when he was eight years old, it was because he had been hiding, had needed to simply... disappear... and he did, by virtue of turning himself into a mouse and scurrying into a hidey hole until those whom he had been hiding from had given up searching and gone away.

"And then what?" I asked. "You just decided to be you again...?"

"Sure," he said. "If you like."

I had thought that there were no shared memories between the forms. That the human lived as a human and did not recall the things that the animal form knew and felt and did while transformed – the same entity but two completely different ways of looking at the world. Everything Were was governed by the phases of the Moon – you Turned when it rose, full, in the sky above you and you Turned back to human three days after that, like clockwork. It was all written, it was all done by the book, there were laws.

Except... except if what Chalky said was true, then for him it was different. It had to be different. For him to turn at will, both forms had to share a memory – because if the animal form did not remember that it was human there was no law to turn it back into one when it was time. It all had to be conscious, and done by an act of will, and that meant that he could remember everything.

I tried to ask him to explain. But I didn't have the words, the concepts. And he was either unwilling to articulate what occurred, or as unable to put it into a coherent narrative answer as I was to put the question. I had had to learn many new things when I came to my new world, in order to survive in it – and Chalky – well – I just took Chalky to be the outer limits of what was possible. I still had everything in front of me, after all, and there was no reason to suppose that anything out of the ordinary would mark my own transition into full adult Were.

But that was then.

The years that followed... showed me that I could never expect anything to be a sure thing, that nothing at all was to be taken for granted. It was as futile to have hopes and dreams and plans as it was to try and help others achieve theirs – because life was what happened to us all while we would be making those plans, and life would laugh at us.

I was twelve years old when everything that I had ever known crumbled around me in one moment of senseless tragedy.

I knew about Adaptadyne by then, of course. Stay, the wonder drug. The thing that arrived from the Were administration like clockwork every month, one prescription per Turn for three pills, no refills, expiring at the re-Turning of the named prescription holder to his or her human form. I knew about it in broad terms only, of course – I was just a kid – but I knew that one pill could delay a Turn for up to six hours, and could be used as an emergency measure to do this if necessary, a last-ditch thing to be used only when no other alternatives were possible and Turning would be catastrophic – or at the very least vastly inconvenient. Sometimes the Were worked for employers whose needs might not match their employee's biological imperative, and if a deadline needed to be met... there was the drug, to do it with.

If you filled a prescription and had any pills left over by the end of the Turn you were supposed to get rid of them – but people hoarded them, everyone knew that. My father who worked for a bank which sometimes required him to delay a Turn because of urgent business at the office. So there was an emergency stash at the house. I knew where it was kept it would not be difficult to raid it.

Celia knew that it existed, too.

She did not have her own supply – not yet – you were technically permitted to take Adaptadyne to delay a Turn but although Turning age was on average fifteen, the legal majority was not reached until the age of eighteen (for mundanes – it was actually as high as twenty one for those of us who had been born Were-kind. If you needed access to Adaptadyne in between those age brackets you were supposed to get it only through your parents.

But you could get it if you wanted it, on the black market. Everyone at school knew about Adaptadyne – the mundanes knew it as Stay, and for them it had value other than the practical applications the drug had for its Were recipients. You could sell Stay in the school bathrooms, to not-our-kind, for whatever you cared to ask for it – and the Were kids in our classes routinely used pilfered pills to delay their own Turns so that they could take some essential test – there were teachers who deliberately scheduled tests so that Were kids would be unable to sit them, being some other creature at the time of the exam, just because they could – just because they wanted to make their lives harder.

One of those teachers, whose name I was to learn to remember, was my sister Celia's malicious bane, a Mr. Barbican Bain. The first time my parents had found out she had taken a handful of Stay she had obtained from a friend at school, I was a fascinated witness to the confrontation that followed.

Celia had taken the pills at carefully measured intervals so that she could keep pushing her Turn back six hours at a stretch. By the end of that particular course of tablets – in order to take an exam she did really badly on anyway, despite the recourse to the pills or maybe because of that – she was a wreck, pallid, her skin the color and consistency of wax, her breath coming in gasps and her heart apparently beating almost hard enough to punch right through her ribcage.

"What were you thinking!" Mom yelled at her, afterwards, when everyone had safely Turned back into their human forms and she learned of Celia's transgression. "There's a reason those pills aren't given to children! How many of them did you take?"

"Only five, Mama, don't fuss. But I got the exam done, and it was an important..."

"Only *five*?" Mom spluttered, all but incoherent with rage and fear. "I'm taking you to the doctor, right now, to have you checked out! Heaven alone knows what damage you might have caused – five pills – you're *fifteen*... Where did you get hold of Adaptadyne, anyway?"

"You can buy them at school," I volunteered helpfully.

Celia shot me a reproachful look, but it was too late. The consequences were already set. One was that Celia was made to promise – to *swear!* – that she would not touch Stay again. Another was that I had made the final connection – seriously, until I said what I said I had not quite made the mental bridge between those things – that there was an actual market for these things in the schools and that kids who had whatever access they could manage were potentially able to make themselves valuable to other kids who did not, and wanted it. I had no doubt that Chalky would know how to find a market for Stay – and I knew for a fact that I could get a few pills here and there without anybody being the wiser, really.

So Celia soldiered on with Mr. Bain and his dirty tricks, and I managed to earn a few bucks by grabbing a handful of pills from the household stash.

But then Bain pulled the dirtiest trick of all. Celia's favorite writer was scheduled to come to the school for a visit. During a Turn so Celia would not be able to be there. Not without Stay.

But in order to be there, she would not need to just postpone the Turn, she would need to skip it entirely and would have to take twelve pills. Her friends at school might have been able to slip her a few, but not that many. She couldn't even be sure that she could buy that many on the black market at once, without raising red flags.

Being Celia, it did not even occur to her to wonder about Mom's secret stash or where it was kept. She did things by the book, and she would never have even considered it – and particularly not after she had given her word that she would not use the drug again.

But there was the Emily Winterthorn visit. And the fact that she would be kept from it, by virtue of the fact that she was Were... even though Emily Winterthorn's appeal was to just such readers who were Were.

I could see the injustice of it burn her, eat at her, from the inside. In some ways Emily Winterthorne was who Celia wanted to be when she grew up... and now she would not even have a chance to have a glimpse of her, of the real writer behind the words that meant so much to her – no chance to perhaps speak to her, to ask all the questions that she wanted to ask, to tell her thank you for everything that those stories had given her.

And I loved my sister. More than anyone will ever know.

I knew that her friend Karen had given her a couple of pills. I had overheard the transaction in the school corridors. I knew that it was not nearly enough for what she needed, for what she wanted.

Well, Mom had neglected to make *me* swear in blood.

Two days before the fateful Turn, seeing Celia backed up against a wall,

I spoke up.

"You could get it from Mama's stash."

"Mama is watching me," Celia said.

"I can get it for you. How many do you need?"

She stared at me, obviously at war with her own conscience, but I saw her lose that battle, allow defiance and raw courage to beat down her misgivings, and said just two words.

"Do it."

The morning after that conversation I went into her room and pulled a double handful of pills out of my grubby pocket – I had never taken so many at once, this would probably be missed, but it could not possibly be put at Celia's door. Like she had said herself, she was too carefully watched. I had not been. The ones that I gave her were not all the same – some round, some lozenge-shaped – but I had thought nothing of that, and neither did she.

"You probably shouldn't have done that," she said, staring at the little pile of pills on her bed.

Well, that was obvious. I asked the practical question.

"How are you going to get past Vivian?"

Vivian was the New-Moon Were who stayed at our house and acted as our babysitter while our parents were in their Turn.

Celia told me she had a plan. I didn't know that it involved taking all the pills I had got for her, all of them, at once, just before her Turn began. Just to make absolutely certain that she would not Turn during that particular Full Moon. We didn't know, either of us, that the differently shaped pills had been different doses, some single-dose 50mg pill and others an extended-release 200mg tab.

Perhaps it is guilt that wipes my memory of specific events after this, because all I remember is a series of images that are burned into my brain.

My sister, laid out on a gurney.

A bunch of paramedics in dark jackets, leaning over to adjust a plastic mask over Celia's face, talking quickly and quietly over her prone body.

Celia's hand, lying palm-up on the blue-sheeted gurney right beside her hip, twitching uncontrollably as they wheeled her out of the house – as though she was trying to tell me something, to signal something, in language I could not understand.

Driving to the hospital as we followed the ambulance with its flashing lights, my younger sister Jazz in the front seat, myself and Vivian's son Charlie in the back, all of us keeping very quiet.

Mom's face, in the aftermath, as life without Celia began in our house. Dad's wordless, never spoken-of, bone-deep pain.

Perhaps I should have confessed my part in all of this, right away, in the first black days after she died. But the silence that descended on the matter in our family circle was impossible to break. They could not bear to talk about it, so I said nothing at all, and by the time Jazz began to wonder, and to ask questions, and try and get me to talk about the sister she had never really had a chance to get to know properly – by that time, it was way too late. And there was a part of me that resented Jazz's very presence in that house, as though it was her fault that Celia was no longer there, as though she had somehow deleted Celia through her own existence, a new sibling born in the new world.

I should have said something. Probably.

But they all blamed themselves, and not me – and it was easier that way. I let Mom believe that it had been Celia, after all, who had somehow raided that secret stash, and not me. And it wasn't an issue, after that, anyway, because she threw them all away. Every single one of them in that stash. I watched her do it. If there was a time... it might have been then... but she didn't want to know anything in that moment. She was too wrapped up in Celia right then, she didn't have time to sit down and listen to anything I might have said, she didn't have time for anything I might have done, or wanted, or needed. There just came a point at which telling her anything would have been – well, just unkind. Even cruel. Especially after I watched her, month in and month out, rip up the envelopes with the Stay prescriptions that kept on coming from the Administration offices. She just destroyed them – she *killed* them, violently, as though she was intent on wreaking her revenge on them for Celia's death.

Maybe I shouldn't have shouldered Jazz aside, in the years that followed – but she was too much of a reminder, really, and every time I looked at her, I could see that she was not Celia. It was not her fault, of course, and after a while she became wary of me and just stopped trying. A part of me might have been sorry, but another part had reached the simple conclusion that if I never loved another sister as much as I had loved Celia, if I didn't put my heart out there, I could not get it broken. It was as simple as that.

Jazz was only seven years old when Celia died, maybe way too young for her to understand why I resented the simple fact that Mom decided that she would not risk sending Jazz to the school which had destroyed Celia. She could not let it happen again, and she could make sure of that. Jazz would be taken off the grid, homeschooled, wrapped in cotton wool, protected and overprotected, tied down with golden ropes, pinned where Mom could make absolutely certain that she was 'safe'... and that she had no life at all, locked inside four walls like some medieval princess who was being kept from a fatal curse.

My own response to become even wilder. It was too late for them to trammel me, I was already loose, and I pushed out even further. I became angry, brooding, silent; they knew better than to try and make me into a social and civil human being at home, I could not spend much time with my family because every time I looked on them all I knew what I had done, that I had had a hand in Celia's death, and the guilt was simply too heavy.

I know that Jazz saw me as the only real living bridge between her and Celia – but I could not be that for her. I could not bear it. She dared to ask once if I wanted to leave home, and all I said in response was simply, *Wouldn't you?* – but of course she could not hope to understand where that came from. All she knew – all that she thought she knew – was that somehow, despite all the freedom that I apparently enjoyed and which she was denied, I was feeling trapped in that family circle, that I didn't know what I wanted to do or where I wanted to go so long as it wasn't what I was doing right then and that it wasn't right there, and that I was happiest when I was away from the rest of them. And she was right, of course. But it wasn't because I hated them.

It was because I loved them all. Because I needed them and could not reach out to them. Because I felt I did not deserve them. Not anymore.

I didn't think things could get any worse, until they did.

I celebrated my fifteenth birthday. From here on, it was supposed to get easier. I would Turn, on schedule, and become a full-fledged Were – which would somehow make me a full substitute for the lost Celia and re-center my family, which would somehow make me an equal to my accomplished friend Chalky who had never had to wait this long. It was with great anticipation that I was locked away for my first Turn in the Turning Room reserved for me in our basement – trying hard not to look too hard in the direction of the one that Celia would never occupy again – with a thoroughly sedated wolverine in the room, chained to a strong iron bar just in case it decided to wake up and take exception to me.

It wasn't an issue. The Moon rose, and sailed across the sky, and I did not Turn. The guy from whom my father had rented the wolverine came and got his animal before it ever had a chance to wake up from its nap.

No matter, they said. It doesn't always happen the first time.

But it did not happen the second time, either. Or the third. Or the fourth. Or the fifth. Or the tenth.

My sixteenth birthday came and went. And then half a year after that. And still... the moon rose, the wolverine slept, and I stayed myself.

By this point it was obvious to me that I was being punished by the Universe for what I had done, for my sins and my silence, for the price that Celia had paid instead of me. It was with an almost philosophical calm that I accepted the simple fact that the wolverine was getting to be an expensive indulgence, and my potential primary form was reduced to a much cheaper rental – a weasel – they're from the same family, my father said reasonably enough, a weasel is just a smaller wolverine, in a way. It stung – it diminished me – I knew, I just knew, that Jazz and Vivian's son Charlie (her bosom buddy) were laughing at me while I tried to stare down the weasel every Turn without success.

Seventeen.

I was already the oldest un-Turned Were that I knew of in my own generation. People were beginning to point, to laugh, to talk. All of it behind my back of course because I would give anyone doing it in front of me a bloody nose – and it all served to focus me even further into darkness. I became a polished card-shark, and I knew how to cheat when the luck wasn't running my way. I became someone whose path you did not cross in a way I did not like if you wanted to escape potentially very unpleasant consequences. I learned how to *hurt* people – or at the very least how to inflict physical harm (I kind of figured there was little left for me to learn on how to do less visible but more insidious damage to people who trusted or even loved me).

And then – well past seventeen years old, closing on my eighteenth birthday, still unturned – I emerged from the Turning Room yet again in my own shape with the wretched weasel sulking in its corner... and learned that the Universe wasn't done punishing me yet.

Jazz had unexpectedly Turned. Before she really should have.

Into something impossible.

Into a *boy*.

I thought I had built myself a good solid bad-ass armor, that I had figured out a way to let nothing in, that I had successfully set myself up not to care, given myself the magical ability to not get hurt. But this... this slipped through some tiny crack somewhere and lodged straight in my heart, a piece of fiery steel still white-hot from the forging.

It was worse than being hurt. It was being betrayed. I had no idea how much I would be expected to pay in order to expiate my guilt for my part in Celia's death – but something in me cried out *TOO MUCH!* at this particular installment of that debt.

I was nearly eighteen years old. It was my time, damn it all. It was *my Turn*.

I couldn't look at her, when I came out of that cursed room with the weasel still in it and came upstairs and saw her... him... *it*... sitting there in our living room. I was bitter. I was in a black funk. My jaw was clenched so hard that it was practically locked together; I could feel a small pulse beating in my face as my heart fought to beat in a way that wasn't either leaden or threatening to make it beat itself against my ribcage into a bloody pulp.

I couldn't accept this. I could not. It was too much.

If the fabled laws of this new land were to be obeyed to the letter, she – Jazz – the thing that used to be Jazz – ought to have been locked up downstairs in that Turning Room, not sitting in the living room of my house eating pizza. It was bad enough that she had Turned at all, Turned first, Turned before me – but this – this – she had Turned into something that gave her freedom. No weasels for this girl. She could walk the streets when Turned. Unlike me.

A chance that Celia would have died for.

Did die for.

Everything sane, all my senses, told me I was looking at a strange boy I had never met before. And yet, underneath this new skin, I could still see *her*, my little sister, Jazz. I could see how bewildered and frightened she herself was at this change, that there was not that much I could do to add to that, but oh, how I wanted to in that moment.

I had never loved her more, nor hated her more, in the same moment of a feeling so molten and incandescent that I had no name for it at all. I spat out the poison. I suggested that it would be best if we simply gave her... him... *it*... to the authorities.

That was received with the predictable recoil that it deserved. But it was all I had right now. I flung out into the stark bitter world where I could be Bad Mal with impunity. I found Chalky and spilled it all out, and he had the sense not to ask questions, not yet, not at that moment, but instead simply produced enough alcohol to get us both drunk enough to finally pass out.

By the time I came back to some semblance of sanity the Turning days were almost over and I crawled back to the house to face the family. And everything else that needed to be faced.

When she came back, when she Turned back into Jazz, I was there for the gathering. I could see my parents trembling on the brink of this new catastrophe, and I waited for the cards to be thrown, not yet sure what was in the hand that I held – other than a burning question, staring at Jazz. *Who are you? Where did you come from? How is this thing even possible?*

Jazz was just as much at a loss as I was.

"Hi, Mom. Hi, Dad," she said into the silence that greeted her as she walked back into the living room as herself. "I'm fine."

I actually almost laughed out loud at that. It was a game try.

They wanted an explanation and she gave them one, as best she could. I listened – with anger and the dregs of that sense of betrayal, yes, but also with something that astonished me by the fact that I could only really call it envy. I was *jealous*. Of my *little sister*.

But it all finally came out on that day. The thing that happened to Jazz... and the thing that happened... to Celia. The truth. And my part in it.

They did, in the end, call in the Were authorities – in the shape of the man we all knew as Uncle Peregrine, who had been the one to meet us when we first arrived here, who had been our family's friend since our first hours in this new world. He brought in other people, who poked at Jazz and prodded at her and tested her and asked her questions.

He said he himself wanted to be there for the next Turn, so that he could observe matters for himself. At the next full moon, I dutifully went into my own Turning Room yet again - and came out as Mal a couple of hours later to learn that Peregrine had tricked my little sister into proving she was a pure-blood Random Were. He Turned her into a mouse, for the duration of this second Turn, simply by showing her a mouse as the last warm-blooded creature that she saw before the Turn took her.

So that settled that. They would register her as a True Blue Random Were, and register her primary as the mouse, and they all agreed that the less said about the real nature of things the better. There were people who would have to know, but not everyone would.

We passed in the corridor, after the family pow-wow that followed her mouse Turn. She could see it on me, maybe, like a shroud – a feeling of bleak surrender, of just being ready to give up.

"Are you all right?" she asked – she actually asked me that, and it was at once an awkward sympathy and a sort of apology which she didn't quite know how to put into words.

I made a chopping motion against my throat, below a mouth that split open into a slightly manic grin.

"Never better," I said brightly. "Thanks for asking."

"Mal... seriously..."

"Seriously, little sister?" I said, knowing that I was about to give her the truth, that the truth would hurt. "*Seriously*? I've kind of had it. Had it with waiting. I'm riding on fumes, here. I have nothing left. I've been waiting for so long... and frankly... that's the thing that is killing me. The waiting. The hope. If I just knew that it wasn't going to happen, I might be able to find a way to live with it, somehow. Although..." And there it was again. For a moment it was just impossible to look at her, to hold her gaze. "Jazz, it would probably break that last bit of my heart that isn't already broken. But at least it would be *over*."

I made my escape into my room. And then I heard her go back into the living room, back into the kitchen. Don't ask me what made me step back out into the corridor and lurk like a spy just outside the door, eavesdropping crazily to things I probably should not have been listening to. But then, there you have it. One less secret in a house which had been thick with them until not so very long ago.

Dad was still in the kitchen, drying and putting away some dishes.

"Hey," I heard him say softly, as Jazz must have walked in. "You okay?"

"Daddy, can I talk to you for a sec?"

"Sounds serious," Dad said. "What is it?"

There was a pause, and then she said it, the reason I knew I had come out here in the first place.

"It's... Mal, Dad. I kind of feel... as though I... stole his... Dad, he hates it, you know. He *hates* it. The whole lock-me-up-with-a-weasel thing. It's killing him."

And how would you know, I thought, pressing my lips together.

"Have you guys talked about this?" Dad asked.

I heard Jazz hesitate before answering. "No. Well, yes. Not really. But you know, a little."

Little liar, I thought.

"None of this is your fault, Jazz." You didn't pick the time and the place, the context, the consequences..."

"Yes... but... what happens when he is eighteen? As soon as he's of age, he'll just go, and I don't want to lose him too."

I actually had to swallow a lump in my throat at that. And again, there was a cocktail of emotions that threatened to erupt – fury and betrayal and anguish – what do you mean, *too*, kid? You never lost Celia – you never had her – but she was still talking.

"How long does he have to keep at this?" she asked. "To have to keep enduring it? What's the oldest age that anyone ever did? And what happened to that person?"

"I'd have to look it up," Dad said. Too carefully.

I could hear the unwillingness in his voice, I could hear it two rooms away skulking in the corridor, but he answered her.

"To the best of my knowledge, twenty two. There are rumors of even older, but I am not at all sure that they are to be trusted. It was a young man... he didn't live to see his twenty fifth birthday."

I heard Jazz ask why. I heard Dad answer that there had been... various explanations given. But it had been as though he'd thrown a pail of ice water at me. I was cold, cold, cold standing there listening to this. It was a death sentence, of a sort. If I didn't do this thing soon... if I didn't Turn... well, it would be the end apparently.

"Dad, can't you just... let him go? Let him decide? If it hasn't happened by now..."

"But it *will* happen. If it isn't to be here, in the room downstairs, safely... he knows the alternative is worse."

I whispered it with her as she said it. The evil fairy tale of our lives.

"The Turning Houses."

"Yes," Dad said, after a short pause. "Those... were a reality that your mother and I never wanted any of our children to see."

"But Dad..." she wasn't letting this go, she was a little terrier, worrying at it until it gave. "I don't know how much more of this he can take."

"But what would you have me do?" Dad asked. "I can't just say 'let's stop it' and let it end there. You don't just stop being Were-kind, just by wishing. And there are laws here, and we live by the laws. And the law says that a young Were cannot leave home before he reaches his majority, and not even then without provision being made for a safe Turn elsewhere"

"But he hasn't Turned," she interrupted.

"Not *yet*," Dad said. Implacable. I wished I could have laid claim to the same kind of certainty.

"What if he just isn't meant to be a weasel?"

"As opposed to what? Like you were meant to be a boy? Or that mouse that Peregrine lobbed at you just before you Turned into it? Jazz, if he were meant to be something else – something that was not Random – he would certainly have done that by now. And if not even the Turn-prompt animal will trigger it in a Random Were, what makes you think that he's ready to Turn into anything else at all?"

"But what if he doesn't? Can you keep him locked up in a Turning Room every time the phase of the moon changes, for the rest of his life? That's prison..."

"I don't know, Jazz. I don't know what the answer is. All I can tell you is that I hope, every time I walk into my own Turning Room, that I will walk out again and be able to slap Malcolm on the back and congratulate him at finally crossing that bridge. And there is nobody more disappointed than me when it does not happen..."

"Yes, there is," she said, almost too softly for me to hear. But I heard, anyway. "Mal. I wish you could just... leave him alone. I wish you could make it stop," she said, her voice breaking slightly.

"So do I, sweetie. So do I."

I couldn't bear any more. I slunk back into my room like a thief. It felt as though I had literally stolen this conversation, as though I had had no right to it at all.

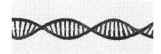

The day after that, I told Chalky about it. And something came out that I hadn't expected at all.

"He made it sound as though a choice was possible," I said, having related my father's words to Chalky and having heard an odd nuance in them that I had not really registered the first time. "As though it was *I* who had the choice. I mean, not just by picking another animal. That I could somehow... choose. That there might be a clan I had a call to. I mean, it's hardly likely that I would Turn into a Corvid, or an actual wolf..."

And there it was. It stuck. I could not get rid of it after that, no matter how hard I tried to put the ludicrous idea out of my mind.

Wolf.

What if I reverted to our most primary form of all? The form that began it?

But I knew nothing of Lycans. Nobody did. And it was damned hard to find out, as it turned out, because either there was very little to find out in the first place or else they were doing a very good job of hiding in plain sight.

But Chalky was very good at this sort of thing. I had said it, and he heard it, and he took it upon himself to do his own research. And the next time I drifted over to his room, he opened up his laptop and showed me what he had discovered on the Lycan Clan.

"Where do you *find* all this stuff?" I asked, not sure if I felt admiring or irritated at the ability of some people to delve into the cyberworld and come up with information which most of us – me included – would never discover if we searched for a thousand years. Chalky had a nose for stuff – it wasn't just he was able to *find* things, he was also one of the few people I knew who instinctively knew where to look – which was half the job, of course. Others wasted so much time looking in all the wrong places. Any place Chalky turned to... had pay dirt in there somewhere. And he looked in places that other people didn't even know were places.

I scrolled down the screen on Chalky's laptop, URL after URL, most of them looking exotic and unrecognizable.

"It's a gift," Chalky said laconically, and reached out to stop me, scrolling back up a couple of lines. "This one, for instance. Click on that."

I did, dutifully, and was rewarded by a tightly typed screed in a language I did not immediately recognize although some of the constructs seemed similar enough to my own cradle tongue for me to squint at it with a feeling that I *should* be able to make sense of it if I worked at it for a little while.

Which did beg a question, and I asked it.

"How do you know what this says?"

"We have ways," Chalky said, and reached over my hand to type something complicated on the keyboard. At which act, the screen threw up a blue bar across the top which said "Translating..." and after a moment the page I had been looking at blinked twice and then reappeared, this time rendered in a form that I could understand.

"How do you do that...?" I said irritably, and then brushed him off as his face broke into a smug grin that I was beginning to find all too familiar. "Never mind. What am I looking at?"

"Way back when," Chalky murmured. "That right there, that's it. That's the mushroom that the goats ate. That's where it all began."

I frowned up at him. "Okay," I said carefully, my tone an invitation for him to keep on explaining.

"That's the chemical, right there. The actual chemistry, that came later. Over on this side of the water. When they ground up that mushroom to make up the early versions of Adaptadyne. Back there, they probably knew all about the mushroom's properties – I have absolutely no doubt that you'd have found people who chewed the actual thing itself to get at what it could do. But then – then – it came over here, and it was recognized for what it was, for what it had the potential to be. And they brought the herbal old-wives-tale concoction into the lab – and the rest is history. It, uh, you might say it mushroomed, after that."

"This is serious, Chalky," I said.

"I know. Sorry. But there – that thing – that tells you how it started being what it became. And *who* started it. The Lycans... go back a long way. They existed back there in those same mountains that the original mushroom came from. They knew – long before anyone else figured it out, they knew – and they got the jump on everyone else. The original pharmacological patent for Adaptadyne... it was filed by the tiny seed company of what is now a pharmaceutical empire, an empire that was founded on this thing. And that original company was founded by the Alpha of one of the major Lycan packs, and he brought in the rest of the clans. The Lycans developed this thing from nothing. They knew what the raw material could do, and they knew that they could make it pay. Somehow. The Lycans know how to land on their feet."

"They used to be the dominant clan, sure," I said. "But I don't think I've ever even heard of one in a good long time. I certainly don't think one has ever crossed my path, that I know of."

"Probably have," Chalky said. "They went into the shadows, they didn't disappear. There may be fewer of them than there were, to be sure – but that doesn't mean that they're any the less powerful for that."

"You sound as though you've been investigating them," I said.

"I have, sort of," Chalky said, surprisingly. "Whatever they used to be – bogeymen to frighten children with – they're scientists now. They don't advertise the fact of their identity but a few of the top researchers in the big universities... are Lycans."

"And how do *you* know?"

Chalky shrugged. "If you look, it's easy to find," he said. "And anyway. It isn't just that. I know that they've got facilities of their own where they do... God only knows what."

"What, you don't know *that*? You know everything else, but you can't figure out...?"

"They're firewalled. By people who know how. I tried, believe me. I know *where* to look, but there's nothing for me to see there and once they caught me snooping and I had to burn my way out of there pretty fast – and they almost had me by the tail before I could escape."

"They're perfecting Stay?"

"I'm sure they've got much more interesting projects than that going on," Chalky said. "I'd love to know what, actually. But it's either having somebody on the inside who's willing to dish the dirt – and they're *wolves*, it's a pack, that's not going to happen – or I have to be better than their best. That hasn't happened yet."

"But if you had the data... what would you do with it?"

He hesitated. "I have my own questions," he said at length, after a long pause, "and I would like to see if I can't get my own answers. Besides, the world would probably be better off knowing about some of their hush-hush stuff."

"I could always change my mind and start asking for a wolf," I said. "For my primary, you know. If I were a wolf I could just..."

Chalky was shaking his head. "Just try it," he said. "You'd find yourself nattily stonewalled. I think that a wolf is off the list of acceptable animals which you can choose, for your Random transformation. If you tried, you'd probably get a visit from someone who wouldn't necessarily give his name, only a warning to stay out of their playground. If you tried it again there wouldn't even be that much of a courtesy before they took you out. Like I said, they went into the shadows – there may be fewer of them than there used to be once – but they didn't give up their power. Don't test them."

"But how would they even know if..." But before I could fully finish framing my question – how would a pack of true Lycans even know if one of their number was a 'fake' wolf who had only Turned into one because he was a Random whose gift was to Turn into whatever he looked at last before the change hit him, Chalky was already shaking his head.

"You aren't listening. They're a *pack*, They're family. They aren't like you or me. They aren't even like a flock of Corvids – it would be easy enough to hang out on the outskirts of a flock, they have communal aviaries and they'll share the space amicably enough during the Turns – they'll open the aviary to a visiting Corvid even if the human was a passing stranger – but the wolves... they'd be harder to crack. You'd have to *be* one of them before they would let you near them, before they would ever trust you to approach – they would put you down first, they don't waste time asking questions if they think you are a danger to them."

"But what if I really... was one...?" I asked slowly.

Chalky stared at me. "What do you mean?"

"Well... how does one become a Lycan? You can be born into it, of course, like most of the clans breed true to species and I suppose they do too. But you said there were fewer of them so that means they can't be having that many members of the new generation. So they have to keep up numbers – so how do they do it? It used to be that you got bitten, and you changed..."

"It's more complicated than that," Chalky said. "You'd need to find two of them who'd be willing to take that bite, and even then they might not be all that gentle about it."

"What do you mean, two of them?"

"That's the way the bite thing really works," Chalky said. "You'd need to be bitten by two wolves. The alpha pair of a pack. The male and the female. And even then, if you didn't already have the predisposition to Turn, even if it was just a distant memory in your genes, you'd probably just die rather than become Lycan. But these days – with the laws – they're locked away when they're wolves, and they keep themselves to themselves – and if you tried going in there to glad hand them into giving you that courtesy bite they're more likely to fall on you and shred you before they'll just take that genteel nibble that you need."

"I do have the predisposition," I said slowly, an idea coming together in my head, an idea so huge and probably so bad that I didn't really want to take the time to examine it too closely because I would talk myself out of it. But if it worked... if it worked... it would solve so many problems, really. My own problems – the failure to Turn for so long – maybe I could jump-start it... and then, if it worked at all, perhaps being that inside man that Chalky wanted...

But he was staring at me, with a frown etched into his forehead. "Are you seriously thinking what I think you are thinking...?"

"I think so," I said, with a grin.

"Bad idea," he said, shaking his head. "And just where would you go looking for the wolves that you would need to..."

I tapped him on the shoulder. "Right here."

He actually did a very satisfying double take. "What – you want *me* to..."

"You said you could Turn into anything you wanted."

"Yes, but a wolf...? Actually, technically, *two* wolves...? One of them female...?"

"What, you can't do what my sister did? Just Turn into a different gender?"

Chalky paused. "Believe it or not I simply never tried," he said. "All I ever did was change my outer skin, inside I always remained... well... *me*. The fundamentals didn't change. I didn't think about changing into a girl any more than I considered changing into a baby, or an old man. Age and gender... just seemed to be fixed."

"Are you saying you can't?"

"I'm saying I never tried, and I'm saying I have no idea how – and if – it will affect what I *can* do if I tried it."

"You think it would hurt you?"

"I wouldn't *think* so," Chalky said carefully. "Maybe if I just made myself *believe* I was a she-wolf, just for a second, just for long enough for the juices to work... on you. But all that aside you're asking me to change into something with lots of sharp teeth and to use those teeth on you..."

"If there is no other way, yes," I said.

"I could damage you," Chalky said. "I could, you know. Without even meaning to. A wolf's bite is a weapon – it's supposed to be one – I don't know if I can..."

"It's my choice," I said stubbornly, all the more committed to this crazy idea. The more Chalky threw up the obvious obstacles the more determined I became, somehow.

"Like you chose the wolverine...?" Chalky asked softly.

I didn't even know why that hurt. But it did. It stung. And I lashed out. "Like that was a choice," I said savagely. "It was a prayer – an increasingly desperate prayer – and now there's just the weasel, after all that, and *if and when* I eventually Turn at all that's all I'll ever be. Nothing more than that. Just a stupid little weasel. I know, it's been a privilege of a sort to have been offered a choice at all – in the first place – but if I couldn't actually land the choice and it got snatched from me like this one was – it's no longer a choice at all. I am what I am, I was born Were, in the end I will either Turn like all my kindred and into something that I don't even want to be."

The rest of that sentence, unspoken, hung between us: *or else I'll just live out my days, however long my life turns out to be, as a wretched failure, a dud, the Were child who couldn't even fulfil that part of his genetic heritage. Weak, useless, outcast.*

I went on. "At least this way... if we try... look, it may not work at all in which case nothing has been lost. If it works out badly, Chalky... well... I've had it with waiting, with living my life from Turn to Turn and watching everyone's expectations crumble at every cycle, I can't even bear the thought of it any longer. So if it ends, it might as well end like this. And if it works..." I paused to draw breath, and Chalky nodded, into the silence, just once, accepting my words.

"Are you sure?" he asked, one more time, just one more time, but his eyes were steady on mine.

"You say you remember yourself when you're changed," I said. "You will remember who I am. You probably will hurt me some, that's inevitable, but I don't believe you'll give in to a pure murderous instinct to rip me apart. In theory it doesn't even have to take very long. Just long enough to draw blood. Long enough to pass it into me, the change trigger, and then, after that, all we can do is wait."

"If this works, they *will* come for you," Chalky said. "They'll find out, and they will come for you. If they know you Turned into a wolf... you, a Random who cannot have Turned into anything that he hadn't observed and they knew you had no wolf to imprint on... they will know that it was a Lycan Turn. And they can't afford not to bring you into the fold."

"You get your inside man," I said. "I swear, I will be a fount of information."

"That is not why you are doing this," Chalky said. "Or at least not why you *should*."

"It isn't," I said. "But if what you said is true and it is they who created the thing that eventually killed my sister – the thing that I gave to her myself, unknowing – then I will find out just what they did, why they did it, and how they think their accomplishment helps them... do... whatever it is you think they are trying to do..."

"What makes you think I think they're trying to do anything specific?" Chalky said, a strange little smile playing around the corners of his mouth.

"If you didn't have ideas," I said, "you wouldn't have wanted an inside man..."

I had once asked him to prove that he could turn into anything he chose. And then took it back. And that had never really been brought up again. The truth of it was, on the matter of his being able to do what he said he could do, all I had ever had was his word on it – perhaps part of the reason behind this was my own problems, was just that Chalky had shied away from rubbing my face in the simple fact that he could Turn on a whim, without any rules at all, the thing that I could not do. But now – now – he was about to prove to me without any doubt the truth of who he was.

If this didn't work, all that I would be left with in the end would be a possibly debilitating bite wound and ripped up muscles... and undisputable evidence that I had tried everything, even this, and I had failed it all. We were both wary – but at the same time I felt released, as though I had finally rolled my last dice throw and gambled everything on it. One way or another, it would end, my torment. It would be over.

It wasn't something I was looking forward to, frankly. It wasn't something I particularly wanted to do. But I knew – and so did Chalky, despite his own reservations – that it was probably something that I *had* to do.

I had never *watched* someone Turn. Oh, I saw the Before and the After – I had seen my parents go into their Turning rooms as my parents, and then later I could look in and see them there in their Were forms – but I had never stood and watched them change. In all my days, as a Were child, as a young Were boy, this was something I had taken for granted. It happened but I had never observed the moment of it happening.

Now, for the first time, I did.

Chalky held my eyes for the longest time, and then I saw it begin –a ripple in the air, his outline blurring, as though I was suddenly seeing him through wet glass – and then he... kind of ... melted... and the lines of his body began to change. He fell onto all fours, his head hanging down, his eyes now on the splayed-out palms of his hands which were spread out on the floor... and then the hands twisted into something narrower and longer, the fingers curling into paw pads, a dark gray pelt shimmering into existence over them. His back arched; his legs twitched, lifting his rear into the air, and when it all came down again it was *different* – and then he lifted up his head, and his face was gone, and in its place a long gray muzzle pointed in my direction, a pair of golden yellow eyes staring at me like twin lasers.

I knew it was coming. I was expecting it. I was waiting for it. And still my breath came ragged and short and I had to fight an instinct to turn and run. I was alone in a room with a closed and locked door... with a wolf. A *wolf*. A wolf who might once have been my friend, but in whose intelligent gaze I could find no trace of Chalky.

The wolf's muzzle lifted a little, revealing long and sharp white canines – and I thought about those teeth meeting in my tender flesh, and began to question this whole thing – but of course it was way too late for that.

I wanted this. I reminded myself that I *wanted* this.

I tried to remember all of the things that had led me to this place. The fear and frustration of my own failures. The guilt and regret and the unhealable wound of Celia, the sister who had always loved me and had my back, whom I had only wanted to help, whom I had destroyed through ignorance and innocence. The feeling of bitter betrayal after Jazz had Turned, my younger sister, forever leaving me behind – and Turned into the crazy thing that she became. The whole cocktail, the poison of all my days, and this was the draught which, if I could only be brave enough to drain it all to the dregs, would save me... or confirm that I was beyond saving.

"Do it," I said to the wolf, hoping that Chalky was still in there somewhere, that he was listening, that he could hear me. "Just do it. Get it over with."

A low growl answered me. That could mean anything. I closed my eyes, and in that self-inflicted blindness I could hear the click of claws on the wooden floor as the wolf came closer. And then – pain – incandescent pain – the feeling of those canines sinking into my right calf.

I howled.

You can brace yourself for anything but there are things that go beyond your ability to brace for them. That's what wolf teeth in your flesh feel like. The stab of agony; the horror of feeling muscle tear; the sensation of warm wetness spilling down your limb as the blood comes. And then there was the second bite, weaker than the first but even more agonizingly felt as the fangs shifted in my leg – the second bite, the potentially crucial one, the one from the *female* – and a blackness washed over my vision, the pain almost making me pass out.

It did not matter that Chalky's control of the whole moment was nothing short of exquisite – the bite lasted no longer than it absolutely had to, barely had the teeth closed for that second time than he was out of it, a human once again, backing away, tangling into his now blood spattered clothing which hung awry and shredded on his frame, wiping at his mouth with the back of his hand and grimacing at the taste which still must have ruled his tongue. He glanced over to where I was trying to staunch the bleeding from my leg with the remains of my torn jeans, and tossed me a towel which had been draped over the back of a chair nearby.

"Here, try not to bleed over *everything*," he said. "Do you want an aspirin? I'll just throw on some clean clothes, and then I think we'd better run you over to the ER. You might need stitches for that. Sorry."

"Did it... work...?" I managed to grind out, through clenched teeth.

He had started to rummage through a closet whose innards looked like a clothes bomb had exploded inside, and half turned to look at me at that question, a semi-clean (or at the very least unbloodied) T-shirt in his hand.

"How would I know?" he asked. "Wait till the next full moon and see. In the meantime, how are you going to explain that leg at home?"

"They don't inspect me for holes every night," I snarled. "Ow, ow, ow, if I had known it was going to hurt *this* much..."

"Dude," Chalky said in a voice of such sweet reason that I really wanted to clock him with the nearest blunt object. "You asked a wolf to take a chunk out of you. What did you think was going to happen?"

I did need stitches. Five. My leg was mopped up and put back together, with a cobbled together story of how I had played too rough with a friend's dog (that, because we could both swear that the dog was domesticated and not stray and had had all his shots, and I could at least hope to escape the indignity and further pain of a rabies counter-measure being forcibly injected into me). The nurse wrapped a bandage around the wound, gave me a topical antibiotic ointment, told me to watch the gash for signs of inflammation and to make sure to get prompt attention if it started acting up, and told me off roundly for being a prize idiot.

Chalky helped me get home. I limped badly for a little while, but maybe it was just part of Were physiology – we really do heal faster. When my mother asked what the matter was, I could honestly say that I'd hurt my leg but it was going to be just fine. It had been a clean bite, apparently, and it didn't fester or anything. I hobbled around for the next week or so but after that I was almost back to normal, with just a freshly healed jagged wound on my leg which looked as though it would heal into an interesting scar.

And then it came around again, as it always did, as it had to. The full moon, And the moment of truth, for me.

The stupid weasel was already in the room, tethered in its corner, when I walked in there in my Turning cloak and settled down cross-legged on the floor. I heard the door close behind me, I heard the lock snick shut, like I had heard them dozens of times before. And then... I waited.

And the next time I opened my eyes... and knew myself to be myself, Mal, the one who had yet to Turn, who might never Turn... I took in the room I was in, smeared with unspeakable things on the walls, feeling my gorge rise at the sharp ammoniac smell of urine combined with the stench of blood and excrement which assailed my nostrils. The weasel was nowhere... unless some of the blood that decorated the place belonged to that poor hapless beast. Part of me hoped so, anyway.

My Turning cloak was torn, and even as I gathered up the shreds of that and what was left of my dignity around me I looked up and saw faces peering into the room through the glass panel on the door. Their expressions told me everything I needed to know.

"It worked, Chalky. It worked," I whispered to myself, even as I began to struggle to my feet and the door swung open to permit my father to enter, bearing a clean cloak and offering a steadying arm.

"I need a shower," I said, suddenly conscious of what I had to look like, smell like.

"Let me help you," he said. "Lean on me."

I did not meet anyone else's eyes as I stumbled past them and up the stairs from the basement, shamefully abandoning the problem of that room and the state it was in for others to deal with. My father and I did not speak again; he left me at the door to the bathroom and retreated, and I climbed into the shower and stood under the sluice of water as hot as my body would bear it for as long as I could – until I knew that I had to get out of that sanctuary sometime, that they all had to be waiting for me, and besides, all that talk about always being hungry after Turning... was beginning to catch up to me. My stomach growled insistently until I could not ignore it any further.

I dried myself off, padded to my room for clean clothes, rooted out a pair of black jeans and a black T-shirt bearing the emblem of some long-defunct heavy-metal rock band in faded but still lurid green, and walked reluctantly, barefoot, into the living room where the rest of them waited – my family, and Peregrine, the man who had been our friend and our contact with the Were-authorities since we had set foot in this country – who was here to observe Jazz's preposterous transformation, not mine. But there it was, now. It was I who was, after all, in the spotlight in the center of the stage right now.

Nothing was said until I had folded myself into one of the armchairs, aware of a posture at once defensive and defiant, and finally looked up at everybody.

"All right," I said, my voice hoarse to my own ears, as though it was not quite my own. "Here I am. Hit me."

And they did. Hit me. With a boatload of information they thought I might not know – but which had *led* me here, had been the cause of this transformation, rather than being discovered because of it. They told me that we, the Were-kind, were once literally known as Werewolves, because that was all there was. But a handful of centuries ago *something happened* and things changed. Were-kind differentiated. Wolves, were able to hold on to their top spot on the totem pole but their numbers dwindled. Peregrine had the same statistics that Chalky had shown me, that the wolves now comprised about one percent of the total Were population. As Peregrine put it, they still bred true but sometimes they didn't breed at all and fewer and fewer of them remained to hold on to power. What was left of them... did what Chalky said they had done. They pulled back, into the shadows. They let the Corvids assume the visible seat of power and become the top clan. But Chalky knew – I knew – I think everyone knew but weren't talking about it – that the Lycans hadn't abdicated. The deeper in

WOLF

the shadows they were the more dangerous they had become, and the more mysterious and enigmatic their true agenda.

"I have to report this, Mal. I have no choice," Peregrine said. "You *Turned into a wolf*. Into a form that is *fixed* for you, apparently, not Random at all, because of that weasel that was present in the room with you when you Turned. A true Random would have had no choice but to Turn into that form – and particularly you, for your first Turn. But you – you Turned not only into a form that is fixed, but also into the form that once used to dominate our kind and which is now remarkable for its rarity value. It's a fluke which I cannot begin to tell you about just how improbable it is. And there is an authority, where you are concerned. One which I am obliged to report your unexpected existence to. The Lycan Council of Alphas."

I saw my mother's shoulder stiffen, but I could not spare her my attention just then. What Peregrine was saying was my map into the now very different future from the one which I had faced when I had walked into that Turning room at the rise of the full moon.

"You are *rare*, Mal. Rare as rare can be. And I have to let the Prime Alpha know you are here. Trust me, if I do not, he will find out even without my assistance. There simply isn't a way of hiding a wolf, not even in a Random family like this. Special arrangements would have had to be made anyway – as I think you found out already, to your cost, down in that Turning room this time round."

"What special arrangements?"

"The Lycans will have a say in that, I suspect," Peregrine said.

"What will they want with him?" Mom said. I stole another look. Her hands were clasped in her lap, and her face looked *stiff*, as though she was holding on to a calm expression by pure force of will.

"I will have to speak to the Prime Alpha. Right now, that is all I can tell you," Peregrine said. "But now that this has actually happened – it all fits, looking back. The pattern as we currently know it, for Lycans, for their Turn – they might never have shown such a dramatic decline had they not already been showing all the symptoms, if you like, that Mal might have been exhibiting. They don't advertise this or even allow it to be widely known but we have archival studies that show that Lycans have been reputed to Turn much later than any other Were-kind did, and when they do Turn it's violent – I'm betting your insides are feeling a little raw right now, Mal?"

In point of fact, they were – but I could not actually say that I remembered anything at all of the manner of my first Turn. There was just a sense of being ripped apart and reconstituted – but I had been under the impression that this applied to almost every Turn, especially the first one, the most traumatic one. However, the question did remind me of something else. I was still hungry. Vivian had passed over a plate of food when I had settled into my chair, and somehow I had already cleaned that out – she caught my glance towards the empty plate, and rose to her feet, reaching for it.

"I'll get you some more," she murmured.

"How... how could this have happened?" my father said, and his voice was far too steady. It was a voice that was carefully modulated and controlled. "If what you say is true and he's such a rare... form...?"

Peregrine lifted his hands in a gesture that was an admission of defeat. "We don't know, and if they know they aren't telling us," he said. "Why are there so few of them left? We have no idea. But the numbers tell their own story. It may be just that this new modern world is not good for them, or to them – something that interferes with their birth rates, or Turn rates – something that changed in the first place to allow for transformations into creatures other than wolves."

"Do they still pass it on if they bite somebody?" Jazz asked.

I stared at her, and she appeared to think better of pursuing that line of questioning, subsiding back into her chair.

Peregrine took over again. "Until such time as I hear back from the Alpha... I don't know how long that is likely to take, but I do suggest one thing – for the next Turn cycle, if they haven't contacted you yet, make an arrangement for Mal at one of the specialized facilities – there are ways that large predators can be cared for during a Turn, and I can give you some contacts, but you'll probably agree that you don't want him Turning inside that cramped little room any more often than you can help it. Those rooms are perfectly adequate for the rest of you, but I don't believe they were ever built with a wolf in mind."

I could not ignore my mother any more – she was ready to lose it, her eyes brimming with tears, and I was acutely aware of what she was thinking – that she had lost us all, now, Celia who had died, Jazz who had gone and turned into a Were-*boy* and thus something utterly incomprehensible to her – and now me, the wolf, not, by the very definition, a part of her own family any more.

"Mom, stop it," I said sharply. More sharply than I had intended, but it was turning tragic, and I couldn't handle much more of it. "Just stop it. It's finally happened, okay? I've Turned, I've crossed the damned river so there's nothing more to weep and wail about now. I'll be fine."

I pushed myself off the arms of the chair and rose to my feet – admittedly, I felt a little wobbly, but I covered admirably, and none of them reacted other than to raise their eyes to look at me.

"If it's all right with everybody," I said, "I'd like to go and think about things for a bit. Alone."

"Of course," Peregrine said. "That's completely understandable."

I walked out of the room without staggering, but outside, in the corridor, a wave of weakness washed over me and the bad leg – the bitten leg, the one that had brought me to this in the first place – threatened to buckle from under me. I leaned against the wall, suddenly light-headed.

I really didn't want any of them near me right now – but she had somehow followed me, the pesky little sister, and had materialized beside me there in the corridor.

"Are you all right – are you really all right?" she asked. It was sincere enough, one recently Turned sibling to another – she could have no idea of what I had gone through, but she knew what it had been like for her, the experience was still very fresh, and she probably figured that I must have been feeling pretty wretched.

I tried to reach for anger, for the fury and the sense of betrayal that I had felt at her Turning before me, but there was nothing where those things had used to live. I was tired, and overwhelmed, and blank. My head was beginning to throb, and I rubbed at my temples with my fingertips.

"I had not realized," I said, "that it would be so…"

"So… what?" she said after a moment.

I had not meant to go even that far. I did not know how much she knew, how much I wanted her to know. I actually flushed, as though I had been caught in betraying some confidence. "Nothing," I said abruptly. "Nothing. Look, if you don't mind, I think I need to go and…"

I took a step back, and then turned away, and she said nothing, and let me leave, let me go into my room and shut the door.

I needed time. I needed to think.

I needed to call Chalky and let him know. I didn't know how much time I had left, out here in this world which was the only world that I had known, until the Lycan pack reached out for me. And there was so much to do.

We managed one meeting – a short and rushed and woefully inadequate one – in the two weeks that it took for the knock on the door to come. I had hoped for another opportunity, but the Lycan response was swift and uncompromising.

I actually heard it, from my room – an authoritative rap on our front door, demanding entry, not a casual or random passer-by, someone who meant business.

Jazz answered the door. I heard voices, but did not emerge from my room – I was expecting a summons which, when it came, was a single soft knock. Jazz. I growled a response, and she opened the door, just a crack – we had an unspoken understanding, she and I, that a closed door meant 'go away' by definition and she usually respected that under ordinary circumstances, but these were far from ordinary circumstances.

"Mal?" she said. "You'd better come. The Lycans are here…"

I flung the door open all the way, steadying Jazz on her feet as she all but fell into the room at the grand gesture and stalked past her with just a single long look exchanged, not quite trusting myself to speak.

I didn't know what I expected to see, but the man waiting for me in the living room was sufficiently taller than me to necessitate my actually tilting my head back to look him in the eyes – and the eyes in question were almost, *almost*, a wolf-gold shade, even in his human form – but the height was no more than just a physical manifestation of a sense of power and presence which he would have exuded even if he had been no more than Jazz's height. He was wolf, all wolf, definitely wolf, and I suddenly felt like an impostor, here under a series of false pretenses any one of which would get my throat torn out by those who had the right to punish me for reaching for them.

But he did not go for my throat – or at least not right away. He gave me a long apprising look, to be sure, but his first words to me were no more than formality.

"You are Malcolm Marsh?" he said in an accent which was just present enough for the ordinary words to acquire an exotic and perhaps a little dangerous air. I almost didn't recognize the name at all, but some instinct did kick in and I responded automatically.

"I go by Mal," I said.

"I am Yuri Volkov. Lycan Pack Prime Alpha. Are you ready?"

The Prime? He came himself?

"Ready for what?" I said, covering my astonishment at his identity.

"You are now part of the Pack," Yuri said. "We are your family now. I am here to take you home."

"What is going to happen to my son?" Mom asked.

"Mrs. Marsh, this is not really an invitation. I am here for him, and he is leaving with me. There are no options or choices here."

That was it, that was all he had for my mother. He was here to get me, and his next words were to me, directly. "You may pack a bag, if you wish. No computers, no cell phones. You have five minutes."

"Half an hour," I said, hoping for enough time to at least reach out to Chalky.

"Fifteen minutes." The bargaining was over.

"Mal..." Only that, from Mom – only my name – in a voice that was brittle, broken. I couldn't give her what she needed, in the end. I had made this happen, and everything that had followed my initial choice had been developing exactly to plan, but I don't know that I had planned on this kind of goodbye. On the whole I would have preferred to have simply slipped off by myself in response to a summons, or something. Now I was forced to be a witness to this, to her pain, to her loss, knowing that there was no longer anything I could do about it.

"Mom. Mom, I'm going to be fine. It's what I am. I... I have to go."

I left her standing there – I didn't have much time – and stepped into the corridor... and right there, by the half-open door to my room, was Jazz. I jerked my chin towards the door.

"Don't have much time," I said. "Come with me."

She followed me into my room, where I had rarely invited her before, without asking any questions.

I had been expecting this summons, of course – and there was a gym bag which was already half packed with the things I had considered to be essential necessities – one of them was that notebook which nobody had ever seen, the sketchbook which contained my memories. The bag was out and already open on my unmade bed as Jazz stepped into my room, and I was stuffing one or two last-minute afterthoughts into it. I paused as she came inside, wondering if I really should bring her any further into any of this, but then realizing I had no choice – I would have no chance to tell Chalky about what was going on, not with my new Lycan pack leader

WOLF

waiting for me outside.

I took a last look at my laptop, no time to do anything with that! Instead, I scribbled something down and thrust the page at Jazz. "This is a friend's email. He'll know who you are. Write him a note, just tell him I'm gone. And tell him why."

"Mal..."

"I don't have time for this," I said, grabbing hold of my hand and crumpling the paper into it. "Just do it."

I finished stuffing the last item into the bag on the bed, and then zipped it closed. It was a gesture that spoke volumes, and Jazz understood it for what it was – I saw her flinch at the sound.

"It's a life," I said. "It's mine. I'll deal. But..."

"Good bye," I said. I had no more than that left to give. I flung the bag over my shoulder and walked out of the room, without looking back, leaving this familiar place – this family – this world – walking blind into something new and unknown, with no guarantees if the gamble I had taken had gifted me an entirely unlooked-for kind of existence or a short and painful road to rapid discovery of my ruse and an exit which would be made with little fanfare and probably with nobody I loved being any the wiser.

He was standing on the sidewalk outside our house, Yuri Volkov, very still, waiting, a cigarette smoldering between his lips. He took it out with an economical little motion as I emerged from the house and threw it down on the sidewalk, grinding it into powder with his foot. Behind him, a black car with its engine running was parked next to the curb.

I hesitated for a moment, and then strode down the steps from our front door and down towards the street.

"Okay," I said. "I'm ready."

The Second Mask:
A Spirit by Any Other
Nature

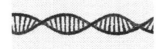

Call me a wolf...

I had not really thought past that moment, the moment where I Turned and became that wolf in spirit and in name, and crossed over into a shadowy world I really knew very little about. There were no manuals for this, no rule books, no training wheels – and what laws there were, governing this particular event, I had probably not so much broken as smashed into shards and then ground the pieces underfoot into dust. In that car, with the duffle bag – which suddenly seemed filled with irrelevant flotsam and jetsam of a past which I was already in the process of forgetting – at my feet, facing a future of which I knew practically nothing, all I had was that moment. The present. The fraction of a second that I was literally *in*, the amount of time that it took for an incoherent self-reassurance – something along the lines of, *It will all be all right* – scrolling across my otherwise empty mind like a marquee.

Yuri Volkov sat in the front passenger seat, next to a silent driver whose face I had never really had a chance to take a closer look at. I had been stuffed into the back, with my bag, and in a way, I would have been quite content to have skulked there in silence, ignored and forgotten.

I spoke up, once, about ten minutes into the drive.

"Where are we going?" I asked. It seemed as though it was a reasonable question, but it was a long time before an answer came – so long that I had been *this* close to just assuming that I wasn't going to be spoken to at all.

"The First Western Compound," Yuri said at last. As though I should have known this already, and the significance of the information.

I had assumed that I would be assigned to a Lycan Pack, but if I had interpreted what was said and what had been left unspoken correctly, it looked as though I had been assigned to Yuri Volkov's own pack. He wasn't just the Prime Alpha, he would be *my* Alpha, my pack leader. Watching his half-profile from the back seat, the set of his jaw, I caught myself wondering whether it wouldn't have been better to have waited and turned into that weasel... instead of opting to have it for breakfast.

Too late now, of course.

We kept driving. There was a break for something to eat, at a nondescript roadside diner, and then it was back on the road, in silence, with the driver and Yuri occasionally exchanging a few words in a language I didn't understand. They did not speak to me if you didn't count necessary instructions.

I think I slept, eventually, curled up on the back seat with my head pillowed on my duffle bag.

When I woke, disoriented and bleary-eyed, the car was no longer moving, and it was full dark outside. The car sat parked under a floodlight in what looked like a solid concrete underground parking garage, surrounded by several other cars of similar make and color, and Yuri Volkov loomed over me.

"We're here," he said. "Bring your things, and come."

The two of us were alone; the driver seemed to have vanished. I obediently scrambled out of the back of the car and followed Yuri through a somewhat battered and scratched door, that looked as though it needed painting, into an empty anteroom with scuffed lino floors and what looked like a security camera brooding ominously in a corner.

Yuri paused at another, inner, door, which he accessed by punching in a code on a numerical keypad. The door snicked open and he gestured for me to follow him. We went into a long corridor which was carpeted in a good quality wall-to-wall Berber and lit by sconced lights beside several closed doors leading off it. Yuri opened one of them and we walked down another corridor, this one gently curving, one side of it apparently completely made of glass – but looking out into an unlit area, and giving back nothing but reflection; I saw myself slouching along in Yuri's wake, slope-shouldered, my head tucked down and forward, looking anything but wolf-like.

Eventually we appeared to pass into a different wing of the building we had entered, and stepped into a large open atrium which appeared to have a skylight on the roof and three stories of inward-facing open corridors from which you could look down into the atrium over matte black metal balustrades, with doors leading off them as though in a hotel. Yuri stopped at an elevator shaft at the far end of the atrium, half turned to me, and handed me a keycard.

"Room 210," he said. "Second floor, that far corner over there. Don't lose that card, without it you cannot access a large number of necessary areas here in the inner compound. There is a lot for you to learn, but I am not going to start that education tonight. Tomorrow, you will report to the lab for a full work-up, so that we can begin answering some of the questions behind what happened to bring you here. We will discuss matters in greater detail then."

"I... uh...."

"Yes?" he said, having already turned to leave.

"Where... is the lab?"

He pointed economically to a door opening off the floor we were on. "That is the breakfast room," he said. "If you want some tomorrow, that is where you will find it. Someone there will point you to the lab. We will expect you no later than nine – we usually start our work much earlier than that, but we will make an exception for you this once. Tomorrow is your first morning in your new home, after all. Sleep well."

I took the elevator to the second floor and followed the corridor around to Room 210; the place was quiet, it seemed deserted. I didn't know how large this pack was, how many people were supposed to be here, but I might as well have been the only one on the premises that night, a ghost drifting in an empty shell of a building. The card opened the door to Room

210 when swiped through the key lock, and it was with almost a sense of stepping into a cell that I crossed the threshold and closed the door behind me. The room itself was almost disappointingly unremarkable, more like a hotel suite in a reasonably up-market establishment than anything like living quarters – but it was a reasonable studio apartment. It had a tiny kitchenette, a sitting area with two comfortable armchairs and a flat-screen TV hanging on the wall like some strange blank work of art; behind a curved wall, hiding the area from the front door, was a double bed and a small efficient desk flanked by an empty bookshelf against the far wall. A half-open closet door faced the bed, and beyond that another door led into a tiled bathroom with a gleaming glass shower cubicle and a number of pale green towels stacked neatly on a small wooden table in the corner.

I wasn't sure what I had been expecting. Possibly anything I found would have seemed strange. But I had the bizarre feeling of having arrived here for a pleasant vacation rather than a sense of having come to a place which would be home.

They had questions, to be sure. I had no real clue what kind of answers I could possibly give them that they would be satisfied with; I had no doubt that 'a full work-up' meant exactly what it said and that every molecule of me that they could get their hands on would be examined very closely indeed – and as far as that went, the process and its results might turn out to be quite exciting for them, I had very little idea of how my Random Were DNA and Chalky's wild-card genetic contribution would pan out in their tests. I could only hope that I passed at least adequately enough to be accepted. The alternatives... I didn't really want to think about. I had questions of my own, and I had a feeling that I probably wouldn't like the answers to some of them all that much.

But that was for tomorrow morning. I figured I might as well try and get some sleep. Unpacking could wait – I took only one thing out of my bag, my sketch book, and tossed the rest into a corner of the closet. The notebook I tucked, with pathetic faith that nobody would search there, deep under the mattress of my bed. I'd find a better place to keep it, eventually, if everything worked out and I stayed here as a fully-fledged young Lycan. Some secrets I wanted to keep. I had no idea what they'd make of my sketch of shapeshifting Chalky.

Although I thought it would be best to try and actually get some sleep to be fresh for the next day's developments, I didn't think I would ever be able to fall asleep. But I surprised myself, and when next I opened my eyes to my surroundings it was full daylight that streamed in through the windows whose curtains I had failed to close the night before. The clock by my bedside told me that it was a few minutes past eight o'clock; if I wanted to get anywhere by nine, I had to scramble. I fell into the shower, threw on a clean T-shirt which I dug out of my bag, and was out of the room and trotting down the stairs (it seemed ridiculous to take an elevator for one floor) within a commendable twenty five minutes of waking up.

I could smell food through the open door to what Yuri had indicated was the breakfast room, and that made me realize how hungry I really was.

But I hesitated, nonetheless. This would be the first encounter... with a stranger... with somebody who belonged here. An experience I was not particularly looking forward to, but it was inevitable, in the end – and I squared my shoulders and walked into the breakfast room.

A dark-haired young woman was pouring coffee into a pretty ceramic mug as I stepped inside, and looked up at my entrance.

"Hello, new guy," she said. "Can I get you some coffee?"

"Yes. Thank you. I mean, I don't really have time. I'm supposed to get to a lab by nine..."

"Relax. I'll take you there," she said, reaching to grab another mug out of a cabinet above the coffee maker. "I'm Anna Cotton, by the way."

"Mal," I muttered, sounding churlish even to myself, skating very close to outright rude. It would have been even more rude if I had gone on to ask her just who Anna Cotton was and what her relationship could possibly be to the taciturn Yuri Volkov – but either she could read minds or else the thought was plain on my face because she actually laughed out loud as she handed me the steaming mug of coffee.

"I'm surprised they haven't left you a copy of the family tree in your room. For the record, I'm Second Family. It'll all be explained, eventually. Here, coffee. How do you take it? There's cream over there on the table if you want it. So tell me, since I have you to myself and I got to corner you first, before you spill it all to official record-keepers, what's your story?"

"I Turned," I said, my back to her, pouring a dollop of cream into my coffee. "It happened to be into a wolf. And here I am. Believe me, that's about as much as *I* know."

"So you're technically a floater?"

"A what?"

She grimaced. "That's what we call the ones who aren't necessarily affiliated – and you're about at an age where you might, if you'd been born into a pack, be offered as an exchange into another pack, a different family. They take genetic degeneration and interbreeding fairly seriously in the Lycan families because there are so few of us, after all – so an exchange of genetic material is always looked on as a good thing."

My heart sank a little. It had all seemed like such a great idea, back in Chalky's room... back in the Turning Room with the weasel staring me down and wearing me out. A good way out. The only way out. But in so many ways it had been an impulse, and I had blundered into the whole thing blind, fueled by fear and guilt and frustration. I had thought that once I got to the Lycans' home base I could trust momentum to keep moving things forward. Now... that seemed less than certain. The way forward was far less clear than I had expected... or even hoped. "So I might not stay here at all?"

"We don't know that yet," Anna said. "They might well choose to hang on to you – as far as fresh genes are concerned they don't come fresher than you, I'm guessing. They might jump at the chance of new blood."

The way she was looking at me, with an oddly measuring gaze, instantly put me on the defensive. *New blood?*

"So, you're to join the pack," she murmured. "Maybe."

I shrugged, taking a sip of the coffee. It was good coffee. "Who decides?" I asked warily. "I have absolutely no idea. All I know is that the first thing that everyone squawked about is that the Lycans had to be told... about what happened. And someone told them. And here I am."

"Poor boy," she said. "You do realize that if you come on to the roster you'll be the outsider, the lowest rung, the omega? Your first wolf Turn here could be rough on you. My brother Rory will take entirely too much pleasure in the fact that he is no longer the most junior in the pack. You'll have to take a whole load of punishment before they are all certain that you know your place."

"I know how to take care of myself," I said.

"Lesson number one," Anna said gravely, "forget everything you know. Fight back, and it'll get bloody. You have to learn how to take it, at least at first, until you get established. You're a wolf now. We live by different rules. There's a bagel over there, if you're starving – but maybe you'd better eat and walk. If they told you to be there at nine, you don't want to keep them waiting."

I got the quick tour on the way to the lab – by way of Anna's breezily flinging her hand in this direction or that as we scurried down corridors and past various rooms – *that's the library, and over here on the other side are the study halls... down that wing it's the pharma labs, they're generally kept under strict security, don't wander down there unless you're invited or have business... cafeteria is one floor up, those stairs over there, remember that, you'll get hungry eventually, the bagel won't hold you forever... if you keep going thataway you'll come out into the enclosure – it's generally kept locked in between Turns – and beyond that it's the wolf sanctuary... the biochem and genetics labs are to the left...*

None of it made any sense. I supposed it would, eventually, if I kept my eyes and ears open. That, or something would roll out of a side corridor and eat me. I was starting to be rather philosophical about that. But the only way out... was through.

The lab complex turned out to consist of a knot of rooms and a couple of walk-in incubation areas kept at different temperatures which were shown in digital displays above their entrances. Anna led me straight past all of that and into a short corridor, home to four glass-walled cubicles which turned out to be small offices, and then through a more solid door into an anteroom from which two rather more substantial studies opened laterally, one to each side. One of those proved to house Yuri Volkov, who waited for me seated behind a large and frighteningly tidy mahogany desk. He wasn't wearing a lab coat but two other people in that room, seated in chairs before Yuri's desk, were – a man who looked rather too much like Anna not to be her father, and an older woman who wore her long blond hair in a complicated old-fashioned style with braids arranged in a sort of severe and aristocratic crown atop her head.

"I brought him," Anna announced, letting me past her into the room and then stepping back outside again.

"Back to work, now," said the man I had pegged as her father, with a quick wink in her direction. She grinned at him, gave me a final sympathetic glance which might have been offered to a gladiator about to be pushed into the arena with the lions, and withdrew, closing the door behind her.

The cup of coffee in my hand suddenly seemed like a dangerous liability; I had devoured the last of my bagel just a few moments before, but I was uncomfortably aware that I should have probably kept my hands clean of food... and that I was still chewing a last piece of bagel, which seemed to be very disrespectful. I swallowed it hurriedly and it almost stuck in my throat, threatening an embarrassment of epic proportions if I started having an attack of the hiccups. Thankfully I managed to force it down, and covered whatever discomfiture there was by appearing to take a moment to obey Yuri's imperious gesture to take the last remaining chair before his desk, in between the two white-coated scientists who were looking at me with disconcerting avidity. It seemed rather too disrespectful to simply park my coffee cup on that desk uninvited so I tucked it as unobtrusively as I could on the floor by my feet and perched on the edge of the chair, feeling rather as though I had just been thrust under a microscope.

Not without cause.

They wanted me to tell them the whole story about what had happened. How it had happened. Where it had happened. And then they had me tell it again. I knew they were looking for any deviation, for any possible stumble, if there was a lie to catch me in they wanted to close the trap as soon as they found one. But the Turn into a wolf was too well documented to be staged, and the cover story that Chalky and I had concocted held up well enough. What had ostensibly happened might have been rare, but it could hardly have been unprecedented; at some point, after all, there had to be a 'first' real Lycan, one who simply was what he was without any outside influences that could be explained away – and for the Were, there was always that loophole. We didn't come out of nowhere. There were origins. And sometimes, if we'd skated too far from our origins, there could be throwbacks.

It lasted for almost two hours, this interrogation, but in the end, Yuri sighed and sat back in his chair, crossing his arms over his chest.

"Well. All right, then. I am going to hand you over to Dr. Cotton and Dr. Berezhnoyeva. If you will follow them, please, they will escort you to the infirmary – we will draw some blood for tests, and we will do a full genetic workup on you in our labs. While that is going on, and until we have the results that will determine what will happen next, tomorrow you will start here in the labs as an assistant, with responsibility for such jobs as may be assigned to by the researchers. They will begin training you to perform the necessary tasks. If your tests come through satisfactorily, you will also begin more advanced training which should eventually lead to a higher position in our facility. Your position in the pack will become clearer when we have some solid data."

"Come along, then," said the man Yuri had called Dr. Cotton. "The nurse is waiting for us. Sooner it is done, sooner it will all be finished."

The woman, Dr. Berezhnoyeva, merely inclined her head at Yuri, and then at me, and rose from her seat with the gravitas of an empress, preceding Dr. Cotton and myself out of the room.

"What happens if..." I began, but Dr. Cotton, ushering me out of Yuri's office, lifted an index finger to silence me.

"Let me talk, son," he said. "It'll save time. This is all probably utterly confusing to you, but hold on, it'll shake itself down. For now, you need to start learning the way the pack is put together. You have met Yuri, he's the Alpha and he's in charge, he's also the current Prime Alpha, the head of the Lycan Council, that is to say the whole Lycan clan in its entirety, not just this pack. His word is law around here, and don't you ever forget it. Dr. Sofia Berezhnoyeva, here, is the female Alpha of this pack – you may not have much to do with her directly, because her responsibilities do not concern you personally, but she is Yuri's peer, and she rules this compound. She is also, as it happens, our head genetics researcher, and she will be in charge of your tests so in that way I guess you are answerable to her – but I'd let your DNA do the talking there."

He glanced at me, to see if I was paying attention, I guess. "I'm Sam Cotton, Second Family, and you've already met Anna, my daughter – what this means is that we are the second and junior pack family, Yuri and my wife Caitlin share a grandmother, the Alpha of her time, another Anna. Someone will explain the line of descent to you eventually, but for now the easy way to remember where you're at is that anyone with a Slavic moniker is probably from First Family and senior, anyone with names that trace Celtic are Second Family and the junior family, and then there are those who sound foreign and so probably are, who may have come here from different packs, who are on loan to the labs for a specific project, or floaters who are temporarily with the pack but not permanent family members. You...."

"Yes, Anna told me already," I said, a little more snappishly than I might have intended. "I'm the lowest of the low. She seemed to think that I might be part of the pack eventually and that this would give great pleasure to her brother."

Sam smiled. "My youngest, Rory, is the Omega of the family pack," he said. "If the pack adopts you into the family, you will rank well below him – you won't even be Second Family, you may be assigned a separate grouping altogether, a sort of resident floater..."

What had Anna called me? *The outsider, the lowest rung, the omega...*

And that was the *best* of the possible outcomes. That was assuming that all of this had been worth something, that I would be accepted into a pack. I would be worse than useless to Chalky as his 'inside man' if I weren't even the omega of an established pack but rather just tossed hither and yon as the packs pleased. As, if I understood matters correctly, nothing more important than a donor of fresh genetic material for the packs.

"Just call me a floater and toss me out as flotsam and jetsam," I muttered, a little bitterly.

"Would that be hard for you?" Sofia Berezhnoyeva asked, turning her regal head just a little, but without breaking stride.

"He said I belonged to the pack now," I said. "Yuri. When he came to get me. He said that becoming... a wolf... changed my family."

"But it did," Sofia said. "He spoke the truth. You are here."

"I thought he meant..."

"We are all the greater pack," Sam said. "That's what he meant."

The sharp stab inside me was unexpected. I missed Celia. *I missed Jazz.* I missed... no matter how much I had pulled away while I had them, I had still had a tight knot of people I had called my family. That... didn't seem to apply so much anymore. At least not in any way that I understood family.

I looked up just in time to catch Sofia's thoughtful glance back at me before she looked away again.

"Your family is wolf now," Sofia said, in that soft lilting accent that made everything she said somehow sound silkily dangerous. "All wolf. But we shall see what else may be true. In here, please. This is the infirmary."

Sam and Sofia escorted me into a well-equipped doctor's surgery and handed me inside, where a nurse waited with a crisply starched hospital gown and instructions to strip down to my underwear. I did this thing and sat on the couch dangling my stockinged feet until she returned with a formidable collection of paraphernalia. She took what seemed to be half the blood in my veins and also made me swab a stick inside my mouth, for a DNA sample, like I'd seen it done on forensics TV shows. She was hatchet-faced, politely professional, and the procedures were all done efficiently, silently, and without fuss. After she had gathered up her samples and left, her absolute opposite walked into the surgery – a man wearing a white coat and a stethoscope around his neck, a pair of horn-rimmed spectacles pushed up on top of his head.

"Hi Malcolm," he said conversationally, pulling up a stool so that he sat beside me and reaching for my arm with a practiced gesture to slip on a blood pressure cuff. "I'm Dr. Mason. Welcome to the family."

"I rather got the impression that depended on your report," I said. "And I go by Mal." It seemed as though I would have to repeat this last piece of information several times before everyone knew what not to call me if they wanted my attention.

"Sorry. So noted." He glanced up from the cuff readout, met my eyes, and gave me a ready smile. "As for the rest of it... you're here. Few people are here without good reason. So I suspect that my report is only going to serve to confirm what we all already know. But humor me. Tell me all about yourself. I gather your family isn't exactly... from the Lycan fold."

I fought down the temptation to tell him to go ask Yuri about it because I had just spent two hours telling the story in that imperial office, but I doubted if his avuncular attitude would survive that much sass. I wondered if *he* was Lycan, the doctor – if all of them here were. If so, if there was a pack this large, then Peregrine had woefully underestimated the true numbers of the Lycans in the Were family. But I was not yet the one who

268

was asking the questions. I *was* the question. "My family are Random," was all I said.

"Interesting," he murmured, and slapped the business end of his stethoscope on my chest. "Breathe deeply, please. So how does a Random Were end up in a Lycan compound...? No, don't talk. Another deep breath please. I guess that's what we're here to find out. Okay, then, let's get the boring formalities out of the way. It shouldn't take long." He rolled his stool back towards the desk and tapped on a keyboard until a rapidly morphing screen on his monitor displayed the thing that he wanted. "You seem to be in prime physical condition, so we'll just run over a quick medical history and be done with it, for now. At least until your test results come in." I could see his eyes rapidly scanning the data on his screen, and then he turned back to me with another disarming grin. "No allergies, no major surgeries... I see there was a recent ER visit on you record, what was all that about?"

Oh, he was good.

"Dog bite," I said, straightening my leg out and pointing to the pale puckered flesh of the almost healed bite on my calf.

"Oh?" he murmured. "Let me take a look at that."

He scooted his stool back over to me and tilted my ankle a little so that he could get a better angle. His fingers probed at the bite, and the questions, although offered up in a light and disarming voice, were sharp and precise. How long ago the bite had happened. How fast it was healing. What kind of dog it was. Whom it had belonged to. What had happened to it. The detailed timeline of everything, including inquiries of anything... unusual... had happened at any time following the bite.

I told mostly the truth, actually – about everything other than the fictitious dog, whom I had conveniently disposed of so that it couldn't be tracked down and subjected to other strenuous tests of the same ilk that they were deploying on myself. I explained yet again, with commendable patience, I thought, about my Random family, about my non-Turning, about the wretched weasel (and its eventual fate...) and about the unexpected arrival of the wolf.

"And a very short time after that... Yuri Volkov came to get me," I finished off the tale, in what I thought was a nice flourish. "So I'm here. I'm still trying to figure out the 'here', how things work... are you one of..."

"Oh, I'm not part of the family," he said, turning away again to tap some notes into his computer. "I just work for them here in the clinic. I'm Were, myself – were-sheepdog, if you want to be precise – but no, not part of the family, not even Lycan. Not everyone you meet here is part of the core family group – although probably to be safe until you've safely met and identified all the Lycans of this pack it's better to assume that someone is rather than they are not."

"So tell me about the family," I said.

He glanced back over his shoulder with another of his quick smiles. "You'd better talk to one of them about it," he said. "If you're to Turn here, there are protocols you need to know. I'm sure someone will be along shortly to explain all that to you. In fact, I think Dr. Cotton is still here, waiting for you. That's a good place to start."

"Are we done, then?"

"For now," he said. "I'll let you know if there is anything else we need. Those blood tests should all be in within a few days. We'll talk again then. I'll leave you to get dressed."

He tapped at a final key on his keyboard, and the screen dissolved into a screensaver. I had been dismissed.

I discarded the hospital gown on the couch, put my own clothes back on, and stepped out into the small waiting area just outside. Dr. Sam Cotton looked up as I emerged.

"All done?" he said. "I thought we'd grab a bite to eat, I'll try and answer any immediate questions, and then maybe I could take you back to meet Katya. That would be Caitlin Manion Cotton, my wife, she's the eldest daughter of the Second Family."

"I think I need a family tree," I muttered.

"She'll have one somewhere. If you want a detailed breakdown you'll probably have to speak to Tanya or Zoya – that's Yuri's wife, or his oldest daughter – they're the heads of the two genetics labs, and they've got it all mapped out. The First Family is very much the genetics branch. The Second Family is more into pharmaceutical research. You'll probably be expected to join one or the other division, if they work out the logistics and you stay in this pack."

"What, I'll be Third Family?" I asked, and I was being facetious, but he considered the question seriously, his head at a thoughtful angle. "I'm not sure if that would apply," he said after a pause. "You'd be folded into the families somehow. They'll find a proper mate."

I must have looked properly startled at that idea, because Sam actually chuckled out loud.

"That would be the way to integrate you, and you don't have to look all that panicked about it. I don't really think that Yuri would consider you an appropriate mate for Shura, who's his youngest and of an age for her to be a possibility for you, because she's his way of cementing a closer alliance with some other pack. My Anna is mated already, which – if they weigh the possibilities and decide to inject your own genetic contribution into revitalizing the core family – then leaves one of my nieces, Sorcha or Seonaid, of the Second Family, and even that will have to wait a little while, the girls are barely two months past their fourteenth birthday.. and then there's Asia, but that would be an indirect route – she's Sergey Berezhnoy's acknowledged daughter but he was never married to her mother, and that has its own problems... although, given her own actual background..."

"Stop," I said. "My head hurts."

He laughed. "I wouldn't be a bit surprised," he said. "In here, that's Katya's office. After you."

Katya Cotton turned out to be a fine-boned woman who wore her years lightly – but once I took a closer look at her face I could see the fine crow's feet that radiated from the corners of her eyes. It was hard to judge age accurately with the Lycans. Like almost all the senior people in either Family, it seemed, she was another Doctor.

She was, in fact, the one in charge of the pharmaceutical wing of this operation.

If Adaptadyne – the drug we all knew as Stay – hadn't been wholly developed and produced here, these labs had had input into the research that led to that drug. Katya was the guardian of that knowledge. I might have even gone so far as to call her the reason I was here in the first place.

She was nothing like Celia, the beloved sister, but the Adaptadyne was a potent bridge between them. I could see my sister's ghost looking out of Katya Cotton's eyes.

"They tell me I'll have to pick between your labs and the genetics crew," I told Katya.

Her lip curled a little and I had a sudden sinking feeling that I might have gone a step too far. But this was the pack, and even as a rank junior outsider it seems I had some standing. When she responded it was in surprisingly civil manner.

"Over there might be interesting, right now," she said. "One of the projects they will be working on right now is probably *you*. It's a rare chance, to be a part of something that, when you break it down to its most basic principles, is actually focused almost entirely on researching just exactly what makes you into yourself. Not that our work is any less interesting – but that's for another day. In the meantime, there's far more practical matters to attend to. I just wanted to put a face to your name – but I'll have Anna take it from here, and give you a tour of the wolf sanctuary, and the Turning enclosure."

"She mentioned that, earlier," I said. "You run a wolf sanctuary out here?"

"And why not?" she said, smiling. "We get to do something good for creatures which represent that side of our nature. And during Turn times, all that happens here is that there are potentially extra wolves out there for the visitors to look at. They never know the difference. It's safe, for us, and we keep it interesting for the normals. And the entrance fees go towards our work here – researching wolves and Lycans and simple humans alike. It all fits together. Anna will give you an idea of what you might expect, come Turning time."

So it was back to Anna, the young woman who was the first Lycan face I had seen that morning, in the breakfast room.

"This way," she instructed me, heading off down a side corridor which ended in a door with a security numeric keypad next to it. A light glowed forbiddingly red just above the pad; Anna keyed in a six-digit code and then pressed her hand onto a glass panel underneath the keypad. The light blinked twice, and changed to green; the door unlocked with a soft snick and she pushed it open.

"We each have our own code," she said, "and it is keyed to the handprint. You need both – to get in here, *and* to get out, after. Yuri will make sure you have the right access information, before it is time."

"Time for what?" I asked, stupidly, before it fell into place. This was the equivalent of my family's Turning Rooms in the basement. There, we needed Vivian Ingram to run the household while we were all locked up in the rooms for the duration. Here, it seemed they didn't trust anyone else to do that – they policed themselves, with security codes and high-tech identity recognition. With this in mind, I began to pay a closer attention to my surroundings. The door out of the main compound led into a short stretch of an outside chain-link fence tunnel which had another security gate at the end of it before it gave into an open grassy space edged on the one side by a fringe of woods and on the other a stream that ran through a gully out of a range of a gently swelling bank of hills. Straight ahead of us, some way away, I could see sunlight glinting on metal. Another fence...?

Anna saw me squinting in that direction, and threw her arms open to indicate the space around us.

"This is ours," she said. "This whole area. It isn't huge, not a wolf's real natural range, but it's a solid acreage – and we generally don't get in each other's way. It isn't like there are pups to defend. There are never pups out here."

I thought about this for a moment. There wouldn't be any wolf young, of course; the Lycan females, like every other Were, carried their children as humans, and by the time the young humans Turned into their wolf form they were already well past that first pup stage. I remembered Mom being pregnant with Jazz. She Turned and she Turned and then, when the pregnancy was established, she stayed in her human form for the duration, until Jazz was born. I had never really given it much thought before but now, when I was facing a whole new future which hadn't seemed entirely plausible before, everything was significant. I wondered, now, what governed that particular instance of Were physiology. But Anna was still talking, and I turned my attention back to what she was saying.

"That far end, that's the wolf sanctuary enclosures," she said. "The real wolves. The ones the visitors come to see. During the Turn, some of us sometimes join them out there, in our own separate enclosure – the sanctuary itself is always closed on the third day of the Turn, just in case somebody changes back right before the humans' eyes. They'd get a little freaked out at that, seeing it happen."

"Wouldn't they just," I muttered, remembering the transformation I had witnessed with Chalky.

Anna took the comment at face value. "Yeah, most of us young ones saw it happen in here," she said. "We knew we were all in for the same thing, when the time came. Some packs make it a point never to have the children present at a Turn, because it's strong stuff – but this pack never kept secrets from its young. Or at least not this secret. Before we knew what it felt like, ourselves, we saw our parents and our older siblings change. And it might be scary, the first time, because sometimes it's a violent shift of form... but then you accept it, and when your Turn comes it isn't frightening any more. We know what is coming, what to expect, what happens, and it doesn't scare us." She gave me a sympathetic look. "You, of course... it must have been quite a thing, for you."

"We all change," I said, a little defensively. "I'm Random; I would have Turned eventually. Into something."

"But you Turned into a wolf," she said softly. "And that means that you aren't a Random any more... if you ever were... that's what they will be trying to unravel back in the labs. Your entire genome is going to be mapped out and poked and prodded, you know. We in the families – and the other packs, the floaters that get exchanged between the packs to ensure a proper genetic balance – we all know our genealogies to the nth degree. We know who our ancestors were, where they came from, I know where every single one of my genes came from, generations back. You're a wild card. Wild genes. If you're true, if you're Lycan – you're a genetic jackpot to the pack that gets you. Unless you... but yet, you *are*. It's no wonder Yuri pulled rank to get you here."

This was news. "Yuri wanted me *here*?"

"Of course. If a case can be made that you are indeed a neo-Lycan, someone who somehow flash-changed into a genetically true wolf, you're a prize. The pack that has you has access to a fresh genetic influx from a brand new source. Your children will strengthen the pack, and through the pack, eventually, all the packs, once the next generation is properly matched..."

"Wait a minute," I said sharply. "All this stuff about using me as breeding stock..."

"You're probably going to be for one of the younger cousins," she said, ignoring my outburst. "And of course you're breeding stock. We all are. They've been trying to..."

She stopped abruptly and I halted, waiting for her to stop walking and turn back to look at me.

"Trying to what?" I asked.

"Well, but there's time enough for that," she said. "You'd probably need to bone up on a lot more genetic background to understand any of that background. In the meantime, come and look at the others. I've made some quite good friends out there, I think, when I'm in wolf shape."

"You think?"

"Well, we don't *remember*. Exactly. But I come back to myself with a soft spot for certain of the true-wolves, and that can only mean that in wolf-form they and I got along pretty well. Come look, they're just beyond the fence there."

I followed her across the field of grass, to the fence on the far side. It took us a little while to get there, it was a substantial open space. At that far end of the Lycan habitat (the word had popped into my head full-formed; that was exactly what this space was, a habitat, a place where the family retired to when they ran on four legs and howled at the full moon) there was a double gate at the fence, connected as the security access at the building end had been set up, separated by a short chain-link fence corridor, but at this end there were no special security precautions, with the gates being secured with physical padlocks.

"You mingle? During the Turn?" I asked, intrigued despite myself.

"Sometimes. We have handlers on the far side who sometimes open the gates, and visitors get a rather larger pack to view than they realized. Only, of course, they never realize. They don't make the connection, mostly."

My mind was still on the genetic stuff. "Can *they* – you know – have..."

"Oh, yeah, sometimes," Anna said breezily. "The wolf females have had several litters sired by a Lycan male when in wolf form."

"And they don't...?"

"No. A Lycan capable of the Turn needs human genes from both his parents – or else he is just a wolf, a natural-born wolf who will never change."

"And a Lycan and a human...?"

"That can get complicated," Anna said, "depending on the genotype of the non-Were parent. There's papers in the library, if you really want to know."

I met some of the rest of the family, the First and the Second branches, over the next couple of days – during which I was really rather in limbo, until the results of whatever tests they were doing came in and were processed to everyone's satisfaction.

Seonaid and Sorcha Manion, two of my potential 'mates' in the family genetic jigsaw puzzle, turned out to be a pair of engaging red-haired fourteen-year-old twins – and I did try and look on them with an eye to our possible shared future but it was no use, all I could see were a pair of kids given to infectious giggling and a penchant for practical jokes. They were not that much younger than Jazz, my own younger sister, but unless they were just putting on an act for my benefit the Manion twins (who belonged to Tom Manion, Katya's younger brother) they were still, to use terms which seemed appropriate to the context, very much pups. Wolf children apparently stayed children, right until such time as they were considered adult, at which point they switched modes and became grown-ups overnight. Anna seemed like she belonged to an entirely different generation from her not *that* much younger cousins.

The other name that was mentioned in the same context as the twins was someone called Asia – and although we were introduced, briefly, in one of the labs I didn't get much from her at all. All I was offered was a comprehensively apprising sideways glance from long-lashed moss-green eyes and a murmured greeting before she excused herself to go back and tend to an experiment in progress. Anna, who had performed the introduction, provided the details.

"Her mother is Veronica Adema, she works in Zoya's lab," Anna said. "She came to the center as a floater, on loan from another pack because we needed someone with her skills in the lab, and then she stayed, because she and Sergey took up together, and, well, Asia. That was more than twenty years ago. But of course they never married, and then he died..."

"I'm sorry, why...?"

She gave me an impatient look. "Sergey Berezhnoy. Sofia's husband.

The Alpha, before Yuri. Keep up."

I was trying to. But it was going to take a lot more time and effort before I was sure I had the whole thing straightened out in my head. Until then, no matter how much it annoyed the people I was pumping for what seemed to be general information that *everybody* already knew, I would keep asking questions.

"So – as Alpha – privilege," Anna said. "And Veronica was... well. She was a looker, when she was young. She was like you, in one way, you know."

My ears perked up. "Like me? How?"

"She was a Lycan throwback, of sorts," Anna said. "Both her parents in fact registered were-canine – they were different dog breeds, as I recall, but still, both dogs, not wolves – but Veronica Turned Lycan when she was sixteen, and was then handed to the packs. She was in a different pack altogether at first, and then she came here, as a floater female, when she was twenty or so. And she and Sergey liked the look of one another, although of course he already had a mate, and the Alpha female at that, and so Veronica could never be more than what she was – the mother of his daughter. Asia is part of the First Family, technically, through Sergey – but she isn't in the line of succession."

"Asia is what, technically half-Lycan...?"

"There's no such thing as *half-Lycan*," Anna snorted. "But she's only first generation true-wolf, born-wolf, through her mother."

Class lines were in places I would least expect them. "She's kind of second rank?"

"There's no such thing either," Anna said. "She's Sergey's daughter. Just not in the Alpha line. He never did have daughters with Sofia – there were the three boys, and then – well – he was already quite a lot older than Sofia when they married, and then he died, when their sons were all not yet ten years old, not adults... and Sofia was still Alpha, but did not wish to take another mate.... so that's when Yuri took over, her brother, and it's temporary, anyway, until the next Alpha..."

"So her oldest son would become the Alpha...?" I asked, trying to understand this complicated family system.

Anna gave me an exasperated look. "No, Mal, it's the female Alpha through which the succession goes – and she picks her male counterpart. Usually a husband. Sometimes it's a common-law mate. Sometimes, like here, a brother. But the sons don't get a direct place in the succession. The young males generally accept a subordinate role in their home pack and then they often go off to other packs – initially as floater members, but then as mates in their own right – and if they choose, or are lucky enough to get, a female who is in line of succession then they might get to become an Alpha male and a pack leader in their own right. When the female Alpha of a pack dies, it's up to her successor to pick her partner."

"So if someone like Yuri had wanted to start a new pack – their own new pack – "

Anna waved her hand impatiently. "The males don't start new packs," she said. "Yuri's position in this one is because of Sofia; he's a good Alpha, and he's even worked his way up to being the Prime in the Council, he's made this pack something to be reckoned with. But it isn't *his* pack. It's Sofia's. And his status here is because of hers. If he were not her brother he would have been long gone, probably – like two of Sofia's sons have gone, out to different packs, seeking their own place. It's important for the genetic basis to be as broad as it can be. There aren't," she said, reiterating what I'd heard repeated before, "after all, that many of us."

They did keep saying that.

I thought back to Peregrine's estimate. "I heard someone say that there were about a thousand of you out there."

"Oh? Who were you discussing Lycan business with?" Anna said.

"This was... straight after I first Turned... they were trying to help," I said defensively.

"Well, a few more than that," Anna said, her dimples showing as she broke into a grin I could only describe as coy. "We don't advertise the true numbers. Particularly as they are the subject of an on-going and intensive study, within the families. Ours aren't the only genetics labs that the Lycans are running their tests in – but Yuri has made sure that ours is one of the leaders. This is the one the floaters try to get into if they're given any kind of a choice about the pack to which they are sent. But we don't really talk about it to outsiders."

"Well, I'm not an outsider," I said, a little exasperated. "I'm kind of in it up to the neck. And boiling."

She laughed. "In which case you'll be told what you need to know, and quickly," she said. "I suspect that they'll start you out washing the lab glassware and making reagents for the *real* scientists, in the beginning, just to teach you humility. True humility is a valuable resource to have at your command during your wolf days. You'll find out. But you'll probably be put on an intensive training course which will eat up all of the copious free time that you think you're going to have. Don't take today as a typical day; you're allowed to do this aimless meandering because you *are* still an outsider, kind of, and I've been let off the leash – at least right now – because you need a minder – and that's today, maybe tomorrow – but it won't last. They'll find a way to make you pull your weight around here. We all do."

The first test results came through the next day, and then they took some more blood, and more tests were run, and before I knew it almost two weeks had somehow gone by and I was beginning to shake down into a routine. Initially there was more in the fabric of my days that impacted directly on establishing my own personal medical and genetic footprint – but as that waned, other things took over. Anna was right in that she didn't get to spend quite so much leisure time babysitting me after that first day – and she was also right about the shape of short-term future at the compound.

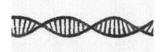

I became chief bottle washer for both the genetics and pharma labs at the research center, and I was given a 'recipe book' for the commonly used reagents in the labs which it became my duty to prepare and keep an adequate supply of on hand. It was a moderately boring existence, to be sure, and I didn't exactly take to it willingly or happily – but then, I didn't get the feeling that I would remain in that menial position forever, or even for long, once I got my security clearances and my actual status in the pack was finally cemented. I'd started to sort out the members of the core family of this pack by then and none of them were low-status. If I made the pack, I would not be where I had started out for long.

And in the meantime, two days after my arrival at the compound, Sam Cotton took me to a study carrel at the back of the library. A folder with my name on it in large black letters waited for me there, beside a shiny new laptop computer whose screen currently showed an image of a dark-haired man with horn-rimmed spectacles. A live link, I corrected my initial impression, as the man stirred and lifted an arm to greet us as he obviously saw us come into his field of vision.

"Mal, meet Dr. Samir Goswamy," Sam said. "He's going to be your contact at the University, and your first tutor – you may find that you have plenty of useful resources in the people who actually work in our own labs, but any questions you have that we can't immediately answer, Dr. Goswamy is your man."

"I have questions," I said. "Er, contact? At the University? Tutor?"

Sam nodded at the folder beside the computer. "You'll find your curriculum in there," he said. "Along with other useful information, and your registration papers. You've been enrolled in an accelerated study program which will give you a basic grounding across a range of relevant disciplines – and then we can consider narrowing our options from there."

"I can fill you in," Dr. Goswamy said equably. "I'm here for our first session, and I have ninety minutes set aside for the orientation chat – we can make an appointment after for further meetings as we judge them to be necessary."

My initial idea about joining the Lycan clan had been loosely about infiltrating their ranks and finding out what agenda they were pursuing behind the shroud of secrecy behind which they hid the truths about their identity and their existence. To accomplish this, something along the lines of what they had just presented me with would be a necessity. But I found myself resenting the high-handed way it had all been done – nobody had even *asked* me. They had simply trotted me out here and plumped me down before an academic advisor for a course of study I had had no idea I was about to begin.

To be perfectly honest about it, I had never been one of those people with a vocation, a calling, I did not ever claim to know (as some do) from an early age what I was going to do, or be, when I "grew up". I more or less went to school because I was required to, and did the absolute minimum I needed to do to skate through what was needful without inconveniencing myself to the point of having to repeat grades or drop out. It wasn't that I didn't care about anything at all, it was that I didn't much care about anything in particular. I never went beyond learning what I needed to know, no more and no less. So in that sense the direction in which I was now being pushed to go was not something that I had never had any interest in or had absolutely never wanted to go into – as far as any of that went, this was as good as any – but the flip side of that was also that I had never had any particular interest in it. Which meant that I had no background knowledge. No base. Nothing to build on. I would have to start from the beginning, and build from bedrock.

I'm not sure that anyone had explained any of that to my new tutor. We had a few false starts, he and I, until we came to a more complete understanding as to just how much I did not know. I ended up enrolled in several college-level courses – I could play catch-up with the required math and statistics courses, but I would also be starting out on organic chemistry, biochemistry, and the basic principles of genetics and molecular biology.

"That will do to start with," Dr. Goswamy concluded ominously, after piling on enough of a workload to keep a full-time student busy for an entire semester, quietly ignoring the fact that I was also expected to put in my hours at the labs at the compound, not to mention the fact that very soon now the next Turn would come and with it, I supposed, the cementing of my position in the pack and in the family hierarchy, whatever that turned out to be (and I fully expected the social aspects of my assimilation into the Lycans to be just as much of a full-time job as anything else I might be expected to do during the same period).

What the actual results had been of any of the tests they had conducted on all that blood and saliva they had taken, I was not told – not before the moon swelled again, and Sam Cotton came to me with a new set of protocols to remember.

"Your code for the gate is 1389," he said, after he had taken me to the security gate into the habitat to take my handprint and encode the system for a new wolf who'd be coming in that Turn. "Don't forget it. You don't have the clearance to change or alter this; it's system assigned. If you are caught on this side of the gate post-Turn, in your wolf form, things can get pretty unpleasant – and we've all learned that the hard way. You know, you start an experiment and you think you have time, just a little more time, and then – well – you don't, and you're wolf, and the security crew have to deal with it. It's tranq guns if they can get away with it – but even those are no fun, the hangovers are brutal when you're back to human, trust me, I know from experience – and if it comes to the worst, they do have live ammo. They are supposed to shoot to incapacitate only, but eh, if a wolf is coming at you, I wouldn't blame them if they got an itchy trigger finger. Remember the code, and most importantly, be through that gate before the full moon is completely up. You *have* to change when you're inside the enclosure. This first time here for you – well – Sofia said she'll delay Turn until you're inside..."

"She just wants to watch," I said.

"Of course," Sam said. "Yes, we know you've Turned into wolf already – the once – in a way that points to the probability that you will do so again, here, without anything untoward happening – and we have the evidence for that – but there's nothing like eyewitness testimony, in the end."

Evidence. That was the first mention I'd heard of my test results. My ears pricked up.

"Evidence?" I asked.

"All will be settled post-Turn," Sam said. "It's that eyewitness account that we still want in the file."

But they were certain. They were already certain. I would not still be at the compound, I would not have been permitted into the labs, I would not have been enrolled in courses which were obviously aimed at furthering my career and cementing my future in those labs, if they had had the slightest doubt about my right to be here.

One way or another, I was Wolf. It was confirmed.

They did keep a careful eye on me, that first Turn. Anna Cotton and Tom Manion both escorted me when I took the tunnel into the habitat at twilight of the day before the full moon rose into the sky, and stood back to make sure that I could deal with all the security that was required. I dutifully entered my code and hand-printed my way through the gate, and they followed me in. And then we were all through, the three of us, and on the far side Tom was the first to shrug out of his Turning cloak and hang it on a hook on the wire. Anna was starting to peel off hers. I goggled.

"In here, it's wolf country," Tom said, in response to that look, completely at ease with his nudity. "These, the cloaks, they're for modesty out there – back in the building – when the wolf days are over and we step back into that world. Not everyone in the compound is one of us. But in here... it would be hard to keep us in cloaks if we were to hang onto them until such time as other people's sensibilities demanded. We're wolves. We don't change into some quiet gentle pussy cat who can fall out of a cloak and then curl up on it and go to sleep – we'd shred the things. Every time. Naked we Turn, and so naked we go into the Turn. You'll get used to it. I guess it's strange and embarrassing to you now but trust me – you'll see them all – young bodies, old bodies, men and women, and after a while you don't pay that much attention. At this moment, it's all about the wolf, not the man. Come on, off with yours."

I couldn't help an admiring look in Anna's direction – she had a trim waist and lovely long legs and small but well-shaped breasts – and then I tried to make myself as invisible as I could, making my way to the trees in the small wood on the one side of the enclosure and skulking naked amongst them.

I watched the change begin, the Turn in the wolf enclosure, as one by one they became their wolf selves. I could see it even more clearly than I had done with Chalky, because here there were no clothes in the way, and I saw the human give way to the beast. It was only when my own moment came, when I began to see stars from the pain, when I began to lose myself in that other mind, that I realized that I, the watcher, had been watched all this time. A little away from me, in deeper shadows, the pack Alpha, Sofia Berezhnoyeva, stood in the deeper shadows, waiting. As best as I could figure it – without verifiable evidence – she must have been a woman at the very least in her late fifties, but there was something about her that impinged on my consciousness just as my mind faded from human into wolf and such ideas became unimportant to me; I tried to tell myself to remember this, later, not to let it be erased by what had to come next. I did not have the time, right in that moment, to work out just why it was an important piece of the puzzle but I retained enough awareness to know that it was, that it was worth remembering.

The wrinkles and folds on where the once young and supple skin stretched over shoulders and belly and thighs, the thin and papery fragile skin I had noticed – but had not given that much thought to – on her hands. The deep crow's-feet that sprayed out from the corners of her eyes. The drooping breasts that were turning to dugs, hanging shapelessly over her ribcage.

She looks old. That body is old. We age so fast. We die so young.

Sam Cotton, modestly clad in his Turning cloak, waited for me at the inner gate into the compound at the end of the third day – after I had Turned back into my human form somewhere in the woods and came loping out of them, naked, on my way back into the human world. The rest of the habitat seemed empty, deserted.

"Am I the last one out?" I asked, glancing back over my shoulder.

"Not quite. I think Veronica is still in there. She likes to hide somewhere by herself, towards the end, and sometimes even falls asleep in here, afterwards. We've had her come out a full six hours after everyone else once or twice. It's of no importance, she'll be out in her own time. How are you feeling?"

"I... fine. I guess. Hungry."

He laughed. "The young ones are always hungry. If you're absolutely starving it won't be the first time that we've had someone come into the cafeteria still in their Turning cloak and empty their larders of whatever's there – there was one time that one of Sofia's boys ate every single pickle they had on the shelves after a Turn. Otherwise, if you want to go back to your quarters for a shower and a change of clothing, I can have a proper dinner waiting for you in forty minutes, and we can talk."

I was willing to endure a growling stomach for that long; it seemed like a fair trade-off for information. "You've got a deal," I said, shrugging haphazardly into my own Turning cloak. My voice sounded like an odd croak to me, and I cleared my throat several times, shaking my head.

Sam was nodding. "There's that, too. Your throat sometimes feels as though someone tried to cut it, after. Honey helps. You should probably have a supply of it in your room, the liquid kind, the stuff you can drink out of the jar. I'll see that some is delivered to you."

"Thanks," I said. "So – as far as first times go – how did I do?"

"You did fine, cub," Sam said, grinning. "Go, get your shower, I'll start your dinner. Meet you in the cafeteria."

He gave me forty minutes. I took almost half that time to retrieve my sketchbook from its hiding place (I had found a better one than the one I had resorted to on my first night here) and draw from memory that thing that I had told myself that I should remember. I drew the body of the old woman in the woods, waiting to Turn into her wolf self; her face was a blur, not Sofia's, that didn't matter. What mattered was the vision of just how fast the human body of the Were aged. I had not, admittedly, seen the naked bodies of many women of any age before I had walked into the Turning habitat of Yuri's pack – but if I'd been presented with Sofia, not knowing her, not knowing anything about her, I would have guessed her to have been fifteen or maybe even twenty years older than what had to have been her physiological human age. I tried to remember my own grandmother, the one I had left behind together with my family history and my true name when we fled the land where I was born – but I had been too young for a real memory to have stuck and I wasn't at all sure of how accurate my remembrance of my grandmother's face and shape still was. All I could safely swear to was that I was completely certain that she had been an old woman. And yet... she might have been young, in relative terms, she might have been younger than Sofia.

We age so fast.

We die so young.

Sam was waiting when I turned up at the cafeteria, some forty five minutes after I had left the Turning habitat, and they must have been keeping my dinner warm in the back because at a quiet signal of Sam's they brought out my plate, piled high with pasta smothered in meat sauce. My innards, reminded by the sight and smell of the food of just how hungry I was, growled audibly – I wondered briefly, if this truly was the norm post-Turn and if Turning into an apex predator like a wolf affected the size of the appetite, what the food budget was for this compound – and Sam chuckled as he watched me dive enthusiastically into the spaghetti.

"Well, you haven't been too much of a pest over the last couple of weeks although you must have been wondering about a lot of things," Sam said, "so here's your reward."

"Actually, I've been spying on the genetics labs for all I was worth," I admitted. "Didn't they notice that every time they had a conversation about this, I was underfoot resupplying the reagent cabinet?"

Sam laughed. "They haven't mentioned that, no," he said. "Did you learn anything useful?"

"I think I'm starting to get the gist of it," I said.

"Well, good," he said approvingly. "There's the academic stuff – the basic background knowledge that you need to have to make sense out of it all – but there's an instinct, too, and that's just as important, and maybe you've got it, lad. In any case – they've pretty much put your DNA through the wringer – if you ever want to see a detailed map of your own genetic makeup, there's a fat file of data with your name on it back in Zoya's lab."

I *knew* that. I'd glimpsed it. I hadn't quite stretched so far as sneaking a look inside, even if I'd been completely confident of understanding the important stuff in it, which I wasn't. But Sam's statement implied that the information was there if I wanted it, that far from keeping me away from the file in question and shrouding it in secrecy they were quite open to having me dig through it – which... took me a little by surprise. I had latched onto the basic idea that the Lycans were all about secrecy and covert operations, and that anything I could learn from them I'd probably have to be savvy about stealing. I kept on forgetting the one important fact – that I *was* a Lycan, now. That technically I was on the other side of that veil, by definition. "They'd let me?" I asked, before I was quite able to stop the surprise from escaping.

"You may not understand a great deal of it," Sam said, still grinning. "Sure, they'd let you. It would be just like letting a curious boy who wanted to know more about Homer have a copy of the Odyssey in ancient Greek – the stuff's in there but you'd need a certain background to understand it. However, if you ask nicely, they might well explain it to you..."

"Well, can you summarize?" I asked practically.

"You're wolf," Sam said. "That's what it boils down to."

"I saw Sofia watching me in the Turning area – back when – "

Sam nodded. "Yes. She made that report. You make a fine young wolf, by her account. Apparently you got into a bit of a scrap with one or two of the others – but that's only to be expected, you're the stranger in the pack and they were only asserting their own authority..."

I swallowed my current mouthful of pasta. "I didn't notice any new scars in the shower..."

"Young Rory's got a fresh one or two," Sam said. "You don't let yourself be disrespected. That's a good attitude to have but watch it around the senior wolves, pup. Even someone with your talents will get put in their place if they try to sass the likes of Yuri. Or Tom. Or even myself. And we won't even talk about the women."

I started to give him some sort of wiseass response to that but thought better of it – not because of who he was, but because his comment made me conscious all over again about how the 'women' of this pack might shape my own future, whatever I thought I had to say about it myself. I wanted to ask Sam if that file in the lab, the one with my name on it, held far more answers than just my genetic identity – if in fact it might be the metaphorical tablet of stone on which the life that awaited me was already etched into, where my future mate and my future children were also already decided and described, and how all of us fit into the future which the Lycans were shaping for themselves and their world.

But I didn't ask.

And if he was aware that I had held back, he did not acknowledge it.

We left the cafeteria after I was done eating, with Sam rattling off something about my schedule for the following week and myself barely paying attention to begin with... and then not at all, as a slender vision in scarlet motorcycle riding leathers caught my eye and drifted across the far side of the hall we were crossing, heading for the living quarters.

Sam caught me staring, and stopped talking long enough to follow my riveted gaze, and then frown.

"She's a wild one, that one," he muttered. "I wonder if she signed out this time like she was supposed to."

"Signed out?" I echoed. "Who is that?"

Sam glanced at me. "Asia. Asia Adema. That one... her genetic background is interesting; her mother... was more like *you*, actually, she came to us Lycan-Turned from a family with good Canid genes, to be sure, but they were dogs for all that. But she was full Lycan, just like you are, and her daughter certainly had the impeccable genetic pedigree of the Berezhnoy line injected into her lineage – she's part of the future of the pack, in that sense, not to mention that she shows promise of becoming a gifted scientist in her own right. She's only twenty two, and she started work on her Masters degree this year, and making good headway with it from what I hear."

Asia Adema. It was one of the names on the roster of my own potential 'mates' in the pack. I craned my neck to see more, but she had already passed out of sight, just the afterimage of the scarlet leathers remaining behind in the hall like a lingering scent.

Beautiful, brilliant, a little intimidating, so far I had barely exchanged a few words with her – or, to be more accurate in that report, she had barely exchanged a few words with me. Guarded and wary. Like a wild thing. Like the wild thing that she was. Wolf-born.

But Sam was still talking.

"...bought herself a motorcycle last year. And that riding gear. It's as though she *wants* everyone's eye on her..."

I blinked at Sam. "I'd think that wouldn't be hard to accomplish," I muttered.

Sam clicked his tongue against his teeth, a small sound of disapproval and frustration. "Yes, but it isn't really *policy* that the Lycans... I mean, we keep a low profile, for good reasons... and that one, she takes the motorcycle and tears around the country back roads like some sort of superhero..."

"And does what?" I asked, unable to help myself. "Where does she go?"

"Sometimes nowhere," Sam said, frowning. "Sometimes she just takes the motorcycle and rides around for an hour or two, in circles. Often after a Turn. It's as though she feels... like she's still trapped behind the..." He shook his head, breaking the train of thought. "No matter. I'll have a word with Sofia about it. In any event, cub, welcome to the pack. You're really one of us now."

I don't even know if it was ever a conscious decision, but after that first Turn, what with that aspect of things settling down into the first beginnings of a routine, the rest of it began to fall into place as well. When I had talked about this with Chalky it was the origins and development of Adaptadyne that I wanted to pursue (and quite possibly, although the idea was very hazy and nebulous in the beginning, perhaps destroy) – but whether it was the fact of the thorough investigation my genes received in the Lycan labs, the inklings I was beginning to get about life in the pack and the genetics of Lycan propagation , the way such procedures and protocols affected everyone else in the pack and most particularly how they would very soon affect myself (all right, how it would affect myself in terms of the possibility of sharing kids with someone like Asia Adema), it was to the genetics labs that I gravitated as my personal placement in the pack. They did nothing to influence me in any direction, or assign me to a specific work team. They let me drift until I found my own level, my own place. And in the end that place turned out to be as the junior lab tech in Zoya Volkova's lab.

I surprised myself by how hard I worked at my academics, much of it online learning with Dr. Goswamy and other tutors, the practical aspects taken on in Zoya's lab under the guidance of herself and other senior scientists. In the beginning, to be sure, I was more of an observer and a gofer and a records keeper than a hands-on scientist, but I was a quick study, in the end. I always was, when it came to things that interested me. And this was beginning to fascinate me.

Asia was polite to me, but short – and much to my annoyance I was entirely too aware of what potentially lay between us and suddenly very conscious of the years that separated us – she was all of twenty two to my nearly eighteen and it shouldn't have mattered *that* much, but somehow it did, she was the adult and the smooth, elegant, polished one while I was the bumbling boy forever tripping over my own feet whenever she came into view. I knew I was doing it, I could see it start happening every time I laid eyes on her, I knew she probably thought I was a prize idiot, and I could not help it one little bit. It was incredibly aggravating, and sometimes I'd go back to my room and literally snarl at myself in the mirror because of my latest trip or drop or fumble in a situation where I would have absolutely not succumbed to those things had I not been acutely aware of Asia watching me under those long lashes.

If I didn't know better, I would have sworn I was developing a crush on an older woman.

But part of my obsession with her was not just her identity and all that it meant for my own future. There was also a genuine envy of what seemed to be an unprecedented amount of freedom. That motorbike.

There had been, from the very beginning, a distinct encouragement to think about the pack (and by extension other Lycan packs) as the one and the only circle of family and friends. Lycans were a secretive and almost incestuous bunch, witness the care they took of their genetic pool; they had to, with a limited supply of genetic material which would ensure a true-bred Lycan they didn't want to jeopardize their chances with too many crosses of too-close DNA. But what worked for the vast majority of people who had been born into this clan or had been brought into it somehow through the Lycans' own initiative was not necessarily true for an outlier like me, someone who was here only by what they saw as happenstance and accident, someone whose loyalties before I entered the Lycan fold had of necessity been given elsewhere.

It was a given that I should not be discussing anything that happened within the fold of the pack outside the walls of the compound – and that included my work in the labs, the stuff that hadn't been codified and published by senior members of the research team. I didn't *know for a fact* that they were, or could be, keeping tabs on my communications, but I was wary enough of the possibility that I shied away from doing so. There was always, in the back of my mind, the fact that I wanted to figure out a safe way to get in touch with and stay in touch with Chalky – after all, that was part of the reason I had done this thing in the first place – but I did not trust that the laptop which the pack had given me was entirely free of some sort of spyware that could trace or even read any email I sent out on it, and I emphatically did not want the Lycans on Chalky's tail.

The physical compound itself was inconveniently a little way off the beaten path, and I lacked discreet transport to the nearest place that would allow me to indulge in things that were out of the Lycans' supervision. And there were several things I badly wanted to send to Chalky – I had done several drawings that I really wanted him to see, and I had been keeping notes to myself, in hard copy (again with the computer) and I might have sent those – but again using the compound's own outgoing mail system would mean leaving a traceable address out in the open, leaving a way for them to find Chalky if they wanted to.

So I hoarded my notes and drawings, and waited for an opportunity.

And the opportunity, eventually, came from none other than Asia Adema herself.

I'd been concentrating on some paperwork, head down at my desk in the corner of the lab where I had been set up, when her voice brought me sharply out of that bubble. I looked up, startled, to see her standing beside my desk.

"Field trip," she said. "Gina was supposed to come with me, but she just called in sick, and I need a backup – so tag, you're it today, Wonderboy. Come on, you're up."

"What?"

She rolled her eyes. Just a little. "I'll explain on the way. Come on. We need to get going. Grab a cup of coffee for the road if you want. I'll get the car, you'd better be out there and waiting for me by the time I drive around the front to pick you up. I'll give you fifteen minutes – meet me out front."

She didn't wait for an answer, turning smartly and marching off.

Sasha Berezhnoy, true-born son of Sofia and her late husband Sergey and Asia's half-brother through their shared father, looked up from his own bench across the lab, his face splitting into a sympathetic grin.

"Better not keep that one waiting," he said. "She's got a temper on her."

"But I'm in the middle of..." I began, gesturing at the pile of papers on my desk.

"I'll tell them you were co-opted," Sasha said. "You heard her. Go."

I slouched off resentfully to my quarters, annoyed at being dragged from my own work at someone else's whim, particularly Asia's. I had no idea what was going on and where I was headed – but I detoured to my room and picked up, just in case, the envelope into which I had stuffed things I wanted to mail to Chalky. Maybe there would be a chance to do that on the sly somewhere on the road, while my 'supervisor' wasn't watching.

She was already there when I emerged out of the front door, behind the wheel of a silver sedan, tapping impatiently on the steering wheel with long fingers. She barely gave me enough time to settle into the passenger seat and click my safety belt in place before the car took off down the drive, spraying gravel.

"Where are we going?" I asked, a little sullenly. "Do I at least get to know that?"

"I need some new samples," she said. "We're going to a different Turning House this time, and there's going to be a... what's the matter with you?"

I reacted as though I had been touched by an electric cattle prod. "*Turning* House?"

She turned her head briefly to give me a startled look. "What?"

"My parents... had to go to one of those, when we first came over," I mumbled. "I was... very young then. The stories they told – the things they were careful not to tell us – my father built special rooms for us, in our house, in the basement, just so that us kids would never have to see the inside of one. Those were the monster stories of my childhood."

She drove in silence for a few moments, her eyes on the road ahead.

"I forgot," she said quietly, after a moment. "Now that you've been at the compound for a while... it's hard to remember that you aren't just another floater from a different pack. You aren't really one of us. You're from *outside*."

That stung, far more than it had any right to – seeing as it was no more than the truth. But there was also the fact that she was herself only a generation away from being from *outside*, and if she thought that the wolves considered her their absolute equal, she wasn't listening to them when they talked about her. More than two decades with the pack, and the first thing anyone ever mentioned about Veronica Adema, Asia's mother, was her inferior genetic background. Mere *dog*. Asia herself had been wolf-born, true wolf, but her mother's heritage was a shadow that still haunted her.

"What have you got to do with the Turning Houses?" I asked, after a moment's silence of my own.

She hesitated, glancing over at me again. "I brought a folder with me," she said at length, indicating the back seat with a toss of her chin. "I don't know how much background you've already got in any of this, but you can read through that later, if you want. But to summarize... that's my Masters project. I'm working on what happened... how it happened... the people there now, the ones who have lost the ability to Turn..."

"Half-Souled," I muttered.

"What was that?"

"That's what they... that's how I heard them described. The Half-Souled. The lost souls, literally."

"Yes," she said, after another brief pause. "I've heard the term."

"What do you have to do with any of this?"

Asia clutched the steering wheel convulsively with both hands for a moment, and then drew a deep breath.

"Someday, maybe, this will make a whole lot more sense to you," she said. "But you've been wasting your time in the compound to a far greater degree than I think you have if some of this hasn't started to percolate down to you. The history of it all. Where it began. How it began. What it all means, on a blueprint level. How are we different from them?"

"Who is *we* in this equation?" I asked carefully. "Lycans? The Were as a whole?"

"Yes," she said, and then took a moment to glance over at me and offer a wan grin. "What I mean is, yes, all of the above. Look, you meandered into the Lycan circle by happenstance – it doesn't happen all that often, granted, or at least not any more, not since the packs have been sequestered during the Turns – but okay, that's how you turned up. For the rest of us – even for people like me, who is drawn in from a periphery into the core families – we're the aristocracy, we're the oldest, we're the original Were kind."

There it was again. She identified Lycan, completely Lycan, she was turning a blind eye to her own origins. *People like me*, she said – but that was her point of view. I'd heard more than one member of the core families speak of Asia, and although they certainly accepted her as part of the pack there was still – always – there would never not be that thin edge of distancing themselves from someone whose grandparents were not genetically pure. Asia seemed utterly unaware of all of this – or perhaps she was hyper-aware of it, clinging to her Lycan identity like there was nothing else, like there could be nothing else. True Lycans had nothing to prove to the pack; Asia's loyalty was tested at every turn, and met with protestations of true faith. Much like she was doing now, in that car, to me.

"There was a time there was nothing out there that was Were unless it was Lycan – these were two circles which were absolutely overlapping, and anything outside of them was not relevant to us at all," she said, still in lecture mode.

"Okay," I said, "and then...?"

"And then," she said. "Then the Divergence happened, somehow, and the Were splintered into all the other species, and somehow the Lycans became more and more rare. And it was more and more difficult to keep the first true Were strain from actually becoming extinct – the natural birthrates for Lycan bloodlines has been dropping over centuries and these days a Lycan woman if she is lucky is going to bear maybe three children in her fertile years. More often than not it is two, or just one. Sometimes she'll have four, five miscarriages until a live birth occurs – it's tough to bear a true Lycan baby. And then all too quickly it's over and she's old and – well – you may have realized that there is no such thing as a Lycan who is over sixty. Our average life expectancy is maybe fifty years. That isn't a long time."

I felt my life narrow down into a tunnel before me. This, I had not known. Perhaps if I had I would not have made some of the choices that I did.

Asia stole another glance at me. "Look, we may as well talk about it," she said, and her voice was suddenly pinched, awkward. "You... for all your raw and recent and improbable provenance, whatever else you might once have been... you're still a true wolf now, and you're a genetic prize for the pack, an influx of fresh genes, they'll want to keep you in this family, and let's face it, I'm the prime candidate to be your mate."

"They mentioned the Manion girls, too," I said, baring my teeth in what might have passed for a smile.

I had wanted to take a jab at her, and it worked – I saw her flinch, a little. And then she bore down again, with brutal honesty.

"They might have mentioned them," she said quietly, "but if you're being logical about this, you can work it out. One, Sorcha and Seonaid are young enough for their mating not to be a priority – and there's time to arrange for them to cement really good alliances if they're given to the right pack as mates. They have the potential to become Alphas, they're from the main lineage, even if they are a good long way down on it. You're too young and too untried; they'd be wasted on you, no matter how much they wanted to keep you in the pack."

"But you just said, they're young. They'd have to wait – those two haven't even Turned yet, never mind anything else – and there's still years to prove..."

"Sure," Asia said, "and when those years are gone, you're still an outsider with no connection to bring and they are Inner Family. With pure lineage tracing back generations. They would be a prize."

"I've been told I was a prize, too."

"I'm not putting a value on it," she said. "But they are a legacy prize. That's a different thing altogether than the sort of thing you bring to the table. They're royal-born, if you like, and you... you're just Wonderboy. If you'd been a second generation neo-Lycan, maybe – but there's a flip side to all those fresh genes you're bringing in. Sometimes strange things come out in the wash genetically, when such DNA is brought into the mix. There's a question mark on whether they'll want to risk someone like Sorcha or Seonaid to be the one who will bear whatever children get to carry those fresh new genes."

I stared at her, unable to figure her out. There was so much that was contradictory inside of her – the fierce loyalty to the Lycan clan and identity, the clinging to that as the only thing about herself that really mattered... and yet... I was wrong, she did know that they somehow looked down on her. And hated it. She was Sergey Berezhnoy's daughter, she could have been, should have been, part of that inner circle... except for the inconvenient identity and heritage of her mother.

"So you see, I'm the only real choice," she said. She was trying to keep the bitter taste of those words bottled up, but some of it leaked around the edges, I could not help but feel the burn of it. "They're too young, and they have too much potential for the pack to risk on a mating like this. Whereas I, if anything, am almost too old already. So far, I've escaped the trammels – yes, I know my genes belong to the pack and that my duty lies there but dammit my body and my soul are my own – and my life is going to be a Lycan-short one – and there was so much that I wanted to *do*..." She bit her lip. "Well. Anyway. My time is running out, here. If Lycan women don't bear their children by the time they're twenty five, twenty six, the odds drop. By a lot. I managed to escape being paired and being kept pregnant by diving into my work, by being so good at what I do that they traded the chance of procreation and keeping the Lycan line going for whatever I could bring to the table as a scientist, as a researcher. And I've busted my hump trying to prove myself to them. Until you. Until you came. And now – what I can do, I have to finish fast, because once they... once we..."

"Have they said anything to you?" I said, startled. "Is this a done deal, then? Because nobody has said a word to me."

"You've barely been cleared," Asia said. "They haven't had time. But they will. You've Turned now, in the pack, and you're part of that family – and they'll reel you in, fast, before some other pack gets wind of you for real and demand that you be released as a floater into the Lycan population, taking the genes where you can. Yuri will want you sealed into his own pack before that happens. That means it's likely to happen at any time, really."

I wasn't sure how I felt about all of this, but there was a part of me that responded with pure ego – she was basically recoiling from the whole idea of me as a possible mate, a possible husband. The only potential mate, in this instance, was me. Although my interactions with her so far had made it perfectly clear that I was somewhat in awe of her, it still didn't sit very well that I had the distinct feeling that if she had the chance, the choice, the option, she would run as far and as fast as she could.

Then I remembered something else – the drawing that even now sat in the envelope meant for Chalky which was secreted into my backpack on the back seat of the car.

We age so fast.

Sofia. With her old woman's body, there in the Lycan woods in the shadows.

"Asia... how old is Sofia?" I asked carefully.

She looked at me a little strangely. "Sofia's going to be forty-nine in November," she said. "Why?"

"God," I said. "I thought that she was... that she had to be..."

"That will be me," Asia said, clutching the steering wheel again with a white-knuckled grip. "Before I've lived as long again as I've lived to this hour, that'll be me. And between now and then... I am expected to provide the pack with at least one true-Lycan progeny to continue the line, the pack, the clan." She glanced over at me again and her cheeks had flushed feverishly – but the color left them even as I watched, leaving her very pale and composed. "So, Wonderboy," she said. "When should we make the wedding?"

I did not respond. And the silence was heavy between us.

And it would be like this. For the rest of my life.

For the rest of what might be a very short life.

We recovered, a little. Or at least tried to. It took an hour or so, but we were actually talking, almost normally, avoiding shop talk about what we were out here to do or discussions about the possible inevitability of a shared future, right until the moment when Asia consulted the GPS in the dashboard a little more closely and then flicked on her indicator and turned left into what seemed to be an arbitrary country road which stretched out anonymously for a little way looking like it led nowhere much.

"There are no signposts," I said stupidly.

"Why would there be?" Asia asked, a little testily. "For those who need to know what is here, they know. For those who do not need to know, what point is there to having a sign for the rubberneckers to follow to gawk and stare? These are not *zoos*."

"The pack runs a wolf sanctuary," I reminded her.

Her lip curled a little; if she had been in wolf form it would have been a snarl. "That's different. And you know it."

I zipped it, after that, just staring at the road, aware that I was instinctively turning into that thing that I had always been so damnably good at, the observer, the recorder. The details of the area leapt out at me, etched themselves into my consciousness. The flat barren land that lay to either side of the road, with apparently nothing growing there except stubby yellowing grasses. The texture of the road, its tarmac rough, patched in places, in need of more repair here and there where new wounds had appeared on it – it was obviously not a road which was being kept in shape by public taxes, but a private or semi-private thing which was being maintained sporadically.

Then, eventually, a line of short pillars which looked like they might have been raised to support a fence – but there was no fence between them, just the evenly spaced pillars marching in a wide curving arc in both directions, a ring around something in the middle of the area they encircled.

"No fence?" I asked, nodding at the pillars.

"Oh, there's a fence," Asia said. "Just because you can't see it..."

We drove through the ring of pillars, and then past them, and I turned to crane my neck to look back at them. There were red lights, like baleful eyes, gleaming on the backs of them, glaring back into the center.

ALMA ALEXANDER

"What *are* those things?" I asked.
"They're electronic readers," Asia said. "Trackers."
"Tracking what?"
"Your Half-Souled. The ones gathered up in here. You'll see when we get there. They're all chipped, just above the left ankle there's a subcutaneous chip implanted, and the microchip signatures are registered on those pillars. Nobody gets past that perimeter, from the inside, heading out, not without authorization, without the chip being identified, singled out, neutralized by a supervisor, if necessary. Nobody gets by those posts who shouldn't."
"So it's a prison after all," I said. "It's like those invisible fences they use for dogs. What happened to these people? Don't they feel like they're being kept in jail here? What happens if they try to get out?"
Asia bit her lip before answering. "Those posts... are also weapons, if they need to be," she said reluctantly. "There have always been attempts to leave – but really, these people are here because they need to be, not because anyone wants to keep them locked up. They can be kept in a confined place, and kept comfortable there, and cared for..."
"And controlled," I said.
"Don't get pious," she barked, back to full-fledged Lycan imperiousness. "Like I said, you'll see in a minute. They aren't permitted to come and go as they please because of very good reasons. Those who try to run – well – it can get messy. But most of them... don't know anything other than... have absolutely no compelling reason to try to leave. There is nothing for them out here. They don't have a reason to go seeking nothing. Many of them are depressed, and I mean clinically depressed, and on medication for it; there are some who are literally close to catatonic. They would not last long on the outside, even if they made it there. And anyway..."
It was a second thought, and cut off – but I wasn't having it. "Anyway what?"
"There are two things that can happen, here," Asia said. "There are some out here who simply do not age as fast as the rest of us do. They are – at least in theory – probably capable of reaching the kind of old age that the humans can expect. And there's a scientific basis for that. There has to be. *Something* has changed, when the Turning went away. And yet... there's the other... they just don't live all that long."
"I thought none of us did," I said, the vision of Sofia flashing back into my mind's eye.
"Even relative to that. It might be nothing to do with anything at all that I can investigate, or pin down. But it might be... I don't know. My area of concern is the genetics, not the psychology – but I am told by those who care for the mind rather than the physical body that there is a kind of.... insanity... here. I can understand that, actually. The wolf is a part of me; I don't know, I literally cannot know, I can't begin to understand, what it would mean to be suddenly severed from that – after having that other half of me, knowing it, experiencing it, even if my memories while in that other skin are not necessarily freely available to me, right now, as myself, as my

human self. But the severing of those two halves – I can see that unhinging a certain kind of mind. It would be like suddenly going blind in an unfamiliar space and spending the rest of your days blundering about in the dark with your hands outstretched trying to feel for that missing thing that you know should be there but that you can't find, can never find again."

"So it's an insane asylum," I said, appalled.

Asia shook her head violently. "I said *some*," she said, "and even then, it might not be... but I am not qualified to speak to that. Don't push me."

"What is that you have to do with them?" I asked. "Why are we here? You said, they don't live all that long – but that doesn't – "

"The complexity of genetics is beautiful," Asia said. "There are multiple levels of triage involved here. The first is how the severing between the human self and the Were-self occurred. If traumatic enough, the circumstances of that can affect everything that goes on afterwards. So there are the personal medical and social histories of each individual to consider. But then there are other ways of winnowing out – and there are some rare individuals in these places who are the negative equivalent of you, if you want."

"How's that?"

"If you waltzed onto the Were stage a fully-formed Lycan out of nowhere with no way to predict your coming... there are also some for whom the reverse happened and they simply stopped Turning for no discernible reason – and I am investigating why. There are others for whom it was a chemical thing – they ingested or were otherwise exposed to some substance which altered their genetic make up to the point that they stopped Turning. I am investigating *that*. And the reason that I am investigating those things is partly because some of these people, the latter kind, those that do not go catatonic or insane or try to escape and get... fried... by the grid... something has changed, deep inside them. If it is possible for people like this to live longer. I want to know why. I want to know how. I want to know what it is about the Turning that cuts our own lives so short. So I research them, and I follow them, and I find them, and I take physical samples, and I run genetic tests. I'm after nothing less than the elixir of youth, maybe. And also... here..."

There was more buried in the vault of the Lycans' secrets than I had ever known. And then more still. There had been something else that she had been about to say, and I was already pushing past every boundary I had ever crossed before.

"And also here what?"

"There may be a hint about just why, just how, the Divergence happened in the first place," Asia said, almost reluctantly. "Lycans were the first and the only kind of Were when it all began, or so the histories say. And then suddenly we had splintered into hundreds of Were species, and we were all over the map, and the true Lycan genes went into eclipse. It was as though we were the ones standing closest to the edge, and something or someone pushed us. I want to know what. I want to know why. But Yuri wants to..."

She stopped again as the car came to a gate and stopped. Asia reached out through the driver's window to swipe a plastic card into a slot on a somewhat battered-looking old-fashioned card reader setup and then punch in a numeric code into the keypad beside it. The gate unlocked with an audible clang, and automatically retracted back against a tall fence of interlocking iron bars. I could see lighter metal on the joints of the bars, and narrowed my eyes at it as we drove through.

"Silver?"

"Touches of it, yes," she said.

Yes, there had always been the myth of the silver bullet, the only thing that would kill a Were. But Chalky had always dismissed that as a fairy tale. Admittedly I had never tested it, myself. And yet... here, now...

"Really?" I said. "Silver works?"

Asia actually laughed. "Don't believe *everything* you're told," she said. "But it isn't comfortable. It... hurts, in a way. I know, I tried putting on a silver bangle. Once. It almost left scars. It didn't leave me dead on the spot but it did something, it... burned. Exposure, prolonged exposure, will do that to all of us, I think. Most of us know it and avoid it. Some of us don't know it, and that ilk finds out the hard way."

The drive beyond the gate, which closed behind us with an unnerving clang that made me shiver, was graveled rather than paved, and the closer we got to our destination the more cultivated the grounds became. There were flower beds now. Ornamental trees which clearly had not originated here. I could even glimpse my first people, some of them kneeling on the ground digging at weeds or watering bits of the garden.

"Are those...?" I began, and Asia, following my gaze, nodded.

"It isn't just an asylum where we tie them into straitjackets and put them in padded rooms," she said. "We don't just lock them away and forget about them. In every Turning House, we have the higher-functioning ones in charge of the whole Turning aspect of it all. It is they who meet the Were who come here to spend their Turn days, it is they who see to the disposition of these people, who care for them while they're in their alternate form, who feed them and clean their spaces – stalls or cages or whatever is necessary – they're the custodians of the place..."

I watched one individual walking across a lawn towards a main building which we ourselves seemed to be heading for, and we were now close enough for me to see the expression on the man's face, and it froze me to my marrow – there was a blankness there, a mask of what almost looked like serenity until it became clear that it was merely emptiness, a sort of contentment rooted in having absolutely nothing left to care about.

"But... they know, don't they?" I blurted.

"They know what?"

"What they once were... who they were... that they no longer can... you're telling me that you've got the people who have lost a key part of their own identity acting as jail guards to those who are still that thing which they no longer are – that they are made to stand there, and watch

293

while those that can Turn do it before their eyes, and then take care of the animals knowing that the animals are really humans just like they used to be... it just seems a harsh sentence...they're forced to stare their own loss in the eye, over and over and over again... and you wonder why they go insane?

"There are *too many of them*," Asia said, her voice tight. "What do you suggest as an alternative? That we institutionalize *them*? Who's to take over that? The whole reason behind the Turning Houses was because the normals were too terrified of the idea of a Were creature loose in the night in their own world to countenance that happening – that's why we're all fingerprinted and documented and administrivialized to death, they have to know exactly who we are when they meet one of us, just so that they can avoid touching us if they can as though what we have is a transmissible disease, as though just being in our presence contaminates them."

Clearly I had hit a nerve. "We all had to be locked up, and safely out of sight, so that we don't scare their children, when we're in our Were form... for three days, *three days*, out of every month of our lives. And that's what goes for what they consider to be the productive Were, the ones who work in their businesses, serve them their food in diners, toil in their factories – the *useful* ones. Do you think they would have taken the responsibility of caring for those of us who are wounded or damaged or sick? What do you suppose would have happened to these people in the normals tender hands?"

There was nothing to answer to that, or way too much, and while I struggled with the possibilities Asia brought the car to a halt in a parking space a few paces away from the front door of the main building.

"At least come in and see what's really happening, before you are so quick to make judgments," she said. "It may not be ideal, but there are too many of these people out there for us to either ignore them or expect others to take care of them. And the best that could be done was to make the places which already had to exist by law, to keep the rest of in line, into some sort of refuges for them."

"Reservations," I said, unable to stop myself.

"Whatever. It's a *life*. At least they are given some sort of a useful existence to lead, here. You may call them jailors if you like. I'm sure most of them don't see it that way. I popped the trunk; bring the kit from the back, please, when you come around."

I was not convinced, and some part of me still quailed at the thought of setting foot inside one of these things. It was with an almost superstitious dread that I trailed Asia into the house.

The first two people I saw, sitting across from one another on a window seat built into the alcove of a bay window, seemed to absolutely confirm and justify every iota of the terror I had of this place. Two women, one of them quite young (what sort of catastrophe had brought *her* here?), the other with graying hair pulled back into a severe chignon at the nape of her neck; the younger one was sitting curled up in the corner between window and wall, head turned to stare vacantly out of the window, holding out her arms out like a mannequin doll with a skein of blue yarn resting loosely between her wrists while the other seemed totally focused on winding that yarn into a ball, humming tunelessly as she worked, her movements mechanical like those of a wind-up doll as she went through the almost hypnotic motions of following the yarn with the motion of her hands as she wound it off the skein stretched between her companion's arms.

There was a third woman, of indeterminate age, curled up in an armchair beside the window; at first I thought she might be frankly asleep, but her eyes were not completely closed, only half-lidded, and she looked drowsing but somehow on the alert, like a cat who was only pretending to nap. The whole tableau raised hackles on the back of my neck.

"The Half-Souled," I said. "It's as though it's the human half of the soul that they lost, not their animal avatar. They know... how to exist... but it's like they could only keep one part of themselves, and they snatched at the wrong part... it's just instinct, here, they keep breathing, and they eat, and they sleep, but does that one who looks so asleep actually dream human dreams anymore?"

"Now you're just being melodramatic," Asia said, but there had been the briefest of pauses there and it was enough. I had heard it. She had to believe what she had been telling me because there was no other way of dealing with the issue – but she was far from being an evangelist for the idea.

I shifted my grip uneasily on the kit I was carrying and she saw me do it.

"Come on," she said, "the sooner we get started the sooner we can get out of here. Yes, it creeps me out too. But there's nothing at all I can do about except perhaps use it to get some answers – so – that's what I do, and try to look past the rest. The infirmary is up the stairs, and they know we're coming, I called ahead."

"To who?"

"There's a doctor," Asia said.

"One of *them*?"

"There are some who are quite high-functioning, in here, whatever you want to believe," Asia said quietly. "But in point of fact, no, he's one of us. Truly one of us, really. He's a Lycan scientist himself. He helps me with the harvest sometimes."

"The *harvest*?" I repeated, swinging my head back to stare at her.

She shrugged. "He sends me prospects," she said. "I'm here today to get DNA from three good specimens – and yes, I *do* have to think of it like that. I can't go back to the lab and start calling my samples Joe and Jenny and Annie, you'd go mad yourself pretty fast that way. So they're specimens. I record their names and after that they're just numbers to me. Genome number AA124. No more than that. I can't... get involved. They'd suck the soul from me."

It was the most honest she'd been so far.

Her doctor was waiting for her in the infirmary, together with the three Half-Souled individuals whom he had picked out for her. They exchanged formal pleasantries over my head, but I'd stopped listening, stopped hearing, a rush of white noise in my head – I was distanced, detached, almost watching this whole scene from the outside with myself just another stock character in a small drama unfolding as a silent movie all around me.

I laid out Asia's equipment, trying to avoid looking at either her or the man she was speaking to, or at the three sitting quietly on three plastic chairs against the wall and waiting for whatever they had been brought there for to be over.

Two men and an older woman – but now I was no longer even sure that I could trust my judgment on age. She might have been thirty. She might have been fifty. I had absolutely no way of knowing.

The doctor had handed Asia folders on each of the three candidates he had lined up for her; I watched her scan the files, her eyes flickering over the contents, and then she handed one of them back to the doctor and tucked the other two into her messenger bag. One of the men, at a touch on his shoulder from the doctor, got up with an almost mechanical precision and slipped out of the infirmary; the other two remained, their expressions unchanged. Asia swabbed the insides of each individual's cheek and dropped the sample swabs into tubes, closing them up with an expert flick of the wrist and handing them to me to label, while she prepared to draw a blood sample.

Her movements were precise and economical, like she had done this many times before. I met her eyes at one point during the procedure, as she handed back a tube containing a blood sample, and it was there in her face, too, that weird disconnection, a blankness, her pupils wide and black and windows into an empty darkness, a place in which she did not want to shine too much of a light, as though she knew that she might be afraid of the thing that such a light would show her.

Our fingers touched, across the tube. For a moment she was back, the warmth of a familiar expression washing over her face, but then the doctor said something... and at the sound of his voice she shut down again, responding automatically, with politeness and outward grace, doing her job.

A thought coalesced – *just like me... when I came to the Lycans*. It was the same ritual. The same efficient collection of samples. These samples, the ones I was sorting and labelling for Asia, might wind up in the same labs where my own blood and spit had been tested. There, but for a twist of fate, stood I, myself...

I tucked the sample tube away into a safety rack inside a small cooler box, and scrambled to my feet.

The motion brought the doctor's attention to me, and then, after a moment. Asia's.

"I need some air," I said, hearing the desperate note that had crept into my voice, and then turned and yanked the door open, stumbling out of that room, leaving Asia and her samples in my wake.

It wasn't until I was standing outside, gulping great breaths of that air that I had said I needed, that the brain-fog began to clear, and normal sounds began to impinge on my consciousness once more. I heard a bird singing somewhere close by, an insistent chirping; its fellows were wheeling about overhead against the clear sky flecked with innocent powder-puff white clouds. I'd somehow taken a wrong turn inside that house and had emerged through a different doorway than the one I had entered by – I realized I had stepped out into the back of the property, and the view was that of a well-ordered farmyard. A large barn stood across a broad courtyard, its doors half-open; a strong smell of horse came from inside. Next to it, a covered passage led off to mysteries beyond – and next to that a smaller, longer, lower L-shaped building edged the corner of the courtyard. I could hear bleating from behind it – goats, perhaps. A large enclosed poultry yard took up space in the field that opened up beyond this second barn, and in it I could glimpse chickens scratching around in the dirt, and maybe a couple of ducks sitting next to a small open pond in the midst of the enclosure. A ginger cat was sunning itself on top of one of the pillars which held up a low fence between the field and the courtyard, in which a gate hung half-open. The field beyond was empty; on the far side a hayloft half filled with an untidy mess of hay took up one corner. Out of sight, beyond the buildings, I could hear a dog barking intermittently – curiosity, perhaps, or a game, not alarm.

It was pastoral. It was like a painting of a farm. It reminded me a little of the things I had no right to remember at all – anyone would tell you that my mind was way too young to hold coherent and 'true' memories when I had been snatched away from the place where I was born and brought to this country, with its Turning Houses which tried to emulate the very thing I had left behind – but I remembered hay. I remembered farmyards. I remembered how they smelled, the kinds of shadows that they cast. And the weirdest thing was that I didn't really know that I remembered until I stepped into this one, here, now, half a world away.

Celia would have remembered.

Something rose in my throat and threatened to choke me. Breathing itself became difficult, as though I was trying to gulp air through a blanket. My eyes teared up as I fought for that breath, my mouth open, trying to drink in enough oxygen for my heart to keep beating...

"Can I help you?"

The voice at my shoulder made me collect myself sufficiently to turn around in response, my eyes still prickling with tears.

"I... uh..."

The young woman standing beside me wore rubber boots suitable for mucking around farmyards in, with loose trousers tucked untidily tucked into the boots and blowsing over the sides and a denim shirt with its sleeves rolled up above her elbows. Her hair was scraped back into a braid down her back, with tendrils snaking free to fold themselves along her cheekbones and curling into the small gap between her shirt collar and the back of her neck.

She might have been anyone, we might have been anywhere. But we were here, and there were few here who were other than who she must have been.

I stared at the first Half-Souled creature I had ever seen up close, and tried to decide if I would have recognized her as one of her kind if I'd met her in an anonymous city streets.

I wasn't sure.

There was something about her – something in the expression in her eyes that gave me the impression of serenity, but not the enviable natural kind, rather the sort that was achieved via pharmaceutical means, happiness in a pill. There was a sense of *now*, of the moment she was in being all there was, as if there had been no past, as if there could be no future.

But she had spoken to me, and perfectly coherently, and there was no sign that she was in any way catatonic, or anxious, or otherwise insane.

She stood waiting for her answer, and I struggled to find the words to reply to her perfectly simple question, and couldn't seem to make any familiar syllables come out of my mouth in a comprehensible sentence.

Asia saved me.

"He's fine, he's just feeling a little faint," Asia said, from the doorway of the house I had just left. I turned around, ashamed at the stab of pure gratitude that tore through me, and the farm girl nodded calmly as if those words explained everything in the world.

"Okay, then," she said, and stepped away without another word, heading across the courtyard and into the barn.

"Thanks," I muttered. It was pretty much all I could muster.

"Come on," Asia said. "Let's go."

"Are you done...?"

"Pretty much."

I never did know when to keep my mouth shut. "Was that it...? Didn't seem worth the trouble of dragging extra baggage like me around – there's nothing much that I..."

The expression on her face stopped me, and then she turned away.

"We have to come to these Houses in pairs," she said. "It's protocol. And even if that wasn't the case... given your reaction to the whole thing, you of all people might begin to understand why I wouldn't want to come here on my own anyway."

"Ash." I had no idea why her name came out like that. It was – just – there, between us, something new, something shared. She looked up, startled, and somehow I had taken the few steps over to her and gave her a brief, awkward hug. "I'm sorry. Thank you."

After a moment she disentangled herself from the circle of my arms around her and brushed her hair back from her face, without meeting my eyes.

"We'd better start back," she said. "It's a long drive home."

She turned back into the house and I started after her, and then paused, taking one last look back into the courtyard over my shoulder.

"It looks so quiet," I said. "So peaceful. So... ordinary."

"I wouldn't want to be here the day before the first night of the full moon," Asia said abruptly. "I'm betting it's a very different place."

I actually shivered at the thought, and then squared my shoulders and followed her across the threshold.

The drive back was the color of silence, in all its many shades. There were moments in which I thought it was the soft silence of companionship and understanding, perhaps the beginning of something that I had no real name for yet, that thing that had brought forth the 'Ash' contraction of Asia's name, an acceptance of a path into a future, perhaps. Other times, I was not so sure, and the silence was a rough gray wall and I knew that if I tried to breach or scale it I would be as squarely zapped by lethal force as those hapless escaping Half-Souled escapees had been by the invisible artillery that surrounded the Turning House. I thought I could sense it morphing from one aspect to another if I concentrated, but then there were also instants which were sharp boundaries and I had no way of knowing what had triggered the change. Needless to say I never asked her to stop for a clandestine mail drop; Chalky's envelope returned to the compound with me. It was already dark when Asia dumped me at the front door of the main house and drove off, without a word, to return the car to the carpool garage. I practically sneaked back into the compound, trying hard not cross anyone else's path, and made my way back to my quarters where I spent most of that night lying on my bed, fully clothed, unable to sleep, staring at the shadows on the ceiling, trying to put that day into perspective.

Asia made no mention of the day trip in the lab the next day. She handed me tasks if she had any for me to do, and otherwise left me alone, at Zoya's beck and call. Part of me wanted to sit down and talk to Asia, really talk to her, about a whole lot of things… and another part told me to leave well enough alone for now. It would be easy to say that it was the latter instinct that triumphed in the end and it was that which made me into the kind of 'better man' who simply knew how to respect the distance that was being put in place – but perhaps it would be just as easy and perhaps more honest to admit that Asia took the choice away from me and that I was given no real opportunity for conversation even if I had pushed for it.

My second Turn in the compound came, and went. And the day after all the Lycans had returned safely to their human forms, I was summoned to Yuri's office.

It was with a sense of inevitability that I saw Asia already waiting there when I arrived.

Sofia, who was also there, showed us our genetic charts. We were educated on the potential genetics of our unborn children, and of the importance of those children to the continuing wellbeing, if not existence, of the Lycan clan. It was presented as a duty; not once was either of our problematic genetic backgrounds mentioned, or the fact that they had partnered us because they wanted to lose neither of us, because they wanted both our genetic legacy in the pack, but they didn't want to put their own pure genetic bloodlines at risk without a guarantee of at least one generation's true-breeding of the Lycan line – we were both wolves of this pack, but we were on the fringes, and it was entirely possible that only our children would earn the full right to completely belong here.

We were given a date, later that summer, when we would be expected to marry... and the unspoken directive was that we should begin trying for those children as soon as possible after that event.

Asia said very little, looking pinched and resigned, her skin stretched too tightly across the bones of her face, eyes darting around the room trying to find something safe to look at... something, anything, that was not me.

After she left, I tried to say something. But Yuri and Sofia let the words slide off them both as though I was throwing them on a smooth wall. There would be no discussion on this.

I had made a choice to become a Lycan. She had been born one. We would do what was necessary for our clan.

The wedding date was set for August, after the Turn was over. I was dizzy with the speed of it all; in the space of less than a year I had completely changed my identity, from the core, and this was just another layer accreting onto this strange new skin that I was wearing, that I barely had time to adjust to before it became stiffer and heavier and more permanent. Our lives were apparently short – but mine also appeared to be moving at a greater speed than I had believed to be possible. I seemed to be in dire danger of living out my entire short life in one rapid incandescent blast and then – what – I could get snuffed out like a candle... with only the potential children which were supposed to come out of this marriage to show that I had been here at all.

The Were, as a whole, and the Lycans in particular, had a rich and ancient history – and I found myself wondering how on earth it had ever accumulated, if the lives of every individual within that history were as ephemeral as my own seemed to be right at that moment.

I had managed to mail my Chalky envelope – with the stuff that had been inside it at the time – but that was before the big announcement, and thus I knew that he remained ignorant of the current situation. So did my birth family, for that matter, there was no indication that they would be invited to the wedding. So far as the Lycan clan was concerned, they were permanently out of my life. My children would never be grandchildren to my parents.

There was little I could do about that. In the aftermath of the wedding banns having been read at the compound, I found myself incommunicado with the outside world once again. I found a calm center of the universe in knuckling under to my work and my studies, and tried to stay out of Asia's way as much as I could until such time as that became impossible. I didn't know what her destiny in the pack would have been had I not turned up – but the fact of the matter was that I *had* turned up, and the choices I had made had ended up turning her own world upside down, and for what that was worth, I regretted it. But there seemed to be little point in sharing those regrets. It had been a cool and calculated choice on my part to become a wolf, to be in this place, to learn the things I could learn here – and short of blowing all that up now by doing something stupid I had painted myself into this corner all by myself. If I was sorry that my choice had trapped someone like Asia in the same corner... that had to be my own burden. Things were what they were.

On the morning of the Saturday following the August Turn, Asia and I met outside the doors to the main hall of the Lycan compound and waited for our signal. She had her hair up, which emphasized the thinness of her face, and three small white rosebuds had been threaded into the braid which was wrapped around her chignon. She was beautiful.

If she had looked up at me at all, she could have read that thought on my face, in my eyes. But she did not. She kept her eyes downcast, resting on a spare bouquet of white roses and a spray of some tiny white flowers tied together with a lace ribbon which she dangled loosely in her right hand. It was only as the doors opened before us, our signal to enter, that she finally looked up, and met my eyes, briefly. What was in them was something that burned quietly deep in the background - defiance, resentment, even anger – a strong feeling but one which was banked, and buried, and was being dealt with as best she knew how. But there was also something else, something that I wasn't expecting, something that rocked me back. A touch of pity.

"Well, then," she said quietly as the doors began to ease open, "here goes."

Her eyes had slid away again, but she offered me her free hand, the one minus the bouquet. I took it almost automatically; our fingers closed around each other's, and I felt her give me a brief, perhaps reassuring, squeeze. And then she stepped forward and, perforce, if I didn't want to make my entrance stumbling into the room while being dragged by my bride like a small child purposefully directed by its mom, fell into step beside her. We walked down the length of the room, past chairs in which the rest of the clan was sitting in silence, and stopped before an officiant standing beside a folding table on which rested the impedimenta of the occasion – a handful of fat white candles, a book with a white satin bookmark, a small wooden box which stood open to reveal a pair of rings on a blue velvet cushion.

I think I remember the moment when the rings were exchanged – Asia's long competent fingers slipping mine onto my left hand, my own fumbling and unsteady scramble to do the same to her in return – and then it was done, and I stood there feeling dizzy and disoriented, barely hearing the final words that sealed this new reality into being.

Asia lifted her head and brushed her lips against mine.

"It will be all right," she whispered against my mouth.

And then we had to turn, and face them all.

It will be all right.

The words were searingly familiar. It was what I had been thinking while I sat in the back of Yuri Volkov's car on my way to the compound, that first time, to begin a new life. That new life appeared to have looped back to yet another beginning. And the words, again. This time in another voice. The same promise.

I found myself wondering, walking out of that room with Asia at my side, if either of us really knew what those words even meant.

There was a buffet lunch laid on for the occasion, and family members – this was my family, I was now literally related, if only by proxy, to at least Yuri's half of it – milled about balancing plates and wine glasses. Asia was swept away from me by her mother Veronica and the Volkov girls, Yuri's daughters, with Anna Cotton, the senior Second Family daughter, on the fringes of the circle. I somehow found myself being surrounded by the senior members of the pack – Yuri and Sofia, Sam Cotton, and Tom Manion, who might have been my father-in-law had the choice of my mate fallen on one of his twins instead of Asia.

Sam, setting his plate and glass down on the nearest flat surface, fished out a keycard from his inner jacket pocket and presented it to me. "Your new quarters," he said. "You and Asia have been assigned Number 301, over at the east corner. Your stuff has already been transferred; you can drop of your old key any time, just leave it on my desk."

I had anticipated something like this would happen. My sketchbook, the only thing of value that I did not want to lose, had already been taken out of my room – I had left it, not without some trepidation, under a pile of papers I was working on at my desk in the lab, taking the chance that it would be perfectly safe from prying eyes for at least a short while until my inevitable change of residence gave me a way to make a new hiding place for it, if that would even be possible in a place I shared so closely with someone else; but I figured I would cross that bridge when I had to.

"Would you like another glass of wine?" Sofia asked, in her soft accent. I stole a glance at her; there may have been an edge of something smugly triumphant in her expression, the Alpha female who had just done something of potentially great benefit to her pack, but she also looked just a little bit sympathetic... or maybe that was just imagination and wishful thinking.

"Sure," I said, and she smiled, stepping away to fetch one.

"We will let you two settle in for a few days," Yuri said. His expression had not changed at all, he looked just as inscrutable as ever. "You have a leave of absence, you will not be expected in the labs until Monday next. It is time you can use to learn to share your lives together. I know that it might all have gone a little too fast for you, but it is for the best. For you, and for her, and for the pack."

It will be all right.

I looked across the room, at the knot of women on the far side, and caught Asia's eyes on me. I managed a small smile, and after a moment so did she, raising a hand in a little wave of acknowledgment before turning away again.

I don't know how much later it was that I realized that she was no longer there.

How she had managed to slip out without general notice – the bride, the supposed center of attention on a day like this – I'll never know; it was just Asia. She was good at unexpected things. My own attempts to do the same thing didn't go quite as well, but eventually I succeeded in convincing Yuri and Sam that I'd had a lovely time at the party, thanks, and that now it was time to go.

I swung by the lab on the way to the new quarters whose key was burning a hole in my jacket pocket, and it was thankfully deserted – everyone else was apparently still at the revels – and retrieved the sketchbook from underneath the papers on my desk. It did not look as though it had been discovered or investigated, and probably it would have been quite safe if I had just left it there, but they did tell me that I was on furlough for a week and I didn't want to trust it out of my direct control for that long. I didn't quite know what I was going to do with it if I found Asia in our new apartment when I turned up there with the sketchbook in hand – we might have just been married but I was far from ready to reveal the sketches to her – but I thought I could deal with that if I was faced with it.

But Asia was not in the apartment.

I found a spot to stash the book away, at least for the time being – it could always be fine-tuned once I learned Asia's habits more closely – and then explored this new place for a little while. It was itchy, like a new sweater, not comfortable yet, not known. My feelings still ran more towards those of a wary visitor careful not to disturb anything because the real owners might return and be very annoyed at me than they did to a sense of being *home*.

It was finally borne upon me, however, that I had been alone here for more than an hour, on the aftermath of my wedding and my own wedding reception, and that I had absolutely no clue where my new bride was, or if she was ever coming back to this new *home* that we were supposed to be sharing now.

It will be all right, she had said. She had whispered it like a shared secret. Right there in front of them all. I could only hope that sometime between that moment and now something had not happened to change her mind... and I refused to entertain the possible fallout of that, for either of us.

I considered, very briefly, the idea of going out to try and look for her – and then dismissed it. I would not know where to begin, and it would not look well at all if the bridegroom of the day was found drifting alone through the corridors of the main compound, calling his wife's name. Until it became impossible to do so, all I could do was wait... and hope.

At some point I became aware that the tension I had been carrying in my shoulders for days now had been tipped, by this latest issue, into a full-blown tension headache which gripped my temples and the back of my neck in a vise which tightened with each passing moment. I paced; and when that became too much because it hurt to move, I lay down on the couch in the new apartment's small sitting room... and then I must have simply passed out, fallen asleep, closed my eyes and had time slip away from me, because when I blinked back into some sort of consciousness it was full dark outside, there was a single lamp lit in the sitting room that cast a diffuse glow of warm yellow light, and Asia was curled up in the armchair next to the couch, staring at me.

Her hair was down, and she appeared to be wearing nothing more than an oversized faded pink T-shirt which must have come to halfway down her knees when she was standing, now draped across her body in soft folds which spoke of a well-loved garment softened by many washings. In the yellow half-light, her eyes were huge in her face, the green irises almost obliterated by the black holes of her pupils.

"Hi," she said.

I sat up on the couch, swinging my feet down to the floor, at the same time rubbing the bleariness out of my eyes. The remnants of the headache were still there, a darkness behind my eyes. "Hi," I said, very carefully. "I was... sorry. I think I fell asleep. Where have you been?"

I regretted the question as soon as I uttered it. I did not want to start things on this note. But she took it at face value.

"Walking," she said. "I'm the one who should apologize. I should never have left you dangling out here by yourself. It isn't your doing, any of it."

"I never heard you... when did you... how long have you been back? Why didn't you wake me?"

"Long enough," she said. "I've been watching you sleep, actually. There was a frown line etched into your face for a bit, and then you smiled, just a little... what were you dreaming about?"

"I can honestly say I have no idea," I said. I didn't have any recollection of having done so I must have taken my watch off my wrist at some point because it was not there when I stole my habitual glance at it. "What time is it?"

She actually laughed softly at that. "Later than we both realize, probably," she said. "Are you coming to bed?"

I felt the blood rush to my cheeks at that innocuous phrase, I could not help it. Here, in this place, in this moment, those words buckled and cracked under the weight of all the baggage that they carried.

Asia uncurled her long bare legs from the chair and got to her feet, holding out a hand to me.

"Come on," she said. "This night has to happen. It's probably best if we just close our eyes and jump in."

"Do we have to close our eyes?" I asked.

We actually exchanged a smile, at that. A real one. Perhaps the first real one we had shared.

The Lycans did things differently. The first time I had taken part in a Lycan Turn, here in the compound, it had been embarrassing and awkward because I was so used to modesty being preserved by the Turning Cloaks in which we were all ceremonially clad back in the Turning Rooms my father had built at the house. I'm afraid I must have probably broken protocol in many ways I was not even aware of because I *must* have stared, because it was so foreign to see all the members of the pack, from first-Turned to grizzled elders, step naked into the Turning habitat without even thinking about it. But it made sense, in this context, in the context of the pack, and it had quickly become something I completely accepted and became a part of.

Asia and I had seen each other naked. Not for long, certainly, and only for the less-than-handful of the Turns I'd shared with the pack since I became Lycan. But on those occasions... it had been – or it had very quickly become – something completely irrelevant. We were not two naked human beings; we were two creatures on the cusp of becoming two wolves, our mind and our spirit already on the way to that crossover, our human skins no more than that – just skins, just an outer covering, a shape that became less meaningful with every second of the Turn until it ceased to be relevant at all.

It was electrically different in this bedroom, our new bedroom, on this night, when she pulled her pink T-shirt over her head, and then wearing nothing but her own skin, peeled away my own clothes. Wolves were nowhere; we were deeply, vulnerably, *nakedly* human, just the two of us, alone together, alone, together. Asia's body was astonishing – she was slender but full-figured for all that, with curves in all the places which needed curves. Her skin was sun-warmed where it had been touched by sun and wind and rain, but an unexpected shade of pale cream in hidden places I had not really looked at before; I traced the thin white line of an old scar than curved down the side of her left knee, and marveled at the softness of the skin on the inside of her wrist, on the curve of her hip, in the hollow of her throat. Her fingers, strong and gentle, mapped the myriad of scars my own body bore, from all the battles I had been in the alleys behind the school, in the streets; she questioned, with a wordless touch, the lump where the bones of my broken arm had knit ever so slightly crooked, and seemed to heal with a brush of fingertips wounds that were content to forget having ever existed for the reward of her touch. We did not ask questions of one another, not this night, nothing that had gone before really mattered in the darkness of the room with only that golden light from the sitting room ghosting in through the bedroom door. We did not have to face the future until the sun rose into a new day in the morning; our past was a different country whose borders we had just left behind; there was nothing except the two of us, tangled together in that bed, where finally we slept the sleep of the exhausted in the dark hours before dawn.

It was back to a certain amount of wariness the next day, when we woke almost in the same moment, wrapped in twisted bedclothes and each other. Asia looked at me, from under the circle of my arm which lay across her shoulder, and smiled, pushing wild curly hair out of her eyes.

"I'll make breakfast," she said.

It will be all right.

We adjusted. We were not ready to make grand plans, if we ever would be, and we had certainly not told one another all our deepest secrets, and might never do so – but on a day-today basis we were now a mated pair in Yuri and Sofia's pack; Asia's status, no matter how suspect it might have been in some respects, had rubbed off on me and I was already a step up on the hierarchy ladder, which meant that Rory Cotton was back to being the Omega of the pack, and didn't much like that.

I was working on the rest of it, on my own, working hard both at my studies and in the lab, and perhaps that was made easier in a way because I now had Asia on hand to ask about concepts which were difficult for me to get my head around. At any rate, I made sufficient progress for Sam Cotton to make a point of telling me that Dr. Goswamy had reported being astonished and delighted at the rate of my progress.

If anyone expected Asia and I to produce an instant family, a child whose genetics the Volkov labs could investigate and index and annotate, the child who would prove that both Asia's line and my own were genuine and true Lycan bloodlines, they remained disappointed. Another Turn came and went without anything to report in that department, and then, maybe a week before the Moon reached full in October, Asia came looking for me in the lab again.

I was in the incubator room, poring over some cultures, when she opened the heavy insulated door a crack and motioned me outside. I sighed, put the culture bottle I had been inspecting back in its rack, and emerged into the lab proper peeling off my gloves.

"What?" I said, a little testily. "I need to get this done by..."

"Field trip," Asia said. "Sorry. You're it. It's an overnight trip, this time – I have the RV. We leave in an hour."

A chill finger touched me right there at the top of my spine, and I shivered. "Turning House? Again?"

"I need..."

I glanced outside. "Ash," I said, "you're talking about an overnight trip and the Turn is just around the corner. Maybe this isn't the time..."

She glared at me, the way only Asia could. "I leave it until after the Turn, I lose two weeks' work," she said. "We'll be back in plenty of time. I said it's an overnight trip, not a week's junket – we'll be out of here today, we'll spend the night at the Turning House – comfortably, in our own RV – and we'll be done there the next morning, and back here by tomorrow night – and even if we have to stop over another night on the way, in a worst case scenario, we're still home with three days to spare. Now come on – the sooner we go the sooner we get back."

She strode off without waiting for a reply, and I rolled my eyes at nobody in particular and then turned to Sasha Volkov, who was working at his own bench a few paces away and had of course once more been witness to the whole thing, and Wilfred Sand, the taciturn floater Lycan who had joined our team only a handful of days before and about whom I knew little else other than his name and an almost obsessive work ethic.

"I have stuff..." I began, gesturing at the incubation room, and Wilfred nodded brusquely.

"I'll keep an eye on it," he said.

I scribbled a few hurried notes of instructions and left them on Wilfred's desk, shrugged out of my lab coat, and stomped off to the apartment to throw a change of underwear and a clean T-shirt and my toothbrush into a bag. In what was almost a replay of our previous expedition, Asia waited in our vehicle by the time I emerged from the front door to the compound. I climbed into the passenger seat, not in a very happy mood, and slammed the door a little harder than perhaps I had intended.

"What now?" I said. "Ran out of genome?"

She eased the RV into gear and turned it into the driveway, heading out.

"Actually, there are apparently a number of people in this particular House – all of them recent arrivals – who match my criteria perfectly," she said.

"It couldn't wait? Really? You're cutting it very fine, and if you start Turning on the road, I can't drive this thing."

She laughed. "Well, since you'd be wolf, too, no, I would guess you would find driving difficult," she said. "But like I said. Plenty of time. And if I get back quickly and start something going before the Turn I'll have results by the time I get back to the lab after the change. And I'm *this* close to something, and I can't wait another two weeks to start this protocol." She glanced at me out of the corner of her eye. "I'd better warn you, though, this one's different than that other one you saw. Bigger. More people."

"How many?"

"A couple of hundred, here, I think," Asia said.

I flinched. "How many are there?" I asked quietly. "In all the Houses? All of them? All the...Half-Souled?"

"Hard to say," Asia said. "Numbers change, quickly. But there are *many* Turning Houses. A lot of damaged people live there. Sometimes they're the only 'staff' on the premises, in some of the smaller Houses – and every Turning House has to have a minimum staff of at least forty warm bodies to run it. But that's the bare minimum. I don't think there are many that have *just* the minimum complement. Sometimes... like with this one, where we're headed... about a year ago, when I was last there, it had some seven hundred people living there. It's a little village, all by itself."

"*Seven hundred?*" I echoed, and a convulsive shiver shook my shoulders as I stared out at the road unspooling ahead of us. "How do seven hundred people end up... like this? What on Earth happened to them all?"

"Things happened, and things keep happening," Asia said. "I don't know what the turnover is, how many of the ones I've seen there before are still there now. But it doesn't stop. New people are always coming in – here, at all the Houses."

"Is anybody studying *that*?" I asked. "I mean, look at this, we are losing true Were into this weird half-dead state, all the time, and you're telling me that it just keeps happening and nobody knows how, or when, or who? Could it just ... happen to anyone? To you? To me?"

"Probably," Asia said. "There's never been a cause nailed down. It's different for most everyone."

I watched the world out of the window in silence while Asia drove. On the trees that lined the road we were on, the leaves were turning; we were in the middle of Golden October, as Celia used to call it, once upon a time, so long ago, back when we were children together and I was still young enough to like it when she told me stories. Stuff she made up, spun out of the air, just kept talking – it was something that calmed me in those early days when Mom and Dad had to leave us, to go to the Turning Houses. I hadn't thought about that for years, but the combination of the season and the nature of my destination, not to mention the fact that I had quickly realized that we were headed almost directly towards the town and the house which I had last left as a new-hatched young Lycan on my way to the compound, had shaken the memory loose from some hidden shadowed place and it was vivid, sharp, unexpectedly painful. I felt tears spring into my eyes, and blinked them furiously away, keeping my head turned so that Asia would not see.

I had not told her about Celia. I was not ready to start telling her now.

The October day, gloomy with a bleached-looking sky through which light but not sunshine filtered down into the world, eventually faded – first to a muddy grey dusk, and then into an impenetrable darkness barely pierced by our own headlights or those of the occasional car coming from the opposite direction which loomed large and then passed behind us into the night. I stirred, in the end, and stretched, stiff from the long drive.

"Are we there yet?" I asked, in the whiny voice of a bored two-year-old.

"Almost," Asia said, sounding tired. "The GPS says another half hour or so."

It was closer to an hour, in the end, but eventually we turned into another unmarked side road just like the one that had led to the other Turning House we'd visited. This one also led past a circle of that outer perimeter fence, its red baleful eyes even weirder and scarier than they had been in the daylight in the other place, and then through a gate in an inner fence, and onto a road that quickly began to have low bungalows to both sides of it, buildings with bright lights above their front doors and at each corner of every house, some showing glimmers of inside lights through not-quite-closed curtains. Asia threaded her way through these until we were finally past them and headed towards a complex of bigger, multi-storied buildings with parking lots, now largely empty, before them. Asia maneuvered the RV into a spot where it would cause the least possible obstruction, and turned the engine off with a sigh of relief.

"That's the main administration building," she said. "They have been told to expect us; I suppose someone is waiting. I'll go check in with them, but we'll start real work in the morning."

I got up from the passenger seat, pressing the palms of my hands against my own temples.

"Fine. I need to stretch my legs."

"Don't wander off," she said. And somehow the words, innocuous enough in themselves, assumed an air of warning when uttered in this place, in this dark hour.

"Don't worry," I muttered, "I wouldn't dream of it."

She was away for twenty minutes or more; I walked a little way – but not too far – across the grass lawn bordering the parking lot and peered into the darkness; the moon was not full, but it was waxing, and somewhere off in the near distance I thought I could see it glint off water. I was still peering at this and trying to parse the shadowy landscape by the time Asia returned and called me back into the RV.

She slept, there beside me in the narrow double bed of the RV, but something kept me awake for a very long time. I lay still, trying not to toss and turn too much and wake her up, but my mind was restless and almost preternaturally aware. I could hear sounds outside the RV – the cry of a night bird, something that might have been a distant chorus of frogs. If I closed my eyes, images danced against my closed eyelids, memories I did not want to deal with, insistent and strong enough to trigger the echoes of associated sound (Celia's voice, children's laughter...) and taste (cookies and milk, the thing that they used to bribe me with when I was young and fretful and loath to let go of my nightmares and go back to sleep). It must have been hours later that I finally drifted off into a restless sleep, and a very short time after that that I was gently shaken awake.

"I made coffee," Asia said. "There's bagels."

"I'll be right there," I said. "Let me wake up."

She drew back, into the kitchen area, fussing with something on the counter, and I crawled out of the rumpled bed and cast around for my clothes. I was handed coffee and half a bagel smeared with cream cheese. As I made myself presentable, I grumbled because Asia insisted there was work to do.

"You said you just needed a day," I said grumpily.

"Yes, and you were the one worrying about what would happen if we ran late," Asia said. "So come on, get a move on. The sooner we start the sooner we're out of here."

"I still wish you'd left it till after the Turn," I muttered, gulping down the last of the coffee.

"On the bright side, they're used to dealing with Turned Were in this place, come the full moon," Asia said. It was black humor, and I shook my head, without turning around to look at her.

"Don't. Even."

"No, I'm not going to let them have a go at my wolf," Asia said. "But I do have a contingency plan. I brought a supply of Adaptadyne that can..."

Before I knew what I was doing, I had spun around to face her and my hand had lifted, open palmed, to strike her.

I froze, mid motion, and she recoiled and then did the same. We stared at one another, shocked, and then I dropped my hand, reached out to her.

"Ash..."

She took a step back, raising both her hands in a warding off motion; she was closer to the door, and another few paces would have seen her fleeing the RV – and I knew that if I let her do that something irreparable

309

would have lodged between us, something that we might never have shifted. My hand shot out and closed around her wrist, but gently, and I said,

"Wait. Listen. There are things you do not know about me. There are things... Adaptadyne... I had a sister. Back when I was not yet a wolf, back when I was just that Random boy who could not Turn. My older sister did, and she... it's a long story... I ..."

She snatched her hand loose and stared at me, her eyes still dilated with shock.

"What's that got to do with anything...?"

I dropped my hands to my sides. "For some reason I've been thinking about her a lot, just as we were coming here. Our house is only a few more hours' drive away from here, and it all came back, all the... Ash... she needed to stay, to delay a Turn, and it was me... I raided my mother's supply of Adaptadyne. I didn't have the first clue about what the different kinds of pills meant, I grabbed whatever was there – I only learned afterwards that there were tablets and then there were the extended-release tabs which were four times the dosage – but I gave them to my sister, and she took them... and she died. It nearly broke us, Ash. It nearly destroyed my family. And it was my fault. And it was Adaptadyne. I don't want to see you... I don't want to..."

"We'll talk about this later," she said, through bloodless lips, and her eyes slid away from mine. "Get the kit. It's in the closet."

This time, when she turned towards the door, I made no move to stop her. Instead, I obeyed her instructions, and followed her outside.

We didn't speak as we trudged across the parking lot and into the main building, not as she began her work with the dozen or so men and women who had been lined up for her, barely (and then only the essentials) as we shared a lunch that had been brought for us while we took a break from the sample collecting and collating, and again not at all as she finished up with the remaining Half-Souled candidates after the break. It was in silence, hurting and knowing she was hurting but not knowing how to bridge the sudden chasm between us, that I helped pack away her paraphernalia when she was done.

This was not the way I had wanted her to find out about the darkest thing I had done in my life. Not by compounding my errors by compromising what might have been a rare good card that had been dealt to me in the chaotic and what sometimes seemed outright malevolent hand that had been my life so far. There had to have been a better time and place for spilling dark secrets than the moment in which this one had happened, in which I had only barely stopped myself in time from delivering a flat-palmed slap the force behind which – I knew, I could feel it behind the swing of my hand – would have snapped her head back on her shoulders if it had connected. Guilt and pain could give great strength if they were allowed free rein, and the load of guilt I carried had been a crushing one for years.

I had never forgiven myself for Celia. I could not. And I could not forgive anyone else. In one way my going Lycan was a path to gaining knowledge that might work to erase some of that guilt. In another way, it was my penance for what I had done.

But all of that was a great wordless cloud inside my mind. I quailed from even looking into its depths, never mind distilling something coherent from that soup, something I could use to lay in front of Asia and try and at least explain.

When I heard a voice off somewhere behind me as we were walking out of that building, a voice which was calling out Celia's name – no, not *Celia's* name, her other name, her cradle-name, the name by which I had first known my older sister – I actually thought for a moment that I must have gone so deep into the guilt that I was literally hallucinating.

But no.

It came again.

"Svetlana! Svetya! No! Come back here!"

I stopped dead in the corridor, my head swiveling from side to side, trying to pinpoint the direction from which the voice had come. Asia, aware that I had halted, paused and turned her head, just barely, just enough to glance back over her shoulders.

"What?"

"Wait – I thought I heard – "

"*Svetya*! Leave that!"

I laid the kit I was carrying, with all of Asia's samples, very gently and very deliberately at my feet.

"What is it?" Asia demanded again, impatiently.

"Did you hear that?"

"Did I hear what?"

"The voice – that name – "

"I heard someone call – "

But I was already running, running back the way we had come, past doors I had ignored as I had walked past them. A number of them were closed, but one... one of them... it was ajar, just enough ajar to allow a voice, perhaps, to carry out into the corridor...

"Where are you going?" Asia called out after me, but I did not even break stride. I pushed that door open wider, stumbled into the room, and stared at the tableau inside.

A woman was sitting on a narrow bed against the far wall; crushed between her hands was a length of knitting, held awkwardly, stitches falling off one needle. Another woman knelt at her feet, trying to extract the knitting and the needles without inflicting injury on either herself or the one who clutched it.

The kneeling woman turned to look as I pushed the door open. The one sitting on the bed did not lift her eyes. Her face was partly covered by a strand of hair, escaping from one of two untidy braids which rested on her shoulders, but I did not need to see her face. I knew her. I *knew her*, and this could not be true.

This could not be true.

Celia was dead.

Svetlana, my older sister, who had once chosen the name Celia by which she would be known when she set foot in the strange new world to which her parents had taken her, was dead.

She could not be sitting here, in this room, on this bed, all these years later – all these years after I had lost her, in which I had never stopped mourning her, missing her.

"Celia." I said hoarsely, staring at her. "Celia. It's Mal."

She did not respond, and the woman kneeling on the floor rose to her feet.

"Her name isn't Celia," she said.

I tore my frozen glance off my sister, my impossibly alive sister, and let it rest briefly on the one who had spoken.

"You're right," I said, and stepped inside, going down on one knee before Celia, folding my own hands over hers where they curled around the knitting. And I spoke to her in our own language, using our old names, our true names. I called her Svetya. I called her, as Goran, her brother, from the old country.

And she responded. Slowly, very slowly, her eyes lifted from the knitting, and she released it; unheeded, it slid from her lap into an untidy unravelling heap on the floor at her feet. She whispered a word, a single word. My name. And then she reached for me, and her arms fluttered down almost nervelessly around the back of my neck as I gathered her into my arms and rocked her gently like a child.

Over the top of her head I met Asia's shocked gaze as she stood framed by the doorway. I could barely make her out, my eyes were so full of hot, desperate tears.

"What are you *doing?*" she asked, staring.

"Ash…" I managed to get it out, through a jaw so clenched that I could barely form words. "This… is my sister. *My sister is alive.*"

The Third Mask: Dead and Alive

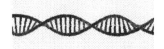

Call me Celia's brother.

I had never thought of myself as defined by that relationship – but it was more because it was so natural and instinctive, like breathing or the beating of my heart, than because I had taken the time to sit down and think through the relationship between Celia and myself in the same way that, for instance, the Lycans went about mapping out their complicated family relationships.

I tried to explain that to Asia, after she had managed to pry me away from Celia's side (if only because she made profligate promises that it would not be for long). Back at the RV, she had made a pot of strong black coffee and had then laced it with a dollop of brandy from a bottle I had not known she even had (between that and the Adaptadyne she had mentioned earlier, she'd certainly come here prepared) which, according to the letter of the law, I was certainly not old enough to drink. But the fire of it burned down my throat, and perhaps ignited an already inflammable cocktail of emotions.

She sat beside me on the hard and narrow bench beside the built-in dining table next to the RV kitchen and held one of my hands, her fingers laced through mine, to stop me from a nervous agitated gesture of dragging my hand through my hair until it was standing on end in punk-like spikes about my head, resembling nothing so much as a cartoon of a man who had just been electrocuted... and perhaps that wasn't too far from the truth. I held on to the coffee mug with the other hand as though it contained the very elixir of life.

I was very aware that that I was babbling now, that it was coming out through a breach in the dam, words gushing out and falling over one another, all the anguish and the guilt and the pain. The whole massive sense of loss that had been carefully walled away, even from myself. All the things that I had never really spoken of to anyone before. But I did not know how to stop myself.

"It was the two of us against the world," I said. "We were both so young – I was barely more than a baby – when we came here – and then, before my father solved that problem, when my parents were still bound to the Turning Houses by the law, back when it felt like I was being abandoned every time they just *left* – I was too young, way too young to understand why, laws meant nothing and places like Turning Houses could not possibly have been explained to me –and my sister and I stayed behind with strangers to feed us our supper and tuck us into bed – and it was Svetya who was always there for me. The only one who was. I learned to call her Celia, we all did, just as she dutifully called me Malcolm, especially when there was anyone else to hear – but when we were alone we used our cradle names, and talked between ourselves in the language which we had brought over with us from the old country, the only thing that we still really had from that place. I know she would have done anything for me – the same way as I would have done anything for her, *anything*, including the thing that I did, the thing that I thought all these years had killed her..."

"Adaptadyne," Asia said. "Can you tell me what happened?"

"I thought that... that I had her back, that's all. "I thought I was helping..."

And I told her about the teacher who went by the name of Barbican Bain, his petty acts of discrimination against the Were kids in his classes and his malice, how he scheduled important tests and all kinds of interesting educational activities for precisely those three days of every month that the Were students could not be attending classes. I told her how he had denied her a chance to meet the writer she admired and how she used Adaptadyne to delay her Turn for long enough to make sure she could be at that author's school visit. How I had raided my mother's stash to give Celia the pills and of what followed.

"She was afraid," I said.

"Of what?" Asia asked gently.

"Of blowing this chance, on the face of it. But it was greater than that – it was a fear of it being... like that... always," I said. "Of never being in control of her own life. Of being a puppet who danced to someone else's music, of having no *choice*, of being pushed outside into the cold and banging on a locked door all her days asking to be let in... just because someone else wanted it that way, just because someone else wanted to keep her out, and *could*. This place – this place to which we came, to which we had to adapt, which became ours because there was nowhere else to go and nobody else to be – this is a cruel world..."

"It's a cruel world everywhere," Asia said. "That's the way the world has always been."

I shook my head violently. "No. You don't understand. It was almost better, back where we were born – yes, our kind had to hide, and wear a disguise of being 'one of them', one of the normals, if we didn't want them to turn on us. We were hated, and we were feared, and they wreaked vengeance on us if they found us out. The Were lived in the shadows, we had to be careful of where and how we Turned, and if we were caught we often died – but that was a covenant both sides understood. They were afraid of the secrets which we kept – which we had to keep, if we wanted to survive! – but at least it was out in the open, there. Out here – in the land where we walk openly amongst the normals – there's an illusion of almost being one of them, almost being accepted, almost being equal, until it begins to get too close to them. And when it does then it's Turning Houses, and special ID cards, and anything to keep us branded and apart. They still hate us and fear us. They're just hypocrites."

"That's why they're in the Turning Houses," Asia said. "The ones you call Half-Souled. The ones like... like your sister. Think of how kind that world you're describing would be to them, if they were out there."

"But she was dead," I said, sounding pitiful even to myself. "She was dead. We mourned her. *I helped kill her.*"

"No," Asia said, squeezing my hand. "No, no, you did not. This was not your fault. All of this was way over your head, out of your control. But Adaptadyne..."

She paused, too long, and I finally turned to look at her. "Adaptadyne what?"

"It... the side-effects..."

"I know," I said savagely. "I read the warnings, after."

But she was shaking her head. "No. Not the stuff that made it onto the scrips that went out with the pills. There's always been more to Adaptadyne than it was considered appropriate for anyone out there to..."

"I knew that," I said. "Somehow, I knew that. That's what I came to find out. What that 'more' was. I had to know what my sister had..." Her brow furrowed, and I halted. "What?"

"What you came to find out?" she echoed.

But I shied away from *that*. It would all come out, probably – all of it – the stuff that all the careful prying and testing back at the compound couldn't get out of me I would spill willingly, because everything had changed now, everything was different – but not yet, not yet, not yet. There were things now that were more urgent, far more important.

"I have to get her out of here," I said, pushing the coffee away, feeling the fever in my blood, driven by a horrible sense that I was wasting time, wasting every moment, that Celia was still locked into that awful place – and she was *not dead*, but alive alive alive and I had to do something to get her out...

But Asia stared at me. "Get her out? Where would you take her?" she asked. "You saw – she is not even one of the more highly functioning ones – that is what sometimes happens when..." She bit down on whatever she was going to say, clamping her lips together; I knew that whatever it had been she'd been about to utter was probably important and I should pursue it but at that moment I was too focused on Celia herself.

"You think I can just *leave* her in there? Like that? Now that I know...?"

Asia grabbed for both my hands, made me subside back onto the seat from which I had almost surged.

"Let me find out a bit more," she said. "You have to realize – I know, I know, she is your sister but you saw what she was – she's there for a reason, now – let me make some inquiries – oh, we don't have *time*, the Turn is coming – we can't stay here too long – we have to be back in time for..."

I heard her words, but I seemed to be a step behind her because as she spoke them they made no sense, and I had to struggle to understand what she was saying, and when I finally did it still made no sense at all.

"Go back...? Right now? I would want to..."

"Mal," Asia said. "There is no choice in this."

"There is something I have to do first," I said, after a moment, stubbornly, digging in my heels. "I have to get home. I have to tell them. I have to let them know."

"*Now*?" Asia said. "Days before the Turn?"

"What, you think they'll let me fly back here afterwards?" I demanded. "I have to tell my family..."

"We *are* your family," Asia said sharply.

"She's my sister," I said, after a moment. "I'm sorry. But she came long before the wolves. I love her. I owe her. I cannot abandon her."

"But not now," Asia said desperately. "If the Turn catches us..."

"You were the one who wanted to rush this before the Turn came," I said.

"Well, finding out after this Turn would hardly have made a difference!" she flared, her temper catching. "But even so – although taking you back there, in the state you're in, you're liable to kill someone in that enclosure if you Turn in this frame of mind – "

"I thought we didn't carry over memories from shape to shape," I muttered.

"We don't, but we may carry emotions," Asia said, "and right now you're murderous – and I don't want to risk any of them being blindsided by a young wolf trying to pick a fight, and the pack would turn on *you* if you tried..."

"Ash," I said levelly, "I'm going home. My old home, I mean it, I have to. Maybe there's time, before the Turn. I don't know. But if you won't drive me – it's only a couple of hours away – I can't drive this thing but I'll find my way there some other way, myself. I'll *walk* if I have to. I have to do this."

She bit her lip savagely. "*Fine*. Maybe it'll calm you down, just enough. Let's go, now, and get it over with."

"What were you saying, before, about Stay and side effects?" I said, as we both stumbled towards the front of the RV, latching on to something she had begun to speak about but then turned away from.

She hesitated. "Not now," she said. "Make yourself useful, if you insist on doing this, and put your address into the GPS."

The GPS informed us that it would take two hours and seventeen minutes to get from the parking lot of the building in which I was leaving Celia – and fully a part of my soul – to the front door of my old house, and if I'd had a choice about it I would have spent that entire time pacing restlessly up and down the RV while Asia drove. She insisted that I keep to the passenger seat, buckled in and restrained, instead, but I couldn't keep still even while sitting there tied down by my seatbelt. And even if I appeared to be doing so everything in me was quivering and racing and crumbling under the emotional and physical overload. My heart was racing, and my blood roared in my ears; I caught Asia stealing glances at me from time to time and she looked worried.

"If you start to feel really weird..." she began, and gripped the steering wheel harder before going on. "Mal, it's been known for a Turn to be precipitated by agitation of some sort and you're floating on adrenaline – this is such a bad idea – "

"I'll be fine," I said, and then clenched my teeth to stop them from chattering.

"You'll tell me if you...?"

"I'll tell you," I said, although it was far from clear just how her definition of 'agitation' really differed from what had me in its grip and what she planned to do if a premature Turn *was* precipitated by something like it.

I knew this was not the world's best idea. I understood that. But I was utterly beyond caring about the consequences at this precise moment.

I directed Asia myself when it came to the last few turns, but when we finally came to a stop in the street outside the house, I could do little but sit and stare at the front door for a second or two, shivering.

"Are you all right?" Asia asked.

"Fine. I'm fine." I clicked off my seatbelt with cold stiff fingers, and pushed open the door. "How am I supposed to tell them...?"

"We can still..." Asia began, but I shook my head.

"No. I have to – I'd better just – "

I was out of the RV, stumbling down onto the road, grabbing at the front of the vehicle for support as I rounded it and scrambled past the kerb and onto the sidewalk, onto the path that led to the steps leading to the door of the house. I heard the other door slam behind me, Asia's quick footsteps as she came up behind me, and for the first time stepped back from the wheel of fire in my mind that was Celia and her fate for long enough to wonder briefly just how I was going to explain Asia to my family. But then I was at the door, and ringing the doorbell seemed to be way too inadequate for what I felt, for what I had come there to do. So I hammered on the door, with my fist, hard, as though I planned to smash my way inside.

For a while it seemed as though I was knocking in vain – as if the house was empty, with nobody inside to receive the news I had come there to bring. But then, in between two hammer blows on the door, I heard the click of the double bolt being unlocked; the door began to open, very slowly, just a crack, and then it was thrown wide by my young sister Jazz who stood there staring at me, her mouth open and her eyes wide with shock.

If I looked on the outside anything like I felt on the inside, I knew I had to be a picture to scare young children with; I was still wearing the same crumpled clothes I had had on when I'd held Celia in my arms, and I hadn't shaved in a while, and my eyes had to be rolling like a wild animal's. My hand, when I glanced down at it, was still balled into a fist, and I forced myself to relax it.

"Jazz? You on your own?"

My voice sounded hoarse, unrecognizable even to me.

"Dad's been called in for work, and Mom stepped out for supplies – Vivian's coming tomorrow, for the Turn – what are you *doing* here?" she gasped. "What's the matter? Are you all right?"

I started to take a step towards her, into the house, but staggered under

319

the wash of an unexpected wave of weariness and reached out instinctively for support. My hand closed around Jazz's wrist, wrenchingly thin and fragile in my grip, hard enough that she winced – but I was beyond caring about that.

It wasn't supposed to be this way – she wasn't supposed to be the first person to find out – she was way too young for this – but I could not stop it.

"Jazz," I said. "Jazz... I found her. I found her. She isn't gone. She..."

"What are you talking about?" she said, looking really frightened now.

I crumpled to my knees before her, on the doorstep.

"Celia," I whispered hoarsely. "I found Celia. *She is alive.*"

I heard Jazz take in one long ragged gasping breath, and then hold it, long enough that I staggered gracelessly to my feet, still holding her arm, and gathered her up into my arms. She was rigid, frozen, stiff with shock. But the act of that awkward hug broke the stasis – we had never been huggy, not really, and the strangeness of that far more humdrum act somehow broke her out of that other, deeper, shock. She squirmed in my grasp, and I let her go, and then we stood on the doorstep staring at each other wide-eyed in blank silence for a very long moment before Jazz managed to find the strength to move her feet.

"You'd better come inside," she said, and only then did her eyes slide off me, and by my right shoulder, and land on Asia, who had been standing a few steps behind me and watching the whole thing in silence.

I glanced back at her, suddenly realizing that I had brought more than one shock home to roost, and then decided that there really wasn't time to be delicate about it.

"Ash," I said, "this is my younger sister. Jazz... this is Asia. My wife."

Jazz goggled at Asia, her mouth open, and Asia, more composed, stepped up with a strange little half-smile playing about her mouth.

"I think we'd best take this conversation off the street," she murmured.

Jazz blinked, and gathered herself. "Yes," she said. "You'd better come inside."

It was strange, coming back to this house. I hadn't left it that long ago, in purely chronological terms, but already it felt like it had belonged to a different existence, an entirely different me. But I could see the ghost of that other self in the shadows, scowling, silent, choosing solitude, keeping at an arm's length the family I had now come back here to... to do what? My mind balked at it. To gather up the wreckage and glue it all together and hope that the cracks didn't show? What was I doing – what could I possibly do to change everything that had already happened, that was already part of my family's history?

But Jazz, who had closed the door behind us, now turned on me, somehow released from her stasis. Asia, at whom she stole one more long appraising glance, could wait. There was something else that had been said, something that had burned her almost as deeply as it had affected myself.

"What do you *mean*, Celia is alive...?" she demanded, grabbing one of my arms with both hands.

"The Turning House, about two hours from here," I said faintly, not entirely sure how or where I was even to begin. "She's there. I saw her."

"What were you doing at a Turning House?" Jazz demanded. "I thought you wolves..."

She stopped, darted another glance at Asia.

"Yes, we're both Lycan," Asia said. "My work involves... subjects at the Turning Houses."

"My sister?" Jazz gasped.

Asia hesitated, and shook her head. "I don't think I crossed paths with her before," she said carefully, "the girl your brother saw, whom he believes to be your sister..."

I threw her a burning glance, and she threw up her hands in a defensive gesture.

"Look," Asia said, "Mal filled me in, on some of it – and I don't know the details, or how or when she ended up there – but I have an inkling about why – the Stay cases..."

"*Cases*?" I said. "There are others?"

Asia's shoulders dropped a little, in resignation. "That was what I was trying to tell you," she said. "There are things about Stay that aren't really general knowledge. It can do everything they say it can do, but it is utterly important for the dosage to be carefully controlled. Because overdoses..." She was clearly struggling with this, it was something that was not supposed to be discussed with those outside a charmed circle, was not meant as general knowledge. Even I, as Lycan, was too new to this to know, maybe – and Jazz was certainly not inside that select group of people. And yet, clearly, even with all that as a given, Asia felt that whatever she was trying not to say was important for us to know, under the circumstances.

And suddenly I found myself in full agreement with her. "Because overdoses what?" I said, my voice sounding oddly and flatly dangerous.

"Doctors and hospitals are mandatory reporters, when it comes to anything to do with Stay," Asia said, after another long pause during which she seemed to have come to a break inside herself. She was not happy doing this, clearly, but she would do it. "Remember I told you that some of those you called Half-Souled had got there through chemical means – well, it's partly this. Stay is a great servant, when administered properly, and under medical supervision. But it's one lousy master, if it's let loose without proper oversight."

"But they send out pills in the *mail*," Jazz said. "People get their pills, and they have them, and they take them, and there aren't usually doctors living under everyone's beds."

"Yes, but those dosages are measured," Asia said.

"No, they're not – or they weren't," I countered. "There were definitely two different kinds of pills in my mother's stash. Two different dosages."

"Yes, and they were probably sent out for good reasons – but in general Stay is meted out to the public in an overwhelmingly hidebound way –

there's more rules and regulations than you even know. And it's all because it's so very useful, in so many ways, when grimly kept in check. But let it off the straight and narrow – and overdoses..."

"They can make it permanent, can't they," Jazz said, her voice gone oddly cold.

She had leaped to it faster than me, but I was not far behind. "It delays... I know it delays the Turn... Asia, what does that thing really *do*?"

"It's complicated," Asia said. "But in really basic terms – it goes back to how a Turn is triggered – "

I knew a lot more about the genetics of this now than I had mere months ago. I had been born Were but I had not really known the basics of what defined me until the Lycans pointed me at my college courses and slapped me down in the messy middle of things in the lab. I was still feeling my way around the vocabulary and the definitions, but it had not taken long for me to become fascinated by the process of it all.

Our human DNA hummed along in quite an ordinary human way, reproducing itself faithfully into replicas of itself every time a cell divided, being read and transcribed into the building blocks of the proteins and enzymes and hormones that ordered our lives, and if we were only human, merely human, that was all it would ever do.

But in the heart of the nucleus of every Were creature a small ticking time-bomb – triggered by the full moon for the great majority of us, the new moon for a few – quietly waited for three days of every month. A particular set of genes woke into brief life during this period, a transcription signal changed, and certain regions of our genome, which were under normal circumstances open for business as usual, became blocked off and completely inaccessible to transfer-RNA and messenger-RNA molecules... and our entire genome was accessed and read in an entirely different way.

For the Were-kind, the vast stretches of genetic material regarded as 'junk' DNA in an ordinary human being suddenly assumed an entirely different meaning when the genome was being read from a different starting point. We carried the genetic blueprint of an entirely different creature inside us, that of our alter ego, our other avatar, our animals selves. The 'Were-operon', as it were, went silent again after those three days, and we returned back to our human form.

"Stay... shortcircuits the entire Turn by stopping that alternative genetic reading," Asia said. "The trigger operon wakes up, produces the blocking RNAs... and finds that the drug binds them before they can bind to the proper parts of the genome to enact the necessary blocks which would lead to the change."

"That's not what it says on the thingy that comes with the pills," I said, trying to remember what I had read about the way Stay worked. I couldn't have repeated it precisely, not verbatim, but I was pretty certain that it did not mention the genetic component at all.

"Don't believe everything you see," Asia said. "There are reasons that the details aren't more widely disseminated. People might not be as ready to use the drug when it is necessary if they're scared stupid about what its method of action actually is and are not capable of understanding the details."

"I think you're underestimating people's intelligence," I said. "If it was explained..."

"She's right," Jazz said, interrupting me. "Tell someone the drug they're taking is *messing with their DNA*, and they're not that likely to volunteer to take it."

"Thank you," Asia said.

"It wasn't meant as justification," Jazz said. "Or an excuse."

Asia gave my suddenly very precocious younger sister a long look, and then dropped her gaze down to her hands, which lifted in a tiny, helpless gesture. "In any case," she said. "Stay has a carefully coded pharmaceutical half-life, not a genetic one, and so you can calculate exactly how long a specific dosage will last in preventing a Turn; if there's a natural molecule in play and the Stay wears off the natural signal is still there and it can still trigger that alternative reading. A Turn can still take place. But if Stay is present in too great a concentration, or for too long... this was originally a natural substance, not a lab-manufactured drug, and it already has a certain relationship with our DNA. Enough of it, for long enough, and that trigger operon shuts down. Permanently. It's a feedback loop..."

"Irreversibly?"

"As far as we know."

"So she might as well be dead," Jazz said, her voice so lost and full of anguish that I flinched at it as if it had been a blade cutting into my flesh. "If she can never be... herself... again..."

"That's why it's a mandatory reporter thing," Asia said. "This is... they try to scotch it before it becomes widely known."

"So they end up in the Turning Houses?" I asked.

"Some. Most. And they make perfect subjects for study, for how our genes work, we may be able to figure out what went wrong, and that will tell us a lot about what happens when the process works according to plan... and your family... she's Random... those genes..."

She clamped down again, but this was new, and I latched onto it. "What do Random Were genes have to do with it?"

"Damn it," Asia said, angry tears in her eyes. "This isn't what it sounds like."

I reached out and closed my hand around her arm. Hard. "Tell me," I said.

"You're hurting me," Asia said, wrenching herself out of my grasp. "All right, if you have to know – with Were, each of us of a certain kind carries that particular creature's genes within our own. A wolf, for you, for me; a dog, a cat, a crow. We're human, and...and *that*, that single specific other. And that's complicated enough. But a Random Were... you're.... you're potentially *everything*. And Randoms are not as commonplace as you might think. And a chance to study one..."

I lashed out at her. "You're telling us someone *took* Celia? After the Stay

323

incident was reported? Stabilized her, faked her death so that she wouldn't be looked for and there would be no commitment or consent forms to extract from a potentially reluctant family, and took her off so she could be *studied*? Like a specimen?"

Asia's head came up, a gesture of defiance. *"She had already overdosed,"* she snapped. "At least that's what you said. Nobody forced the drug on her, not the amount she took. At the levels that she must have had in her system it was already too late. She would have had to have been institutionalized somewhere, somehow, anyway. Sometimes... it is kinder..."

"Who makes these decisions?" I demanded. "You said that the reporting was mandatory – to whom do these doctors report?"

"The Lycan Council," Asia said heavily. "The Lycans control the manufacture and distribution of Adaptadyne. They are the only ones doing research in that area. We hold the patents to all of it."

I actually had to back up a few steps and subside heavily on the arm of one of the armchairs in the living room. Patches of black swam before my eyes.

"Did Yuri... know... about Celia... and who I was?" I managed to ask.

"I have no way of knowing that," Asia said. "But it's possible."

"Mal..." I had almost forgotten that Jazz was there, and her voice came as something of a shock. I shook my head to clear it, and tried to focus on her; she looked ashen, and her eyes swam with tears. She slid down to her knees at my feet and wrapped both her hands around one of mine, looking at me in earnest appeal. "Mal... you can't... you simply cannot slam Mom and Dad with this thing, not this close before a Turn... and honestly, if you present Vivian with the prospect of presiding over yet another of this family's Turn disasters, I think they'll lock her up permanently in a padded room and leave her gibbering in a corner..."

"I have to get her out of there," I said. It was a blunt statement of fact, and I had absolutely nothing to back it up with. No plan. Just a vow.

But a couple of things were already beginning to coalesce into a sense of startling helplessness as I tried to sort and assimilate all the things I had learned within the space of the past twenty four hours. One of those things was that I could trust absolutely nobody. If the Lycans were directly involved to the extent that Asia said they were, I would get annihilated if I tried to get in their way. And if the Lycans were involved then the Were authorities had to know to at least some extent of that involvement, and they would not want to tangle directly with the Lycan council either – it would be far easier to simply sweep someone like myself off the board and forget that a potential incident was ever even whispered about.

It went without saying that the normals authorities would wash their hands of the whole matter altogether. And closer to home – what Jazz had said was absolutely right. I could not involve anyone else, for the same reasons – we were all too small, too irrelevant, and if we made enough trouble probably too disposable. If I presented Celia's existence to my parents, particularly now, on the eve of a Turn during which they could do nothing in any event, I would merely be expanding the sphere of helpless fury which already held me in its grip. The shape of the person – the only person – to whom I could perhaps turn to was something that apparently came to Jazz and myself in the same instant.

"You could call your friend. The weird one. Saladin."

Yes. Saladin. Chalky, who had helped me become who I was, who was part of the reason I had found out about Celia in the first place. Chalky, who knew so much, who had connections, who might know where to jump next.

Jazz had said it first, but the name had already trembled at the edges of my own mind. I instinctively reached for my phone, and then, glancing at Asia, thought the better of it.

"I'll call him from the landline," I said. "I don't want anything on this phone... that the Lycans can trace."

Asia actually flinched and dropped her gaze to stare down at the toes of her shoes. I knew I was punishing her, for everything, just because she happened to be one of *them* right now and because she was here and available; I knew I was being unfair. I felt a stirring of a distant need to apologize for that. But if I had to grovel, I would do it later.

In any event, she wasn't the kind to stay down for long. I had barely got the phone in my hand before she crossed over to me and put a hand over my own where it cradled the phone.

"Mal. We don't have time. Not now. Do you realize just how close we're cutting it...? Full moon rises tomorrow night; if we leave *right now* we can't get back to the compound before late tonight, if we leave much later we'd have to drive through the night just to make sure to get there in time and even then there's no guarantees... and in any event..." She bit her lip, dropped her hand. "You're on the edge," she said. "You are so close to the edge. High emotions can sometimes do that, and you – you're – I'm not even sure I'd completely trust you not to Turn sometime during the drive back, right there in the RV, and go for my throat... it may be too late even now..."

"There's the Turning Rooms," Jazz said, wide-eyed.

"Yes, and you know how well that turned out last time," I said, wincing as I remembered the state of the Turning Room after my own first wolf Turn in it. And now there would be two wolves – or perhaps one wolf per room in two rooms – either way, the mess would be exponentially worse.

I hesitated for a moment, and then grimly dialed Chalky's number. Perhaps he'd have an answer for this, too. But Asia...

"I'm sorry," I said. "This is just something – if you want to make a run for it, go. If I have to make a plan..."

"Don't be silly," she said, staring at me. "I'm not leaving you here like this."

I heard the phone click, and a mechanical female voice inform me that the person I had called was not available, but if I left a message... But Chalky always screened the calls he received, even on this phone number, known only to people who really needed to know it.

"Pick up," I said into the phone when the beep told me that I could talk. "It's me. And it's urgent."

It took almost too long – almost long enough for me to think, with a sinking feeling, that this one time Chalky really might have meant it about leaving a message. But then I heard another click, and his voice.

"Dude," he said. "What's up? Where are you?"

"I'm at my old house. But I have to get out of here, fast, before my parents..." I glanced at the clock on the kitchen wall, inexorably measuring out seconds with a ticking bright red second hand. "Can we meet?"

"Food court. Fifteen minutes."

"We'll be there."

"We?" Chalky said, in a raising-his-eyebrow kind of tone.

"Explain there. Go."

He did not waste any more time. The phone went dead. I handed it back to Jazz.

"Thanks," I said. "Better get going."

"You can't just *leave* me..."

"I have to go, you yourself said we don't want Mom and Dad blundering into this, or Vivian. But if I need to..."

"Dammit, Mal!" Her eyes darted from me to Asia, and then back again. "Look, if the worst comes to the worst – promise me you'll come back here – we can sort out something downstairs – "

"I'll call you," I said.

"No. I'm coming with you," Jazz said obstinately, her face flushed. "You can't walk in here and tell me that Celia... that we... and then walk straight out again, without any... you *can't*. I'm not staying here and waiting – you'll *never* call me back, you so know you won't – and I need to know – "

"And when Mom comes home?"

But she was already scribbling a note on the back of an envelope which had been lying on the kitchen counter – I glimpsed large sloppy capitals as she propped it up against the coffee maker – GONE TO MALL WITH NELL.

"Really?" I said. "This close to Turn?" Things had changed in this household if Jazz could just waltz out of here with a note on the counter as the only explanation for her absence.

"We don't have time for this," Asia said. "Who's this guy you're calling?"

"A friend. We'll make the time. Come on, we need to get that RV out of here."

Asia stared at me mutely for a beat, and then turned and walked toward the front door, sorting her keys out in her hand.

"I will pay for this one," she muttered.

"Not your fault," I said, falling into step behind her.

"Oh yes it is. This is my responsibility. *You* are my responsibility. This is my research trip and whatever happens it's my screw-up."

Perhaps the time was now, after all. "Asia. I'm sorry."

"Don't be," she said, without looking at me. "Do what you have to. Just do it *fast*."

She didn't understand. How could she? But she was standing by me – even if it potentially meant facing down the rest of the wolves when we got back to the pack, and taking the heat for this sudden irrational compulsion of mine.

We might have been an odd pair, mismatched and mated by others, but in that moment something warm and unexpected surged through me. Gratitude, maybe. I did not know if it would be presumptuous to call it love.

We all piled into the RV and I directed Asia to the mall where we were supposed to meet Chalky. It took us a few extra minutes to find a parking spot for the rather bulky RV, and that made us late – Chalky was already waiting as we walked into the crowded food court. He looked relaxed, almost bored, slouching at the table and apparently playing with his phone with a half-drunk soda in front of him – but I, who knew him, could tell that he was hyper-alert, and in fact we had barely stepped into the food court hall before his eyes, laser-like, zeroed in on us, and met mine.

"Mal," he said by way of greeting, as Asia and I took our seats across the table from him, taking a brief moment to glance sideways at Jazz as she slid onto the bench on the far side of him and give her a slight nod of acknowledgment. "I didn't expect to see you back here. Not for a while anyway. Not in person. How are the wolves treating you?"

"Hi," Asia said, a little testily. "I'm one of them."

Chalky gave her a long apprising look, one of his mobile eyebrows halfway to his hairline.

"And what are you two fine Lycans doing so far from home so close to Turn?" he inquired.

Asia lost the staring match, taking the time to glance back at me.

"As to that," I said, "we were hoping you had some ideas. We are kind of cutting it very fine, here. But Asia's a researcher back at the Lycan genetics labs."

Both Asia and Chalky reacted to that bald statement, in their own way, but I had no time to tiptoe around any of this. "It's her work that brought us out... we were at the Turning House, the one about two hours' drive from here.... Chalky... Celia is there. She's alive. She's... damaged... she's lost the ability to Turn... Ash says the Stay overdose... but I'll fill you in on that later."

"Hey," Asia said sharply, leaning forward. "Look, I have no idea who you really are – but Mal – some things – "

"The Lycans know how to keep their secrets," Chalky said, "but there are people out here who already know more than you suspect. And I do mean to..."

"I need to get her out of there," I interrupted. "I need to... make a plan. Somehow. If you have any ideas on that subject – but it's going to have to wait until after – Ash, how much time do we – "

She shook her head. "I don't know. I really don't know if we can make it back. The precise moment of Turn... is not an exact science. And right now, nothing is too certain."

"Wait, do I understand that you two are skating close to Turn... and are out of the Lycan nest?" Chalky said, sitting up.

I exchanged looks with Asia, mine helpless, hers resigned. "It's all my fault," I said, "after I saw Celia it was all I could think of to come here, to come home, to tell Mom and Dad about it, to let them know that she's alive and that all those years of mourning could be put away at last... but Jazz is right, at the very least my timing is appalling. I can't do it now, not right before the Turn, and then leave it hanging, and then Ash said something... about the whole set-up... I don't know who I can trust any more, who needs telling, and if anyone at all can do anything about any of it...I have a horrible feeling that whatever I do now I can only make things worse..."

Asia reached out and briefly covered my hand with hers. Chalky noticed – he never failed to notice anything – but chose not to comment on it. Instead, he focused on the more immediate problem.

"So you need a safe space to Turn?"

Jazz, white-faced and obviously hating herself for even saying it, whispered, "But you were already at the Turning House..."

I flinched, instinctively, but Asia was already shaking her head. "They aren't set up for the likes of us."

"They have predators," Chalky pointed out. "It would be a matter of adjusting..."

"No. Wolves are... kind of special. I would never get the clearance to go to a Turning House for a Lycan Turn. And if I'd made the decision to stay there, to do that anyway, there would have been *consequences*."

"Is there another pack nearer than yours?" Chalky asked quietly. "Somewhere you can beg for sanctuary?"

Asia shook her head.

"And you don't think you can make it back before it's too late...?"

"It might come down to me driving the RV down the highway while trying to fend off a frustrated wolf," Asia said. "If it didn't come down to nobody driving the RV at all because both of us might have... we'd kill ourselves. I don't know – " she stole another glance at me, and her gaze was worried. "I don't know if I can trust him not to stay unTurned for another day."

"But if you're right, that means no public option. No Turning House. Not even a large predator center – yes, there is one of those around here, they don't exactly advertise, for obvious reasons, but those who need to know where to find it are kept in the loop."

"Large predators?" Jazz asked.

"There aren't that many of them," Chalky said. "But yes. I believe they cater to a number of large cats, for a start. Maybe a couple of bears."

Asia was staring at him, frowning. "And are you one of them?"

"Sometimes," Chalky said laconically, and left it at that. I could see Asia's mind trying to latch onto this but fail. But Chalky's secrets were his own and besides this was no time to go into long personal histories.

"There's always the Turning Rooms, back at our house," Jazz said. "But Mal already said – and then there's the fact that we'd have to let Mom and

Dad and Vivian in on the whole thing anyway – I just don't know if they can safely do it, there, two of them..."

"Then we need to find somewhere that is big enough to contain..."

"Wait," Jazz said, flatly interrupting Chalky as though she had been completely oblivious that he was speaking, whipping out her phone and dialing frantically. "If anyone knows, the Corvids will – they're in charge, they'll run things, and if there's an alternative – Nell? It's Jazz. Listen – no, wait, don't talk – I need to ask you..."

Chalky turned away from the conversation, leaning forward towards Asia and myself and dropping his voice.

"*Celia*," he said. "Tell me. Was this something your lot had anything to do with?" That last, directly to Asia; and I suddenly felt moved to rise up in defense.

Not, perhaps, of the Lycans themselves. But of *her*. She and I... were a team, no matter how much rationalization had gone into the match in the first place.

"Hey," I said, "they're my lot now, too."

"You weren't supposed to go native," Chalky said.

Asia laced her fingers together, tilting her head at Chalky in a manner that signified that she was willing to meet him on a battlefield – but there was something about the set of her shoulders that spoke to me alone – there was a set to them, a rigidity, that said volumes of how much it was costing her to maintain the position of defense and defiance.

But Jazz had shifted the phone, putting her conversation on hold, and reached out to tap my hand.

"Nell says her Uncle Sebastian owns a summer house, lakeside, up in the hills," she said. "It's got a few other cottages scattered around, but mostly there's lots of room – and there are woods directly behind, national forest – and it's empty, this time of year. Or mostly empty. Few enough witnesses, anyway. And most important of all she can get the keys – she says they aren't too happy about her leaving the house right now, too close to Turn and all that, same problem you two are having, but we can pick them up at her place, just give her half an hour..."

"I know the area," Chalky said, "it might do. But you're not getting up there in an RV, not on those narrow roads." He fished out a battered notebook, tore out a page, and looked up expectantly. "Anyone got a pen? Thanks. Jazz, tell Nell I'll be by to pick up the keys. Mal, here, take this – " he thrust the short note he had written on the notebook page in my direction, and the pen back at Asia, who had supplied it. "Take the RV to the campground, you know where it is. Give that note to the guy who runs the place, ask him for the last hookup spot at the back, the last one in the long-term positions, the one out of sight behind the trees – he'll know. He's a sort of friend of mine. Go there, and wait – I'll swing by with the keys and the car as soon as I can, and we can go straight up there."

"What about *me*?" Jazz said.

"You go home; I can drop you off on the way. *Everybody* go home and find a space to lie low. I seriously don't want to be riding herd on a bunch

of rowdy just-Turned Were loose in the streets. As for the rest of it..."
Chalky gave both Asia and myself a long steady look. "Let's get this sorted
out," he said. "We can discuss... everything else... when we aren't quite so
pressed for time."

Jazz looked mutinous, but Chalky was right, we all needed to pull in the
same direction

"Do you think we should call them, back at the compound? To check in?
To try and stall?" I asked Asia quietly, on our way out of the mall.

"Probably," she said wearily, "but I can't possibly explain on the phone
and if they tell me to ignore everything else and just get in the RV and
drive then if I don't then it'll be disobeying a direct order from Yuri and
that would probably be *worse* than when I go back and try to blame it all
on the lack of my own better judgment..."

"Asia... what *are* you going to tell them? How much of it?"

"You mean will I spill about your sister?"

"Could she... be in danger?"

Asia looked at me helplessly. "I don't know, Mal. Honestly. I don't
know."

Chalky whisked Jazz off to his own car as we came out of the mall into
the parking lot. I directed Asia to the RV park as directed, and then we
waited. It took Chalky almost forty five minutes to get there, and he barely
stopped long enough for us to come out of the RV and lock it up and pile
into the back of the car before he spun the wheel and drove back out of the
park and then towards the north of town, out to where the road climbed up
towards the lake.

There wasn't much talking, each of us preoccupied with our own
thoughts; I barely noticed the miles slipping by, still sifting through my
options, determined to somehow rescue Celia from the Turning House
fate, coming up with plan after plan which I then discarded as too wild and
farfetched, wrestling with the lack of choices, with more secrecy that had to
be piled on top of what had already been layered onto Celia's story in our
own family.

I was almost startled when Chalky rolled to a stop and turned the keys
in the ignition.

"We're here," he said, into the silence.

Asia wordlessly opened her door, and slipped out of the car; I did the
same on my side, and stared around me. We were parked next to a two-
room wooden cabin which was maybe a dozen paces away from a small
sliver of shingled beach at which tiny wavelets lapped from the pewter-
colored lake. There was a glimpse of one other house, away through the
trees and on the curve of the shore, but it looked empty, deserted. Behind
the cottage, a handful of dark conifers brooded amongst a forest of trees in
full autumn foliage which thickly covered the slope of the hillside.

Golden October. Celia haunted me, even here.

There were no other cars in sight, no other people.

"Will this do?" Chalky inquired, after Asia and I had the chance to look.

"Nothing is ideal, under the circumstances," Asia said. "But it's better than it might have been."

But I could see problems. "This is not exactly a contained area," I said. "What if we wander too far – we'll be in wolf-mind, with no true memory to rely on, we won't know where we end up – "

Chalky stared at me.

"It's time you learned, then," he said. "Find a bridge. Something to keep you linked to your other self. You're a wolf – use a wolf's senses – find a smell, find a taste, use it to anchor a visual memory of where you've been, what you've seen –" He grabbed my arm, in a swift, unexpected movement, too fast for me to respond, and somehow there was a pen-knife in his other hand and he had nicked the exposed skin at my wrist, just enough to make a bead of blood well up.

"Hey!" I yelped, snatching my offended limb back, instinctively bringing it to my mouth to suck at the cut, to staunch the seep of blood. The taste of it flooded through me – subtle, not overwhelming, but enough, enough – Chalky was grinning at me, and the grin was more wolfish than anything that you might have found on the face of a real wolf.

"*Remember that*," he said. "And remember it in this place, in front of this house. If you get lost, remember these two things and come home – here – the thread of memory will attach to it, and you will know your landmarks, as a man or as a wolf."

"How do you know all that?" Asia demanded rounding on him "Who are you, anyway?"

"That's what he was supposed to help me find out and confirm," Chalky said, glancing at her and then back at me, suddenly serious again. "From the inside, as it were. I have *always* thought the Lycans had a hand in it all. But eh – less than three months in, and he's gallivanting around the countryside with a pretty girl, and he's not – "

"Leave my wife alone," I said. "It isn't her doing."

Chalky's mobile eyebrows shot up again, and I remembered I hadn't exactly told him about my relationship to Asia.

"*Wife?*" Chalky said. "Wow, dude. That didn't take long…"

"That's for the pack to decide," Asia said.

Chalky's gaze sharpened. "Oh? My bad. I suppose it stands to reason that they'd practice on their own before they cast their net wider out there."

They both obviously knew something that I did not; there was a churning subtext to this conversation that I could sense, but not understand. Chalky was the one to break it off, taking his eyes off Asia to let them rest speculatively on me for a moment, and then he fished a set of keys out of his pocket.

"Well, let's get inside," he said. "In theory, you'll be okay for tonight – it's tomorrow that things will start getting interesting – but in the meantime, there's a box of supplies in the trunk, you guys go get it. I figured there would be nothing out here – it's been closed down for the season, I think the water's been turned off, I brought a case of bottled water just in case. And something to eat. Won't be a feast but at least you won't Turn hungry."

"Are you sticking around?" I asked.

He shot me a grin over his shoulder as he turned to climb the three steps to the cottage's front porch and open up the house. "*Someone's* got to keep an eye on you, dude."

Asia had ducked into the car to pull the lever which opened the trunk, and I went around to gather up Chalky's box. She followed me, and there, shielded from view from inside the house by the open trunk lid, she reached out an urgent hand to keep me from immediately stepping back into view.

"Who *is* that guy?" she demanded, in a low intense voice.

I grimaced. "For now... he's a friend," I said. "He's partly... the reason that I'm... who I am. He's had my back for a long time."

"Yeah, I can see that," Asia retorted. "Like the way he just stabbed you. What does he mean, he'll keep an eye on us? Is he not Were, himself?"

"Not... exactly," I said.

She clicked her tongue against the roof of her mouth, a small sound of exasperation. "I'm trying to understand," she said. "But if you're keeping stuff from me..."

"Not now, Asia," I pleaded, leaning forward wearily to balance the box on the lip of the trunk. "It's not for me to tell."

Her hand dropped from mine. "Someday," she said, "you're going to have to decide whose side you're on and who you're really willing to trust."

It was not a comfortable evening. Asia was silent and withdrawn, I was torn between all my conflicting loyalties and penned in by them until I was too afraid to make a move in any direction for fear of making a bad situation worse, and Chalky actually excused himself and went off somewhere after a couple of hours – and I could imagine that he had simply decided to change into something else, anything else, and spend the night exploring the woods by himself rather than linger in the cottage. Asia eventually curled up on the bed and went to sleep, as the light faded, and although I lay down beside her and tried to do the same, sleep would not come for a very long time. I suppose that at some point I just passed out from sheer physical and emotional exhaustion, and then, somehow, it was morning.

And although it should have been hours still before dusk, and the full moon rose that night, Asia's concerns proved bitterly correct, because it was barely past noon that I felt it begin in my bones, that stretching, racking pain that heralded the Turn.

I tried to smother it, to delay it, to control it – but if there was a way to do this, I had never been taught it. I could not keep on top of it for long, and Asia turned sharply as a gasp of stabbing agony was forced from me before I could stop it from escaping. One look, and she knew.

Chalky persisted in his absence as Asia hustled me out of the cottage door, even while she was helping me peel off my shirt. My feet were bare, and the wooden planks of the porch were cold as I stepped outside; the sun was out, but it was an October sun, and it didn't do much to warm up the cool autumn air that made me shiver as it curled down my spine and across the goose-pimpled flesh of my forearms.

"Asia – what are you going to – " I managed, through a mouth which was already finding it difficult to mold to human speech.

"Hush! Quiet! I will no doubt follow soon! Oh, *God*, this is exactly what I was afraid of..."

This last, because the transformation that was upon me was the swiftest and the most brutal that I had known so far. The pain was almost unbearable, so overwhelming that it blotted out everything else; I could hear deep gasping breaths and it was with a sense of shock that I came to realize that it was myself who was making them. I was barely free of my clothes than I was on my hands and knees on the cold ground in front of the porch, my back arched, my hands digging into the earth, letting out a howl that started out from a human throat and by the time it ended it was coming from the wolf and not the man.

The taste of blood flooded into my mouth, Chalky's words, fading in semantic meaning but deeply felt for the sense and context of them, chasing memory – *remember it in this place... remember these things and come home ... the thread of memory will attach to it, and you will know your landmarks... as a man... or as a wolf...*

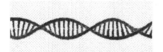

T he wolf days were usually shielded from us. The memories of the wolf were not given to us to keep. But this time... this time I fought that wall. Every time the human mind threatened to become subsumed into the wolf mind the taste of blood would come, that, and the name – Celia – *Celia* – the name that was given to this season all around me was still Golden October, even in my wolf-shape. I could not forget, could not put this from my consciousness. Even as the wolf, I had a lost sister who needed me.

The taste of blood. The taste of memory. There were – there had to be – huge chunks of time that I lost, running on wolf feet through the autumn woods, I don't know for how long I was alone but very quickly I had her by my side, the she-wolf, my mate. *The taste of blood*, as we trotted through the trees together, her description registering as memory on the human part of my mind. We ran and ran, and the nights were cold and clear, and the full moon shimmered in the dark starlit sky through the branches which were shedding their golden leaves. It was a dizzy, delicious kind of freedom; we knew no fences, we knew no borders, we knew no boundaries. For those hours we spent wolf-roaming the woods, if it was possible to qualify such a thing as a wolf, we were able to glimpse a sense of what it might mean to be purely happy.

The taste of blood. The taste of memory.

We ran. We played. We hunted. We ate. We slept.

And on a cool grey morning, three days later, I woke, human once more, naked and cold, curled up in a hollow under a tree root, with a wolf sleeping at my feet.

My breathing still ragged from my own Turn back into human form, I watched her sleep – her paws curled underneath her and occasionally twitching as if she dreamed of running, her flank rising and falling with every breath, her fur silver grey with touches of elegant black. And then I watched it begin, the return, the change from wolf to woman. I watched her face transform, I watched her mouth open in a grimace that was pain, I watched her eyes flicker open and swim from sleep to full conscious focus, to awareness. I saw her see me, and I saw her look at me, warily, guardedly, through a veil of reserve, with a question in her eyes.

It was borne upon me that there was no way forward for me from this place that would not involve hurting someone that I loved – and that yes, I did love her. I loved the way she had stood by me – trying to understand my motives, struggling with my passions, going against her own best judgment, but staying loyal, loyal to *me* over her older and far stronger loyalties to the pack. They may have mated us for whatever reasons made sense to them, but the pack had given me a treasure they did not even know they had... and there were still things I was keeping from her, because I was afraid of what she might do with those secrets.

"Ash," I said hoarsely, just that, just her name, just the name that I had given her, and reached for her.

And she came to me.

We clung together, shivering, for a moment and then I realized something. Not far from us sat a neat little pile of blankets and a small bag beside which rested two pairs of shoes, hers and mine, the ones we had been wearing back at the cottage when we Turned.

Holding Asia against me I probed the woods beyond with a sweeping look but nothing stirred; whoever had brought these things to us – Chalky, I presumed – was not here now. But the blankets were a gift and I murmured something against Asia's hair as I twisted to reach them, grabbing the top one and draping it over her bare shoulders, taking a moment to shake out one on the ground so she could roll over onto it, pulling a third to cover myself and then her with another layer. The ground was still hard and cold but the situation was already improved, an order of magnitude better.

"Tell me the truth," I said. "Would it help if you went back without me? Without being answerable for me?"

She reared a little away from me and stared at me. "Why would you ask that? What would you do?"

"I don't know," I said helplessly. "I just don't want this to land on *you*. It isn't something you should have to be punished for, if that's what they would do. You could tell them whatever you wanted, I would not argue against anything."

"That ship's sailed," she said, after a pause, letting her head fall back down and lie on my chest, tucking the top of her head under my chin. "I'm here, right now, and that's already too much to explain. And I'm not going back without you."

"What would you have me tell them? The truth? What would that do to Celia?"

"Mal... they may already have dealt with that... your encounter with her was witnessed... and they may have put that together." She paused. "They may just move her somewhere else. Somewhere where you couldn't find her."

"I'll find her, if they moved her to the moon," I said softly.

"I know," she said. And wrapped her arms tightly around me.

It was not romantic, or born out of duty to pack or clan – when we came together that morning it was out of something raw, almost brutal, a mutual need, a sharing of strength, a commitment. I had not told her everything... but I would. She had not put everything on the line yet... but she would. I might have made my choices because my loyalties were so strongly rooted into the family I had been born into – but hers, made here, now, on this morning, were made because of the family she had chosen. Because she had chosen me.

We were breathless, laughing, stealing what tiny fragment of joy there might have been before all sorts of reckonings had to be faced out in that other, wider, world, the one that included all the fractured realities which included people that were not either of us.

It will be all right, she had said, she had promised, on our wedding day.

She couldn't know how true, how prophetic, those words would be.

But the outside world had to be faced, eventually, and it was finally I who stirred in our nest of blankets and smoothed her hair away from her face.

"We'd better get dressed, and get going," I said, reluctantly and with regret, but we couldn't stay out here in these woods indefinitely, tangled up in these blankets and in each other.

"Get *dressed*?" Asia echoed, rearing up and away from me, and then she caught sight of the bag and the shoes and her mouth fell open into an almost comical O of surprise. "Where did *that* come from? How did you manage...?"

"Not me," I said. "Chalky."

"Your friend? But how did he...?"

"He has his ways," I said. "They have a lot to do with how I landed in the lap of the Lycans in the first place. I'll explain later – but we'd better move. I think the weather's turned, while we were out of it. We have to get back to the cottage. And we'd better get something to eat."

She sat up, reaching across me for the bag. "Now that you mention it, yeah, I could eat," she said. "Is there any food in that bag? Here, these are yours."

She passed me a shirt, pants, socks, a sweatshirt; underneath, she

335

unearthed her jeans, a t-shirt, a sweater. A handful of energy bars lurked at the bottom, and Asia, once dressed, devoured one of them in short order. Still chewing, she tried to drag a small hairbrush (which had also come with the bag – Chalky had been quite thorough) through her tangled hair, working out a few knots with her fingers as she went.

"Where are we, exactly...?" she asked worrying at a particularly stubborn one.

I lifted my head, sniffed at the air, trying to penetrate the woods probing glances. For a moment I had absolutely no idea, but then... *taste of blood... memory...* there was a particular shape of a fallen tree that looked familiar. And then, beyond that, a V-shaped trunk of another tree. And then a rock, jutting bare and grey through the carpet of fallen leaves.

"That way," I said, with absolute certainty.

Asia looked at me strangely, but did not object. She finished with her hair and stuffed the brush back into the bag, pulled on her shoes, and scrambled to her feet.

"On our way, then," she said.

By way of reply, I reached out and closed my hand around her wrist. Warned, she came to attention, turned to look where I was looking, and froze as she stared into the yellow eyes of a wolf standing only a few paces away from us.

"Is it....?" she began, but a slow smile was starting to spread on my own face.

"Don't worry," I said. "I think I know that wolf."

It was time. And if Chalky was here, had elected to show himself – he didn't have to let himself be seen – it meant something, it meant that he had made the same decision.

"Come on, then," I said to the wolf, pulling off the blanket I had draped over my shoulder and tossing it in the wolf's direction.

"What are you doing?" Asia said in a low voice.

"Just watch," I said, and she did, and saw Chalky change, saw the wolf limbs flow back into human arms and legs, saw the grey fur vanish as his back arched into bare skin covering the bones of his spine as he crouched on the ground with his head down and tucked between his shoulders and his hair falling forward to hide his face. And then he moved, reaching for the blanket that I had thrown at his feet, and draped it around himself as he rose to his feet in a single fluid motion. When he lifted his head to meet Asia's eyes, a ghost of a smile hovered around his mouth.

"Ash, meet my friend Saladin van Schalkwyk. Better known as Chalky."

Asia was staring at Chalky, her utter astonishment plain upon her face. "So you *are* Lycan...?"

"On occasion," he said, wearing the blanket with the aplomb of a Roman Emperor draped in his toga.

"He isn't anything that you can categorize with a clan or an affiliation," I said. "I called him a shifter, once. He can... he can Turn into anything. Be anything. And he doesn't have to wait on the moon to be able to do it."

"But... that is..."

"He is also," I said, "the wolf that put me in the pack."

Asia's eyes flickered from me to Chalky and then back again, several times, and then staggered back a few paces to collapse onto the edge of the large tree-root under whose protective overhang we had woken earlier from our wolf dreams.

"He... *how?*"

"Do you think you might be able to wait for the rest of it until we get back to the cottage?" Chalky asked, shifting from foot to foot. "It's cold out here and getting colder, and I might point out that you two are now wearing shoes, something that I hadn't quite planned as far forward as having had the foresight to bring out here for myself. By your leave, fair lady, I will switch back into something a little more... appropriate... and I'll meet you guys back by the lake. The stove has a fire going, back in the cottage, I'll have coffee ready by the time you get there, and I popped down to the shops and got a few more things that are fit for a hungry Lycan's breakfast – and perhaps we can discuss matters further over that. Do you need me to lead you home? It's going to be a bit of a walk, I'm afraid..."

"I know the way," I said, and something flashed in Chalky's eyes as he looked at me, a curious sort of pride, that of a mentor who had just seen a green and inexperienced protégé graduate and become a master.

"I'll see you there, then," he said. "You can fill her in on the basics on the way, Mal."

"Hey," I said softly, just as he was beginning another transformation out of human shape, "thank you."

He could no longer speak, but his eyes told me he understood. And then he was done, Chalky was gone, and in his place, struggling out from underneath the folds of the blanket that had fallen about him, stood a large raven. It shook its head and ruffled its feathers, inclined its head at us as though in farewell, and took off, flying low between the trees.

If he'd really wanted to freak Asia out, he could not have done any better than this; I knew his gifts, and I could understand perfectly why he'd chosen a winged form this time – after all, he had already told us it was quite a walk. But this was the first time Asia had ever seen anyone just *Turn...* at will... into anything he chose. Her eyes were quite round as she stared at the crumpled blanket he had left behind.

"What is he?" she gasped. "I don't even think I could have *imagined...* You know about this – all the time – and you never said anything – "

I squeezed her hand in reassurance, and then stepped up to shake the blanket out and re-fold it and then swing it back over my shoulder where I'd had it before Chalky had turned up.

"I couldn't say anything," I said. "It wasn't my secret. It was his. He may be the only one of his kind, for all we know – but he has his ideas about his origins. If he's chosen to trust you this far, he'll tell you. And oh, Ash, it's Lycans all over again. They've got their fingers in everything. Back when I Turned into the wolf, I was at the end of my rope – you don't know the full story behind this."

"I'm beginning to think I am woefully ignorant on too many things," she said.

"Come on," I said. "Let's start walking. We aren't going to get any less hungry waiting around here. *That* way."

"How can you be so certain...?"

"I know. I know how to know, now. I'm just as ignorant... but I'm learning. All sorts of things. All the time."

It took us just over three hours of brisk walking to trudge back to the house by the lake – we had apparently gone quite a way into the forest (Chalky would later inform us, quite cheerfully, that he had been keeping track of us – that we'd actually been much further in than we were when we Turned back into our human shape, and that we were lucky that we hadn't ended up fully a day's hard hike away from the cottage). We were footsore and a little grumpy and a lot hungry – that handful of power bars didn't go very far when you're a post-Turn Lycan – by the time we got there but Chalky was as good as his word. He might even have been monitoring our progress in his bird-shape because everything was just about perfectly ready when we arrived. And just the smell of food and fresh coffee as we opened the door and stepped into a warm and comfortable room, out of the cold October day, was enough to lift our mood immediately. Chalky had the good sense not to get between us and our delayed but greatly appreciated breakfast, but once we were done and were settled down with a second cup of coffee, he cleared his throat.

"Okay," he said, "before we get into everything else... your RV broke down."

"What?" Asia said, rousing.

"Your RV broke down," Chalky repeated, and gave a big innocent shrug of his shoulders. "You hit something on the road that you barely saw or noticed or you thought was just an empty box, whatever, but then you hit it and it was something solid enough to give you a puncture, and your spare was flat, and it turned out that you'd bent something in the wheel well anyway when you drove over the obstacle, and you were kind of stuck. That's what happened. Don't worry, it's all on record. All I need to nail it down is the number of the credit card that you would actually use to pay for this repair – once I plug that in, the story is solid and it will stand if they challenge anything. That's simply what happened – you left the Turning House in good time, you had an accident, and you were stuck trying to fix it."

"He's a bit of a hacker," I said to Asia, by way of explanation.

She blinked a couple of times. "Okay," she said slowly, "but we didn't get in touch..."

"You were in an area with bad cell service – that much is true, actually, you'd know if you tried to use your phone out here – and anyway, your phone battery died, and you, Mal, lost your phone."

"No, I didn't," I said, startled.

"Oh, yes, you did," Chalky said with a conspiratorial smile. "It happens. If they replace it with another one, that's all for the good, you get an upgrade. But this one – the one you 'lost' – " I realized he actually had my phone in his hand, waggling it in my direction. It took me a moment, but then I got it.

"You've hacked that one," I said.

"It's clean now, and if they get you the same make and model they'll never know which phone you're actually using if they see you using it. I don't have to put my number on there – you know it, and it won't hold a memory of it if it's dialed – and so even if anyone gets hold of it the thing will yield nothing, they don't have a trail – but if we need to speak, we can, on a secure line. And given the 'everything else' we're about to get into... it might be important to have that line of communication open."

I glanced at Asia.

"So we're going back," I said. "And I'm still... undercover?"

"That," Asia said, her hands curling convulsively around her coffee cup. "Before we go anywhere else... that. What really happened, Mal? How much of what you told us, back at the compound, was just a lie?"

"I told enough truth for it to matter," I said. "There's roots to this – one of them is Celia, and everything that happened with Celia, and everything that I took from that and carried. I couldn't get away from the knowledge that it was I who handed her the thing that killed her. And then Chalky told me that the Lycans were where Stay had started, and they held the keys to what it was, what it did – and that if I could get on the inside I could find out more information, and – I don't know, I don't even think I thought it through to the end – make amends, somehow. To her ghost, at least. Except, now..."

"We'll get back to Celia," Asia said. "You said roots. What else?'

This was difficult to talk about. I had been in such a dark place, back then. But just as I didn't spill Chalky's secrets, he would not now speak of mine, not until I did – and so I haltingly, reluctantly, told Asia about that tainted past that had dogged my footsteps. How I was the oldest unTurned Were in my generation. How close I was to the end of my rope, how I just wanted to *end* it – and how, when the idea of Turning Lycan came up, I had latched onto it as a last resort.

"And so... you met the wolf," I said, at length, nodding in Chalky's direction. "I had the potential to go Lycan – I had the genetic background for Turning, after all. All I needed was that push, the key to it, and that could come... from the bite. And I knew what Chalky was, what he could do. So I asked him... to be the wolf... to bite me, as a true werewolf. I didn't know if it would even work – or if it did, how it would stand to scrutiny – you'll never know what it was like, those first few weeks at the compound, waiting for the lab to come down with the test results, hoping that some genetic hiccup wouldn't trip me up or give the lie to what I was telling them..."

"No, you're Lycan," Asia said faintly. "I worked on some of those tests myself. I know. But wait – that still doesn't make sense – a bite transfer hasn't really worked properly for a long time – it's a pack thing, it needs... a male and a female... to..." She stared at Chalky, suddenly confused. "It takes... two bites..." she said. "How could you..."

Chalky gave a small shrug. "We didn't know if that part of it would work at all," he said. "I know it's hard to believe that it never occurred to me to try, but it's true. But after Jazz Turned into Jesse, I knew it was technically possible for me to… what? You didn't tell her about that, either, Mal?"

"What now?" Asia said, sounding genuinely alarmed. "And who's… Jesse?"

And just like that, I was back there again – back in the same dark place where I had once threatened to hand Jazz over to be dissected by bug-eyed scientists in a lab, straight after that first disastrous Turn into Jesse, the were-boy.

Asia was *exactly* the bug-eyed scientist to whom Jazz might have been sent for analysis. I may not have really meant it back then when I said that I would tell the authorities all about Jazz, but I was still about to do it. Exactly that.

Chalky knew exactly why I hesitated.

"You're going to stop now?" he asked. "Mal, there's too much that she already knows, that you should never have said if you didn't trust her…"

"You can't tell them" I said to Asia, desperately. "You can't tell the Lycan labs. You can't – they'll take her too…"

"Tell them *what*?" she said, spreading her hands in a gesture of pure frustrated fury. "Mal, I'm drowning out here. Unless something starts making sense to me soon, I'll just go under…"

So – for Celia's sake – I told the truth about Jazz, unwillingly, unhappily, knowing that the pack was probably already putting out all of its substantial resources to find out just what had happened to two of its missing members, that the longer all of this took the harder it was going to be to re-integrate back into that other reality which had only just begun to feel like something I might belong in and which may have already been irretrievably shattered for me.

I had succumbed to an impulse to try and set right an old wrong. It was starting to look as if all that the impulse had led to was a morass of impossible choices and even deeper possible disasters than the original one which had been driving me – and saving Celia was just as far away as ever, and just as out of reach.

I wasn't happy about going back to that time, that place. It was the nadir of everything that I was – the bottom of a pit of despair and jealousy and dark impulses of pure distilled malevolence. But worst of all, I had felt as though I had somehow brought it on myself, that I had deserved it. That what had happened to Jazz, and had *not* happened to me, was a punishment for the part I had played in what had happened to Celia.

Asia had no way of knowing any of this. Nor could I explain it to her, not really, not in a way that she could hope to understand – or at least hope to understand and come out on the other side with some feeling for me other than a disgusted recoil. I was aware of a simmering terror even as I laid my sins bare before her – the fear that in the end it would all turn to dust in my hands, and not even the revenge and retribution I had maybe perhaps planned, in however nebulous a manner, would remain to me to hold on to. I would lose everything. Everything. Even the things I had never hoped to be allowed near. Things like Ash, and continuing to have the right to call her mine.

At the end of it all, Asia summed it up by counting items off on the fingers of her right hand.

"Let me get this straight. One of your sisters has come back from the dead and is living a resurrected life in a Turning House with little real memory of what has been lost; another sister has Turned into an impossible thing which makes her a genetic treasure map for those who know where to look and what to look for and which should have been immediately reported to the proper authorities but which has been hushed up because, amongst other reasons, of that first sister's death, which is now moot – and you, yourself, are a Random Were who was on the verge of resigning your Were card completely but instead chose to cheat your way into the ranks of the most closely guarded Were-kind of all – how am I doing?"

"When you put it that way..." Chalky said, with a twisted little smile.

"And I thought my family was trouble," Asia said, dropping her hands to her sides.

"If you guys are planning to go back to your pack, you'd better do it soon," Chalky warned. "Give me that credit card number and I'll finish cooking up your alibi. And then, if you're going, you'd better go. And hope they don't raise too much hell about it."

Asia stared at the both of us for a long moment, and then sighed, rooted out her wallet from the depths of her pocketbook, and handed over a card to Chalky. He took it and went to work on his laptop

I faced my wife.

"Ash. You can't tell them about Jazz."

"I can't tell them about any of this," she said sharply. "Not without sounding like a complete lunatic."

"I still need to find out if I can manage to spring Celia out of..."

"Yes, think about that," she interrupted. "Think about it a lot. It may come to you how useless and hopeless a thing that is. Just what would you do with her, out here, if you did 'rescue' her?" I could all but hear the sarcastic quotes she had put around that word. I felt the blood rush into my face, feeling rather like a guilty child who was being brought to account by a stern elder. "It's not as if you could *cure* her..." Asia added, as an afterthought.

For some reason those words fell into a pocket of silence as deep as a well, and echoed in there. I sat up, my head tilted at a slight angle, staring at Asia; Chalky, aware that something electric had just happened, paused mid-type, hands poised above his keyboard, and turned to pay attention.

"But what if she could be?" I said.

"Don't be silly," Asia said. "There are hundreds, thousands, of people just like her, some even worse than her, living out their wretched lives in those houses. If anything could have been done, don't you think that someone would already have..."

"No," I said, "I don't. It's entirely possible that nobody's really bothered to try because everyone knows that it is impossible. But what if someone began to think about what it would take...?"

"You don't know nearly enough about it all," Asia said, extrapolating my words directly onto myself. But I kept staring at her, the beginnings of a small smile starting to tug at the edges of my mouth.

"No," I agreed easily to her somewhat trenchant dismissal of my abilities. "But *you* do."

I was perhaps expecting any reaction than the one I got. Her eyes sliding off mine. *Guilt.*

"You *do*," I said slowly. "You already do. For real."

"Not like that," she said. "And not me, not really. But..."

"But others? Other Lycans? And like what, then, if not... *that*?"

"Asia," Chalky said, leaning both elbows on the table and resting his chin in his interlaced hands, "what *does* go on behind the locked doors of those labs? Our young friend here thinks that Turning Lycan was entirely his own idea – which it was, up to a certain point. But it worked, for me, too. Because I have a shrewd suspicion about my own origins. Just how much of Were genetics and genealogy *are* the Lycans controlling?"

He paused and gave her back her credit card. "It's an accepted thing that Were-clans breed true, and that two parents of the same were-ilk will produce progeny that is the same Were-ilk – Corvids breed Corvids, Felids breed Felids, Canids breed Canids, Were-parrots or Were-owls or Were-rats will produce children who themselves Turn into parrots or owls or rats, and two Random Weres will produce little Random Weres, you have this crazy family to prove that."

He tossed his head in my direction, Exhibit One. "But I've found traces," Chalky continued, his voice dropping a little, becoming more intense, "nothing firm, nothing I can use to prove anything – but there are definitely tracks that I've followed a certain distance before they got buried again – of there being a social program, back some two or three decades, where *different* Were-kind were mated, a sort of experiment. Because there was no way of predicting, or so they thought, that their progeny would be. In the handful of cases that I have been able to follow to any degree, some of the F1 generation ended up dead after short and painful lives – or no progeny was produced at all, or there were serious complications with the pregnancies which were either never fully carried to term or resulted in stillbirths. It was a disaster, in fact, as far as that went, and as far as I've been able to find out it was quietly... discontinued. But not before *some* were born, and managed to survive. Some, perhaps, just like me."

"You think you're the result of a breeding experiment?" I asked incredulously. He had never gone into this detail of it with me.

He shrugged. "I know for a fact that there was little between my parents. My father was a Were-dassie – that's a kind of a rock rabbit, they're related to elephants, apparently, there's something to ponder when you look at that wee bundle of fur – and he disappeared when I was no

342

more than four or five. He left me nothing except the legacy of my admittedly rather grand name. I barely remember him – and even what memories are there I don't really trust because there's just so little there to remember, and I was so young. My mother was a Were-serval – that's a kind of a cat. Perfectly run-of-the-mill were-critters, both of them... but *different kinds*. It would appear according to the best available evidence that they married very shortly after they met – which would imply a grand passion, in the greater scheme of things, except that they barely stayed together long enough for my mother to carry a child to term. I was the second attempt, incidentally; I found out that my mother had had a miscarriage before me, a bad one, and that I gave her plenty of problems myself while yet in her womb. But barely was I breathing with my own lungs and had a chance to begin using my brain to think for myself that the man who fathered me – I can barely call him my 'father', he deserves the name so little – was gone."

He paused, shook his head and went on.

"I grew up alone with my mother, who was rapidly falling apart – by the time I was seven years old I was taking care of her, when her Turns came. And then, at about eight or so, I discovered...what I was. What I could do. By accident, really, but I was never a child, I never really had a chance to be a child, and once I got an inkling I pursued it until I was sure. But by that time... my mother was already psychotic. She was clinically depressed, and could get manic, and when she got into one of her rages – well – let me just say that it was one of those that triggered my initial discovery of my gifts, it was a self-defense thing to get out of her way. Telling her about my abilities... would have probably been... suicidal. I shut up about it and soldiered on by myself, for a little while."

Asia was staring at him, her eyes round with shock. "Couldn't you get help?"

"For her? Yes. There were medications. When she remembered to take them. And if she forgot, if I could get her to do it before the worst of it kicked in. For me...? Just who would have helped me, and how? I didn't know then the half of what I know now, and from what I know now... I wouldn't have run to the people who engineered me, would I? And who else was there?"

"What happened to your mother?"

"I don't know," Chalky said, his voice flat. "When I was ten, I knew it was beyond me. So I called an ambulance one time when she was passed out on the couch, left the door of our apartment open for them, and just... left."

"And went where?"

"To school," Chalky said, with one of his grins. "Not an official one, of course. But I learned everything I know by figuring out how to survive, and then I made it my business to start finding out more about what made me, what brought me into this world, if I was in fact the only such critter alive..."

"Are you?" Asia gasped.

Chalky waggled his index finger. "I'll tell you that when you get *me* some of the answers I still haven't got," he said. "Now, are you kids going home? Because I'm sure by now they've missed you... and they'll be plenty mad without you being any later than you already are..."

I roused. "But what about Celia...?"

"I will keep an eye on that Turning House," Chalky said. "If anything happens, I will let you know. It's just the Lycan computers I can't hack into – Turning Houses are embarrassingly easy, by comparison. I will keep tabs, I will keep you informed. And you two lovebirds had better go home and talk this through. And then let me know what you want to do next."

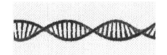

We did talk, on the way back to the compound. Some. But we were both feeling wrung out from recent events and at the same time bracing for what was to come when we got back and had to face the music, and conversation was desultory at best. In addition, we were fretting about different things – me about the situation I was leaving behind, about how I could not help but feel as though I had been maneuvered into abandoning my lost sister and then found her again. Asia appeared to be steeling herself for what she was about to face when we set foot back in the compound again.

I had a bit of a plan about that – which I didn't tell her because she would probably have argued me silent if I had. When Asia finally brought the RV to a halt in the parking lot outside the front door, Rory Cotton was waiting for us in the entrance hall to tell us that we were to present ourselves immediately before Yuri and Sofia to explain the days we'd gone AWOL.

I spoke before any of them had a chance to, before Asia could incriminate herself by trying to figure out which lie to pick, before Yuri or Sofia began asking questions she could not answer. And like all the best lies it began with an absolute truth.

"It was my fault," I said. "Turning Houses have always been something of a nightmare to me – it's something that I've carried from when I was very young, when my family first came out here, and the Turning Houses took my parents from me – I was too young to understand, and all I knew was that they were horrible, and my parents told us as little as they could get away with but what they didn't say left an impression. I hate those places. But I didn't realize just how much of a problem it was going to be this close to a Turn. Asia told me later that emotional stress can bring it on early – and that's pretty much what pushed us into trouble – we had an accident on the road out from the Turning House, and the spare was flat, and I was on the brink of Turning and things could get really messy if I did on the road – and we were close enough to the town I grew up in. I knew people... who could help. So we went there to weather this. And then we got the RV fixed and came straight back. It was my fault."

"No," Asia said faintly, "it was probably mine. I never should have gone out this close to Turn. I was just trying to get a jump on work I didn't want to have to wait to do – I'm sorry. It won't happen again."

"These *people*," Yuri said . "The ones who you said... could help. Who are they? How did they help? The Lycan clans have withdrawn from the public eye... for a reason. You did not have permission or authority to reveal hidden things about ourselves or our ways to those who are not our own kind."

"There was no other pack close by to whom we could have gone for asylum," Asia said. "Not near enough to matter. There was the option of returning to the Turning House but I had no idea what sort of facilities they had for someone like Mal or myself, or if it would be worse to put ourselves in their hands during our most vulnerable time."

Yuri considered this in silence, and it was Sofia who spoke in reply.

"Perhaps this is so," she said. "But no contact? You could not let us know you were in trouble?"

I sat up. This was something we had no real answer for. Unless we bluffed it out. If they didn't call our bluff. But it was something else I could take on – drawing fire, if fire was to be drawn, away from Asia. Technically she was the senior, in charge of the trip and of making command decisions, but I could derail that. Asia shot me a warning look, but I chose to pretend I had not seen it.

"With all due respect," I said, "we had one cell phone with us. Asia's. If I had mine, I don't know what I did with it, and was not in the frame of mind to look for it. And hers didn't have signal for a little while at the critical moment, and after that we were far too busy trying to solve the problem than trying to report it. We did the best we could. It isn't her fault, like I said. It's mine. I am not... as stable in the Turns as I might be, apparently. And maybe the Turning House was the tipping point, and then... but whatever. I'm sorry. There came a point when we hadn't called, and we were past the point of calling. There was nothing you could have done, at that distance."

"We could have offered guidance," Yuri said. "At the very least."

"Or perhaps given us orders which we could not follow, given the circumstances on the ground, and which we would have wasted time trying to," I said, feeling far less brave and confident than I came off sounding. "I was already on the point of the Turn..."

"But there was Stay, no? You had a supply?"

This was skating too close to dangerous territory... but they had to know about my family background. They *had* to. They would have investigated that much. They knew, at the very least, the cover story – the story in which Celia died.

"I have... a history with that," was all I said.

345

"I think, no more excursions for the time being," Sofia said softly, gently, but it was a royal decree. We were grounded, Asia and I, for the rest of our natural lives... or until the Alpha saw fit to release us. "And I will have a report, in writing, from both of you, and in detail, of exactly what happened, and how, and where, and who knows about it. And I will think further on it, and perhaps once that report is in, we will speak again."

That was left to hang over us as we were dismissed.

"I'm sorry," I said to Asia as we walked down the corridor towards the labs, "I tried to..."

"Thanks for trying," she said, managing a small smile.

"What do you supposed they will do?"

"I might find myself bumped down the queue when it comes to requisitioning things I need for my work," Asia said. "Funding is always a way to get you. I'll miss the rides, though."

"The rides?"

"I don't suppose they're going to be quite as happy to let me out on the motorcycle by myself again, any time soon," she said. "I haven't shown myself... *responsible.*"

"I'm sorry," I said again, and genuinely meant it that time. I had an inkling as to what those brief moments of freedom meant to her, and I regretted any part I might have had in taking that away from her.

She shrugged, and looked away. "I'd better go and get those samples organized, hard won as they've proved to be," she said.

I reached for her arm, just as she turned to leave. "Ash."

"What?" she said, lifting her eyes to mine again.

"You aren't going to... you know, in the report..."

I was pleading with her. Actually begging.

"What do you hope to accomplish, keeping you sister under wraps?" she asked, lowering her voice a little. "You have to realize that it is practically impossible to do anything about that. You *have* to know that."

"I was hoping that maybe... that you can tell me... If it's a known effect, maybe there's a way to restore – I mean – if the genetic function has been impaired, then why can't there be gene therapy of some sorts available to – you know – *restore* – "

"What, exactly?"

"Bring her back," I said, desperately. "Ash, I don't know. I'm asking *you*. Has there ever even been an attempt?"

She looked trapped, actually, far more trapped than even the admittedly difficult corner I was painting her into. "You don't understand," she said.

My hand tightened around her wrist; I was starting to get a bad feeling about this. "Try me," I said. "What aren't you telling me?"

Asia freed her hand, a little desperately. "Just because she's your sister doesn't make it easy, or right," she said. 'The truth is, we've been... it's been tried – there have been experiments, several batches, where the introduction, or re-introduction, of genomic sequences was attempted.... of *Lycan genomic sequences*. If we could get one of them to revert to true

Lycan, through gene therapy..."

"Wait," I said, trying to get my head around this. "You've been using the Half-Souled as... as some sort of lab rats? To create Lycan Were from... creatures who were never wolves?"

Asia looked around almost furtively. "We really shouldn't be talking about this out here."

"You could have explained back in the RV," I said, a little desperately. "But you didn't, and now we're here, and you have to tell me – what's going on in those Turning Houses...? What happened... to those people? To the subjects?"

"It was a failure," she said. "It never worked. *It never worked*, Mal."

"No," I said slowly, putting together a few pieces in my mind, coming up with a picture – Chalky had always said I was particularly good at that. "But you were trying to do something very specific and that didn't work. And because that didn't work, you guys... just left it there... if they couldn't be Lycans, there would be no attempts at anything else, right? But the fact that it was done means that the technology exists, Ash. It exists, and maybe it could be adapted."

"To do what?" she demanded.

"To bring her back," I said. "To bring *her* back, my sister, not as a rank-and-file Lycan for your army of wolves but as her, as herself, to return her to what she was before the Stay took it from her."

"You're not listening. It never worked. There is no reason to suppose that it would be any different, with non-Lycan Were DNA."

"Was it ever tried?" I asked. "Ash, it's my sister."

"You'll just get into more trouble," she said desperately.

"I'm getting her out of there," I said. "One way or another."

Asia took a step back from me, flinging both hands up in a gesture of surrender. "Fine. "You do your dreaming. But we'd better get back to work. I don't know about you but I have samples to deal with, if they haven't been lost through this whole mess – and in case you didn't hear them I won't be going back to gather anymore any time soon. You won't be going anywhere either, so live with it. We're going to pay for this Turn, one way or another – and until they've extracted that price your sister may as well *be* dead for any use you are to her."

"Ash, wait..."

"No, not now, not here. I'll talk to you later."

It was reckless and rash to talk to her about any of this here in the open corridor. Just how rash was borne upon me when I turned away from helplessly watching Asia walk away from me... and met the eyes of Sorcha Manion, one of Tom Manion's red-headed twins and an erstwhile candidate for my mate here in the pack. She'd be turning fifteen soon, Turning soon, taking up her rightful place in the pack hierarchy... which, I was uncomfortably reminded was quite a high rung, relatively speaking. She was part of the core families. Close to the heart of the pack.

The pack, from whom I had wanted to keep Celia's astonishing, heart-stopping resurrection into my life a deep and dark secret. And I had just poured it all into Sorcha's ears, free for the talking. It took all I had not to utter the trite, clichéd phrase, *how much have you heard?*

It was she who broke the silence first, in the end.

"I didn't know you had a sister," she said.

I decided on going as far as I could on the truth, and cross the bridge of lies only when I had to.

"I had two," I said. "One younger, one older."

"It must have been hard, leaving them. To come here, I mean."

Oh, you don't know the half of it, girl-child, I thought, a little savagely. But all I said out loud was just, "Yes."

She nodded, with complete understanding. "I can't imagine leaving my own sister behind anywhere," she said quietly. "But you said... she wasn't Lycan?"

She'd heard plenty, it seemed.

"No," I said. "She's not. Neither of them are. I was... an anomaly."

"Talk to Wilfred," Sorcha said unexpectedly, and then turned away and, with a skip and a small smile, was gone.

Talk to Wilfred? Wilfred Sand, my taciturn lab-mate? To whom I had barely spoken a dozen words, outside of the required shoptalk over experiments and procedures in progress, since he had arrived at the compound? Granted, that was only a short while after me – so technically we were the two newest wolves on the premises – but that hadn't seemed to create that much of a bond, really. If anything, the exact opposite. We were both on the fringes of the pack, myself a little deeper in because of Asia and him just a general floater young male on loan from another pack, but still novices and untried, and feeling our way around to find out where we stood in the hierarchy. What did Wilfred Sand have to do with any of this?

But Sorcha wouldn't have said that without a reason. So while Asia went back to the lab to try and salvage the remnants of the work that had driven her on this ill-fated expedition in the first place, I went to the library and looked up Wilfred Sand's profile on the computer.

He was twenty-nine years old, an only child and then an orphan (at the tender age of only fifteen, just about as old as Sorcha was now) of a couple who themselves were apparently not all that high on the social scale in their own pack, with a record of having been a floater in two other packs before he had come to this one. He seemed a bit of a cypher, really, nothing that I could pin him down on... until I looked at his work record, and Sorcha's words fell into place.

I had access to some things, from these firewalled inner-sanctum Lycan compound computers, that I probably would never have been able to find from the outside, and one of those perks was a work record, a history of interests and accomplishments. And Wilfred's particular focus, at least for the last handful of years... was gene therapy. In particular, work on the vectors used in the introduction of foreign genes into human subjects.

Asia's words came back to me – *it's been tried... the introduction, or re-introduction, of genomic sequences... of Lycan genomic sequences....if we could get one of them to revert to true Lycan, through gene therapy...*

Those people who thronged the Turning Houses, the ones whose ability to Turn was gone, the poor lost and dispossessed crew whom I knew as the Half-Souled, dead already to both their own kind (because they could no longer lay claim to being Were) and to normals (because they had once been Were), unwanted, unprotected, the ones who had no voices to speak for themselves and nobody to speak for them. They were...numbers. Nameless bodies. Nothing more than human-shaped lab rats – convenient research fodder for the Lycan scientists who could wade in amongst them as though into herds of cattle and cull out the ones they found useful for their work. There was barely a hint of any ethical misgiving in the tone of the Lycans who had worked on them – even Asia had not said much on that subject – and in the papers that bore Wilfred Sand's name...

They'd tried to *vaccinate* these people with Lycan genes, in the hope of creating a spark that would return them to the Were fold, perhaps – but as Lycans, as wolves bound to the packs, a way to build up the decimated ranks of the true were-wolf bloodlines. The Lycans were working for a return to the age before the Diversification, before all the other different Were-kind came to be... an age in which Random Were, such as I had been born as, such as Celia was, had not even existed.

And now that I knew what I was looking for, I could see it. There was a thread in the research that I was reading, a thread that valued Random Were above all others as raw material, as subjects for the purposes of experimentation. With a species-committed Were of any kind the Lycan genes would literally have to supplant and overwhelm completely the genes for whatever that other creature was that the human Were avatar carried. With a Random Were – well – we potentially carried *everything*. If any genome could be tweaked, prodded or bullied into producing Lycan phenotypes, it was ours.

It was Celia's.

I was all too aware that my knowledge of this particular subject was horribly inadequate – I had made some good inroads, since I had started intensive study here at the Lycan compound, but there were vast areas that were still just a jumble of words to me. I had a certain instinctive understanding born of the simple fact of being Were-born myself, which gave me an ability to extrapolate a little from the basics of which I was reasonably certain, and in some ways, although this had been an even shorter time span than my studies as a whole, my exposure to Asia's knowledge and experience since we had been thrown together had not gone completely awry. The point was, I knew and understood more than I had thought I would. And the things I was beginning to know and understand scared and horrified me.

One thing *was* clear – Wilfred had been involved in a lot of gene therapy studies in his career so far. From what I could find of him in the trail that he had left behind in research literature, he could have been a real expert on the subject and know far more about it than even Asia, whose expertise I had learned to respect. But my pattern-seeking eye soon found one in the profile that I was looking at, and it was an interesting one – Wilfred's published research came in concentrated chunks, and the time periods of his greatest productivity came when he first joined his packs as the floater and researcher. His first position was as a young man straight out of grad school, with a smallish pack out on the coast – there was a batch of published research papers with his name on them which dated from that period, for about a year and a half or so. Then things went silent for a short while, and Wilfred next surfaced at a different pack, with a different research group, and a different batch of papers, at a pack whose base was far distant from the first. That lasted about two years or so, and then he disappeared off the research radar again for a bit, and now he was here, with Yuri's pack, still too new here to have published much but apparently starting again from scratch. It was an odd profile – it was as though he was just *blocked*, as though he got to a place, gave it his all, got to a certain point, and then something would happen to displace him and send him off again in search of a new beginning.

The problem, of course, was that I could hardly saunter into the lab and start a casual conversation about any of this. This was a man with secrets.

But I had a sense of urgency now that was a physical ache, something that made me square my jaw and clench my teeth against it. I could not forget Celia's eyes as they followed me out of her room there at the Turning House. Eyes that were hollowed out, lost, eyes that knew me and were trying to remember, eyes that were windows into a spirit that had been burned and maimed and wounded almost unto death.

I had left her behind. There had been other priorities, more immediate ones. But I had meant it when I said that I would get my sister out of that particular hell. And if that meant learning how to circle around the likes of Wilfred Sand until I could extract the information I needed, then that was what I would do. Whatever it took, I would do it.

It actually proved to be easier than I had thought it might be – because I'd forgotten that he had technically volunteered to keep an eye on experiments in progress when Asia had come to kidnap me from the lab for her research trip. And as it turned out one of the experiments I had left in his care had managed to fail rather spectacularly during my days away from the lab, and that gave me the opening I needed – from complaining about the failure it was a short step to asking him, as a more experienced colleague, for his opinions and advice, and it was easy enough in that context to introduce the subject of a broader scope of research, as well as a personal comment or two about how Turning Houses had always given me nightmares anyway.

"Never wanted to get any closer than I had to," I told him. "Not after the stories my parents told. And to be perfectly honest about it, there was something personal in it – given that I took my time actually Turning, I was starting to think that I might just end up there, amongst the incurables..."

He gave me a sour sideways look. "Incurables," he said. "Interesting way of putting it."

He had practically handed me my opening on a plate. "Oh? You think it's curable, then?"

"Some people think they have *a* cure," he said dryly. "I don't know that it's *the* cure. But who am I to argue? I'm just the lab-serf, hardly a policy setter."

"What *are* you talking about?"

"Nothing," Wilfred said, turning away abruptly. "Forget it."

But the door was open, now. And I had the tools to keep it that way. Wilfred was something of a perfectionist, and was given to correcting a rookie's mistakes, often sharply, when he saw them. All I needed to do was give him an opportunity to 'correct' me – and I found it the very next day, after a night of uneasy silences shared with Asia, when I straightened up from something I had been doing on a lab bench while rubbing my back and smothering a huge yawn.

Wilfred pounced on it.

"Pay attention," he admonished me, from across the bench. "This stuff needs focus and steady hands You can't work properly if you're sleepwalking."

"Maybe I'll go get a coffee," I said, "just to wake up the brain a bit more. Had a bit of a night, actually. Didn't get nearly enough sleep."

He snorted, but made no comment.

"Want to take a break? Come join me?" I said.

"I can't just drop everything in the middle..." he began testily, looking up with a frown.

He really was a prematurely presenting curmudgeon – if ever there was evidence that the Were aged too fast and died too young here it stood in the flesh. His actual chronological age might not have been that vast but he was, in Lycan terms at least, well past middle age. And it showed.

I had never been big on boyish charm but apparently I had some remnant of it somewhere – because I offered up a tentative smile, and after a moment Wilfred straightened, running one hand through his hair.

"Well, a cup of coffee wouldn't come amiss, I guess," he grumbled.

I raised the subject of gene therapy – something he had been working on in at least one former lab of his, and something that I saw as a hope and a possibility as far as rehabilitating Celia was concerned – when we were perched on our white plastic chairs in the cafeteria, nursing our coffees.

"They're talking about switching me to that, kind of full time," I said. It wasn't true and he was certainly going to find out it wasn't true but it seemed a good gamble at the moment. "Maybe they're moving me to working more closely with Asia, now that they've got us together in private they want to make us a professional team as well, or they will once I actually get some credentials under my belt. But I've been reading up on it. Your name kept coming up."

That appeared to be a tactical mistake, because his brow clouded. "Yeah," he said. "Worked on it some."

"It's complicated," I said, persevering. It was as good a chance as I was going to get. And maybe I could bet on his inability to let an error go unchallenged. "Seems to me that no matter what you do you're courting the possibility of wreaking havoc. I've read you can use the common cold virus to deliver the new genetic material – which frankly freaks me out because of the way we all get colds, what if someone who doesn't need the gene tweak breathes this stuff in? What does it do to your own gene-stuff?"

"Please," Wilfred said, sniffily, "one takes a reasonable amount of care with such things. And Adenoviruses – the kind you're talking about – they've got their pros and cons, anyway. The pros definitely include a certain ease of administration – they're equally at home in both actively dividing cells and ones which are not – but they *can* cause an immune response in the patient, which is bad, and also the genetic payload they carry doesn't integrate into the host DNA so it doesn't get replicated when the cell does. It is only actively expressed for a week or two before the cell discards it. You're literally confined to 'catching cold' twice a month if you want this therapy to continue doing anything on a long-term basis. It can carry a decent-sized chunk of stuff – some seven and half thousand base pairs of DNA – you can pack a fair wallop into that but it's all very temporary."

"And if you wanted something more permanent?" I said. "Those Adeno-associated viruses…"

Wilfred lifted a hand. "No, that's something different," he said. "Those don't cause illness in humans, common cold or anything else – they carry single-stranded DNA, and they *will* integrate the payload into the host genome – but they can only carry about 5000 base pairs, and they need 'helper' viruses to replicate themselves inside host cells, and when they integrate they'll almost inevitably do so in a very specific region of Chromosome 19 in humans – which is great because you know they won't disrupt anything important, like a Retrovirus might do – but if you want a target outside that particular region you may have problems."

"Common cold is one thing," I said. "Retroviruses can be nasty. I wouldn't want any accidents with those."

"They've been known to be used as the vector of choice for a more permanent solution," Wilfred said. I think he was actually enjoying himself, as far as he was able. He was the professor here, and I was the junior acolyte at his knee thirsting for knowledge. "They'll carry a comparable payload to an Adenovirus – that's the common cold one, not the associated ones I've just been talking about – some eight thousand base pairs in all – and they will integrate into the host genome at their destination, so that when the cell that's been introduced divides is going to get replicated together with the host DNA. But there are other problems with those."

I really had done my background reading, and I actually knew my stuff here. "They can cause immune responses, too," I said. "Not to mention cancers."

Wilfred was nodding. "Exactly. But like I've just been saying – there's also the fact that they are unpredictable. They will integrate, yes, and they will replicate, yes, but they tend to integrate completely *randomly*, into any place they might fall, rather than into some pre-determined useful spot where they can do some good. And if they integrate right in the middle of some other important gene – they can wreak a pretty piece of havoc."

"What if you wanted something like that, though – something that does insert into a specific location...?"

It was a step too far. Wilfred paused, tilting his head at me quizzically.

"You're picking my brain," he said. "And it's about something very precise and defined, if you're talking about genotype specific preferential insertion. Nice line of questioning, lad, but what do you really want to know?"

Well, but perhaps it was time to get direct.

"Can you kickstart a stalled Were?"

"Can you what, now?" But that was a startle reaction, and the scientist in Wilfred was already leapfrogging the initial confusion and into the next level. "The Turning Houses. You're talking about the Project, aren't you?"

"The Project?" I had heard the capital P in that word, but my own confusion was genuine. This – at least not by that name – I had not encountered in the literature.

Wilfred was staring at me in a funny way. "You're either very good – at what, I'm still not entirely clear – or you're a genuine innocent and you're standing on very thin ice and don't even know it. Just what has Asia been telling you?"

"Not that much," I said. "Not nearly enough. Not enough for what I need to find out."

"And what is that, exactly?"

"Whether you can... I don't know... vaccinate someone who has lost the ability to Turn. A re-Were shot, as it were."

"It's been quite an ongoing thing," he said. "Without much success. Trying to twist the lost souls at the Turning Houses back into good little Lycans. It just doesn't seem to work, no matter what the vector they use to deliver what they believe to be the crucial bits of genetic information. They don't... what?"

I was shaking my head before he had got halfway through that speech and he finally took notice of that, and broke off.

"Not into Lycans," I said. "Back. Into themselves."

He leaned forward, cupping his chin in his hand. "Oh?"

I felt the blood rush into my cheeks. It felt as though I was indulging in yet another spot of betrayal – except that by this stage I was not quite sure any more whom I was betraying.

"I just... I need to know," I said. "Is it doable? Remotely within the realm of possibility?"

"This is something personal," Wilfred said.

There was no point in denying *that*. "Yes," I said. "Very."

"And just who sent you straight to me...?"

I hesitated, but not for long. "One of the Manion twins," I said. "Sorcha."

"Sorcha Manion told you to talk to me," Wilfred said. "This gets interesting. Does she know your reasons?"

"She... overheard something... Asia and I were talking about. That's all she knows."

"So *Asia* knows."

"She was there," I said, and instantly wished I could bite my tongue because I had just said more than I wanted just then. And Wilfred was too sharp not to pick up on it.

"It's something from this last disastrous trip," Wilfred said. "It's something at that Turning House you two just went to. No... it's *someone*." He thought about it for a moment, putting the pieces together in his head. "That's the reason Sorcha responded," he said finally, after a long pause, dropping his voice a little. "It's... you have a sister?"

The ground trembled underneath me. Everything could fall into ashes, right here, right now. How badly had I botched this?

I said nothing, but he was still watching me, and he read on my face what he needed to in order to confirm his hypothesis.

"You should tell me more," he said, pushing back his chair and gulping down the last of his coffee as he got up. "But not here. And not now."

It was subtle – and maybe a year ago I would have been too frustrated and too angry to notice such a thing – but somehow I knew that I was looking at an ally. He would say nothing of this conversation to people who might use it against me. He was willing to help. If I asked.

And I would ask.

"Wilfred."

He turned, a few steps away from the table already, one eyebrow raised in mute question.

"Come to our place," I said. "Come tonight, after work. I'll tell you what I know."

"All right," he said. Only that.

It was enough.

In the beginning, back when Celia and I were young, back perhaps when we were still Svetya and Goran to one another, two lost children from a different world, we were everything to each other, we had one another's backs, we were the only true allies we absolutely knew we could count on. When she went – when I thought she was dead – I had been *left alone*, and there had been a great yawning black hole where Celia had been. I had allowed it to all but suck me in completely. But not quite. In the beginning it had been Celia and I against the world... and now, all of a sudden, I had tapped into that world, drawing in friends, people who were willing to help me at least try to reclaim my sister from the abyss into which she had been flung. Everything had changed and rearranged, and I was feeling a little dizzy and disoriented with it all, but for a boy who once didn't trust anyone at all and liked them even less, I was learning how to forge alliances. Learning that I needed to forge alliances. Learning that I was not – that I did not need to be – alone.

Asia was less surprised to see Wilfred show up at our apartment than she might have been. I think she had already figured out that part of it for herself. She looked vaguely worried – I knew her tells by now, and the incessant gnawing at her lower lip while we talked over coffee that night was a dead giveaway – but she was also reaching a plateau of something that was almost serenity. There was an inevitability to this that almost took my own breath away.

Wilfred had brought a folder of notes, and he had pushed it over at me once we got into it. But it was Asia who picked it up and began poring over its contents.

"You don't *want* one of the viruses," Wilfred said. "You need something different. Something new enough to be almost experimental. They're called 'virosomes' – it's there in that folder..."

I glanced at Asia and she looked up. "In a nutshell," she said, "they're little bags of fat covered with viral surface protein to get them into the cell. They can carry a bundle – they've all the advantages of specific DNA inserts, like on plasmids, on bits of introduced DNA, but with the efficiency and specificity of delivery that only a real virus can give you. They'll interact with the cell, directly, at the membrane, the viral proteins shaking hands with the ones on the target cell, and the virosome will simply fuse its inner lipid membrane with the cell and dump its contents inside. You might say they're hollowed out viruses, with all the viral stuff dug out and replaced with what you want to put into the host DNA."

She paused, glancing at Wilfred. "There *has* been some work done with these – with Lycan genes – and you know how that went."

"But you'd need target-specific genetic material in order to re-start a specific Were potential," Wilfred said. "And that might make a difference. With the Lycan stuff you were still introducing foreign matter, similar enough perhaps for you to hope that it might trigger a Lycan transformation but different enough for the original genetic code to reject it as not-self and it never did get expressed. You'd need to find a specific kind of, well, of ex-Were, in a Turning House... and then find some 'live' genetic material from a working Were of the same ilk. Like, an ex-Were-rat, and a true Were-rat for the transfer DNA."

"How would you administer the thing?" That was me, the rookie, asking the most basic of questions.

Wilfred gave me a somewhat pitying grin. "That's the least of your problems," he said. "A simple intramuscular injection would do it. But you need to line up your test subjects first.

"I know someone I could get the right DNA from," I began, thinking of the very simple equation that presented itself for Celia. Our father was Were-cat, just like she had been. It was the correct DNA and it had the added advantage of being close family genetic material which lessened the possibility of problems.

"You don't want to use her as a guinea pig," Asia said. "You'd need to test this. On someone. On someone *else*."

Wilfred's face clouded. "That's the part that I always fall at," he said. "I hate the idea of using these people as lab rats. I hate it. Always have done. It's ruined my career twice over already because I'm fine doing the work in the lab as long as I don't think about the ultimate destination – and then I simply can't bring myself to go there, when it comes to the finale. I've balked at using the Turning House crew for experiments."

Asia looked up. "I never think of them as people," she said softly. "They're numbers."

"But you take your samples yourself," Wilfred said. "You just went to the Turning House where you found... someone unexpected. But you went. Yourself. You faced them, you took their blood, you looked them in the eye."

"Yes," Asia said, "but I don't interact and I don't engage. And when I leave those samples are labelled only with numbers and after that I make myself forget which number goes with which face."

"Ah," Wilfred said, nodding knowingly.

"Don't get all superior on me," Asia snapped. "I do what I must."

"Rat," I said suddenly, and they both turned to stare at me. "If you can find an ex-Were-rat, I know someone who could probably supply the live DNA."

"Your friend Chalky," Asia said. A flat statement.

"He can do most anything that's needed," I said, aware I was setting Chalky up for this but perfectly certain that he'd be there if I called him for it.

Asia lifted both hands in a helpless gesture. "But we're grounded," she said to me, looking past Wilfred. "Until further notice."

"Like I said, administering the thing is the least of your problems. If you can find me the stuff I need to work with... I can build you a virosome. We can figure out the rest from there."

We talked about it later, Asia and I, after Wilfred had left, lying side by side on our bed.

"You really have no idea what you're getting into," Asia said. "And getting others into, potentially. All of this... if Sofia or Yuri gets a whiff of it..."

"I have to," I said. "I'm sorry."

I always seemed to be apologizing to her for something.

"I know," she said. She meant on both counts. "But Mal... this can't be a *thing*. It can't be open ended, from now until forever more until some result that you like comes out of it at the other end. For a start, it will be utterly impossible to keep it a secret for that long – I mean, look at how many people are already involved, hip deep and wading through it like I am or just skating on the fringes like Sorcha when she heard us talking, before. Sooner or later one of us will do something, say something, let something slip, and we're all going down for it then."

"If you ever need to choose," I said carefully, "I mean really choose, if it comes down to surviving in a pack or just me... you can just..."

She put a hand over my mouth, lightly, stopping the words from tumbling out. "Oh, Wonder Boy," she said. "I've already crossed *that* line, in case you haven't noticed."

"What about your own work?" I asked. "All the research into life expectancy, and all that?"

"This might help, at that," she said, with a watery grin, "even though I could never directly use the data from the underground experiments. But it might give me insights, at that. I could be weeding out all that so-called 'junk' DNA – and perhaps get an inkling in what goes on during genetic development – we know that there's stuff in our DNA that maybe *used* to get expressed, in the history of our species, but then stopped getting expressed for whatever reason – maybe that is what gave us the Diversification, when we began Turning into all the different Were kinds – "

"Maybe we were *all* Lycan once, in the beginning of time," I said. "One First Pack, roaming around at the dawn of history. Maybe everyone was a half-wolf, and then lived short sharp brutal lives, and someone's genes tried to jump the rails – and first got it wrong and changed into all kinds of different creatures instead of just un-expressing altogether – and then figured it out properly, and ditched the Were genes altogether to make a more stable human being..."

Asia sat up. "Keep talking..."

"Ash, I'm pulling this out of thin air..."

"Inspiration sometimes strikes in the weirdest places," she said. "You understand more than you know, perhaps. But it's making sense. Keep talking."

I rearranged the patterns again in my head. Perhaps it really was my superpower.

"Look, it's' obvious," I said at length, almost ludicrously astonished at how clear it all seemed to me now. "The way genetics work now isn't the way they've always worked. Things used to be *different*, you could *see* that. I mean, look at certain historical eras – the times when Bigger was Better, the times of absolute gigantism in everything, from insects to dinosaurs. Everything was huge. But then environmental changes happened, perhaps – or whatever else might have played a part – and all those genes for The Big got lost or silenced somehow – it just triggers a genotype change in the end. Maybe a small section of the living things in any given era get to keep a Big Gene, like for instance an elephant, a fragment of a population that gets to keep the ancient types – and the rest, well, they find something better or more useful and they just *adapt*, and the world changes..."

"Mal, you're brilliant," Asia said slowly.

"I know that but nobody ever gives me enough credit," I said, taking refuge in sarcasm, but I could feel myself actually flush at those words.

"It makes sense. It all makes *perfect* sense, really. Look at us – we're your 'Big" remnant, if you like. Maybe we *were* the originals. But we were flawed in fundamental ways – we had the ability to shift, to become the wolves that were our second halves, but we paid for it with short lives, a lifespan that made us old when we were barely fifty, few of us reaching ages much greater than that. So nature tried to shift gears – "

"What, changing us into Were-Rabbits and Were-Weasels and Were-Rats?"

"Well, it was a shot that had to be taken," Asia said. "It's scientific method at its finest. You experiment, and then you eliminate."

"But the other-kind Were didn't get eliminated," I pointed out. "They're still out there."

"Yes, but instead of *us* being offshoots of the normals, maybe they're offshoots of *us*," Asia said. "They call what we are – what we have – a 'syndrome' – "

"Lunar Trans-substantiation Syndrome," I said, recalling what I had read on the Stay leaflet once upon a time.

"Exactly. They had to call it something. But in effect... they're calling their own ancestral form diseased," Asia said, sounding almost amused. "I could play merry hob with the accepted published papers on this, if I could make a case for going exactly backwards from where most people start – there being so few Were compared to the normals it seemed to be perfectly rational to assume that we were the offshoot, the minority, the ones with the 'syndrome'. But there are few of us because we have a harder time breeding true, we have fewer offspring, and we die younger. We don't have the time to establish numbers. I think I have some reading to catch up on." She leaned over and kissed me, lightly, playfully. "Like I said. You're brilliant."

"Really?" I said, reaching over to wrap an arm around her shoulders and keeping her close to me. That catch-up reading could *wait*. "Show me..."

But as much as the night was a gift, the day project – the conspiracy – reasserted itself the following morning.

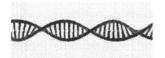

All the talk about lab rats had focused us all in an unexpected way. Asia seemed unable to help herself, and announced two days later that she had been in touch with some of her contacts in the Turning Houses and there were, in fact, two good Were-rat candidates in two separate Turning Houses available for testing the possible reawakening gene therapy injection. This was a good thing – there would be only one such patient per House, and any untoward attention would not be drawn to the fact that two similar subjects had suddenly been selected for an unsanctioned (that would have been easy to discover) experiment.

For the sourcing of relevant functioning Were-rat DNA I turned to Chalky, who assured me that it would not be a problem.

Turned out he delivered it himself – in changed form, wearing a different face. I did not know it was him when this delivery man in the uniform of the scientific supplies company we favored turned up a handful of days before our November Turn, with an official-looking cooler filled with dry ice and medical samples addressed to Asia and requiring a signature. Somehow he managed to engineer it so that I was the one stuck with signing for it, and while we were shuffling the paperwork between us the stranger grinned at me and said,

"I've dug up one or two things. Be in touch soon. Stay safe, Mal."

He was gone before I had time to muster a coherent response. A response that would have been – at least initially – a pure undiluted astonishment. It might have been Jazz's transformation that had given him the inspiration to try Turning into a different *human* rather than just a different creature – but hot damn, he had done it. And he had carried it off. And that thing that Jazz had discovered by accident – that it was possible to carry memories over from one form to another – he'd just proved it. I didn't know what this would do to the Were world if Chalky's new skills were revealed to them. I had a feeling the Lycans would rip him apart molecule by molecule to find out exactly what it was that made him tick the way he did.

But as for right at that moment, once I had got over his rabbit-out-of-a-hat appearance in the lab, now I knew what the cooler contained, and I took it straight to Wilfred instead of to Asia.

"Rat," I said, passing the cooler and its contents over to him.

"Right," he said, without missing a beat. "On it."

He left the cooler sitting there for the longest time, simply ignoring it, and all the while I was trying not to watch it too closely or to bring attention to it or to indicate in any way to anyone else who might have had their interest piqued that it was in any way important. But it was precisely the right thing to do because he was treating it as neither more nor less than something that was boring and routine and anyone who *might* have had suspicions about anything must have quickly decided that this particular cooler was not the one they were looking for. When he eventually left off doing whatever he had been busy with and took the cooler off to stow it somewhere, that was no longer anything that it was worth taking note of.

I didn't know what he was doing, precisely, or how long it would take, or what came next – but in any event we all left things unfinished for the Turn days, and it was only some ten days or so afterwards that Wilfred brushed past me in the lab and said laconically, "Your experiment's ready."

It took me a moment to understand, and then my heart thumped painfully against my ribs.

"Right," I said. "Thanks."

Asia and I were still grounded, by Yuri's fiat. Wilfred, however much he had been willing to risk in preparing the genetic material, was simply not going to be the one who would go to the Turning Houses to administer the necessary shots – he had made it fairly clear that the refusal to do that had been part of what had dogged his entire research career with the Lycans so far. We had to make do with another layer of subterfuge and concoction of a passel of lies and half-truths, and I called in Chalky again. It was he who came to pick up the 'vaccine' when it was ready; it was he who delivered it to the relevant Turning Houses, together with instructions for administration to the first selected subject and the address to which a report of the results should be sent. And then all we could do was wait for the following Turn, and what it would bring; if our theory was right, the subjects injected with the live Were-rat DNA virosomes would Turn in the usual way when the next full moon rose, into the rat-avatars they had once been.

If that happened, we might have some explaining to do. To *somebody*. If anyone was watching. But I hadn't planned that far ahead, and there were still two weeks to go, so all of us conspirators knuckled down to other work that we had to do and tried to avoid the subject altogether in casual conversation.

When the reports came back from the Turning Houses, three days after the December Turn, they were devastating.

"I don't understand it," Asia said, visibly upset and pacing the floor, at a late-night meeting at our place. "If it went wrong as drastically as this, it should have gone wrong *in the same way*. How can the exact same thing have two completely opposite reactions? How could one have dropped dead, and the other one show zero response at all? It's either deadly or it's not; it either affects the trigger gene or it does not; if it kills they both should have died and if we made an error somewhere and rigged it so that it failed to have an effect at all then neither should have had any reaction. How can one drop dead and the other not be affected at all? It doesn't make sense!"

For the moment, at least, she was in full scientist mode, completely focused on the result of the experiment, to the point that she was completely unable to retain an awareness that the one who had 'dropped dead' was in fact a human being. That we had, in blunt practical terms, literally just killed somebody.

Wilfred's expression spoke volumes about his own inner conflict – he at least could not divorce the experiment from the subject in his mind. But this time he was in way too deep, and some part of him was trying to shake the ethics and the morality of it loose so that he could concentrate on the science of it all. So that perhaps he could learn something from this disaster. Make sure it wasn't repeated. "Maybe the trigger genes are far more specific than we knew," he said, trying to work through it all, going back over what he had done and what he might have left undone. "Maybe only very specific DNA can fix things – generic genetic material just doesn't hack it – that would go a long way to making sense of why none of the plans for making neo-Lycans out of these people never met with any success. It just wasn't what the individuals responded to."

"But that makes it impossible," I said, dizzy with failure. "You can't have this be tied so intimately to every single person. It just can't be done – there are too many of them, and there would be way too few resources to deal with all of them…"

"Do you have any of her own genetic material? Your sister's?" Wilfred asked abruptly.

"Actually... yes," Asia said. I looked up, startled, because I had been unaware that she had collected any – as far as I knew Celia hadn't been one of her own test subjects. She met the look and waved it away with a gesture of dismissal. "I asked for it. A few weeks back. Don't worry, not just hers. I know better than light a neon sign over her head right now. I asked for a few individuals from that Turning House. And yes, hers, amongst them."

"Let me take a look," Wilfred said. "Maybe I can noodge an idea or two into ripening. But it might take some time..."

But time, as it turned out, we were running out of – if we had ever had any to begin with.

On the heels of the Turning Houses reports came a phone call from Chalky, on the clean phone that he had left with me.

"There's something you probably need to know," he said. Too carefully. All my hackles were up immediately – this was not going to be good.

He had phoned late at night, and Asia was curled up on her own side of the bed, woken up by the phone call but only able to hear my side of the conversation.

"What is it?" I asked, and Asia's eyes were wide and steady on mine.

"I finally got hold of your sister's records from the House. All of the records."

"And you found something?"

"Not good," Chalky said.

"Spit it out," I said sharply. "You're starting to freak me out."

"There's no easy way of telling you this," he said. "I found out that Celia... had been pregnant, there in the Turning House."

"She was *pregnant*?" I repeated, incredulous. Asia sat up in bed.

"At least twice, in fact. At least one pregnancy was on record as having ended in a miscarriage – a pretty bad one, as far as I can gather from the notes in her case file, quite late in the pregnancy. There were... complications. There are hints of other instances, less life-threatening but nevertheless on record. The final one..."

"The *final* one? How many...? Do I even want to know...? What happened with the... final... one?"

"That's just it. I don't know," Chalky said. "There's a record of a live birth. That's all I can find in Celia's file. I know its date of birth, and I know that it was a girl. No name. No indication as to what happened to the baby after Celia gave birth."

"Who was the father?"

"No record of that either," he said. "Not in this file. I'll keep digging. But I thought... you needed to know."

Asia reached out and wrapped a cold hand around my arm.

"What is it?" she demanded, after I thumbed the phone off and laid it down on my lap.

"We have to get Celia out of there," I said, through bloodless lips, trying to stop my whole body from being jackknifed by deep shudders. "I have no idea what really goes on in those places, not anymore, but Chalky says...

that Celia had a baby. That she was pregnant, multiple times, that she lost all the babies through bad or worse miscarriages, and then managed to bring one of them to term. She gave birth to a girl... and then the child disappears. What are they *doing* with those people in the Turning Houses? How could she have been pregnant? She was a kid herself when she went in there – she's pretty much your age, now – how can she have been pregnant? And with not even a name recorded for a possible father to that child – those *children* – and heaven knows if that was all that happened – oh *God*..."

I buried my face in my hands, and then felt Asia's arms go around me and her head come down on my shoulder.

"This wasn't the way I wanted to tell you," she whispered against my ear. "I was waiting... for a good moment... and before you jump all over me, I've only really been sure for a few days. I think that I'm pregnant, too. And this one too you can probably lay at the Turning House doors. To the best of my calculations it must have happened that October Turn in the wild woods, on that last morning, when we..." her voice faded, and for a moment there was only her breath in my hair.

And then I uncoiled, reached up, gathered her to me and kissed the crown of her head where it ended up tucked under my chin.

"So," I said, laying my cheek against the top of her head. "When do you want to tell the pack that the cub is on the way...?"

She tensed in my arms, a little. "And you?" she said. "Are *you*...?"

"Of course I am," I said quietly.

But it complicated matters. On the heels of that other news, being happy about a child of my own after hearing of what must have been a hellish life that my sister had led – being happy that I was contributing a new member to a Lycan bloodline at least some members of which may well have known about or even brought about that life for Celia – it just felt like another layer of betrayal. I more or less felt like bursting into tears, but I was not exactly sure just what it was I would have been crying about. But the tears came anyway; I closed my eyes against the hot prickly rush of them, trying not to let Asia know.

She stirred in my arms.

"About Celia," she said quietly. "About the whole... project. I may have an idea."

The Fourth Mask: A Place in the Pack

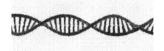

C all me... something new.

With the arrival of the new year in January, I was suddenly out of time – out of time to think carefully, to lay down precise and detailed plans. Everything was up in the air, and I knew that failure – by this time – did not just mean failing Celia for a second and perhaps final time but now also meant that I was gambling with the careers (perhaps the existence, when it came to someone like Chalky) of people who had trusted me and whose help in my feverish quest to save my sister had marked them in the eyes of the Lycans, Not to mention playing a game – with loaded dice – with the future of my wife and my child.

All of a sudden, I was not who I had used to be, no longer the angry young man out for blood. There were responsibilities. And if I wanted to accomplish what I had set out to do – get Celia out of the Turning House and the clutches of whoever had landed her there – I would have to work very fast.

Asia and I held on to the secret existence of the child, for just a little longer. We got together with Wilfred, the day after she had told me about the baby, and we said nothing to him – instead, Asia talked about the idea she had mentioned to me on the same night that she had told me about the child.

"It's been done," she was saying to Wilfred, poking her finger at a copy of a research paper that she had passed on to him and which he was scanning as she spoke. "And it *worked*."

"Asia. It worked in yeast," Wilfred said, his voice full of doubt. "A considerably less complicated..."

"*No*. Perhaps the organism is more complicated but the principles are the same. And let's face it, nothing else has done that much good. What do we have to lose?"

"All right," I said, a little impatiently, "I know you two know all about it, but would someone please try and explain it to me?"

"We aren't just messing about with a few important genes, or a handful of areas we know to be essential in the Turn," Asia said. "We'd simply be creating and implanting an entire artificial chromosome. With everything we want on it already. No messing about with insertions of the DNA that we want exactly in the spot where we want it, no potential problems with interference with other genes we don't want to screw up, just a simple single elegant chromosome and we can insert that and watch it start working its magic."

"If it works at all," Wilfred muttered.

"If it doesn't, we haven't lost much," Asia shot back. "Nothing *else* has worked, anyway. And In the yeast..."

"What happened with this in the yeast, then?" I interrupted, my eyes flicking from one to the other as if I were watching a tennis match.

"Everything," Asia said. "The new chromosome - well – it didn't seem to have any detrimental effect on the yeast cells in which the thing was implanted other than the yeast now having abilities – coded for on the new chromosome – that the host yeast did not."

"And this was permanent?"

"As far as they could see," Asia said. "The paper speaks of smooth replication across generations and the new abilities are solid."

I turned to Wilfred. "Is this doable?"

He hesitated. "In theory," he said, "yes, but there are..."

"With your virosome things? Can you put a... a *fixed* chromosome... into one of those and get it in place and make it start functioning instead of the one that was damaged, that Stay wrecked? One that will give her back her natural ability to Turn?"

Wilfred spread his hands in a gesture that was at once incoherent and eloquent. "I wish I could tell you that I could," he said. "I wish I could sit here and tell you that this is a solution to all our problems. But I have no idea if it will work. It's never been done before." He raised one hand to forestall an objection from Asia. "In human beings, it hasn't. Look, you wanted to test gene therapy in the Turning Houses pool of potential subjects —and we did – and it didn't go well – do you want me to set up another test? With something like this?"

He sounded reluctant, and unhappy; he had compromised his own principles, in one sense, to be a part of my quest to save my sister and it had all worked out exactly the way he had feared it would. Now I could see how he might feel as though he had trapped himself into this. There was no way back, no way out of this, no way to disavow what had happened or his part in it. The only way was forward.

But I was starting to feel something electric in the air, something that told me that my window was closing, that something was going to slam down on me soon, that if I didn't do something, *right now,* I might end up never having another chance.

"No," I said, and both Asia and Wilfred looked up at the flat denial, startled. "No. This works, or it doesn't work. When can you have something ready?"

"I'll have to work on it on the side," Wilfred said. "Zoya just slammed me with a big project, and that's going to take a huge amount of focus and lab time."

"Can you have something by the next Turn?"

"This one? In January? I don't know. I have no idea what I'm doing, I'm going to have to make this up as I go along – and you're going to have one shot at this, if you're planning on going directly to her, to your sister. You don't want me to cut corners. No. Probably not by this Turn. I'll try, but..."

"Do what you can," I said.

Asia stared at me after Wilfred left. "You look like you're running a fever," she said.

"I am, I suppose," I said.

"What if it doesn't work?"

"I'll have tried."

"All right," she said. "All right, then. But what... after?"

"I don't know," I said with a watery grin. "I haven't thought in terms of *after*. Although... I suppose it's time I did." I laid a hand on her belly, still not really showing her pregnancy. "I don't know how I am going to do right by both Celia and by *him*."

"Him?" Asia said, grinning.

"Her. It, The baby."

"I liked 'him' better. Let me take care of him, for now."

"Ash. Thank you."

"I will be glad," she said, after a pause, "when this is done. But you do realize, don't you, that you've just chosen the straight path and if this doesn't take you there... nothing will. You've left yourself no retreat at all."

"None of it was supposed to be like this," I said. "Nothing has turned out the way I expected. For good or ill."

"Well, thanks," she said dryly.

"You're the good part," I said.

The days slipped by, with an agonizing oily slowness that comes with *waiting*. I would catch Wilfred's eye in the lab every so often, and he'd respond with a tiny shake of his head – *nothing, nothing yet*. And I grudged every day that passed without the breakthrough that I wanted, because I was starting to get a horrible itchy feeling between my shoulder blades that felt as though I was in someone's sights and that at any time there could be a bullet in my back. I didn't want to jump the gun and spring Celia without having a plan; I couldn't make a plan without knowing that everything was ready; it was exhausting and it made me wretched and irritated and I even snapped at people like Asia, who deserved it so very little, because my temper was riding its frayed edges – patience had never been one of my virtues. But I could not make things happen any faster, and the January Turn was upon us before I realized that it had come.

Never before had I so grudged those three lost days I spent in my wolf skin. And I suppose Asia was right in that we at the very least carried our emotions into the Turn with us, because when I came out of this one it was obvious that I had picked at least one fight that I had not come all that well out of. The doctor – the same one who had examined me when I had first arrived, tut-tutted over me as he patched me up, post-Turn, and dealt out double handfuls of well-meaning exhortations not to mess with senior wolves in the enclosure during the Turn.

I licked my wounds, metaphorically, and waited.

But when the thing broke, it wasn't with Wilfred coming to slip into my waiting hand a virosome with a clean chromosome with the potential to bring my sister back to life.

It was Asia, scurrying almost furtively into the lab where I was working some two weeks or so after the January Turn, and calling me out into the corridor on a flimsy pretext. Sasha merely looked up and gave us a somewhat salacious grin and a thumbs-up. Wilfred appeared not to react at all, but I could see his shoulders tense under his white lab coat.

Something was wrong.

"She wants a report," Asia hissed as we stepped out of the lab. "Sofia. She wants to know what I've been working on for the last two months. Exactly. In detail. Mal, it isn't going to add up. If they look at what I've done and the time I've taken there will be questions asked."

"Has Wilfred said anything to you about where he's at?"

"Almost, but not quite," Asia said. "But I just don't think there's any more time. I can stall but not for too long."

"Okay, then," I said. "Okay."

I phoned Chalky on the 'clean' phone that night.

"Any further news to report?" I asked.

"I haven't been able to find out that much more," he said. "Why? Something up?"

"I may have to get Celia out of there," I said. "Quickly."

"They starting to sniff around? The wolves?"

"They may be. I have to..."

"Leave it to me," he interrupted.

"You can't do it alone," I said. "All the security... and the chip in her leg... and you can't let yourself be seen or recorded or recognized..."

I could hear the smile in his voice when he spoke again. "Remember who you're talking to," he said. "They won't recognize me. They can't. The person who goes to get Celia out will never have existed. And don't worry. I may have assistance already planned. All right, I'll figure on setting something up... for the next Turn. That's the best time – everything is that much more chaotic at the Turning Houses at those times, and a lot of things may slide under the radar if I play things right. I'll take her up to the woods. You know, the cabin."

"How are you going to get the keys again?"

"I made a copy, last time," Chalky said laconically, as though he was not admitting to what was practically an act of burglary. "Are you any further with the cure?"

"They tell me it's close," I said. "It all has to be done on the quiet, in between, in the cracks, shuffled into other more legit stuff – and that isn't ideal."

"Will you have something by the next Turn?"

"I have no idea. I hope so."

"We'll have to figure out what to do next," Chalky said. "I mean, all this is very well. Do you have a plan, for afterwards?"

"I haven't thought that far ahead," I said. "I know. I'd better come up with that too."

"We'll talk," Chalky said. "I'll keep an eye on movements and communications. If it becomes necessary to move things forward I'll let you know. Otherwise, I'll plan on the February Turn."

"Chalky... Don't let her..."

"I'll take care of her. Trust me."

"I do," I said, and I meant it. I trusted him absolutely.

I trusted him with Celia's life. And possibly my own. And maybe Asia's, too.

I considered distractions. Perhaps announcing that Asia and I were about to become parents would have drawn the pack's attention away from what was going on in the labs – but I didn't want to throw that out there, not like this, not waste perhaps the only good card we had left with the pack – so we all stalled as best we could. Wilfred was suddenly deluged with extra work; perhaps that was a coincidence, perhaps they really were onto us all and were simply trying to put a stop to everything without getting any of it out into the open, but whether or not it was a deliberate sabotage it put a spoke into the wheels of his progress on our secret project and it wasn't until almost literally the eve of the February Turn that he finally responded to my daily wordless questioning look with a slight, almost invisible, nod. It was done.

I called Chalky to let him know; he said his plans to snatch Celia from the Turning House were in place, but he wouldn't tell me more than that, he said the less I knew about it the safer he would feel going in. He was giving me plausible deniability. And then I had to have a hard talk with my wife, only a handful of hours before the full moon was due to rise and we had to report to the enclosure for the Turn.

"First thing, after I come out of there, I'm taking Wilfred's stuff... and I'm going," I said. "Ash, you don't have to come with me. There is still time to..."

"Are you telling me you don't want me anymore? Or the baby?"

"Of course not," I said. "You know better. It's just..."

"Then I'm coming with you," she said. "Look, you might think there's still time, but the truth of it is that we're standing on a bridge that is already ashes. You and me both, don't think you're on it alone. I'm actually surprised that it hasn't fallen in from underneath us yet."

"I'm going straight to the lab to pick up Wilfred's kit and then out to get a car, as soon as I come out of the Turn," I warned her.

"Get one of the diesels," she said. "I'll pack an emergency bug out bag. I have a safe place in the garage where I can hide it. I'll meet you out there. Don't you *dare* leave without me, Mal. I mean it."

"I was just trying to..."

"I know what you were trying to. It's way too late for that. But there's one other thing you should consider, while you're at it."

"What's that?"

She folded her hands over her belly. "Mal... if anyone is paying real attention... we haven't told them yet but they'll know. Some of them probably suspected already, last Turn – I should have told you, but with everything else – I barely *flickered* last time. I was last in, and I was out of the enclosure by the end of the first day. My body is responding to this – you know that after the first trimester, at the outset, a pregnant Were woman no longer Turns until the birth of that child – and this time... I am not feeling it, Mal. I may not Turn at all. And if I did walk into that enclosure, they'll probably know, just by looking at me. It isn't as if they weren't watching for any signs that we're on our way to starting a family – that's what they brought us together for in the first place. That game may well be up."

I hadn't even thought about that – but of course, she was right. And we should have said something long before now. But if she didn't Turn this time – we wouldn't have to say anything, any more, not really.

Perhaps it was just my guilty conscience screaming but I felt as though everyone's eyes were on me that Turn. I got to the enclosure at the same time as the Cotton family, and it wasn't as though Anna didn't always make a point of greeting me and smiling at me or Sam didn't (almost) always come over to have a word or two before the Turn took us all – but this time all of these small gestures acquired a sort of brittle, sharp significance, as though they'd never happened before, as though they would never happen again. I was almost taciturn in response, saying as little as I could get away with; I don't know if that didn't already send a signal that something was off, but I couldn't help myself.

I tried to hold out until Asia got there, if she got there, until I could see her enter the enclosure – but I could not, in the end. She had not come in before the wolf took me that time. I did see that the Manion twins were here for the first time, Sorcha and Seonaid, ushered in almost at the last moment of my human awareness, looking both eager and self-conscious – their first Turn. Their first three wolf days. There was a part of me that almost felt... regret... because I genuinely liked those girls. And what I was about to do might well have consequences that could mean that I never talked to them again.

There were a couple of Turning cloaks missing from the hooks on the fence when I came out of the Turn – some of us had already left the enclosure, there was no way of telling who, or when. If Asia had been right, she had never been inside at all this Turn - but either way, she was already waiting in the garage when I got there, carrying the precious cargo of Wilfred's reconstructed chromosome. Celia's chance of life, maybe. I clutched the cooler containing the virosomes with white-knuckled hands.

I was under no illusions that I was breaking all the rules, all the laws. That if I ever came back here it would be to consequences I could not begin to think about. I caught a glimpse of Asia's face, in the unguarded moment before she was aware that I was there, and I could see the knowledge of this written all over her features, too – but she schooled her expression when she saw me coming, and lifted a hand from which a set of car keys dangled.

"Got the keys," she said. "The bag's in the trunk. Let's stow that thing and let's go."

"Ash..." I began, my heart thumping painfully. "Did you..."

"Shhh," she said, placing long fingers briefly over my lips to hush me. That was no answer, but it was answer enough. She had not Turned. The pregnancy was established, and it was now out in the open. "We'd better get out of here before they come looking for us. Come on."

I tried to get hold of Chalky while Asia was driving, steadily and in silence, but he wasn't picking up, or else cell phones really did have trouble with signal up near the cabins where he was supposed to be with Celia, if all had gone well. I was increasingly and uncomfortably aware that I had taken him completely on faith – there had been no message to tell me if the operation had been a success – I had put Asia's life and my own on the table, high stakes, assuming that there would be something worth the sacrifice at the other end. She did not ask any questions, and I was grateful, because I would have found it hard to give her any kind of answer that could have reassured her.

The long drive was made even longer by the ratcheting tension in the car as we drew close to the cabin in the woods. I could see Asia's hands gripping the steering wheel fiercely as she pulled the car up on the graveled patch outside Nell's uncle's cottage. There was a dark SUV, slightly shabby and very nondescript, already parked there; I did not recognize the car. I could only hope that it didn't belong to Nell Baudoin's Uncle Sebastian himself and that he hadn't taken it upon himself to go back up to the lake on the spur of the out-of-season moment. Technically, on top of all the other rules and laws that we were breaking, our being here was really breaking and entering even if Chalky did have a copy of the key. We weren't exactly sanctioned to be here, this time not even by a remotely administered fiat by the owner's niece like on the previous occasion.

"Is that his car?" Asia asked, echoing my thoughts.

"I don't know," I said. "One way to find out."

I got out of our car and stood for a moment with my hand on the door, frozen. If this had all been for nothing... But before I had a chance to move, the cabin door was flung open... by someone I had *not* been expecting to see there.

"Jazz?" I said, staring. "What are *you* doing here?" And then, looking closer and noticing that she had been crying, more sharply, "Is everything... all right? Is...did Chalky..."

"She's here," Jazz said. "She's here, and she doesn't even seem to know me. Not really. But she doesn't seem to be upset – that we took her – she seems to be – oh, *Mal*. That is a horrible place. And she is broken. She is so broken..."

"How do you know? Wait, Chalky took *you*?"

"Of course," Jazz said. "Well, he took *Jesse*, really. And 'he' didn't take me, technically. He... he's a little scary, Mal."

Asia was beside me, reaching for my hand, her other closed around the handle of the cooler containing the genetic infusion of Celia's potential reincarnation which we had all risked everything to bring here. And then my vision swam into a white haze.

"Where is she?" I said hoarsely. "Show me."

Jazz beckoned me forward with an urgent motion, and Asia and I followed.

My breath caught in my throat as I stepped into the cabin. Chalky was leaning on the kitchen counter, across the room, and sitting in a chair in front of the woodstove, wrapped in a blanket, her hands wrapped around a mug of tea which she seemed to be ignoring completely while staring over its rim into the far distance, was the sister whom I had thought dead for so many years.

For a moment I could not speak at all, my voice seemed to have dried up to a husk and blown away on a high wind. And then it came, a single word, the only thing I could bring myself to say out loud, the name of the little girl she once was.

"*Svetya...*"

Her head turned, a little; her eyes slid slowly off the point where they had been fixed and slowly, ever so slowly, came to rest on me. Her lips curled up at the corners, a movement almost too tiny to be noticeable – but it was the beginning of a sweet, hesitant, uncertain smile.

I dropped Asia's hand and strode across the room in two long steps, falling to one knee next to Celia's chair and wrapping both arms around her, burying my head on her shoulder and trying to control the wracking sobs that had begun to shake me. One of her hands left the mug she was holding and fluttered up until it came to rest, like a tired butterfly, on one of mine.

They let me have that, the rest of them, there was silence in the room and not one of them came to interfere with the two of us. But then I glanced down and saw the bandage around Celia's leg, the seep of blood that showed on the edges of it.

"She's hurt," I said, rearing back, flinging an accusing look at Chalky. "What happened...?"

"The chip," Asia said faintly.

I had already remembered, a moment too late, about the tracking chips embedded in the flesh of those who were locked away inside the Turning Houses. Of course. They would have had to remove that.

"It's okay," Chalky said. "I knocked it out with an EMP – and then it was only just under the skin. There was a small scar, we knew exactly where it was. There'll be a somewhat bigger scar there now, I'm afraid, but it can't be helped. I can do basic field medicine if needs must. A surgeon I am not."

"What did you do with the thing...?"

"Smashed it. Threw the mortal remains into the lake when we got here. Don't worry, nobody will be tracking that, not ever, not anymore."

"You took Jazz in there," I said to Chalky, accusingly. "Anything could have gone wrong..."

"Actually, very little," Chalky said. "And besides, she insisted."

"She *insisted*? How? She didn't even know..."

"I emailed him," Jazz said. "You gave me his email. There was no way he was going in there without me."

I was shaking my head. "If anything had happened to *you*..." I managed to wring out, barely coherent. But they all understood. If anything had happened to Jazz that would have been two sisters that I would have been responsible for having come to grief. Yes, it was probably selfish – I was appalled at being selfish right now, but there it was. I was terrified, actually, in this hour – afraid for all of us. It was partly because, with Celia actually here with us, I had begun to realize just exactly what it was that I had done – that it could not be undone – and that I had very little idea about what to do next.

It was Asia who asked the question I wanted to ask, but could not find my way to through the silence.

"What happened?"

"We took her," Jazz said. "We just went in and..."

"Rewind a little. Start at the beginning."

"Jazz emailed me, like she said," Chalky said.

"And you told her everything?"

"Most of it," Chalky said laconically. Jazz actually turned to stare at him, but he ignored her, still focused on me. "Mal, she had as much right to know as you. It's her sister, too."

"But she is..." I swallowed it. This was not the time to blame the one person who could have sprung Celia or to question his methods. "Tell me," I said instead, straightening up, one hand still resting on Celia's shoulder. I had to keep touching her. To reassure myself that she was really here.

"There isn't that much to tell, really," Chalky said, shrugging. "I had the paperwork ready, and that got us through the gates. And sweet seventh circle of hell, that place is a complete screaming mess during Turn. The noises that were coming out of everywhere – the crowded pens and cages and stalls – the ever so slow movement of the people who were taking care of them, as though they couldn't hear the urgency, the stress in the cries – it was freaky."

"Mom and Dad were right," Jazz said faintly. "It's everything they never wanted to tell us about. It's like a bad dream, Mal. A very, very bad dream."

I closed my eyes briefly, imagining Celia's life there, the years of this that she had endured. "And you found her?"

"There was actually a moment," Chalky said. "We'd found her in her room – we had her between the two of us, supporting her like she was a marionette with her strings cut, and we were almost out of the main house when someone came along and found some small discrepancy in the papers. I had Jazz – Jesse as was – stagger out by himself with Celia out to the van I'd brought for the getaway, while I double-talked my way through that – but I was all but expecting to have to bull my way through the gates at this point, maybe. But in the end the administrative busybody decided everything was on the level, after all, and I got to the van, and zapped the ankle, and hoped that would be enough to blow the chip's signal and get us through the fence, and it worked well enough. We were out of there without further incident, anyway."

"They just... let you take her out of there?" Asia said, staring at him.

Chalky grinned at her, his irrepressible quicksilver smile. "My paperwork came straight from the Lycans," he said.

She roused. "How on earth did you..."

"I'm talented that way," Chalky said. "But all the same... that place did give me the willies. It was all I could do, actually, not to floor it, getting out of there – but I drove a slow steady respectable speed all the way up here, giving nobody any reason to suspect anything at all. And then we finally got here, and I dug the thing out of her leg and tossed it, and she's... pretty much been like you see her, since. She eats if you put food in front of her, and she drinks if you put a cup in her hand, but she has barely said half a dozen words – she's just this sweet empty shell with nothing left inside..."

"She doesn't know who I am," Jazz said, choking on the words. "Not really. I can see her looking at me and there's nothing there – *nothing* – "

"She might not, at that," I said. "Remember, you were a child the last time she saw you. And now, the first time she laid eyes on you, you weren't even yourself."

Celia murmured my name – my real name, the name of the child who had crossed the ocean with her, the baby brother whom she had loved and cared for and protected when she was barely a girl herself.

She remembered *me*.

I tightened my hand on her shoulder, fighting back the tears that threatened to come again.

"She remembers older memories," Chalky said. "At least that is what it looks like. It's just as well that she doesn't really remember any of these Turning House years. It isn't a memory anyone would want to wish on her." His eyes warned me. He had not told Jazz the whole story. Not about Celia's children.

Asia stirred, in the awkward moment, and reached out to put the cooler she still held on the table beside her. Chalky's eyes turned to that, and then to Asia's face.

"Is that what I think it is?"

"It's our last chance at it, I think," Asia said.

"You think it'll work?"

"I hope so," Asia said, after a brief but telling hesitation.

Jazz looked up, her eyes burning. "Let me do it," she said, pleading. "Let me give it to her."

"How much *did* you tell her?" I asked Chalky sharply.

"Enough, for this," he said. "She understands what you're trying to do. That's why she wanted so much to be a part of it. To help."

Asia was looking questioningly at me. I wasn't so sure about it – Jazz was so young! – but in the end I bit my lip and grimaced a sort of consent. Asia fumbled with the catch to the cooler lid and extracted a syringe from within, a plastic safety cap on the needle. Jazz reached for it, and Asia reluctantly gave it up.

"Show me," Jazz said. "Show me what to do."

"Best in the upper arm," Asia said. "Slip off the sleeve. Here's an alcohol wipe; clean the place where you're going to inject..."

She took off the protective plastic sleeve as she spoke, and the needle glinted sharp and wicked in the amber-colored light in the room. Celia put up no resistance whatsoever as her cup was taken from her and one of her arms freed from its long sleeve. Jazz tore open one of Asia's wipes and smeared it on Celia's limp arm. Asia looked unconvinced as she stared at the needle and at the child who waited to administer it – and for some reason she looked very much a child, Jazz did, in that moment. Frightened, determined, on the verge of bursting into tears all over again.

I knew a split second before she did that she could not do it, just before she sobbed quietly and quailed at Celia's blank empty stare which rested upon her.

"I can't," she whimpered. "I can't, I can't, she doesn't know me, she doesn't want me..."

Asia, who was the closest, reached out and gathered Jazz against her with one arm, removing the syringe with her free hand.

"It's okay. Give it to me."

And I realized I knew something else, too.

I reached out and gently closed my hand around Asia's wrist.

"No," I said. "*You've already given too much.* This is mine, I landed us all here."

I took the syringe from Asia even as she whispered, "Are you sure about this?" over the top of Jazz's head.

I gave her a ghost of a smile. "If not this then it's all been sacrificed for nothing..."

She gave up the syringe after holding onto it convulsively for an instant longer, and folded both her arms around Jazz, who was now openly crying with her head tucked up against Asia's shoulder. I held the syringe in my right hand and stared at Celia.

I barely saw her. What I saw was... a palimpsest beneath which all of her other selves were hidden. The young girl, no more than a child herself, who had tried to hold me and comfort me when I was a frightened little boy – frightened of the Turning Houses and how they snatched our parents away from us and left us alone, her and me, until they could return after their three days of captivity there. The older Celia, the one from our early lives in this city, the one who had first crossed Barbican Bain's path, the one who stumbled on that path, and fell, and was lost. The one whom I had pushed, maybe. The one whom I would never forgive myself for having hurt, no matter how young and ignorant I myself might have been at the time. The one whose death had shadowed my life and left me dark places in which to lurk and hide – the moment which had shaped me, and twisted me, and drove me to doing everything I had done in order to stand here in this place right now.

The one whom I might have been the one to condemn to the shattered existence I had not even known about until that moment – the loss of her very identity, the grim Turning House years, the bearing of children she was not capable of wanting or loving, the spirit I remembered erased along with her memories.

I became aware that my hand – the one holding the syringe – was shaking, and fought to steady it, to control it, as I murmured something incoherent and went down on one knee beside Celia's chair. And then she whispered something I couldn't make out except for my name, and reached out, laying one of those pale limp hands on mine.

I heard a strange sound, like the moan of a mortally wounded animal, and did not even realize it was me until I felt another hand come to rest on my arm.

"I can't," I said, in a low and helpless voice, my eyes too blurred with tears to see straight. "What if... what if this doesn't work... what if it kills... I can't do this, I can't do it *again*, I can't kill her twice, Ash, Ash, are you sure – are you sure this is going to work – are you *sure*..."

"Enough," Chalky's voice said into my ear. "You are all too close. Give me the thing."

"But you..."

"Give it to me," he repeated. "If you want to help, hold her hand. It seems to calm her, to have you near her."

He took the syringe, which I had no strength to hold on to, and I collapsed on both knees beside Celia's chair, folding one of her hands into both of my own. I knew there was an instant of time when the needle went into her arm because I felt her hand flinch a little, but that was all, and it seemed to be so small, such a tiny reaction, to something that could be this enormous and life-changing.

"Done," Chalky said quietly. "All done. You can pull the sleeve back on now. What happens next?"

That last, to Asia, who was still standing frozen by the table on which the cooler rested, with Jazz still in her arms.

"Next?" she said, her voice oddly inflectionless. "Well, where she is concerned...it's a waiting game. We don't know if it works until the Turn signal comes – and then it either triggers that Turn, or it does not, and if it does not... I don't know if there is anything left to try. There's another syringe in here, already prepared; Wilfred said he thought another injection, maybe a week before the Turn, might help to kick in the function of the new DNA, help the Turn come. But I don't even know if that is an issue. It might help, it won't hurt, but if it doesn't happen, I don't think that it will change the outcome much one way or another. From here on... it's on her. It's in her body, in every cell, in every strand of her DNA. Mal... we've done what we can do. There is nothing left, after this."

"I have to think," I said, my mind still mired in a fog, blundering about blindly, trying to find a way. "I have to figure out... to keep her safe..."

Chalky cupped his hand under my elbow, and I allowed him to raise me to my feet.

"You've got other things to figure out," Chalky said. "I am reasonably certain that your absence without leave has been noted, and that your activities are being scrutinized even now back at the Lycan fortress. Are you going back? How are you going back? What are you going to do when you go back? There have been lone wolves before now – it's in the histories – but they tend to live short sharp and brutal lives – and do you want that for your family?"

Asia's head lifted sharply, and Chalky nodded once, knowingly.

"No, I didn't know," he said, "but I do now. Mal, you have to think about *this* family, now. You have to leave Celia to me. I will take her somewhere safe, don't worry about that, and I will watch her, until that next Turn. And yes, if you leave that second syringe with me I'll even make sure she gets that second dose when she needs to. How much of this do you want your parents to know? The rest of the Were hierarchy? How much do we have to – how much *can* we – hide and hope that nobody notices? I know how to cover my own tracks, at some point someone *will* notice the fake paperwork trail that I had to leave behind in order to spring Celia from that place, if they haven't already, but there is no way to trace any of that back to me. You guys, however – *this* stuff – " He gestured at the cooler and its contents "This is traceable. You couldn't do this in a vacuum, and in fact you were doing it literally under their noses anyway, deep in the heart of their realm, it always was a matter of time. They're probably waiting for you, right now."

"It'll probably be the full Tribunal, this time," Asia said faintly.

"What happens at a full Tribunal?" I asked, collecting myself sufficiently to look at her.

"It's – we'll be facing the whole Pack," she said. "It's kind of Lycan Judgment Day. Isn't often invoked, especially for lesser sins – but when it is, then it carries considerable clout."

"What can they do?"

"Anything they want," she said. Her hand curled protectively in front of her belly.

I hesitated. "Do we have to... go back?"

"We can't stay on the run forever," Asia said.

"Well, then," I said. "The sooner the better. Nothing worse than waiting for something; at least let's get it over with."

But I hesitated, looking down at Celia, and then at Jazz.

"Leave it with me, then," Chalky said. "I'll take the kid sister home and then Celia and I will hole up somewhere quiet until the next Turn. I'll find a way to let you know. And here, I have something for you." He took a few steps over to the counter on which he'd been leaning earlier, and retrieved a sealed envelope, handing to me. I took it reflexively. "About... the other matter. That's all I know, so far. Still have feelers out, but I managed to ferret out some more bits and pieces. I wouldn't," he added, after a small hesitation, "let the Lycans know how much you know."

"About this?"

"Well, about anything, really," Chalky said laconically. "They can do their own homework, I'm not about to do it for them."

"Are you going to be all right?" Asia asked, with unexpected concern.

Chalky appeared a little nonplussed at the inquiry, but took it in his stride. "I know how to keep swimming," he said. "So long as I know that there's sharks in the water and where they are, I know how to avoid them. I'll be fine."

"And Celia?"

"Well, in the end, it's going to be one of two things," Chalky said.

"Either nothing is going to change or everything will. Either way, I'll have it covered. Do we want to let your parents into this? What happens if she *does* Turn? Somehow, Mal, I think you are going to have to think this one through to its conclusions – I can deal with it, short term, but I can't take her on as a permanent dependent. I need to be able to move or disappear at any moment, and it would be next to impossible to do that with someone like your sister in tow."

"Can you ever bring her... home?" Jazz asked.

"Can your parents handle this?" Chalky asked carefully. "And if she does go home – oh, man, this could get really complicated really fast. If the Were Authority got wind of the situation – whether they decided to run a full investigation or not – I don't know whether to wish for it or hope that they can be tricked into looking permanently in the other direction. We may have to end up creating a whole new identity for her. I know how to do that, it won't be an insurmountable task, but if that's the endgame then I need to know sooner rather than later because even though it's doable it *does* take some work. Especially if it turns out that it's a new Were identity that she needs. Remember, if she regains her faculties, it's going to be back to a Random – and that might prove to be problematic in itself..."

"Let's just find out... first... if it worked at all," Asia said.

Chalky shrugged. "Fine. We can do that. Leave the girls with me, and you two, get out of here. Let me know how it all pans out. You have my number."

I felt ripped in half as I stood there, Asia on one side of me, Celia on the other, Jazz standing a foot or two away staring at me with a mix of emotions playing on her face. And Chalky, steady and calm, the eye of this storm, reaching out to grasp me by the shoulder and look into my eyes.

"There may be a time when you can find a way to be all the things you need to be to all the people you think need you to be those things," he said, "but dude, right now, you have to make a few breaks. There isn't enough of you to go around. Trust me, I'll make sure she is safe."

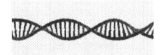

And so we left them – I left both my sisters under Chalky's care, knowing that it was the only thing that I could do. We got back in the car, Asia and I, and she turned us back towards... I had thought of it in terms of 'towards home' but the sense of dread I felt was hardly something that you could lay on a place you could call by that name.

Asia saw them first, as we pulled into the driveway and came to a halt outside the main building – Sasha Berezhnoy, John Cotton, and Tom Manion, waiting for us at the front door, their faces grim.

Asia nodded as she studied their expressions. "It's the Tribunal," she said. "Look at them. You'd better brace yourself."

I gave her a noncommittal grunt in response. I had been bracing myself for the duration of that whole long drive. This was the moment when the consequences of all the choices I had made in my life came home to roost.

"I wonder if they already nailed poor Wilfred to the wall," I said.

"They might want to wait to get all of us," Asia said. "They were never ones for wasting effort."

I searched for the right thing to say, but nothing helpful came to mind except the words that I had said to her so often before. "I'm sorry, Ash. About all of this."

"I'd like to think," she said, "that I would have done the same thing, in your shoes. I've never had a sibling – and my family, here, has always been... well, not what you have with your own sisters, anyway. But if I'd had a sister...I hope I would have had the courage to go against the whole world for her sake, too."

"You did," I said quietly. "For *mine*."

We linked fingers, briefly, there in the car, and held tight onto one another's hand. And then she shook me loose and sighed.

"Time to go into the den," she said.

"What do you think they're going to do?"

"Anything is possible," she said. "We're part of the pack, and we went against the pack – they have us cold on that..."

"No, we didn't! We just went around them – and anyway – we aren't really core pack, are we? Either of us?"

"As to that..." she hesitated, and then looked thoughtful, and then shook her head as though to dismiss a bothersome idea. "Neither of us were floaters," she said. "I was blood-linked, straight through the Alpha line, despite not being in the legitimate line of descent; and you were adopted into the core pack – through Yuri and Sofia's own word, through linking you into the families by marrying you to me – however tenuous, that is a bond, and it was meant to bind. At least that's the way they will see it. Come on. They're waiting for us, We're out of time."

The three Lycans that waited for us stood stonily by the door as we got out of the car and approached the building, side by side.

"Yuri and Sofia are waiting for you," Tom Manion said. "With the rest of the family."

He turned and led the way; the others waited until we had passed them and then fell into step behind us. It definitely felt as though we were being escorted to a court. Perhaps to an execution.

They took us to a room I had not seen before – deep in the heart of the complex, a hexagonal room with no windows, just a round skylight high in the vaulted roof. The room had seats along four walls; the wide double doors of the entrance took up the fifth, and a raised dais on which two separate chairs, which bore an unnerving resemblance to two thrones despite their apparent simplicity, had been set. Yuri and Sofia occupied those. Tom motioned Asia and myself into two other chairs, set squarely in the empty middle of the room, and then withdrew to take his own seat in the tiers along the walls.

"We are not here to hear a confession," Sofia said, in her soft and dangerous voice. "Most of it, we know. The reason you are here now is you, Malcolm Marsh, were only a few months' warm in the Pack before you broke the Lycan Law; and you Asia Adema, were instrumental in enabling the breaking of that Law, and in you we are extremely disappointed. You were raised in the bosom of the pack, the daughter of the Alpha wolf. We expected better from you."

Neither of us attempted to speak.

"Given the current situation we now have to distrust everything – we are certain that the events that took place during the first time you and Asia vanished on what was supposed to be a routine research trip to a Turning House bear very little resemblance to those you presented to us in the reports that you were asked to produce upon your return. And we were lenient, then. Perhaps too lenient. But at that time we did not know how deep the sedition went – and it went far deeper, because there was a conspiracy to use the assets and resources of this pack in order to pursue an unsanctioned agenda. Is there anything that you wish to say to us? Please do not indulge in a hope that it might be used in defense – that is futile. There is no defense. Only a calling to account. The Law is first, and the Law was broken."

I had no idea how much they really knew; I had not had a chance to look properly around the ranks of the seated Lycans, and I did not know if Wilfred was in this room or if it really was just the Families. But I didn't exactly want to volunteer anything – not least because Chalky and Celia were still out there, still potentially vulnerable. But Asia stirred beside me, lifting her head.

"You knew," she said to Sofia, "when he came here, you tested him and found him true Lycan but you knew he came from the outside, he was an adult, and he came with baggage. He already had a family, before he came to you. They were his family before you were; he went through things with that family, in the *years* that they lived together, which he didn't have a chance of making up for during his *months* here with us. Loyalty is valued by the Lycans. You cannot now fault one of your own for being the very thing that you hold so highly."

"Loyalty to Lycan Law," Yuri said.

"Loyalty is freely given," Asia said passionately.

"We thought we had yours."

"You did," she said. "You gave me in marriage, in mating, and I went where you commanded. Because of loyalty."

I felt my jaw clench a little, at that. It implied that she might not, at the very least in the beginning when her taking me on as mate was first mooted, have been entirely willing after all. But she had not finished speaking yet.

"But there are layers of loyalties, Yuri," she said. "And I am first and above all Lycan because that is all I have ever known. But then there is the loyalty to a mate. And when that mate is in a crisis of pain – which I myself may have had a hand in precipitating – loyalty finds a new level. I owed him."

"You owed the pack," Sofia said. "It is us you owed that loyalty to, first."

"To my family?" Asia questioned softly.

"Precisely," Sofia said.

"Like he did?" Asia asked. "To the birth family that he could not exactly pretend he had never had?"

"We thought we could trust that the Lycan came first," Yuri said. "As it does with all of us. As it should have done. I told him when I went to bring him here after he first Turned that we were his family now. I thought that was understood."

I could not let Asia fall on this sword.

"Stop," I said. "If you want to blame anyone, you can blame it all on me. I did what I had to do, what I was driven to do, and I used whatever means were available to do it. That is partly a road you showed me; before I came to this place that I knew very little about what made us tick, what made us Were, and how much of that could be lost, and how much it mattered."

They clearly knew about Celia's identity and existence or there wouldn't have been that much emphasis placed on 'family' so I wasn't really giving that up here. I gave them more – just a little bit more.

"I saw a sister I had thought dead. Dead through something that I myself might have been responsible for. I could no more have walked away from that than... than any of you could renounce being wolf, right now, and be believed if you offered up some of that thing that you called loyalty to some other form or creature. Dead... and she was alive again. And once I knew that I would have walked through fire to rescue her."

"We are told that she was taken, your sister, but the persons who took her have not been traced and cannot be found. I may, then, safely assume that you know their identities as we do not. This knowledge we will have from you."

"No," I said softly. "Because to give that up would be to give her up. And I may already have sacrificed too much to surrender now."

"Then Asia will tell us."

Asia shook her head, just once.

Yuri frowned.

"It may be that we made a mistake, mating you to each other," he murmured. "Highly strung and yet raw, one only a second-generation Lycan despite an exemplary line of descent through the father, the other barely Lycan at all. It may be best for all involved if this marriage were ended, and Asia, at least, bestowed where it would benefit the pack."

"No," Asia said. "You cannot do that."

"It is in my rights," Yuri said heavily. "And Sofia's word, also. We are Alpha. We speak for the pack, and do the things that must be done to make the pack strong."

"And I can claim a right, too," Asia said, and rose to her feet.

I looked up at her, startled. If she had planned anything, she had not told me of it, and I literally had as little idea as anyone else in that room about what would happen next.

"I have to thank you," Asia said, speaking directly to the two on the dais but somehow lifting her voice so that it carried into the rest of the chamber, "for gathering the entire pack here today because I need to do what I have to do in front of all, and it would have gone hard, I suspect, for myself to have rallied the pack to gather and listen."

Her chin lifted, and she held their eyes with her own defiant gaze.

"But according to an ancient right, and rooted in the Law to which you hold so dear, I stand before you and step out of the pack of my birth in order to form my own. I am Alpha, of a new pack; and in that capacity I have broken no rule because I do what I do for the benefit of my own pack now."

"You cannot stand alone," Yuri said, his scowl deepening. "This too is the Law."

"I do not," Asia said, and turned to me. "I am one of a mated pair, and you mated me. I have my Alpha male wolf beside me, and in this gathering and in this hour I claim a seat for him in the Council."

My heart was suddenly beating very fast. It was a brave and unexpected thing to do – and she really had chosen me. Above all else.

I stood, and stepped forward until I was next to her, shoulder to shoulder.

"You cannot be serious." That was Tom Manion, from the side seats, aghast. "The boy has barely been Lycan, and now you claim a seat for him in the Council? As an Alpha? He doesn't have the first clue how to lead a pack – he's barely stepped up from the Omega position, and *that* was due to marrying a daughter of a pack Alpha, even one not in direct lineage – and now you're giving him this kind of influence? He was just brought here because *he broke the Law* – now you're talking about seating him in a conclave which was formed to preserve and protect it?"

I suddenly flashed back to a conversation I had had with Anna Cotton on my first morning at the Lycan compound. On a day when I still knew... practically nothing at all about what I had got myself into. I had asked, then, about packs. I had assumed an Alpha leader formed one – but I had been wrong about how it all worked. I remembered an impatient wave of Anna's hand at my ignorant blundering about. *The males don't start new packs*, she had said.

The males didn't. The female Alpha did.

As Asia had just done.

And the Alpha female of the pack then chose her mate, the Alpha male, the outward face, the one who would speak for the pack to the world outside while the Alpha female got on with handling the internal matters of the pack and the direction in which it would go, how it would function, its hierarchies and its layers and its family relations.

As Asia had just done. She had claimed a seat for me... in the Lycan *Council*. I would technically be Yuri Volkov's peer.

"If Asia names me, I will stand," I said, my voice surprisingly steady, given the circumstances. "I know I would be the Omega among the Alphas. But if she trusts me to speak for her pack, I will."

"You don't *have* a pack," Yuri growled. "You cannot be a pack of two."

"Three," Asia said, folding her hands over her stomach. "Our child will be born in the summer."

"And this too you have kept from us," Sofia said. "I knew. Because of the last Turn. I knew that your condition was already advanced enough to keep you from the wolf form. But I was expecting you to tell me of this, as your Alpha and your leader, rather than let me find out for myself through rumor and observation."

"I was not certain," Asia said, "and then there was no proper time. But be that as it may. In the summer, there will be three. And that is a family. The core of a pack. It is the Law."

"*Four.*"

My head snapped around at the sound of that word, and I saw Wilfred Sand rise heavily from a seat in the far corner of the room, right next to the doors, and begin walking across the floor to come and stand just a pace or so behind me at my right shoulder. "I am a floater, and not part of any permanent pack. But I can ask to join one, if they will have me. It is my right. And I request permission to become a part of yours, Asia. I pledge to accept and follow you and Mal as my Alphas, and to be a faithful member of the new pack."

"I accept," Asia said. "And with gratitude."

"Four," Tom said, ripping the word from his throat. "That's still..."

"Five," a new voice said.

"And *six*," another added.

I hadn't known that Wilfred had had the standing to be in this room, but the only surprise there was that he had in fact been present; I might have anticipated him choosing to stand with us, here, especially given the role he himself had played in recent events. But these two other voices were an utter surprise, and I literally stared as first Sorcha and then Seonaid Manion stood from their seats and stepped forward towards us also.

"Sorcha! Seonaid! Sit *down*!" Tom Manion said sharply.

"No, Father. We have Turned; we are of age. And we can choose. And we choose to go with them."

Wilfred was one thing. As he said, he was a floater, and had no strong ties. But these two... they were core family. They were part of the heart of this pack. This defection was unexpected, and at least according to the expressions on the Manion family's faces, completely devastating.

"I pledge to accept and follow you and Mal as my Alphas, and to be a faithful member of the new pack," Sorcha said.

"As do I," her sister echoed.

"I *forbid* this," their father spluttered, and Celine Adams Manion, their mother, half rose from her seat and held out both arms to her daughters.

"Come back here," she said cajolingly. "Come on, girls."

"No, Mother. We have made our pledge."

"*Why*?" Celine said, her voice breaking.

"If it were my sister," Sorcha said, "I would have done the same – I would have done whatever I needed to do. And I know that Seonaid would have done the same for me. I will follow that kind of Alpha."

Asia appeared nonplussed for a moment, but at those words a small frown that had gathered on her forehead cleared.

"I can't ask you," she began, and Sorcha, who seemed to be remarkably self-possessed for a young girl of her age, lifted a hand to forestall her.

"We made the pledge," she said. "Will you have us?"

"I will be honored to have you," Asia said.

"And what will you do with this pack? You need a place to safely Turn, and to pursue whatever it is that you will do to keep yourselves fed and sheltered – and where do you intend to take these children?" That was Tom, frantic, his face flushed and frantic.

"As to that, we can help," Sorcha said. "Father, if you were to see us married, you would give us a dowry. If you want us safely sheltered, you will give us that dowry to help us secure a shelter for our new pack."

I could not help a smile which curled the corners of my lips up. If it hadn't been for Asia – one of these two had been mulled as a potential bride for me. And I was somehow proud of that, that I might have even been considered for someone like Sorcha, with this much heart and spirit, with this much courage.

"All that can be discussed at another time," Asia said, as the twins completed the crossing of the floor and stood with us in a loose knot, just behind Wilfred. "I also intend to put out word that for the foreseeable future at least I will need a floater base to keep us fully functional, until the core pack is properly established. The rest... we will build, with time."

"That still leaves the matter before this gathering," Yuri said.

"With respect, no," Asia said. "Whatever was done, whatever you hold objections to, now the Law is followed – because it was this pack's Law that was being obeyed. Your jurisdiction therefore ends."

"You had not declared secession," Yuri said. "You cannot retroactively..."

"They declared by deed," said an unexpected voice from a seat to Sofia's left. Her son, Sasha, with whom I had worked in the lab, stood up to speak. "I know the Law as well as any of you. This, today, was a public declaration – but Mother, I think you made this pack the moment you mated the two outliers and gave them a unified front behind which they could stand together. You might have seen this coming."

"We will consider..." Yuri began stonily, but Sasha Berezhnoy raised his hand.

"It was done as it should have been done, Uncle," he said. "There is nothing left to consider."

For whatever private reasons of his own that he might have had, Sasha seemed to be rather enjoying the chance to cross his powerful seniors. It did occur to me, if the letter of the Law was followed, that he himself was just a little trapped in his position – as the son of the Alpha female, the leader of the pack, he ranked high in the family hierarchy but he was very unlikely to ever get the opportunity to rise to the Alpha position in his birth-pack. He might have entertained a passing thought of jumping ship right along with us and running with Asia's breakaway pack which was coalescing right here before his eyes – his chances of advancement might be marginally better in such a company, Asia was his half-sister after all – but he would start there at a hierarchical position that would be an order of magnitude lower than the one he currently held. Privilege already held, no matter how impossible it was to rise above a certain level which that privilege offered, was probably a better bargain for someone not absolutely driven by ambition than the potential of some nebulous privilege in the future which may or may not have come his way. So he contented himself with greasing the wheels of our passage, without joining our ranks. I could understand that. I could even respect it.

He caught my eye, and gave me a slow nod. It was as though he had read my thoughts, and was confirming them.

"Then, if that is all, we will retire from the Tribunal," Asia said, and only because I knew her, did I realize what an iron control she was exercising over her voice so that it didn't shake as she spoke. "There is much that needs to be done now."

Yuri said nothing, and after a moment Sofia sighed deeply and lifted a hand in a gesture of assent. Asia turned to face us all, her new pack – myself, Wilfred, the twins – and nodded at us all before she walked down the middle of the room, with the rest of us falling in behind her, until she passed through the doors on the far end.

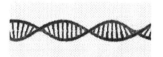

I
t was only after those doors closed behind us, leaving the rest of our former pack behind them, that Asia stumbled and leaned hard against the nearest wall.

"Did you walk in there intending to do that?" I asked, hurrying over to slip an arm around her waist and help her down on a nearby bench built into the walls of the corridor leading up to the Tribunal room, obviously there for the benefit of some poor creature who might be expected to wait out here until their fate was decided in the council room beyond. It might very well have been us, if Asia had not pulled this rabbit out of her hat.

"I had no idea if I could actually do it," she gasped out, leaning against me. "I kind of *volunteered* you – maybe I should have asked – and the rest of you, whatever made you do what you did, I am grateful, you gave me the legitimacy..."

"We'll get something out of Father," Sorcha said. "Maybe he will dither and give us only a bit of what we're supposed to get – but we'll get something. And it'll be a seed."

"Sorcha… Seonaid… are you absolutely sure about this?" Asia asked, lifting her head. "You are in the line of succession, here. You are core family. You had status."

"We are Second Family," Seonaid said. "We're way down in the line of succession. We don't matter as much as you think."

But they had mentioned dowries, and that came with a wedding – and so far, there was only Wilfred who might have been an option for one of the sisters in this tiny proto-pack. And on top of that they were both still so young, of age in Were Law because they had Turned but certainly not old enough to marry, either in the Were Law or the secular laws of normals that applied. That would have to wait a good handful of years. And until then there would be no core family except Asia, myself, and our own child…

I shook my head to clear it. I was infected with this already, the hierarchies and the lines of descent and the family relationships; it was what the Lycan clans, at least, seemed to thrive on. And now it was my problem.

Alpha. Asia had named me Alpha and pack leader.

It was a long way to come from a rookie wolfling who had blundered into this whole mess without thinking twice about the consequences of it all.

"They'll want us out," Wilfred said laconically. "Luckily we have a little while until the next Turn, but we'd better find somewhere to land before then. I don't think the enclosure will be open to us, here. We could guest at my natal pack, they will have us for at least that first Turn, until you can find your feet, Asia."

"Set it up," Asia said, lifting her head. "We will go there as soon as we may."

"We'll go pack," Sorcha said. "Come on, Seonaid. We'd better get a move on."

"Hey, you two… thank you. Again."

"We might still be a burden," Sorcha said with a small smile. "We aren't trained, like you guys are, and we still need to put in a lot of time and effort and school to be able to pull our own weight in terms of contributing to the pack properly."

"I'll find a way to make it work," Asia said.

"We thought you might," Seonaid said, echoing her sister's grin almost exactly. Twins could be that disconcerting. "The two of you."

"They won't toss us out tonight," I said, with more conviction than I really felt. But it seemed to reassure the others, and so I went on, "Let's plan on moving out tomorrow."

"I'll get transport organized," Wilfred said.

"Okay," Asia said after a pause. "Do that. And everyone come to our apartment tomorrow morning, and we'll go from there. I guess it's a question of take what you can carry, for now at least."

"We'll see you then," Sorcha said. "Let's see what we can do before the rest of the family comes home, Seonaid. I'm pretty sure that Mom at least will be up all night, anyway, and we probably are, too. She'll try and talk us out of it."

"Dad might actually try and lock us into our rooms," Seonaid said.

"Well, if he does, we'll call the Law on him," Sorcha said to Asia. "We pledged, you accepted, he doesn't have the right. And now that you can get Mal to sit in on the council, if he throws that down before them they'll have to side with you or break their own law. One way or another, we'll be with you."

We separated, went our ways to our respective quarters, with maybe hours to pack for exile. I had come here with a single duffle bag and I had no problem with leaving here with that bag – but this had been Asia's home for a lot longer than that, and it was trying to decide what was important enough to take with her that began to bring home the magnitude of what she had just done. She was actually crying as she threw things together, or turned something over in her hands contemplating abandoning it here, and she was working herself up into such a state that I eventually made her take an aspirin, drink a cup of herbal tea, and go to bed.

I stayed up, and hauled out that sketchbook which I had brought here as my own personal treasure when I had first arrived. My book of memory. I flipped through the pages, looking at my drawings, taking my mind back to this moment or that one, tracing the road that had brought me to this hour, to this place. And then I began drawing something new, something I had never done before – instead of memory, I drew hope.

The sleeping woman lay stretched out on the bed, her shape only hinted at by the sheet that covered her, draped over her hips and the long legs bent at the knee. One of her arms was tucked under her head, her wild curly hair spilling over it. The other, stretched out over and across the sheet that covered her, was curled protectively around the child that slept beside her.

The woman's hair – her narrow face, her generous mouth curled up in a secretive little smile over something she was dreaming about – were all Asia. The Asia I had seen sleeping this way dozens of times. If there was anything different it was a hint of a tear that was caught by her long closed eyelashes, the tears that she had shed this night, over the things that had come to a head in the Tribunal Room.

The child... the child's face I could not find. Yet. The figure in the sketch, curled up against its mother's

*belly and under the sheltering curve of her arm, was
still unformed – still a ghost from our future, not yet
born, not yet here. I did not know the shade of its hair,
the shape of its face, the color of its eyes. In the
drawing its face was almost blurred, its features not
defined, just a child, asleep. But its small hand was
curled inside its mother's, and I could see it in a kind
of detail that made my breath catch – the vulnerable
little hand of my son or daughter (I was completely
unable to make a decision as to which I was drawing)
with its small pink nails, its thumb curled inwards
slightly as though it still held a memory of being
sucked while the child had still been a baby in its
cradle.*

*The sleeping child. Hers. Mine. Ours. The one who
would come. The one whom she had used to anchor
the existence of the new pack which she had stepped
up to lead.*

*I drew them – one right here, whom I loved fiercely
right now for everything that she had said and done
because of my own needs and wishes, and one I was
yet to meet, still months away from being real. In its
physical form, anyway. In some ways, the spirit of
that child was already here, already with us, alive in
our shadows, in the sudden shards of our lives, in this
sketch. The child was... a memory too... a memory of
the future...*

I thought it best to try and leave Asia to a decent few hours' sleep, but I
had fully intended to crawl into bed myself eventually to snatch a couple of
hours there myself. Instead, I actually fell asleep on the couch, the
sketchbook still open on the table before me. And the next thing I knew, I
was blinking myself awake and she was there, Asia, perched on the edge of
the coffee table and carefully examining the drawings in my book.

I had never showed it to her. It had been my last secret. But I said
nothing, watching her through half-hooded eyes, knowing that she was
aware that I was awake now and observing, until she flipped back to where
the thing had been left open when I fell asleep – the last drawing, the
sleeping woman and the sleeping child beside her – and looked up from
that directly at me.

"I never knew you could draw," she said.

"I needed to," I said, fully opening my eyes and giving up even the
pretense of not being fully alert. "It's the way I remember."

"You don't remember this," she said, her fingers fluttering over the final
drawing.

"No," I said. "It's a new world – since I came here, since I found Celia,

388

since I met you. Maybe I am starting to draw what will come rather than what has been. Maybe that's what I came here to learn, really. To stop crouching in the corner piling up the past like barricades between me and everything that's out there, and try and be ready to meet what is still to happen."

"You never showed me," she said.

"No," I said. "I probably should have done, a long time ago. I'm sorry."

"Draw this new pack," she said, and the tears glittered again. "Draw it *real*. Draw it so I know that when the morning comes... I will be someone else entirely..."

"Oh, Ash. Of course you won't. You've never been more yourself than you were in that room yesterday."

"But I made *everyone* choose..." she began, and I sat up, taking the sketchbook from her hand, folding my fingers over hers.

"Yes," I said quietly. "You did. And I promise I'll do whatever I can to have your back, from here on. Whatever happens. I probably don't deserve having you stand up for me the way you did, but I'm grateful."

"Don't be *grateful*," she said. "I didn't do it for the thanks."

"But thank you, anyway," I said. "And why are you up? It's still dark out there. You needed your sleep."

"I woke up," she said. "You weren't there so I... came to find you."

"All right," I said, getting to my feet and drawing her to hers, letting the sketchbook fall on the table. "Let's both go to bed for another hour or two. God alone knows what's waiting in the morning."

I glanced back at the sketch as we left the room. Maybe it *was* only in my own imagination, but that child's face suddenly had more definition. When it woke, and opened up those sleeping eyes, they would be Asia's eyes. And – somehow, weirdly, without any real reason at all – I saw my sister Celia's smile curve its small mouth.

Wilfred did not appear to have slept that night at all. In the morning, he came to Asia to tell her that there would be a van for us outside the front door before noon, and brought news of at least a temporary potential home for the new-fledged pack, a house with some acreage which belonged to one of the elders of his natal pack and which that elder had indicated he would be willing to let us rent at a reasonable rate for the time being. We had a means of transport, and a destination. He also delivered into her keeping half a dozen notebooks and logs about work that had been done on Celia's behalf in the labs.

"Technically, this is work done on the issue which caused the splintering of the pack – so you were leading it, as new Alpha," he said. "It is not work done under Sofia's jurisdiction. And there's some potentially important stuff in here."

"We haven't the facilities to pursue any of it, yet," Asia said morosely. "That's something I haven't even begun to figure out yet. It costs money to set up a lab of our own. There's so much that we'd need."

"It'll come," he said, sounding completely convinced of that, speaking as if it wasn't even an issue. "In the meantime, hang on to these. They might prove useful."

Only three members of Sofia's pack were there to see us leave. Sasha, who had come to shake Wilfred's hand and my own, and wish us luck; Anna Cotton, who seemed ambivalent, and did ask her cousins Sorcha and Seonaid if they had really thought through what they were doing; and Yuri's second daughter, Lara, who did not speak to us but appeared to have been sent as an observer by the elders of the pack. We had surprisingly little luggage among the five of us, to the point that Sasha actually volunteered to send on a few other things we had not been in a position to carry if we told him where anything like that needed to be delivered. But it was freeing, traveling light. It would be a tough ask, but we had everything to build yet. And we needed to build it on our own, not drag it around like a burden. Our future was still settling into its permanent shape. We didn't have space for too much of the past in there, not until we could figure out how much room there would be for it in the new place we were making for ourselves.

And so, we ended something, and began something, and it was Wilfred who took the wheel of the van while I rode shotgun and Asia went into a huddle with the Manion girls in the back. They had insisted they were absolutely certain, but Seonaid, at least, had not been entirely dry-eyed as we drove away. They were still so very young, those two, and now I was responsible for them, in a way – they were my new family, this motley crew, under Asia's law and my care.

Our new house was isolated, at the end of a long, graveled drive, and in need of a little loving care. Asia and the Manions set about making the inside of it presentable, and Wilfred and I immediately began work on setting up a fenced enclosure where we could Turn safely. It was not an insignificant task, and we only had a very short time to accomplish it. Wilfred did enlist the aid of a couple of Lycan young men from his old pack to help us be done with it in good time. But we did it, the fence was complete and secure a week before the Turn was due, necessary supplies for the Turn were laid in, and I even had a caretaker lined up.

Jazz, with whom I had been in constant contact since I left Yuri's compound (just in case Chalky had checked in with her), had volunteered without my asking to come out and stay in the house during this first Turn in a strange new place, just to keep an eye on us all and make sure everything went down properly. I was hoping that I would have a little more of a chance to work out the details of it all, after this first Turn, after I could get us safely through that much.

She had no word about Celia, no contact from Chalky. He seemed to have taken our sister and vanished from the face of the earth.

Which was good... in a way. If we had no idea where they were nobody else probably did, either. And that meant that Celia was still safe.

I had not had too much time to obsess on what might have been the results of the virosome injection that Chalky had given her, back in that cabin in the woods. But the closer the Turn came, the more my thoughts bent that way – because as important as this Turn was for our group, our new pack, it was a vital one for Celia. It would be the Turn which showed whether we had succeeded in what we had set out to do – whether this place, this position we found ourselves in, the precarious ledge we clung to as a brand new Lycan pack and one which had formed under such controversial circumstances, could even be justified at all if the biggest thing that had led us here, Celia's rescue and the restoration of her Were self, turned out to have failed. I kept my phone on me at all times, barely letting go of it long enough to recharge it during the night, but there was no word from Chalky. And of course there wouldn't be, not before the Turn, not before the full moon rose and either triggered Celia or did not.

I went into the Turn with this on my mind.

That – perhaps betraying my new pack and my responsibilities – was the first thing that I thought of when I came back, going straight to Jazz, asking the question wordlessly with burning eyes. She merely shook her head.

There had been no word. Nothing from Chalky. Only silence.

I had not been prepared for the devastation that this tiny small gesture would open up inside of me. The possibility that it had all been futile, and useless, and for nothing – that I might have risked Asia and our child for failure, and had led others to follow us on that wasted path – it was too much. I felt it come on me, like it hadn't done for a very long time –that solid black fury and despair that had ridden me for so many years when I was growing up in the vicious world where I was different, the Were among the normals, and then afterwards in the aftermath of Celia's death. I could not look any of them in the face. I stumbled out of the house, by myself, into the woods, pretending I had not heard Asia's voice call my name as I fled into the woods.

Far enough away so that nobody could see me, I collapsed to the cold ground underneath a still- leafless tree – it was only March, after all – and buried the heels of my hands into my eyesockets, hopelessly trying to hold back the tears, and failing. I cried alone, in the forest, like a child – with fury, with fear, with grief, with guilt – I had no idea how long I was there for, but the light had changed by the time I looked up and wiped the back of my hand over my swollen eyelids.

"All right then," I said to myself, softly, bleakly, out loud just so that I could hear my own voice. "All right."

The world was what it was. Nobody had promised me that it would be fair. And I had other responsibilities now. The first Lycan Council meeting that I was supposed to attend, as Asia's representative, as Alpha of the new pack, was due in only a week – and it would be my first meeting, one where the existence of the new pack would be ratified by the Alphas of all the packs, one where I would have to present a strong front, to speak for Asia's courage and her actions. Whatever else had happened to leave the scorched earth that was at the heart of me... would have to wait.

Jazz had filled them in on the important facts of the matter, apparently, before I returned. They didn't try to offer up platitudes or comfort, and for that I was grateful; the only thing I could bear to accept was the squeeze of

Asia's hand, given in silence and in understanding. If it threatened to become too heavy, if I could feel it crushing my shoulders and bowing my back, I would pause to clench my teeth and ball my hands into fists until my nails left half-moon impressions in my palms and the pain brought me back to more immediate matters. I survived like that for almost three days.... until my phone rang unexpectedly, on the late afternoon of the third day. And it was Chalky.

"Dude," he greeted me easily, as if nothing at all was the matter. "So. What's up?"

"What's... *up*...?" I almost spluttered. "Well, Asia called them on the finer points of the Law and split us off as our own pack, so we've gone our own way – and now we're kind of hanging out on the ragged fringes of the Lycan clan, trying to figure out how to survive there."

"Let me know if you need anything," he said. "I have people I can call."

I closed my eyes, centering myself, the hand which wasn't holding the phone curling into the familiar fist, inflicting the familiar pain. "Just tell me," I managed at last, the words wrung from me. "Please. Just tell me."

"Where are you, exactly? I'll come out and see you," he said. "No, Mal, trust me. It is better if we talk face to face. Give me an address and I can be there tomorrow."

"You don't even know where 'there' is," I said.

"It doesn't matter. I can be there tomorrow, wherever it is. Text me an address, and expect me. Gotta go – I'll see you soon."

"Chalky..."

But he was already gone. Gritting my teeth, I typed out the address of our temporary sanctuary and texted it to him as he had instructed.

Jazz, who had stayed a few extra days, had been on the point of returning home – but when she heard that Chalky had called, and that he was on his way, adamantly refused to leave before she saw him, too.

"But what happened?" Asia said. "He said absolutely nothing?"

"Better if we talk in person," I muttered darkly. "He'd better talk fast when he gets here. Before I *strangle* him. Nothing, Ash. He said nothing. As though it means that little to me. He didn't even say..." I hated it when my voice broke, but it did, on that word, on that thought. I took a deep breath before I spoke again. "I don't even know if she's all right. He could have told me that. He could have said that much."

"Mal." Asia said. "Whatever happens tomorrow, it cannot possibly be any worse than what you have already tormented yourself by imagining. And if you want to hit something, there's a loose stair outside on the porch. Go hammer a few nails into it."

The following day we were all on edge – myself brittle and sharp, Asia looking white and stressed, Jazz strung so tight that you could almost see her vibrating, and everyone else walking on eggshells around us. And it almost broke me when we all crowded out onto the front porch to watch the dark car pull in at the front of the house, and I realized that Chalky was not alone.

It was Jazz who whimpered first, actually, realizing who Chalky's companion was – but I was not that far behind, and I reached out and clung to Asia's hand, hard, for pure support.

Chalky got out of the car first, and then walked around to the passenger side to open the door. Celia stepped out, and straightened, and looked up at the house.

"Oh, my God," Asia whispered. "Look at her."

I was. Oh, I was. I was staring, gulping her down with my eyes. Because she was different – *different* – she looked – she looked – *alive* again. There was something in her face, in her eyes, that had not been there on that day that we had seen her in the cabin in the woods, on the day that she had received her shot after the escape from the Turning House.

Jazz grabbed for my free hand, and clung to it with both of her own. I suddenly realized that she was sobbing quietly.

"Mal – look – it looks like she actually *knows*..."

Chalky slammed the passenger door closed behind Celia, and then guided her gently, with a hand under her elbow, up the steps to the front porch (the same ones I had taken out my demons on the day before at Asia's command) and to where we waited for them.

He was smiling, damn him. Just a little. Just the faintest ghost of a smile. But it was there. It was *there*. And that told me – told me everything – and it was all I could do not to cry out with the weight of that knowledge.

"I'm sorry," Chalky said. "Things... worked out just a little unexpectedly, and I'm sorry that you went through what I know you went through over the last few days. But I honestly could not do anything about that... until yesterday. Until she actually... Turned back."

Asia let out her breath with a little gasp. "She..."

I finally managed to find the strength to look straight into Celia's eyes, and they were bright with tears.

"Hey," she said softly. "I'm back."

Somewhere behind, I heard someone begin to cry – Sorcha, or Seonaid, or both. I stood for a moment, frozen, and then gently freed my hands from Asia's and Jazz's grip, and stepped forward, and wrapped my arms around Celia, and stood there holding her tightly and my whole body shaking with the sobs that I myself could not quite release.

Her arms came up around me and held me to her, like she had done so many times before when we were young.

There were no words. There could be none. There was nothing at all that I could hang onto for long enough in order to say it out loud.

"You'd better come in," Asia said, from beside me but out of sight. "I've got coffee on."

I heard them leave, the sound of footsteps on the porch, the sound of the door opening and closing, and then I knew we were alone out here, Celia and I, that Asia had herded them all away so that we could have a moment.

"He told me you came to get me," Celia said, after we had come apart, just far enough to still cling onto one another's elbows with both hands. "He told me you were willing to wreck everything to come and get me."

She threatened to make me cry all over again. "When I saw you – when I first saw you, in that place – I thought I was dreaming – just how much *do* you remember?"

"Fragments," she said. "Like my mind was frozen, and now someone came and chopped up the ice, and it's all bits and pieces and nothing quite fits, and I feel as though I've been asleep for years. Like Sleeping Beauty, pricked my hand on a spindle and fell asleep as the world changed around me. Maybe I'll never remember. I am missing... whole chunks of my life."

Some of those, knowing what I knew about them, it might be just as well if she never got back. But I wasn't about to tell her that now.

"But what happened?" I asked. "The last I heard... Chalky had taken you and he hid you somewhere – I had no idea if you were alive or dead or okay or lost all over again – no word –"

"Perhaps Saladin had better do the explaining," she said. "I certainly don't remember enough detail about it. Let's go inside."

"Saladin," I said, with a weak laugh. "I swear, I let him out of my sight for a month and he gets delusions of grandeur..."

There was a quiet murmur of conversation as we walked into the large kitchen of the house, where everyone had gathered. It stilled as we walked inside.

I skewered Chalky – I suppose I'd better learn to give him his full name, *Saladin* – with a gimlet stare as I stepped into the room.

"I could throttle you. Thank you. *Spill*."

He finally allowed that smile to flower.

"Well, for a while it looked like there wasn't anything to tell you except for bad news," he said. "And then..."

"Start at the beginning," Asia said. "After we left you."

"I left straight after you," Saladin said. "Took Celia to a safe house I knew, with a woman I knew I could trust. Then we waited, really."

"The second dose," Wilfred said. "Did you give it?"

"No," Saladin said. "I decided that either the thing had worked – in which case it was all moot – or it didn't, and if it didn't there didn't seem to be much point in torturing her further. So I just let it go. And then the full moon came... and I waited, right there in the room with her... and *nothing happened*."

Sorcha caught her breath.

"Oh, no," I said, "You don't do that. By 'nothing happened' what exactly do you mean? What did happen?"

"Nothing," Saladin said. "Literally, nothing. I sat in the armchair by her bed and watched her, and she slept, the moon came up and she was still there, sleeping, as herself, no Turn, nothing. And I thought... that was it. That would have been the end of it. Unless one of you laboratory types had come up with some other bright ideas. Of course, I couldn't let you know – because it was full Turn by then, and you were all presumably somewhere out there on all fours howling at that full moon... then something took me by surprise."

I actually growled at him.

He grinned wider, and continued.

"I had left the room in order to get something to eat, on the evening of the first day after the full Turn," he said. "I fully intended to call you the next morning. She seemed to have evaporated – turned into thin air – into a ghost. That is, right until I heard the meow from under the bed."

Jazz's eyes were sparkling. "The cat?"

"She Turned, all right," Saladin said. "Exactly into what she was supposed to Turn into. But somehow whatever you did – maybe it was the timing of that injection – it screwed up her temporal settings. She Turned *three days late.*"

Wilfred and Asia exchanged startled looks. "That shouldn't have mattered," Wilfred said. "You think this is a permanent thing? Or just something that is going to work itself out as the kinks get straightened out?"

"Next Turn will give you the answer, no doubt," Saladin said. "Anyway. I provided the necessities, and she waited it out as the cat in that room, for the three required days, and then... when she came back... she was someone else entirely. I had never met this creature before. She was simply no longer that empty puppet whom we had snatched from the Turning House. It was as though some kind of spirit had come back into her, and made her whole again. And then. Well, anyway. Here we are."

"Thank you," I said, in a voice that shook only a little. And then it shook a whole lot harder as I looked at all of them, sitting there, their faces lit up with this revelation. "All of you. Thank you. I owe you all – *we* owe you – more than we can ever say."

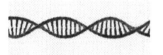

T he rest... was logistics. There was a question of what would happen next, of course, but it was barely a question at all.

"She must stay here, of course," Asia said firmly.

"But if she's back to being fully Random, what if she just Turns into a wolf from here on because that's the last thing she sees before Turn?" Jazz said. "Or if she Turns into a cat – what if one of the wolves makes her a snack...?"

"Well, technically, she seems to have Turned into cat only after we all Turned back from wolf," Wilfred said. "And if that holds – then the staggered Turn means that there is no danger of that."

"And anyway," Asia said, "for the next few months... I'll be around to supervise. I won't be Turning again until this child is born."

Celia's eyes leaped from Asia to me. "Saladin didn't tell me *that*," she said.

"You're going to be an aunt," I said laconically. And then winced internally, wondering how much of her own history she could really remember, if she would ever recall that she had – at least once – been a mother herself.

"What about Mom and Dad?" Jazz asked, clasping her hands together.

"They lost a child," Celia said, and bit her lip. "I am not that child any longer. They would not be getting back what they lost, even if went home with you right now, Jazz. I want to tell them. I do. I want to go back and hug Mom and tell her how sorry I am, about everything... but I just don't know. I don't know if I can do it to them or to me. None of us are the same people that we were... when I disappeared. And they have already mourned me, would it make it better if they suddenly had all that undone and had to face the consequences of all of this? How much would you explain to them? How much could you explain?"

"And you have to realize that if this goes public – and it will if you go home – you have everyone to reckon with," Saladin said soberly. "You have to think about that – all of that. The Lycans, the Were authorities, the normals lawmakers who won't know what to make of you... and then your whole family goes under the microscope – you, and Jazz, and Mal... there will be a whole lot of scrambling to explain, to figure out a chain of command, of who was responsible for what, who knew what, who lied, who said nothing when they could have spoken up... there are a whole lot of secrets buried here, and not all of them are your own, and some of them people might do... horrible things... to protect."

"She'll be safe here," Asia said. "Nobody who doesn't have to know need ever know. And if things change... maybe, later, there might be a chance to make it right."

"All right, then," Saladin said. "Then my work is done. And now there are a few things I should probably do to clean up after me, just so that nobody traces the wrong things..."

"You can't *leave* yet, you only just got here," Asia said.

"I've done what I came to do," he said. "She's healed, she's here, she's safe. It's up to you now. And I have to find a new place to hide."

"You're just going to disappear again?" I said, incredulous.

He grinned at me. "I'll stay in touch," he said. "Never fear. It may come, someday, that I might need help or sanctuary from *you.*"

Asia stood. "In any house where I am," she said, "in this pack, where I stand Alpha, you will be welcome."

"Thank you," he said. "Appreciate it. I should probably be on my way, then. Mal, a word, before I go...?"

Asia gave me a faint nod, and I got up, impulsively leaning over to kiss Celia on the top of her head.

"I'll take care of her," Asia said, with a faint smile. "Go."

I followed Saladin out onto the porch, where he was waiting for me.

"Well," he said, "you've come a long way... from picking fights in back alleys. And when you crossed into the Lycans I have to confess I never expected you to end up with a seat on the Council one day."

"Nor I," I said. "Asia... happened. She was not part of the plan."

"Sometimes the best things that happen are those you never planned for," Saladin said easily. "I should know, really, I never plan anything that much in advance. And stuff... happens... anyway. I never planned to help you out in that scuffle, you know, that first time we met. It just seemed to be a good idea at the time."

"What are you going to do now?"

"Well, I found out a few things I didn't know through all of this," he said. "There are still leads I am following, so it isn't over yet. There are still... things that I haven't quite figured out yet. So there's that. I might still call now and then, to pick your brains – yours on what goes on inside the Lycan inner sanctum, your wife's on what goes on inside the cells of my own body. Maybe she'll help me figure out what I am, in the end. Who knows. And besides, I have to keep an eye on that girl. I've kind of... become rather attached to that sister of yours, over the space of the last few weeks. She's part of my answers, anyway. You take care of her."

"I will. And once again... I don't even know how to begin..."

"Then don't," he said. "I understand."

He reached out, and so did I, and we clasped one another's arms, forearm to forearm, like the knights of the Round Table did of old. And that's exactly what he was, a paladin, a solitary hero, a knight in shining armor full of power and mystery, an enigma, about to ride off back into the darkness by himself.

"Take care, dude," he said.

"And you," I whispered.

He held my eyes for another long moment, and then nodded, once, released my arm, and turned away. He did not look back as he crossed the drive back to his car, got into it, turned the key in the ignition, and swept out of the graveled patch before the porch and back down the long driveway.

I don't know how long I stood there staring after him. It was only Asia's gentle touch on my shoulder that brought me back. I glanced down at her, and reached out to slip an arm around her waist, drawing her closer to me.

"Come on back inside," she said, "it's getting dark. And they're waiting." And then, after a small hesitation, "Is he gone, then?"

"Saladin...?" I said, staring down the long empty drive down which his car had disappeared. "I don't know. He's in the wind."

THE
W E R E
CHRONICLES

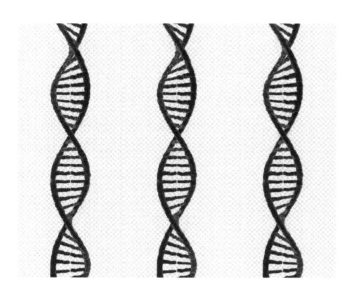

BOOK 3: SHIFTER

Part 1:
Chrysalis

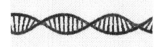

I must have dreamed it.

Those were the words she often used, my mother. I was cajoled with them and blackmailed with them and bullied with them because they were the wall she used against anything that she couldn't handle, that she could not or would not believe was real. If she could not cope with it, that's where it went – into the dream hopper. Where she didn't have to deal with it.

When I was very young, I accepted the truth of it without question. But I very quickly began to question the whole idea. If I had dreamed a life for myself, I would have done a better job of it. I would have dreamed that I was like everyone else, that I fit in, that people liked me, that there were those in this world whose job it was to protect me and to take care of me. I would have dreamed of someone who was not the complicated thing I discovered that I was, and someone who had not been given a name that painted a target on my back, or occasion a double take every time someone tripped over the full glory of its improbability.

I would have been someone other than what I was. If I had had any choice in the matter at all, when I was that child trying to find solid ground in the quicksand of my beginnings, I would have chosen to be nothing less than *ordinary*.

But I was not.

My name is Saladin van Schalkwyk. And in a world divided between Were-kind and normals, I belonged in neither camp, alien and threatening to both. I am a Shifter.

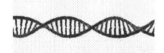

I measured my life by the moments which I recognized as crossroads even before I understood just what that idea meant. My early memories are nebulous, as they would have to be, being formed in the mind of a baby who still had no yardstick by which to measure and understand the things I was observing. They were there, and even with all of their fuzzy edges they were real.

Quite simply, I remembered growing older. I had a sense of time passing which, as I came to understand later, was quite unheard of in a child of that age. My first milestones involved seeing two faces – one male, one female – bent over my crib saying goodbye, and then a few days later, saying hello again. I told my mother I remembered this, once, and she told me that I could not possibly have done so because I was only a couple of months old then. Because she dismissed it, I didn't speak of it again, but I always knew I did remember.

Later, when I had the information with which to underlay those memories, it became clear to me that I was remembering the Turns that my parents made when I was still a baby. I was defined as Were, from the cradle. I knew of Turns long before I knew what they actually were. Three days of every month when my parents, and others like them, changed into their animal forms. They lived as those beasts until the shadows began to nibble at the edge of the full moon and it began to diminish again. They then returned to being human, without any memories of their lives as animals.

In those early months of babyhood I spent those Turn-days in the care of a woman whose name I do not know now, if I ever did – someone who may never have spoken directly to me at all because I remember nothing of her voice, just a round face under an untidy fall of shaggy dark hair. She did not mistreat me. She did not particularly care about me, though. She was a babysitter and I was a job to do.

I do remember voices. Not the babysitter's, but theirs, my mother's and my father's. I remember arguments. Words which stuck – meaningless at the time but with meaning accreting to them as I grew older and mulled them around in my mind. Words like *I can't do this anymore*. Or *It's over. This time it really is over.*

Very occasionally, there was laughter, but more often there were tears, hers, and silent absences, his. For a while, he always came back, no matter how badly the argument had gone, no matter how long he chose to stay away. He returned. But one day – I had just turned four years old – I remember his face, his expression, clearly saying goodbye. I remember that he kissed me, on the forehead, and ruffled my hair; I remember how bright his eyes were – but there were no tears, not quite. And then I remember him walking away.

I never saw him again.

After that, things got a little difficult. Tighter.

There were boxes, one day, in the small house that I thought of as home. A lot of stuff in the house did not end up in the boxes which were packaged up and hauled out of the front door, and into a small truck. I hesitated in the doorway, looking back, knowing I was leaving this place but bewildered by all the things that were still there, still in place, still an anchor tying me to a different world.

Mamma slipped an arm around my shoulders as I stood there and held me tightly to her side for a moment before leaning down and planting a light kiss on the top of my head.

"It's okay," she said. "It's just you and me now. There's a new place waiting."

So we moved, Mamma and I. The new place turned out to be a tiny little one-bedroom apartment in an intimidating building that was high, and wide, and full of windows behind which lived other people. I spent my days in a gloomy small-windowed room with a clutch of other children of like age, all of whom seemed to me to be barely more than larvae. They staggered around on unsteady feet or crawled on the floor which was covered by foam squares in bright primary colors, building things out of blocks, or smearing crayons over outlines on pages of coloring books without regard to where any edges went.

I had more of a clue about it, somehow, but perhaps happily still lacked access to the dexterity that would have been required to betray that fact and so I smeared my crayons with the rest of them. My mother came to pick me up every day, in the late afternoons looking tired and drawn. I was usually the last child there. I quickly learned that her patience was very thin, and did not try it. I must have been the quietest, best-behaved four-year-old, ever, but all I knew *then* was that I was being careful, and somehow doing what I could to steer my universe along safe and calm waters.

I should have started school at six years of age, but somehow... that never quite happened. I outgrew the room with the red and blue and yellow floor, but I never graduated to anything *else*. Mamma seemed to have forgotten about me, other than a background responsibility. She would feed me; sometimes she would even read to me, from books which I quickly learned by heart; other times she would talk to me, over our food, as though I were another adult, and I would understand maybe one word in five but it seemed to soothe her that she had someone there to listen and so I did that for her.

I did other things, too, because it was at about this age that Mamma Turned unexpectedly in the apartment.

I was six years old and this had caught me by surprise; I had been asleep, and when I woke, I was alone in the apartment. Alone, that is, except for a large cat which I had never seen before, and which stalked, hissing and spitting in the tiny confining space it had found itself in. Perhaps I should have been quicker on the uptake, but I failed to connect the large cat which was suddenly *there,* in a solid way in which my mother failed to be *there*, with the fact that Mamma was gone – she was often gone, after all, and I was used to her absences. But this time she didn't come back, and the cat growled and prowled and scratched at doors and windows until I finally, not knowing any better and not being able to think of any alternatives, helplessly let it out. And then I was alone in the apartment. Mamma had vanished.

I was a self-sufficient kind of child and I was not afraid of being alone. But I didn't get into my pajamas to go to bed when night fell, sleeping fully dressed on top of my bed with only my shoes kicked off onto the floor.

And the next morning, she wasn't back.

I ate, when I got hungry, whatever I could get my hands on – a couple of stale bread rolls which had been left on the counter, bowlfuls of the sugary cereal which I was partial to and which Mamma always had on hand. I could be trusted to eat that even when I turned up my nose at anything else that she put before me, and, once, our neighbor noticed me hanging around and offered me a bowl of soup and a nice grilled cheese sandwich.

But I was pretty hungry by the time Mamma did turn up again – rather spectacularly. Early in the morning of the fourth day of her absence she rapped on the door to the apartment, which I had managed to lock. The knock continued until I finally broke down and opened it to have my wild-eyed, snaggle-haired, and very naked mother all but fall inside.

"Close the door!" she hissed at me, and stole a frantic look over her shoulder. "Did anyone see me come in?"

"I don't know," I stammered, pushing the door closed behind her as instructed. I goggled at her. She had interesting scars on her back which I had never seen before. And a large mole on her hip.

All this, in the space of a handful of breathless seconds, before she ran, half-crouching, down the corridor towards the bathroom.

"Don't make a sound!" she flung at me over her shoulder as she slipped into the bathroom and closed the door behind her.

In this commanded silence, I heard the shower running, followed by long minutes of a total absence of any hint that she was still there at all. I sat, quiet and frightened, and waited – and eventually the bathroom door opened again and she came out again, hair damp on her shoulders but less insanely wild than it had been when she had come to the door, wrapped in a fading pink towel. She was more herself again, and I began to relax a little.

"I don't suppose there is much to eat in the kitchen," she said. "I for one am starving – and you – I'm so sorry, I really didn't mean to – well, but, anyway. I'll go get dressed and then we can go out for pancakes. You like those. How about that?"

"Okay," I said.

"Go look in my purse," she said, as she disappeared into the bedroom. "See how much money I've got in there."

There wasn't much, but I helpfully added a handful of pennies which I had collected while burrowing into the furniture during the three days of her absence, and in the end there was at least enough for breakfast. We went down to the local 24-hour pancake shop which I liked and she ordered two adult portions of pancakes, four large ones on each plate.

I drowned mine in maple syrup and wolfed them down, cleaning my plate before she had barely started on her third, and she passed her last one to me after she saw me eyeing it and sat there watching me mop the remaining syrup up with it.

"You shouldn't have let me out, Salah-al-Din," she said, picking at her food, giving my name that lilt that only she did. I was Saladin to everyone else – but I thought of her version, the *Salah-al-Din*, as my true name, that nobody except the two of us was allowed to know. "You should never have let me out. It was my fault – I let the time slip away – I should have started out for the Turning House long before anything had a chance to – but there you go, I was late from work, and you were whining that you were hungry, and I was trying to get something together for your supper, and it all just got away from me – and it ended okay, anyway – but if anyone really saw, if anyone was paying attention, then we could be in trouble..."

"Was it a secret? Don't they know you're Were?" I asked, kicking my heels against the hollow booth to produce a satisfying hollow noise which seemed to irritate the people in the booth across the aisle from us no end... which made me all the more eager to keep on doing it, to keep the reaction going.

"Of course they know," Mamma snapped at me. "But I don't go by my real name, and they don't know where I am or how to find me... or you..." She looked around the anonymous pancake house, furtively, as though it was filled with spies.

Me? Someone was looking for me?

"I gave up so much," Mamma continued, almost oblivious of my presence by now. She was justifying something to herself. "When I took the child they wanted and ran away, the money that they paid – the child support – that all went..."

There were times she made too little sense for me. I was happy with the pancakes, that time. We didn't get much further than that.

But that was the first time, and after that things started to trickle out when she wasn't careful.

The first development was simply that Mamma suddenly formed a paranoid aversion to the Turning Houses where she had been going for her mandated three-day retreats during her Turns. I discovered that she had in fact been going to different ones every Turn, hiding her identity, running from something that I could not understand but running, cowering, scared. The next Turn she stayed away from the Turning House, too, and I took care of her as best I could inside our apartment. It was messy, but I learned. The Turn after that, it was better. And after that it was simply understood. She would be a sandcat for three days, and I would take care of her. Then she'd Turn back into Mamma and take care of me... as best she was able.

There were the good days, like the time she decided that something needed to be done about my book-learning – but instead of school I got a library card. I remember the morning that we went to our local library, a low red brick building a couple of blocks away from our apartment, and she presented me to the librarian at the desk.

"And how old are you?" the librarian asked me with her best placate-a-small-child smile.

"Nine," I said instantly. And could see that she was skeptical in the extreme about that. So I backtracked, just enough to be believable. "Eight and three quarters," I said, my lower lip thrust out in a sulk.

Mamma smiled. "Eight and three quarters in a month and a half," she said, the lie coming as easily to her lips as to my own.

The librarian still looked unconvinced, but in the face of that united front she couldn't exactly call us both liars, and calling for my birth certificate seemed a bit extreme. And then Mamma made it better.

"Actually, he's already finished all the books in our house," she said, which was perfectly true, although the librarian could have no possible clue as to just how limited that selection was. "So I was hoping for something – I don't know – do you have a Teen Card?"

The librarian looked even less convinced. "The teen section can have a lot of material that – he isn't – you say he's going to be nine soon?"

She was buying into it, which was good – and once she did that it was not *that* much harder to get her to cave on the Teen Card. The bonus to that was the Teen Card came with computer privileges. It was the first cracking open, just enough for a sliver of light to shine through around the edges, of a door that would take me into conquering a world that was always meant to be mine.

But first, I had other lessons to learn.

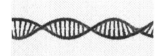

T he first time I stepped through the veil... it was into a bird.

I had taken care of Mamma through many Turns by the time I was eight years old, and things were not getting better. The good days were fewer and fewer, and she grew more secretive, more paranoid... and more violent. A couple of months after my eighth birthday, I didn't have something that she wanted quickly enough after she came out of one of her Turns. She slapped me so hard that my head snapped back on my neck and one of the loose milk teeth I was in the process of losing that year literally rocked in its socket. After the slap I ran from the apartment to get away from her and as I slouched down the street with the hood of my sweatshirt pulled up over my hair and as far over my face as I could make it go I was able to simply pluck that loose tooth from its socket. The future stretched ahead of me, grey and bleak, unchanging. I was way too young to do anything other than knuckle under and endure. I was already infected by Mamma's wariness towards everyone else, her treating every other soul out there as a potential enemy, and it did not occur to me that there might be an option of actually asking for help. I wouldn't have had the first idea who to ask, anyway – if *she* was hiding from the Were I couldn't run to them and I already understood that those who were not like us, the majority of the people out there, would wash their hands of someone like me fairly quickly by quite simply not accepting me as their problem.

Maybe it was just that on this particular day I was more sunk into misery and self-pity than usual. Perhaps I was wrapped into myself deeply enough to trigger something without knowing – but I found myself watching a couple of crows picking at something unspeakable on the tarmac in a half-empty parking lot in a drizzly sort of rain...and wishing I was *like them*, with nothing to worry about but carrion.

And something happened.

To say I have no memory of what actually happened would be lying. I do. I remember that it *hurt*, agonizingly so, that it was human screams that merged with a crow's caws in the end. I remember that I felt the feathers break my skin, every one of them a shot of sharp pain – as though I had just been fallen upon by a company of knife-wielding thugs intent on stabbing until there was no life left in my body at all. I remember that the light dimmed behind my eyes, into greyness, into blindness, and when sight returned it was different somehow, that things now stood out in sharp focus that were not so before. I remember stumbling, unbalanced, falling down with wings... *wings*... spreading out to catch my fall. Crying out. Crying. Crying. Staggering on two thin trembling legs, my mouth open, screaming – *caw caw caw* – until finally some instinct made me stretch the wings and beat them and I was somehow airborne., I was unsteadily, weaving through the air just above the ground but flying – I was *flying* – I had no right to do this, no knowledge of it, no sanction, I was still a child, this should never have happened to me. It was way too early for a traditional Were Turn, it was not the full moon, and I didn't just Turn into a bird and forget my human self. I retained full self-awareness. *I knew who I was.*

It was all so wrong, so utterly wrong.

Except that it was not. It was right for *me*. My wings suddenly remembered the mechanics of something they had *never done before,* and I finally rose into the sky and circled above the parking lot. And the cries changed – the fear, the panic, the confusion had somehow shifted into something else, into something that was joy, almost triumph. I could see, down on the ground below me as I circled, the pitiful pile of rags which was the clothing I had been wearing, which my body had shed as it had changed. I braced myself for never seeing any of those items of clothing again (and it wasn't as though I had clothes to spare, lying about at home) and for the technical difficulties of somehow dealing with getting home later, naked, in just the skin I was born in.

I remembered everything, in fact. I was a crow, but inside that bird's head... I was still me. My own thoughts, my own memories, I recognized things that had belonged to me-the-boy when I saw them through the eyes of me-the-bird.

I was very young but that didn't matter – there were things you knew about being Were, simply by being Were, no matter what age you happened to be. I knew about Turning Houses, and I knew that they had been built to keep my kind away from the non-Were, ordinary, normal human beings during the times that we changed into our animal shapes. The thinking behind this, the reasoning, the justification, was that when we Turned we lost our human mind and became all beast and therefore could not be trusted not to act out of pure animal instinct and prove dangerous to unsuspecting humans crossing our path. It was common knowledge, a common wisdom, and I had never heard it refuted or read

SHIFTER

that it was wrong, that we Were carried two distinct things in ourselves, our human forms and our Were forms, and that those two things did not communicate.

There were supposed to be no shared memories.

The human-shaped Were being knew and saw and understood things; the animal-shaped Were knew and saw and understood *different* things; they were only supposed to be able to make sense of stuff from one of those two worlds at a time. In other words, as the crow, the pile of clothes on the pavement should have meant nothing more to me than a jumbled mess of fabric. I might have been moved to investigate underneath it for possible hiding of potential food sources but nothing beyond that. I should not have been able, as that crow, to look down on that pile and know it for what it was – the discarded clothes which I had been wearing, as a boy, moments earlier.

There were laws about this sort of thing. Natural laws. Laws that I should not have been able to cross.

Then there was the fact that the Were Turned at age fifteen, on average, give or take a few months. I was at least six years younger than that average. In the absolute terms of an eight-year-old mind, my Turning was a lifetime away – I would have to live almost as long as I had already lived before I would even have to consider thinking about the idea.

Then there was another natural law of the Were – that we Turned when the moon grew full, except for the few who Turned at the new moon, and Turned back three days later. Our world was like clockwork, perfectly tuned, ticking along in the manner that it had always done. And yet. And yet. And yet. There I was, boy-crow, coming down in a somewhat awkward, but nonetheless perfectly serviceable, landing on top of a wall just above my clothes. Emphatically Turned. And absolutely aware of both my identities – and I somehow knew that I would just as surely remember the things that I had seen as Crow when I Turned back into Boy...

If I Turned back to Boy. For the first time a touch of unease. Would I even be able to do that? Ever again?

I considered my position, staring at the clothes pile, my bright-eyed crow head tilted at an angle that someone walking past might have grinned at and described as "thoughtful". What if I was stuck, as the bird...? What if I *never* went back to being the human child...?

I remembered Mamma, and the slap that had driven me out of the apartment. I did think for a moment that it might be better for everyone if I never Turned back into Saladin van Schalkwyk, the human misfit who was so very wary and lonely and alone in that life. Perhaps I could just stay as this bird, from now on, and I might never have to think about any of that other stuff again. Nobody would ever hit me, or look at me as though I was the cause of everything bad that had happened to them. They wouldn't resent me or think of me as a burden or a nuisance, or even a reminder of things that might have been but never came to pass. I would be free.

But just for a moment.

There were whole worlds that were not open to a bird that would be to a boy. A boy who would grow up; who had already grown far older than his chronological age would present him to an uninformed outside eye. A boy who had one eye on the future already, on everything that might be, could be, would be.

No sooner had I coherently formed that thought, the thought that *I want to be ME again,* when... well, suffice it to say that as a boy I was not nearly as good at perching on top of a narrow wall as a crow had been. Quite aside from the stab of agony that spasmed my limbs uncontrollably, my center of gravity was suddenly *different,* everything spun out of control, and I tumbled bare ass over head, on the other side of the wall, opposite to where my clothes were. I landed hard, in a tangled and ungainly heap, with a force that knocked the breath from my body. For a moment or two I sat there trying to at least whimper but only small gasps came out as I was trying to gather my wits and my faculties. When I finally collected myself enough to investigate the consequences of this new change and the fall, I discovered that I appeared to be scraped and bruised and smarting but nothing was broken or even sprained when I tested my limbs. When I finally found enough breath to whimper, I did, but it was both pain and relief. I chalked this one down to experience, making a mental note to myself to ensure that I could handle my environment properly in the moment of change before I attempted a Turn again.

Because that was all it took, all it needed to take. I had done it once, by purest freaky accident; I had done it again, by a blundering and uncertain grope-about-in-the-dark conscious decision (possibly ill-timed and misguided as to the precise sequence of events but still – a *choice* I had decided to make). And now the existence of that choice, for me, was no longer in doubt. I understood that I would be able to do this again. At will. Full moon or no full moon, of age to Turn or not, this was something that was mine, and under my control. It would need fine tuning, of course... but it was there now, locked inside of me. The knowledge of it. The certainty.

I itched to go back to the library, the computers, and find out if this sort of thing had happened before. But before I could do anything at all there was the small problem of those clothes, of being on the wrong side of this wall, and on somehow getting home (if I couldn't get hold of the clothes without incident) and into the apartment without being noticed.

How was I going to explain any of this to Mamma...?

Again, it was a passing thought, and one that crossed my mind only once... I knew the answer to that question was that I could say nothing at all, at least not right now, not until I knew more. She was not stable enough to deal with this. I did not want a panicked over-reaction which could result in any number of roads I did not want to travel on. What if she came to the conclusion that I would be better off locked up permanently into a Turning House? No, there were things I needed to know first, before I said anything about any of this to anybody. And least of all, to my mother.

But first there was the problem of getting home to Mamma in the first place.

This side of the wall, the grass was high and unkempt, full of weeds and

411

dandelions; the area looked almost abandoned, it certainly didn't seem as though I was in imminent danger of discovery, but it was definitely *the wrong side*. I'd have to get out of this enclosure to get home. The wall was too high for me to jump, in my current form, and I had no idea whether it had any doors in it through which I might pass to get out, or if they would even be open to my trying to do so in the first place. If there was a high wall, it stood to reason that it might contain doors which were kept locked. The advantage was that on *this* side it didn't matter that I was small, naked, bruised, and a little bloodied. But how could I avoid attracting the inevitable and unwanted attention on the parking-lot side of that wall?

"Think," I told myself sternly, nursing a particularly raw and smarting scrape which I had somehow managed to inflict on my heel; that alone would make walking, let alone running, somewhat interesting, in this boy form. "You have to *think*."

The plan, which I snatched out of thin air in tiny little jigsaw pieces, eventually proved to be simpler than I had thought.

First I Turned back into that crow once again. I had thought, perhaps, that the second time it would go easier, that now I "knew how to" – or that I would not care as much. It was just as agonizing as the first time, and once again the child's cry merged into a bird's as I shifted form. I caught a stray thought of *I don't want to do this anymore* as it skittered across my consciousness, but then I was through it once again, and in crow form the pain was gone.

On black wings I circled the wall that penned me in, looking for a way out and discovered that on the far side it was not a solid wall but rather a wire fence which I could, with a little effort, scale with my human limbs. Exit planned, I returned to the parking lot, where (for a wonder) my clothes still remained in their pitiful jumbled little heap. There were few people out there – but there were enough to notice if anything really weird started going on. I didn't know which would be worse – naked boy materializing beside a pile of clothes, or a bird trying to gather up those clothes and fly off with them – but on the whole people tended to ignore the street wildlife far more readily than they ignored odd people doing strange things. So I opted to stay the bird, for a little longer. I hoped that nobody would be watching and that those who might glance that way would not pay too much attention – but one by one I picked up individual items of clothing with my feet or my beak and lifted them over the wall. I nearly lost it with the jeans, they were heavy, and they were difficult to get a solid grip on, but eventually I dragged them over. I couldn't handle my shoes, they were just too awkward, but there was no putting those on anyway, not with that heel scrape. I would just have to come back for them if they were still there and carry them home. In the meantime, after moving my clothes over the wall I fluttered back over into the sanctuary of the tall grass and Turned back into myself.

I had done this too many times in too short a period of time, with zero prior experience in any of it – too fast, too hard. Less than an hour ago I had not had the faintest clue that something like this was even possible,

412

never mind that it was in my power. Now I had Turned no less than four times – boy to bird to boy to bird to boy – and my body felt as though it was about to disintegrate into a pile of gloop. I ached all over. My limbs didn't seem to know whether they wanted to be wings or hands and I was all thumbs getting dressed again.

It was a little while before I could make myself move at all and the mere act of simple walking, of dragging one foot in front of another, seemed to be more than I could handle. Scaling that wire fence was a far more painful exercise than I might have ever believed possible, and I had to will myself to make every necessary small movement. Even so there were frozen instants when I was hanging on the wire, literally unable to move at all, just hanging on by fingertips and bare toes until I could force myself to inch forward again. I all but fell down the final few feet, letting myself drop, and crouched there beside the fence panting. I was in a cold sweat, my hair plastered to my temples and the back of my neck. I could feel my heart throwing itself violently against my ribs.

It took me several long, fraught minutes before I could move again, but I knew I had to. I dragged myself upright and forced myself to walk. I did look around to see what kind of a place I had been fenced into, but it seemed as though whatever purpose that walled-in area had once actually served, it no longer did. There was a building that fronted the property, but its windows and door were boarded up with old plywood, layered with graffiti and tags. I recognized one or two of the sigs, the beetle that marked the work of someone we all knew only as Scarab, the tiny cartoon shark that showed that someone who went by the name Mako had been there .I had seen that guy, once, in the middle of tagging a concrete wall with a spray-paint can. He was a tall, stringy, almost skeletal, Asian character who hid his face under a waterfall of lanky black hair. I had not lingered to introduce myself.

Underneath its own share of street art, the sign that was still hanging out front was no more than a faded gray peeling oblivion now. At one time it might have been some sort of shop, a mechanic's maybe – but it was nothing now. I felt grateful that I'd had that oasis, abandoned and secluded, to deal with things without any prying eyes. I had somehow managed my escape without being seen, and I even managed to retrieve one of my shoes from its spot in the parking lot (I looked and looked but could not find the other. If anyone had taken it I was at a loss as to why they would take just one and leave the other – but it was just gone, and I was too spent to look for it for long). In the end I limped home, my clothes dirty and bloodied, my hair standing on end, my eyes wild and bloodshot, my feet bare and leaving a dribble of blood from my wounded heel in my wake.

If I worried about having to explain any of this to Mamma, I could put my mind at rest. She was not home when I got there. I did what I could about the filthy clothes after peeling them off my back, cleaned up my scrapes, and crawled into bed thinking I could sleep for a hundred years.

When I woke, it was almost dark, and Mamma was passed out cold in the grubby old armchair in the sitting room in front of a flickering TV with the sound turned off. If I had had any illusions about perhaps talking about any of this with her, she had just confirmed how inadvisable that would be. It was an almost physical pain for me to realize that there was no way I could trust my own mother with a secret of this magnitude.

There were three slices of cold pizza leftovers in the fridge and I wolfed them down, but I was still starving when they were gone and the pickings in the kitchen were slim – so I took a twenty from Mamma's purse on the floor by the front door, and slipped out to our weird little corner glory-hole store. It had random things like assorted and mismatched buttons, duct tape, dusty silk flowers, laundry detergent, and plastic action figures of comic book superheroes, all rubbing shoulders with such staples as cheese and cereal and the weird-smelling rack of exotic spices in the back. I couldn't find much of anything that would be considered healthy that I could actually get for my wrinkled $20 – a packet of sliced pepperoni, a couple of granola energy bars, a bag of crisps – but it took the edge off the unnatural hunger. There was a part of me that was keeping a running tally of all these new things – the pain at the Turn, the exhaustion, the hunger – things I would have to learn to handle and to deal with in the future if I were to attempt this particular feat again. I knew I would... as I knew I would be driven to.

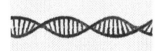

I rewrote the code for 'Epidemic' when I was just a couple of months' shy of my tenth birthday.

It might be hard to understand why a computer game about a disease that wreaks havoc on the world, with dead bodies piling everywhere and with survival options increasingly narrowing down to a point where player had kill or be killed, eat or be eaten, would be such a draw for someone like me. But those games on the elderly computers in our hopelessly inadequate and gently decaying neighborhood library were an escape, an escape from a reality that was every bit as grim at times as the worlds the games depicted.

And the reality was getting to be pretty grim, indeed. I was never entirely certain what Mamma's actual job was, what she did and where she did whatever it was that she got paid for, or even when she did it. Her hours seemed to fluctuate from day to day and I could not count on knowing that she would be at home at any given time of day or night. I was not even sure it was the same job for any two consecutive months running, but she managed to bring in just enough to keep the rent paid and the lights on. We ate a lot of noodles and quite a few individual specimens of canned goods which were probably a little questionable as far as their sell-by date was concerned, but we scraped by – and one of the side effects of that life was simply knowing that I was *on my own*. Oh, she squawked out a peremptory 'Where are you going?' if she happened to be at home as I made for the door, but she didn't really need, want, or even expect an answer. And even if she exerted her parental prerogative to lock me up and deny me permission to go out, all I had to do is crack open the window and Turn into a small enough bird to fit through the tiniest of gaps, and I was free to do what I wanted. I actually kept a secret stash of clothes in a safe place, out there, for just such an occasion, and used it more than once.

As to what drew me out – well – I had no interest in falling in with any one version of a bad crowd, and I had my pick of those in our neighborhood, or pursuing unhealthy obsessions of any sort... if you excluded the computers in the library, for which I quickly developed a compulsive interest in. Part of that was the dawning idea that computers, even these horrible ancient monsters, were tapped into an information net which was out there to be mined and explored at my will; the other part, of course, were those games that had been loaded onto the Teen Section computers.

I quickly discovered a couple of things about the computers.

One was that I was considered way too young, by the other users, to be there at all, and I could be (and usually was) booted off any given computer because some older teen wanted a crack at it. I solved that by sneaking in sometimes, in the form of something small and unobtrusive like a mouse (no building is completely mouse proof) and then sitting there in the deserted library at night. With a threadbare thing which Mamma had referred to as my "baby blanket" (which I had spirited away from home and stashed at the back of the broom cupboard for occasions such as this) draped over my shivering bare shoulders, bathed in the eerie bluish glow from the monitor like some Phantom of the Library, I played my games without rude interruptions.

Another thing was that I was actually better at these games than most of those older teens.

There was a scoreboard which displayed at the beginning of every game session, and all the players had fanciful monikers – a guy who went by the name of Emperor Six (I had to wonder what had befallen Emperors One through Five) was a consistent top player with scores that were frequently a couple of thousand points higher than his nearest competitor. But once I started in on the games (I was Coyote on the scoreboard) I quickly caught up – and remained steady in a position that hovered for a long time just below Emperor's. And then I beat the top score, one night, during my solitary play.

I happened to be there, in the library, when I found out who Emperor Six really was.

"I don't believe it!"

The outraged explosion came from the computer banks while I was in one of the nearby stacks, trying to decide which of two choices I would check out – I was only allowed so many books at a time, on the card that I had, and I was only one book away from my maximum. But, intrigued, I re-shelved both books and peered around the corner of the stacks towards the computer desks.

An older boy – he was old enough for a faint shadow of beard to show on his chin – was staring at a computer screen, with a couple of his friends crowding around him and peering at the screen over his shoulder.

"Who is this Coyote character?" Stubble-Boy, obviously Emperor Six, demanded incredulously. "Where did he suddenly come from? And when did he get *that* score? It took me more than an hour to crack 25,000 points – and he's passed me? I haven't seen anyone else playing this thing for nearly the amount of time it would take!"

Actually, it had taken me under an hour. I gave myself a quiet fist pump in the privacy of my own mind, without allowing any outward reaction.

He was in a high dudgeon, the Emperor, and had taken this as a personal challenge. Nothing would do but he had to beat the score I had posted, and as soon as possible.

He was fired up and outraged, and he made stupid mistakes. I watched him go down in flames with low scores twice (and took careful note of some of the language he flung at the computer for failing to cooperate, words I had not heard uttered before) but then he got the glow of the zealot in his eyes and cracked his knuckles and settled down to a serious session. I left him to it, but when I crept back into the library that night, I saw that he had done what he had set out to do. He was at the top of the scoreboard again.

By ten points.

I played my session that night, and ended up with almost eighty points above his. And then practically lived in the library until he came back in again, waited until he inspected the scores, and watched his face turn an ugly shade of purple.

He beat me again, by a narrow margin, after playing the game obsessively for almost four hours.

I passed him again, in a night session, and hit 26,000 points.

And he couldn't beat that. He nearly killed himself trying, but that seemed to be the top playable score, and Coyote owned it. The best he could do was draw level; there we were, at the top of the score board, sharing it, 26,000 points apiece.

Now that I knew exactly how, staying at this level was easy. It began to be boringly easy. But this was the most complex game available on the library menu, and everything else on offer was even worse – all the same, it began to annoy me that I was spinning my wheels and not going anywhere at all. And so on my next night session I decided not to play the game so much as tinker with it – I had been reading books on code and programming, some of them quite complicated and definitely not meant for my Junior Library Card. I found ways around that, and I decided to see if tweaking the code produced a rise in the score. I discovered a line of code which limited the number of corpses a player was allowed to accumulate during 'Epidemic', and my obvious solution to that problem was to simply remove that cap. It was entirely possible that the game ought not to have functioned at all after I was done but for a wonder it did – and it worked exactly the way I wanted it to work. I played it for almost two hours after I was done fixing it to my satisfaction, and Coyote ended up posting a score of 43,057.

I was there the next time Emperor Six showed up, and watched with glee as his eyes bugged out of his head when they lit upon the scoreboard on the computer monitor. By this stage I had investigated him and knew all sorts of things about him. His real name was Luke Barnes – he was Were like me (as best I could establish, his family were registered as Were-owls); he was almost seventeen, with two younger brothers, no father in the picture, and a vaguely unstable mother (she had an actual official record on file with the police) who bore a remarkable resemblance to mine. In some ways, I felt a kinship there, of sorts – but this, this was war, this wasn't Luke and Saladin and their broken families, it was a battle in a different world altogether between Coyote and Emperor Six, and Coyote had just not so much scored an extra goal or two but had moved the goalposts.

"This... isn't... even... possible," Luke said, apparently finding it difficult to form articulated words all of a sudden. "There's a high score. You can't get a score above the high score. He cheated. I don't know how but he cheated."

I ambled over, innocently enough and got snarled at by the older kids as I drew near, even as Luke was still muttering something about cheating.

I took an entirely unnecessary look at the screen, mouthed a *wow* which I thought quite believable for the utter insincerity with which it was offered, and deliberately lit a metaphorical match under Luke.

"Well, if he cheated, it doesn't matter," I said. "It's a cheat and you still won. But still... he's got the highest score..."

"Who asked you, pipsqueak? Anyway, not for long," Luke snarled and attacked the keyboard. He knew his way around computers as well as anyone, and he didn't care who saw him doing what he did – with just as little difficulty as I had had to tweak the scoreboard, he somehow moved into the game code and erased the entire board, zeroing it completely. He might have noticed my changes, if he'd gone just a little deeper into the code, but he didn't. It had still not occurred to him that his nemesis Coyote had gone that far.

"Right," he said. "So we start all over again."

He played the way he always played, and that was conservatively. Because the cap was removed he managed to cross his original 26,000 by quite a bit – but he had still not reached that high score that had triggered all this by the time he picked up his stuff to leave the library at closing time. I watched him leave – already a mouse, hiding underneath the lowest shelf in the stacks, closest to the computer bank. I saw him hesitate twice, turning back to look, reluctant to abandon the computer on which he had played, almost ready to sneak back in and stand guard over it twenty four hours straight if that's what it would take to keep Coyote away. But the librarians ushered him and his clique out, busied themselves with closing time tasks, and finally left, turning out the lights.

I barely waited an hour before coming out to play… and posted a score of almost 50,000 before I was done for the night.

The game was not the actual *game* anymore, it was positioning myself to be in the right place and the right time to observe Luke's taking the bait that I was leaving for him. The game was simply being better than someone who considered himself the best. For now, the anonymous one-upmanship was highly satisfying… but I was beginning to glimpse a time in which it would become important for the people I beat to know who had beaten them.

As it happened… I wasn't there to see Luke's response. Because things began to go downhill at home, fast, and for a while I had my hands full playing quite a different game, in real-time, with no possibility of cheating by rewriting the code at all. But before that came to a head, there came a turn in the road which might, looking back, have followed logically from the game in the library – but which, at the time that it happened, seemed to me to be a gift straight from the Gods. I met Hikaru Shimura.

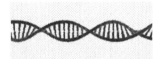

Shimura's Computer Shop was a tiny shopfront on a side street which branched off the road I always took between home and the library. The store sign looked hand-painted and by a meticulous hand which – once I got to know the man behind that name – made me reasonably certain that it had been his own, although I never straight-out asked him about that. I had noticed the store, in passing, glancing down the street, a number of times. But it was in the aftermath of my re-writing the computer game at the library that I really paid attention to the subtext on that sign. In smaller letters, underneath the shop's name, it said "Buy – Sell – Fix". It was that "Fix" that suddenly attached itself to my subconscious. Computers had become of interest – and now I was curious to know just how they functioned. Physically. And I could hardly take apart the library computers to study their innards.

I began to hang around the Shimura shop. Initially I couldn't see any real sign of life there except for a rather surly character who manned the front of the shop – one who didn't like me loitering there, and made that clear. He was older than me, and I found out later that his temper and the 'attitude' came from a chip on his shoulder which arose from a tangled genetic heritage which included Jamaican, a couple of generations of inner-city urban black, Polish Jew, and a smattering of Native American. He also had a proprietary interest in the shop and perhaps it was pure instinct that kicked in when he first laid eyes on me – because he instantly saw a rival. And it turned out he wasn't wrong.

I sneaked into the heart of the establishment through the back door. I myself couldn't have told you exactly why – but once I got past the couple of dingy blue dumpsters shoved up against the dirty brick wall on the opposite side to the alley I was richly rewarded for my adventuresome impulse by discovering the open back door, which led into an enchanted cave of a workshop in the back of Shimura's shop. Hikaru Shimura himself was perched at a bench littered with the innards of computers, patiently putting them back together and resurrecting machines which had been brought there, supposedly at death's door, by panicked customers.

I hung around for a while, watching him, before he noticed me there; he had actually lifted his head and looked out of that back door, in my direction, a number of times before he actually focused on me and realized that I was there. But when he did register my presense, he did precisely the opposite to what the young man at the front of the shop had done. He did not yell at me and tell me to go away; instead, he beckoned me closer.

"What are you doing there?" he asked, his hand in mid-motion, holding something that went inside a computer and made it function, something I didn't recognize.

"Watching," I said.

"Why?"

"I want to know how they work," I said, and it made no sense at all, and it made all the sense in the world.

"What is your name?" he asked, his lips stretching into a thin smile.

"Saladin."

"Well, Saladin, there is another stool in the corner over there. Bring it closer. If you do not distract me while I am working, you may watch, if you like."

It might have been the kind of offer that would have made any other boy my age run for their life. But I was not any of those boys. I dragged that second stool to the other side of his bench, in silence, and perched there, while he bent back down to his work, the smile still ghosting around the edges of his mouth.

I don't know how long I was there. He worked steadily, all the while I watched. We didn't speak. I don't even know if he noticed when I finally slipped off that stool and scuttled away – but the unspoken invitation to come back had been there. I took him up on it and returned – again, and again. I sat there watching his steady hands fitting together pieces of computer guts until he had reconstituted any number of machines, patiently retrieving data from compromised or damaged drives. I had started to get a real sense of how things connected, of how and why things worked, without him ever having spoken a word of anything that might have been understood as instruction on the matter at hand

I began to fiddle with spare parts on my own, parts I didn't even know. Perhaps he left them there on the workbench deliberately, to see what I would do with them – and at first, I carefully kept my hands away from anything lest I damaged it. But the parts were there, and I could hear them whispering to me, and eventually the temptation to handle them and rearrange them and understand their form and function instinctively and directly through my fingertips became too much. I started to play with them on the bench with my silent mentor apparently doing his best to studiously ignore me. Although there were moments that I would look up occasionally after I'd completed some connection or hook-up and catch his eyes resting on me and he would give me just the slightest, most imperceptible of nods before looking down at his own work again. We had exchanged few words on the subject and what brief conversations did occur were mostly due to me scraping up enough gumption, on a handful of occasions, to do what he had expressly said I should not do, distract him. I piped up to actually ask a question about the thing he was working on at the time – and he had answered me, concisely and exactly, not volunteering any more information beyond the thing I had asked about.

I'd addressed him as Mister Shimura, at first, and he took that as it came, but it didn't take him very long to put a stop to it.

"You can call me Oji-san," he said.

That wasn't his name, so I asked the obvious question. "What does that mean?"

"Uncle," he said, in his succinct and economical manner of speaking. He did not elaborate. I did not ask, But I looked it up later, on the Net (I was getting better at finding the stuff I wanted to know rather than being buried under a deluge of irrelevant information if I phrased a query wrong) and I was rewarded, this time, by a site that explained a little bit about not just the Japanese language but the culture in which it was embedded. Being invited to call Mister Shimura my uncle turned out to be quite a big deal, apparently, and meant that he really liked me. But it was Josh, the guy from the front of the Shimura shop, who told me why.

Josh loathed me. That much was obvious. The first time he popped his head into the workshop from round the front – to get his boss for a customer who had asked for him – and found me there, he had been startled, and then something dark and sharp had flashed in his dark eyes and they felt like stone knives on me as he slowly stepped back into the store front. It was the early days, then, and as Mister Shimura – I had yet to be invited to call him Uncle – rose from his perch to follow Josh into the shop he murmured, politely but firmly, "Don't touch anything." This scenario repeated itself a few times, and then several small things changed.

Oji-san said, "Don't touch anything, Saladin-chan," as he left.

Josh heard him say that.

The time after that, Oji-san said nothing at all as he left the workbench.

And Josh heard that, too. The silence of omission.

As it happened, I took that silence for permission to slip off my own stool and go over to the far side of the bench where the real work was being done, peering at the current project on the go. I had not been told not to touch anything, not that time, but I might have been expected to understand that instruction as read – except that I didn't. Oji-san had been re-building a computer and there were a few connections I could see needed to be made but he had not made them – so I did. And then, hearing his steps as he made his way back to the workshop, fled from his workstation and back to my own side of the bench.

He returned to his own stool, glanced at the workbench, paused for only the briefest of instants, but said nothing. It was on the tip of my tongue to blurt out I was sorry, but he didn't seem to expect an apology and so I didn't offer one. But as I slipped off my stool to leave, that time, he lifted his hand to stop me.

"I have something for you," he said. "Over there, on the third shelf. Please go and get it."

Curious, I crossed the small workshop and reached up to the third shelf, which was roughly at my eye level, and brought down a cumbersome, thick-bodied, older model laptop computer.

It was in sorry shape, on the outside, with its shell scraped and scratched – but this was Shimura's workshop, and I had seen him resurrect computers before my eyes, and I knew that if this one was here it must, despite its appearance, be a decent working machine.

My heart thumped, holding the computer. I had never had one of my own before.

"This?" I asked faintly, holding the laptop up with both hands.

"That," he agreed. "It was left here for me to sell, but I would not get much for that machine if I tried to put it in the store. I can fix what the man thought was wrong with it, but I cannot fix how he treated it. But that does not matter. It is an older machine, and a little slow, but it works."

"Why?" I asked, unable to expand that question into a hundred smaller questions which it contained.

Oji-san gestured to the eviscerated computer in front of him on the bench. "You understand," he said. "The hard drive has been reformatted. It does not have much inside it. Next time, I will show you code. Programming."

I would like to believe I said thank you. I don't remember if I did. I left the workshop, clutching the computer under my arm... and practically walked into Josh, waiting for me on the corner of the alley that led to the back.

"I know what you're up to," he snarled at me, with his lips drawn back over his canines like a furious and cornered dog's. "You slip in here, and you think you can just take it from me, just like that? I worked for this place. I've been with him for years. You think I don't see what you're doing? I watched you – you don't go to school, you got no real family 'cept that crazy mother of yours, I know where you live – you think you can just sneak in here and find a better feathered nest? This place is mine, I tell you. *Chan*, he called you. He called *you*. He never called me that, not ever. Just because you're the same stupid age as his stupid son when he..."

I had not known just *why* Josh hated me – but the idea that he "had a place" and that I was trying to "take his place" hadn't really crossed my mind. I stared at him, probably looking bewildered, and that just seemed to build his head of steam. He reached out to try and tug the battered laptop from under my arm.

"Give me that!" he snapped, but this was a treasure and I wasn't giving it up. I knew how to fight dirty, and I was silently and bitterly preparing to, when another voice cut into the conversation.

"Pick on someone your own size, Josh," the voice said, and Josh snapped his head around to look. So did I; the voice had sounded familiar. For good reason, it turned out. I found myself staring at Luke Barnes. Emperor Six, from the library.

"Butt out," Josh snarled. "None of your business."

"Laptop yours?"

It wasn't clear whom he was addressing, but I answered first. "Yes. Mister Shimura just gave it to me."

"Lying little rat," Josh said.

"We could always ask Mister Shimura," Luke suggested with a slippery grin, tucking both his hands, finger-deep, just catching the edge of the fabric with the web between thumb and forefinger, into the front pockets of his jeans. The gesture might have been a disarming one, apparently taking fists out of the equation, but for some reason it was as threatening as they came, and Josh let go of the laptop, scowling blackly.

"I've come to pick up my stuff," Luke said easily. "You said, a week. You have it?"

"No idea," Josh said, still surly. "I have to check deliveries."

"Well, go and look," Luke said.

Josh gave me another black scowl and turned to stomp back into the store.

"Thanks, Emperor," I said, without thinking – and then could have bitten my tongue out.

Luke's eyebrow rose. "Emperor...?"

"You're Emperor Six," I said helplessly. "The library..." Trying to deny anything at this point would be stupid and just turning and running would be churlish.

"You play that game, pipsqueak?"

"Yeah," I said.

"I kind of remember seeing your mug around there, now you mention it. You any good?

I really could not help the smile from tugging at the corners of my mouth. "Yeah."

"You made the board...? How old *are* you?"

"Yeah, I made the board," I said, a little warily, choosing not to admit to my age.

"Well," he said. "There's something. But how did you know I was Emperor Six?"

"Watched you, that time Coyote beat you," I said.

His face darkened a little, into a scowl that wasn't anywhere near as thunderous as Josh's had been but was still a gathering thundercloud. "*That* cheat," he muttered.

422

"Wasn't cheating," I said.

His eyes glittered. "And just how would you know?"

And finally, at long last, my feet decided that it would be a very good idea if I was elsewhere right now – and I turned to run, still clutching my precious laptop. But not before sealing my fate, seemingly unable to keep anything from being blurted out loud today.

"Because *I'm* Coyote," I threw back over my shoulder, and fled.

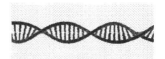

I don't remember when Mamma began to talk to invisible people– but I do recall stumbling into a room in response to her voice raised in argument and finding her sitting in the armchair, both hands clutching the arm-rests with a furious intensity. Her head was turned a little to her right and she was staring intently at empty space while she attempted to convince the ghost she saw there of something that obviously meant a lot to her, judging by the expression on her face and the flickers of sheer desperation that danced in her eyes. I did nothing – what could I have done? – other than leaving her to it.

That time. The next time it happened, I listened to some of the one-sided conversation, and what little I understood of it chilled me. I could not be *certain* – I was still too young to be as adept at reading between lines – but she seemed to be talking about an unbearable burden, and there were hints that the burden was *me*.

All the things she had given up, all the things she had had taken away from her, because she had given birth to *me*.

All the things she had lost.

All the things she had been forced into, bullied into, tricked into.

She had never loved or wanted my father. She seemed ambivalent, at times, when I stood there frozen and listening, as to whether she had wanted children at all. Perhaps she might have wanted the ones she had lost before they were born, before I was born, whether or not she had ever wanted me, in particular.

She seemed to think she had done well by me just to have snatched me from *them*, from the nebulous people who seemed to have had a hand in my very existence and who might have had designs on me. She had loved me enough to take me away and hide me, in whatever way she knew how, keeping one step ahead of the chase and then she wondered whether it was all worth it, in the end. Could she get anything out of it all, get anything *back*, if she went tamely back to the people she had been running from all of this time and handed me back to become somebody else's problem, not hers, not something she was responsible for, had to take care of?

I was... too hard.

I listened. I waited. I did not know what to do next. My tenth birthday came and went unnoticed in this fog of fear and dread. The only oasis of peace I knew was in Shimura's workshop, or huddled over the laptop which he had given me.

It was maybe two months after that birthday that I finally heard her make up her mind – or sound as though she was ready to do so.

"Tomorrow," she was whispering, over and over again, lying sprawled in our armchair, her eyes closed. It was hypnotic, watching her, looking as though she was just talking in a restless sleep – right until her eyes flew open and she looked straight at me, although I didn't think that it was my face that she saw. "Tomorrow," she said earnestly. "I will call them. Tomorrow."

I stood there staring at her until she finally did pass out, or fall asleep. And then I gathered up a handful of possessions that fitted into my small battered backpack and, with that slung on my back and the precious laptop clutched in my arms, I left the apartment.

There was a public phone booth on the corner of our street, the last remaining one for that city block. Too many people had cellphones now; these booths were going the way of the dinosaur; even this one had long ceased to accept coins to make any actual phone call to a real person, but it was still useful – and often used – for emergency calls. I slipped inside, picking up the black Bakelite receiver sticky with God alone knew what, and hesitated.

I had a choice. There was 911, the straight emergency number. And then there was another number I knew, a number that was code, that would get you emergency help... but of a specialized kind. 9119 – or 911W, if you looked at the phone buttons – got you to a Were emergency hotline.

The full moon was maybe three days away. There would be plenty of time for them to find out about Mamma, the hard way. Calling the Were line felt almost as big a betrayal as hers would have been of me. It might have been the very same number she would have called, if she'd chosen to turn me in for some sort of a reward that she imagined that she was long past due. All the same... she was Were. She would need specialized help in only a few short days. And I was no longer there to watch over her.

When the dispatcher at 9119 asked what my emergency was, I gave them our apartment's address and told them that there was a woman there who needed help. And then I dropped the phone, leaving the sticky black receiver dangling at the end of its cord while the dispatcher desperately tried to get me to tell her who I was and where I was – I could hear the echo of her "Hello?... helloo?" in my wake – and I walked away from it all.

My first instinct was to go to Oji-san's although I had no real idea as to what would happen after that – I could hardly turn up on his doorstep and announce I had come to stay. But in any event the world seemed intent on blocking me at every turn – because when I got to the familiar shop the front door was firmly closed and there was a sign on it: "CLOSED DUE TO ILLNESS". I tried the back, without much hope, but the back door was closed and locked. I could have broken in and claimed a sort of sanctuary, but I didn't think that would be a good idea. In the end, I walked away to the other place that had been a haven to me. The library.

And perhaps the Universe *did* have a hand in guiding me to where I should have been because Luke Barnes was there, loitering just outside the front doors of the library, bantering with his crew.

After that encounter in front of Shimura's shop, when I had flung the identity of Coyote at his feet and ran for my life, I had succeeded in actually avoiding him for a few weeks. If I glimpsed him at the library, I made myself scarce; I ducked behind other people and scurried into shadows if I saw him coming down the street. He'd helped me there at the shop, but that was *before* he knew about Coyote. And all that rivalry... mattered. I just didn't want to face him properly, to explain.

But I couldn't avoid him forever – while ours wasn't the sort of neighborhood that encouraged cordial relations and chats between chums who ran into one another unexpectedly while out walking, and everyone knew to mind their own business, it was still a small enough pond for the fish in it to bump into one another by accident every so often. I had my own laptop now but that didn't mean I had given up on the library full of books and of course it was inevitable in the long run that Luke should be there at precisely the wrong moment. Eventually.

When that happened, it was almost ludicrous – I had literally walked out of the stacks with my nose stuck in a book and stumbled straight into him. We both rocked back, he reached out a hand to steady me, and then we both became aware of one another's identity at the same moment.

It was close quarters – shelves on either side of me, no real room to turn, Luke squarely in front – and so I just squared my shoulders and stood my ground and looked up at him, meeting his eyes.

To my surprise, he was actually grinning.

"Well, if it isn't Coyote," he said. "You've been making yourself scarce."

I mumbled something in response, trying to keep it noncommittal.

To my surprise, he kept grinning.

"I looked at your handiwork, dude," he said. "That was quite a number you pulled."

"I didn't *cheat*," I said rebelliously.

"Well, I don't know about that," Luke said. "But even if I said you did, it was cheating on a whole different level. Dude, that was *good*. How old did you say you were?"

"I didn't," I muttered.

Luke laughed. "Well, when you grow up some," he said, "come get me if you want a job. I can fix someone like you up with something pretty sweet."

I said okay, then, hoping he'd just go away, unconvinced that he meant a word he said. For the time being it was just a relief that he had chosen to take the Coyote revelation in the way that he had.

But now, only weeks later, having left Mamma behind for good, with Oji-san apparently down for the count and that avenue of escape closed to me, without any place else to go, I saw Luke by the library door and I remembered what he had said.

I hesitated, and he turned and saw me, and I made a small hopeless gesture with my chin – *can I talk to you?*

He understood the signal, and said something to his mates that made them laugh and look at me in a way that made me want to run again, but I stood my ground as he broke off from his group and ambled over to me.

"Hey, Coyote," he said. "You look like a month of wet Sundays. What's up?"

"You said when I grow up some I should come to you for a job," I said. His gaze sharpened. "Oh?"

"That still open?"

"I meant a few years, not a couple of *weeks*," he said.

"Now, or never," I said. My voice was steady enough and I held his gaze, but I had to concentrate on not letting my hands tighten into a white-knuckled grip of desperation on the laptop I was carrying. "I... need a place to go. I can't go home."

He studied me for a long moment, and then stuffed his hands into the pockets of his jeans in a manner I was already learning to recognize was Luke Barnes girding for battle.

"Well," he said, "maybe you might as well meet the Collective. If they're okay with things – well, nobody on the Net needs to know that Coyote is still a cub. Give me ten minutes and then meet me by Joey's Diner. I'll walk past you; when I do, just follow me."

"Okay," I said.

He turned without another word and sauntered back to his mates who were still loitering by the library door. One of them said something, Luke shrugged broadly (his hands still in his pockets), and they all laughed, at least one of them glancing over at me.

I knew when to make an exit. I dropped my eyes to the cracked pavement and followed the cracks, one foot in front of the other, until I fetched up outside the grimy windows of Joey's Diner about a block and a half from the library and leaned against the wall by the drainpipe, keeping an eye out for Luke. I half expected him not to show at all, and was almost ready to flee by myself to whatever destination awaited at the end of an unknown and treacherous road ahead, when he turned up on schedule, about ten minutes later, and walked by the diner and past me without any sort of acknowledgment.

I fell into step behind him, at a discreet distance, as instructed, and hesitated only briefly when he disappeared down a side alley and then through a wooden gate set into a two-story-high brick wall which looked like it had been raised to guard a palace. The gate led into an unkempt back garden – a postage-stamp-sized piece of lawn, and a weedy flower bed that abutted the inside of the wall to the street.

On one side of the lawn rose a three-story brownstone. On the far side, against the wall that faced the back alley was a peculiar structure which gave the impression of somebody having pulled up an ordinary suburban clapboard bungalow up by the roof until it distorted into two stories high and half-a-house wide – an elongated building with no two windows on it quite the same size or shape, including an odd and asymmetrically placed dormer window jutting out of the steep roof. The entrance featured a wide and sturdy door that looked like it was solid oak and framed by a narrow edging of elegant stained glass. The house had once been painted green, but it was faded and peeling in places. Two steps led to the narrow porch that graced the front of this extraordinary building but the second one was missing and so access to the front door, necessitated an awkward half-skip to the level of the deck.

Luke negotiated this with practised ease and then turned at that fabulous door to look at me over his shoulder.

"Well, come on then," he said. "I called ahead, they're expecting us. Welcome to the Green House Collective."

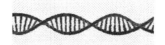

The Green House Collective turned out to consist of four individuals who were living off the grid while hidden in plain sight in the green house at the bottom of the garden. There was Luke, and his girlfriend LuLu – another Were-owl, as it happened, and of mixed blood, very mixed blood. A soup of European genes combined with a mix of Chinese and South East Asian thrown in, with the tawny skin and thick straight black hair of her Asian heritage and the rangy height of a Midwest cowboy. The two of them, despite both of them still being under twenty, seemed to be the leaders of the group and it was LuLu's stamp of approval that I had to get before I was permitted to take my place amongst their ranks.

Another member of the Collective was Imogen Cooper, who seemed to be surgically attached to her earbuds and the music player that hung on a lanyard around her neck. She didn't seem capable of verbal communication other than grunts and sighs, although I discovered later that she could wax very eloquent in online forums on subjects she cared deeply about.

The fourth member was Tucker – I never did find out if that was his first name, last name, or only name – whose prematurely receding hairline, at war with his acne-scarred face, together with a pair of large spectacles framed in thick black plastic (which seemed distantly related to the stuff the telephone receiver in the public phone booth was made of) made it impossible to accurately guess at his age.

Imogen and Tucker barely paused to lift their heads when I stepped through the door, one sitting at a messy desk in the corner of the great room, which ran the length of the front of the house, tapping at a keyboard and staring intensely at a pair of monitors almost crowding one another off the surface of the desk, and the other lounging on a sagging sofa with a laptop propped up against his knees and studying the screen with a frown. Luke introduced them, offhandedly – "Imogen... Tucker..." – by waving a lazy hand in their general direction, and then guided me through the room and into the kitchen where I was to face my real inquisition.

LuLu sat at the kitchen table like a queen about to grant an audience, her face impassive.

"This is the cub," Luke said.

"He's just a kid," LuLu said. "He's a liability, Luke. Someone will be hunting him before long."

"They'll never find me," I said, with a flat certainty. All I would ever have to do if I was cornered was shift into something, and scurry away with nobody any the wiser – but I was not about to tell anybody about *that*, not yet, anyway. All I was willing to offer was that certainty. And it was genuine; LuLu heard it in my voice, and could not help but believe it.

She stared at me. "That tadpole rewrote the code on the game?" she asked Luke, without taking her eyes off me. "You sure?"

"Wasn't *me* that did it," Luke said. "And I had so little expectation that anyone else in that library would have the chops for it that I never even looked for it... until much later. If we can point him in the right direction – I think he's already on fire. And Lu – he doesn't need to pull an equal share until he puts in an equal share."

"What about your family?" LuLu asked me, speaking directly to me for the first time.

"Only my mother," I said, caught by surprise by the stab of pain that the words, the image, the memory, brought. But that was what it was, a memory. Already a memory. I didn't need to explain anything any further, but they did have a right to at least the basic story if not the details and rationalizations. "She's always been... difficult. It's been me taking care of her when she needed to – during the Turn days, anyway – for years now. But I can't help her any more. I called the services on her, and I left. I can't go home. Not again. There *is* no home any more, I suspect. I can't see them leaving her to fend for herself. She can't."

I looked at Luke. "I went to Shimura's, first," I said. "He wasn't there. Nobody was. It said, closed because of illness. I don't know what the matter is, or even where he is, or where Josh is – the place is closed. If you won't let me stay, can I at least crash here tonight? I'll leave in the morning, if you want."

"And go where?" Luke asked, after a pause and an exchange of eloquent looks with LuLu. There was a laptop on the table, in sleep mode, and Luke reached over and spun it towards himself, waking it and rapidly typing something, watching the screen, typing some more, and then studying the screen intently with intermittent stabs at the keyboard for some minutes.

"Got him," he said at last, having completed something to his satisfaction. "Your Mister Shimura is in Mercy General. Heart attack, yesterday morning. He seems not to be doing so well. Might be the end of that store. Pity. That was a useful place and Josh was a useful tool."

"Tonight," LuLu said. "We'll give you a little test, tomorrow. Then we'll see."

Imogen and Tucker had bedrooms on the second floor of the house – those, and a bathroom between the two rooms, were the only rooms on that level. But a second staircase, steep and made out of fire-escape steel, led up a further level, into the room with the dormer window facing the yard between the green house and the brownstone. That room was shared by Luke and LuLu.

But there was a closet-sized space off on the far side of the house, with a tiny casement window opening onto the narrow alley at the back of the house and with a dirty brick wall which seemed barely an arm's reach away as its only view. It was filled with boxes and mops and other junk but Luke helped me haul all that stuff out on the landing and provided an air mattress and a blanket to go into the makeshift bedroom instead. It seemed like a good sign – there didn't seem to be much point in cleaning out a space for me if it was only to crash for one night – they could have just dumped me on the sofa which Tucker had been occupying down in the great room if it was just for the one night. I allowed the thinnest tendril of hope to grow, hope that I had somehow managed a soft landing after almost literally jumping out of the window of my life up to that point. I shared their supper – plain fare, but decent – and when night fell, I tucked my precious laptop under the lumpy pillow Luke had also scrounged up for me, and let myself sleep without keeping one eye open.

They made me do stuff the next morning – fiddle with code – but my knowledge was mostly instinctive, with a few pointers that had stuck from the time I had spent with Oji-san. LuLu's verdict was that I was raw and had a lot to learn but that she thought I had the mother wit to do that, and that I could be of some use. They still didn't quite tell me what it was that the Collective did, but it didn't take me long to find out, and to become a part of it.

They were hackers for hire. They worked anonymously, under screen names, for the highest bidder, and the jobs they took on were not always, strictly speaking, *legal*. They were good. And they were paid very well for their work.

I learned the ropes quickly. It didn't take me long at all to catalogue the Collective itself. Imogen was definitely at the bottom of the totem pole, with a single towering talent – she could burrow into the Net, and anywhere it had tendrils, and find people or things with a touch that was fine enough not to leave a trace. It was something I knew I could use, and I studied her techniques, especially over her shoulder when she wasn't aware I was there. That was easier than it should have been, but between her tight focus on her work and the fact that she couldn't hear anything past the music that constantly streamed into her ears from her player it was hardly difficult to keep a weather eye on what she was actually doing. Then I'd go in and retrace her steps and discover just where she had been and how lightly she had passed there.

If she found lost things and lost people, then Tucker was the wizard who could create things and people who had never existed. From nothing except electrons and stray bits of information he would make it look as though they were creaky with age and the world could not possibly ever have lived without them. He could create a new identity from *nothing* and slip it into filing systems which had chugged along for decades, so seamlessly that the system would probably have disintegrated with alarums if anyone had attempted to actually remove the fake entry from within its coils.

This was a lesson very much worth learning, and I was his avid disciple – it flattered him, I think, to have the Cub (as I was promptly dubbed inside the Collective) hanging onto his every keystroke. It was under his tutelage that I created my own first alter ego – a creaky one which would not have passed too close a scrutiny but which served as a springboard from which I created a dozen others. The name of Saladin van Schalkwyk was soon buried deep. I had told LuLu that they would never find me, anyone who wished me harm, and I was learning quickly how to make absolutely certain of that.

LuLu was the wizard of the group – she was quite simply brilliant at anything and everything. She could break through any wall, hack through any protection. At her side I walked ghostlike into the vaults of banks and the carefully guarded towers of academic learning and the offices of government intelligence. I learned that there were very few places I could not go... and I tried not to let that knowledge go to my head. I also instinctively did not tell LuLu that I was learning far more than she knew she was giving away.

Luke was hardly a slouch in the hacker world, but only when he chose to be. What he brought to the Collective was that much-needed outside face, and he made that into a bigger game than we had ever played on the library computers, back in what now seemed like a prehistoric era. It seemed weird to me, actually, after I had spent a little time with the Collective, that he would ever go to a place like the library to play their silly little games at all – after all, he had unfettered access to much better games right there in the Green House, and over and above that there was the real world in which stuff went on all the time that put dinky little library computer games with bad graphics to shame. I asked him about it once, in the early days.

"I muck around, outside," he said. "That's my cover – I'm just a stupid geeky teen who likes playing around with computers, and if anyone ever came near enough to smell our trail that's where it would dead-end .They'd end up with me, and sure, they'd have a computer geek on their hands, but they'd have no real idea that I was just camouflage and that the real work goes on behind me in the shadows. If they found out something possibly incriminating, they would discover I buy computer parts on the cheap from Josh at Shimura's and fiddle at building computers. Just enough smoke to hide the bigger fire. They'd quickly figure that any information they might have on anything they thought I was involved in had just enough half-truth to it to make it a real truth, and also not worth pursuing. Kids like me are a dime a dozen out there. And besides..."

The besides was all Luke, really. Out there, with his posse of other teenage boys, he could expend very little effort at being the best at stuff. Those games in the library, he had ruled that world. He'd basked in the admiration and envy of the less able, in his entourage. That is, right until he met Coyote, which rather threw a grenade into the whole thing. He told me, a little aggrieved, that it was that idiotic game of one-upmanship that I'd forced him into that had taken the shine off the whole thing. Gradually he had stopped seeing that library gaggle at all, had withdrawn from the library. His favored cover now was more along the lines of sitting in a coffee shop with earphones on and pretending to tap on his laptop, while eavesdropping on both meat-space and cyber conversations all around him and snatching at potentially useful tendrils to bring back and lay at the feet of the Collective.

It was still moot what my contribution would be. For the time being, for a little while, they seemed to accept that I was learning, and they would wait until I was ready to start repaying the investment they were making. I had never been in a formal schoolroom – but in one sense I was getting one now. I had gone from complete chaos into a period of unscripted but still intense education.

It was the conversation which had to be had, given our backgrounds – Luke at least knew I was Were – that launched me onto a project that I had not really thought about tackling before, the vexed question of my own identity.

I had explained about my mixed Were heritage, and Luke had asked what kind I was, or thought I would be when I eventually Turned in my allotted moment. None of them knew about my shifting abilities. That, I was holding close. But it was a legitimate question, given that there were two owls on the loose in the house during the Turn days.

"We're Free Were," Luke said, "Lu and I. Yes, the law is that we should be in a Turning House – but I've been, a couple of times, and I won't go back again, and Lu has managed to avoid it altogether and doesn't want to find out about what goes on there from any closer than she has to. We pass the Turns here. Free. But if your mother was a cat, and you Turn here, we may have to put procedures into place."

"I have no way of telling," I said, honestly enough. If this had even been an issue, I couldn't have told them what they wanted to know. But I was suddenly intrigued. "What usually happens? With mixed parentage like that?"

Luke stared at me. "You know, I have no idea," he said. "I don't actually think I ever heard of such a mating, before you. I have absolutely no inkling about which form would take precedence – if either – or why…"

"You aren't telling me I'm the first – ever – to be born of two Were-kind parents who are of different clans?" I asked, genuinely taken aback.

"I guess you can't be," Luke said. "Logically. But I can't say I've heard it talked about. At the very least, it isn't a common thing."

"But the Random Were – they can be very different things – and their children…"

"Their children are also Random," Luke said. "That lot, they're weird, it seems to be a question of anything goes. But the point is, there isn't a *this* kind and a *that* kind, all of them are potentially *everything*, they may have different primary forms which they got when they first Turned, but they're able to Turn into anything at all across the board – and the children are born with the ability to do that, to choose – they're the only Were who can actually pick their form, if they're lucky enough to be able to be in the presence of their chosen creature when they first Turn. And then they stick to that. But they don't automatically Turn into their mother's form or their father's."

He frowned, as an idea tickled the back of his mind. "I wonder if that's how the Random Were got started?" he muttered, almost to himself, as though he had momentarily forgotten that I was even there. "Two different Were kindreds, and the child born of that union is so utterly confused by the whole genetic mess that they just Turn into... anything they can? It's complicated."

"Well, it's years until I'm supposed to Turn properly, traditionally," I said.

"Yeah, I suppose we can cross that bridge, and all that," Luke said. "Just have to be careful, that's all. I can't have you hunting Lu or me down when none of us are walking on two legs."

That's when I started digging into my background, for real, for the first time – and because I was so young, it sounded so *cool*. I began to gather up everything I found into a secret cyber information vault I called "The Evidence Locker" – it was random, and organized, if that word applied at all in any context, according to topic. I was not building a structure. I was building a *net*.

I still had a little while to go before I would meet my first true Random Were and begin to understand, from his perspective, what that clan's peculiar burdens were – but I began to research Were history and mythology and the science that stood behind us all. And long before Mal Marsh came into my life, I would learn three things.

The first was that there was indeed very little out there on lineages such as mine – and what there was, at least the stuff that I could get to without showing my hand, was often buried deep and well.

The second was that the picture that *was* beginning to come into focus for me was that I – and possibly, although I was finding it hard to run this down to a certainty, others similar to myself were *made*, not naturally born or selected; that we were the product of carefully engineered cross-breeding, the purpose of which I remained ignorant.

And the third was that the whole project – the whole breeding program, if I had to call it that – seemed to have its roots deep into our own kind. The case might have been made that the normals – the ones who controlled the world we lived in, who outnumbered us dramatically, and who still feared and misunderstood us all the way – could have been the ones to begin researching something like this, in order to dissect us, to comprehend us, to make sure that we were properly tamed or at least hobbled and tethered and existed on terms that they, the normals, set for us. But it was not them. This had been done by my own kind. It was the Were who had initiated this project.

It came from deep within the heart of us.

Someone – or a faction of someones – at the core of Were-kind had their hands in our genes, up to the elbows, and were letting Were DNA run through their fingers like threads... from which they intended to tease out the strands they wanted and weave a whole new thing.

But before I got too deep into that... I crossed paths with Malcolm Marsh.

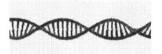

I was maybe twelve, and by this stage starting to truly pull my own weight in the Collective, when I first saw the boy in the alley, facing down three circling opponents who were clearly intent on pressing their advantage, it should have been a no-brainer, really. It was not my problem.

I had observed fights in streets and back alleys before, and had always steered clear of them. The physical world of fisticuffs; black eyes and bloodied noses was just not my arena. I wasn't built for it. I was always the stringy scrawny kid – contrary to what people with training in this or that martial skill like to say, size and weight and reach *do* matter, especially when you're young – and I knew where my advantage lay. I fought my battles with my mind, with my fingers on a keyboard, with a ghostly presence that walked at will through the cyberworld if I needed to. But this time... there was something about this time, *this* particular boy, that made me pause, and take another look.

Perhaps it was the expression that twisted his features as I watched. I had felt that helpless black rage, myself, I saw it and greeted it as an old friend, but I had never quite seen it so clearly drawn on a human face before. It was as though I had suddenly looked into a mirror – and the face I saw reflected there was not my face, but the feelings that it threw back at me were my feelings, my emotions, my fears, my failures... and all of a sudden it was a fight I could not quite walk away from, after all.

He looked like he had grown up scrawny, like me – but he also looked like he was starting to grow out of that phase. Give him a few years and a chance to actually bulk out those muscles, and he could be formidable. But right now he was still a kid – I judged him to be perhaps just a little younger than me – and there were three of them ranged against him in that alley. And it just wasn't fair.

He asked me once, later, what it had been – had I known him for what he was? A Were-kid? One of my own (if I stretched the concept) kind? But

I did not. All I saw was himself, not the masks of identity that he chose to wear. It didn't matter why he fought. It mattered that I decided that whatever his reasons were, whatever had painted that black scowl on his face, I could see myself being haunted by them.

I watched, for a little while. I saw one of the three bruisers land a blow, right on the cheekbone, and I winced, knowing that there would be a price to pay for that – but I also saw him, *my* boy, my miniature gladiator, use the opportunity which that blow had given him to land one of his own, one which landed just as hard. He gave as good as he got. I had drawn close, by this stage, and I could hear them all breathing hard, and I could see that he was actually holding his own against two of his opponents. He fought physically, yes, but I could also see an instinctive understanding of strategy here, and he actually used his opponents against one another at one point, ducking fluidly out of the way while one of them landed a hard thump on the other. I could see the swift half-smile that blossomed on the face of that kid, just for a moment, just before he turned at the ready and waded into the fray once more.

He was too focused on the two in front of him. He had left the third guy out of the equation. The third guy, who was even now sneaking up to his rear, waiting for a chance. I could see his thoughts, his plans, as though they were hanging above his head in a thought bubble like you'd find in a comic book – *If I can get him, right there, I can land one good blow to the kidneys and he's down...*

"Oh no, you don't," I muttered suddenly.

And without quite having planned it, my foot found its way to where the thug's feet slapped the pavement, and he was down – and I landed a blow to his kidney. Oh, I knew *how*. I was just not convinced that it would have been to my own advantage, ever, to pick such a fight. This – this seemed like a good payoff. But I wasn't going to go any further than that.

I leaned over to where the thug I had felled was still lying on the ground, wheezing; he wore a jacket which had a name tag stuck on it, and I took note of that name. I would remember it. I whispered into his ear, conversationally, "I'd just leave, now, if I were you, *Randy Coleman*. And if I get wind of you sniffing around again... you'll never pass a class test again. I can fix that for you. I know where your grades are stored."

He didn't have the breath to answer me. First he had also looked up and met my eyes, and knew that what I had just said was no idle threat – and then, rolling his eyes like a spooked horse, he noticed that his two friends were missing – at some point my alley boy had landed the decisive blow in this fight and his pair of opponents had chosen the better part of valor – retreat, and fight another day. My own victim, there on the ground, was the one who was alone now, against possibly two of us, and he did not have the kind of courage that took. He scraped himself off the ground, somehow, and slouched off down the alley and behind some dumpsters, bent double with his arms wrapped around his middle, trying to catch his breath as he made his escape.

I straightened, and realized that the victor of the alley scuffle, left in possession of the battlefield, had finally become aware of me. I saw him brace himself, first, his shoulders tensing, as he turned to face what might have been an assault from a different angle and a fresh adversary. I could see a couple of things warring in his expression, a blazing triumph that had washed across him briefly as he had realized he had won this particular scuffle, followed by a bleak resignation to the victory perhaps being a fleeting one and there were more enemies waiting for him. An easy to read look came next – that he didn't have what it took to face a new attack, and was prepared to get the snot beaten out of him by an unbloodied opponent. But I saw him take me in, as I stood there, and size me up, and come to his own conclusions about me, and I saw his shoulders relax. Just a little.

And then I saw something else, something I had not been entirely expecting, but should have done. Resentment. For a moment, there, he had *won*. By himself. Now he was running the scuffle over in his mind, and realizing that there had been an extra dimension to it – that he'd been at least marginally aware of that third guy in the back – that he would never have won if that third guy had not been taken out... by someone else. Someone who had thus taken the shine off his victory.

This, too, I could completely understand, though.

He was still looking at me as though I was just another predator, though, and so I just grinned at him, shrugging my shoulders.

"I saw them jump you. I hung around in case you needed help."

"Do I know you?" he spat out, forcing the words out between breaths that were still coming in uneven gasps. The unspoken second question that hung between us was, *Did I ask you to help?*

But I knew when to bow out. I shoved myself off the wall which I had leaned against as he spoke to me, and stuffed both hands into the pockets of my jeans – it served, if nothing else, to get my hands out of the equation and show him I had no intention of picking a fight myself. I ducked around the corner and away.

I could have sworn, before this particular encounter, that I had never seen that particular boy before – and maybe I hadn't, at that, because we lived in different worlds, really. Mine were the wild streets of the seedier parts of the city, places where people went to hide in plain sight, which had suited my mother at the time she dragged both of us there with me barely more than a toddler.

His was the quiet tree-lined suburban streets with pocket-sized lawns outside modest detached houses, where kids rode bikes on grass-verged pavements and family dogs wagged tails at them from behind picket fences. It is entirely possible that we might never have met... except that even when the world of computers and all the knowledge of the Net opened up to me, I had a sentimental attachment to libraries – real libraries with real books – and the one in his neighborhood, about five blocks away from his school, was far better stocked and equipped than my own local branch. I didn't mind the bus ride it took me to get there – it was spent with my nose in a book anyway – and I liked the feel of the place, so I visited that library, *his* library, at least once a week.

Maybe it was just that the run-in that we had in that alley had etched his face in my subconscious and now I couldn't stop myself from glimpsing him, and recognizing him. He seemed to be aware of me, too, and we'd pass, sometimes, in places where neither of us would have looked for the other, and our eyes would meet, and then we'd kind of find something else to be busy with. I wouldn't say I was out *looking* for him – but somehow I found him now constantly. On several occasions – sometimes he saw me, and sometimes he did not – I found myself in the background of one of his back-alley battles, and helped out in what small ways I could without trying to take any of his victories from him. He seemed... annoyed at this. Even in the moments when I saw something like gratitude flash behind his eyes before he'd look away to hide it. He didn't like the idea of being assisted, but there was something about someone out there who had your back – particularly if you'd spent your entire life so far without a hint of that.

After a few of these encounters we started exchanging slight, almost non-existent, acknowledging nods while *not* in the throes of a fight. After a few of those, it became silly to pretend that there was nothing going on. There was a connection there, somehow, somewhere – but I had already crossed a certain line, by involving myself in that street fight. My instinct for keeping myself solitary, for knowing I was always better off alone, was at war with my sense of kinship, here. And he – well, I never saw him with any other kid, he was always by himself, unless he was in another fight somewhere. We were two isolated people, wearing our solitude and proud self-sufficiency as armor, and neither of us wanted to acknowledge a breach. But in the end, he did. He crossed that line first. I'll give him that.

He saw me coming out of that library I liked, his local branch, one Saturday afternoon, and he simply planted himself at the bottom of the steps that led from the front door, where I would have to pass.

I came to where he was standing, and stopped.

"I'm Malcolm Marsh," he said abruptly.

"I know," I said. I had already investigated him. But now I hesitated, suddenly, because I had been so many people already, worn so many names. Which one should I give him...?

In the end, it took me less time than I thought it might to decide. I'd gone only as far back to learn that he had been an immigrant child, brought over as a toddler – he would tell me later, himself, about the true-name he had left behind. But for now, all I had on him was the name he went by as his current self – he only had one name, as far as I was concerned, and he gave it to me. So I discarded years of mask and pretense and hiding, and told him the truth.

"I'm Saladin," I said. "Saladin van Schalkwyk."

I might have known there would be a double take. It *was* a mouthful, even I had to admit that.

"Spell it."

I dutifully did, unable to stop a grin. I could see him piece it together in his mind, trying to wrap his tongue around it.

"S-c-h-a-l-k..."

He tried. He really did. But in the end, he simply found the easy way out.

"I'll just call you Chalky," he announced.

I didn't much like it. I didn't have to. I wasn't asked. That was the way it was going to be.

In return, I gave him the identity he adopted as his own. I had not been the first one to ever call him 'Mal'- Celia had done that, his beloved sister. His parents carefully used the full name, Malcolm, and had never shortened it. As a consequence, he had guarded the 'Mal' thing ferociously – it was a precious and intimate name, one he shared with the only person whom he had ever seen as being completely on his side. Outside his house, he had stubbornly insisted on introducing himself to everyone else by the full name and nothing else, and it had hung heavy on a ten-year-old. I heard someone try to attack him with 'Colly', calling the weird and totally non-intuitive invented diminutive of his name after him one day in the street – and he had exacted his price for that, and after that fight (one I chose to offer assistance in, with a particular relish) nobody called him by anything other than Malcolm.

But then I took leave of him one fateful time with a cheerful, 'See you, Mal!' without really thinking about it, without (yet) knowing the Celia connection – and he accepted it, from me. And then consciously chose it as his new face to the world. He stepped into that particular diminutive, and wore it like a cloak. It was a persona, someone called Mal was suddenly the kind of person that he could comfortably accept being out in the world. It was as though my using it had somehow vindicated it in his eyes – people who cared about him called him that, and it gave the name strength – and it was hard to tell, in the aftermath, if he had been waiting for his proper name (for Celia to bestow it and for me to confirm it) all this time or if he had simply been growing into the name that had always really belonged to him. It was more than just something for the world to refer to him by – it was a sort of connection, a belonging, a seal, a mask he would wear to the rest of the world and behind which he could be himself.

I can't say I ever felt quite the same way about 'Chalky' – but it was his name for me, and in the end, I accepted it from him. It was a binding, and we had named one another; we were blood brothers of a sort, after.

We fed each other's hungers. He envied what he saw as my freedom, my being responsible for myself, not that much older than him but untrammeled by anything or anybody, free to do what I chose and go where I pleased.

I envied him for what I had never had, a family. The Collective had been... a sanctuary, not a family. We had found one another useful, in the Collective. We had even liked one another, perhaps. But in the end we were solitary beings (with the possible exception of Luke and LuLu) who happened to share, for a short while, the same space of existence. They weren't a family to begin with and they couldn't replace the family I had never had – which meant that in a very real sense I had never had a family at all.

Until I met Mal.

And, in my heart, called him my brother.

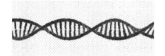

We lost the Green House the year I turned fourteen. It was a miracle that it had lasted as long as it did – it was only metaphorically invisible, after all, not literally so, and it *did* exist in the back yard of a building occupied by other people who were not completely blind or insensitive. It was the sort of neighborhood where everyone minded their business – and the turnover in the brownstone apartments was sufficiently high that nobody was there long enough to do more than wonder about the Green House. But in the end we began to feel distinctly watched, and people like us have a finely honed instinct for this kind of thing.

Tucker disappeared first, just gone one morning as though he had never been there, the air closing around his absence and leaving no hole. And then, when I was out on one of my library jaunts, I got a text from Luke on the cell phone that I'd been given as part of the Collective-issued equipment.

Lu and I have gone to ground in a safe place. Don't go back to the house. Stay in touch.

He didn't mention Imogen. I never did find out what happened to her, if she'd been at the house when its invisibility field had faded, if she had been caught in the glare of a sudden spotlight and had been burned up by it. But I had my laptop with me, and that's where my world lived; anything else at the house was just ephemera and all it took for that ephemera to cease to exist for me was to simply forget it had ever existed at all. I had a couple of temporary boltholes where I could hide out – and in the longer term, thanks to the Collective and to my share of the rather astonishing income that came in for the jobs to which I had contributed my growing skills, I wouldn't have to worry about money, at least not for a very long time, if ever.

It took me less than a week to find a more permanent home, and it was actually an old haunt.

Shimura's buy-sell-fix computer business had folded not long after he had died in that hospital where Luke had found him – if Josh had tried to keep it running by himself he had obviously met with little success. The shop had become, in turn, a copy shop, a vintage clothing store, and business premises for a notary public. And then the building itself was damaged by a fire, and the place got emptied out and stood boarded up for a little while. I had noticed that it had sprouted a couple of signs tacked to the plywood covering what had been the shop window – one "For Sale", and one "For Rent" – but those had been there for a little while, and were both starting to fade by the time I started looking around for a place of my own. I inquired about the "For Rent" (via email, by proxy – they were hardly going to rent to a fourteen-year-old) and discovered that the owners were renting out... the back of the building. Shimura's old workshop, and the tiny little studio apartment just above it reached by a narrow stair at the rear of the building.

I could have taken the rental. But in the end I gave in to a sentimental impulse. The whole place was for sale, after all – and I had the money – and in a strange way this was the closest thing I had had to a place I could call home – and I just bought the whole thing, lock, stock and barrel.

I wondered if Oji-san's spirit would still haunt the place, but I found it clean of any such lingering shadows when I took up residence. And this place was mine, in a way that the Green House had never been.

Mal had never seen the Green House. But he came to see me here. Often. It was a place where he could come after one of his street battles to clean up a bloody nose before he could go home. It was a place where he could come when he was in a blue funk and either sit sullenly in a corner in stubborn silence until he had worked things through or spill it all out to me and get whatever he needed at the time – somebody to laugh with him and mock his enemies or someone with whom he could share his fury and frustration without getting judgment or pity in return.

It was Mal who brought the ghost which this bolthole would be haunted by, not me. It wasn't Shimura; he had been here, and touched it lightly, and let it go. The spirit that stayed... was Celia's.

Mal was twelve years old when he stumbled into my room, hollow-eyed and bleak and buckling under the weight of guilt and horror. He might have been a hundred.

It was a while before I could get past him repeating, "She's dead, Celia is dead, and I killed her..." to the details of what had actually happened, as best he was able to convey them.

He told me about Celia's desperation to delay her Turn so that she could remain Celia long enough to see an author she loved come to speak at her school, and how he had raided their mother's stash of Stay for her, how she took too many and died.

I had never met Celia. It had been Mal's prerogative to keep his blood-kin and his friend in two separate universes – and his instinct. He had good instincts. I trusted them. But he had spoken to me of Celia, often, and it was as though I had known her, as though a part of me (through that part of me that cared for Mal) had loved her, too.

I was astonished at how much of a kick in the gut the news of her death was to me, how much grief I myself carried, how much deep and bitter resentment welled up inside me aimed at this Barbican Bain. A teacher charged with the care and welfare of children who were all supposed to be treated as equal – but a teacher who had seemingly had very little scruple about deciding that some children were to be cherished and protected while others were fair game for him to hunt as best he was able. I had a list – a list of people whose names I would not forget – there were few on it. I was not one to hold grudges or keep resentments at low boil on the back burner, but Bain made it. He made it not only because of what he had done to Celia, but of what he had done by proxy to her family, to her brother, who was the closest thing I had to my own.

It nearly broke Mal. It did break him, to the point of damaging him permanently – I watched him try to deal with the aftermath of Celia, I watched that deep fissure that had been opened inside of him harden and scar, I watched him change and close himself off to anything other than the shadows. I saw him arm himself with sarcasm and with words he knew bore edges sharp enough to slice apart those at whom they had been flung.

He suggested, once, that he should just run from his home and what remained of his family and live like I did, on my own, fending for myself, alone – but for all that he was of a Random Were kindred, he was traditional Were and held the traditional values that went with that. He might have survived – he probably would have – but it was not the kind of life that I myself would have chosen, had I been given a choice at all, and I told him so.

"You *have* a family," I told him. "It's something I never had. You still have a family. They've already lost one child. What about your parents? How about your other sister?"

He turned those haunted eyes on me. "Jazz would probably be safer with me nowhere near her."

"Mal," I said, for the hundredth time. "You could not have known – it was *not* your fault..."

"She took the Stay from my hand," he said.

That could not be changed. That was the fixed point in that story. It had been love that had made him do that so he had turned his back on love, then, because it could not be trusted. Because when he wanted to do something good, he had killed, instead. I could see the recoil inside of him when he thought of Jazz, his younger sister – when he thought of her in the context of Celia. It was safer not to love her. It was safer not to care at all.

Except that he could not help it.

So the only way out that he knew was to keep his feelings hidden and buried deep – to rebuff and reject any kind of warmth or affection that might have been either offered or sought – he stayed with his family, in the end, waiting for his Turn and until he was reckoned fully adult in the Were world. I could see him watching the coming of that Turn while holding his breath. It could not come soon enough, and then he would be free. Free to be alone. Free of the crushing responsibility that love brought to bear on him.

We talked of that Turn, he and I, as the Turn birthday approached. We hadn't discussed it before, not in detail – I knew he was a Random, and he knew I was Were but not what, and for the most part he didn't care. But as his own Turn came closer and the problems of being a Random Were began to sharpen in his focus, that conversation did come up – and when it did bend to that subject, I found myself, a little to my astonishment, being completely truthful with him.

He misunderstood at first, and thought I too was of his own kind – a Random, just like him. I said I was not.

"So then what?" he asked. "What shape are you supposed to Turn into?"

"Anything I choose," I said.

"Yes," he said obstinately. "Like me. I am Random. I can probably change into anything, too, if I lay eyes on it at the right time."

He didn't understand and I didn't push it then.

"But you get to pick your primary," I reminded him.

The one thing that he had found to focus his passion on was finding out that here, in this new world to which his parents had brought him, he was permitted to choose – and he had chosen his primary already. There were people out there who would hire out an animal which someone like Mal, a Random, might have in front of him at first Turn. According to Random law, he would Turn into an image of that beast because that would be the last warm-blooded thing that he would see as he Turned – and that form would then remain his primary form, the default form, the shape which he would Turn into ever after unless another warm-blooded creature scuttled into his range of vision just at the right point of the Turn.

It was entertaining, in fact, to play with scenarios of poor Random Were individuals and the endless practical jokes that could be played upon them – or the risk of very real accidents which could have permanent consequences. One of those accidents had rendered Mal's own mother into a Were-chicken (unfortunate farmyard accident). And it would be easy enough to trick a Random into Turning into anything somebody chose, if they were close enough and adroit enough to produce the creature they wanted that Random to Turn into at exactly the right moment.

But the primary, that would be his choice. And he had chosen – he had picked a wolverine. I was skeptical about this – he lived in a city, and he was very much a city boy, and a wolverine was not exactly the kind of creature it would be easy for anyone to deal with in an inner city environment. But he wanted something big and powerful and it was this animal that had captured his imagination. His father had said mildly that a wolverine would be expensive to rent on a regular basis until such time as Mal deigned to Turn and it was no longer necessary – but he hadn't said no, not in so many words, and Mal clung to his choice.

"And you don't get to pick a primary?" he asked me, trying to get his head around the laws that governed my own Turn. Which, he was starting to understand, were *not* the same as his own.

"I don't *have* a primary," I explained patiently. "I don't, really, have a Turn. Not as such. I can tell myself to change, and I do. That's all."

"Into *what*?" he asked, mystified.

"Into anything I want."

"Anything?"

"Well, I guess the usual rules apply," I said. "The kind of creatures that the Were Turn into. I don't think snakes or cockroaches are an option, although, on second thought, I don't actually even know. I don't think I've ever tried."

"When the full moon comes, you just..."

I was shaking my head and he didn't finish the sentence. "No. Not just at full moon."

"When, then?"

"Any time. Whenever I want. Whenever I say so."

"Prove it," he challenged, clearly unconvinced. And then I saw the thought clarify itself in his mind, and he hastily took the challenge back as he recalled the realities of Turning with which he had lived his entire life, after all. That there were no convenient Turning cloaks around and that he'd have to contend with me shedding my clothes right there and then. All that, on top of the wild change – the very idea that I could simply *shift*, at will, right there in front of him, without any kind of law or trigger governing any of it. He assured me he believed every word I was saying, although I could see the shadows of his doubts still linger about him; I could see that once again I had something that he could not help but envy, the freedom to be what I wanted when I wanted without anyone else's permission. And I could also see something else – a coming of maturity, perhaps – an understanding of what it all meant. Of how, if any of this was really true, alone and different and *out there* I was. How I wasn't really a Were at all... and he confirmed that, by re-defining me in a single word.

"You're not Were," he said. "You're a *shifter*."

I hadn't classified myself, but it made sense. I didn't argue the point. Strictly speaking I had come from Were-kind but I was no longer that – not even a Random, something that was capable of being pushed into any form by the right trigger, but which still needed that trigger. I literally was exactly what he had named me, a true shifter who had come perhaps, from out of two perfectly boring and ordinary Were parents.

I remembered my own research. I was sought. I was pushed for. I was *created*. I still did not know for what purpose.

Although it wasn't the Turn that he would experience, it was still a Turn, a change, and he knew that it had happened to me already, despite the fact that I had been well shy of the accepted age at which it usually happened to Were kids. With his own Turn approaching, he found his curiosity stirred and finally did get around to asking me about how it had been, for me, that first time – and I cast my mind back, and told him about the moment at which I had taken flight on crow wings.

"Yes, but how...?" he demanded, perplexed. "Just like that?"

"Just like that." I agreed. And damn, it had hurt. I suppose I should have told him about that part of it. But pain... you will usually find out about in your own time, on your own terms. Besides, I had no way of knowing if it hurt that much, for a proper traditional Were, Turning in his own good time and appointed hour. For all I knew, it was just peculiar to me and to my own weird initiation.

"And then what?" he persisted. "You just... decided... to be you again?"

"Sure," I said, again omitting the pain.

He was not satisfied. He could tell I was keeping something from him.

He didn't Turn after he passed his fifteenth birthday. Nor his sixteenth. He had to scale down his vision from wolverine to weasel, a kind of grim inside joke – a wolverine was the largest member of the weasel family, after all – and hunkered down to wait. I could see the waiting begin to hollow him out as the months passed and his Turn did not come.

And then all the waiting seemed to come to an end all at once.

But before the world turned far enough to release Mal from his holding pattern... he had to take a first step. To acknowledge the things he did not want to think about. And the way the Universe chose to teach both of us that lesson... was his little sister, Jazz.

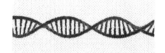

J azz had been sheltered and over-protected, an understandable overreaction to Celia's death. But she was a bright and intelligent spirit and it was inevitable that she would begin to chafe at that shelter, which she perceived as captivity.

Mal mentioned something to me about her unexpectedly making friends with Nell Baudoin, the high-profile daughter of one of the most high-profile families in the Were world. He sounded a little nonplussed about it. Nell was a bird of a very different feather to Jazz (oh, but how being Were played havoc with language and its metaphors...) and their worlds were as unlike to one another as it might be possible for them to be – but the thing that Jazz found in this friendship was a vision of freedom and she took it as a license to pursue that freedom. She was kicking over the traces, a little at a time, and it was Mal, the older brother who had sworn off loving her for her own protection, who was there to witness as his present and his past collided, the dead sister's world with the one in which his living sister still inhabited, as a malevolent ghost stepped back into their lives.

We'd met in the library, he and I, one perfectly ordinary Tuesday night, as we sometimes did, and we were standing across from the smaller of the two meeting rooms, talking, when I suddenly became aware of the fact that he was no longer listening to me at all. He was staring at the door of the meeting room as it opened and began to disgorge its occupants. His jaw was locked, and his eyes, cold and flat and implacable, were fixed on a man who was just walking out of the room accompanied by an adoring teenage acolyte babbling something worshipful at him.

Mal had said enough to me about the teacher who had been Celia's nemesis, but even if it had not been for his own visceral physical reaction to what emerged from the meeting room, I would have known this man anywhere. He was made of a peculiar kind of unctuous malevolence. Not large enough to be physically imposing, but he seemed filled with a black light. His small skull was outlined precisely by his slicked-back dark hair, his teeth small and perfect and vicious in his thin-lipped mouth. His eyes were veiled with meekness and calm tranquility but I saw him through Mal's eyes, through Celia's eyes, and could see the bones that grinned behind that innocuous mask.

Barbican Bain, in the flesh.

He must have felt the weight of Mal's stare on him, because he looked up – still smiling that small smile of his that put my hackles up like nothing I'd ever seen before – and met Mal's eyes. Just for one long moment. But long enough for recognition. A finely arched eyebrow lifted; and then he cradled the book he carried more closely to his chest and turned to walk away with the grand sweeping gesture of a High Priest who was dismissing the unworthy from his presence simply by ignoring their very existence.

A girl I had never met was the next to walk through the door. and I knew her instantly. This was Jazz, the little sister, and the thing I was getting from Mal, radiating from him like waves of heat, was fury. And worry. And fear.

I reached out a hand and laid it on his arm. "Mal..."

"I'll call you later," he said, in a low voice that I barely recognized.

Three long steps that took him from my side to stand before Jazz – and another girl, a friend who stood close beside her, protective, terrified.

Nell Baudoin. I had seen a photo or two.

Jazz looked... frightened. The eyes she raised to meet her brother's were huge and haunted.

"Mom knows... I'm with Nell," she said, very faintly.

I heard Mal's one-word reply. "*Here?*"

"I'd... better get home," Nell said, sounding rather fragile herself, but still, it was a courageous attempt to break the moment between Mal and his sister – for whom, I knew, he was suddenly terrified. The ghost of Celia stood between them, a solid presence, in that moment.

I saw Mal's head turn, just a fraction. His voice and his words were cold courtesy. "We'll make sure you get there safely," he said to Nell. "And then I'd better take Jazz home."

He turned back to me, long enough for me to meet and hold his gaze, and his eyes were frightening. I didn't know what he would tell Jazz on the way home that night, but my heart went out to her, because Mal was in no mood, and in no shape, to be kind.

I didn't ask him about it, when he finally came to see me the following night. Not directly. But the thing sat there between us, awkward and huge, and he spilled it all of his own accord anyway.

"I cannot believe she could be so reckless," he said. "Going there... like that..."

But I had done a little bit of looking into things, and there was at least one thing I knew. "She didn't know he would be there," I said. "Bain. That group is usually led by somebody else altogether."

"That doesn't matter," Mal said sharply. "The point was, he *was* there. She said she never even gave him her surname – but I'm sure he knew exactly who she was. He had to have done. And he can... do damage. He has the power to bring down the Inquisition on my mother. I don't think Jazz was ever really *officially* exempted from being in school."

"How did he know Jazz?

"I don't know. He didn't have a file on Celia. Not the kind that lists her closest family and Jazz never crossed his path. She wasn't on his radar. Now she is. Now we all are. He has agendas, that man. He's always had them."

He drew a ragged breath, and dug his fingers into his hair in a gesture of pure anguish. "She said... Jazz said... that he *killed* Celia. How does she know that? How could she know? She was pulled from any kind of school – *out* there – the day after they buried Celia. She was kept from that. Far away from all that."

"She can't be kept locked up forever," I said quietly.

He actually laughed, throwing me a grimly amused look. "Yeah. That's what *she* said last night. Jazz. That she had to have air. And I told her that she had opened the door wide enough to let *him* in with that air. And there was no knowing which way he was going to jump."

"What did you tell the poor girl?" I asked. "If you looked anything like you look now, you scared her out of her wits."

"I hope so," he said. "I hope that is enough." He paused, and then looked up at me again. "I think I even brought up the specter of the Turning Houses..."

"Oy," I said. He had told me a little of what those had meant in their family history.

He shrugged helplessly. "She cried," he said.

"I'm not surprised."

"And I told her... I told her..."

"What?"

"That I'd take care of it. I told her not to worry, that I'd take care of it." The hand buried itself in his hair again. "I don't even know..."

But I followed him already, to the place which he didn't know how to properly approach. And I opened the door to him.

"Can I help?"

"I don't know," he said faintly. "Can you?"

"Maybe I can think of something," I said.

He looked up, too quickly, and I smiled, and threw his own words back at him.

"Don't worry," I said. "I'll take care of it."

And what's more, I was going to *enjoy* it.

I wasted little time in putting the operation in motion. This was probably going to hurt me – at least in terms of flesh and blood – more than it was going to ever hurt him; it was never going to be about a physical confrontation. A man like Bain would wear traces of physical violence like a badge of honor, they would serve to prove his point, to offer up as evidence for his faith – Were-kind could not be other than what they had been born to be, violent, animalistic, and the bruises and cuts and scratches would prove that for all to see. No, if I was to get a point across it would have to be aimed at his mind – at his fear, at his faith, at his prejudices.

I took only the barest minimum of time that I was willing to spare to learn what I could about Barbican Bain – about his habits, about his movements, about the places he went and when he went there and how long he spent there... and when he came home, when he was alone. When I was ready, it was trivially easy to gain access to his house – it was locked down, tight, to be sure, but that was against two-legged burglars and large strays. The place was no proof against a determined mouse that wanted in.

He had been to one of his *Vox Verae Hominis* meetings, on the night that I was ready for him, and by the time he came home it was well dark. The outside light on his house, motion activated, still worked as expected as he stepped lightly to his front door and unlocked it, slipping inside.

The light switch in the hall would not respond to his touch as he toggled it. He tried it a couple of times, and made a small exasperated sigh, and started forward into the house – and then I saw him realize something.

The light in the hall was not working... but there was a light on in his kitchen, which, by the expression I glimpsed on his face, he was suddenly certain that he had not left on. It was the only light that was on in the entire place. Carefully, but with the inevitability of a moth being drawn to the candle, he moved forward towards the kitchen, his hands clenching into fists at his sides.

He found the typed note I had left on his kitchen counter – "WE ARE WATCHING YOU. TAKE ANOTHER STEP IN A DIRECTION WE DO NOT LIKE AND WE WILL BE THERE TO STOP YOU. THIS IS A WARNING. IT IS THE ONLY ONE YOU WILL GET."

I could see him staring at it, holding it in one hand, the other gripping the edge of the counter. Trying to figure out how it had come to be there. And then, finally, feeling the prickling between his shoulder blades, the sensation of *being watched*. He put the paper he was holding back down on the counter, very slowly, and turned around.

Sitting in the doorway of the kitchen, staring at him, was a cat, its gaze steady and emerald green as it met his own.

He did not own a cat.

I saw his eyes change, as a nebulous comprehension began to flood through him. And it was about then that I had my first real pang of misgivings.

With a combination of the sublime arrogance of the invincibility of youth and a cold furious loathing that had driven me too quickly to action. I had done some preparation, but I had not rehearsed any of this prior to being here. I knew what I wanted to accomplish, and how best I thought I could do that – but my plan necessitated doing something I had never done before, and I suddenly realized I had no idea of whether I was able to do it at all – changing from creature to creature, without *ever* changing back into my human form in between.

I had had enough practice, by now, for the change itself to be quick, and fluid, and as relatively painless as it was possible for it to be. But that was the change between animal form and human form. Animal to animal... I'd never attempted before.

Oh well. It was too late now. I had his attention and I had to seize the moment.

I willed the change. The cat in the doorway grew, shifted, its outlines blurring and folding into a new shape – still a cat, but a much larger one, a maned one, its paws immense as it stood staring at Bain with yellow lion eyes. I showed him my teeth, pulling my lip up over large canines. I took a step forward, and roared. The plates in his crockery cabinet shook in response, and I saw him flinch, cringe, but damn the man, his courage held. His eyes were still locked with my own.

I changed again. It was hard; I had to fight for this one. The lion rose on its hind legs, its muzzle lengthening, its eyes growing smaller and sharper, the claws on its front paws long and scimitar-like. The bear had to duck his head to fit into the kitchen, and its own roar was enough to rattle the crockery all over again. A great paw reached out to claw at him, and he reflexively staggered back, fetching up against the far counter in the small of his back.

And then again. Shrinking in shape but not in power. The muzzle turned into a wicked curved beak which opened to emit the scream of a hunting raptor; the paws blossomed into wings; I was airborne, and it took me only a moment to orient myself into a stoop, my taloned feet towards him as a powerful beat of my wings knocked a few items from open shelves. I heard shattering glass in my wake. And he broke, at last, crumbling into a crouch against the counter with his arms crossed across his face and above his head to protect himself against the talons...

But I was past him, and through a doorway, and into another room. And out of his line of sight the eagle was gone in an instant, and a tiny mouse scurried into a shadowed corner, and watched.

I had never taken so many shapes in quick succession – different sizes, different weights, different physiologies. It had taken a lot more out of me than I had expected. My heart was racing, it felt like a wild bird trying to break out from captivity through the bars of my ribcage, and there was a roaring in my ears as the blood rushed through my body.

There was a trade-off when it came to Were changes. Things had to be kept in balance. If the new shape weighed roughly the same as the human form, the balance was even, and the metabolism wasn't affected. But changing into forms that weighed much more, or much less, than one's own carried consequences.

Much smaller creatures – like for instance a mouse, the shape I was in now – paid for the loss of mass by an increase in metabolism – we were hypercharged mice, if you like. Our heart rates were much higher than an ordinary mouse. The wear and tear on our insides was enormous; we literally had to give up physical substance to drop into something that could weigh one hundredth or less of our human form, and that had to go somewhere. We paid for it with an acceleration of energy and metabolism. Our small forms lived faster. If we stayed in a small form for too long we could – probably literally – explode our hearts.

On the other end of the spectrum, the very large creatures – like for instance the grizzly whose form had graced me only moments ago – were that much *slower* than their original counterparts. A human male who weighed about 120 pounds who then turned into a bear weighing several times that much was *slow*. Bain did not know this but he could have probably taken the time to turn around, look for a nice-sized kitchen knife, walk up to me at a leisurely pace, and stab me twice before I could react enough to injure him in return. Well, close, anyway. Our big forms were slow, sleepy, we moved almost in slow motion and our heart rates slowed to just enough to keep the big animal alive and moving.

I had mucked around with shapes and weights and sizes too much, too fast – and it was all I could do to hold on to consciousness. But I had to see what he would do next. To know if I would have to come back and do it again.

There was no movement from the kitchen for a long time, or for what seemed to be a long time. Then I saw him walk into the room I was in, and head for a cabinet against the far wall. He opened the cabinet, took out a bottle, and filled a large glass. He was white as a sheet, and his eyes were rolling wildly like those of a spooked horse. But his hand was steady, and the glass did not shake as he lifted it to his lips.

I waited until he had collapsed into the nearest armchair, his glass hanging precariously from the fingers of his left hand, and closed his eyes, drawing in a few ragged breaths. With ebbing strength, I scuttled quietly along the wall, out towards the back hallway, and through a tiny crack in the corner wall through which I had gained entry earlier that night. I managed to get through that, and out, and then I found the neatly folded stack of clothes I had left in a quiet corner of someone else's garden, turned back into my own shape, drew on sweatpants and a hooded jacket, and managed to drag myself home through the empty and silent streets. By the time I finally crawled into bed, I was half blind with exhaustion, waves of blackness washing over my vision – if I had not made it home, just barely, I might actually have passed out on the pavement somewhere. My innards felt churned up, as though all my major organs were still deciding where they properly went after they'd been forced to play do-si-do in various body forms with such intensity over such a shatteringly short period of time.

I had the uncomfortable feeling that it wasn't over, that at least one return visit to Barbican Bain's house would be necessary in order to underline the message I had just left for him.

But it was not until Jazz unexpectedly Turned... into something unlooked for, impossible... that the idea for that second visit began to take shape.

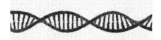

T hat Mal's was not an ordinary family, and not given to crises that were less than catastrophic, was underlined by Jazz's unexpected and just a little bit premature Turn. In the true tradition of Random Were and their tendency to fall prey to, um, *accidents...* Jazz had outdone herself.

Not only did she beat Mal to the Turn – which he, when he came over to my place after once again failing in his own attempt, found it almost impossible to either believe or forgive – but Jazz had been alone when the first Turn came upon her, the Turn when a Random was supposed to establish their primary form – alone, that is, except for one single companion.

A boy.

Another human being.

So, obligingly, being Random and under the thumb of her peculiar genetic imperative, that was precisely what she had Turned into.

Another human being.

I was still trying to get my head around that during Mal's initial rant. Once he was past the white heat of rage and an irrational sense of betrayal, he had settled on the cold fury setting; if he'd found Jazz at the library at Barbican Bain's side this day instead of when he did, he might have been less inclined to allow the protective instinct to kick in, and far more ready to give his *second* sister over to Bain's tender mercies.

It took me a while to actually grasp this – even me, the shifter who might have been expected to have hit upon this myself as the obvious extension to my abilities – but so unthinkable, so unprecedented, so never-before-seen was this thing that Jazz had just done, that I found myself blinking at it in sheer incomprehension the first few times I tried to focus on it.

A Were-boy. A Were BOY. A human being who was a Were who then Turned... into another human being.

There was a part of me, standing back and observing all of this through a cold and objective lens, that suddenly quailed at the potential backlash against the Were – how much worse all the fear and hate that had been traditionally levelled against the Were by the normals would get if they ever thought that the Were could Turn... into one of *themselves.*

But I shied away from that, for now – and after I'd made myself stop circling around the concept of a Were-boy, I addressed Mal's underlying concerns. The more immediate and personal ones.

"What are you really afraid of? That you've been overtaken in the race?"

He deflated, quite suddenly, into bleakness.

"That I've never been *in* the race," he said.

"It's unheard of that a Were of proper lineage fails to Turn...

449

eventually," I said.

He looked at me, and just for a moment the look was fire, just before I saw it fall back into cold ashes. "That's rich," he said. "Coming from one who fell into his full potential and Turned at eight years old..."

"I didn't..." I began, but he raised a hand to stop me.

"Yeah," he said. "I know. I know. But at this stage... I just wish I could give up, and throw it all in... I don't know how much of this I can take. In that house. With that family. With that history. With what I obviously am – a dud. I guess there's a bad bullet in every pack of ammo, and I'm the blank."

"You can't be sure of that," I said.

"When proof keeps coming at you all the time, you can get pretty sure," he said, with a brittle little laugh. "Honestly, there have been times that I have been seriously tempted to tear that stupid weasel's throat out. With my bare hands, if I can't manage teeth."

He had come to me, to pour out the poison, but even here, even with me, he was folding up and closing in. I had never seen him this alone, this isolated... this defeated. And he was right – being who I was, I could hardly offer advice. It would all come across as patter and platitudes.

I could listen, and I did. But then he left, and dragged his unwilling feet back to his home again, and I was left alone... to think.

I had turned myself into any number of creatures – but I had never attempted to turn into a different *human*. It had simply not even occurred to me. In the beginning I was just another Were, a slightly different Were, but we turned into animal forms and that was that, and I had accepted that as the law and I hadn't pushed it.

When I had first gone to Barbican Bain's house, I had had to leave him that note – because I knew I would be shifting into the kinds of creatures which could not otherwise communicate with him. And I thought I had reached him... but I had not completely achieved my objectives. But if this thing that Jazz had done was possible – and it *was*, because she was living proof that it could be accomplished – then I suddenly had the makings of a new plan. One that would possibly nail this particular danger down far enough for it not to be a threat to Mal's family any more.

This one, I practised. In front of a mirror. And it was deeply disturbing, even to me, who was used to transformation.

I stood there, naked, and stared at my natural self, at the form and shape and body and face and hair which I knew as *me*, as myself, as the things I had been born with. And then I conjured up an image of a different human in my head – someone whose hair was a sun-bleached blond, whose eyes faded from my odd and unusual dark green to a faded blue, who was taller than I was by a head and a half, who wore shoes three sizes bigger than my own. And I watched myself... flow... into that image, there in the mirror. Then I changed the image, and I watched that tall blue-eyed blond morph into a stocky, solid dude with big hands and ears that stuck out at a crazy angle and skin as black as midnight. And again, into a bronze-skinned man with long black hair and deep-set dark eyes and a pair of canines almost sharp enough not to be human. And again. And again.

It worked. I could change my face. I could change my body. I could change *me*. All I needed to do was *want* it.

I allowed it all to fade and watched as I finally turned back into myself, and I caught my own gaze in the mirror, full of speculation.

If this didn't freak Bain into retreat... I didn't know what would.

I hung back for a few days, strangely hesitant to beard the man in his den again, but in the end I persuaded myself that it had to be done, I had to be sure, I had to finish what I had started – there was nothing worse than leaving a job like this half-done, just poking at a dangerous beast for long enough to get it upset but not making sure that it was really conquered before I turned my back on it.

As soon as I had come to that conclusion, I slipped into his house the same way I had done before, made a few preparations, and waited for him to come home.

He noticed an untidy pile of blanket in the middle of his living room as he came in, and frowned, because he must have been aware that there had been no such thing in there when he had left his house only a few short hours ago. But before he could nut this out in his head, I seized the initiative – and the mouse that had been hiding underneath the blanket rose to its hind legs and changed, growing into a human being. One who was not the natural me. The man I became stood up in Bain's living room, and casually draped that blanket around his nakedness before he looked up and met Bain's frightened and bewildered eyes.

"We came back," I said, and the voice was deeper than mine, more gravelly, "to make sure you understood the warning we left you."

"What warning?" he demanded, and his own voice sounded high-pitched and almost squeaky next to the one I was using.

I was pretty sure that he had already destroyed all trace of that note that I'd left for him, last time, so I had printed out a new one, and lifted it from a small pile of papers which lay on his coffee table.

"This one," I said.

He probably couldn't read it at that distance, but he recognized it there in my hand, and I saw his fists clench. "How did you get in here?" he demanded. "You are one of... I can call the police..."

I laughed, and *changed*. The blanket fell into place around me... differently. His eyes began to bug out a little as an entirely different human being faced him. "Can you show signs of a break-in?" the new voice asked, almost gently. "Without that... you *asked* me in. If, that is, they could find any evidence of *me*. But I repeat. I came back to make sure you understood our message. And oh, because of one more thing. Have you got a pen...?"

He clutched at his shirt pocket, and then dropped his hands, a gesture of defiance. "No."

"Doesn't matter, I brought one," I said, and *changed*. Bain's lips parted, and his breath began to come a little ragged. I backed up and sat down in one of his armchairs, and pointed at the coffee table. "There's a piece of paper on the table. If you would sign it, please."

"No," he snarled. "You are an abomination, a complete anathema, a heresy that walks on two legs. You are a creature of darkness. I will not bow..."

"You will sign it now," I said, "or we will keep coming back, until you do."

I *changed*.

Bain blanched. "Stop it," he said, through bloodless lips. "Stop *doing* that."

"Never," I said, quite conversationally. And pointed to the table again. "Paper. Pen. Sign."

"No," he said, crossing his arms across his chest. But I had seen his hands trembling, and it was a gesture that was not so much rebellion as a way to conceal that shaking from me. He did not want me to see a weakness.

"We can wait," I said.

He glanced at the table, reluctantly, plainly against his own will.

"What is it?"

"A confession," I said. And *changed*. I was enjoying this entirely too much, watching his entire body flinch at every changeover. But I was starting to sweat; it took a lot of energy and willpower, this, and I couldn't keep it up indefinitely.

"I have nothing to confess," he said.

"Oh yes you do," I said softly.

And lost it, just a little. I changed, all right, but it was into *me*, the original me, the face and form I habitually wore. The best I could do, and I tried to do it to the best of my ability, was to act as if this was just another mask. But it increased my own vulnerability for just a moment, and damn him, he was fast on the uptake for that. I saw his shoulders square as he gathered his own powers of defiance again.

"And if I don't...?"

But I had it in hand again and I changed into the most threatening thing I could think of – someone twice Bain's size, with muscles like anacondas, and I could see him shrink as I rose to my feet and, in this form, towered over him.

"Then it is like I said, we will return. Again. And again. And again. And again. You will never know peace from us. You will never feel safe again. You will never know which stranger out there... is one of us. Where the blow will come from."

"This is... this.... You can't do this," he said, and I could hear him clamp his jaws on that last word. "You – your kind – you're not supposed to be able to – "

"You're right," I said. "Not many of us can. But some of us can, and it could be *any* of us."

I had forgotten my own earlier conclusions, from before, that it couldn't be physical threats or physical violence that would bring Bain to heel. It had to be a hit to his inner core – to his faith, to his belief system, to himself. But I had remembered in time, and it was with a slow smile that I changed again... and flowed into his own likeness.

I heard his breathing stop as he stood there facing himself. His hands dropped to his sides, and his jaw went slack. His eyes were wide, and unblinking.

"Sign," I said, in his own voice.

As though hypnotized, he took a couple of staggering steps towards the coffee table, fell to his knees before it, picked up the pen I had left beside another sheet of paper lying there, and nervelessly signed his name at the bottom of the page. And then dropped the pen and sat there staring at the thing he had just signed, all the bravado gone out of him for the moment.

"Don't forget," I whispered into his ear as I bent down to pick up the signed confession – of what he had done to Celia – and roll it up into a tight roll, and secure the roll with a rubber band which had also been lying on the table. "We *will* be watching. Even when you look in the mirror."

I walked out of his front door still clutching the blanket around me, dropping it only after I was out of direct sight.

As a crow I watched from the branches of a nearby tree, the rolled-up scroll carefully wedged in beside me, until he emerged a few minutes later, already looking a little more like himself, a little more color back in his waxen cheeks. I didn't think he was going to take this as a mortal wound – neither he, nor the *Vox Verae Hominis* higher-ups to whom no doubt this entire episode would be carefully repeated – but at least I had a club to hold over him. He was still a viper, but I had defanged him. What the organization he was a part of could do, however... that was another matter.

But I had unveiled a secret I'd kept for more than a decade now, the secret of my existence, the existence of someone like me. And trust me to do that in flashiest way I could muster – by painting a target on my forehead. Up until now, I had managed a decent obscurity by simply not stepping out of the shadows which I'd drawn around myself – but now they knew, the people who hated my kind with a fiery hate and burned with the urge to destroy us to keep the world pure and safe for themselves, they knew of the shadows, and then they had glimpsed me. The shadows were no longer a safe place to hide. Now I had to learn another strategy – I had to learn to *run*. Because now... now I was something to be hunted.

Now I was prey.

Intermission I:
The Evidence Locker

1.ORIGINS

The origins of the phenomenon of the Were transformation are lost in time, too far removed in temporal terms to ever be accurately or systematically documented. The mythology that grew up around it, rooted in the fear and incomprehension of the non-Were majority, has long since erased any trace of its real historical roots. But there are a few things that we can salvage out of the morass of misinformation, fear-mongering propaganda, and misconceptions that grew up around the beginnings.

The first of these is the simple fact that the Were are not aliens from another planet, nor are they mutants, strange incomprehensible beings that somehow arose in the midst of the human population as a sudden and explosive event.

They have always been with us, and amongst us.

In early accounts, based on populations where early European civilizations began to keep records, the Were transformation seemed confined to a tight and focused single interspecies link - that between man and wolf. In fact "Werewolf" was, for a long time, the only reference to what had been observed by the record-keepers of the time - because no other animal form had ever been observed to be taken by those who Turned at the time of the full moon.

It was not until the first Werewolves – they later become known as the Lycan clan – crossed the sea fleeing persecution in their lands of origin that they first crossed paths with peculiarly new-world forms of Were they had not encountered before – the so-called 'skinwalkers' of the Native populations (who appeared to be rare enough, but to be rather different than the Moon-driven Were in that they were self-triggering shifters) and then the New Moon kindred, more similar to themselves, who Turned on the advent of the new moon rather than the traditional full moon and who favored the bat as their own dedicated animal avatar.

The incidence of the skinwalker-type subspecies – or at the very least reports of their existence – seemed to decline in direct proportion to the increase in Lycan numbers in the New World; some studies of the phenomenon have discussed the possibility that the newcomers had taken steps to clear the new habitat for themselves, and had had a direct hand in that decline. But if that is so, then they targeted only one kind of shapeshifter, and not the other. The New Moon kindreds were never numerous but they never showed such a proportional decline in numbers. The relationship here quickly assumed a more symbiotic form.

Perhaps it was the discovery of these new kinds of Were that originally triggered what became known as the Breaking, the cusp at which the Were differentiated into the species-specific clans known in more modern times (Corvids, Felids, Canids, Mustelids, the clans that became bound to forms like owls, or deer, or sheep, or horses). The genetic basis of this morphological shift have not been well elucidated to this day – but it was one specific clan, the Werewolves or Lycans, who pursued the issue and evolved into accomplished scientists in the fields of pharmacology, genetics, and the origins of their kind. In one sense – perhaps inevitably, given that their clan was tied to the iconic wolf – they led the way in Were-themed research as well as, by inference and extrapolation, the broader field of human genetics as a whole.

The Lycan clan – for reasons they did not see fit to share widely with the world at large, although many inferred what they could from the clues that the Lycans left available for those determined to discover them and knew where to look – themselves dwindled in both numbers and in apparent importance as the Were kindred continued to evolve into their many clans. It was the Corvids who took on a leadership role in the Were Authority, although it was widely suspected that despite their withdrawal deeper into the shadows of their world the Lycans continued to direct the affairs of their kind in a more indirect way, from a position of knowledge and deeper wisdom accumulated over the centuries of their existence. Their agenda has always appeared to be survival – of their kind, and specifically of their own clan – and there have been more than a few rumors of the Lycans having not exactly the highest of moral ground when it came to this.

For instance, although few would have called them this to their face, there are those in what became the Were Authority (the governing body of the Were-kind) who have, at one time or another, seen the Lycans as betraying their own kind. Such individuals have sometimes spoken out in public about being less than happy with what they saw as the Lycans collaborating with the non-Were humans in the general government, sometimes to the apparent detriment of Were clans OTHER than specifically the Lycans themselves. What privileges the Lycans gained for their own clan, in exchange for what might have been hitherto protected information or through actions which provided useful tools or weapons to the non-Were governing bodies with whom they had been cooperating, it has never been easy to run to ground in a verifiable form and as such much remains in the realm of rumor and hearsay.

"Myth and History: The Were World" - A.D. Henderson and Lisa Nightingale

2. TURNING HOUSES

2.1

The first laws specifically applying to the Were demographic appeared on the books at roughly the time that the Were became a statistically significant measurable national minority, which happened sometime after the splintering of the Were into different clans which bore the forms of different animal avatars. Before this event, the population of Were was not regulated and their recorded numbers probably do not accurately reflect the actual number of Were individuals extant in society. The native forms of shifters (the aboriginal 'skinwalkers' and the so-called New Moon Were, with Turns triggered by the New Moon as opposed to the Full Moon as for traditional Were) have not been well documented in the historical record, and many of the early accounts of their presence and existence has been tainted by hearsay, rumor, and outright fabrication – but they have always been very rare. At best guess, when population census records began to be kept, the number of such individuals has always been well below 1.5% of the general population.

This changed with the wave of immigration which brought a large number of the more traditional Were from countries of origin where they were persecuted because of their nature. Initially, a significant number of such immigrants were known to be Lycan (or, as better known, "Were-wolves"), and in these early days the Lycan newcomers swelled the numbers of the Were to between 2.0 - 2.3% of the general population. With the advent of the splintering into the various different clans, the issue of statistics becomes complicated by the multiplication of the KIND of entities who self-identified as Were, but the Were percentage in the population quickly climbed to above 3.5%.

Increased incidents of conflict began to creep into the record as the unregulated Were population began to interact more frequently and sometimes more violently with their non-Were neighbors.

Initial laws centered on registration and identification of the Were populace, with special identity cards – with an identifying watermark sign in the form of a paw print in deference to the original Lycan nature of the emerging Were population, a document that Were-kind were obliged to carry at all times. The "paw cards" or "paw passes" were very much disliked by Were-folk, who saw them as a form of blatant discrimination.

The nature of the change underwent by the Were was reasonably well established – its timing (at the rise of the full moon) and duration (three full days) were both thoroughly documented and well known. Responses by the general population to unregulated Turns, particularly those of larger predator-type animals such as the wolves, large cats, bears, and the like, became increasingly and understandably fearful and defensive. Police blotters are full of incidents occurring between Were-kind in their Turned state and non-Were populations defending themselves against what they perceived as a threat with an escalation of violence (from both sides). When the first laws which cracked down on the Turns were proposed, this was done with the rationalization that both Were and non-Were lives and property needed to be protected if the Were kindred of any kind were to be permitted to live – as any kind of protected minority – amongst those who did not Turn. Such laws were proposed on the grounds of "public safety".

Initially the laws mandated simply that Turns had to be properly regulated, and that it became illegal for Turned Were to roam the streets without restraint or supervision in their animal forms. Because some forms were easier to legislate than others (it was easier, for instance, to deal with aviary forms – all that was required was a large enclosed communal space where like species of birds could spend their three days in their Were form in a flock) proposed laws quickly became bogged down in logistics and trammeled in legal language which became too dense for even lawmakers to properly understand – and it was easy for an otherwise law-abiding Were to break half a dozen laws simply by going on with his or her ordinary everyday existence. It was in this period that the idea of the Turning Houses was first mooted, although it is no longer on the official record as to whether the concept was proposed from the Were or the non-Were side of the divide – an important distinction, in the sense that it colors the way the Turning House was perceived.

In their most basic form, Turning Houses were large government-owned properties where all Were who could not prove that they had made proper arrangements on their own, were now required by law to report on the day before their Turn and stay there for the duration in suitable confinement under properly supervised conditions. As most things of this nature do, the issue quickly became very much more complex.

Because of the large numbers of people who were now required to present themselves at these facilities and their wide geographical distribution, a very large number of Turning Houses had to be provided, so that Were population (which, at the advent of Turning Houses, was nudging 5% of the general population) could have access to one without requiring that any specific individual would need to spend more than five hours in order to reach one. Larger population centers had to have a large number of Turning Houses, because no single one could be overloaded with residents during the Turning days (particularly in the light of the fact that the Were had splintered into so many different species and arrangements needed to be made for both predator and prey species, large and small species, and limited funds and indeed limited suitable properties were available for this purpose.

It was perhaps inevitable that ownership of these properties, the establishment of Turning Houses on those premises, and the actual day-to-day running of those Turning Houses, quickly passed from being a government project into private hands – and it was not always obvious who the new owners actually were although many clues pointed to, at the very least, a large number of them being Were-kind. As for the running of the facilities under the new management, the Turning Houses began to shake down into something that wasn't quite what the original laws had in mind.

In addition to being places where it was mandated that the Were who lacked other facilities had to be interned during their Turns, the Houses became places where a semi-permanent population of crippled, damaged, or otherwise handicapped Were-kind began to be established – people who were sometimes colloquially referred to, in Were circles, as the Half-Souled (because for many of them the handicap involved a loss of the ability to Turn into their animal avatar, hence a loss of half their identity/half their soul). Some of these individuals were in need of long-term care facilities themselves (physical or psychological) but a sufficient number were high-functioning enough that the basic tasks of the day-to-day running of the Houses began to be their responsibility. There were occasions when the direct results of this state of affairs became predictably chaotic, and sometimes horrifying. And because of the ambiguous legal standing of the Turning Houses themselves and what they needed to represent in the strictest letter of, and in the spirit of, the law of the land, it was sometimes difficult to find.

World Encyclopedia, 47th Digital Edition

2.2 *REPORT FROM THE TURNING HOUSE COMMITTEE*:

Purchase of two more Turning Houses in the North West Sector (both medium-sized, on outskirts of large population centers) and one each in the North Central (small, central urban) and South East (very large, rural) Sectors. The SE Sector House suitable for housing of large animals and/or specialization for predator species, with the possibility of supplying adequate range for several species for implementing suitable behavioral studies while inmates in Were shape. One more purchase (also in North West Sector) is pending, but a speedy resolution is expected. It is acknowledged that there is a cluster of new Houses in a single sector, but several properties came ripe at the same time in that sector, and the committee considered it prudent to step in with bids to secure those properties. The advantages of having a large pool of new subjects in the North West Sector for any research projects currently in the planning stages was also a factor in our decision.

These purchases bring the total Houses under Lycan ownership to twenty-three. The total population now resident or employed by Turning Houses under Lycan ownership and/or management is now approaching 44,000.

Keeping the mandated 10% of those subjects as a control group and free from participation, only about half of the rest of the Turning House population is committed to participation in currently approved projects. The committee is open to proposals for allocating subjects and Turning House resources to new projects – paperwork (in duplicate, to this committee and to the Research Project Approval Committee) should be submitted within six weeks for any projects which are scheduled for launch in the new year. No further selective breeding or genetic marker inheritance research projects will be launched in the next available funding window, though, until such time as results from projects currently in progress or recently concluded can be collated and evaluated; research requirements and new directions will be made public in the first trimester of the new year and any new programs in these areas will be discussed in more detail at that time.

Transcripts, Lycan Council
Source: confidential informant, leaked from classified files in Lycan Council Archives

3. PARTIAL REPORT FROM GENETIC RECONSTRUCTION PROJECT 133463L

Subject 1
Mother: classical full moon Were, pure-blooded Middle Eastern descent
Animal form: sandcat
Father: classical full moon Were, white, third-generation African-born (southern Africa)
Animal form: hyrax/rock rabbit/dassie (local name)

Subject: male, first live birth to these parents after three (known) previous attempts resulting in miscarriages. Pregnancy: difficult with potentially life-threatening complications. Mother under hospital supervision for the last trimester; child born twenty three days before expected due date, without further complications. Early medical records reveal no problems other than the slightly premature arrival. Heart strong, all other scores normal. Original genetic tests and bloodwork confirm parentage and genetic recombination; some interesting variation observed. Placed on Watch List. Siblings desired.

NOTE ON REPORT: Parental partnership dissolved prematurely. Father abandoned family and returned to original country of residence. Mother and baby escaped custody and are still being sought. Priority one for recovery of child. Mother now believed to be unstable; recovery desirable but non-essential. Please refer to the identity file for updates on the boy's current age and possible appearance as he reaches developmental milestones, as projected by our artists.

Subject 2
**Mother: classical full moon Were, white, genetic heritage
includes Eastern and Southern Europe, possibly some Celtic**
Animal form: fox
**Father: classical full moon Were, white, genetic heritage
includes German/Scandinavian**
Animal form: rabbit

Subject: female. Mother proved unable to carry a fetus to term, but a product of this genetic cross (predator/prey) highly desirable for further study. Surrogate pregnancy resorted to after several attempts at a natural pregnancy failed, and further attempts would have endangered the life of the mother. Through human error, surrogate carrier of this important first-generation cross was NON-WERE – this introduces a possible wild element into the pregnancy, and warrants further study, but the error was discovered only after surrogate mother – and the child she carried, and bore through an otherwise uneventful pregnancy – were lost to the study as they removed themselves from the sphere of Were physicians and researchers and into the non-Were circles of the surrogate mother – especially after the legal complications resulting after the surrogate mother refused to give up the child as arranged preferring to raise it herself. The female progeny of this experiment was then thrown into the foster-care system, and further removed from the reach of Were scientists, by the mother's untimely death when the child was five years old. Attempts to recover child unsuccessful.

Child adopted from foster care shortly after mother's death. Surveillance has been close and constant but at a distance. Further developments awaited, particularly as Turning age approaches. Adoptive parents have been apprised of child's potential heritage and problems which may arise from this, but other than accepting information, the parents have not been cooperative in permitting full medical access to their adopted daughter. Some genetic work done from partial and incomplete samples has intriguing possibilities, but further study is required. Girl herself to be approached as soon as possible.

Subject 3
Mother: classical full moon Were, white, Celtic/Norse
Animal form: fox
**Father: classical full moon Were, white, Asian, South East
Asian genetic heritage**
Animal form: orangutan

Subject: male, third attempt at mating. Heart problems at birth; immediate corrective surgery; Child deceased, age 3. No further attempts at breeding from this pair.

Subject 4
Mother: classical full moon Were, black, EastAfrican genetic heritage
Animal form: hyena
Father: classical full moon Were, white, Spanish genetic heritage with Northern African Arab admixture
Animal form: dog (appearance: Shepherd breed)

Subject: female, fourth attempt at mating. Child born alive but died from respiratory complications twenty four days after birth. No further attempts at breeding from this pair.

Subject 5
Mother: classical full moon Were, white, Spanish genetic descent
Animal form: crow
Father: classical full moon Were, white, Spanish/French genetic heritage
Animal form: cat (appearance: gray mackerel tabby)

Subject: no live births were achieved with this coupling.

Source: confidential informant, leaked from classified files in Lycan Council Archives

Part II:
Seeker

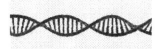

After that last failed Turn, something had cracked in Mal. He was so full of anger and frustration when he came to my apartment that I could see it coming out of his pores. He sat kicking the legs of the chair he had straddled, his hands spasming on the scarred wood of the back as though he wanted to strangle it.

He'd overheard Jazz talking to his father about him, showing pity. He could handle a lot of things, but not that, not pity from his little sister.

Where the idea really came from, I am not sure – whether she really planted it, or if Mal had stumbled upon it by the sheerest of accidents, but there it suddenly was.

"He made it sound as though a choice was possible," Mal had said, regurgitating this overheard conversation as though it was something that had stuck in his gullet, something that he needed to throw back up before it choked him. "As though it was *I* who had the choice. That I could somehow... choose. After all. That there may be a clan I had a call to. I mean, it's hardly likely that I would Turn into a Corvid, or an actual wolf..."

We didn't pursue it. Not then. But it stuck in my head, because of the Lycan connection, and I could not but wonder how different it might all be if I had someone on the inside of that fortress that I had been trying to breach all by myself for all this time. And obviously it was an idea which he couldn't quite get rid of either.

Wolf.

What if it was actually possible...?

It was I who did the research, though, and I who brought it back up. We didn't make small talk about it, the next time he dropped by, but I had it ready for him, on my laptop – everything that I had found out since he had planted the word in my mind, the seed of a preposterous plan.

"Where do you *find* all this stuff?" he asked, a little peevishly. He was quite good enough himself, when it came to finding things out on the Net, but the Lycans were a special case.

Unlike the *Vox Verae Hominis* crowd, the "Voice of True Men", Barbican Bain's crew, who might not be totally open about their membership but who nevertheless did all they could to shout their message for anyone to see, the Lycans knew how to hide. It took someone like me. Someone who did as little blundering as necessary, who had the instinct to follow a blood trail in the water without leaving one of my own, who had the knack for finding stuff out. Mal told me more than once (and it wasn't always a compliment) that I knew how to look in places that other people didn't even know were places.

I'd put together a list of sites that might have been relevant, and Mal scrolled down on the screen, from one URL to the next, frowning at what he was seeing.

"It's a gift," I said, and reached out to stop him as he scrolled past a particularly interesting item. "This one, for example. Try this."

He dutifully clicked on it, and his face was everything I hoped it would be. He was presented by a busy screen of tiny type, in a language close to his own cradle tongue but just *this* side of comprehensible. He stared at it, frowning, until he finally gave up and said, peevishly enough, "And how do *you* know what that says?"

I couldn't help it, sometimes he was fun to poke a stick at. I was grinning as I reached over his hand to tap out a command on the keyboard. "We have ways," I said, just as the screen threw up a blue bar across the top which said, helpfully, *Translating...* – and then the screen blinked on and off and the text rearranged itself, in a language we both understood. It was an imperfect translation, to be sure, but it was sufficient. Mal scowled at the computer, careful to avoid meeting my eyes because he knew that I was laughing and he wasn't in the mood to be laughed at.

"How do you *do* that," he muttered in an annoyed voice, and then made the mistake of looking up after all and seeing a smug grin spreading across my face which I was not quite able to smother in time. "Never mind," he said, "what is this stuff? What am I looking at?"

"The mushroom," I said. "That right there is the mushroom that the goats ate. That's where it all began."

"Okay," he said carefully, in a manner that told me he was keeping a tight hold on a flash of temper.

I took pity on him, and tapped the screen at the relevant part of the screed.

"Right *there*. That's the chemical. The development – the actual chemistry, the biochemistry – that came later, over on this side of the water, when they ground up the mushrooms and made the early versions of Adaptadyne."

Mal lifted his eyes from the screen and stared at me in silence. That word – that was his magic word, the key to the guilt that drove him. God help me, I knew that.

I pressed on.

"Back there – back in the mountains, with the goatherds – they probably already knew all about that mushroom's properties – I have zero doubts that the early human 'trials' were the actual goatherds who munched on the stuff themselves, once they figured out what it could do, partly just for the normals – they aren't just willing to pay the big bucks for this stuff for nothing, it does a doozy on the ordinary human brain somehow. But later – ah, later – it came over here, and they recognized its real potential, and they brought the herbal old-wives'-tale concoction into the lab – you might say it mushroomed, after that."

"This is *serious*, Chalky," Mal said, without smiling.

Tactical misstep, it broke the mood, but it had just been such an obvious joke. I regrouped.

"I know," I said. "Sorry. But there – that thing – it tells you how it started being what it became. And *who* started it."

"Who?"

"The Lycans. They stalked the same mountains where that original mushroom came from. Before anyone else figured it out, they knew – they had known all along. When the science came along to make this useful... they had the jump on everyone else. The original pharmacological patent for Adaptadyne is public record – it was filed by the tiny seed company of what's now a pharma-empire, founded on this, on this one thing. Adaptadyne is huge. What's less easy to ferret out is that the original company was founded by the then-Alpha of one of the major Lycan packs, and he brought in the rest of his clan. The Lycans developed this thing from nothing. They knew what the raw material could do, and they knew they could make it pay. Somehow. They've always known how to land on their feet."

"They used to be the big-boss clan, sure," Mal said, hesitating. He had his own Were catechism, the knowledge that he had acquired by simply being born into a Were family. "But I haven't heard of one in a long time. I don't think one has ever crossed my path, that I know of."

"Probably more than one," I said, and he frowned, trying to come to terms with that fact. I seized the advantage. "Look, they went into the shadows, they didn't just vanish. There may be fewer of them than there used to be – but that doesn't mean that they're any the less powerful."

"You sound as though you've been researching them," Mal said.

"I have," I said, no more than the truth. "Whatever they used to be – bogeymen to frighten small normals children – but they're scientists now. They don't advertise it, but some of the top researchers in the big Universities are Lycan. And that's just the tip of the iceberg."

"If they don't advertise it," Mal said, "how would *you* know?"

I shrugged. "There are tells," I said. "If you look in the right places, the truth of it is easy enough to find."

"What do you mean, tip of the iceberg?"

"They've got facilities of their own," I said. "Places where they can do things without any oversight at all. Places where they do... God only knows what."

"What, you don't know *that*?" Mal said, tilting his head at me sardonically. "I mean, you know everything else, apparently, but you can't figure out..."

"They're firewalled," I said, biting the words off. It had been a source of endless frustration and annoyance, and he was picking at a sore spot. "By people who know how. I tried, believe me. I know exactly where I should be looking but either they've left nothing for me to find or they've honey-trapped the sites – at least once they caught me snooping and I had to burn my way out of there pretty fast. And even then they almost had me by the tail before I could escape. They've got some good people working this thing."

But hacking one's way into deeply buried truths on sites which ought to have been inaccessible to any mere mortal – the fact that I had got *that far*, at least – meant nothing to Mal. He dropped the subject, circling back to his own obsessions.

"They're perfecting Stay?"

"They've probably got far more interesting stuff going on now," I said carefully. "Stay is old news for them. I'd love to know what's on the drawing board now, actually. But it's either learning to be better than their best... or it's having someone on the inside who's willing to dish the dirt – and they're *wolves*, it's a pack, they're tight, they aren't going to turn on each other for the likes of me."

"But if you had the data... what would you do with it?"

I had thrown out the bait, and he was nibbling on it. But I hesitated, right now, in the endgame. This was Mal. He was my friend. He was the closest thing I had to a brother. And I really was angling to throw him to the wolves... or, worse, to think that it had been his own idea to get thrown there.

"I have my own questions," I finally said, "and I would like to see if I can't get my own answers. Besides, the world would probably be better off knowing about some of their hush-hush stuff."

"I could always change my mind and start asking for a wolf," Mal said. "For my primary, you know. If I were a wolf I could just..."

And there we were. I had him. But now I was actually wincing at seeing this through, and playing devil's advocate came naturally.

"Wolf is off the list of acceptable animals which you can choose for your Random transformation. If you tried, you'd probably get a visit from someone very serious who wouldn't necessarily give his name, only a warning to stay out of their playground. And if you tried it again there wouldn't even be that much of a courtesy before they took you out. They will act to protect themselves if they have to."

"You're telling me they'd cheerfully *kill* somebody...? That would be just a little obvious, wouldn't it?"

"Don't test them. You'd probably never see them coming."

But Mal had the bit between his teeth now. "How would they even know if..."

"They'd know," I said. "You can't use a wolf for a Random turn. Period."

"But what if I really... was one...?" Mal asked slowly.

I stared at him. He was actually *serious* now. I had pushed this snowball down the hill and now it was gathering momentum all on its own.

"How do you mean?" I asked carefully.

"How does one become a Lycan? You can be born into it, of course. But if their numbers are shrinking... It used to be that you got bitten, and you changed..."

"That's complicated," I interrupted. "You'd need to find two of them who'd be willing to take that bite, and they might not be all that gentle about it."

I told him about the necessity of having to be bitten by an alpha pair. "And they aren't gentle about it."

I could see the idea coming together in his head. If it worked it would solve so many problems, really. It would break his own curse, to be sure – the failure to Turn for so long. And I saw it when it also occurred to him that I would find it useful, too. That inside man I had said I wanted.

The devil's advocate side was in full flight. "That's probably a very, very bad idea," I said. And just where would you go looking for the wolves that you'd need to..."

"You could do it. You said you could Turn into anything you wanted."

"Yes, but a wolf...? I have never tried. Besides, there would still have to be *two* wolves, one of them female."

"What, you can't do what my sister did? Just Turn into a different gender?"

I never had. Yes, I had Turned into different *people* when I went to scare the daylights out of Barbican Bain... but they had all been male people of my own age (other than that last, when I Turned into him). But although it might have been the crowning achievement when it came to freaking Bain out... it had simply never occurred to me to try a girl. Not even given that it was Jazz's Turning into a *boy* that had triggered the idea of becoming different humans. I had not dabbled with any other variables.

"Believe it or not, I simply never tried," I said slowly, in response to Mal's question. "All I ever did was change my outer skin, inside I always remained... well... *me*. I didn't think about changing into a girl any more than I considered changing into a baby, or an old man. Age and gender... just seemed to be fixed."

"Are you saying you can't?"

"I'm saying I never tried, and I'm saying I have no idea how – and if – it will affect what I *can* do if I tried it."

We talked it over for quite some time. "You're sure?"

"If there is no other way, yes," Mal said. "It's my choice."

Well, it wasn't. Not really. Not after I had planted it... but the more I threw up the obvious obstacles the more determined he became.

"It's no longer a choice at all. I was born Were, a Random, in the end I will either Turn like all my kindred and into something that I don't even want to be..."

The rest of that sentence, unspoken, hung between us: *or else I'll just live out my days, however long my life turns out to be, as a wretched failure, a dud, the Were child who couldn't even fulfil that part of his genetic heritage. Weak, useless, outcast.*

"At least this way... if we try... look, it may not work at all in which case nothing has been lost. If it works out badly, Chalky... well... I've had it with waiting, with living my life from Turn to Turn and watching everyone's expectations crumble at every cycle, I can't even bear the thought of it any longer. If it ends, it might as well end like this. And if it works..."

He paused to draw breath, and I nodded, into the silence, just once, accepting his words.

"Are you sure?" I asked, one more time, just one more time, but his eyes were steady on mine.

"You told me you remember yourself when you're changed," he said.

"You will remember who I am. You probably will hurt me some, that's inevitable, but I don't believe you'll give in to a pure murderous instinct to rip me apart. In theory it doesn't even have to take very long. Just long enough to draw blood. Long enough to pass it into me, the change trigger, and then, after that, all we can do is wait."

"If it works, they *will* come for you," I warned. "A Random who cannot have Turned into anything that he hadn't observed ... they will come for you."

"You get your inside man," he said, and the grin that spread across his face with those words actually stabbed me to the heart. "I swear, I will be a fount of information."

"That is not why you are doing this," I said, stricken with a sudden attack of pure guilt. At this point if I could have talked him out of this I would have. "Or at least not why you *should*."

"It isn't," he said. "But if they are who created the thing that killed my sister, then I will find out just what they did, why they did it, and how they think their accomplishment helps them... do... whatever it is you think they are trying to do..."

"What makes you think I think they're trying to do anything specific?" I said, a strange little smile finding its way to my own lips.

"If you didn't have ideas," he said, "you wouldn't have wanted an inside man..."

He had once asked me, back when we had been very young, to prove that I could Turn into anything I chose. And then took it back. And that had never really been brought up again. The truth of it was, on the matter of my being able to do what I had told him that I could do, all he had ever had was my word on it.

It was not a topic we had discussed lightly, anyway, not back then when it was pure curiosity on his behalf and even less later on when his own Turning dramas began to twist his perception of what it meant to be Were, and the importance of that Turn. I, for one, was hardly keen to talk about something that could not help but seem to be rubbing his nose into the fact that what I could do by a pure act of will while breaking all the rules... he could not accomplish at all, even following all the rules to the letter."

But now we were back to that, the two guys who had bonded, who had chosen to somehow trust each other, laying down the shields that we carried born of a legacy of having to be tough to survive and that meant trusting nobody at all. He had just asked me to prove what I could do, once again – and this time, he was not about to take it back.

There were so many layers to this. So many. We were both gambling with high stakes. What if it all went south, and Mal got hurt, or even died, or, worse, if it all came to nothing after all? This – the friendship, the closeness – this would never survive failure, and I could well lose him completely, we were mucking about with things that neither of us fully understood. And as for Mal... if this thing he was now so desperate to try did not work... he could be left with nothing at all. Only proof that he had failed completely, that he could not Turn even when pushed as I was about to push him now, and a nasty bite wound, and probably a bitter scar, to remind him ever after of the ultimate failure of his life. I seriously doubted if he could face me again, in the aftermath of that.

We had nothing to lose... except each other. And that suddenly seemed to be a pretty steep price.

But this now seemed like a fixed point in time, from which any number of futures could unfold. And the only place they could unfold from... was from the far side of this pact.

Although we were both wary, I could see in his eyes that he knew that something had relaxed in me, that something I had held close and tight had released. And there was some of that in him too. One way or another, it would end his torment. It would be over. He wasn't looking forward to it, clearly – I could sense him bracing for what was to come – and that was entirely sane; I had my own reservations about the pure mechanics of it. But there was something that had hardened inside him, a sense that this was something that he *had* to do.

"All right, then," I said softly. "All right."

"Now," Mal said. "Do it now, before I lose my nerve."

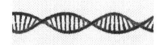

I had never done this before with someone watching me. It had been a private thing, something I did when I was sure I was alone, not meant for anyone else's prying eyes. But I had seen Mamma do it, in front of my eyes, when I was still taking care of her, and to me there had been no mystery. The only surprise had been just how much it had *hurt*, when it had happened to me.

But there was something in Mal's face – something tightly coiled, a curiosity, a fear – that suddenly made me realize that it was a very real possibility that he had never actually seen anyone Turn before. Not the act of it, the moment of it. He might have been too young to care, initially, and then when his own Turn age approached, he had simply never been in a position to do so. He would have been locked away in his own Turning Room while the rest of this family was going through their own Turns, elsewhere. Sure, he knew about the results – he had seen plenty of Turned Were-kind in his time – but not about how it all came about, how it all *looked*, and certainly he had had zero experience in how it *felt*. What I had on my hands was a true Turn virgin, for all that he was Were.

This was going to be traumatic, whatever I did, and there was no way to soften any of it for him.

I held his gaze, trying to think of the right words – an apology would have sounded really lame at this point – but in the end there was nothing to say. I reached for that place in my mind where my trigger lived, and told myself what I needed to be.

He saw it begin, I could see his expression change, and then I didn't see much more of that initial reaction, being too busy with my own transformation. But when it was over, and I looked up at him out of my wolf eyes, I could see him trying hard to control his breathing, and his eyes were wide with something that was close to shock. It was just beginning to dawn on him that he was in a locked room with a *wolf*. I could see him frantically searching my eyes with his own, trying to find any trace of humanity in there, but it would not be visible to him.

He flinched, just a little, as I lifted my head and bared the long, sharp white canines. They were about to close on his own flesh and he was understandably rattled at the reality of the whole experience now that it was in full flight. But it was already way too late for any second thoughts, any regrets. And he came to the same conclusion, after I had seen a flurry of expressions cross his face – a reminder to himself that he had wanted this, asked for it; his fear, and his frustrations, and his guilt, and his regrets, and even that unhealed wound that was Celia, the sister whom he could not forgive himself for having destroyed through ignorance and innocence; the betrayal of Jazz's Turn coming before his own, something that would *always* be there between them. All of it – all of the poison. And I was the only thing, now, that could heal him, by tearing him open.

"Do it," he said, in a low voice that he was only barely able to stop from trembling – speaking to the wolf, to a creature he was far from certain could hear his words, could understand. "Just do it. Get it over with."

My answer came in a low growl, deep in my throat; I could see him try to interpret that, to make it into something, anything, that he could understand, could glean the faintest inkling that I had actually understood *him*. But there was no communication across this chasm, no bridge that both man and beast could tread at once, and finally he closed his eyes and clenched both fists by his side.

My claws clicked on the wooden floor as I approached him and I could see him tense at each small sound – I wished I *could* speak to him, to tell him that it would go worse for him with his muscles tensed up as tightly as he had them, that I would have no choice but to rip and tear – but by the time I stopped right next to his right leg it was too late for warnings anyway.

Well, I could try and wreak the least damage I could, under the circumstances.

My teeth closed in the fleshy part of his right calf and he screamed in pain as the taste of his blood flooded into my mouth; and then I released, just a little, and *reached* again – I have no real idea if my *female, be female* command had any real effect because I felt only a faintest tinge of change, if any, but I closed the jaws again, the second bite.

It was all that was needful, all that had been necessary, and I released the bite and stepped back. He didn't see me Turn back into human again, he had his eyes closed and was shuddering in agony, which was just as well because the thing had devolved into something that was almost comical –

with the drama of the moment I had forgotten about the clothes that I had still been wearing when I had Turned into the wolf and they now hung about me in tattered and bloodied rags. His eyes did open, filmed with pain, just in time to see me wipe the blood – his blood – from the corners of my mouth. His first instinct had been to staunch the bleeding from the bite with the ragged remains of his pants leg, but he wasn't doing a very good job of it; I looked around for something useful, in the midst of the usual state of entropy that my room perpetually existed in, and grabbed a towel off the back of a nearby chair, tossing it at him.

"Here, try not to bleed over *everything*," I said, resignedly, as he managed an awkward catch and wadded the towel against his leg. "Do you want an aspirin? I should have some somewhere. I'll just throw on some clean clothes, and then I think we'd better run you over to the emergency clinic – there's one around the corner, they know me there. You might need stitches for that. Sorry."

"Did it... work...?" he managed to grind out, through clenched teeth.

I'd already started to rummage through the controlled chaos that was the inside of my closed, but I turned at that question, clutching a T-shirt whose only real virtue was that it was whole and had no actual blood on it.

"How would I know?" I asked, reasonably enough. "You were never going to instantaneously Turn into that wolf right here and now in front of me. Doesn't work that way. Wait till the next full moon and see. In the meantime, how are you going to explain that leg at home?"

"They don't inspect me for holes every night," he snarled. "Ow, ow, ow, if I had known it was going to hurt *this* much..."

"You asked a wolf to take a chunk out of you. What did you think was going to happen?"

He just clenched his teeth and hobbled to the door.

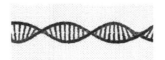

Did I expect it to work? I constantly swung from wild optimism to black doubt. In the end I wasn't even sure whether I actually *wanted* it to work – because if it did, miraculously, then it would all be on Mal. It wasn't me who would be ducking into the wolves' den.

The fateful Turn came, and went. I had had no word from Mal, and we had already agreed that I would not call him first, not before the thing played out. That silence from him could have meant anything, though – if our ploy had failed, I could see him having a good reason to avoid me. If it had succeeded... well, it stood to reason that he couldn't have phoned me during the three days of the Turn. I hung out in a few places where I knew he went, during those three days, and I didn't see him there. But again, that didn't mean anything at all.

On the second day post-Turn there was a text message on my phone.

The weasel is dead.

And then, moments later,

We need to talk. I'll be around later.

It took every ounce of self-control I had not to phone him back immediately demanding to know what had happened – but if he was texting me in these shorthand and cryptic ways, that could very well have meant that he was in no position to indulge in extended chats. I waited. I had a job going on which I could have been getting on with, but I was finding it predictably difficult to concentrate on that, and I was riding on the fumes of my patience when Mal finally turned up on my doorstep. The expression on his face was an interesting one, and when he didn't speak, for just a little too long, I finally lost it completely.

"What. The. Blazes. Happened?"

He told me.

I had no idea how or why all my memories stayed intact through changes and shifts, but that couldn't be the case for the likes of Mal, regular traditional Were.

He said the last thing he remembered was the pain – and when I winced and made a face he snapped,

"You could have *told* me."

"I could have told you nothing," I said, truthfully. "Yeah, it hurt. For me. That first time. But..."

"Does it get better...?"

"Yes... or you get used to it. It's something you live with," I said, then snapped at him, "Now tell me what happened?"

"They told me I ate the weasel," Mal said, with a grin that sat well on a new-minted wolf like him. "I don't *remember* that, which means that it wasn't a conscious act of revenge, maybe I was just hungry, when I Turned, and it was unlucky enough to be meat and to be *there* – but when I came back to myself, afterwards, and they told me about it, it was hard to feel sorry for it."

"Wolf," I said, underlying that, because he still hadn't said that in so many words. "You're *wolf*."

"Yeah," he said. "It worked. And you're right about the implications of that. I've already been warned about the Lycans. That they will come. And soon."

"Did your friends tell you where they think the Lycans will take you?"

"They told me a lot of what I already knew, thanks to you and everything you found out," Mal said. "I guess I will find out everything that you didn't know... when I step into it."

"We'll have to figure out a way to stay in touch," I said. "I don't particularly want them tracing you back to me."

"I've no idea about any of it. I guess I have to wait and see, where I get taken, how much room I have to maneuver. I've been doing some more work, I've got stuff on my laptop."

"You'd better be careful about all that," I said. "How much stuff?"

"Plenty," he said.

"They may want access to the laptop," I said. "And even if you wipe it, you can't get all traces of this out of there. You should probably bring me the whole thing, and maybe they'll give you proper new equipment once you're inside the den. And then we can see how we can set up a line of communication."

"I should have brought it with me," Mal said, sounding chagrinned. "I wasn't thinking."

"Ask me if I'm surprised that you've got other things on your mind," I muttered. "Wolf, eh? Well, this ought to be interesting."

He couldn't stay long – he was on a fairly tight leash, now – but we made arrangements for him to drop off the laptop within a few days.

Only, he never quite managed to find time to do it. And then a week had gone by, and then another. And then I got an email, from an unexpected source.

The Lycans took Mal, Jazz wrote. *He asked that I let you know. He's already gone.*

I had barely finished reading the thing before I hit "reply" – a short response, only three words long.

Can we talk?

I actually sat waiting for her to answer, literally staring at the screen. It took a few minutes, a few very long minutes for me, and when the email came in it was almost as terse as mine had been.

What's there to talk about?

But this wasn't the time for small talk. There was something I needed to know, and I needed to know it *now*.

Did he take his laptop with him?

It's sitting on his desk, Jazz answered.

I hit the keys hard enough to make my fingertips sting. *BRING IT.*

We set up a time and a place – one calculated to make her feel safe about meeting this weird stranger with her lost brother's laptop in tow – lunchtime, on a weekend, in a busy mall food court which would be swarming with people. She never did ask anything about how she would know me, and I wondered if she actually remembered me at all – she had only, as far as I knew, seen me once, and that time she was under Barbican Bain's spell – but it didn't matter, I'd know her, and I could be the one to make the contact. But when she came into that food court, carrying Mal's laptop in its battered case under her arm, it was as though she was looking for me – whether she remembered me or not, she *knew* me when she saw me. Our eyes locked, and I gave her a small nod from the table I had commandeered; I could feel the weight of her curiosity and, yes, judgment, as she gave me the once-over. And then she dropped her gaze and picked her way over to me.

When she stood beside the table, and I looked up to meet her eyes again, I could see her expression shift slightly as though she had to suddenly revise some initial impression of me. But she remained wary, like a gazelle approaching a watering hole knowing there might be a lion waiting in the reeds.

"Have you got it?" I asked without preamble, nodding towards the laptop which was still under her arm.

"Hi," she said, an edge of sarcasm sharpening her voice, "I'm Mal's sister. Nice to meet you too."

Oh, they were related, these two.

But I couldn't help an eye roll. Just a small one. Well, two could play this game, then. "Oh," I said. "Social niceties. I see. Fine." I leaned forward, sticking a hand out across the slightly sticky surface of the food court table. My voice dropped into the syrupy accent of an upper-class British toff. "My dear, let me introduce myself. Saladin van Schalkwyk, at your service."

She laughed. They *all* laughed.

"Saladin van Schalkwyk? Really?" And then she made the connection. "Oh. *Chalky.* You're Chalky."

"Yes."

"But you're the one – you are..." She was struggling with the memory, and I could see that night in the library come flooding back to her.

"If you're thinking of a certain ex-teacher, right now, yeah. Mal asked me to fix that problem."

"What did you...?"

"What did I do?" I said, my voice barely above a whisper. "I dealt with it. I don't think you need to fear that ghost anymore."

"Is he... did you..."

"Don't worry, he's alive and well." But it was time to change that subject. I raised an eyebrow in the direction of the laptop case. "That Mal's?"

She kept her hand on the laptop case, still looking a little rattled. "Yes, but hold everything. How come you want this so badly? What's on here?"

"Stuff," I said. "He told me he had some research on there. Things he might have been able to save."

"Research on *what?*"

I stared at her. "You two really didn't talk much, did you."

"He never seemed to have the time or the inclination for heart-to-heart chats." She sat back, crossing her arms in gesture that was almost belligerence, and said, "Who are you, exactly, and just what is going on?"

I echoed her, crossing my own arms and leaning both elbows on the table. "This Turning business," I said. "Mal wasn't having much luck with it."

"Tell me something I don't know," she muttered, sounding exasperated. "Actually, I always thought that was part of the reason he was such an ill-tempered brute."

It was my turn to be startled. "Mal? Ill-tempered? Brute?"

"Are we talking about the same guy?" she snapped.

"I suppose he was a little... twisted about stuff. It got worse after you. After you Turned. Just like that. After he had spent his entire life waiting for that to happen. I suppose he can't be blamed for thinking it was all such

478

a *waste*, him sitting there staring at his chosen beast and hoping that the Turning Gods would finally smile and let him become something... *anything*... and then he could be free..."

"But that's not how it works," she said, interrupting me. "You aren't Were... are you?"

I couldn't help a twisted little grin. That kept coming up, with this family. "Of sorts," I said, yet again. And then wrestled the topic back to where we'd had it. "My point is, Mal had no choice. He was *this* close to breaking."

"I know," she said. This was a sore point, for all of them. And then she gathered herself again. "But you don't just stop being – you can't just decide not to be Were any longer – he had no choice – "

"Actually, he did," I said. "Look, all I can tell you is that he was ready to do murder – he knew very well that almost anyone in your entire precious Were society could name him in a heartbeat if they were asked who the oldest unTurned Were kid was. He was a poster boy for failure. Did you ever wonder why he picked fights so often?"

"But there wasn't anything he could do about it," Jazz said stubbornly, if bleakly.

"There was," I said. Well, it would have to come around to this, eventually. "Once he made a real choice. Once he found a purpose, and started to figure out the Lycans."

"Mal was researching the *Lycans*?"

"I was helping," I said, feeling almost defensive at this point. "I have... certain talents he lacks. I could get him behind firewalls, if he needed that, into sites from which lesser mortals are comprehensively excluded. I am good at that sort of thing." I grinned at her, taking back my advantage. "Like, I read your blog."

The effect of that alone was almost worth coming here for. I could read her face – she couldn't hide her emotions – and I had a feeling that I was a hair's-breadth away from having Mal's laptop smashed over my head. And then, on the heels of outrage, came something that was almost horror – a recoil – a palpable sense of violation. Celia – their Celia – was so *private*, and there I was, sweeping aside her barricades like they were made out of chiffon, reading that protected blog without leave, without invitation...

And then I saw her circle back to Mal, and her face changed, and I took the chance that was offered.

"That was never your blog you were thinking of, just then," I challenged.

"That's not important," she said. "Tell me the rest of it."

"Give me the laptop."

She hung onto it protectively. "Oh no," she said. "Not until I get the full story."

"That's where it *is*," I said impatiently, and gestured for the laptop.

She hesitated, but in the end, she gave in and pushed the thing across the table at me. I powered it on, and stared at the indicators. I busied myself trying to retrace Mal's movements, following him through

479

cyberspace. I could feel Jazz staring at me as I was doing that, and it annoyed me, but I did promise her a story, and so I began a running commentary as I typed.

"You do know what it is that your brother's particularly good at?" I said. "He *puts things together*. He's the ultimate puzzle solver – he doesn't get these huge original ideas but give him six things that don't go together, and he'll find a way to make a pattern. He never quite knows where to begin looking, but he knows how to look, and more importantly, how to find. That's a gift."

"But *you* are the ideas man," Jazz said slowly. I shot her a glance and caught her staring at me speculatively, and flashed her a quick grin.

"Well," I said, "when I'm inspired."

"So what inspired you this time?"

She was sharp, this one. But this was a cards-on-the-table moment, and she got an honest answer.

"Mal," I said. "His own troubles and frustrations. When it came to the point where he was either ready to jump off the nearest bridge or do murder... and when he brought up something you'd said... well, I kind of threw in the Lycans."

"Something *I* said?" she repeated, sounding bewildered. "I know nothing about them. I don't remember ever uttering the word."

"There was a long chat you had with your father, apparently. About his Turning. Anyway, it was something you said – and then he put it together, as he does – and I threw in an idea. The Lycans. And he came up with a theory and plan. The Lycans – they're scientists, they're rare, they used to be the Last Big Thing before they went into decline... and, well, other things. They were potentially useful."

"Useful for *what*?"

"If nothing else, then giving Mal a purpose," I said. "Here, look."

I turned the laptop around to face her. I had half a dozen windows open, minimized – they showed glimpses of the road Mal had taken. Some of them I recognized, my own research, and others had been new to me and unexpected – but I could begin to see the pattern there. It was clear, however, that Jazz was lost.

I snaked a hand between her glazing eyes and the screen and poked at individual things.

"*Here*. Look. A bit of history, and then a bunch of old wives' tales, and you can easily see the stepping stones which led from one to the other. Silver doesn't really kill a Were-wolf, all those silver bullets of legend were an awful waste, but it does poison them. Slowly. They might well die from it... anyway. In time. None of the Were handle silver all that well, really."

She squinted at me, staring at my ear. I wore a single simple hoop in one ear, an affectation, really, but I could see the question forming.

"The earring..."

"Steel," I said.

She grasped that like a drowning girl at a spar. "So, you *are* a Were."

"Like I said, not exactly. But that's irrelevant right now. Pay attention.

Back here. This site talks about theories of Were-wolf procreation, the creation of new Were-wolves."

"I asked him, I think, if they still did it by biting," she said, and gave a watery giggle. "He seemed... put out by the question."

I grinned at her again. "That's because you're right. There are actually two ways of doing it. One is for two Were-wolves to have a natural child – it *is* carried genetically, like with all Were, and they *do* breed true, like the rest of the fixed clans – there are sites that explain the genetics of this whole thing."

"You said two ways," she said.

"Well – yeah, you're right, it can traditionally be passed by a bite. But here's where it gets interesting. Some of the more esoteric and classified sites will tell you – "

"You've been to classified sites?"

I gave her a look "Of course I have. How else would I know the important stuff? You think they just leave it lying around to be picked up by anybody wandering past?"

"Sorry," she said. "You were saying...?"

"Here's where it gets interesting, actually," I said. "It's more complex than just a wolf taking a chunk out of any off-the-street generic human. Three things – one, there's the hunt for a new victim, a new pack member, and that would have to be done by the whole pack. It's a collective decision. In theory. Because, two, it isn't just one bite that is needed. It's two bites. One each from the alpha pair. The male *and* the female. And three... well... not just *anyone* will do. Many people, ordinary people, would just die and that would be the end of it. The victim... er, the new pack member... has to already have an underlying predisposition to being Turned."

I saw her working it out. "But the new laws," she said. "The Lycans are locked away now, when they're in wolf form. Just like every other Were is. So, no more pack hunting."

I gave her a nod. "Right."

"And if one of them – or two of them, like you said – managed to get out... they'd still need to find the right prey."

"Right."

"And... Peregrine said..."

"Who's Peregrine?"

"He's... I don't know. He's Were Authority, I think. Someone quite high up in the hierarchy. When I Turned, it was he who smoothed it all over..."

I nodded. "High enough for cover up," I said. "Okay. What did Peregrine say?"

"Well... the Lycans...they don't have enough true-born descendants to maintain the pack numbers..."

"Right again."

"But what has any of this to do with..."

I tapped the computer again. "Look. *Look.* I told you they were scientists. They do research – genetics, biochemistry, molecular manipulation of basic DNA. Anything to figure out how to get out from underneath a grim sentence."

"But what has any of this to do with Mal?"

There were moments she was Mal's true sister, and things just seemed to fall into place for her, patterns forming, stuff coming into focus. But she was struggling, here, and I could actually understand why. The parts of the pattern that she could grasp, they were abstract, and she could handle them – and then it all broke against the rock that was her brother, and she couldn't fit him in there.

She understood, though. She just didn't know that she understood.

"Mal... was stuck in his place," I said slowly. "Well past the age of Turning, almost eighteen, of genuine Were-stock, but still unTurned. Some of those symptoms are actually very Lycan. If you're to believe some of the stuff that's out there, a significant number of them traditionally Turned at an older age than the rest of the Were. Like I said, he was about ready to start gnawing on people himself by this stage, or he was certainly eating himself hollow, knowing that he was the laughing stock of anyone who spoke his name, amongst his own kind. He was hanging on to the end of his rope, waiting for something to happen. And then he put the pattern together, and decided to *make* something happen. And then... there was the other thing."

"What other thing?" she asked. And the genuineness of the question almost undid me, because the 'other thing' was the thing that I had done. The trap that I had laid for her brother, and watched him willingly walk into.

"Lycans are scientists," I said at last. "I spit it out. "Jazz... the Lycans invented Stay."

She suddenly saw it fall into place – or thought she did, without knowing my own part in it. But as for Mal – it all fit. It all made sense for her now. Yes, it was partly pure frustration. But it was also... payback. It might have been something for Mal himself, to see himself Turned at last, and achieving the thing that had eluded him for so long... but it was also for Celia, the vanished sister, the one who was the empty heart of that family.

"Are you telling me... that he deliberately... set out to become Lycan?" she whispered.

"Well, bingo," I said, taking refuge in a bit of sarcasm. And then I was immediately sorry, because I had thrown a bit of facetiousness her way (which was my own defense mechanism) but I could see her really struggling with the idea.

"But... he wasn't... he was just a Random, like the rest of us... so if he wasn't *born* Lycan —and if they're as rare as they say they are – and if Mal was stuck behind closed doors, at the Turn, and so were the Lycan packs... *who bit him?*"

I actually squirmed under her direct gaze. "Well," I said at last, "as to that, *me*."

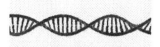

That blew Jazz's mind. I was ambivalent about telling her everything, but Mal was already gone, and Jazz could prove to be the lifeline strung between him and me, and so it was important that she understand. At least the broad picture.

"Look," I said, "it comes down to genetics, again. As best I understand it, I'm a genetic freak. On several levels. Not least being that I don't have that switch-off trigger that classical Were have, the thing that switches off the change when the Moon stops being in the correct phase and returns you to being, well, *you*. Or maybe I do have it – but I have it under my own conscious control, somehow, and not just keeping track of where the Moon's at. But I've always been this way. And the truth of it is, I simply *do not know*. But I have reason to believe that the Lycans may have had a hand in it."

"In what?"

"In... me. In my being what I am. I was hoping that *this* might be one of the ideas that Mal can find the pattern for, while he's in there. In their den. In their labs. In their computers, into which I cannot go without getting my tail set on fire."

There was resentment in her expression – she understood, correctly, that I might have had a hand in pushing her brother into this enemy camp. But she was also, against her own better judgment, getting curious. "What's he supposed to be looking for?"

"Anything. Everything. Secrets. They have plenty of those to go around. And if none of them prove directly useful to me– well – there are always those for whom the stuff he finds might be relevant, and people are always willing to buy knowledge, especially if it's knowledge that's hard to come by. Well, that's my part of it, anyway. Mal... well, it's his job to simply get inside the keep when they lift the drawbridge and absorb information like a sponge. What he does with his share of it – that's his business."

We didn't mention Celia. Very carefully.

"Still," Jazz said, after a moment of thoughtful silence, "It's Mal – I probably ought to tell Peregrine..."

I laid a hand across hers – it looked like just a touch, but it was a gesture of warning, and I could see her face change as my fingers dug into her skin.

"Say anything about any of this to anyone like Peregrine and you might kill Mal," I said. I didn't *know* this, but I did know how far Lycans would go to protect their secrets. They would not treat what they saw as Mal's betrayal lightly.

"As long as they really believe it was a fluke – and miracles happen, that's how things always begin – the Lycans will accept him, train him, teach him, they'll give him the answers we both want. If they suspect him as an outside agent who's somehow slipped past their barricades and is there to spy on them – Jazz, they're *wolves*. Think about that. Look, crazy or not, it's done, and if this thing works according to plan it might be spectacular. But it's need-to-know, and the only way it can *work* is if none of us go blabbing about it to people who Don't Need to Know."

"That makes me an accomplice," she said, looking almost scared.

I couldn't help it, I smiled. It wasn't a particularly pleasant smile, at that, because it was mostly a baring of the teeth aimed at myself. In some ways this was my fault, too, involving this kid in the whole scheme – but that was the way things had fallen out, that was the way it had to be.

She was looking at me as though I had suddenly turned into one of those wolves I had invited her to think about.

"You are that," I said. "We're all accomplices, now. Look... there are reasons... he may not be able to contact me. At least not soon. But you – it might be different, you're family, you're his sister. If he gets in touch, let me know, would you? That email he gave you for me, that will always work."

"And if I don't....?" she said after a small hesitation, a tiny plume of defiance coming out, like a baby dragon trying to breathe fire. But I heard her voice tremble, just a little.

"I'll find a way," I said. "I'll find out, anyway. But you're his sister, and he loves you – it would be nice if you'd help him..."

"*Loves* me?" she burst out. "When he was still around he spent half his time ignoring me and the other half sniping at me – sure, we had a few conversations that mattered, that we..." She stopped, her teeth clamping onto her lower lip as her eyes filled with tears.

Yeah, Mal had his reasons, and far be it from me to give family life advice... but this kid loved him, that was for sure, and he'd not done well by her.

"And yet he does," I countered quietly. Maybe Mal was the one who should have told her, but he was gone, for better or for worse, and now there was me. "Wouldn't be the first time a friend knew someone better than his family ever could. But...

And there it was, again. That name. The lost sister whom this family could not forget.

"He never really forgave himself about Celia," I said, as gently as I could. I knew this was painful. "But he was too young to understand, back then. And then, when he thought he'd grown up and he understood things better, well, he never quite got around to forgiving anyone else about Celia. And as for you..."

"Yes," she said. "I know. I was an echo."

"He told me stuff, about their escape, their journey here. Long before I read about it on your blog, in Celia's diary. The things that happened to them on the way, and then after they got here. It was always the two of them, him and Celia, against everything and everybody – your parents made them reinvent themselves when they got here, and made them into quite different people... and Mal was just better at it than Celia quite managed to be... or maybe worse... well, I read the diaries you posted. She was quite somebody, your sister. She had great courage."

"Stop it," Jazz said, but weakly, like a kitten hissing.

"But she did," I said firmly. This, too, it was important that she hear. "It takes great courage to admit that you're afraid. And that's something that Mal never quite did, to anyone – and if anybody called him on his bluff it was fisticuffs all the way. He always reacted to things. Now Celia – she had both hands in the dough, and she was trying to shape her life into something that was hers, hers alone. And until this – until the Lycan thing – Mal just rolled with it, took it as it came, never making the hard choices himself until he had to. And then... there's you."

"What about me?" she demanded, and the tears still stood in her eyes, ready to spill. She probably hated me right now. For knowing all this. For knowing all this *better than she had done*. For making her feel, perhaps, that *she* might have failed *Mal* in some weird way.

I gave her a crooked little grin, the best I knew how, the one that was meant to be reassuring, kind. I told her the things she had never known... the things she should have known... the things Mal ought to have told her... the things she needed to hear.

"You're no echo," I said. "If anything... you're a hybrid of the two of them, you took the best of them, the child of *this* land, one who was born knowing the way. You're... Jazz." I closed the laptop, and slid out from the table, the computer tucked under my arm. "Mal thought you were pretty amazing, by the way," I said, and that was no more than the truth. "He was probably jealous of you. And not for the reasons you might think. Well... if he calls, let me know. It's nice to finally meet you, Jazz Marsh."

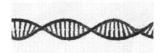

After that meeting, everything slipped into a sort of limbo. There was nothing but a very loud silence from Mal; not just to me, Jazz emailed me at least twice to tell me that he hadn't been in touch, almost begging *me* to tell her why. But I knew as little as she did. I received one piece of mail from him, at the post office box which I used as a mail drop, and there was a lot in that (including some of his drawings, which were often more eloquent than his words) but that was all.

Right until three months later, until the moment my phone rang. The 'clean' one, the one whose number very few people knew.

I let it go to voicemail – I always did, even with this phone, where I could be fairly certain that the caller was somebody I might want to talk to

– but the mechanical voice of the recording had barely finished saying that the person who had been called was unavailable and asking for a message when I heard Mal's voice, and he sounded brittle, ragged, tired.

"Pick up," he said. He knew I was there, listening. "It's me. And it's urgent."

I reached for the phone and killed the recording.

"Dude," I said. "What's up? Where are you?"

"At my old house. But I have to get out of here fast, before my parents get back... can we meet?"

"Food court. Fifteen minutes."

"We'll be there."

My eyebrow rose. "*We?*"

"Explain there. Go."

I did. In fact, I was already halfway out of the door. The phone went dead.

I was sitting at an empty table I had commandeered at the food court, waiting, when Mal walked through the mall doors. We had always had that connection, right from the beginning, and he found me almost as fast as I saw him. We locked eyes, and then I looked past him. The 'we' of the phone call turned out to consist of Jazz... and a striking young woman whom I did not know.

Jazz slipped into the seat next to me as Mal and the other girl took the seats across the table. I turned slightly to give Jazz a slight nod of acknowledgment, and noted that she looked wide-eyed and anxious. And then I turned back to look at my friend.

"Hey, Mal," I said. "Didn't expect to see you back here for a while. Not in person, anyway. How are the wolves treating you?"

"Hi," the young woman at his side said, with a touch of asperity. "I'm one of the wolves."

I gave her a long look from underneath a raised eyebrow. "And what," I asked, conversationally enough although every nerve in me was on alert, "are you two fine young Lycans doing so far from home this close to Turn?"

Mal's companion couldn't hold my eyes, dropping her gaze to the table and then turning her head marginally to glance at Mal. Interesting. She was looking to him for a lead.

"As to the Turn," Mal said, "we were hoping you had some ideas. You're right, we're cutting it very fine. But in a nutshell... Asia works back at the Lycan genetics labs." That sentence brought another interesting reaction from the girl he had called Asia, but I myself found my interest piqued, and sat up. "It's Asia's work that brings us out here. We were... at the Turning House... the one about two hours' drive from here...Chalky... Celia is there. She's *alive*. She's... damaged...she can't Turn... Ash says that Stay overdose... but I'll fill you in on that later..."

"Hey," Asia said, leaning forward, reaching out a hand to stop him talking. And caught my eye again. "Look," she said to me, warily, "I have no idea who you are – but... Mal..." She glanced sideways at him again, clearly worried. "Some things..."

"There are people out there who already know more than you suspect," I said, addressing Asia. But Mal, shaking off her hand, leaned forward towards me himself, his eyes burning with passionate intensity.

"Chalky. I need to get her out of there. I need to make a plan. Some kind of plan. If you have any ideas on that... but it's going to have to wait until after... Ash, how much time do we have...?"

She shook her head, looking helpless. "I really don't know. I have my doubts that we could make it back to the compound in time – the precise moment of the Turn is hardly an exact science, but everything is up in the air right now anyway. Even if I could give you a more precise time, under normal circumstances, right now – the way you're using up energy – "

"Wait – you two are really skating close to Turn and you're out of the Lycan fold?" I said, suddenly grasping the full magnitude of their predicament.

Mal and Asia exchanged a look, and then he drew a deep ragged breath. "It's all my fault," he said. "After I saw her – after I saw Celia – all I could think of was coming here, coming home, bring the news to Mom and Dad, to tell them that all those years of mourning.... But Jazz is right, Asia is right, at the very least my timing is appalling. I can't do it to them, not right now, not right before a Turn, and then leave it hanging like that. And then Ash... said something... about the whole set-up... frankly, I don't know who I can trust anymore, who needs telling, from whom it needs to be kept, if anyone at all can do anything about it... and I have an awful feeling that anything I do will just make things worse."

I saw Asia reach out and briefly cover his hand with hers, a reassuring, loving gesture. Mal saw that I saw. But there were more pressing things to discuss.

"So you need a safe space to Turn?"

From the expression on her pinched white face, Jazz hated the very sound of the words she was about to say, but said them anyway. "But... you were already at the Turning House..."

Mal winced, but Asia was there to take up the defense, already shaking her head. "No. They aren't set up for the likes of us."

"They do predators," I pointed out. "It would have been a matter of adjusting..."

"No. You don't understand. Lycans are... wolves are kind of a special case... I would never have got the clearance to use a Turning House – *any* Turning House – for a Lycan Turn. And I would have had to answer for it, if I'd made the decision to that by myself, without the leave to do it."

I asked the obvious question, although I already knew the answer had to be no – because otherwise they would probably not have called me. "Is there another pack nearby? Nearer than yours? Somewhere you could beg for sanctuary?"

Asia shook her head mutely.

"And there's no hope of getting home before it's too late?"

"Let me put it this way, it might come down to me driving the RV down the highway while trying to fend off a pent-up and frustrated wolf," she said. "Unless there were two pent-up and frustrated wolves, in which case there would be nobody driving the RV at all. We'd kill ourselves." She stole another sideways glance at Mal, and I could see the worry etched into the lines that had cut themselves into her face. "Frankly, I don't know if I can trust him to stay unTurned another day. It might be *hours*."

"Right, so that means no public option. No Turning Houses. Not even a large predator center – yes, there actually is one of those not too far from here. They don't exactly advertise – the reasons are obvious – but those who need to know where to find them are kept in the loop."

"Large predators?" Jazz asked.

"There aren't that many of them. But yeah. I think they've got a number of the big cats. Maybe a few bears."

Asia was staring at me again. "And are you one of them?"

"Sometimes," I said, and left it at that, watching her trying to work it out.

"There are always the Turning Rooms," Jazz said, a little desperately. "But Mal already said... and then there's the fact that we'd have to let Mom and Dad and Vivian know... and I just don't know how safe it would be down there, for the two of them..."

"Then we need to find somewhere that is big enough to contain..."

"Wait," Jazz said, fumbling for her phone, interrupting me as though she had barely been aware that I was speaking. "If anyone knows anything, the Corvids will. They run things. They're in charge. If there's an alternative... Nell? It's Jazz. Listen –no, wait don't talk, this is urgent, I need to ask you..."

I left her to it, leaning forward towards Mal and Asia across the table between us, and dropping my voice.

"Tell me," I said. "*Celia*." I was looking at Mal, but my next words were aimed squarely at Asia. "Did your lot have anything to do with any of this?"

"Hey," Mal said defensively, "they're my lot now, too."

"You weren't supposed to go native," I said.

Asia looked as though she was ready to do battle, but we were all saved by Jazz and her phone conversation. She reached out to tap my hand, and I transferred my attention to her.

"Nell says her Uncle Sebastian owns a summer house, lakeside, up in the woods in the hills." She gave us the details.

"I know the area," I said. "It might serve. But you mentioned an RV... You aren't getting up there in that. Not on those narrow roads." I fished out a notebook from my back pocket, tore out a page and scribbled on it. Thanks. Jazz, tell Nell I'll be by to pick up those keys. Mal – take this – " I thrust the note I'd scribbled down on the torn-out page in Mal's direction. He took it reflexively. "Take the RV to the campground – you know where it is – just give *that* to the guy who runs the place – ask him for the last hookup spot in the back, the last one in the long-term positions – he'll know. He's sort of a friend of mine. Go there, and wait – I'll swing by with the keys and the car as soon as I can, and we'll go straight up to the cabin from there."

"What about me?" Jazz asked.

"You... go home," I said. "I can drop you off on the way. Seriously. *Everyone* just find a place to lie low. I seriously don't want to be riding herd on a couple of frisky new-Turned wolves in the streets of this town. As for the rest of it..." I turned back to Mal and Asia again. "We can talk about... everything else... when we aren't quite so pressed for time."

Jazz looked properly mutinous, I expected nothing else, but they all knew I was right – the best thing we could do right now was for everyone to just pull in the same direction.

I dropped off Jazz at her house after a silent drive, and it was only once I pulled up at the curb outside her house that she turned to me.

"Call me," she said desperately. "Let me know. I'll... be Jesse... I can take a phone call. Let me know that he's all right."

"It'll be okay," I said. "I will get them there. I'll take care of them."

She held my gaze, looked as though she was about to say something else, and then decided against it, simply giving one sharp little nod and slipping out of the car. She didn't look back as she strode back to her front door with her shoulders hunched up about her ears.

Nell Baudoin had slipped the leash long enough to sneak out of her house and run to my idling car, dangling a set of keys from a metal key ring – but it had taken her a little bit of time to accomplish that. She and I had never met, never spoken, but Jazz had told her to expect me, and she trusted that. She hesitated only a little before she handed over the keys.

"I'll get these back to you as soon as I can," I said. "Nell. Thank you. This is a lifesaver."

"Glad I could help," she said faintly. I could see her standing there as I drove away, a solitary figure in my rear-view mirror, her hands clasped together.

I was glad to know that Jazz had such a friend.

I stopped in a supermarket, on my way back, figuring that there probably wasn't going to be much by way of supplies up at the cabin which had already been closed down for the season. Just the essentials, but it held me up, and it took me close to an hour to get back to the RV park. If Asia was right we were seriously running out of time – and I only stopped long enough for them to pile into the back of the car before I spun the car on the gravel drive and drove back out of the park and then north out of town, out to where the road climbed into the hills and the resort lake. There wasn't much talking – I was busy driving, the other two sat in the back in silence. I glanced back, periodically, but Mal seemed very far away and Asia was preoccupied, sitting drawn up into the smallest possible space, her legs curled up on the seat and her knees resting on Mal's thigh.

Interesting, again.

I startled them both when I finally came to a gravelly stop and turned the keys in the ignition. Mal looked as though I had just woken him up from a bad dream.

"Well," I said, "We're here."

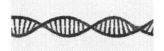

We all climbed out of the car, and took stock. I'd parked next to a small wooden cabin, maybe a dozen paces away from a coarsely shingled beach. A small cold breeze stirred the waters of the lake, gray under the heavy skies, and small wavelets broke and whispered on the shore. There was only one other building in sight, half hidden by now-bare branches of shrubbery I imagined must provide quite a bit of privacy in the full green lushness of summer, but there was no vehicle near it and it looked deserted, which suited our purposes very well. Behind the cabin we had come here to borrow there was a hillside of nothing but woods – a few dark conifers standing out amongst an army of deciduous trees in full golden autumn glory.

So," I said, after the other two had had a chance to look around, "you think this might do?"

"Less than ideal, under the circumstances," Asia said. "But it could have been worse. Much worse."

But Mal frowned. "It's not exactly *contained*," he said, "is it? If we just take off – we'll be wolves, this is open range, we will have no human idea of distance... We won't have the memory to guide us back here. No true memory. We might get lost, with no way of knowing how to get back here."

I turned to stare at him. This was one of those Were things that I found it hard to understand, because my own experience went utterly against accepted wisdom. But if I could do this – retain the memory into a different shape – surely there was really no good reason that he could not.

"Well, maybe it's time you learned," I said. "Find *something* – find a bridge – something to keep you linked to your other self – it should be easy enough, you're a wolf, use a wolf's senses, use smell or taste, use it to anchor some sort of visual memory..." I had not thought this through, it was pure impulse, but I grabbed his arm as I talked and the pen knife I always carried was in my other hand and I had nicked the exposed skin between the edge of his long sleeve and the heel of his hand. Not hard. Just enough to make a bead of bright blood well up.

"Hey!" he yelped, more in surprise than in actual pain, and instinctively brought the damaged wrist to his mouth, sucking at the blood. I could see the taste of it go through him, and I knew I was grinning at him because this might just work, at that.

"*Remember that*," I said. "And remember the place where you first knew it, here, right in front of this house. If you get lost in the woods as a wolf... when you come back to yourself, as a man, remember these two things, and connect them, and you will be able to come back here – the landmarks you noticed as a wolf will come back to you, guide you home."

"How do you know all that?" Asia asked sharply, looking at me as though she was about to call me a witch. "Who are you, anyway?"

I still wore that grin. "That was one thing he was supposed to help me find out," I said. "From the inside, as it were. As to the question about who I am – I have reason to believe that the Lycans had a hand in the answer to that. But, eh. Less than three months in, and he's here, gallivanting around the countryside with a pretty girl, and he isn't..."

"Leave my wife alone," Mal said. "It isn't her fault."

Well, *that* was something he had left out. Watching the two of them together, I had figured out that there was a romantic link involved, that they were some sort of couple – but I hadn't gone so far as to think marriage. I stared at them with my eyebrow climbing practically into my hairline.

"*Wife*?" I said. "Wow, dude. That didn't take long."

"It was for the pack to decide," Asia said.

I looked at them both, my gaze sharpening. "Oh...? Well, I suppose it stands to reason that they had to practice on their own, before they cast their net wider..."

Asia had decided to clam up on whatever she knew, and Mal was starting to look a little at sea, and I decided that this conversation was best pursued at a later time. I broke the moment by fishing in my pocket and bringing out a set of keys, the ones that Nell had handed to me at her house.

"Well, we'd better get inside," I said. "In theory you have tonight, unless something critical goes wrong – it's tomorrow that things should start getting interesting in earnest, isn't it? There's a box of supplies in the trunk, I figured there would be nothing out here to speak of, it's been closed down for the season – do you mind bringing the stuff in? I brought a couple of cases of bottled water as well, if this thing has been winterized they might well have turned the water off. It isn't much, but I didn't think you should go into Turn hungry..."

Asia turned back to the car, and Mal hesitated, just for a moment. "Are you going to stick around?"

I turned, from the steps to the front porch, and flashed him a grin. "*Someone*'s got to keep an eye on you, dude."

The swift mountain dusk of October was upon us by the time we had ferried all the supplies in the house and settled in. There was nothing to do but wait, now, and the weight of that settled heavily down on all of us. Asia retreated into silence and solitude, Mal was twitchy and sharp, and I eventually retreated outside, leaving my clothes neatly tucked into a V-shaped split of a nearby cedar and taking to the air on an owl's wings, flying through the dark woods by myself. By the time I came back, it was dawn, and the two of them were asleep, side by side on the bed, not quite touching but with their hands close together on the covers as though just the proximity of the other's fingers gave them comfort of sorts. Mal's lanky body was twitching restlessly on the bed like a puppy – or like a wolf cub having dreams of chasing lunch down in the forest; Asia was curled up on her side, her lips slightly parted and her face twisted into a slight scowl – whatever *she* was dreaming can't have been pleasant. And dreams were the least of it – what would come in the cold light of the next day, that was a whole different realm, and that was reality, and had to be faced awake...

...but still...

I watched them sleeping for a moment and then something hit me unexpectedly and shockingly, like being doused by cold water.

Jealousy.

Despite his whining and complaining, in spite of all the tragedies and dramas in his past, this was something he had always had – this sense of family – and it was something I had never really known. There was almost... an entitlement to it. Mal had *walked into a wolf's den alone...* and came out with a family. With a wife.

The Collective had been the closest thing to a family that I had ever had, until Mal. That sense of trust that had made me tell him the truth about myself where I had kept that even from my own mother. I'd needed him. Now, watching him sleep with his fingers curling towards those of the girl beside him... I wondered with a sudden taste of bitterness if he had ever really needed me, in the same way.

I didn't wake them. Neither could I linger, not in my present mood; if Asia was right, the next day – at some point – should trigger the Turn, and my presence would be a complicating factor. I left them a short note on the table in the kitchen and hoped they'd find it before things overtook them and they had other things to worry about, picked up the car keys, and drove back down into town for breakfast. Alone, as usual.

I didn't much care about where I went or what I ate, so I just stopped at the nearest roadside greasy spoon place I happened upon. Hashbrowns and a cup of that strong black roadside coffee would do – I needed something raw and warm and familiar, to ground me back into my world and to settle that wash of turbulence that had crashed over me earlier.

They had the morning talk shows on the flat screen TV that hung in a corner above the counter, turned down low, just as background noise, and I kept an eye on it as I sipped at the coffee out of one of those really badly designed mugs with tiny handles that made it impossible to hold them properly and drink from them without looking ridiculous. I could barely hear the sound, but something suddenly caught my eye – something – and I focused properly, sharpening my ears.

The show host was interviewing somebody, a man who (despite bearing no physical resemblance to him) suddenly put me in mind of Barbican Bain. And as it turned out my instincts were unerring. The next time they came up for a station break and then returned to the studio and (as they always did) reintroduced the guest for all those people who might have forgotten who he was during the few minutes of commercials, I heard the host brightly welcome back his guest... Marcus Moresby, the self-styled Vicar General of the *Vox Verae Hominis*, the "Voice of True Men", the movement that Barbican Bain himself had ties to.

I lost the first few lines of the re-introduction as I was shuffling the facts in my head, and by the time I craned my neck and began to listen properly Moresby was in full flight, his eyes shining with outrage and fervor.

"Our Founder said it," Moresby said, lifting a book he held in his right hand as apparent corroborative evidence for what he was talking about. "There can be no true human soul in a creature which lives part of its life in the body of a lower form of life, an *animal*. And this new abomination – oh, it was carefully hidden! – but it is an abomination, and it is a mockery of true men. This is truly from the dark side, that they can take the shape of another human being, that they can *fake* being a *man* instead of a *beast* – this is beyond anything that..."

He went on in that vein for a few more minutes while I stared at the TV and let my coffee grow cold between the hands I had cupped around the difficult mug. So Bain had... told what had happened? Was this because of what I had done? Could it have blown up so quickly, got out so fast?

The host was speaking again, trying to soothe Moresby who sat on the edge of his seat with his book clutched in both his hands as though it was the only thing that kept him from the pits of Hell itself and staring into the camera with eyes full of the wild and earnest passion of the zealot.

"I'd like to bring in another guest," the host said smoothly, with one of those practised showbusiness smiles. "Joining us from our sister studio, please welcome Iris Crowder, member of the highest council of the Were Authority, of the Corvid clan. Welcome, Iris. You have heard the allegations which Mr. Moresby, our guest here in the studio today, brings to us. As the representative of the Were Authority, what is your response to his statement?"

"It's arrant nonsense," Iris Crowder, a willowy brunette with deep-set dark eyes and angular cheekbones, said crisply. I could see a tiny muscle in her cheek jumping; she was holding her jaw clenched hard. Her hands were out of sight, out of frame of the screen that showed her head and shoulders, and I was willing to bet that she was clutching something in a white-knuckled grip trying to keep a rigid self-control on the air.

"With all due respect to the tenets of anybody's faith, Mr. Moresby has been out for Were blood, on behalf of the *Vox Verae Hominis*, for some time. He is our outspoken enemy, working against the Were in every way that is legally open to him. But this crosses the line into outright scaremongering, and slander."

She paused a beat and then rushed on as Moresby started to retort. "What the Were do, what we are, has been well known and documented for generations, for centuries. It has been enshrined in the very laws of this country. We Turn at specified times, and into specific forms, and no, we do not Turn at will into another human being. *This is impossible*. And I would have to say to Mr. Moresby, with all due regard for the freedom of speech which allows him to say whatever he wishes with impunity especially if it masquerades as the zeal of a true faith, that if he cannot substantiate his preposterous allegations, he has this time crossed a very dangerous line..."

I became aware that my teeth were actually clamped around the edge of the mug, and I had no idea for how long I had been doing that. But I was hearing what was being said on the TV, and re-evaluating my own actions in the light of what now appeared to be happening, and this... could have some evil fallout. I had underestimated Bain and this organization that he belonged to.

I had done what I had done. I had revealed myself to Barbican Bain to scare him straight. And I thought I had. But It was done in gleeful arrogance, because I could, because it was a brand-new game. Part of it was justifiable as a response to the things Bain himself had done but part of it was just complete and undiluted fun. Sure, I knew I had torn the veil from the secret of my own existence, from the things that I could do. Sure, I knew what that meant – that Bain would hate and fear me all the more for having seen what he had seen, and that there was a real possibility that he might go to the higher-ups in his organization with it. Eventually.

I had not counted on it being so soon, or that they would take it on a *public* warpath. I had known that I would become prey; I just didn't know the hunt would be on so quickly, and so aggressively.

I had been playing. But I had been playing with matches while standing in a puddle of gasoline and now my feet were on fire.

I finished up the coffee, left half my hashbrowns on the plate, threw enough money to cover the bill on the table, and hurried out of the café.

"Stupid, stupid, stupid," I snarled at myself under my breath. I had to work out what came next, but I was effectively on notice that the hunters were gathering and were ready to let loose the hounds at any moment. I had to think about covering my tracks. I knew I was good at that, but it stunned me that I had not seen the fallout of this before I had stepped full in it.

I had all but promised Mal that I would be keeping an eye on things, up at the cabin, and now I was feeling guilty, on top of everything else, for having abandoned the two of them up there to pursue my own demons. I figured I'd better get back there fast. If the Turn hadn't happened yet, it was imminent, and Mal did have a point when he had said that the woods were woefully wide-open to their incursion. It was entirely possible I would need to go looking for them at Turn's-end.

They'd be hungry after the Turn. I decided to be practical about things; I was already down here, in civilization, and I stopped off to replenish the few supplies I had got earlier. It took a little while, because I visited several stores, reluctant to buy a lot of things in any one place lest the quantity be remarked upon and I didn't want to draw attention to myself right now. Halfway back up to the cabin, my phone rang.

There was no cell service up by the lake. I must have been riding the ragged edges of it now. But very few people had this number, and most of those were already involved in this whole adventure and would have no need to phone me. The call was anomalous, and right now anything out of the ordinary made all my antennae quiver. I pulled over to the side of the road, hoping to stay in a pocket which had signal enough to talk, and reached for the phone.

It had gone to voicemail, as usual. I toggled that, and listened to the message.

Whatever I had been expecting, whoever I might have guessed would call, it would not have been Jazz – and it would not have been Jazz speaking in a voice that sounded thin and close to panic.

"Saladin? If you get this, give me a ring...I think Nell said something about no phones up at the cabin... but maybe you can get your messages... how are things going up there....and... uh... I'm kind of freaked out... call me..."

I hit redial, and the phone was picked up practically on the second ring.

"Hey," I said. "On my way back up to the cabin, supply run to town. Nothing to report yet. Got your call. What's up...?" There was a silence, and I added, warily, "Can you talk...?"

"Yes," she said, after a pause. "I'm sorry... I just don't know who to ask – Dad's already Turned, and Mom would freak, and if I drag Vivian into it again, not that she has anything to do with it... this is kind of a family thing..."

I have to admit it, that came down like balm on that wound that had driven me down the mountain in the first place. It was a family thing. And she had called *me*.

"What is it? What's happened?"

Another hesitation. "I... got a call from Peregrine," she said. She was being very careful with this. "It was... about... he sounded angry, actually. He wanted to know... if I had been indiscreet. If anyone who shouldn't know... about Jesse... somehow got wind of it. If I'd changed in front of anyone who shouldn't have seen it."

I should have seen this coming. I should have seen a lot of things coming. I had done what I had done, with Bain, amongst other things to protect Jazz – and it might turn out that my ill-considered and impulsive actions had ended up putting her in danger instead. They didn't know about *me*, in the Were Authority... but some of them, at least, knew about *her*. And when the Vox Verae Hominis had come up with the 'changing into other humans' abomination story... she was the first person they had gone to.

"I saw it on TV," I said grimly. "Just now. Jazz, there's nothing I can do about any of it right now. We're all in the middle of something, and it's hard to get out from under it – even Peregrine will be out of it for the next three days – I have Mal and his Lycan friend to babysit – just sit tight, would you? Don't leave the house, for the rest of the Turn. Don't show Jesse's face in the street. Just in case. When I come back down to town, when all this is done, we'll talk. I'll see what I can do to sort things out. Lie low, and stay quiet, and I'll be in touch as soon as I can. I don't know if the phone will work up there but the voicemail always will. If you need to leave a message, do it. I'll come down low enough to get signal at least once a day over the Turn days and if there's an emergency let me know and I'll make a plan. But I have to finish taking care of the Lycan problem first."

"Okay," she said faintly. "I'll do that."

"Did he say anything else?"

"Something weird," she said. "He said that he'd probably have to move 'the project' forward now."

"What project?"

"I have no idea."

"I'll find out," I said, my fingers tightening around the phone. "I promise you I'll find out. Let's just get through the Turn and then we can deal with whatever comes."

"I'm afraid," she whispered.

"I know," I said, staring blindly out into the woods, one hand wrapped around the phone and the other curled tightly around the steering wheel. The phone crackled, and went dead; the 'Searching for Signal' circle began turning endlessly on the screen. "So am I," I said into the dead air.

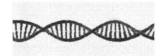

Mal and Asia were both gone by the time I got back to the cottage, and my note was still where I had left it – so it was possible that whatever had happened had come on suddenly and they had not even been really aware of my absence. It took me a little while to find them, circling in crow shape (it was my first form, and still a favorite) above and through the trees – and they were good looking young wolves, the pair of them, who actually seemed to be having quite a good time out there in the wild woods. I followed them, off and on, through the Turn, taking time out to drive down the road a ways and touch base with Jazz, Jesse now, and I knew I was nearing a moment where I would have to make a decision when it came to Asia. Mal knew about me, Jazz knew about me... the 'family' did. But she – although she suspected something was *different* about me – did not know. Not for sure. Not without a doubt. And I would have to make a choice as to whether I would let her in, or not.

If I chose to keep my secret so would Mal. I knew that. He would never tell anyone whom I had not unequivocally approved. If anyone spilled this to Asia, it would be me.

She was Lycan. She... her crew... might have been what had *made* me. She would have those loyalties – Lycan, scientist, bound by commitments which might take precedence over my own situation. On the other hand, she was *Mal's* Lycan. She might have been mated to him by the command of the pack, but she was... there it came again... family. And the fact that she was here, with him, flying in the face of that pack and its commandments, was saying a lot, and quite loudly.

I was still weighing my options when I packed a bag for them (a couple of small blankets, clothes, emergency rations for post-Turn hunger) and took it up to where I left the two of them sleeping – curled up against one another in their wolf form – on the last night of their wild Turn. And I wasn't sure until I saw them both change back, into Mal and Asia, and reach out for each other with a kind of blind trust which finally settled onto one side of the scales and tipped the balance for me.

It would have taken days to explain. Best to show, not to lecture.

I waited in the shadows of the woods, in my own wolf shape, until Asia was done straightening herself out after the Turn, and lifted her head, looking out into the forest.

"Right," she said, "I suppose we'd better be on our way…"

But I had stepped out into the open, and Mal saw me. He stared at me for a long moment, and then reached out and carefully closed his hand around her wrist. It was a warning gesture and her head came around, to look where he was looking. I saw her freeze – the girl who had herself been a wolf a scant hour before – as she met my eyes.

"Is it…" she began, in a low voice, and then stopped as she saw the slow smile that was starting to spread on Mal's face.

"Don't worry," he said. "I think I know that wolf." He took his blanket, which he had folded and flung over his shoulder, and tossed it towards me. "Come on, then," he said to me, "if you think it's the right time."

"What are you doing?" Asia demanded.

"Watch," Mal said. And she turned back to me, and saw me change, saw the muzzle of the wolf flow back into the human face, the limbs lengthen and straighten as my stance turned more into a human crouch rather than a four-legged animal standing its ground, the grey fur fading into bare skin. I reached out for the blanket that Mal had so considerately thrown at me and draped it around myself as I rose to my feet. Mal was still smiling; Asia was staring at me with her mouth open and her eyes wide in unblinking astonishment.

"Ash," Mal said, "meet my friend. Saladin van Schalkwyk. Better known as Chalky."

"So you *are* Lycan…?" Asia said, bewildered.

"On occasion," I said, with the blanket draped around me like a toga.

"I called him a shifter," Mal said. "He isn't anything… *Were…* specifically. He can Turn into anything. Be anything. And he doesn't have to wait on the moon being in the correct phase to be able to do it."

"But… that is…"

Mal sought permission with his eyes, and I nodded, very slightly, just once.

"He is also," Mal said, "the wolf that put me in the pack."

I could see her trying to work this out, her eyes flickering from Mal to me back to Mal again, and then she took a few unsteady paces back and collapsed onto the edge of the log under whose protective overhang she had just woken from her wolf form.

"He… *how…*?"

But I was getting cold. "I'll meet you guys back by the lake. I started a fire in the wood stove, and I'll have coffee and a proper breakfast ready by the time you get there. Do you need me to lead you?"

"I know the way," he said, and smiled.

The lesson had taken, then. The first tendrils of shared memories. I may yet have something of value to teach the Were.

"I'll see you there, then," I said. "It's going to be a bit of a hike. Maybe you can fill her in on the basics on the way, Mal."

I turned into a raven and rose into the sky. The last thing I saw before I left them was the utter consternation on Asia's face.

It was more than three hours later that they eventually turned up at the cottage's doorstep. Mal was grumpy. "Asia has a blister, and I think I twisted my knee somehow."

"It could have been worse," I pointed out. "There was a moment that you seemed to contemplate going right up into the mountain, and if you had it would have been the best part of the day, walking back on human feet. But you're here now, so sit down – breakfast is ready, and the coffee is hot."

The smell of that coffee and that food had already worked its magic. Mal's mood was lifting as he fell on his breakfast like a good little wolf and practically licked his plate clean. He was almost back to just his normal level of grumpy by the time he was done, and had settled himself with his second cup of coffee cradled in both hands.

I piled the dishes in the kitchen sink – we could do the clean-up later, and decided I'd better get the logistics out of the way. I hadn't been wasting time, waiting for the two of them to shed the wolf skins.

"Okay," I said, turning back to the now rather more relaxed and sweet-tempered pair of Lycans in the living room, "before we get into everything else... here's what happened. Your RV broke down."

"What?" Asia said, frowning.

I laid out the cover story I had put together, ending with:

"You were in an area with bad cell service," I said. "Your phone battery died... and you, Mal, lost your phone. I've got you a new one."

"You've hacked that one."

"This one's clean, yes," I said. "It's a secure line, now, and if we need to talk, we can. And given everything else that we're about to get into... a clear line of communication will be important."

I didn't say anything about the witch hunt that was about to descend on my head. Not now, not yet. There was far too much else to deal with at the moment. Time enough, when it became necessary.

"So," Mal said, accepting his phone, "we're going back? And I'm still undercover?"

"*That*," Asia said firmly, her hands curling convulsively around her coffee cup. "Before we go anywhere else... that. I think I deserve to know. What really happened, Mal? How much of what you told us was a lie?"

"I told enough truth to make it real," Mal said. "The roots of all this... may be with Celia, and what happened to her. There's no getting away from it, for me, that it was I who gave her the thing that killed her. And then, when Chalky told me about Lycans and Stay and how they held the keys to it all... and I could find out more if I got on the inside... and in a way... I don't know, I think I wanted to make amends – to Celia's ghost, even – "

"You said roots," Asia said. "Plural. What, then, besides Celia...?"

Mal had not told Asia about his darkest hours. But now, reluctantly, the story came out – of his failures, of his anguish and anger as he got older and older until he became the oldest known unTurned Were of his generation. How close he was to despair, to giving up, to giving in – and how, when the idea of the Lycans came up, he was already at the point of having nothing to lose.

I let him talk. His version of things wasn't mine, not exactly, but it was his and Asia was his and it was his prerogative to tell the story as he saw it.

"And... well... you met my wolf," Mal said to her at last, nodding in my direction. "I had the potential, the genetic background – all I needed was the key, the push, something to help me take that final step... and that would come... from the bite. You'll never know what it was really like, those first few weeks at the compound, waiting for the test results to come down from the lab. Hoping some tiny genetic hiccup I had simply known nothing about and could not plan for would not come up at the last moment to trip me up or reveal the lie..."

"No," Asia said faintly. "You're Lycan. I should know. I worked on some of those tests myself. But it still doesn't make sense – not even – the bite thing hasn't worked properly for a long time, it's a pack thing, and it's really hard, under the new laws... if passed by bite, it takes *two* bites, the male and the female... how could you have..."

I shrugged. "That part of it, I didn't know if it would work properly," I said. "I know it's hard to believe that it never really occurred to me to try before Jazz Turned into Jesse, but it was technically possible... what? You didn't tell her about that, either, Mal...?"

Because Asia's face was starting to scrunch up into a frown of confusion again. "What now?" she said, with both weariness and a genuine alarm in her voice. "Who's Jesse?"

It was hard for Mal to talk about this. He had kept it bottled up, hidden and in the dark, because he didn't like this part of himself much at all. But he had always had courage, and he was honest. He told her everything. "You can't tell them," he said at the end, a desperate attempt to stop the leak in the dike. "Ash, you can't tell the Lycans about this. You can't – they'll take her too, they'll take Jazz too..."

"Let me get this straight," Asia said. "You chose to cheat your way into the ranks of the most closely protected and guarded Were-kind clan of all of them... how am I doing?"

I *liked* this girl. I could not help grinning at her.

"Well, when you put it *that* way..." I said.

"Wow," Asia said after a moment, dropping her hands to her sides. "And here I thought my family was trouble."

"If you guys are planning to go back to the pack, you'd better do it soon," I said. "Give me that credit card, and I'll finish cooking up your alibi. And then I can drop you off at the RV park and you can get going. And hope they don't raise too much hell about it."

Asia pulled out her wallet and passed a card over to me. I busied myself with the laptop for a moment, and only barely registered the peripheral conversation which had carried on in low voices between the lovebirds as I worked. I heard Mal mutter something about springing Celia, again (he was obsessing on that. He was circling back to that subject, no matter what else had been discussed.)

And then Asia said something that created a pool of charged silence, and I looked up from the computer.

"It's not as if you could *cure* her..." she said.

"But what if she could be cured?" Mal said slowly.

"Don't be silly," Asia snapped. "There are thousands just like her, worse than her, in the Turning Houses living out what's left of their lives. If anything could have been done don't you think that someone would already have..."

I had grown up needing to be able to read people, to know how to react, to know when they were telling the truth... and watching Asia now I was aware that she wasn't exactly *lying*, not outright, but she was definitely hiding something.

Mal had apparently latched onto the same kind of instinct.

"No," he said, "no, I don't. Nobody might have bothered to try, because everyone's been told how impossible it is. But what if someone began to think about what it would take?"

"You don't know nearly enough about it all," Asia said, throwing Mal's words back at himself, shaping the narrative to fit *him*, only him, personally.

But he was looking at her with the beginnings of a strange small smile playing at the corners of his mouth.

"No," he said, finding nothing to deny in Asia's dismissal of his personal abilities. But two could play at this game, and he lobbed the same thing back in her direction, aiming squarely at *her*, this time. "But *you* do."

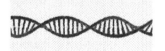

I saw Asia's eyes slide off Mal's; I saw him notice, too, and I knew he had come to the same conclusion that I had. *Guilt.*

"You *do*," he said. "You already do. For real."

"Not like that," she said, her voice oddly faint, like an echo from somewhere deep underground. "And not me. Not really. But..."

"But others? Other scientists? Other Lycans? And like what, then, if not...*that*?" Mal demanded.

Okay, this was my turf, too. It was past time I joined in. I leaned forward across the table where I'd been sitting with the laptop.

"Asia," I said, "what *does* go on behind the locked doors of those labs? If we're putting cards on the table – and here's yours back, by the way, speaking of cards, that's all settled – Mal... sorry... Asia, Mal might think that this Lycan thing was entirely his idea. And up to a point... sure... but I fostered it. I encouraged it. I have suspicions about my own origins, and the lines of inquiry all dead-end at the Lycans' door – Mal's going on the inside was on my behalf, too. Just how much Were genetics and genealogy *are* the Lycans controlling? I mean, we have the accepted wisdom, as we all know it. Were-clans breed true. Two parents of the same Were-ilk will produce progeny of the same Were-ilk – Corvids breed Corvids, Felids breed Felids, Canids breed Canids, Were-owls or Were-rats will hatch out owl chicks or pop out baby rats. Even Randoms stick to form – two Randoms will produce little Randoms, you have your own husband's family to prove that."

Mal growled at me. But I would apologize properly later.

"But there are tracks that I've followed, when it comes to myself," I said. "There's nothing firm, nothing I can call complete evidence although I've found plenty of pieces that seem to be part of the same jigsaw puzzle – back some two or three decades, and up to maybe only a few years ago if it isn't still going, there was a social and genetic program."

A social and genetic program that flouted all the laws and rules, official and unspoken, society contracts long honored and accepted.

Different kinds of Were simply... did not mate. This was a well understood and tacitly practiced taboo almost as strong as that against incest. There was of course no law against attraction – different Were did flirt, and even date, but when it came to marriage, to procreation, to progeny... they mated their own kind, and perpetuated their own clans.

The Lycan scheme... had gone against that. Coldly and deliberately.

Two Weres of *different* kinds were deliberately mated, an experiment of sorts. Because there was no way of predicting what their progeny would then turn out to be.

I hadn't worked it all out, not in detail, not yet, but I had begun to piece it together, from all the evidence that I had. "In the handful of cases that I've been able to follow to any degree," I said, "a large percentage of the F1 generation seemed to end up dead – either they are stillborn or lead short pitiful lives full of weird disabilities. There were lots of pregnancies that never got carried to term at all. I figured that it was some sort of pseudodominance that is going on, where a particular combination of genes turns out to be lethal – but I honestly don't know enough to make a claim of that as the cause. It might be only a part of the answer. I don't know if it is still ongoing – if it is they're covering their tracks well and if I had to swear to it I could say that I believed that it had been discontinued – but I don't know, I haven't been able to prove it. But it was a disaster. Catastrophic."

"But you think there were some successes," Asia said.

"Some were born, yes. And survived. Some, perhaps, in some way just like me."

"There's more than one of you?" Mal murmured, unable to stop the sarcastic remark. But then he dropped it and sat forward. We had talked of this before, he and I, but not in this kind of detail, and now we had a real scientist with us. "You really think you're a result of a breeding experiment?"

"I know my parents never got together for love," I said grimly. "I barely remember my father. All I have of him is the preposterous name. Were-dassie, as they call them where he came from, a kind of rock rabbit furball improbably related to the elephant on a genetic level. You can look it up. My mother was a Were-sandcat. Perfectly good Were, both of them, of their own kind... but they were *different kinds*. Best I can figure it, they married pretty much the day after they met or shortly thereafter which might imply a grand passion, but I remember no trace of that. In fact they barely stayed together for my mother to carry a pregnancy to term. I was not the first attempt, but I appear to be the first, and the only, successful one. My father certainly didn't stick around for long after that. It was as though producing me was a duty and once that was done, he disappeared as fast as he could. And whether it was as a result of any of this or not I don't know, but my mother spiraled downward after that. Some of her problems might have been imaginary but she ran for a reason, and hid me for a reason."

"But why would they want to do this?" Asia asked.

"I was hoping you could tell me," I said. "I'll tell you what I know when you give me some of the answers I still haven't got. But we can't do that now, or here. Are you kids going home? Because by now I'm pretty sure that they've missed you – and they'll probably be plenty mad, without you being any later than they already are..."

Mal sat up, squaring his shoulders. "But... what about Celia...?"

"Were you seriously thinking of just going back out there and walking out with her in tow?" I asked. "And then what, take her back to the pack? You need some sort of a plan – or at least a better plan than *that*. You need a place to land."

"But I know she's in there," Mal whispered, and I could see the thought eating at him like acid. "I'm supposed to just *leave her*..."

"Leave it with me, for now," I said. "If you jump the gun everything so far will have been a waste – you won't help her, and you can seriously damage your own situation. Don't say anything to the pack. I'll keep an eye on that particular Turning House and if anything changes, I'll let you know. The Lycan computers I can't quite hack, but the Turning Houses have revolving front doors, by comparison. I'll worm in and find out what I can, and I'll keep tabs. I'll keep you informed. I promise. You two lovebirds had better go home and talk this through. I'll call you when I get the lay of the land, and you can let me know what you want to do next."

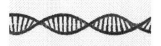

Apparently they wanted to go nuclear, and it didn't take them that long to take that plunge, but before Mal called me about Celia's situation I had his other sister's predicament to figure out.

I got in touch with Jazz – concerning the mysterious 'project' that this Peregrine fellow wanted to 'move forward'. It seemed that Peregrine, who was instrumental in investigating (and then quietly burying) Jazz's unprecedented Turn into human boy, had always meant to call in his chips on that particular favor. And the chips turned out to be deeply grounded in politics.

The government had committees in place to discuss Were affairs. The Were Authority – the governing body of Were-kind – could have non-voting observers at the meetings and could formally submit their opinions or their objections to any piece of legislation being discussed, but they had no voting rights. But that pre-supposed their knowing about everything that was being discussed. And it turned out that the Barbican Bains of this world had learned at least some of their tricks from the most powerful politicians of the land.

Some of the most important government meetings were deliberately held at such times as to make direct Were Authority observation and oversight nearly impossible. 'Emergency' meetings were often held during the precise Turn days that most of the members of the Were Authority were locked into their animal forms. To be sure, there were Band-Aid measures that could be applied. When proper notification was given, new-moon Were could be sent in to observe. But there were definite areas where the two different kinds of Were found their interests did not wholly overlap. There were also – there had always been – sympathizers to the Were kindred who were not themselves Were-kind, and who could sit in as observers at any time – but for all their protestations they were not Were themselves, the Were Authority was not entirely happy about trusting such intelligence completely.

And it went without saying that any observers who were actually paid for their time and their reports were, by definition, for sale, and the Were had always (and for good reason) been a little paranoid. Everyone had their price, and it had happened far too frequently that somebody had met the price that the Were had been paying, and raised it. Were-kind had discovered – the hard way, and often too late – that the people whose services they had thought they had been paying for were no longer working for them at all.

The Were and the humans coexisted – shared a world – shared a society – but there was no love and precious little trust between them. There were some areas where the Were held power or a position of influence – the Lycan scientists were way ahead of the cutting edge of human genetics research, and didn't share *everything* they learned with their human colleagues – but the numbers were against them. There were simply too few of the Were to maintain the kind of influence over their own affairs which they believed to be necessary, even essential, to their survival.

And then destiny – or pure entropy – had pressed a gift into the hands of at least one high-ranking Were. In the shape of a true Were who could pass as human.

Someone who could infiltrate the places where Were could not go.

Peregrine had eased Jazz's chaotic Turn, had smoothed her path, had swept as much as he could under a rock – yes, there had been medical examinations, and several people had been involved in that, but I had a shrewd suspicion that at least some of those medical investigators had not been told the whole story. There had been no mention of this favor coming with a price tag, at the time, but the circumstances had been unique, and Jazz and her family had not been in a position to ask questions. They had been grateful that Peregrine had been there to work his magic.

Now, however, it seemed as though he was about to call in his chips.

He had his spy, someone beholden to him, someone who would report directly to him and who could not be bribed or bought for a higher price.

His only problem was that his spy was still a child, and the presence of a child in such a forum would raise more questions than the presence of an unsanctioned Were. He had apparently said something about 'moving the project forward' by implication solving that problem somehow, but Jazz didn't know anything more about the logistics of it at the time that I spoke to her.

I had an eye on the Turning Houses and on Celia, but that did not require constant monitoring, my systems would warn me if anything changed. In any event, I was waiting for word from Mal and Asia on the next step, and I had some time on my hands.

I had always been more interested in digging for knowledge and for evidence rather than playing at politics, but now I was interested – and I, of course, was under no constraints. The Vox Verae Hominis crowd might be baying for the blood of the 'metamorph' but the Were Authority was still denying the existence of any such thing, and they had no way of fingering me even if they were actively looking for me which I didn't think anyone really was, yet. All the noise about it was still just preliminary saber rattling.

So I decided to visit the halls of government, and see what these meetings were all about, and if the Were-kind paranoia about what was going on behind the closed doors was actually real.

I didn't go wearing my own face. It wasn't a trivial matter, turning myself into somebody else and then holding that form for literally hours with only a partial focus on the logistics of that because I needed to concentrate on other things which were the reason that I was there in the first place – but I had worked on building up some endurance in this game, and that stood me in good stead. I only needed to retire to the restrooms once, to take a ten-minute break and release the shape back into myself.

I learned some interesting things – but mostly from the people I chatted with in the public gallery during lulls in the committee meetings. I particularly fell in with one young and eager journalist who was very ready to supply me with fascinating bits of gossip and rumor which he had picked up along the way. He offered excellent profiles of some of the main players in that particular arena... and other interesting people.

One, in particular.

I'd actually felt myself being watched, on several occasions. When unwanted attention is unhealthy, you become hyper-aware of it, that feeling of too-interested and possibly unfriendly eyes crawling over your skin, but I had been unable to catch anyone at it until I finally looked up at precisely the right moment to catch a long lingering glance from a girl with a pair of improbable eyes, somewhere between golden and hazel. She quickly dropped them and turned away when she became aware that I had noticed her looking. But now it was I who could not seem to look away.

She had one of those faces that made judging age impossible – she might have been a young-looking thirty or an older-looking eighteen. Her skin was very pale, and young and smooth, with no telltale lines anywhere to help with an educated guess. But those amazing eyes – what I'd glimpsed of them – belonged to someone much older, someone who had seen and known so much more than anyone living in that unmarked skin had any right to have done. Her face was narrow and almost foxlike, with cheekbones that looked like they were made of diamond, a small sharp nose, and a generous but thin-lipped mouth which looked like it had been trained into an expressionless line by a lifetime's habit of holding smiles too precious to be generously bestowed. That face was framed by a curtain of shoulder-length fox-red hair which only accentuated those features. But I wasn't given an opportunity of any deeper study because once she had noticed that I had noticed her she had risen from her seat and quietly slipped away followed closely by an older woman who wore her hair scraped back into a tight bun at the nape of her neck and had all the airs of a prison guard.

There had been... something... in that look. A hint of a wild thing, trapped. A message, perhaps, which I did not have enough information to read. It meant something. Something I had to think about.

My journalist friend had taken note of this exchange, and grinned at me as my attention came back to him when the young fox had left.

"That one," he said. "I saw that she'd noticed you. I'd be careful if I were you –too much attention from her is not healthy."

"Why is that?" I asked. Maybe he could help me with my sense that something deeper was going on here. I threw out a bait-line couched in easy flippancy. "Maybe she just likes the look of me."

He laughed. "Possible," he said. "But good luck getting her alone. That's her minder, that other one who left with her – and she carries a gun. And won't be afraid to use it. They take great care of their asset, and they wouldn't let you just go up and start flirting with her."

Now I was really intrigued. "Asset? Who is that girl?"

"She's their sniffer," the journalist said. "She's often in the gallery. She has some sort of weird ability to spot a Were in a crowd – and they use her to scan the people up here, when they want to know if any Were are present in the gallery, or to make sure that none are when it's a closed session."

"*She's* Were?" I asked, frowning.

"I don't know," he said, shrugging. "I don't think so, that isn't the impression that I get. It's just that somehow she can... sense them. Smell them. I don't know. It's weird."

"There's only one of them? Only one of her?"

"Far as I know, yeah," he said easily. "Never seen anyone else do it."

"Does she have a name?"

He laughed again. "Smitten, are we? No chance there, pal. Trust me. She might as well be a nun. I don't know her name."

But I found it out.

Her name was Grayson Garvin. She had a job title at the Capitol which didn't bear any resemblance to what my journalist friend had said that she did there, but I had no reason to doubt his word on it. I didn't find much on her out in the open, but I did discover that she'd had a difficult early life, that she was orphaned young and that she'd ended up in foster care and then was adopted. And then I broke through an encryption wall and found out the deeper truth behind her origins.

I might have known. *There is only one of her*, the journalist had said. And when I looked into it, when I looked deep enough and far enough back, she matched completely with another case from my Evidence Locker. Another one who was created by an unnatural mating of different Were-kind, to see what would transpire.

Which made her, in that important sense, almost but not quite completely unlike me... except that she was so like me. Both of us the only ones of our kind. Both *different*. Both with some kind of weird variation on the Were theme. We seemed to have drawn a zero-sum matched set of lottery numbers, though – I, with the ability to shift into anything, and she with the apparent ability to shift into nothing directly, herself, but with an innate sense of being unerringly drawn to those who did carry the power of change inside them. The ability was already being used as a weapon – by the normals, by the government of ordinary humans who were in charge of the Were destiny out there in the real world. But if she turned vengeful or bad, or if factions like the Vox crowd got a hold of her... I was suddenly shuddering at the thought of her potential ability of sheer destruction.

I suppose anyone looking in from the outside might have drawn, *did* draw, much the same conclusions about me. We were both wild cards, unlooked for, unknowns.

And now there were two of us.

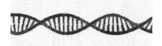

I t was a call from Mal on the safe phone I had given him (the replacement for his 'lost' phone was identical so they never noticed) that brought me back from this new and interesting avenue of research. It turned out that he had managed to infect Asia – and, improbably, another hapless Lycan from inside the genetics labs – with his own sense of urgency and passion, and the three of them appeared to have set out on a dangerous and clandestine conspiracy to find a genetic cure for whatever had happened to Celia, whatever had rendered her only half-alive and stuck in a single body out there amongst the wounded and the damaged and the abandoned relics of the Were world.

He said they needed lab rats. Of sorts. Were (or ex-Were) 'lab rats', of course. More literally, they needed samples of 'damaged' DNA to analyze, from others who had been similarly afflicted to Celia. But Mal and Asia had been confined to base for their earlier AWOL activities, and could not do the collection themselves – and their colleague really couldn't draw attention to himself by doing so – and therefore Mal came to me to provide them with the raw material they needed.

I found them exactly and literally what they sought.

Armed with some creative paperwork, I marched into several different Turning Houses and collected DNA samples from several ex-Were-rats. Then I put on a different face to go with a different uniform, one belonging to a scientific supplies company which seemed to be favored by the labs by Mal's pack, and delivered the goods myself only a handful of days before the November Turn was upon them. The official-looking cooler I carried, filled with dry ice and carefully packaged biological samples that had been requested, bore Asia's name (Mal was still too junior to rate a delivery like this) but I insisted that the delivery had to be signed for.

Mal came out to do that. As we were handing the paperwork back and forth between us, it was obvious that while he may well have had an idea about what the cooler contained he had no clue about the identity of the delivery boy... until I couldn't hold a grin back any more as I caught his eye and I saw his expression change as awareness flooded through him.

He straightened in surprise, but before he could succumb to something stupid I snatched back the final piece of paper from his hand and gave him a tiny half-salute.

"I've been digging," I said, in a low voice. "I found out a few interesting things." His eyes darted from side to side, in precisely the way they shouldn't have done if his intention had been *not* to look like he'd just been caught red-handed at something.

"What are you doing here?" he said, dropping his voice. "If they knew who just walked in..."

"I won't tell them if you don't," I said. "That's it for now? Okay, then. I'd better go before people *do* start paying attention. I'll be in touch soon. Stay safe."

I left quickly. I had come to deliver a set of biological samples; I'd walked into the wolves' den of my own free will, but I had no wish, through some unguarded reaction on Mal's part, to remain detained there and end up being a lab specimen myself.

They couldn't have done much with the stuff when I first brought it, not with the Turn upon them so quickly, but the guy they had working on this was good, and *fast*. I had no way of knowing if it was Mal who was keeping the fire lit under his feet, but it was less than two weeks after I had delivered the initial goods that I got the call-back that there was a product to be delivered back to the Turning Houses. I picked it up myself, again, wearing a different face than before, but it was at the hands someone who was neither Asia nor Mal. I had never met their third man, Wilfred; I assumed that it was him. He was terse, and looked anxious; he gave me the thing that Mal insisted on calling the 'vaccine', together with instructions on how it was to be administered and an email address to which the report of the results should be sent. I accepted the product and the instructions and delivered them back to the Turning Houses which had held the original subjects. But this time... I was not content just to drop things off and wait. I was involved now, up to the gills, and there was a reckless curiosity growing in me.

I knew that the *Vox Verae Hominis* lot had declared an open hunt on me. I knew that the Were (in general) had been rattled by the report that something like me might even *exist*, and that the Lycan scientists (in particular) – or at least those scientists not involved in Mal's conspiracy – would have been interested in far more than that. The Vox people wanted me dead; the Were wanted me found, if I indeed walked the Earth; and the Lycans would want me alive, and available as a guinea pig in experiments which I probably didn't want to think too closely about. In theory this ought to have been a time in which I ought to have pulled my horns in and kept my head down. But it was already way too late for that.

The Lycan experiments were being done for a purpose. To, and for, real people. And suddenly I had to know exactly who those people were.

It started with the 'lab rat' subjects.

If I understood it correctly, what they were shooting for was a complete reversal – when the next Turn came, in theory, the ex-Were-rats who had been dumped at the Turning Houses when they lost their ability to Turn should have presented as cured, and as properly Turned Were once again. Nobody knew if that would actually happen. It was a matter of waiting for the results. I had to wonder if Mal had thought far enough forward to realize that there might be... consequences to this. Someone would investigate this sudden reversion. You didn't have to be as good as I was to trace the origins of it back to Mal and his group; it would not be difficult to do.

But in the meantime it was all still up in the air. And when I delivered the vaccines to the Turning Houses where the test subjects were, I did so in person, with doctored instructions which permitted me to be present when the genetic cocktail was administered. I looked into the eyes of the 'lab rat' subjects as they received their injections.

One of them met my gaze levelly, almost defiantly, almost as though he was burning with an unspoken rebellion, as though he would have hurled the syringe into the air and bolted if he had been given a chance, or even tried to turn the injection in the other direction and attempted to stab the nurse administering the shot with the needle. But he did not do any of those things. He accepted his injection, rolled down his sleeve, and left the clinic room where he'd been summoned to receive it without uttering a word.

The other man rattled me considerably because he was so obviously beyond caring what happened to him at all. He raised his head only once, his gaze brushing mine only briefly, and then he dropped his eyes again to where his one hand, the one at the end of the arm not receiving the needle, rested in his lap. The other hand hung limply from the edge of the armrest where his arm had been laid by the nurse in order to position it for the shot. He had allowed himself to be handled like a marionette, with no real signs of life at all. It was as though everything inside of him was already gone, and his body was just a physical shell that had remained behind, still animated by some strange magic but no longer truly alive.

It was maybe because of him, of that second man, that I suddenly got it into my head to make another visit – one which I might have thought about making before, but never had.

In all this time, Celia had been just the heroine of a horrible fairy tale gone wrong, the princess in the tower waiting to be rescued. She had always been real to Mal, even when she was just a loving ghost, but she had never really been 'real' to me.

In all this time, I had never laid eyes on her, the sister whom Mal had thought dead and who was now somehow alive again.

I made one last Turning House visit, and drove to the Turning House where Mal had seen her, where the sight of her had started this whole wheel of destiny spinning.

I went to find Celia.

The Turning House was a wet grey smear through the windshield of my car as I drove up to the main building, armed with a ton of fake paperwork which identified me as a doctor with permission to examine several residents.

I figured that since I was specifically interested in someone like Celia – who went by her other, older, original name here, Svetlana, what was it Mal had called her, Svetya? – I would attempt to create a pattern where there was none and inquire after several 'patients' who matched the same general set of criteria – a certain age bracket, female. The nurse-practitioner who met me in the clinic immediately assumed that she knew just why I was there.

"I suppose you're here for the assessments," she said. "I thought you'd have asked for Agnes Swift, she's also part of the same general cohort, and I'm a little surprised to find Lydia Hunting on the list, I would have thought she's a bit old..."

"A bit old for what?" I asked, startled into a possible indiscretion. But I knew how to paint over a crack. "I mean, I can understand your concerns, but what specifically do you think the issue is?"

"Well, I would have said, personally, that she was a very iffy candidate – being almost at the end of her useful reproductive cycle..."

"Nurse," I said, and now my ears were fully pricked up and I was wantonly fishing, "we aren't entirely doing this in a traditional way to begin with."

"Of course," she said. "I just thought... well, Svetya's already waiting for you in the surgery, if you'd like to start there, she's been doing okay since she lost the last one, it's been almost six months now, but she has her days... and she's been rather poorly over the last week or so, as it happens. So do go easy on the poor girl. I'll send someone for Lydia while I go round up Isabella Harewood for you. It's this way, up the stairs, third door to your right there off the landing..."

"Her chart...?"

"The latest paperwork is in the surgery, waiting for you."

I didn't know what to expect when I entered the room I had been directed to and carefully, quietly, closed the door behind me. The girl who sat in a char by the window didn't turn to look at me as I came in, keeping her head turned to stare out through the rain-blurred glass. She looked... frayed, fragile, almost transparent, as though somebody had been rubbing at a piece of dark silk until it was almost worn through and only a few strands remained intact enough so that you could still say the cloth did not (yet) have a hole. I knew how old she was, from Mal, but she looked older, with a few strands of silver threading through the hair at her temples.

"Svetya?" I tried, using Mal's name for her, although it sat odd in my mouth.

But she did not respond.

I took a folder which had been left on the desk and flipped through it... and then, casting a swift guarded look at the door, slipped out my phone and took photos of a couple of pages.

It was not a complete record. It only covered the past year, for a start. But I knew I was looking at something that might have been a continuation of my own story, at a woman who had been used as a vessel for the possible genetic programming of new Were generations.

There was more here to find out. Far more. Mal was not going to like any of this. And as far as I was concerned... now it was personal.

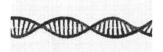

I t was a trivial matter to set up a forward from the email that I had been given to send the results to, and they arrived – in the conspirators' inbox, as well as my own – three days after they came out of their December Turn.

And they were not good.

Something had gone wrong, but it had not even gone wrong in predictable and quantifiable way. One of their test subjects was dead. The other had showed absolutely no response to the 'vaccine' at all.

I knew that was going to hit hard, back at the compound, with Mal and his posse. But I'd been digging deeper into the files – Celia's, and other girls just like her – and things were coming into an even more unpleasant focus there. I didn't want to add to Mal's load, but I couldn't exactly keep something like this to myself. So, late one night, after the devastating news broke about the test results, I called him on the safe phone I had given him, with the other bad news.

It was hard, knowing exactly what to say.

"There's something... you probably need to know," I began. Very carefully. Too carefully.

I could hear his voice tense on the other end of the line.

"What is it?"

"I finally got hold of your sister's records from the House. And before. All of the records."

"You found something....?"

I hesitated. "Not good," I said.

"You're starting to freak me out," he said sharply. "Spit it out."

There was no easy way into this. "She's been pregnant. While there in the Turning House."

"*Pregnant*?" Mal echoed incredulously.

"At least twice. There's at least one clear record of a pretty bad miscarriage. There had been... complications. There are hints of others, but nothing detailed. Still looking into that. The final pregnancy..."

"The *final* one? How many...? Do I even want to know...?" I could hear him breathing, unevenly, raggedly. "What happened," he said at last, through clenched teeth, his voice barely making it clearly into the phone, "with the... final... one...?"

"That's just it. I don't know. There's a record of a live birth. That's all I can find in the file. I know the date of birth, and I know that it was a girl. No name. No indication of what became of the baby, afterwards."

"Who was the father?"

"No name on record," I said grimly. "Not in the file I've managed to get hold of, anyway. I'll keep digging. But I thought… you should know."

There wasn't anything I could do, other than keep investigating, because it was all up to the three of them up in the labs… and it was all taking time. Inevitably. What they were trying to do would not have been easy technically, and they were already fighting with the ethical issues, too. It was Mal's game, Mal's call, but the old year slipped away into the new and then the January Turn came and went, and still there was no word from the compound. I was willing to help and do all the ground pounding outside in the real world – but he needed to tell me what was happening before I could do anything specific, and so I, too, waited in limbo until he could come up with a plan for Celia's rescue that he thought might work. And I knew that all the impatience and frustration that I might have felt, waiting for things to fall in line, was still trivial in comparison to what Mal himself must have been staggering under.

He finally phoned me one night, some two weeks after the January Turn.

"Out of time, I think," he said, grimly. "Asia's being bullied for a report on what she's been working on, and it's all going to come out in the wash eventually. Maybe sooner than we would like to think. Any further news on your end?"

"I haven't been able to find out that much more," I said.

"I may need to get Celia out of there," Mal said. "Quickly. With very little notice. I have to figure out…"

"Leave that part of it to me," I said. "Give me a time frame, and then leave it to me."

"You can't do it alone – all the security – and there's that chip in her leg – and you can't let yourself be seen or recognized…"

I smiled. "Remember who you're talking to," I said. "They won't recognize me. They can't. Even if they remember me perfectly and describe me in detail, after, the person who goes to get Celia out will never have existed. I'll figure on setting something up for next Turn, then. That's the best time – everything is in chaos at the Turning Houses at those times, and a lot of things might be allowed to slide if I time it right. I'll take her up to the woods. You know, the cabin. Nell's uncle's cabin. How far are you with the cure?"

"They are telling me they're close," Mal said helplessly. "They've got to work on it on the quiet, in between, shuffled under more legit stuff they're doing in the lab… and that's far from ideal. But if it's to be done at all it has to happen now, I think."

"Will you have something by next Turn?"

"I couldn't tell you," he said. "I hope so."

"And what happens afterwards?" I questioned gently. "Do we have a plan for that?"

"I'd better come up with one of those, too," he said.

"Okay, then," I said. "I'll plan on the February Turn for the removal, unless you tell me otherwise."

"Chalky… don't let her…"

I remembered the lost and silent girl sitting by the window staring out into the rainy November Day, and my fingers closed tight around the phone in my hand.

"I'll take care of her," I said. "Trust me."

"I do," he said.

That was all.

The next time I heard from him, it was practically on the eve of the February Turn, and the call lasted more or less only long enough for him to tell me that we had a go. Wilfred had finally come up with the goods, apparently. He couldn't help but ask about my plans with Celia and the Turning House, but I told him that the less he actually knew about that the better, and he could see the wisdom in that. But my reasons weren't entirely altruistic. I was feeling just a little guilty. Because Jazz had phoned me, not too long before this, and demanded to know what the situation was with everything that was going on and I had unwisely let it slip that things were rather far advanced and that I was planning on the February Turn for a raid on Celia's Turning House. And she had simply said,

"I'm coming with you."

"You've got the wrong end of the stick," I said. "I'm supposed to be breaking one of Mal's sisters *out* of the Turning House, not sneaking the other one inside. He'd throttle me if he knew."

"But it won't be his sister who you'd be taking in," she said. "I'll be Jesse. And you will need help."

"You're supposed to be lying low," I said, "remember? With Peregrine watching you..."

"I don't care," she said, and I could hear the steel in the voice. There was Mal here, all right. This was him when he had made up his mind, and there was no talking to him. "I swear, if you don't take me, I'm coming after you anyway by myself. And that *would* be a potential disaster."

"*God*," I said. "Mal will kill me if anything goes wrong."

"You'd better make sure it doesn't, then," she said, sweet again. "Pick me up when you're ready to go. I mean it, Chalky." She had taken to calling me by the same nickname as her brother. "If you don't turn up to get me, I'm coming alone."

If she was going to do something stupid, it was probably better if I could watch out for her. "All right," I said heavily. "But I think it's a lousy idea."

"It isn't," she said. "She's my sister, too. I have a right."

I couldn't argue with that. I didn't have to *like* it, but I couldn't argue with it.

My plan was to arrive at the Turning House sometime in the middle of the last Turn day, at the height of the House bracing for the chaos of the resident Turned Were-folk beginning to return to their human forms, trying to deal with finding clothes, food, transport back to their human lives. Those who ran the place would have their hands full. One more set of paperwork might get lost in the crush. Having to factor in the fact of Jazz being Jesse, and not wanting *her* Turning back into her girl-form unexpectedly right there in the middle of the whole affair, made me re-configure things a little bit and it was early on the morning of that third day that I drove up to Jazz's front door.

She – he? It was Jesse, after all – was waiting by the side of the road, accompanied by a very sullen-looking Charlie Ingram, the Marsh family caretaker Vivian Ingram's son. Charlie glared at me, as though this was all my fault. He quite probably thought it was.

"I still think it's crazy," he muttered to Jesse, who looked pained but resigned.

"I'm sorry," Jesse said. "It's something I've got to do."

Charlie turned that malevolent stare back to me. "I should come with you."

"You couldn't really help," I said. "All you would be doing is making sure that there is an identity they can actually nail, if they start chasing this up. Remember, neither of us is wearing our own faces for this, really."

"If Mal..."

"Mal knows nothing about this," Jesse said. "And anyway, he's got nothing to say about it. My choice. I'll be fine, Charlie. We have to go now. Really."

Charlie grabbed at Jesse's hand. "Be careful," he said. "Promise me."

"*I* promise you," I said. "Okay? Hop in, J. We have to get going."

Jesse shook off Charlie's hand, gave him a wan half-smile, and climbed into the passenger seat of the van I had procured for the occasion. We left Charlie standing at the front door of the house, looking bereft.

"There's a uniform in the back," I said. "It might be tight quarters, but you can change in the back there. I hope the size is okay. I had to kind of guess at that. And then, when we get there, all I want to hear from you is yes sir or no sir. *I* do all the talking. If you can't promise me that I swear I'll leave you at the nearest gas station. Clear?"

"Yes, sir," Jesse said.

I stole a look at my passenger. I could only see a profile, but from what I could observe there was an expression of such fierce determination on that face that I sighed and clicked my tongue.

"One more thing," I said. "Please stop looking like you're about to give battle. One look at an expression like that, and the paper pushers get belligerent. You have to keep your eyes down, be calm, be polite. Can you manage this?"

"Stop it," Jesse said, turning to look at me. "You're trying to rattle me into slinking off with my tail between my legs. It won't work. I'll do what it takes. I am not afraid."

I sighed. "Fine. Go get ready."

The uniform fit reasonably well, and somehow it gave the boy who was wearing it more of a look of a young man – it made Jesse look instantly older, somehow. And with the uniform he had also put on a cloak of an almost preternatural calm. I stared at this changed creature for a moment and decided that one could grow afraid of Jesse Marsh, if this was something he could do with such apparent ease.

In some way it made him more of a comrade. I could respect this courage and this spirit.

We drove the rest of the way in silence. I could see the lanky body beside me tense as we approached the gates of the Turning House, hands spasming on the knees – but when I stole a swift glance up the face was unaffected, alert but relaxed, observant eyes taking everything in but without staring.

I had done my homework well. Our entry codes worked; inside the perimeter, as we drove up to the main house, things were already starting to take on a chaotic air. From somewhere at the back of the house, a number of different dogs were yapping, barking, and howling pitifully; in a field off to the side, we could see a couple of horses racing frantically round and round in circles while a lone person tried to herd them through a gate into a more confined area. We were met at the door by a harried administrator who glanced at the provenance of our paperwork (which was really very good, and only a more in-depth investigation would reveal that it didn't in effect come from one of the known Lycan labs) and waved us inside with vague directions as to where our target would be found. Not being a Turning Were, Celia was of secondary importance right now, which was exactly what I had been counting on.

Screeches reached us from somewhere, and something that sounded rather too much like a human scream.

"Birds," I said to Jesse, whose eyes were starting to roll like those of a startled horse. "Parrots, maybe. Possibly a peacock. Keep it together. This way."

He followed me without a word.

The door to Celia's room was locked, but from the outside, and the key hung from the top of the doorframe and down the side of the door attached to an elastic cord. I retrieved it and unlocked the door; inside, Celia and another girl, her roommate, sat on their beds, quietly, without talking. There was a tray with an unfinished meal sitting on a desk in a corner. The beds were neatly made. The room was empty of any personalizing information; even the prints on the wall were meaningless generic thrift-store landscapes. The roommate was in a nightgown, with just a light dressing gown on top of that. Celia, thankfully, was dressed –in a set of dark sweats, and a pair of worn flats on her bare feet.

Jesse stood in the doorway, staring.

"Not *now*," I said with a flash of annoyance. "Help me."

I helped Celia to her feet, murmuring encouragement into her ear; she obeyed my instructions without a word, without the least resistance, passively following where she was led. I heard a strangled sort of noise on the other side of her, where Jesse was helping support Celia with a cupped hand to her elbow, and looked up, catching Jesse's eye as our eyes met over the back of Celia's bowed head.

"I know," Jesse whispered. "I'm sorry. I'll be fine."

"Come on," I said gently to Celia, maneuvering her towards the door.

Outside, in the corridor, I hesitated, and then, with a heavy heart, locked the door again. I knew *this* story, not the roommate's – it wasn't my place to leave the door open and let her wander free throughout the chaos-ridden house right now. She was probably safer where she was. The three of us, Jesse and I supporting a shuffling Celia between us, made our slow and careful way back down the corridor, and across the main hall. I could still see Jesse flinch at every whimper, howl, or animal scream. There were faint echoes of those coming from the back, all the time, and it was impossible to shut them out.

"It's a nightmare," Jesse whispered.

"Quiet," I said.

I was not immune to the creeps, to the feeling of an oppressive weight of something, of eyes on my back. This place had that sort of effect, at the best of times, and these were not the best of times. This was a teetering on the edge of complete bedlam. I could see it, hear it, feel it, and I was all too vividly aware that I was walking a tightrope bridge across it and that I could fall in at any moment.

And indeed, a moment came, with a voice behind us calling for us to halt. I saw Jesse's eyes flash, but I quelled him with a look and brought our shuffling little trio to a complete stop.

"What do you think you are doing?" the voice that had hailed us demanded from my rear, closely followed by the person who owned it stepping around to the left of me until he stood squarely in our way. A different guy from the one who had waved us in.

"Transfer to a different facility," I said.

"Now? Unlikely," he said sharply.

"I have the paperwork."

"Show me."

I sighed. "Hang on. Here, can you take the weight of her…" I turned, ostensibly to transfer Celia more to Jesse, but also so as to block his view with my shoulder and back. "I'll stall him," I hissed. "When I let go, start moving – to the door, out to the van. Clear? Get her into the van."

Jesse nodded, his eyes very bright.

I turned back to the official. "Just a moment. Here, in my pocket…"

"Where do you think you're going?" he snapped, flinging out a hand to stop Jesse and Celia from moving forward. I looked up.

"Would you at least let him get her to some place where he won't let her collapse on the floor?" I said testily. "That one is dead weight, it took two of us to handle her, but now you want papers and there's only him – would you just get out of the way, please? He can't carry her by himself. Here, here's your paperwork."

I distracted him, and he turned back to accept the papers I handed him; I nodded at Jesse, very slightly. His lips tightened, he shifted his grip around Celia's waist, and kept her moving, dragging her feet forward towards the door.

I leaned into the official, hovering over his shoulder, blocking his view of said door.

"There," I said, pointing. "I have two copies of this authorization. The third should have been on record with your office a week ago."

"I don't remember it," he said doggedly, scanning the papers.

"Do you check every single thing that comes down the transom?" I asked impatiently, risking a quick glance over my shoulder. They were almost out. "It might have been someone else who signed off. On a different shift even."

"I should double check..." he began, and I sighed.

"You may," I said, "but the person who signed that document is currently Turned and unavailable for comment. And I have my orders, and my schedule – I can't be coming back here again in two days' time so that you can feel happy about it. She's being transferred – there's the paperwork – if you go back to your office you'll probably find the trail right now – but I have four hours to drive to get her to where she's supposed to go, and honestly, I don't have the time to wait for the Turn to be over before you're happy."

So much for telling young Jesse to be self-effacing, and keep one's eyes politely down. I was being practically belligerent. I was actually on the point of running through Plans B through Omega, ramming my way through the gates with the van and running for all our lives, when the officious fool finally looked up, himself distracted by the noises from the rear of the house, and thrust the papers impatiently back into my hands.

"It looks in order," he barked. "I *will* be confirming things tomorrow."

"Please do," I said. "In the meantime, can I take my transfer and be on my way now?"

"Get out of here," he said.

"Gladly," I said, with feeling, the first word of truth I'd uttered, and walked briskly away from him.

Jesse had managed to drag Celia into the back of the van, and had buckled her into a seat. I slammed the van door closed behind me, and pulled a duffle bag from underneath the seat in front of Celia.

"Couldn't quite get the last bit of the puzzle," I said, "because I would have had to have had someone real provide the deactivation code for the chip. But we can deal with the chip itself later, and for the short term... it's just going to have to be a rather more sledgehammer kind of deactivation." I pulled a sturdy metal anklet out of the bag, and tossed it to Jesse. "Get that around her ankle. Right there, where the chip is."

"Where's that?" Jesse asked, pulling up the sweats and examining Celia's ankles in a jerky, panicked way.

"There'll be a small scar, right over where they inserted it," I said. "You're here, so it's your job. Find it. Make sure the anklet is on over the right spot before we reach the gates. It's a magnet, it'll screw up the electronics. I'd better drive, before they change their mind. Do it."

He didn't answer. I glanced into the rear-view mirror but all I could see was the curve of his back as he worked, bent over Celia, and her own calm, distant, unfocused eyes, staring somewhere into the future.

I turned the key in the ignition and put the van in gear.

"Here goes," I said. "Last chance."

I fought the impulse to lay my foot flat on the gas pedal and drive out of there like a bat out of hell – but I drove at a respectable speed all the way to the gates, slowing down just before I hit the exit to steal another glance into the back of the van. I met Jesse's wide eyes, where he sat next to Celia, holding one of her hands tightly in his own.

"Best I know how," he said, "it's done."

"Soon find out," I muttered, gripped the steering wheel a little more tightly, and... passed through the gates. No alarms went off. Nothing clanged shut before us. Ahead of us lay the open road, and freedom.

I had not realized that I was holding my breath until I released it, driving forward, focused on that road. I would not believe this until we were away, well away...

But we were. We were clear.

The fences were behind us.

"Okay," I said. "That's the first hurdle down. Let's get her to safety, so I can deal with that chip once and for all."

I was tempted to just stop by the side of the road and hack that thing out of Celia's leg as soon as we got out of sight of the Turning House – but I really didn't think it would be that great an idea to have her leaving forensic evidence inside the van which I intended to ditch as soon as I could. I had a car I'd left parked at an inconspicuous strip mall parking lot in front of a busy grocery store where there was a lot of coming and going, and we drove straight there. I stopped the van next to the car long enough to transfer Celia into the other vehicle and then I drove the van around the perimeter of the parking lot, leaving it in a corner outside the liquor shop and the Laundromat, and trotted back to the car. Celia and Jesse were waiting, undetected, and I slipped behind the wheel and drove on, straight up the mountain, up to the cabin. It was in the cabin's kitchen that I finally sliced open Celia's ankle with a sterile knife, and extracted the tiny tracking chip that had been buried just under the skin. I'd got some kind of a special Band-Aid at the store, which claimed to have properties of holding together the edges of a cut, and I slapped that on, together with a cushion of gauze and some bandage tape; I told Jesse to keep Celia's foot elevated, and I went outside and smashed the chip into the gravel driveway with the heel of my boot, several times for good measure, before throwing its mangled remnants as far away into the lake as I could.

And then I held out my hand in front of me, as though it belonged to someone quite other than myself, and watched it begin to shake uncontrollably as the reaction hit me.

I might never really understand just what any of this truly meant to the family bound by blood – to Mal, to Jazz, to Celia herself. In some ways they were the triggers that pulled one another into the whole thing, their lifelines tangled together, whatever affected one was bound to affect them all – Mal wasn't here yet but I knew already how deep the reaction would go when he arrived, and I had already seen how hard Jazz had had to work, back at the Turning House, not to go to pieces at the wrong moment and scuttle the entire operation.

I hadn't been obliged to do anything. It had all been a choice, every step I had taken – until now. From here on I had left choice behind me – I had, by this action, broken both rules and laws, and I was outside both.

For Mal's sake, for Jazz's, for Celia's... and only then, apparently as an appendix to that whole oath of allegiance, on my own behalf. Because Celia's presence in that cottage behind me, the smashed tracking chip that was even now resting at the bottom of the lake, all meant that I had declared war on them all – Lycans, accepted political hierarchies both Were and normals, and outlying crazies who had only been waiting for an excuse to launch a crusade.

A cold wind blew off the water, lifting the ends of my hair, making me wrap my arms around myself and shiver. A reminder that I had consciously and deliberately stepped out of shelter, and now stood alone on the windswept battlefield.

A creak behind me as the cottage door opened brought me back to myself, with a jolt.

There were still things to do. We'd all need to eat something; I had to make Celia as comfortable as possible; Jesse still had to Turn back to Jazz at some point and we had to make provision for that.

And then... there was nothing to do but wait for Mal.

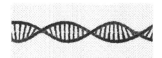

They arrived the next day, Mal and Asia. It was Jazz (she was back by then) who heard the car, and she flung the cottage door open and ran out to meet them before I could have a chance to make her consider her entrance, particularly since her face was still streaked with tears.

"Jazz...?" Mal said, staring. "What are *you* doing here?" And then, as he noticed her tear-smeared cheeks, more sharply, "Is everything all right...? Is... did Chalky..."

"We got her," Jazz said. "She's here. She's inside. She doesn't know me – she has no idea who I am – but she doesn't seem to be upset – she doesn't even seem to realize that we took her or that she's not there anymore – in that place – that horrible place – oh, *Mal*. She is so broken..."

"How do you know about the Turning..." and then he stopped, sucked in his breath. "Wait. He took *you*? Chalky took *you*?"

"*Jesse*," she said. "He took Jesse. And technically... 'he' didn't take me... it's disconcerting... he's a little scary, Mal."

She had dropped her voice, but I was just close enough to hear that.

Mal chose to ignore this particular point. He couldn't think about that now, about the fact that Jazz had now seen me do my shifter thing too. If they had sucked me in, this family, that worked both ways – now they were *all* directly connected to me. Which wasn't altogether a good thing, probably. But at this moment, all Mal could think of was that Celia was inside.

"Where is she?" he asked. "Show me."

Jazz backed into the cottage, gesturing for the other two to follow. I withdrew from the window from which I'd been watching this encounter, across the room, leaving them some space – I saw Mal step into the cottage and then freeze as his eyes fell on Celia. She was sitting in front of the woodstove, exactly where she had been left, wrapped in a blanket, her hands wrapped around a mug of tea which she didn't seem to realize she had been supposed to drink. His sister. His sister, whom he had thought gone. Who had been in every waking thought he had had ever since he had found out that she had not been lost after all. I could see him try to speak, and fail, and swallow hard, and then a word, a single word, a name, the name of the little girl who she had once been.

"*Svetya...*"

My own breath caught a little as she turned her head, just a little, at the sound of her name – and her eyes came to rest, slowly, on Mal's face. And then – maybe for the first time since I had brought her here – for the first time since I had laid eyes on her – I saw the corners of her mouth lift, just a little. In just the barest ghost of the beginnings of a smile.

Mal's hand had been clutching Asia's, but now he loosed his hold and was across the room in two long strides, falling to his knees next to Celia's chair and wrapping both his arms around her, his head buried on her shoulder as his own shoulders shook with sobs he couldn't hold back any longer. One of her hands left the mug she had been holding, precariously, and fluttered uncertainly upwards until it found Mal's own, and then rested there, very lightly.

And then he glanced down and saw the bandage around Celia's ankle, and his head came up sharply.

"The chip," Asia said, faintly.

"I had to get it out," I said. "I knocked it out of commission when we took her but it had to come out – we knew exactly where it was, under the scar – there will be a bigger scar there now, sorry, couldn't be helped. A skilled surgeon, I am not. I got rid of it."

For the first time, Mal took stock of the somewhat larger picture.

"Jazz," he said, directly to me. "You took Jazz in there. It could have gone wrong, and you..."

"It went fine," I said, which was only a little white lie. "And anyway, she insisted. She threatened to come anyway if I didn't take her. I figured it would be better if I was around."

"She didn't even know..."

"I found out," Jazz said. "Of course I found out. And I couldn't have stayed sitting at home twiddling my thumbs."

I saw the moment when it hit him.

"If anything had happened to you..." he managed, and we all

understood the rest of that sentence, the guilt that infused it. If anything *had* gone wrong, and Jazz had paid the price for failure, that would have been *two* sisters for whose fate he would have been responsible.

And I saw it in his eyes. That he was afraid. That the road ahead was shrouded in fog and darkness now.

It was Asia who asked about the details of the operation, and I gave them the bones of it. "And that's pretty much all of it," I concluded, having told it all. "We got here, I got rid of the chip, and she's... been pretty much like you see her now, ever since. She's slept a little. She'll eat if you put food in front of her, and she drinks, sometimes, if you put a cup in her hand and she doesn't forget about it, but she's barely said half a dozen words – just this sweet and gentle shell of a girl, and an emptiness inside..."

"She doesn't know me at all," Jazz said, her voice catching. "There's nothing when she looks at me..."

"You were a child when she last saw you," Mal said. "And this time, when she first saw you, you weren't even wearing your own *current* face. She can hardly be expected to remember..."

Celia's lips parted at this moment, and she whispered a name. *His* name, his own original boyhood name, the name she had known him by when he had been born, when they had been children together. She remembered *him*.

I saw Mal's hand tighten convulsively on her shoulder.

"I think she remembers... older memories," I said carefully. "It's... probably just as well that she doesn't really remember any of these Turning House years. They wouldn't have been pleasant memories." I hadn't told Jazz everything, not the whole story, not about what might have been happening to Celia in the Turning House, and I gave Mal the tiniest shake of my head as he turned to look at me, warning him. He seemed to understand, but the moment of silence stretched, deepened, became brittle and difficult.

Asia broke the stasis by reaching out and putting the cooler she had been clutching in both hands onto the table beside her. I looked at it, and then back at her face.

"Is that what I think it is?"

"It's our last chance at it, I think," Asia said soberly.

"You think it will work?"

"I hope so," Asia said, after a brief but eloquent hesitation.

This much, Jazz knew. What this meant. What was supposed to happen next. But she surprised me by looking up with burning eyes, taking a couple of small steps towards Asia and the cooler.

"Let me do it," she said. "Let me give it to her. Please."

Mal turned to me. "You told her?"

"Enough of it," I said. "Mal, there had to be a reason you wanted Celia out."

Asia was looking at him with a question in her eyes, and I could see Mal grimace as the demons fought inside him – Jazz was so young, still a child

– but he too had been a child, back in that instant that he had handed Celia the pills that had brought her here. Perhaps he thought it would be a fitting bookend if Jazz, only a handful of years older now than he had been then, should be the one to bring her back… if that was in the cards. Asia took it as consent, in the end, and fumbled with the catch on the cooler lid, extracting a syringe from within, a plastic safety cap over the needle. Jazz reached for it, and Asia, seemingly reluctantly, gave up.

"Show me what to do," Jazz said.

"Best in the upper arm, Slip off the sleeve. Swipe it down with an alcohol wipe first, where you're going to inject…"

She took off the protective cap, and the needle glittered in the amber-colored light in the room. Mal took the cup from Celia's hand and put it away; she offered no resistance or response to any of it, to being handled, to the sight of the needle. Asia still looked unconvinced, glancing from the needle to the child who waited to administer the injection and then back again, hesitating.

Mal and I both knew at the same instant, I think, that she could not do it. Just before Jazz herself recoiled from Celia's blank and empty stare, and sobbing quietly into her hands as she turned away, like the child that she so very much still was.

"I can't," she whispered. "I can't. I can't, she doesn't even know me, she doesn't want me to…"

Asia, who was closest, gathered up Jazz into her side.

"It's okay. Just let me…"

And then I saw Mal reach out and close his hand gently around Asia wrist, the hand that held the syringe.

"No," he said. "Not you. *You've already given too much*. I landed us all here. This is my penance. If anyone then me…"

"Are you sure about this?" Asia whispered, over the top of Jazz's head.

"It can't all have been for nothing," Mal said desperately. "We can't have sacrificed it all for nothing."

She held on to the syringe for a moment, and searched his face with her eyes, and then surrendered it into his hand, folding both of her arms around Jazz, who could not seem to stop crying. And Mal held the syringe in his right hand, and turned to look at Celia.

I saw the memories flood him, and shake him. I knew that he wasn't seeing what was there, he was seeing all that had been lost… and all that might potentially still be lost, from this moment on. It was all of it, the weight of all of it, all of the shadows that had been laid on these lives by the choices that had been made when they had all been way too young to choose. I saw his hand begin to tremble as he fought it all, as he came down on one knee beside Celia's chair – and then I saw one of her own pale limp hands reach for him, whispering something I couldn't make out. And I heard him utter a sound like I had never heard from another human being, the moan of a wounded animal.

The moan died into an agonized whisper, as he found words, as he tried to find words.

"What if... this doesn't work... what if it kills... I can't do this... I can't do it *again*, I can't kill her twice... Ash... Ash... are you sure – are you sure this is going to work – are you *sure*..."

And just like that, it was my war, after all. There were stark choices here, standing at the crossroads, and I knew that if I let Mal take one step along the wrong road I would lose him for good. We all would. It was a step too far into that darkness in whose shadows he had already spent far too long. If this did fail, he would not come back from it, not ever. There were some things that no human being should be expected to bear.

There was a chance that it would work, and that too might crack him wide open, raw to the light... and I suddenly knew that there was a very real possibility that by coming so close to it, despite everything that we were to one another, despite everything that I had done to help bring this about, I could lose him anyway – because he might associate me with Celia now, and whatever happened he might not be able to get past that.

But if I was to lose the one person whom I might ever have claimed as my own family, I would rather lose him to that light, than to the darkness.

No, he couldn't do it. *None* of them could. This was Celia. There was too much between them.

I crossed the room, laid a gentle hand on his shoulder.

"Enough," I said softly, into Mal's ear. "You are all too close. Give me that thing."

"But you..."

"Give it to me," I said, taking it from his fingers. "If you want to help, just stay there, hold her hand. You seem to be the only one she knows, and she is happier for having you close to her."

He crumpled to both his knees beside his sister, and folded one of her hands between his own. She flinched, a little, when the needle went in, and I saw Mal flinch with her, but then it was over. And I stepped away.

"Done," I said quietly. "Pull her sleeve back up, now. So. What happens next?"

I addressed that last to Asia, who was still cradling Jazz in her arms, and she looked up at me, her face blank. "Next?" she echoed. "Well, where Celia is concerned... now it's a waiting game, until the next Turn. And when that comes... the Turn is either triggered again, or it is not... and if it doesn't... I don't know that there's anything I know of that's left to try. There's a second syringe in here, already prepped – Wilfred thought it might help, as a booster, maybe a week before the Turn is due, to kick-start the new DNA into action. But I don't even know if that matters. It might help. It won't hurt, but if this doesn't work a second dose won't change the outcome. From here on it's on her. It's *in* her. In her body. In her cells. In every strand of her DNA. Mal, we've done everything we can do. There's nowhere else to go from here."

"I have to think," Mal murmured. "I have to figure out... to keep her safe..."

I wrapped my hands around his elbow and levered him to his feet.

"I think you've got plenty of other things to think about," I said. "Your absence has no doubt been noted by now, back at the compound, and even now, as we speak, they're probably going over your recent activities with rather a fine-toothed comb. Are you going back? How do you intend to go back? What are you going to do – what is going to happen to you – if you do go back? There have been lone wolves before, it's in the histories, but they don't tend to live long or pleasant lives – and that's a choice you have to think about now, for your own family. Leave Celia with me. I will find her a safe bolthole, and I'll watch over her, until that next Turn. I know how to cover my own tracks, but that fake paperwork I used to spring Celia won't stand scrutiny forever. They can't trace that back to me. But you guys – *this* stuff – " I gestured at the cooler on the table.

"This is traceable. You couldn't do this in a vacuum. And the wolves will know. They probably know already. They're probably waiting to call you to account, right now."

"It'll be the full Tribunal, this time," Asia said faintly. It's – we'll be facing the whole Pack, a kind of Lycan Judgment Day. It isn't often invoked – but when it is, it carries considerable weight."

"What can they do?" Mal asked.

She looked at him, levelly.

"Anything they want," she said. One of her hands left Jazz, and curled protectively in front of her belly.

Mal hesitated, weighing his words. "Do we have to return?"

"We can't stay on the run forever. And they'll find us. Eventually. One way or another."

Mal squared his jaw. "I suppose we'd better go back and face the music."

But still, he hesitated, looking down at Celia, and then over at Jazz.

"Leave it with me, then," I said. "Leave them with me. I'll take the kid sister home and then Celia and I will hole up somewhere until the next Turn comes. I'll find a way to let you know. And... about... the other matter." I retrieved a sealed envelope from the edge of the counter, with Mal's name on it. "This is all I know, so far. I still have feelers out. Keep it close; I wouldn't let the Lycans know how much you know."

"About this?" he asked weighing the envelope.

"About anything, really," I said. "They can do their own homework. I'm not about to do it for them."

"Are you going to be all right?" Asia asked me unexpectedly.

It was odd, that understanding had come from *her*. I barely knew her, really. But she had worked it out, that thing that had taken me by the throat and shaken me out there by the lake. She knew. She knew what this all meant to me, for me.

She was Lycan. She understood.

"I know how to keep swimming," I said. "So long as I know where the sharks are. I'll be fine."

"And Celia? Can you really handle..."

"It's going to be one of two things," I said. "It's all or nothing. Either way, I'll have it covered. But what do you want me to do if she does Turn?

Do you want your parents to know? And what happens, next, if it works, if she *does* Turn? I can take it on, Mal, but I'm not a long-term solution. I..." I dropped my gaze for a second, because Jazz had looked up, and I didn't want to sound apocalyptic. "I may need to be able to move... or disappear... at any moment, and it would be next to impossible to do that with someone like Celia in tow..."

"Can you ever bring her... home?" Jazz asked.

"That depends. Can you parents handle this? And if she does go home – oh, this could get really complicated really fast. If the Were authority got wind of the situation... We may have to end up creating an entirely new identity for her. If you did your magic right and it all works perfectly... she goes back to being a Random, with all the potential difficulties of that situation."

Asia gave a small dry laugh. "Shall we just wait and find out if it worked at all?" she asked.

"Fine. We can wait that long. Leave the girls with me, and you two get out of here. Let me know how the Tribunal pans out. You have my number."

There was something incredibly fragile about Mal in this instant, as though he was steeling himself to turn into the teeth of a hurricane, and I reached out a steadying hand, gripping his shoulder, making him turn to look at me.

"Mal," I said quietly, "there may come a time when you can find a way to be everything you think you need to be, to all the people you think you need to be those things for – but right now... take it one thing at a time. There isn't enough of you to go around, not for all of this." His eyes slid past mine, back to Celia, and oh, I knew, she was still in the center of his thoughts. "Trust me," I said. "I will make sure she is safe. That they are both safe."

He met my eyes again, held them for a long instant, and then let his long lashes fall down over them as he turned away, with just the briefest of nods. He held out his hand, and Asia took it; Jazz gripped the other, for a moment, and then let go of both of them. They walked out like that, hand in hand, and I knew exactly how much it took for him not to turn and look back. And then the door closed behind them. A moment later we heard the car start up, and then gravel crunch under wheels as they drove away.

"Well," I said, looking from Jazz to Celia and then back again, "and so it begins, then. Let's clean up and get going. I have a promise I need to keep."

Intermission II:
The Evidence Locker
(Take Two)

1. *VOX VERAE HOMINIS MOVEMENT*

Amar Petrossian, the founder of the *Vox Verae Homins* ("Voice of True Men") movement, was the second son of an immigrant family from Armenia who abandoned their home country because of reasons which are ambiguous. A chain of linked tragic and violent deaths in the immediate family may have been a trigger, but the details of this remain unclear. What is clear, however, is that the young Amar appears to have conceived an early fear and loathing for what he called the 'metamorph', the demographic we know as Were-kind, and in his early writings he implies that it is the 'metamorph' factor that was instrumental in the family tragedy. In his teens, while still at school, Amar gravitated to clubs and societies which held deep conservative views, and very quickly refined his choice of associations to those which were outspoken anti-Were activists. But none of these clubs appeared to have gone far enough for his needs, and what might have begun as a strongly held political position quickly grew beyond those boundaries and into more of a religiously driven creed.

It was while he was still in his twenties, that Amar Petrossian penned the short but intense book which quickly became the kernel of the brand new movement, which became known as the *Vox Verae Hominis*, of which Petrossian himself was the founder and then the leader who styled himself the First Voice. Members of VVH were outspoken in their passionately held beliefs that the Were-kind had been (by definition) created as inferior to the True Men (the non-Were majority of the population) and campaigned against any laws that might have protected or supported the Were minority. After they were censored by public opinion when some of their published writings and speeches crossed the line into what some considered outright hate-speech, the VVH movement, while losing nothing of its vehemence, took a step back and began to work more insidiously from within the system. They are not a secret society, and their existence (as well as their membership rolls, and the names of high-ranking 'clergy' and officials within the organization) has been a matter of open record. They are proud of the fact that they are not, and have never been, in hiding – and it is their continued contention that their views, as described in lyrical but trenchant language in Amar Petrossian's *Scripture*, are a truth that will eventually come to be accepted by all "True Men" and will lead to the eradication of Were-kind from the human demographic.

Source: World Encyclopedia, 25th Digital Edition

1.2 – *Vox Verae Hominis* Credo

"Beware the metamorph! For how can a creature be made in the likeness of the God that it worships when the creature itself is constant flux and change? How can there be a whole soul in a mind and body and spirit so fragmented and broken?

You may well ask, but then, are they here to work against us, have they been sent from the darkness to tempt and pollute and trap us with lies, to lure us from the true path, from speaking with the voice of True Men? That may be so, but one who looks with his eyes open and who sees the truth is in little danger of being misled by them.

All are created, that is for certain – but it is an obvious truth for any True Man to see that these are creatures that have been created lesser than him, these are creatures tainted with the touch of the animal, creatures who can possess no pure human soul because they themselves are not human.

They are beneath us, they have been put onto this world to be our servants and our thralls, to do as they are commanded – any of them who may believe that they have any grounds to be considered a True Man's equal are deluded at best, and dangerously presumptuous at worst.

The courts may maintain that they are like unto us and should be treated no differently – but why then do even the courts require them to carry with them at all times a card of identification by which we may know them? Why require them to hide themselves decently away while they bark and honk and whinney and grunt for three days of every month of their wretched existence?

They may say that the law is on their side – but they are speaking of human law, written and created and administered by human hand, and it is a transitory law, subject to whim and change as it always has been.

The greater Law is the Law which God has put into place for his creation, and that is the Law that states that a human and one who is of Were kind are not, cannot be, cannot ever be, equal to one another – and that it is the right – no, the duty – of the greater of God's own creation to make absolutely certain that this is completely understood. By any means that prove necessary.

It is best if words can suffice, if they can be made to listen and to hear and to understand and to accept the truth of this Law. But if other means are necessary, stronger means, then let it be done. It is the voice of True Men that needs to be heard, to prevail, and it cannot be a sin, then, to obtain the silence in which God's Word triumphs in whatever way you can.

Be True Men. Speak, be heard, be listened to. And know that you hurt nothing dear to God by asserting your right to speak his word in the world, to raise your voice above the clamor of half-men and half-animals, whose domain is short-lived and only of this suffering world, for they will not, can never, follow you into the promise of God's own Heaven to come."

The Scripture of *Vox Verae Hominis*, Amar Petrossian (founder)

2. GENETIC RECONSTRUCTION PROJECT 2235548XB

After a hiatus of almost seven years, the Genetic Reconstruction Project has been revived in several Lycan-run genetics labs. The previous incarnation of this project has met with a limited amount of success but was mismanaged and a lot of the data (including the actual subjects of the first-generation progeny of scientifically controlled genetic recombination between different individual Were subjects) has been lost or is not accessible/available. The new project focuses more on the aspect of controlling longevity and prolonging Were (in general) and Lycan (in particular) life spans, and discovering what determines the low life expectancy of Were-kind and how it can be ameliorated. It will also focus more specifically on the problem of declining numbers of the Lycan clan, investigating methods of increasing our population and the viability of the Lycan genetic bloodlines.

To this extent, many of the genetic matches that have been approved for investigation involve a direct Lycan link. Some lines of inquiry have been kept in-house, involving only Lycan subjects; a limited number of tests along the lines of the original project, mating Lycan individuals to other Were-kind genetic lines and investigating the potential offspring produced through these genetic recombinations; and an experimental line of inquiry involving the introduction of Lycan DNA to individuals incarcerated in Turning Houses, of whatever Were species, who had (for various reasons) lost their own ability to Turn. Several unexpected results have been recorded.

Transcripts, Lycan Council
Source: confidential informant, leaked from classified files in Lycan Council Archives

2.1 PARTIAL REPORT FROM GENETIC RECONSTRUCTION PROJECT 2235548XB

Subject 1
Mother: Turning House inmate, lost own ability to Turn due to overdose of Adaptadyne when quite young, original animal form: cat
Father: Full Lycan, Second Southwestern Pack

Pregnancy: difficult, but carried to term
Subject: female, genetic mapping carried out but inconclusive. Child is being fostered in Second Southwestern Pack, with the father's family, until such time as natural Turn age approaches. She will be placed in isolation for six months before her fifteenth birthday, and kept under close

observation until first Turn. Further recommendations to be made at that time.

3. QUOTES AND HEADLINES (WITH QUICK SUMMARIES)

"IS THERE A ROGUE SHIFTER ON THE LOOSE?"

Unsubstantiated reports maintain that one or more individuals labelled as "shifters" by the media – individuals whose provenance is still uncertain, but who may be rogue Were or genetically altered Were – are out there, amongst us, and they are capable of frightening things. They are not confined by a timetable (the Turn days all common Were are subject to) or a shape (they can apparently Turn into any form, including *another human shape*). Initial reports have caused a measure of panic amongst the population, with some unfortunate incidents where non-Were individuals have turned violent towards card-carrying members of the Were demographic. At least one innocent Were individual has had to be hospitalized from injuries sustained in such confrontations. Authorities are dealing with the situation in a highly unsatisfactory way, putting out scattered fires rather than trying to find out the point of origin and dealing with the matter at its source. Government officials and high-ranking members of the Were Authority, when approached for comment, confined themselves with pre-packaged statements to the effect of that not enough is known at this time for any member of these bodies to supply a full and detailed account of the situation.

"ARE WE BEING SPIED ON?"

Today the Were Authority has submitted a harshly-worded statement of complaint to the government bodies charged with Were affairs after listening devices and other surveillance equipment were discovered in the Were Authority council meeting premises – a place where sensitive and confidential matters are routinely discussed in the expectation of privacy and in full reliance on the degree of autonomy granted to the Authority to govern the affairs of its own population where they fall within its own jurisdiction. Were observers have notoriously been excluded from similar meetings of the government bodies concerned with Were matters, to the point that the Were Authority was sometimes blindsided by legislation directly affecting them, discussed and agreed upon behind closed doors – to the point that there are rumors of the government employing 'sniffers', individuals who are able to somehow read whether or not an observing member of public is Were or not even without recourse to proper identification, with the intent of removing any such Were observers from a position where they might be able to observe or witness any meetings the government did not wish them to see. The questions being asked is who is entitled to what information, and who might have gone too far in obtaining intelligence through unsanctioned means.

"GOVERNMENT WERE SNIFFERS – ARE THESE THE SHIFTERS SOME GROUPS HAVE BEEN WARNING US ABOUT?"

On the heels of the reports of 'monster' shapeshifters who can walk among us undetected while wearing human faces come the new reports of 'sniffers' employed to discover any lurking Were in places where they are not sanctioned to be. Are these sniffers in fact Were-kind themselves? Are these the monsters that groups like *Vox Verae Hominis* have been warning us about?

"LYCAN LABS THOUGHT TO BE INVOLVED IN SHIFTER DRAMA"

Unconfirmed reports are circulating that the so called 'shifter' does, in fact, exist – and that this individual was created in a series of experiments on genetic engineering performed in certain labs at least some of which have been directly linked with Lycan scientists. The Lycans, of course, have been instrumental to many scientific discoveries instrumental to the Were population, and hold the original patents for drugs such as Adaptadyne. On condition of anonymity one such scientist has confirmed that genetic experimentation with Were genomes has in fact been ongoing, but that the intent had been to study the shortened lifespan of the Were as compared to non-Were humans and that the shifter had emerged as an 'accidental side effect'. The scientist would not offer anything further when pressed as to whether there was only one 'accident' or whether there was more to the story than has so far been revealed. The scientist also intimated that the Lycan scientific community – which has been involved in this kind of genetic research for many years, and has accumulated a vast amount of useful data – would be extremely interested in the opportunity to study the 'shifter' individual more closely with respect to shedding some scientific light on these new developments and how much of a danger they pose to the general public.

"THE RACE IS ON"

They all want him – the *Vox Verae Hominis* society and others like them would see the reputed 'shifter' individual permanently incarcerated or even (from some of the more intemperate statements on record) executed. The Were Authority has a vested interest, if such an individual exists, in placing him in protective custody (and possibly obtaining a source for further study of the phenomenon); the government, faced with the inevitable reaction from the majority of the non-Were human populace, would simply like the individual found and suitably removed from a position where he could be considered a danger. His fate would seem to depend entirely on which group finds him first, and after that there could be a scuffle for custody. The unprecedented situation has the explosive potential of destroying the carefully constructed foundation on which the Were/non-Were interactions have rested for so many years now.

SHIFTER

"It's like falling dominoes," a government official told our reporter, "it all depends on which one falls first, but it is bound to knock others down as it topples. And I have no idea which direction it's all going to go."

Part III:
Shifter

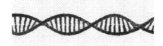

Casa Verona's romantic name bore no real resemblance to the reality of the house which bore it. The house was painted a dingy yellow on the outside, with three tiny windows which looked out directly over the sidewalk. Three steps up from that sidewalk, flanked by ancient wrought-iron rails, the paved path led to an unprepossessing front door with a small sign tacked to the wall beside it bearing the name of the place and proclaiming it to be a 'boarding house'. Underneath this sign there were two hooks on which a second sign, which read 'No Vacancy', sometimes hung – but not very often. The front door gave into a narrow hallway, and two doors led from that.

One was directly to the left as one walked in, and opened into the public rooms of the place (a tiny reception area and office which was usually kept closed up and locked, a sitting room with a TV set in it, a dining room with several small tables which led through into a huge kitchen, and then on through that cluttered vastness into mysterious back areas from which the landlady emerged like a genie when summoned by the buzzer by the door to the office). The other, straight ahead at the end of the hallway, was a double door through which one unexpectedly stepped into a courtyard garden.

One of the walls of the garden, to the right as one stepped into it, was a blind brick casement – the back wall, as it happened, of the gigantic warehouse (now empty for many years) which reared up right next door. One was the inner wall of the public part of the house, with a set of glass French doors that led out into the garden from the sitting room. And at the far end, taking up part of the left-hand wall and the whole of the rear wall of the courtyard, were several rooms occupied by the house's resident boarders.

The accommodation was basic with few frills, but the rent was reasonable and the landlady, Julia Garibaldi, liked to cook and did it well. While meals (other than breakfast) weren't guaranteed, dinners were more often than not available, and the boarders frequently only chipped in towards the grocery bill as their contribution to the household budget. So long as the rent was paid, Julia Garibaldi had no prejudices and asked no questions.

Two long-term residents sharing one of the larger rooms were Laura Stone and Annabel Lawrence, both Were-cats, who wouldn't have known the term 'Free Were' which Luke Barnes had once used to describe himself but who lived by those principles. They Turned into cats quite serenely every month in their room and the enclosed courtyard, and hadn't seen the inside of a Turning House for many years. Laura was happily housebound, and earned a small monthly sum by doing transcriptions for a medical service at home. Annabel should have been retired a century ago, but she didn't feel like quitting her job and nobody was making her do it – so she continued stepping out to the office every morning with her snappy little black cane, to a tiny cubby in the Welfare and Disability Department, where this apparent relic from another age was quite the whiz at computerized records and all sorts of other newfangled technology.

Another resident was Joe Santiago, retired newspaperman, now writing his seventh or eighth unpublished novel. He sometimes sat outside on warm summer days, under the cherry tree that grew in the courtyard, with a straw Panama hat perched on his head and his portable typewriter on a rickety little patio table, happily clacking away at his keyboard, completely absorbed in his work. He didn't like being disturbed but if one judged the moment right and approached with a cold beer just as he was wrapping up, he was an entertaining source of war stories about his journalistic days – and he still had an unnerving amount of connections out there which he was happy to share if he was asked politely.

I kept a room here, in the back, under an assumed name of course, for which I paid Signora Garibaldi a monthly rent and which I visited for a couple of days every so often. In some ways, the rooms-at-the-bottom-of-the-garden reminded me of the lost and vanished Green House, which I still held in fond memory. It was sometimes fun to come here, and let down my guard for just a moment, and eat delicious home-cooked meals. The other residents were always a surprising and entertaining resource. It was also just a fabulous bolt-hole and a convenient safe house where I could be sure of at least a temporary sanctuary if I was ever in need of one. I had learned early the wisdom of having a place to hide if necessary.

It was here I took Celia, after I had seen Mal and Asia on their way to face their Tribunal and dropped Jazz off at home.

They noticed, of course, the regulars – they kind of knew me, in passing, because I dropped by often enough for them to recognize me, but she was new and strange and there was a definite twitch to Laura's curtains as I brought Celia through the garden to my quarters at the back. They were too polite to ask, and it was against the unspoken rules of the boarding house anyway, but the curiosity was natural. I couldn't exactly bring her here and lock her up for a month in my room, and so because it was inevitable that her path would cross that or the other residents I brought her out for breakfast the day after we arrived.

She sat quietly at her place at the table, waiting until I gathered up the breakfast things and brought them to her, and then dutifully ate; Laura happened to brush my elbow, accidentally on purpose, as I was bringing back the breakfast impedimenta to the clear-up bin, after. So I gave her *something*.

"I'm just looking after her, for a little while," I told Laura. "She's been... ill, and she needs some peace and quiet."

"She's so sad and so beautiful," Laura said, glancing covertly back to where Celia had not moved from her spot at the table. 'If there's anything we can do...?"

"To be honest, I have no idea if there is anything anybody can do," I said, and it was no more than the truth. "But there are times I will have to step away and leave her – and perhaps if you can keep an eye...?"

"Oh, absolutely, we would be happy to help," Laura assured me. "What is the poor dear's name?"

"Celia," I said, hesitating a little, "but she doesn't remember it. That's part of the problem. We're hoping the memory will come back but for now... she's very much not herself."

"We'll help you take care of her," Laura said. "Annabel is very good with people who aren't themselves. And maybe I could read to her, when you're not here."

"She might like that," I said. I had no idea if she would or not, but at least she would not be alone, and that mattered. I could not leave Celia alone. In her present state she was utterly pliant and trusting and she would go anywhere with anyone at all – or worse, maybe wander off by herself in her sweet haze and then have no idea where to go back to, easy pickings on the street.

I might have made a case for staying in direct and constant touch with the rest of the family – but there would be nothing at all to report directly on the Celia front until the next Turn broke things one way or another. In the meantime it would probably be best if they knew as little about her whereabouts as possible. I wanted no attention drawn anywhere near her at all. And I particularly did not want any direct connection to Mal – because I knew that he would obsess about this, that there was nothing he could do about any of it, and that, at least according to the truncated and obviously incomplete version of the Lycan Tribunal and its aftermath which I got from Jazz during our single contact phone call during this period, he now had a far greater set of problems and responsibilities in his lap.

I didn't know the exact details but just knowing – broadly – that he and Asia had formed their own breakaway pack as the fallout from their actions concerning Celia was plenty for me to realize that there was far too much to talk about, between the two of us, and not nearly enough either of us could say (with everything being in flux). So, although I knew that it would probably weigh on him, I kept the silence between the two of us until such time as I would either have to break the worst of bad news to him about his sister or bring him the absolution he so desperately wanted in the shape of an account of her first Turn in many years. So far as he knew, as long as I didn't contact him with any actual *bad* news, his sister was safe, and cared for. What would come after the Turn, whatever the Turn itself brought, we would make an opportunity to discuss afterwards.

In the meantime, Laura and Annabel were wonderful, and I actually found myself with more 'free' time than I knew what to do with. I used the gift of those hours to pursue my own research. Which involved, at least partly, the search for Celia's only living baby. I had no idea if she would *ever* remember anything about having had that child or the circumstances in which she had had it – or if she would care – or if her regaining those memories would even be a good idea. But that child, in a lot of ways, was myself all over again. I owed it to all of us – to Celia, to that unknown child, to me – to at the very least find out what had become of it.

I found Celia's daughter being fostered in a Lycan compound – presumably the pack to which her father had belonged. Her name was Petra, and she was now five years old. Her health as a baby and a toddler had not been good, she had had problems with her heart and apparently there had been a number of seizures when she was very young, but she was behind a Lycan firewall and it would take a bit more time and ingenuity and sheer bull-headed determination to get to the bottom of the whole thing – and, for now, the child appeared at least safe and cared for (if you could trust Lycans to do that) and it was the child's mother who was the more immediate priority. I filed my notes, to be pursued after I had solved the Celia puzzle one way or another, and made my way back to where I had left her.

I was back at the Casa Verona two full days before the rise of the full moon and the Turn of March. Laura's report on Celia went on for what seemed to be a long time, but boiled down to, basically, 'no change'. With one eye on the moon and the other on Celia, I settled down to wait.

As it happened, I had an excellent idea as to exactly when the Turn itself was due to begin... because Laura and Annabel themselves vanished, and in their stead two large well-fed cats, one black and white and one orange tabby, appeared out in the courtyard. Celia herself remained unchanged, and went to bed at her regular hour that night without a hint of any transformation taking place.

I spent the night awake, with the curtains wide open on the window, watching the light of that traitorous full moon flow and shift across the foot of the bed – the bed in which the girl slept the sleep of the innocent, the girl who had not changed into any other shape, who had stayed herself. The Turn hour had come... and gone. And still I waited all night, hoping, my eyes wide open and never leaving her, until the light changed and the first bright fingers of day began to wash into a lightening sky.

Morning had come. And Celia was still... Celia.

I had not given her the second dose of the genetic cocktail that Asia had left with me, and that had been a judgment call – Celia had been so fragile, so ethereal, that I figured that either the first dosage worked and the second dosage would make no difference at all or else she was far too compromised to be tortured with a second whammy of something that might not have ever worked at all. I left it up to her own body, to chance, to God. I confess that I stood over her bed, watching her sleep, and my eyes filled with sudden tears – had it been me? Should I have done more? Should I have forced that second dose on her? Would it have made all the difference...?

But all the second-guessing in the world would not help any of us now. The harsh truth of the matter was right there before me. The Turn had come, and it had passed. Celia had not Turned.

All the risks that Mal had taken – everything that he had gambled, and, perhaps, lost – it had all been for nothing. Because she was still here, the shell of a girl, and now we had to make some hard decisions about what was to become of her. I could do a month – and even that had been with assistance from the next-door cat-ladies – but I could not take Celia on full-time. I had never led that kind of life in the past, and it very much looked like I was going to be leading a much more hazardous life in the future, in which there was no place for someone as utterly dependent as Celia would be. Now, I had to call Mal. We had to talk.

But, of course, that would have to wait – because if Celia hadn't Turned, he had. Somewhere out there he was locked away in a safe enclosure, wearing his wolf skin. Asia would be there – but this wasn't hers to decide, for all that she had been so deeply involved in the situation. It had to wait for Mal to come out.

So, we waited it out, Celia and I. She as drifty and dreamy as ever, waiting for the hours of every day to pass and the nights to come, and me heartbroken and regretful, watching over her, keeping vigil, wondering what it would have been like if the world had changed after all. I was resigned, by the end of the third day. Resigned, and bracing for the call that had to come – for the moment I had to tell Mal about this. I told myself that I would call him the morning after the Turn days ended, and I knew exactly when that happened because I walked out into the courtyard from the room where I had left Celia sleeping and exchanged nods with Laura – the woman – as she was slipping into her own room just as I was exiting mine. I was fully determined to do so. I meant to do it. I went out with every intention of punching in Mal's number as soon as I got out of the house.

And then I didn't. I couldn't. I picked up the phone several times, and began entering the number, and then hit cancel and put it back into my pocket. I just couldn't think of how to open the conversation, what to say, how to begin. Telling him without preamble would have been cruel. Starting with silly small talk would be disrespectful. So I walked, for a couple of hours, aimlessly, waiting for my thoughts to gather, and then I went and had a cup of coffee in a nearby coffeeshop, and then I went to a pizza place where the local youth hung out and which had the (at the moment) advantage that they played background music so loudly that you had to practically shout when you had a conversation with someone sitting right next to you which made making a phone call impossible, and then I walked very slowly back to Casa Verona and tried to convince myself that it would be better if I phoned Mal the next morning, no procrastination allowed.

I checked on Celia, and she was still herself, still fine; Signora Garibaldi had made spaghetti bolognaise for dinner, and I stepped out of the room to go back to the dining room and get a plate to bring back to my wounded girl.

I locked the door behind me, as I always did. Laura from next door had a spare key, but Laura and Annabel were both sitting in the dining room having their own dinner when I got there, and I nodded and smiled and they nodded and smiled back over forkfuls of spaghetti.

"How is she today?" Laura asked quietly.

"The same," I said.

She shook her head. "Hasn't left the room, today," she said, a touch of concern in her voice. "She really needs a touch of fresh air..."

"Maybe I'll take her for a quick walk," I said. As if that was going to help.

But Laura nodded and gave me another sympathetic smile. "Let us know," she said, a little arbitrarily. Let us know how she is? Let us know if we can do anything? Let us know if she grew wings?

But they had been kind.

"I will," I said. "Thank you."

Signora Garibaldi handed me Celia's plate and patted me on the hand as she did so, murmuring something about everything being "all right" – I must have looked as tragic as I felt. And then I walked back across the courtyard with the plate in one hand and my keys in the other.

I must have been gone all of ten minutes.

I knew I had left Celia curled up in the armchair by the window. When I came back into the room, unlocking the still-locked door to enter, she was not there. Her *clothes* were – the clothes she had been wearing when I had left her – left discarded on the chair where she'd been sitting, as though she'd dropped them there in a hurry. In the time that I'd had the care of her, she was quite capable of doing things for herself but she had to be pointed in the direction of something before she would do it – if she'd suddenly decided to have a shower, or something of that nature, that would have been a significant change in attitude, the fact that she had made a decision to do something, by herself, and then acted on it. But the door to the bathroom, to the back of the room, was ajar, and there was only silence beyond it. I put the plate down on the counter of the tiny kitchenette and stepped to the side, peering into the bathroom. It was empty.

The door to the outside had been locked – by me, as I left. The window was closed. If she had managed to get out of the room at all (but then, the clothes? Had she gone out wearing nothing...?) she would have been noticed out in the courtyard; there were people in the public rooms, including me as I was waiting to collect her dinner, and there was a clear view into the garden from there – and it had contained no Celia , during the short, the *very* short, time that I was gone.

But the room was still empty. So was the bathroom. So was the kitchenette. So was the closet.

Everything was empty. But Celia was *gone*.

In a heartbeat I had gone from resignation and wretchedness and a touch of self-pity at what awaited me the next morning, to a state of full and high alert. I scanned the room for anything out of place and could see nothing other than the persistent absence of the person who should have been there and now... inexplicably... was not. It was as though Celia had finally fully and completely turned into that ghost that she half-was already, and had decided that her physical body was no longer necessary or relevant, and had discarded it, and the shell had already crumbled into dust.

And then I heard something that burrowed into my brain. A tiny, whimpering sound. A sound that I would have given anything to have heard during these past few days. A sound whose non-manifestation was the root cause for my having to make a hard phone call to my friend the next day.

A whimpering meow.

At first I couldn't place it, there was nowhere in the room I had not looked... and then it came again, and I focused on it, and as I pinpointed its location I dropped to my knees and elbows and craned my neck to peer under the bed.

And there she was. The little brindle cat, her eyes wide, her ears somewhere between the forward of full alert and the laid-back of wary anger.

I collapsed the rest of the way onto the floor, so that I was lying full-length beside the bed, my head pillowed on one hand, grinning at the cat like a complete lunatic.

"There you are," I said, stupidly, joyfully, for lack of anything intelligent to say. "Oh, *there* you are..."

One thing was clear. The plate of spaghetti I had brought for Celia's dinner had been rendered irrelevant. But I had stocked up on certain cat necessities when we had got here, just in case, and although there had been moments during the past three days that I considered doing something practical with them – like giving them away to where an *actual cat* might get use out of them – I had not gone so far as to follow through on that impulse, and was I only happy now that I had allowed my sense of tragic defeat to lull me into that mood of procrastination. Because now I was equipped, at least for the first emergency – I had a pack of three cans of cat food in the kitchen, and I scrambled back to my feet and fetched one, pulling the lid off a shrimp and tuna offering and spooning it out into a small bowl. Before I was done I was aware that the sound and the smell had brought her out and she was sitting a few paces away, just outside my reach, watching me, waiting.

"There you go," I said, setting the bowl down.

She got up, stretched, and then approached the bowl with high-stepping delicate paws, stretching out her neck to sniff at the food, and then deigning to give it the seal of approval by settling down beside the bowl and beginning to work on the contents at a leisurely pace.

I busied myself with other things as she ate – putting down some fresh water into a second bowl, retrieving the still-pristine litter box and pouring in a layer of kitty litter and tucking it into a convenient corner of the small room where it wouldn't be too much in the way. And then I sank down into the armchair by the window, torn between wanting to laugh like a maniac and actually giving vent to what I was feeling by bursting into very unmanly sobs.

The cat finished up her dinner, and then walked over to the armchair and sat down at my feet, looking up at me with a quizzical little chirp. And then it must have decided that I was okay after all because she launched herself into my lap, turned around a few times exploring the territory, and finally settled down draped across one knee and the forearm that I had been resting on the arm of the chair, trapping me effectively. A soft purr I could barely hear but which I could feel against my arm began to emerge as she allowed her eyes to drift closed and her head to fall forward until it was pillowed on a paw stretched out across my wrist.

She looked very content, and very comfortable.

The world was full of trouble and drama and catastrophe, everywhere you looked. It has always been that way. But right then, in that single moment, when something finally just went *right*, I was still on the emotional rollercoaster I had been riding over the last few days. I was exhausted, dizzy with a strange happiness, relieved, and grateful. I closed my own eyes for a moment, just to rest them, and then fell asleep right there in the chair with the purring, drowsing cat in my lap. I may even have dreamed something good, for once.

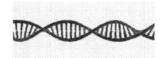

All of this was only half the story, of course, and it meant I couldn't call Mal with the news after all. The full tale would only be told when the Turn had run its course – Celia had Turned three days late, for mysterious reasons I was going to leave to the science people to figure out, but when the three days of her own Turn were over... there was still the issue of what she would then revert to. Would she be Celia again, the old Celia, Mal's sister... or would she simply fall back into the blank and drifting ghost of her former self? If the latter happened... this might well be a one-off, and I didn't want to raise Mal's hopes only to have to dash them again. I waited it out with her, those three cat-days, and it was actually quite pleasant, as far as that went. I was even beginning to think that I might like having a cat, an ordinary cat, warming my feet at night on a more permanent basis.

I didn't know if it would be better if I were present when she Turned back, or if I should leave her to do it on her own – but in the end I decided to err on the side of caution, locked the door and drew the curtains on the afternoon of the third day, and waited with a blanket at the ready to cover up any temporary embarrassment when she Turned back into a naked human female. I watched her very closely, the cat, and at first the animal seemed to be quite oblivious of the imminent change – until, all at once, I observed it lift its head and look around, startled, frightened, and I saw it begin – the elongation of the limbs, the fading of the fur into smooth skin.

I threw the blanket over her, and waited for it work itself out, helpless to do anything but watch and stand ready for... I wasn't sure what, myself. I stood quite still, my heart beating very fast, when it was done and the dark-haired girl lay curled up and breathing a little raggedly on top of the bed. I saw one hand reach out and instinctively draw the blanket closer, before she opened her eyes, and the tiny gesture made me catch my breath – it may have been nothing, but it might mean everything, it might mean that Celia would wake, the real Celia...

She'd had her eyes closed, and when she finally opened them and tried to focus on her surroundings... I knew.

This was someone who was aware of her surroundings. Bewildered by them. Trying to place herself into them. And then, looking up and finding me, to place *me*.

"Celia...?"

She cleared her throat, as though it had gone rusty through not having been properly used for a long time.

"I... where am I? Who are you?"

"I'm a friend of Mal's," I said. "I'm your friend, too. I promise. You're safe. How much *do* you remember of... but wait. Are you hungry? I have soup simmering, and I can put together other stuff if you want to eat. If you want a shower, the bathroom's through there – and your clothes are in there if you want to get changed. I'll have the soup ready by the time you're out. And I'll explain everything."

It took a while, because her memory was spotty in the extreme, and there were things I was telling her that I could see she was finding it very difficult to believe.

"Dead?" she kept on repeating softly to herself. "They all thought I was *dead*?"

But eventually the basics of it were straightened in her mind, and then she cried, and then she dried her eyes and asked me more questions, and tried to get her head around the fact that Mal was now part of a Lycan pack (and quite possibly a Lycan Alpha), and then she cried some more, and then she ate a whole another supper when I called in for pizza, and eventually she fell asleep, exhausted, in the very same bed she had been sleeping in for weeks before this night but, it was clear, a very different girl from the one that she had been then.

And I knew that I could not take this away from Mal, this awakening back into her old self – I could not waste it by wrapping it in words and delivering it in a phone call. They needed the moment. They needed to *see* one another again, to look each other in the eyes and know the truth of this whole immense thing that had happened for something real. I know it made *me* feel like I had just received a gift straight from the hands of God. I could only barely begin to imagine what it would mean to Mal.

And so I phoned Mal, very late on the afternoon of that third day, and the way the phone was answered before the second ring told me all I had to know about what he had been going through in the silence that he had been left in since the end of his own Turn.

"Dude," I said, trying to sound laid back and relaxed, trying to prevent the grin on my face from translating into my voice. "So. What's up...?"

I heard him splutter on the other end of the phone. "What's... *up*?" he said, and it was almost moot as to whether he could say anything else at all, so deep was his outrage at this overture. But two could play at this game, and so he slapped me with a report-back of his own, layered in sarcasm. "Well, as you know, Asia called the Tribunal on the finer points of Lycan law, and split us up as our own pack, so we're on our own... and now we're hanging on the ragged edges of the clan, trying to figure out how to survive... what else do you want me to tell you?"

"Let me know if you need anything," I said, in a manner calculated to rile him further. "I have people I can call."

I knew him well enough to almost see him, on the other side of the phone, probably closing his eyes and counting to ten as he tried to hold on to his temper. In the end, it broke, but not in a roar.

"Just tell me," he said. His voice was soft, almost pleading. "Please. Just tell me."

"Give me an address," I said. "I can be there tomorrow."

"You don't even know where 'there' is," Mal said, hopelessly.

"It doesn't matter," I said. "I can be there tomorrow. Wherever it is. Text me an address, and expect me. Gotta go – see you soon." I had to cut this short because otherwise I would just laugh from the sheer joy of it and spill it all and wreck it. Yes, this would make him dangle for one more day. But oh, when the payoff came. This was going to be beautiful.

"Chalky..." I heard him say, but I toggled the phone off on the rest of it.

Celia had actually asked my name, and I told her Saladin. I didn't offer the surname. There would be *one* of that clan, dammit, who would not be calling me 'Chalky' (or at the very least not before she'd had a chance to connect with the rest of the family and pick it up off the two of them...)

The new pack – plus Jazz, who had been the resident caretaker over this particular Turn in her Jesse shape – crowded out onto the porch of the house they had been offered as sanctuary, as I pulled into the driveway with Celia in the passenger seat. I watched Celia out of the corner of my eye as I drove up, and she was very quiet, very still, with her hands folded on her lap. But I could see that her lips were parted and she was trying very hard for that calm as she struggled to keep her breathing even – it wasn't every day that one was chauffeur-driven to one's resurrection, after all.

I saw Mal reach out for Asia's hand as I brought the car to a stop. We both sat in the car for a moment as I turned the key in the ignition, and then Celia lifted one hand, reaching for her seatbelt.

I touched her arm. "Wait. Let's do this properly. I'll come and hand you out."

I stepped out of the car and walked around the front, without looking at anyone up on the porch, until I reached the passenger side and opened it.

"Now," I mouthed to Celia, with my back to the porch, unable to hold back the grin any longer.

She unfolded herself from the seat, came out of the car, straightened to her full height, and looked up at the house. I turned as she did so, watching the impact on the gathered company on the porch, and I saw Jazz reach out and grab Mal's free hand, and hang on for dear life. She was actually gulping air, as though she was sobbing.

I slammed the door behind Celia, as she stood frozen beside the car, her eyes on her family, and then I guided her gently up to the porch, and then up the steps. The grin on my face had faded to a shadow of itself, but it was a deeper joy for all that, and I said nothing. I did not have to. Mal looked at my eyes, and he knew, he *knew*, the whole story, instantly, and I could see the knowledge go through him like a knife.

And then I finally took pity on him.

"I'm sorry," I said. "I'm sorry you went through what I know you went through over these last few days. But things... worked out... just a little unexpectedly and I didn't want to call you until I was sure. Until yesterday. Until she actually... Turned back."

Asia let out the breath that she had been holding, with a little gasp. "She..."

And oh, it was everything I knew it would be. The moment when Mal actually managed to look straight into his sister's eyes, and she looked at him, and none of the rest of them really existed in that shared look, both of them on the verge of tears.

"Hey," Celia said softly. "I'm back."

One of the red-headed twins behind Mal let out a small strangled cry.

Mal finally found the strength to move, and gently shook off Asia and Jazz on either side of him. He took one small step forward, just that one small step, and wrapped his arms around Celia as though he would never let her go again. I saw her arms slide around him, and up his back, and she held him close like she might have held her little brother so many times before, when they were young.

They did not speak. I didn't think either of them was capable of words in that instant.

This was for them, though. Their moment. Theirs, alone.

Asia sensed it as well as I.

"You'd better come inside," she said to me, and included everyone else on the porch in that sentence, giving Mal and Celia that space that they so clearly needed. "I've got coffee on in the kitchen."

I turned to glance back, as we all trooped through the door and into the house. They hadn't moved.

They were all anxious to hear about it, everything, but we could not possibly do anything about that until the two main actors in this drama walked back onto center stage, so I asked Asia about the new pack and what their plans were – and if Celia had not been standing out on the front porch with their Alpha male it might have been quite a fascinating topic of conversation. But we were all waiting, and we knew it, and not even the new pack was cutting it as filler – and the conversation stilled instantly when Mal and Celia walked into the kitchen a few minutes later.

Mal skewered me with a look. "*Saladin*, eh," he said. "I step out of it for a moment and everyone gets delusions of grandeur." I saw Jazz duck her head to hide a sudden grin. "I could throttle you," Mal said, in the same easy conversational tone, and then his expression changed, and his voice shook, just a little. "Thank you." And that was my reward. The next word, he was back to being Mal. "*Spill.*"

I could finally let that smile come into its own, and it threatened to split my face.

"Like I said, sorry," I said. "But for a while it didn't look as though I'd have anything for you except bad news. And then..."

"Start at the beginning," Asia said. "After we left you at the cabin."

I gave them an abbreviated account of the events of Celia's transformation – Wilfred (the scientist) wanted to know if I'd given that second dose of the genetic cocktail, and I could see his mind making connections when I said that I had not. Oh, I milked it for the drama. I enjoyed the sharp intakes of breath when I came to the night of the Turn, on which nothing happened. And then I told them about Celia's disappearance, the soft meow from under the bed, and all that came after. How she had Turned three days late.

Wilfred was frowning. "That shouldn't have happened," he said. "It isn't a question of... you think this is a permanent thing? Or just a blip because the thing was forced, and it'll settle out into a normal pattern over time?"

"No way of telling – next Turn will give you that answer, I guess," I said.

Mal looked at me, and the raw honesty of that look almost broke me. "Thank you," he said, again, speaking to me alone out of that room full of people, in a voice that shook only slightly. And then I saw the changes that had already started to take root in him – because he took those eyes off me, and looked at everyone, all of them, making every single person in that room feel as though they had given something precious for this to be possible. "*All* of you. I owe you all... *we* owe you...more than we can ever say."

It was finally time to tackle the question of what would come next.

"She must stay here, of course," Asia said firmly.

"But if she's back to being fully Random, what if she just Turns into a wolf from here on because that's the last thing she sees before Turn?" Jazz said. "Or if she Turns into a cat – what if one of the wolves makes her a snack...?"

"Well, technically, she seems to have Turned into cat only after we all Turned back from wolf," Wilfred said. "And if that holds – then the staggered Turn means that there is no danger of any of that."

"And anyway," Asia said, "it doesn't matter, for the next few months... I'll be around to supervise things. I won't be Turning again until this child is born."

Celia's eyes leaped from Asia to Mal. "Saladin didn't tell me *that*," she said.

"Well, you're going to be an aunt," Mal said, with a helpless grin.

And then looked at me, sharply. I shook my head, ever so slightly. The subject of that lost child... was not something I had discussed with Celia. I had figured that she already had enough to deal with at the moment, and that the time for that would come.

Thankfully Jazz, oblivious to that particular undertone but still focused on questions of family, turned the conversation into a different channel.

"What about Mom and Dad?" she asked, clasping her hands together.

This, we had discussed, Celia and I. And it was a hard thing to talk about.

"They lost a child," Celia said, and bit her lip. "I am not that child any longer. They would not be getting back what they lost, even if I went home with you right now, Jazz. I want to tell them. I do. I want to go back and hug Mom and tell her how sorry I am, about everything... but I just don't know. I don't know if I can do it to them or to me. None of us are the same people that we were... when I disappeared. And they have already mourned me, would it make it better if they suddenly had all that undone and had to face the consequences of all of this? How much would you explain to them? How much could you explain?"

I sounded the same note of warning that I had sounded to Celia. "You have to realize that it isn't just Celia," I said. "If she goes back – if this goes public – it's all of you. It's Jazz, and it's very much Mal, all of you get put under the spotlight. There will be a lot of scrambling to explain away who knew what when, who lied and why, who kept their silence when they should have made a report... and they might not be too careful about who they throw under the bus to save themselves – and I mean *everyone*, the Lycans, the Were Authority, the normals' lawmakers who won't know what to do with you. There are a lot of secrets buried here now, and not all of them are your own, and some of them are valuable enough for people to do... horrible things... to protect them."

I didn't mention myself – but of course there would be that, too. Because there was no explaining some of the things that had occurred without revealing the truth of the existence of the 'shifter' monster – and the hunt would really be on, then. Publicly. In the open.

"She'll be quite safe here," Mal said. "For now, anyway. Nobody who doesn't need to know need ever know. And when the time is right... if it ever is... we can fix it. From here."

Speaking of that hunt... I had things to take care of, now. I sighed deeply, and stood up, pushing my coffee cup away.

"All right then," I said. "Then I've done what I can do. There's stuff I have to take care of – clean-up, so that nobody traces the wrong things to the wrong place..."

"You can't *leave* yet," Asia objected. "You just *got* here. And we haven't begun to..."

"Asia. I've done what I can do. You healed her, I kept her safe, she is here now, and the rest... is up to you now. And I – I have to find myself a new place to hide."

Mal stared at me. "You're just going to disappear again?"

"Oh, I'll stay in touch," I said. "The day may well come when I may need to call in my favors. When I might need help, or sanctuary. From *you*."

Asia stood, suddenly very formal, looking much older than her years, and spoke as the new Alpha of a new Lycan clan.

"In any house where I am, in this pack where I stand Alpha, you will always be welcome."

It was an ancient oath and a greater gift than even she knew, perhaps. She was extending her protection...*Lycan* protection... to an outsider.

"Thank you," I said, moved by the gesture. "I should probably be on my way, then. Mal, a word, before I go...?"

I impulsively leaned over to kiss Celia on the top of the head as I walked behind her chair, and she looked up, mute, her eyes full of tears again, trying to find words, and failing.

It was Asia who spoke up, again.

"I'll take care of her," she said. "Go. And travel safely."

I gave a faint nod of farewell to the rest of them and stepped out of the kitchen.

Mal followed me out onto the porch after a moment.

"Well," I said, "You've come a long way from picking fights in back alleys after school. When you joined the Lycans I have to admit I never expected you to end up with a seat on the Lycan Council less than a year later."

He had the grace to look a little sheepish. "Nor I," he said. "Asia... sort of happened. She was never part of the plan."

"Sometimes the best things in life are those you never planned for," I said. "Trust me, I know. I never plan anything too far in advance. And stuff... happens... anyway. Look at that first alley fight. Remember? I never had any plan whatsoever to help you out in that scuffle, the first time we met. It just... seemed to be a good idea at the time."

"Long-term plans aside, then... what are you going to do now?"

"There are a few things I plan to pursue," I said. "For one, I found Celia's daughter. I am going to keep an eye on that, see what else I can learn. And over and above that... there are still a lot of things I haven't really figured out. It isn't over yet. And I may turn up on your doorstep every so often when you least expect me, to pick your brains – yours, on what goes on behind the closed doors of the Lycan inner sanctum, your wife's to help me figure out what goes on inside my own cells..."

Mal flashed a grin. "Still your inside man."

"The old bargain," I said. "And a new one. I still need to figure out who I am... what I am... in the end. And besides... I'll be back to keep an eye on that girl. She may still be a part of my own answers – she's a kind of vested interest for me now, your sister, even if I didn't get kind of attached to her over these last few weeks. You take care of her."

"I will," Mal said, and it was a vow. "This time, I will. It's a gift that I never expected... and you... once again... I don't even know how to begin..."

"Then don't," I said. "I understand."

I reached out, and he reached back, and we clasped one another's arms – forearm to forearm – like a couple of knights out of an old bedtime story.

"Take care, dude," I said.

"And you," he whispered.

We held each other's eyes for another long moment, saying a lot of things that could never be put into words of any kind, because souls do not use language like that to communicate. And then I gave him a small sharp nod, released his arm, and turned away. I did not look back as I crossed the gravel driveway to my car, got into the driver's seat, turned the key in the ignition, and drove away from him into a future I had to walk alone.

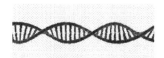

I had promised to craft a new identity for Celia, and I did that when I got back home, but that wrapped up a part of my life which had been a significant focus for some little while... and after I had completed my duties on that front I found myself curiously apathetic, adrift, unfocused, watching the days slip by... waiting for something. I didn't know what.

Life did go on – the births, and the deaths, and everything that went on in between. In the year that followed Celia's rescue, Mal's child was born, a boy they named Alexander; Mal and Asia steered their new pack precariously along a narrow path of survival, with new members coming on board (Wilfred married another Lycan, a doctor named Greta Jung; Sorcha made the decision that she too wanted to be a doctor, and took up with a young floater by the name of Robin Foxworthy, and there was every indication that he would stay on as a permanent member of the new pack when the two of them became an established item by the time she was sixteen; Seonaid attached herself to Asia, second in command).

My mother finally died, alone in the high-security Turning House which functioned as something of a lockdown station for Were with more severe psychological conditions. I had kept tabs on where she was and how she was doing but I had never gone in to see her. She was too far gone to even know who I was. But they wrote, in their reports, which I scanned every so often when I hacked into that system, that she would often talk gently and at length, in her own mother tongue which she had never taught me, to an invisible presence she addressed by my name. I confess to a twinge of guilt, having learned that – but she would not have known the real me. The one she talked to was the lost boy who was long gone. When she went, I could finally feel little more than gratitude that she had been released at last from all her burdens. I wished her peace, but there was only a shallow layer of grief over it all. I had lost her, and mourned her as well as I knew how, long before this.

Celia's daughter, Petra, turned six. Celia herself still had large chunks of her memory missing and Petra's existence remained one of them. Mal had decided to let her come back to that memory herself, or not at all – because there was little chance of her having much to do with this child in the future. Petra – aside from a worrying report of at least two unexplained seizures that she'd had in the intervening year – remained a cypher, a kid who was yet to show any signs of being different from any other six-year-old you could point to.

Jazz briefly stepped out with a high-flying new boyfriend from Nell Baoudoin's clan, a cousin of Nell's, and I got to tease her about having aspirations of becoming a Corvid Princess herself before she dropped the pompous windbag for a more suitable Random escort, one of her own clan. But even that relationship was difficult; there was the Jesse secret to keep, after all. Her benefactor, Peregrine, seemed to have decided to bide his time on the Jesse front, at any rate; that situation did not escalate, although I kept a careful eye on it.

As for myself...I had heard the drums as far as I was concerned, my existence (at least in general terms) was known, but there seemed to be a lull while everyone tried to figure out what to do next. And I coasted in the wake of that, wary, but falling little by little into a trap of complacency. And when the sleeping world woke up and snarled at me, I was blindsided.

Two things happened to change the shape of my life. Well, one may actually have pushed the other over, the first and second dominoes to fall in the rapidly accelerating cascade, but they were the first two, and they were the most important.

Number one was something I had honestly never expected, nor planned for – but perhaps I should have known, all the instincts had been there right from the start. And it was to do with the *Vox Verae Hominis* group, who had sworn to find me (they did not explain how, but they *would*) and destroy me.

The highest official and the public spokesman for the group, the one I happened to catch on the TV talk shows in the beginning, the then-Vicar General Marcus Moresby, died quite suddenly and unexpectedly of a supposed heart attack less than a year after I had first learned of him. The Vox people took some time to announce a replacement, and somewhat surprisingly, when they did make that announcement, it was that the office of Vicar General would be shared (at least for the time being) by two individuals. One was a fiery elder with a shock of white hair and blazing blue eyes full of righteous fury about the indignities that the very existence of the Were had heaped on the True Men of the world, a man by the name of Solomon Waysmith.

The other... was Barbican Bain.

I had not known that his status in the group was so high.

Perhaps I did less research into him than I should have done. Perhaps it was that he was good at keeping a low profile, or that his rise in the ranks was meteoric enough for him to have simply outpaced my investigations. Either way... it had literally come out of nowhere.

I found out about *that* on the talk shows, too, and it was a shock to see that face staring back at me from the TV screen, with his usual oily and viscerally dangerous serenity, the self-confidence and the sheer presence of a man who was absolutely convinced as to the rightness and truth of his own beliefs. A man who saw no action taken in the defense of those beliefs as being in any way wrong... no matter who or what stood in his way.

It was a greater shock to listen to what he was saying on that talk show, because he had transformed his reaction to our previous encounter to something very different to what it had been back then. I knew I had rattled him, back when I had come to him and revealed what I could do. There had been fear, then. There had been shock. I had had a sense of victory, a sense of the thing that I had done being the *right* thing, the *only* thing that would wring from him any sort of admittance of guilt or a sense of penance. And that might have been true... at the time.

But in the months that had passed from then to the present day he had distilled that fear and that shock and any, and unlikely, sense of guilt into something that was almost martyrdom. It now seemed to me that his current stepping up to being co-Vicar General was almost solely due to his having been the only human who had ever really had a significant direct encounter with the shifter, the thing they called the Metamorph, myself, the thing that had become the icon for all the fear and hatred and rage which had ever been levelled at the Were.

I listened to him speak, from the TV screen – the effect that he had was somehow magnified by the borders of the TV frame, focusing attention on him, and it was almost impossible to take one's eyes off him, or to stop straining to catch that almost too-soft voice.

"No," he was saying, with gentle remonstration, giving an impression of a wise elder admonishing a silly child who had just asked a very stupid question, "I would not know his face if I set eyes on him again, not directly – how could I, when he wore several, at our encounter? But I would know the energy which I felt in that room that night. If the Metamorph rose before me right now I would recognize him. Whatever face he wore to try and deceive me."

"But nobody else would know that to be true," said the talk show host, who, to give him credit, was not entirely under Bain's spell. "Which means that you could point to anybody – to a stranger in the street, to myself right here in the studio, to anyone whom you might wish to take down – and proclaim them to be the Metamorph, or at least one of them. Aren't you opening this up to something that can become a pure witch-hunt, with innocent people being accused of something that they could never prove that they were not?"

"Are you saying," Barbican Bain said, with a look of earnest and disbelieving hurt, "that I would falsify my witness on this matter?"

"No, of course not," the host said, backtracking rapidly. Totally immune to the influence, he was not. But still, there was a spark. "I am just saying, that there is a possibility – that you, or someone from your group, might claim..."

He could finger Jazz, if he knew about her situation. Easily. Or anyone else he chose. I had given him a *weapon*, I had put it into his hand myself.

I was the one who had raised Barbican Bain to real power.

It had seemed like such a good idea at the time. And maybe, at the time, it had been one. But its consequences... were difficult to believe.

Mal had heard about the turn of events as well, because it was only hours after Bain had appeared on the television that my phone rang.

"Did you..." he began, without preamble, when I picked up.

"I did," I said, interrupting him. "How is Celia taking this?"

"She remembered... far too many things, seeing that face," Mal said grimly. "This is not going to be easy."

"It was my fault," I said, wringing the admission out of myself. Mal had always had the truth from me.

"Even if you gave him a push, I don't think you took him all the way," Mal said. "He was headed there all the time. The little things led to the bigger things and then straight on to this. If you looked up the word 'inevitable' in an illustrated dictionary I think you'd find his face."

He'd always been honest with me, too. He wouldn't have just been saying this, to make me feel better. But still, it was almost something I could not believe, could not accept, despite the sincere intent. In some ways I had helped to reincarnate Celia, I had helped redeem Mal's own sense of guilt and waste – and now it felt like he was trying to pay me back, lift my own guilt away if possible.

I remembered Bain's certainty on that TV show, his utter and apparently completely sincere belief that he could know his nemesis if ever they walked the same street. And although I could not see how he could possibly be speaking the truth... I could see perfectly how he could shape and twist that truth to fit his own narrative, his own requirements.

At some point – if he fingered some poor idiot, and hauled him up to a stake piled high with kindling, and readied the flames – what would I do? Could I stand back and watch? To – what – save myself? I was looking into a crystal ball, and the future was a roiling and murderous storm through which I suddenly could not see at all.

"There's been talk," Mal said, hesitating. "There will be... something on the agenda at the next Council meeting. Something to do with what *he* calls the Metamorph. I think the Lycans are starting to get very antsy."

"And they're planning to do what?" I snapped. "They can't recognize me any more than Bain could."

"No, but they know that the normals have someone who possibly can," Mal said. "And she's – maybe – another..."

And there was that second thing that I mentioned before. The second domino. Just about to fall over.

Grayson Garvin.

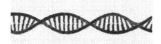

T here was a whole subsection in my Evidence Locker files that ended up dedicated to the individuals whose existence I could connect in any way at all with the program which I was convinced had created me. And Grayson Garvin – the woman pointed out to me as the government "Were-sniffer' by that reporter back when I had first haunted the spectator galleries in government halls of power – had gone into that folder immediately.

What there was about her in the public files only piqued my curiosity. She was... unlikely. Well, that was a description that could easily apply to any of us (just how likely was *I*?) – but in her case it seemed as though unexpected pieces kept on getting fitted into the jigsaw puzzle of her existence, with the result that a coherent image had emerged but one which had very little to do with the target picture which had come printed on the cover of the puzzle box. I had no idea how much I didn't know, or how much even she knew as truth about herself.

She was carefully guarded against chance encounters, as my journalist friend had pointed out. But it was clear that the Lycan scientists had their own ideas and suspicions, and that they had been coldly and deliberately denied access to Grayson herself – she had been a stolen child, in a sense, created by them but then taken out of their control and fiercely guarded against them. My guess was that they had tried a direct approach (there were records of police reports being filed, and one of them actually implied a kidnap attempt when Grayson was twelve) and when that failed they had tried bamboozling with jargon, and none of it had worked. It was not clear how much of the distance being kept between them and their prize was due – at least after she was grown enough to have been asked – from Grayson herself. How much of it was her choice, had ever been her choice, and how much it had all been a matter for whoever had control of her?

What I couldn't find any information about, whether because it was deeply classified or because nobody actually knew, was *how* she performed her trademark talent. What was it about a Were person that triggered recognition? By all accounts she could walk into a room, take a moment or two to observe everyone else in that room, and point out unerringly those who were Were-kind. It was as though, for her, they had neon signs over their heads that lit up when she looked at them.

But I was not at all sure that she had fingered me. That she had known who I was, what I was. I was present in the gallery which she had entered, wearing a different face from my own, changed into something or someone else in the best of Were traditions... and yes, she had caught my eye and held my gaze with her own ever so briefly but she had given no indication that she had thought me anything other than what I appeared to be. Just another ordinary human being.

I wondered if she had made me but had chosen not to say anything. Or if there was something about my own gift that nullified hers. Or if she would be able to pick out, say, Jesse when he was in his Were guise and not the girl called Jazz.

I had a curiosity about these things. It came with the territory.

But it was only when Grayson was thrown into the new mix, after Barbican Bain came to the forefront of things, that the curiosity became something more practical and important.

Because the Lycans had finally managed to find a way into her orbit.

Mal was shamelessly breaking all the Lycan covenants by telling me about the things that went on inside the Lycan Council on which he now had a (somewhat grudgingly granted) seat by virtue of being Asia's mate and the Alpha male of her pack. That was our original bargain, but things had changed vastly, and I could not have faulted him if had drawn back. But he hadn't, and I welcomed the information that he passed on, trying to fit it into the picture that I was building. He had hinted at something being "on the agenda" at the next Council meeting in line, but I don't think either of us expected the thing that the Lycans had proposed.

Mal got back to me the day after the Council session.

"I think this is best not discussed over the phone. Can you come here?"

When I drove out to Mal's compound. Asia simply set another place at the dinner table with nothing more than a welcoming smile, but technically Mal *was* breaking Lycan law, and so the two of us went out for a long walk, so that we wouldn't be talking inside Asia's own house about things that she knew full well I should never have been told.

"So, you said that the Lycans were twitching," I said, once we had got far enough from the house not to be overheard.

"You were right about them having been involved with this Garvin woman right from the start," Mal said. "There was a lot of grousing about how she had been 'kept' from them, and continues to be so – I have some stuff for you, on here." He fished out a thumb drive from his pocket and passed it on to me. "Asia helped me find out some of this, but she knows nothing about it, right...?"

"Absolutely," I agreed, transferring the item I had just been handed into my own pocket and out of sight. "Her ignorance on the subject is profound. Now can you summarize?"

"There's a list," Mal said. "There are three lists, actually. Number one has names of people who are already dead, and whose biological remains the Lycan labs have analyzed, and the data is heavily classified. Number two has names of people who are still alive but who are under Lycan control in some way, or have already been studied and discarded in some manner. And there is a third list, of people who are of interest but whom the Lycans do not have. I have a partial on the drive. Not all the names are on there, but enough are."

"Enough?" I questioned softly.

Mal stole a sideways look at me, a guilty one, as though he was personally shouldering the blame for this.

"Yours is on it," he said. "Your name. On that third list."

"Well, we knew that," I said. "Is Garvin on it? The government bloodhound? Of Were breeding, like me?"

He hesitated. "I've seen the name," he said at length, almost unwillingly.

I tapped my pocket. "Useful." I said. "But more useful would be to know what they plan to do with those lists."

"Some names are starred," Mal said. "The people whom they are absolutely determined to get, one way or another. Yours is one of them." Another hesitation. "That girl. Hers, too."

"So the Vox people want me, and the Lycans want me," I said. "That's nice. But we knew that. What's Garvin got to do with..."

"No," Mal said, after a small hesitation, interrupting me. "It isn't quite what I am saying."

"What? You said I'm on a list of people they want to get," I said.

"Not quite," Mal countered. "You're dropping the important part. The *one way or another* part."

I stopped and turned to stare at him.

"There's something you're trying to tell me," I said. "Stop beating about the bush. Is *one way or another* supposed to mean something to me? To scare me?"

"It should," Mal said grimly. "But there's an unholy alliance being built out there. And you're one of the targets it's aimed at."

"Alliance?"

"You will never prove this," Mal said. "Nobody will. It's all a secret handshake, and meetings in the dark. But they all have a common goal and getting you is going to solve a lot of problems. So long as a Vox trophy hunter can be photographed crowing over your dead body, that's all they're interested in. So long as they get your carcass to play with, dead or alive, that's all the Lycans want. And so long as you're out of the picture – in whatever way that can be made to happen. And that would make life a lot easier for the people in the mundane government. They've all got a stake... and the Lycans are interested in the endgame."

"Who's after me, then?"

Mal looked at me helplessly. "The only possible protection you might have had could have come from the Were Authority," he said. "But they're caught in an untenable position between being loyal to their own kind, even though they're Lycan and a law unto themselves, and keeping the government sweet so that the interests of the Were as a whole are protected. So if the Lycans and the government come to a mutually useful pact, the Authority is going to look the other way and pretend that nothing is wrong – and if this does work and they land you, that's one headache less for the Authority, anyway, because they're off the hook trying to deal with you themselves. And that also means that if Bain and his crew get to you first, they'll respond to the emergency just a little bit too late – so that the Lycans can mop up there, too."

"Let me get this straight," I said. "From here on, I'm the trophy at the end of the hunt. The trophy goes to the Lycans whatever happens. But the Vox people have the numbers and the passion to hunt me...and the government has the means to find me, if their vaunted hunter is up to snuff – which would be great for the Lycans because that hunter would be a great addition to the trophy. Are you telling me the Lycans are in secret cahoots with both of them?"

"I'm not entirely sure they know about each other," Mal said. "And the beauty of this set up is ..."

"I get it," I said. "I'm bait for *her*. And she's an additional prize, or collateral damage, for me."

"You'd better watch your back," Mal said. "I'll try and keep you informed."

"Don't burn yourself," I said. "You have Asia. And Alex."

"What are you going to do?" he asked unexpectedly.

I thought about it while I tried to catch my breath... which was suddenly hard to do. It was as though I was breathing through molasses.

"I think," I said eventually, after I figured I had a better control of my voice, "that I should probably oblige them."

Mal roused, his eyes snapping to mine. "What?"

"What if I let her find me?" I said, allowing a small smile to spread across my features. "And then, when I have us both in a time and place of my own choosing... how about I show up, see what's going on... and then make both of us... just disappear?"

"You've always been good at sleight of hand," Mal said, staring at me, "but are you good enough to take on everyone? By yourself?"

"But I won't be by myself," I pointed out gently. "I'll have Grayson Garvin with me. And maybe between the two of us we can manage it."

"With you? How do you know she's with you?" Mal demanded. "What if she chooses to scream at the wrong moment? What if she *wants* to give you up?"

Good questions, all, but I had something he didn't know about. I had the memory of that look I had intercepted from Grayson herself in the galleries of the halls of government. It had not been a plea for rescue, exactly. Neither had it been the look from someone who was content with her lot. She was just that hard to read – she had been a cross between Were-fox and Were-rabbit, predator and prey, and in her human shape she was sending out one massive mess of mixed signals.

But the answers to it all weren't in the deep background any more. It had all come down to the here and now.

"Details," I said, summarizing all this for Mal with a shrug, still trying to deal with this disconcerting inability to gulp enough air into my lungs. I might have thought that to be an understandable consequence of having just been given the kind of news that Mal had handed me, but the truth was that I'd been getting out of breath lately just walking a city block. I was giving serious thought to paying more attention to basic fitness – apparently a computer-based lifestyle was taking its toll. But I could still muster my trademark quick grin. "All I need is five minutes. To make her listen."

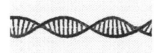

The little ragtag wolf pack had treated me as a strange but acceptable member – not one of them, but a part of the pack lore, and accepted as an integral part of their story. The new members had picked up that line from the original group and Greta, Wilfred's wife, was no exception to that. She was also instinctively maternal – Asia might be the Alpha but it was Greta, both the oldest of them all and a doctor by training, who had evolved into the den mother. When it came to that, because of my dynamic with the pack and because I was so much younger than her, she treated me as just another of the folk for whose health and wellbeing she had made herself responsible.

I must have spaced out over dinner – I had a habit of drifting into these waking dreams, I'd caught myself lately literally 'waking up' while sitting at the computer and not realizing for how long I'd been sitting there staring at the screen without actually seeing anything that was on it – and it was her face, etched with lines of concern, that I focused on when I came back to myself.

"You look tired," she said. "Don't think my colleagues have ever accepted this as a medical term but your eyes look muddy. You been burning the midnight oil a little too much? Looks like you could do with a good night's sleep."

"I do sleep," I protested. I left out some small details. Like the fact that I slept fitfully and woke often, frequently out of some graphic evil dream. More so lately than usual, to be sure, but I'd been afflicted with this since I was a kid. When Mal told me (I don't even remember in what context) that he slept eight or nine hours at a stretch I remember feeling incredulous – but not even he knew of the kind of chopped up slumber that I called normal.

"Well, then, maybe you should let me look you over," she said. "When's the last time you saw a doctor, young man?"

Not lately. But by the sudden flicker of a shared gaze between Asia and Mal I knew what they were thinking. This was a line we hadn't crossed yet. My life was freely shared with the Lycans, or at least this particular pack; my physical self, my body, my cells, my blood, was exactly what the Lycans were in the market to gain control of and if Asia's pack was put in a position where they could get such access, freely offered, and said nothing about it to the Lycan Council it would make for an interesting set of circumstances and probably not particularly pleasant ones.

But Greta had not been with the pack that long, and she did not know all there was to know. She wasn't angling for an advantage. She was just being Greta. Trying to mother another straggling chick.

I defused it, gently.

"You can take my blood pressure if you like," I said, "and if you tell me to take an aspirin I promise I'll call somebody in the morning."

Wilfred had a hand on his wife's arm, shaking his head ever so gently. Greta flushed and looked down. "Sorry," she said. "Maybe not me. But somebody. Maybe."

I did let her take my blood pressure, actually, just so as to make her feel a little better about stepping in it. But it didn't seem to make her happy, and she asked me if I'd always had such a high heart rate. I told her yes, as far as I knew. So far it was just piling on stuff with which I was familiar from childhood, but now that she'd put the wind up me – and with the general fatigue and that weird breathlessness that I had been noticing – I found myself thinking about the whole picture.

The truth was that I had been to the local ER a number of times – twice because of accidents (one time it was a fractured arm, which I'd given myself when I'd fallen off a roof after I changed prematurely from a winged creature to one which was, well, not) and on several occasions because of a slew of other arbitrary malaises (they told me I might suffer from migraines, once, after a particularly evil headache that lasted for four days, very different and much more debilitating than the ones that I got in the aftermath of my shape-shifts – but if that was true then it was a very intermittent thing because such a thing had not happened again since that time even though those smaller post-shift ones never did go away).

But I had not ever really 'seen a doctor', not in the sense that Greta meant. I didn't *have* a doctor to see. And if I had needed to... I would have had to be very careful about it before. Now, it was almost academic. I simply could not trust myself to a medical facility. There was no knowing who might be waiting for me there.

I'd lived by my instincts all of my life. And now, suddenly, there were whispering voices in my head. I had a bad feeling about this, and I realized it had been building up over time, but that I had simply pushed it to the side. It was not something I had the time, the energy, or the luxury of worrying about – or the temperament, to be honest. So long as things functioned tolerably well, I had never paid that much attention to potential health issues. It was an indulgence given to the very young, when everything is still the future and the existence of the future is unquestioned. But in the aftermath of that visit to Mal's place... looking into the kind of future that seemed to be gathering for me... I was no longer so certain.

I had to make a decision to trust somebody, and I eventually phoned Greta, in confidence.

"I understand I'm not the best person to speak to," she said. "Wilfred... explained."

"The problem is with the physical tests," I said. "The problem is that I can't have Asia being accused of, I don't know, withholding evidence, which she technically would be doing if there was anything like a specimen of my blood on site, for instance. But if you told me what tests you would need done – to give me a decent baseline physical – I could spread things out over a bunch of places, and then clear my record, but I could bring the results to you and you can help me make sense of them. If you are willing."

"But the pack..."

"You can tell them," I said. "We won't talk about it. But they'll know that's what you're doing, and everyone who doesn't need to know anything further can look away now. You can even come out to see me somewhere neutral and nothing incriminating would ever make their way into the compound at all."

"Not ideal," she said, in that staccato manner that she had of talking, her sentences rarely complete, as though she thought faster than she spoke and couldn't quite keep up with herself. "But doable."

She gave me a shopping list, and I dutifully compiled it, from half a dozen different and unconnected medical facilities, from which I diligently drew out my medical data and then erased. my ever having been there at all. Armed with all of this, I met Greta in the diner which was the latest thing that occupied the premises of Shimura's old computer shop.

She pored over what I brought her, and looked unhappy. And asked me for some more data.

I provided it.

Greta brought Asia to our second meeting.

I stared at them with a faint frown as they came up to the table where I was already sitting.

"I thought the whole idea was to keep them out of ..." I began, But Asia lifted a hand to silence me.

"It's my pack, and I was told," she said. "And there is... have you got the latest stuff?"

I passed over a folder, grudgingly.

"I didn't want you involved," I said. "For good reasons."

'I know. But your existence cannot be simply rubbed out – I know you and of you and that's already a compromising position. And what Greta has told me... what's in there, Greta?"

Greta looked up from the folder, even more troubled than last time.

"I don't understand it," she said. "It's hard to make it out just from random paperwork – but I've asked for all the pieces, and the pieces aren't making me happy. How old did you say you were?"

"Twenty one," I said.

"The state of your heart, and your blood pressure, and your bone density, and the oxygen levels in your blood, and any number of other small things... if I was looking at this chart without knowing anything else about the patient at all, I would guess that you were forty or even older than that and that you'd led a hard life," she said. "You're *worn out*. Your innards have lived twice your years, and then some. I'm actually surprised that so little of it shows, on the outside."

"So little of *what*, precisely, shows?" I said carefully, feeling the earth tilt a little under my feet. Our kind was not blessed with living to a ripe old age. In the Were, sixty years *was* a ripe old age.

I didn't feel old.

But I had never stopped to think what I was doing to my body, every time I shifted. I had been free with it, reckless, even. I suddenly remembered the relative frivolity with which I'd turned myself into animal and bird when I was young, often, and frequently with no pressing reason, just because I could. And lately, with turning my body into other human forms... who knew what effects that had had on me, physically?

They were both staring at me now, and Asia's eyes were suspiciously bright. Too bright.

I managed a laugh. "Oh, come on," I said. "You aren't telling me I'm literally dying."

There was a silence. A rather awful one. And then I broke it, my voice low, but level.

"Or is that exactly what you're telling me? Greta. I have far too much left to do. I don't have time to die just now."

Asia dropped her eyes. Greta mutely held my gaze.

"Okay," I said, after a beat. "Okay. How long have I got?"

'No way of knowing. Already past projections. Anything can happen."

"You're a doctor," I said savagely. "Tell me how long."

"Wish I could," she said. "Best I can do – look, it isn't as though any of it is going to make you drop dead overnight. But other than that – I might sign off on anything from a year to even ten years... if you don't push it too much."

Ten years. *Ten years.* She was telling me I would not live to be thirty-five.

I didn't know if my sudden dizziness was another symptom, or just a reaction to having been handed a literal death date.

Greta reached out a hand. "There are things we can..."

I shook my head.

"What will happen, will happen," I said. "I'm not about to start playing tag with the grim reaper. Asia. *Asia.*"

She looked up. "What?"

"How much does Mal know?"

"About any of this? Nothing. Greta came to me. I haven't had time..."

"Tell him nothing," I said. And when she began shaking her head I reached out and took her hands in mine. "Please," I said. "Tell him nothing. I will not have him start mourning me before I am gone. He and I still have things to finish. He can't know. Promise me, Asia."

She hesitated. "He's my mate," she said. "He's my Alpha. If this is the pack's..."

"He was my friend," I said, "before he was any of that."

My friend. My *brother.*

Who could not know. About any of this. Not now. Not yet.

Asia finally nodded, her lips tight.

I released her hands, and sat back in my seat. It was odd, given the context and the circumstances, but I could feel the blood coursing in my veins and I could all but feel every one of my neurons firing; the fine hairs on my arms were tasting the air like antennae. In the midst of being told I was actively dying of old age... I had never felt more alive.

"Right," I said. "Well, then. If all I have to leave is a legacy, I'd better start moving."

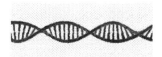

I t was perhaps not all that difficult to understand why I let myself become all but obsessed with the question of Grayson Garvin (and others, like me, but mostly her because she was definitely the highest-profile one out there). It was that, or sit at home brooding about my own impending fate. I might well be setting out on a doomed quest to rescue a princess who had no wish to be rescued but life was a *story*, and I was choosing to make this a story that might matter, that might have consequences.

After all, the worst that could possibly happen is that Mal was right and she'd show me the door. And you'd better believe that I would make sure that there was a door to be shown, I wasn't about to let myself be backed into a corner and locked into a windowless padded room from which there was no escape no matter what shape I chose to take.

So I watched, and waited for an opportunity, one that would hopefully not wait too long to make itself known. And I was rewarded by a huge one.

There had been a definite upsurge in violence between Were and non-Were. It had perhaps been fueled by the *Vox Verae Hominis* rhetoric, which was firing up a lot of ordinarily quiet neighborhoods into acting out the fundamentalists' worst nightmare scenarios, but perhaps it was just something in the air. Were-kind seemed to have become a target – or maybe, to be blunt about it, more of a target than they usually were. While a certain trickle of Were blood was not exactly news, especially in countries where they lived in hiding and were fair game if discovered, things seemed to have gone exponentially worse, everywhere, and the trickle had become a stream. A hemorrhage.

In the manner of politicians everywhere and across all time, the first instinct was, once it became impossible to ignore the problem any longer, to talk at length about it. The first response to the problem was to call a three-day conference on the matter at which those concerned could send representatives and discuss the situation.

The conference was only semi-public in that its existence had been reported in the news – and it was definitely by invitation only, but the full list of attendees had not been publicly released. I had it, of course. Grayson was not officially on it – she was not a conference attendee as such – but she was a unique asset, and there had been internal memos that I had accessed which had indicated that she would definitely be present. I was not sure why; if they had a conference like this and invited Were-kind to attend, they would surely already know that there would be Were present, and having someone who could identify them seemed to be something of an overkill as far as security was concerned – but perhaps it was a gesture to attendees such as *Vox Verae Hominis*.

Why *they* had been invited – and other organizations, similar to them – I could not begin to understand. There was surely little they could bring to the table to make the situation better. If anything, they would be there to fan the flames. But I guess the organizers didn't want them turning up anyway to picket the conference hall and scream that their voices had not been heard. It was perhaps something to do with that old saying that you should keep your friends close, but your enemies closer.

It was here that the peril lay, for my part, if I were to go anywhere near the place – because the Vox representatives would include Barbican Bain. I was absolutely certain that his claim to being able to 'identify' the shifter on sight was ridiculous – but he was always dangerous, and if he saw a way to derail the conference into his own agenda that would be more than enough damage done. Still, he was full of hot air. He didn't even know – *really* know – what I truly even looked like; he had seen my true face, to be sure, but only amongst several others and if he even suspected that one of them was the real me he had no way of telling which it had been.

Still. The danger was there.

Mal thought the whole thing was insane and quite possibly it was, from his point of view, especially since my real reasons were not something I could share with him. If I were going out, I wanted to go out in a blaze. There were quite possibly easier – better – ways of rescuing the girl I had set out to snatch from government control (and keep her out of the Lycans' clutches while at it) than travelling to a foreign place where we would both be displaced and vulnerable. I would probably have to burn up a lot of connections to set up a plan, and use all of my stored talents and knowledge.

And yet... it was irresistible. It didn't seem likely that I would get much of a chance to show off like this again. Why not do it, just once? If I pulled it off it would be something. Something to remember me by. If I failed... well, there wasn't going to be that much time left to regret things, if Greta was right. As things stood, the only regrets I could see having would be if I didn't try.

As these things go, they moved fast – the conference subject matter was an urgent and ongoing one and wouldn't be going away any time soon, so the date was set in the first week of September.

I made my own preparations with every contingency in mind. I made careful travel arrangements for the trip out and the trip back, making the optimistic assumption that I would be in a position to use both; accommodation was booked in at least two separate locations, under two separate names, with enough luggage going to both places to make it look good.

I would have probably denied it if you'd asked me outright, this was all a very serious game, but I was actually having fun.

It was as though I'd been training all my life for a single turn on this particular stage. The irony that the revealed the existence of the 'shifter' – with which vulnerable and gullible populations had been terrified into the actions they had begun to take – was probably the founding reason for this conference was not lost on me, and neither was the fact that the shifter was going to attend the conference called in his name even though he had not been on the list of those invited.

I didn't say goodbye to anyone, when I left for the conference. I'd made a video message, quite a long one, explaining everything – it had been time-locked and scheduled for delivery three days after the conference ended. If I never came back to abort that countdown, it would turn up in Mal's inbox, and it would serve just as well as a farewell.

I hoped he would never see it. But it was made. And ready. And so was I.

It had been easy enough to add myself to one of the delegations, once I'd hacked into the list of attendees, and I picked up my conference ID badge, under the alias of a lowly personal assistant named Santiago Bonaventura, the morning it opened. I had picked a time when a number of delegations would be arriving at once – the concourse where the registration was taking place was busy, crowded, and although security was tight it was stretched by the sudden influx. I was handed the badge without question accompanied by a harried smile and a very quick word of welcome before the young woman at the registration desk turned to the next person in line.

I'd scouted out the venue online and had a pretty good idea about where everything important was, but it was always different when one was actually on the ground, and I took the necessary time to familiarize myself with the layout of the halls and corridors. I had to have a good idea as to where the exits were – and I didn't just note down the emergency doors at the ends of hallways, but also locations where it was possible for tiny creatures to hide and lie low while evading hunters, or find paths where humans could not follow.

The formal opening of the conference involved a series of short addresses to the attendees in a large ballroom set up with rows of identical chairs upholstered in burgundy fabric, into which the audience dutifully deposited themselves to listen. 'Santiago Bonaventura' arrived a little late, and hung about unobtrusively at the back of the hall towards one side, scanning the audience for one familiar face – hers, Grayson's. But she wasn't there, or at least not where she could be seen. It was only after wasting long minutes on this that I realized that she probably wouldn't be among them. She was more likely to be somewhere off to the side, observing, just like me. Once I came to that conclusion I transferred my attention to the edges of the hall, the outer rows of chairs or the few stragglers just like myself who were hovering at the back or hugging the walls trying to be as unobtrusive as possible and not advertise their failure to have presented themselves where they had been expected to be.

She was there, sitting on a slightly set-off handful of chairs, together with her usual minder and a small knot of other people who may or may not have had anything direct to do with her but who were covert security, just like she herself was. She seemed to be paying only half a mind to what was going on around her, staring at the audience (most of whom she could only see from the back or an acute angle which presented little more than a glimpse of the edge of their faces) rather than at the podium where the speakers were. Her eyes were oddly unfocused, as though she was looking but not exactly seeing. I wondered if she was in fact doing her scanning bit – and, again, of what possible use it might be to anyone to know if any Were-kind were in the audience and who exactly they were. She did not look around at me, or even appear to notice that she was under scrutiny. I could still not get a clear read on her, though. It was that predator/prey mix; her shoulders were loose and relaxed, which might mean either resignation to being in a trap or a complete relaxed willingness to be where she was and doing what she was. Her hands were folded serenely in her lap. I could hear Mal's voice as though he had whispered into my ear right there: *What makes you think she wants rescuing?*

I didn't. I couldn't. But there had been *that look*. And I couldn't forget that look, those eyes.

Maybe it was just me. Maybe I had lived my own life almost too freely, according to my own laws, and I couldn't bear seeing another like myself on a leash like this. But all I could do was cut the leash – it was then entirely up to her if she wanted to pick it up again and hang onto it (or tie me up in it and present me to her minders as a trussed-up turkey), or run.

I followed Grayson and her companion – she had two, they took turns – around, and established the exact circumstances of where they were staying, how they were moving from place to place, exactly who had control when and at what points changeovers were made. Grayson was sharing a suite in her hotel with her two protector agents, and one of them accompanied her at all times on the conference floor; she was even followed into the ladies' restroom, where presumably the agent stood guard while Grayson used the facilities.

I figured I would only have one clean shot at this, and that failure would be appropriately punished; it was a balancing act of doing what I had come there to do as quickly and cleanly as possible, and of waiting until a late enough moment in the proceedings that I would have a chance of a getaway without the whole conference coming after me if I revealed myself. So, although I chafed at the wasted time, I waited until the final day of the conference to make my move.

There was a changeover point, during the day when the agent minders changed shifts. On the third day, the roster suited my purposes admirably. One of the agents was a big, solidly built woman whose stony face was set in a single unchanging expression and who looked perfectly capable of knocking me out with one beefy fist. She was far too unlike the slender, small-boned Grayson to be of any use to me in my plan. The second one, her dark hair scraped back into a severe bun at the back of her head so tightly that she seemed to pull her eyes apart, was almost of a height with Grayson herself. This was important. It meant they could wear the same clothes, sort of, without anyone being greatly the wiser.

On the third day, it was the big woman who was on duty overnight and in the early morning, handing over to the dark-haired one after breakfast, after which she would be in charge of Grayson for the day.

The day-shift agent would be alone in the room, just before Grayson's custody was transferred. For just long enough. I left her, secured and sedated, in the closet of Grayson's bedroom in the suite and stepped out wearing her face and her uniform – which included a peaked cap with the security insignia blazoned on the front of it – when the other agent came to change shifts. She saw nothing amiss, and Grayson and I sailed out into the last day of the conference together.

It was the first time I was ever actually this close to her, never mind alone with her. If she did not react the way I needed her to... if she screamed, fought, resisted... I would have very little time to make a getaway, if one was even possible. I would have to time things very carefully, plan what would inevitably be a shocking reveal in a place where we weren't likely to be closely observed or interrupted at least for a precious few moments while I explained things, and then just see if any of this would ever really bear the kind of fruit I hoped for. I had not planned much beyond this high point (and, well, the subsequent escape). I remembered, with some chagrin, how I had urged Mal to have "a plan" for the aftermath of Celia's rescue – and the irony of how little of one I seemed to have for Grayson's.

It is the smallest of the unpredictable things that can throw everything into chaos, and I should have known that. It's impossible to plan for it, by definition, but I should have expected... something...that would throw me. What did, though, was a double whammy of a thing that piled quickly one on top of the other – the occurrence, and then the kick-in-the-belly realization.

The occurrence was simply the lightest of touches that I – in my shape as her escort – laid on Grayson's elbow as I attempted to guide her past an inconvenient knot of chattering conference folk who had chosen to stop for an animated conversation right in the middle of a busy corridor... and the effect of that touch. Incongruous as it might seem, as full as my mind was of her, this was the closest I had physically been to her, ever, and I had never touched her before – this, the first, touch, was almost visible, an actinic arc that briefly connected my fingertips to her arm.

My steps faltered, and she, too, stopped, hesitated, and then turned very slowly to face me, looking at me with those golden-green eyes.

"You're not Marguerite," she said. It was a flat statement, there was no question there.

I sucked in a deep breath, and held her gaze.

"Not quite," I said. "We need to talk."

That's when the second thing hit me, the realization.

The rationalizations I had held out for taking this mad course of action were still valid enough, I suppose – the freeing of a creature not unlike myself who might be held against her will, all the knight in shining armor stuff.

But the underlying reason for it all was far simpler and more real... although I had no real idea just when, where, how, or precisely why I had managed to fall in love with Grayson Garvin.

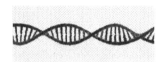

There was an "electrical room" right next to the elevators; it was locked, with a keypad security lock, but it was a trivial matter to find out what the code was. Grayson didn't appear at all put out when I shepherded her to the door I had hacked. When the door unlocked, she pushed it open and walked into the room first, ahead of me. I followed, meekly, shutting the door behind us with an audible snick as it closed and locked again.

She turned to face me, and waited.

I had planned for this moment, but that was before I knew what I now knew, and I found myself uncharacteristically bereft of words for a moment. But then the urgency of the situation reasserted itself, and my practical side shook itself free of the rosy mist that had descended on the rest of me.

"I know you have more questions than you can even think of asking, and we don't have much time," I said, by way of preamble. "We've crossed paths before, and I..."

"Let's start with who you are," she said. "And what happened to Marguerite. And how come you're here instead of her. And how come you've got her face."

I just went for broke.

"I'm the thing that this conference is all about," I said. "I'm the shifter. That's how I'm wearing her face. She's fine, or she will be by the time she wakes up. Which is all the time that I have. I needed to get close enough to you to talk to you, and I figured out a way, that's all."

"You're a shifter." She was staring at me, unblinking. "You... just... Turned... into Marguerite?"

"Technically," I said, "yeah, I guess."

"But you'd be Were," she said. "I can find – it's the only thing that I can – how did I not know, the moment I laid eyes on you?"

"You didn't before," I said. "Or at least you didn't let on that you did."

"When?" she said, frowning.

"It doesn't matter. A little while ago. But I was somebody..."

"You were wearing a *different* face?"

"At the time, yeah."

She reached out, laid her fingertips on my arm. I felt the same small shock as they touched, the same tiny spark of electricity. I wondered how much of that was purely in my own head, a reaction to the two of us touching physically, and if any of it had any actual physiological basis.

"I don't 'see' you," she said. "I can sense the presence of Were. Any kind of Were. But you just – don't – trigger – "

"How *do* you do that?" I asked, fatally diverted.

"I have no idea," she said, unhelpfully. "I just... know. That's all. But I didn't know. With you. Until you..." she swallowed, and glanced at the door. "What... do you want...?"

I noticed that she had absolutely no trouble at all accepting that I was who I said I was. It was both exhilarating and scary at the same time, this being accepted as a completely unremarkable thing. Admittedly the fact that I currently looked like her security handler, although she knew that I was not, was potent evidence for proving my claim – but still. There was an entire conference out there who would have freaked out if I had announced that I was the shifter. Grayson...took it as read. The only thing that bothered her, apparently, was the fact that she could not 'make' me until I chose to reveal my presence.

We really did not have a lot of time, and while I would have loved to discuss everything in great detail, explain every minute thing, tell her everything I knew and everything I suspected, I didn't have that luxury. I had to make my case, and in the next few minutes. Someone would notice that Grayson had disappeared. She might have had a personal minder, but I had no doubt that Marguerite had not been the only one who was charged with keeping an eye on this government asset.

She's asked me what I wanted. The true answer – in a lot of different ways, it now appeared – would have been simply, *You.* But that answer, like most simple things, required a complex explanation.

"I came to get you out," I said instead, and even that sounded lame when I spoke it out loud. "If you want out. This seemed like as good a time as any."

"This," she said. "The conference. The crowds."

"You're *never* alone," I pointed out. "It's much easier to hide in a crowd."

She nodded, giving me the point. "But you don't need to hide," she added, still frowning at Marguerite's face which was obstinately hovering in her sight. "You can be anybody, apparently."

"That was kind of part of the plan," I said. "You would need to..." And then I stopped, and looked at her. "So okay," I said, interrupting myself, asking the question I had needed to ask in the first place. "I may be getting the wrong end of the stick entirely. I may have misread everything. But here's the thing – do you want out? You don't... seem entirely happy to be here. To be doing what you are doing. And you and I – we're more alike than you know – we're part of the same program."

"What program?" she asked. "What on earth are you talking about?"

"That would take too long to explain right now," I said. "I need to know..."

"What, you want me just to make a choice, here and now? Just like that?" she said, with a touch of asperity. "Is it that easy for creatures like you to make decisions about your life? Really?"

"Creatures like *us*," I said. "And no. It isn't. Of course it isn't. This is horribly unfair, and I am an idiot, and I should probably have planned this a dozen different ways which would have made it easier. But in a very real way – and again, too long to explain now – time is running out. For me, at least. If I was going to do something, I had to do it quickly. And this conference..."

"Do what? How were you planning to spirit me away?" she asked, giving me a helpless shrug. "There would be a dozen people riding intercept between me and the door. And besides..."

That besides might have been couched as an afterthought, but I understood somehow, at a much deeper level, that it was the important thing in this conversation.

"Besides, what?" I asked.

She looked at me with complete honesty for perhaps the first time ever, dropping every pretense of a mask, and the bleakness in her eyes almost destroyed me.

"Where would I go?" she said quietly, spreading her hands in a gesture of resignation. "Nobody else has ever wanted me. This is – in a way – the only real home I've ever known."

"More people want you," I said, after I took a moment to collect myself, "than you know. Want you and me, both. You've been kept from your origins, by your handlers, because of their own reasons – not because this is your home."

"My origins? What do you know of my origins?" she said sharply, lashing out. "My mother died when I was five years old. There was nobody else who wanted me, apparently, so they dumped me into foster care – and I remember being trotted out for adoption inspections for several sets of 'parents' before I was seven. And then someone took me, and I suppose they cared for me as much as they can, but somehow when I was about thirteen or so they simply gave me up without a fight – and I was raised by the system, by caretakers and tutors, by minders like Marguerite, until they figured out what I could do, and since then it's been this life, this bloodhound existence – they find me useful, but they're the only ones who wanted me, who took on..."

I shook my head violently. "The woman who gave birth to you, who cared for you when you were an infant, was *not* your mother," I said. "Your real parents were both Were. Your mother was a fox. Your father was a rabbit. The cross was... engineered, because you were part of a genetic investigation program – the Lycan scientists wanted to know what would happen with a predator/prey cross. But they couldn't get your real mother to carry a pregnancy to term so they used a surrogate – who happened to be non-Were – to carry you, to have you. And then she kicked over the traces and decided to keep you, after she had you. And never, apparently, told you the truth at all. You're wrong about nobody wanting you; the Lycans have been trying to get hold of you for years. You're a prize. Same as me. The Lycans who created us want to know very badly how we tick. But the handlers who had you... wouldn't let the Were anywhere near you. Especially after you didn't Turn on schedule and then began to show your very useful abilities. Everything else followed that – but the question still remains – do you want out?"

She hesitated. "Where would I go? What would I do? Go straight to those Lycans you're talking about, and say, here I am, take me?"

At least she was safe, where she was. And in a way so was I, if she couldn't sense me like she could other Were-kind. This could have been pointless. But it had gone beyond that, for me, now.

"I've had quite a bit of experience keeping the Lycans from getting me," I said. "I could do the same for you. I could protect you."

"And what's your price?" she asked. "There's always a price. And at least I know what *they* want from me, the ones who've got me now. I've come to terms with that. But..."

She fingered her throat, as though she could feel a collar there, and I finally knew that I had not been entirely wrong. She was tasting freedom and she liked the taste – but she had been a prisoner too long, and prison had come to mean safety, after all. There might be little I could do about that.

"I have no price," I said.

"So why are you doing this...?"

"Because..." I swallowed. "If you come with me, I'll tell you. Someday."

She actually smiled. "That isn't fair."

"Maybe not. But we're really out of time. Tell me what you want, and I'll do it. I can walk out of here now and you'll never see me again."

"Don't be silly," she said, "I'll see you every time I lay eyes on Marguerite. So what was your plan, then?"

"My plan?"

"For springing me."

"Are you coming then?"

She hesitated again, and then lifted her head, her eyes flashing into a clear gold. "Yes," she said. "Let's say I am. Now tell me how you intend to do that."

I was not expecting this. Not the pure raw courage of it. On the other hand, I had barely expected anything less.

"The plan...?" I said. "Well, *you* can't walk out of here. You're right about that. But this person can – this body – this face that I am wearing. Marguerite. She can step out of here, and go straight out the front door. And nobody would raise an alarm."

"But how does that help..." she began, and then started putting it together in her mind. Her eyes glazed, briefly. "You want... to turn... into me."

She was quick. I smiled.

571

"Here's the thing I planned," I said, inasmuch as I had really 'planned' anything. I was winging this in an appalling manner. "I turn into you. You give me the clothes you're wearing, and I give you the clothes that I am – that Marguerite is – wearing. We walk out of here the same way we walked in, except that I'm you and you're Marguerite. Then you turn and walk out the front door. There's a key in the pocket of this uniform – room 210 at the Metropolitan Hotel. It's some three or four blocks away from here, going south. There's stuff there, and if you find enough that you need you don't even have to wait for me. But when I get there, eventually, I can maybe help. With anything you want help with."

"You plan on getting there yourself? How?"

"All I need to do after I show myself as you is to go somewhere and turn into something else," I said. "I too can just walk out of here, then."

"And if I don't wait for you? Are you going to hunt me down? Or point the Lycans at me?"

"Neither," I said. And clamped my mouth shut.

"And if I wait for you?"

I felt my cheeks – Marguerite's cheeks – flush. "Then we can make a real plan."

"You mean, stay together?"

"One of the options," I said. And for the first time I allowed myself to consider that possibility – going forward *with* her. With her at my side.

In a capacity that might mean more than just...

But now was not the time for daydreaming or fantasy.

"If we're doing this," I said, "we'd better do it. Now. I'm sorry, I should have planned this a lot better than I did – I should have planned it so that you had a chance to think about it, to make a real choice...."

"But you already knew that there was no real choice to be made at all, didn't you," she said quietly. "Okay, then. What do you want me to do?"

"I'll... Turn," I said. "Give me your clothes, and I'll pass Marguerite's clothes back to you. We get changed, we walk out of here, we walk out into the concourse, and then 'you' take 'me' into the busiest, thickest crowd that you can find. And when we're in the middle of it, I'll go one way, and you go for the door."

She fingered a strand of her red hair skeptically. "But I don't look anything like Marguerite," she pointed out.

"People won't be necessarily expecting Marguerite," I said. "When you put on the uniform, you become someone wearing a uniform. Without Grayson Garvin in arm's reach, you stop being specifically Marguerite. You become a security guard. *Any* security guard. Nobody will be looking for a red-haired security guard who happens to be walking out the door."

"And in the meantime, you..."

"I do whatever I need to do, next. I'll create a diversion, if I need to, to keep attention from you. You leave. You go to the hotel." *And wait for me. Or not. I guess I find out when I get there...*

She hesitated just once more, and then turned her back to me, that being as much privacy as we could manage in here, lifting her arms to begin to remove the top she was wearing and leaving me uncomfortably aware that in order to change I would, at some point before I put on a different set of clothes, have to be briefly naked in this tiny room right there beside her. But she was either not thinking about that, or had decided not to care. "All right, then," she said. "Go."

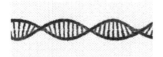

I f anybody looked too closely at the two people who emerged from the Electrical Room, they would be able to observe several unnerving things – the first, of course, was that the dark-haired security guard who went in never did come out; the second (if they took another look) would be that the security guard who *did* step out bore a somewhat remarkable resemblance to the person she was supposed to be guarding – and looked a little spooked. Her charge, however, was calm. Preternaturally calm. Everything that happened from here on would be unplanned and very much taking advantage of the situation as it presented itself – there was absolutely no safe course to be steered at all – and somehow it didn't matter in the least. If anyone had glanced at a readout of my pulse and heart-rate at this point, without knowing the circumstances, they might have assumed I was sitting in an armchair in a patch of sunshine with a good book and a cup of tea. Perhaps it was because of an absolutely bone-deep conviction that I was where I should be, and doing exactly what I should be doing.

It lasted all of five minutes. Until the two of us began approaching the large crowd that I had specified. And as we were getting close to that crowd I registered two things.

One was that the crowd contained the *Vox Verae Hominis* delegation, and that Barbican Bain was part of it, as oily and confident as ever, smiling that evil serene smile of his, completely in control of his world.

The other was the approach of someone else from the other side of the crowd, an individual who had only just entered the concourse at the far end. Someone I knew. Someone who should not have been here at all. Someone whose expression told me that there were memories which had been lost... which had fought their way to the surface of her mind.

Celia had remembered. I could see in her eyes that she had remembered it all.

And whose fault it had been.

"Oh, crap," I said, softly, staring at the impending collision. I had no idea what Celia was going to do but I knew why she was here. It was to confront Bain, the architect of her shattered life. To lay the darkness he had brought at his feet and dare him to look at it. And I could not possibly think of anything worse that could happen, on so many different levels.

"What?" Grayson's head swiveled sharply to look in the direction I was staring at. She saw Celia, and focused on her. "Who's that? Do you know her?"

"That's the closest thing I have to a sister," I said, "and she's about to do something that she'll never be able to take back. No, damn it, this is not what I risked everything to save her for." I looked around, desperate for something, anything, but Celia was coming, inexorable as fate, and the only thing that I had working in my favor was that she hadn't noticed Bain yet. "I need to..."

But it was too late. She had seen him, and had called out his name. I saw him turn, look at her, frown, and then, as she began speaking, put it together.

"You killed me," Celia said. I could hear her clearly, across the concourse; the others had opened up a space between her and Bain, and the two of them stood facing each other across a stretch of open marble flooring, like two elemental spirits. "You killed me, but I came back. And I remember. And it all began with you..."

Something kindled in his eyes as she spoke – was it unease? – she could damage his reputation, and his current standing, and everything he had worked so hard to gain. I don't know if turning into him that one time had given me some insight into his mind and the way he thought, but I knew what he was going to do a moment before he did it... and just as quickly knew what I was going to do next.

I turned to Grayson, and spoke quickly. "Now I need a favor from you. Whatever you decide to do when you get out of this hall. That girl. Her name is Celia Marsh. Something is about to happen that will tear this place apart, and I'm going to try and defuse it – you wanted a distraction – this is the ultimate distraction – when I start talking, don't look back, don't hesitate, go straight to that door... *and take her with you.* You're security, nobody will be surprised. Take her back to the hotel – 210, Metropolitan, remember – I'll try and get there as soon as I can. Do it."

"But you are going to..."

"*Do it,*" I said, watching Bain slowly raise an arm and point a shaking finger at Celia. "Now. Get ready."

"Shifter," Bain said, his voice modulated to that of an ancient prophet making a pronouncement. "It is the shifter. It is the unholy presence that I felt once before. It has come back here to defy me – to destroy me. *It is the Metamorph!*"

A murmur, and then a cry, swept the crowd. I had no way of knowing if Grayson had obeyed me because all my attention was focused on Bain as I stepped forward, staggered forward, and raised my own arm to point at him.

"No," I said, "it's him. He's the one. *He* is the Metamorph. You are the unholy one. You. You..."

The crowd roared, and I took another step forward, and fell to my knees, still pointing at him and mouthing *Metamorph*.

I was wearing Grayson's face. People knew who Grayson was, what she could do. Her abilities were tested, and proven, and had been going on for some time; she was a known thing, a government agent, trusted. Bain... was a new arrival on the scene. True, he had said he could recognize the shifter on sight, but he'd *said* that, he hadn't proved it. And to anyone watching who knew the actors – and everyone at this conference knew the actors in this particular little drama – it was Grayson's trusted word against Bain's untested one.

His people reacted predictably. So did the government people. The crowd swirled together, apart. I could not afford to spare any attention to see what was going on at the peripheries – I was still kneeling there, on the cold hard stone floor, finger pointed at Bain and my eyes on fire, when they came for me, and I felt hands close around my arms, lifting me up, bearing me away.

I allowed myself to close my eyes then, fall into those arms, feigning a dead faint. Someone picked me up and carried me. I dared not open my eyes to see where.

I had no idea what had happened in my wake, or what would happen next.

I hoped they had both got out.

It would be a while before I could even hope to find out.

They carried me back to Grayson's suite, and I could hear the babble of voices all around me as I allowed them, eyes still closed, to lay me down on the bed. They'd found Marguerite, and the high-pitched female voice, verging on shrill, was her, talking about how she had ended up in the closet. A couple of other voices were debating how much my – Grayson's – security had been compromised, and whether it was best to let her – me – come back to consciousness in her own time or whether a dash of cold water in the face was indicated, followed by some sharp questions. I kept my eyes closed and my face still throughout it all, and eventually it seemed as though cooler heads prevailed, and the voices receded, followed by the sound of a closing door and the distinctive click of a lock being turned. So I wasn't far wrong, in that sense, at least. They had decided to let me have my swoon and come back to life whenever it was that I chose to do so but they were still taking the precaution of keeping the door locked, just in case.

I peered out through my lashes, moving my head a fraction to scan the room, and it seemed as though they had drawn the curtains over the sliding glass doors to the tenth-floor balcony, leaving them open just a crack, just enough for a sliver of light to come through. In that light, the rest of the room appeared to be empty except for me. I sighed and stirred, giving a sign of life just to see if there was a reaction, but there was only silence and stillness, and I finally risked opening my eyes and taking a proper look around.

The room had a bathroom opening out from it, and they had left the light on; I could not see inside from where my head was on the bed but I listened intently for the sounds of anyone actually being in there and eventually allowed myself to come to the conclusion that nobody was in there, either.

I was alone.

I wasn't sure for how much longer I would be, and as soon as I came to that conclusion I sat up very quietly and took off the clothes I was still wearing, arranging them carefully on the bed, in the exact same position that my body had been occupying when they had laid me there. It looked creepily as though I had just *evaporated*, leaving my clothes behind right there where I had been – which, in a sense, was precisely what I *was* doing. Naked, I padded across the thick carpet to the sliding doors and quietly, very quietly, opened the locking mechanism – it would be a pity that I couldn't lock the thing again from the outside after I stepped out because that would have been a perfect locked room mystery, but one couldn't have everything. I stepped outside, closed the door gently behind me, and thought myself into a crow. My first shape, and still one of the easiest ones for me to wear, and my favorite.

I suppose I should have just gone straight to the Metropolitan Hotel and started to deal with things there, but I could not help myself – I wanted to be there when someone discovered that bed. I had a healthy sense of the theatric, so there, and I had set up a pretty good piece of theatre. I wanted to see how it played out.

The rewards were not too long in coming. I heard a commotion inside the room, first – obviously I couldn't see inside, a crow peering in through the crack in the curtains would have been a little too much – but even if I didn't get to see the moment of the actual reveal I could hear the chaos break out when somebody had opened the door to check up on me. And then someone flung open the curtains, and the expression on the woman's face was quite enough of a reward for my wait. Like any crow would do when startled, I cast off from the balcony railing where I had been perching, and flew away, cawing. I heard the door open behind me, and as I circled around I saw two of the government suits, then three, then three and a woman who could only have been Marguerite, all crowd out onto that balcony and look around frantically, starting with, reluctantly, down, for the possible sight of a body splayed on the ground below. But that was all I allowed myself. I let my spiral widen out and I flew higher, across the rooftops, towards the Metropolitan Hotel.

The curtains were drawn in the window of room 210 at the Metropolitan Hotel. It was an older building, with no balconies like the modern luxury hotel from which I had just escaped – just windows, overlooking either the busy street or an inner courtyard which held a small parking lot. I had weighed the advantages of those views when I had requested my room – looking out onto the street gave one the advantage of being able to watch that street, if one needed to, but the inside-view rooms had the greater advantage of being discreet. That paid dividends as I swooped in now, hovering just outside the closed-curtained window of the courtyard facing room 210 in a most un-crow-like fashion, tapping at the window with my beak.

I had to do it a couple of times before the curtain twitched and I saw

Grayson's face peering out. She looked startled, and then half-turned, looking back into the room, before finally reaching out and lifting the latch to open the window. She stepped back as I folded my wings and dived inside, landing on the floor at the foot of the bed on which I was relieved to see Celia, and waddling into the bathroom in the most dignified way that a crow could, to change back to human form out of everyone's sight. I had a thumping headache when I was fully Saladin again, and the mirror in the bathroom gave me a glimpse of hollowed-out eyes with dark circles around them. This was taking it out of me, unexpectedly so.

"Hey," I called out softly from the bathroom, from behind a half-closed door, "can you throw me..."

But Grayson was ahead of me, and before I could finish that sentence the things I had been about to ask for were thrust into the bathroom, dangling from the fingertips of her outstretched arm – a pair of sweatpants and a black hoodie.

I pulled both on, and padded out into the room in bare feet. Grayson was waiting, standing in the middle of the room, arms crossed across her chest. She had raided my luggage and wore one of my own T-shirts, and I had to admit it looked better on her than it ever did on me.

"Okay," she said, "that was... spectacular."

"Hey, that was just a bird," I said. "I changed into *you*, remember."

"Oh yeah," she said. "Vividly. And who are you now?"

I managed a grin. "Sorry. Too tired for another mask right now. This time all you get is just me."

"You do realize," she said softly, "that you haven't even told me your *name*?"

I blinked at her owlishly for a moment or two, replaying our conversations in my mind. I didn't think she could possibly be right – if she had been, why on earth would she have ever trusted me enough to go anywhere with me? But unless I was just *that* tired and my memory was shutting down completely I actually could not recall any single instant where I had gone so far as to introduce myself.

"Saladin," I said at last. And then, because there was no point in dancing around it, gave her the full whammy. "Saladin van Schalkwyk. It's a long story."

To her credit, she didn't make any of the obvious cracks. "It's a start," she said. "By the way, Saladin van Schalkwyk, you look like hell."

I ran my fingers through my hair, in what might have been a futile gesture of trying to improve matters. I was pretty sure it did not.

"I bet," I said. "If I look like I feel, I'm sure they can use me to scare small children. After the day I've had..." But the thought of the clothes laid out on the bed, back in the other hotel, did bring a twitch to my mouth. I found myself wanting to tell Grayson all about it, to share a laugh about it, although I did feel a sudden stab of insecurity, wondering whether she found any of this amusing at all. "I'm sorry," I said instead. "I really burned your bridges. If you *wanted* back... I'm not sure you could, any more."

"You burned a lot of bridges, between you," she said, nodding at Celia as she spoke. "There's the next part of that long story. Just who is *she*?"

I glanced at Celia. She was lying on the bed breathing in shallow little breaths, her eyes closed.

"I found some aspirin in your kit," Grayson said. "I gave her two. I didn't know what else to do. She was in a state. I could barely wrangle her here. I think she's cried herself into a stupor."

"I'll sort it," I said, and ran a frustrated hand through my hair again. This, I had not planned for. It was going to... complicate things. "It's another long story. In a nutshell... her brother is someone I've known since we were both children. I honestly think we would probably have done murder for each other, if it had come to that. This girl... she's his older sister. And he went through hell believing that he had been instrumental in handing her the drugs which he – his entire family – thought that she had overdosed on, the thing that killed her."

"*Killed* her?" Grayson echoed, staring at Celia. "But..."

"He found her," I said. "Still alive. Very broken. I helped him snatch her back, and heal her. But there were things from that half-life that she'd led, in between that 'death' and the moment she awoke back into her true self, that she had mercifully lost, buried in the back of her mind, and it was probably better so... until Barbican Bain came back."

"From where?" Grayson said, sounding honestly bewildered.

I couldn't blame her.

"Bain was a teacher, back in the day," I said. "*Her* teacher. And he was a Were-hating little snot even then. But all he could do, as a teacher, is make life difficult or impossible for those of his charges who happened to be of Were blood. It was *he* who triggered that overdose – she was trying to delay her Turn, until she could...oh, long story, *really*. Sad one. Let's just say that she's... special. To Mal; to me. When I saw her in that hall... facing down Bain..." I stopped, shook my head. "I don't even know how she – I'd better phone Mal, let him know I've got her and she's okay, maybe he's got some idea..."

It might have been the idea of calling Mal that made my eyes go to the phone by the bedside, and it was only then that I noticed a little red light flashing insistently on it. I glanced questioningly back at Grayson.

She looked uncomfortable, almost scared. "It rang," she said. "I kind of... let it. I didn't know what I was supposed to say to anyone who might be calling here, or if they'd be expecting anybody but you. So I figured they'd call back, if it was important. And then they seem to have left a message."

"Did you listen to it?" I asked, and she shook her head. "How long ago?"

She shrugged. "I don't know. Ten minutes, maybe? Half an hour?"

I would learn one thing about Grayson very quickly. She had absolutely zero ability to estimate things like the passage of time. With her, half an hour could mean anything from five minutes to half a morning – it didn't matter how long something literally lasted, it was how long it seemed to have taken in her own mind, and that often bore little resemblance to the reality she lived in.

I crossed to the phone, and toggled the message button.

The voice on the other end of the line was female, quiet, almost shaking.

"I don't know who I'm talking to," the woman said. "I am hoping that it is somebody who cares about the girl called Celia, the one who today at the conference centre... look. I overheard the name of this hotel, the number of this room. I got the idea that the person who spoke wanted Celia safe, and I hope very much that I am right. Because I... I know this story. From back when she... when... Look, I may be putting myself in a situation here, one I know absolutely nothing about, but my name is Emily Winterthorn. I wrote books which a young Celia Marsh loved. I was perhaps the thing that caused what I believed to be her death. I named a character for her in one of my books, dedicated it to... I'll be in the lobby. Downstairs. Waiting. If anyone hears this and can tell me anything more."

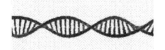

A t some point during this day it had simply become impossible to act on a considered decision. There was no time to consider. Things just kept falling, pushed over one by another, and everything became a matter of trusting one's instincts and acting on impulse.

The phone call from the lobby was no exception.

If there was anything in this world that I had been expecting less than for Emily Winterthorn, the Emily Winterthorn of Celia's heartbreaking diaries, to show up at this particular moment, I could not think of it as I held the receiver of that hotel room telephone to my ear in blank and astonished silence. And then I put the phone down, very slowly.

Instinct.

"There's someone I need to go see," I said to Grayson. "Downstairs. In the lobby. I'll... look, I know I owe you a lot more explanations. I'll do my best when I come back up. Where are my shoes?"

I stuffed my bare feet into a pair of sneakers, aware of the weight of Grayson's wary silence, and headed out of the room. In passing, I caught a glimpse of myself in the mirrored doors of the closet, and realized just what it was that Grayson had meant when she had been so trenchant earlier about my appearance. I looked exhausted, shadow-eyed, brooding, slouching my tired shoulders in their black hoodie, my ankles sticking bonily out of the bottoms of my track pants before they vanished into the tops of my sneakers. My hair was lying on my shoulders, dark and lanky and looking as though it had needed a good scrub three days ago. I had never really showed any great bent towards facial hair so I lacked the semi-unshaven look that some might have had in my place but aside from that I looked like someone I myself would find it hard to trust, a skinny, scary, dusky-skinned and dark-haired waif who might have been a dangerous genie out of some carelessly rubbed lamp. But I didn't have the luxury of the only cure for all of these things – time, time to rest up and get some sleep, or a shower, or a decent meal.

Emily Winterthorn was downstairs, now. An unlikely ghost from Celia's past. If I were to find out anything further about that, I'd have to wade in as I was... and hope that she was the kind of writer who looked past first impressions.

I had no idea what she looked like, a fact which I only really brought to the forefront of my mind as I stepped out into the lobby of the hotel and looked around. But it wasn't as though this was the local resort with one of those busy and cavernous entrance halls. The Metropolitan had a serviceable registration desk, and a small space between it and the front door graced by three overstuffed armchairs around a small coffee table flanked by two potted palms. In this confined area, only one person sat stiffly on the edge of one of the armchairs, staring down into a cellphone she held in her right hand.

She was hardly the type to be glued to a cellphone – not young, not trendy. If anything, she was rather a motherly type, her dark but graying hair up in an untidy knot with strands falling out around her face as if she hadn't had a chance to freshen up lately, her face round and graced with crow's feet spraying out from the edges of her eyes and, currently, a deep worried frown etched into her forehead. Her hand, folded around her phone, was wearing the no-longer-smooth skin of an older woman, upholstering short stubby fingers which made a gallant attempt at elegance with a couple of stylish rings.

She looked tired, too. As tired as I did.

I had no real idea of how to play this, except by ear; her own instincts must have been dialed up into overdrive as much as mine were, though, because she looked up from the phone a fraction of a second after I turned up and paused, hesitating, at the foot of the stairs. Our eyes locked, and a silence that probably felt longer than it was stretched between us. And then I said,

"I got your message."

She got to her feet, very slowly, dropping the hand with the cellphone to her side.

"Who are you?" she asked carefully.

"I'm her friend," I said. "You said you overheard – about this place – where? How?"

"There was a young woman," Emily said reluctantly. "In the conference center. With some sort of a security guard. I don't know her name, I know that she's supposed to be working for the government, I've seen her around the halls over the last few days. I have no idea why she would care enough to want to protect...*her*... the girl who confronted this Bain... but I heard her tell the security guard. The hotel. The room number. And then she – this young woman – she brought all the attention onto herself. She didn't sound as though she was doing it for any other reason except to make sure that ... the other girl... got away."

We were carefully not using names, I understood. Even if things got convoluted and confused. The two of us knew what we were talking about. That was enough.

"What were *you* doing at the conference?" I asked, aware that I was sounding as though I was putting her through an interrogation, but that was one connection that I couldn't make.

She permitted herself a small dry chuckle. "I would have thought I'd made myself enough of a nuisance in Were affairs, in the years since... since I first crossed paths with *her*, in the aftermath of what happened to her... for my name to be rather better known than that to anyone who was paying any sort of attention," she said.

"Sorry. I was rather too focused on other stuff, of late. You said... you know this story. How much of it are you aware of? You might be just scraping the surface of it all."

She hesitated, but apparently she decided to trust me, despite my outlandish and possibly even threatening appearance.

"I got a letter," she said. "Back then. Back at the time. From her sister. Her younger sister. She told me, in broad strokes. And I was appalled enough at what I learned to look into it in more detail. The name – that name – the teacher involved – I have never forgotten it. I shuddered when I learned on the news what... he had become. But I can't say I was surprised, given what I already knew. But she – she – the sister said the girl was dead. I dedicated a book to her – I felt so responsible for that death – I felt as though it had been my carelessness that caused – "

"You were very important to her," I said. "She wrote as much – in her diary – but you – the circumstances just happened to collapse on your head, and hers – if it hadn't been the two of you, he would have found a way to do damage elsewhere, to someone else. You just happened to get in the way of hate and fear and it ran you both over."

Emily clutched harder at her phone. "But... she's *alive*?"

"For a long time, after they thought she died, the 'life' that she had was a hard and appalling one," I said honestly. "Much of it, after her brother and I got her out, she didn't remember. And that was probably good. But then *he* came back into prominence, and once she saw him, it – I don't know – triggered everything. I think she has remembered it all. I never expected her, here, putting herself out there the way she did. That was... I have to figure out a way to deal with it. But yes. She's alive. And right now... I think she is wishing very hard that the original version of her story was true after all."

I wiped my mouth with the back of my hand, a gesture of pure frustration; my eyes must have kindled at the thoughts that roiled in my head because I saw Emily flinch. "God," I said. "*God*. The way she was... when we rescued her. Almost catatonic. Sweet, empty shell of a girl with nothing inside. I thought we'd got her out of that, past it. Now... I don't know how to stop her sliding back in. Or how we would ever pull her out if that black hole closes over her head again."

"If you think it would help," she said carefully, "only if you think it would be of any help... would it make any difference... if I spoke to her? Would she still remember my name?"

"She remembers it all, now," I said savagely, hating Barbican Bain and the long shadow he had cast with everything that was in me. And then looked at Emily Winterthorn's earnest face again, and let instinct guide me again. Instinct made me turn back towards the staircase. "You'd better come with me."

She gathered up a voluminous bag from the floor at her feet and followed me without another word.

Grayson, caught halfway between the bathroom and the bed bearing a glass of water, turned with a startled and instantly guarded stare as Emily and I walked into the room. On the bed, Celia was sitting up, her shoulders hunched and her face hidden by the hair falling forward as she stared at her bare feet on the floor.

"It's fine," I said, "it's a friend."

"She just woke up," Grayson said in a low voice. "Wanted a glass of water."

Emily was staring at Grayson. "You were there," she said. "You were the one who said – you were the one who sent the security person to get Celia – you're the one I overheard – but I saw you pass out, I saw them carry you away, after you pointed at Bain as the metamorph – how did you get here?"

"Actually," I said wearily, "that was me. Wearing her face. The witch they all came there to hunt? That 'metamorph' everyone was accusing everyone else of being... You're looking at him."

"You mean you're real?" Emily asked, staring at me.

"Oh yeah," I said. "Very."

That required an hour's explanation or none at all – particularly at that moment, when the girl on the bed hunched her shoulders ever closer together in a tight knot of misery and appeared to be on the point of throwing up right there on the carpet

Emily, peering past Grayson, already on overload, brought a hand to her mouth in a gesture of raw emotion, her eyes brimming with tears.

"That's Celia?" she whispered. "That's really Celia? She's *alive*? Oh, thank God..."

"Gray," I said, "let her take Celia the water."

Grayson handed Emily the glass, after a startled look in my direction which I couldn't immediately interpret, but then, as Emily accepted the offering and walked forward into the room with it, hung back beside me as we both stood and watched.

"*Gray*?" she said.

"Sorry. Does it bug you?"

"Nobody's ever called me that before. I kind of like it that you did. It's.... new."

A new world. Falling into shape around us, between us.

Her hand drifted sideways, her fingers touched mine, and then twined into them as we watched Emily go down on one knee beside the bed, one hand on Celia's shoulder, the other offering the glass of water, murmuring something soft and gentle as she folded an almost visible wing of nurturing care around the girl. It was what Celia needed – it was so *exactly* what Celia needed right then. I saw her look up, searching this stranger's face with puzzled eyes. Gray drew breath to say something, but I squeezed her hand in warning to stay silent – and it was in that silence that we both heard it.

"I've waited a long time to meet you," Emily said, her voice low but loud enough to reach the two of us hanging back next to the door to the bathroom. "My name is Emily. Emily Winterthorn."

Gray and I heard the words, heard Celia gasp, saw her lips part in a sort of shocked half-smile... and then she burst into tears.

Emily put the glass of water away on the nightstand beside the bed, drew herself up to sit beside Celia, and folded the sobbing girl into her arms, holding Celia's head against her shoulder, rocking her like a child

"Who *is* that?" Gray asked softly, a small smile painted on her lips, her own eyes very bright.

"Sometimes," I said, "destiny sends an angel."

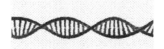

None of us could stand the close confines of that hotel room, once we had all calmed down sufficiently to consider the matter, and so despite it probably being wiser to lay low and keep out of sight we decided that we would go and find some place where we could sit and talk, preferably over a meal – I myself could not remember when I had last eaten anything, and Celia for sure could use something in terms of pure comfort food. We found a nearby café that served pasta and coffee and cheesecake, and tried to pretend that we weren't this mismatched knot of people huddling together in our booth and keeping our voices low. Emily and Celia would not be recognizable by anyone but as for Gray and me I thought a few basic precautions were in order before we could appear in public. I had taken a few moments to change again, into jeans and a dark T-shirt, a baseball cap pulled down over my eyes; Gray, on my insistence, wore dark glasses and had pulled on the black hoodie that I'd been wearing, the hood pulled up to hide her bright hair.

"You may not have been following events, after it all broke loose, because you were all in the middle of it," Emily said, "but you left complete chaos behind. The Vox delegation withdrew immediately, whisking Mr. Bain out of sight – he hasn't actually been seen since, at all, and there's a persistent rumor that he's out, but it isn't clear on whether it's of his own will or by being forced out. Either way, he's been compromised, and he's probably become too much of a liability as a public figure. The Were delegations are in something of a panic, the government people are tight lipped about it all, and I don't even know what the fallout is from Grayson's having gone missing under inexplicable circumstances – what if *she* had been this metamorph all the time? The whole conference just... imploded..."

"Is there anything left to talk about?" Grayson asked, scowling.

"I think, very little," Emily said gravely. "At least on the surface they had something of a common goal – but you've polarized them all now, and nobody is trusting anyone at the moment. I hate to say it, but I think the truce has been not so much cracked as shattered into shards. You may have fired the first shots in a new war."

"What war?" I asked, rousing.

"Human against Were," Emily said. "For a little while, here, they may have tried... to... rein it in. To *civilize* it. To put it under the rule of law. But I'm not sure that law can survive the existence of a true shifter, someone who breaks all the rules from either side."

"I didn't ask to be born this way," I said.

"I know. And it isn't your fault. But you're here, and that's the way things are. I don't think any of them would show you mercy, now. You're the enemy."

"If he's the common enemy doesn't that mean that *some* of the rest of them are allies by way of simply having that common enemy to fight against?"

"In theory," Emily said. "But it never works out that way. There are too many cracks there for there to be a true alliance – they might work together under duress for a single common purpose but as soon as they achieved that purpose – if they ever got you – they'd splinter into a dozen different factions with different ideas about what to do with you."

"So if they keep trying to catch me, we're still okay?" I said bleakly. "I'm the object of the Great Hunt, the white stag, the thing they can mythically chase forever... but if they get an arrow into me – it will be silver, of course, given Were legend – they'll rip me apart and then fall on each other's throats over my carcass?"

"You've so *dramatic*," Celia said faintly.

I turned to look at her, my gaze softening. "And you," I said. "What on earth were you thinking, coming out here?"

"I have no idea," she said. "I really don't. I am not making this up. Yes, I remembered, when I saw him on TV, I remembered... it all... but the one thing I have no clear memory of is how I left the compound, how I got to the city, how I got to the conference center, how I found him at all. It was as though I was on complete autopilot. I sleepwalked here."

"She can't go back to this compound," Emily said briskly. "They'll know who she is..."

"She's got an entirely new identity there," I said.

"Well, they might trace that," Emily said. "If nobody else, the Vox people will want to hunt her down. They will want someone to blame for Bain's downfall. She's a perfect scapegoat."

I didn't want to have to deal with this, not now, not with my own life hanging in the balance like it was – but clearly it was back up to me. I buried my face briefly in my hands, gulping air, my sudden inability to draw an adequate breath back with me and reminding me forcefully of Greta's diagnosis. I had no idea how bad things were going to get, if I could even take on the responsibility. But she was here, and she was Mal's, and she was mine.

"I can change her identity again," I said. "When we get back, I can start to – "

"Sarah Winterthorn," Emily said. "I have a niece... had a niece... she and her friends were in a bad car crash, one night after a school dance, several of them were badly hurt... and one died. Sarah died. She was only seventeen years old." Clearly the memory was a hard one because Emily's throat worked as she tried to swallow, hard. But then she had it under control and looked up at me, resolutely. "I have her birth certificate. If you need an identity – and if you can use this – she can be Sarah Winterthorn. She can come with me. I will take care of her."

Celia was staring at her with parted lips, and so was Gray. But I was tracking the possibilities.

"I'm sorry about your niece, Emily," I said. "But this idea... has its problems... you say Sarah *died*, and it wasn't all that long ago, and there will be living people – family, friends – who will know that she died. If she suddenly turns up again, with you, and doesn't even look like the girl they might remember..."

"I'm a *writer*," Emily said. "There's always a story. I can put together a story for this. It's like something from the witness protection files, really. Sarah's friends – well, none of them kept in touch, much, afterwards. They might not even know about it. Sarah's mother is my younger sister – and losing Sarah was tough for her, when the accident happened – but this would give that senseless death a meaning, for her, maybe..."

"If you think it might work out in practice, on the ground, there are things I can do with the official record," I said. "But you'd better be sure. This is yet another resurrection. You only get so many in a single lifetime."

Emily scrabbled in her enormous handbag and came up with a paperback.

"I'm sure," she said steadily. "Because of *this*."

It was an Emily Winterthorn novel Celia had never seen – it had been written after she was gone. She had not known that she had been immortalized in it, her name given to the protagonist of the book. She had never been told about the dedication inside. Now Emily handed it to her and she held it in trembling hands, staring at the dedication, trying not to break down and cry again.

I had seen the dedication. Jazz had showed it to me. I had been thinking about it when Celia was her empty shadow of a self, mourning the hollowness that the beautiful gesture had become. And now, like some sort of prophecy, it had come full circle and the girl to whom the book had been dedicated had turned into this wounded young woman, and the dedication was there to heal, not memorialize.

I knew it by heart: *To the real Celia, who offered her life as a sacrifice to Word and to Story because she loved them so much – and to Jazz, younger sister, who ensured that the sacrifice would not be in vain.*

"They may be looking for her," I said carefully, trying not to wreck the moment but aware that logistics had to be dealt with. "She needs to be out of the city. Quickly."

"I have my car," Emily said. "They won't be asking for papers, not just yet. If we leave tonight, I can have her out of here and somewhere safe and quiet by tomorrow night. If I give you my email...?"

I pushed my phone at her. "Put your contact details in there," I said. "And take her. Mal and Asia will understand the necessity. I'll be in touch."

While Emily busied herself with this task, I turned to Celia and took both her hands in mine. "I'm sorry," I said. "I thought it might be for the best that you never recall everything that happened."

Celia shook her head. "I need all my pieces," she whispered. "Or I'll never be real again. But Saladin... I remember now... I remember my little girl..."

"I know where she is," I said quietly. "I've been keeping an eye on her."

"Is she safe?"

"She is cared for," I said. "She is considered important. I won't lose track of her. And if ever there is a time I think I can get it done – and if I think that is the best thing for her – I will find her, and I will take her away. But right now, she's very young, and she's an unknown, and you and she... you can't ever play happy families. That's been wrecked from the beginning. It was never the plan."

"I know," she said. "The best I can hope for is to know that you are looking out for her, like you do for us all."

I saw Gray's lashes fall over her eyes at that last remark.

Before I could figure that one out, Emily thrust my phone back at me. "There," she said. "All in there." And then, to Celia, "Honey? Do you have luggage anywhere, something you want to collect, or pick up?"

Celia shook her head. "If I did, I don't know where to begin looking for it," she said faintly.

"Then the only stop we need to make is at my hotel so I can throw my stuff into my suitcase, and we can go home," Emily said. "I'll take care of you. I promise."

We slipped out of the booth and I gave Celia a farewell hug and then, impulsively, Emily one too.

"I'll contact you as soon as I can," I said. "Be careful."

"I can take anybody on," Emily said, smiling, and did look like a soldier in a little old lady disguise. I had no doubt that if anyone tried to say a cross word to Celia they'd have Emily at their throat. "Come on, then, honey. Time we were on our way."

Celia turned, a few steps away, looking back at me. "Tell Mal..."

"I will," I said. "It will be fine."

"I wish..."

"I know. I wish, too..."

She smiled at me, a luminous smile, the kind that Mal would have found familiar. She smiled at me as she would have done on her brother, whom she loved. And then she turned away, and fell into step beside Emily, and the door of the café closed behind the two of them.

I sighed, taking a step back to almost collapse back onto the bench of the booth.

"More coffee?" Gray said. "Or do you just need to find a place to hibernate?"

"I couldn't sleep," I said. "My head's pounding. Coffee might be good."

I looked up, trying to catch the attention of the server, but Gray pushed me back down.

"I'll take care of it," she said. "Stay."

She disappeared, briefly, and I used the moment of solitude to lay my head against the high back of the booth bench and close my eyes. I thought about my long-vanished father and my mother who had buckled under the weight of – well – me. I was the legacy they had left behind – and my own legacy, if Emily was right, would be as the one who had brought down the fragile house of cards in which the Were and the humans both had been sheltering against the storms of the world. Whatever the issues were on the negative side of the scales, the fact remained that for a short and golden time we *did* manage to coexist, somehow, the two kinds, and live together in a cobbled-together truce if not peace.

Of course, it was never that rosy. If it had been, there would have been no reason to distrust each other at all. No reason to be wary of one another. No reason at all for training someone like Gray to do what she did, before I came.

Gray. She was a domino. The one whose fall started the rest. It was for her I came here. If I had not been there – I would never have been in the conference hall – I would never have been there to see Celia confront Barbican Bain and lance all the boils of her painful past – I would never have...

"So," she said, Gray, the one I was thinking about, the one who was the light that had guided me here, as she slipped back into the booth opposite me. "What do we do now?"

I opened my eyes, giving her a weary smile. "We?" I queried. "You're sticking around?"

"Don't you know that saying," she said, "if you save someone's life you become responsible for them. Well, you saved mine."

"Not exactly," I said. "They wouldn't have harmed you."

"Then maybe," she said, and I realized she was utterly serious, "I saved yours."

I looked at her in silence, and she stared back at me – and then the moment broke as the server brought over the fresh coffees she had gone to

SHIFTER

commandeer.

After the server withdrew, Gray gave me a half smile, one that glittered in her golden eyes but barely curved the corners of her lips.

"I came away," she said. "I chose to come away. I chose to come away *when you asked*. I didn't even know your name, remember? I kind of thought that meant you were asking me along for the ride. I might not have..."

To my chagrin, I found tears springing into my own eyes. "I haven't told you everything," I said.

"I figured that," she said. "You said it was a long story and you barely managed a few paragraphs of it so far. I was hoping it would eventually come out. There are things about *me* you aren't exactly aware of, if it comes to that. We've the rest of our lives – those we became responsible for – to find it all out."

"I can promise to spend the rest of my life with you, if you want that," I said. "But I can't ask the same from you."

"Why not?" she asked, her voice bewildered but with a sharp edge.

"Because I have no idea how long I've got," I said at last, laying the truth on the table. "There's so much I want to do – I need to do – and yet – this shifter thing – it seems to be wearing me out. Literally. Every time I change, I hasten the end. A doctor told me I have the heart of an old man. This – " I gestured at myself, at my appearance. "This is not what I am on the inside. I am growing older faster every minute I draw breath..."

"We all are," she said, but I could tell that she was surprised, appalled even.

I had never wanted more to have someone just like her at my side – someone who knew me for what I was and accepted that, who could be my friend and my partner and my soulmate – and I had never felt more selfish for wanting that, for wanting to ask it of her. *I was dying.* How could I shackle Gray to that?

"Not that simple," I said. "I mean, yeah, it's true. But with me... it's got an endgame. And I know it. Oh, I don't know it *exactly* – I could linger for five years, or maybe ten – I'm a stubborn nut, and I might cling to longer than that, through a sheer refusal to shuffle off on schedule – but that doctor who told me all this, she doesn't know, she can't tell me, it might depend entirely if I shift into something else one time too many and just *stop*, right there. And that's not even getting into just how much the damage will affect me, eventually. But I have Celia to protect – and make sure her daughter is cared for – and then there's Jazz – if Emily is right, this will end whatever schemes they may have had for her, and I have to warn her to be careful – and there are others, just like me, whom I need to..."

I stopped, because she was smiling, and the smile was luminous.

"You're a kind of ultimate anti Peter Pan," she said "Not only do you not stay forever young but you grow older faster than any of the rest of us – and yet there you are, gathering together your lost boys and girls, riding in to the rescue, just like you did with me. You're a meteor, Saladin. A comet.

Streaking across the sky, a blaze of light, you aren't there long but while you are, ah, while you are... I seem to have spent my entire life so far hitched up to an ox wagon, plodding quietly in the ruts they pointed me along, never looking up, just going where I was herded and doing what I was told. And now... now I've gone and hitched my own wagon to a shooting star."

She reached out over the table and took my hand in hers. After a moment, I squeezed it.

Something inside of me opened up, and sighed, and suddenly I knew I *could* sleep – I could curl up in a bed somewhere, with my arm around her, and sleep like I hadn't slept for a very long time. Perhaps even dream.

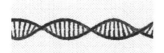

G ray and me, that became a good thing, a solid thing, in an increasingly fraught moment of history.

There was a part of me that had wanted to believe that Emily Winterthorn had been exaggerating, that the world would not go to pieces in quite the way she thought it would. And in a way I was right about that – it didn't. It quickly became much worse than that.

Everything splintered. Into smaller and smaller pieces. And none of the pieces fit together any more.

The *Vox Verae Hominis* group went to ground, after the fateful conference at which Barbican Bain fell (or was pushed), but only for a little while. The circumstances were such that their ideas found fertile soil, and it wasn't long before they re-emerged – but in two pieces instead of the original one. The first kept the name of the parent organization, and most of their ideas; the second, calling itself Aeterna, decided that those ideas hadn't gone far enough and delved even deeper into fear and hatred.

I wasn't surprised to see Barbican Bain's name start coming up in connection with Aeterna in very short order. It wasn't at all hard to see how he belonged there. I actually made him a website called IAmNotTheMetamorph.com which had a brief but fiery existence before it was snuffed out. I would have loved to have been a fly on the wall on the day he first saw that thing on his computer screen. They never *did* find out who did it, of course, he might have suspected Celia.

Both groups continued to promote the subjugation, possible enslavement, or if not that, then extermination-in-self-defense of anything Were.

On the other extreme, the Lycans also underwent a schism, with a formal break in Lycan Council resulting in two factions. One consisted mostly of the older and more traditional packs and came out fiercely in favor of a philosophy which maintained that Lycans were responsible for

Lycans and for nobody else and proposed an increasingly isolationist policy which walled off Lycan clans from the rest of the Were, holding them up as something unique, something primal, something increasingly rare, something worth preserving at all costs even if it meant going it alone.

The other – and not entirely surprisingly Mal found himself in the forefront of this one – argued just as hard that Lycans may have been the *first* Were, but now they had to find a place in the real world that the Were as a whole had come to inhabit and share, and they could not hope to survive at all if they simply pretended that nothing else other than themselves was important enough to exist.

This was a split of some importance because there was a lot of science that had been done by the Lycan labs over the years – some of it, perhaps, questionable in its methods, like the programs that had produced people like Gray, or Petra, or myself, but much of it immensely valuable to understanding Were as a whole – which was now the subject of an internal tug-of-war over who was entitled to access to it. All this on top of the fact that such science, as and of itself, was being targeted by the Vox and the Aeterna factions as being works of the devil and as such something that should be destroyed by definition – which had consequences, if the information fell into the wrong hands.

So much could be lost, so quickly.

In between, caught between the two great fundamentalist rocks and slowly being ground into fine powder, stood the rest of the Were clans (the non-Lycan kinds), and the non-Were human government.

The keeper of Jazz's little secret, the inconvenient Jesse, somehow managed to keep that particular twist sequestered – but Jazz (and Mal, and me) were constantly braced for the fallout of *that,* should it ever come to light. In the meantime, the Corvids did their best to provide responsible and inclusive leadership – but everything was in disarray, and there was a sharp rise in the numbers of what Luke had once called the Free Were, people who no longer trusted the Turning Houses for protection (for a lot of reasons) during their Turn times. A lot of these simply decided that the laws that had applied so far were no longer in force. Many Turns began to take place outside the Turning House confines. The chaos that resulted was probably predictable – and so was the backlash, a return to the fear and loathing of the past from which Mal and Celia's parents had tried to rescue their children. The Were began to go back into hiding.

The human, non-Were, authorities found their house of law and order collapsing rapidly about them, the laws a dead letter on the books, no longer enforceable. Police began to respond differently to calls involving Were – there were incidents even during the days of the law when lawkeepers shot first and asked questions later, but those were isolated enough, mostly frowned on, and even sometimes investigated, and suppressed; in the new era, they became far more common, and far less frowned on. After all, who could blame a policeman for shooting if he believed that someone was on the point of Turning into a bear or a wolf and attacking as an animal would? The mass of the common people did not, anyway.

Part of the fallout of that was the establishment of increasingly segregated neighborhoods as the non-Were moved out in fear or forced their Were neighbors to do so – and the end result of that could get ugly really fast and led straight to ghettos into which the Were could be forced by virtue of the nature of their DNA, or even into concentration camps where they could be rounded up and kept penned in to the point where the non-Were population's fears could be contained.

In the meantime, the human government tried to make deals with whomever they could – and found out the hard way that they could not make and keep treaties with both Lycans and the *Vox Verae Hominis* at the same time. Pretty quickly they developed factions of their own, with pro-Were and pro-'human' groups squabbling endlessly in committee about what needed to be done next, and where, and to whom, and how quickly.

And at the center of it all, there was that primal terror – not of what the Were-kind actually were, but *of what they could be.*

A thing... like me.

So far as I knew I was the only one of my kind, the only true 'shifter' who existed – and I had been an accident of a Lycan program, not selected for or sought or even naturally arising. I was literally an aberration. And yet the fear of... of *me* – of the things that I was supposed to be able to do or to be (and those quickly assumed mythical proportions, the details of some of the wilder imaginings scaring even me) were the central issue of it all, the thing, the idea, that had broken the truce and plunged all of us into this chaos.

Emily had *not* been wrong, I realized bleakly. I had started a war.

In the eye of this storm, knowing (as the rest of the roiling world did not) that my days on this earth were numbered, I tried to make a life.

I honestly had no idea if either Gray or I were even capable of having children of our own – for all I knew the Lycan meddling had produced a generation of offspring who were themselves genetic mules, incapable of bearing any young.

Then, three years after she had spoken of having hitched her wagon to my shooting star, Gray told me that the second generation was not only possible but on its way and I was faced with a whole new set of possibilities.

I talked it over with all the people I trusted – with Gray, with Mal and Asia, with Greta.

"What if there can be only one of you? Only one at a time?" Mal asked, himself falling into the trap of building up the myth of the shifter's existence. "Perhaps that was the reason they never created another shifter. It's you, it's always been you, and just you..."

"That I know of," I said. "I can shine a light into most dark corners, but even I can't poke every shadow. For all I know there's a colony of people like me holed up somewhere. For all I know Barbican Bain *is* one of us.

You can't tell, that's the entire point – that's the reason they're all so scared, you can't tell, if you didn't know who I was you wouldn't have the first idea about what I can do. Anyone can be a shifter. Any stranger you pass on the street."

"I think you'd have heard about that, by now, if it were true," Gray said, her hands folded protectively over her middle where the next generation was getting ready to prove a point one way or another.

Because that was the crux of it, in the end.

Could I pass on, genetically, the thing that I was – at the very least in the same way that the Were attributes were handed down? Would my child be a shifter, like me? Or was I a true aberration, a unique spark that flew out of a flame and would never be repeated? I had taught Mal how to hang onto his memory, taking it with him between human and wolf – but could I pull a much harder trick and pass on my own memories, my own abilities, genetically, down to the son or daughter who would come in my wake?

All I knew for sure was that there was a good likelihood that I myself might not live long enough to find out. Even if it Turned early, like I did, my child would probably have to be eight or nine years old before it did this – and I was very much aware that every day I had was a gift, and that those years that Greta had prophesied for me were only getting shorter with every sunset that I saw.

"Could you tell," I asked Asia, the geneticist, the one whose life's work lay in the building blocks of what it meant to be human, both the normal and Were, "if it would be passed on? If you looked at my innards?"

"I have no idea," she said, "never having come close to taking a look at those innards. There are new techniques every day."

"You spent your life trying to stay out of Lycan hands," Gray said anxiously.

"It's a different kind of Lycan," I said, with a wry grin.

But she was right, of course, and I had spent too long being paranoid about it to give in to the impulse now. I compromised, and I told Asia that she – and only she (and possibly Wilfred) – could have whatever physical shell remained behind after my time ran out, and do whatever they wanted with it. So long as nobody new about the existence of Gray, and of the child which might possibly follow in my footsteps.

When Gray, in the fullness of time, gave birth to not one but *two* babies – twins – things became even more complex and interesting. Would they *both* grow up to be shifters? Would neither? Would one, but not the other – and how would that be determined? Gray named our daughter Sehar, a word that meant 'enchantment' in my long-gone mother's native language; I named our son Gabriel, for no reason that I could give other than the name seemed to fit that small and angrily squalling bundle which I was handed wrapped in the blue blanket after he was born. That was all we could do, for now. That, and watch them and protect them and care for them, and wait. Wait to see what the years would bring.

To see if it was possible for the thing that was myself to go on. For my son, or my daughter, or both of my children, to make better what their father had had a hand in destroying. If it was possible to rebuild and bring back from the ashes the thing that my very existence seemed to have made it impossible to endure. If I could continue to fight my fate, even if the ultimate battle for my soul would be fought by those who carried forward the dangerous inheritance which lay inside my genes and who would fight that battle long after I myself was gone.

I found myself thinking of the thing that my mother had said to me so often when I was a boy, and putting those words, at last, into their true context.

Oh, the life I have had. The raw mystery of the beginning, the richness of the whole muddle in the middle, the transcendence of the end.

I must have dreamed it.

Coda:
The Last Turn

Gray had had a lifetime of practice when it came to living behind a façade, carefully guarding her real thoughts and feelings, letting nothing important show in her eyes, on her face. But either her years with Saladin had mellowed her and made her more vulnerable, or else there was something between Saladin and his friend Mal that had rubbed off on Gray, too, because even though she was almost certain she had schooled her expression well. when she had opened her front door and found Mal on her doorstep, the first words he spoke to her told her that she had not.

"Sometimes I think that you believe I come carrying the plague into your house," Mal said, with a resigned smile.

Gray winced, looked down, but then, because she was still who she was and because of the courage that had always been a part of her, looked up again and met his eyes squarely.

"You do," she said. "The world is sick with the plague and you bring the world to him. When you are not here, I can manage to make him forget the world. For a little while. But you... you always come. You'd better come in. He's in the study."

Mal looked like he was about to say something more, then reconsidered, nodded once sharply in acknowledgment, and stepped past Gray into the house. She paused to look up into a sky heavy with soft, brooding snow-clouds; cast a glance into the trees which were beginning to shiver in a rising wind.

"A storm is coming," Gray announced, to nobody in particular, out into the sullen light of the winter day.

The world did not respond, and she closed the door against it with a sense of futility – she had already invited the worst of it in, after all. Mal usually came with news and updates – he was still keeping up the old bargain, Saladin's "inside man" with the Lycans – and what news he brought was usually not good.

She looked in on the twins as she passed their rooms – Sehar was reading quietly in a corner by herself, precocious in her choice of reading matter, eight years old and well past such books as others her age might have picked, always disdaining picture books in favor of things with words, lots of words; Gabriel was staring into a computer screen, earphones on his ears, his gaze intent on the screen and his thumbs poised over controls as he fought a CGI battle in some computer game.

Beyond the children's rooms, the door to the study was ajar, and she heard voices inside. She knew that she should have walked right by, for her own peace of mind, but she could not help herself. Without her conscious command, her steps slowed as she approached the study, her ears suddenly focused on the softly spoken conversation inside.

"...why you could never get the actual data," Mal was saying. "You might have hacked almost anything, but this was not hackable. It was never on a computer, never accessible online. There is hard copy evidence – and some of it might be the *only* hard copy evidence remaining – and this is a chance to get it, to save it from those who would much rather the truth of things was never completely known, and this time we have a guy – someone on the inside – ”

“Another inside man?” Saladin said, amusement in his voice. “Paying it forward?”

“Learned from the best,” Mal said, with a little bite to his tone. “But that’s neither here nor there. We have the pieces, Chalky, you don’t need to get involved, not directly – but this is yours, this is something you have been hunting for years. I thought you’d want to know. That you might want to take a look. I don’t know what will happen to all of it once we get it – if I can make copies – but if you come, you can look it over before I have to hand it on...”

“Of course I’ll come,” Saladin said. “You knew that.”

Outside, in the corridor, Gray closed her eyes briefly in resignation, and finally passed on by the room into the sitting room.

She did not turn from the easy chair into which she had subsided when she heard the familiar footsteps come into the room. She had no need to. She knew the weight and pattern of them.

“There’s a storm coming,” she said. “It’s going to be a bad night.”

“Gray,” Saladin said, “I have to...”

“I know,” she said. And looked up at last, meeting his eyes. “But there’s a storm coming.”

They both knew she was saying more than the words she spoke, and also that her deeper meaning was a concern which it would have been useless to voice out in the open.

Mal had come. He’d brought the plague with him. The infection was already here, and Saladin was already poisoned with it.

His response to her words was a brief silence, and then he reached out his hand and squeezed her shoulder reassuringly.

“I might be late,” he said.

“I’ll wait up.” She, too, hesitated, and then allowed some of what haunted her to show in her eyes after all. “Please promise me you won’t...”

“There should be no need for that.”

In the first years after the disastrous conference at which he had first directly crossed paths with Gray, when the world went up in flames, Saladin had been guilt-ridden at his own part in all of that. He had pledged his ability to shift at will as to gift to Mal, to be used as it was needed, and Mal had used it, on a number of occasions. Perhaps too many. But after that first wash of taking all the blame, and after the days of his life became more precious to him after the twins were born, he had withdrawn from the front line. He had stopped putting his body through the trauma of the Turn, unless there was no other choice at all in a given set of circumstances.

He hadn’t Turned at all for years now. When they spoke of it, which was not often, Saladin had said semi-seriously to Gray that he wasn’t sure he remembered *how* to do it anymore. And she had been... grateful for that, almost. Knowing that every Turn damaged him further. Knowing that every Turn brought him closer to the end of the days that he still had with her, and with their children.

His abilities had been something that had brought them vividly together, in the beginning; now, she preferred not to even think about what he could do, because she was selfish about the length of the life he still had to spend with her. Saladin was aware that he had been profligate with his shape-changing in the early days. He had done it often, and into many creatures, all without counting the cost. He had been reckless with the gift when he was young because he had not known that he had needed to be careful. But it had started to catch up with him as the awareness of the consequences of it all had come to him, first just as a wary feeling he carried in his mind and then more physically with premature gray starting to silver his dark hair and odd, deep lines becoming etched into his face practically overnight. Before he knew it, he looked years older than he actually was. It couldn't have been plainer than that.

So he had not shifted in years. For Gray, for the twins. He was content to remain only one thing, only Saladin, for them. For as long as he could.

To be sure, Mal had not come (as far as Gray could tell) to ask him to do anything of that nature. It was more of a courtesy warning, a gift he could give his friend, the final proof of his own provenance and parentage and the program that had created him, something that had eluded Saladin for years.

But there was a storm coming.

And something stirred inside Gray, a shivering unease, a premonition – but something she resolutely pushed down until she could safely stop thinking about it long enough to offer Saladin a genuine smile.

"Be careful," she said at last, because it was all she could say.

"Always," Saladin said, taking one of her hands and bending over it in a gallant old-world gesture, brushing the back of it with his lips. "I'll be back as soon as I can."

And he had gone, the two of them had gone, out into the swiftly fading day and the rising wind. It had started to snow when they had walked out of the front door, hunched against the swirling flakes. Gray could still hear the wail of the wind in the trees as she closed the door behind them.

When the power went out a few hours later, plunging the house into a solid darkness and an almost instant drop in temperature, that had come with a sense of inevitability. It was her premonition, given form. Gray built up a fire in the little pot-bellied stove they had in the living room, and sat stiffly in her easy chair by the light of a couple of candles and what little brightness escaped through the stove's grate. Waiting. Knowing that what she waited for was nothing good.

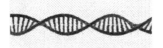

"There," Mal said. "We're here. That's the place."

He had killed the lights of the SUV, and now the car, followed by another behind it, came to a quiet stop just behind the inadequate cover provided by a handful of winter-bare trees whose naked branches creaked and shivered in the rising wind. Between the trees and the building that waited across an open area which might have been a widening of the drive or a parking area, but which was currently just a white drift of unmarked snow.

Saladin gave the place a jaundiced look. "You said nothing about a *castle*," he said.

Because that was the appearance that the building presented. It bore a creepy resemblance to a keep as dreamed up by someone steeped in the romance of the middle ages. A single light glowed over the double-winged front door, which was studded with metal and looked like it had been carved from solid oak. The door looked like it would challenge a good-sized battering ram. There were no other openings on the ground level at all, with the first windows, small and made of what looked like leaded glass, opening halfway up the sheer walls.

"I also said we had someone on the inside," Mal said. "We aren't here to assault the place. But we *are* getting in." He consulted his watch. "Our man said he would unlock that door – just about ten minutes from now. Then we're in. There are only three people in that place tonight, and one of them is ours, leaving only two we have to stay away from while we gather up what we need. It shouldn't take long to..."

Saladin turned his head briefly. "I think your pocket is trying to get your attention," he said.

Mal threw him a quick scowl, and rescued his buzzing phone from the pocket of his windbreaker. He frowned at the number that came up on the screen, and Saladin saw that expression.

"Trouble?" he questioned softly.

Mal raised a hand for silence, and spoke softly into the phone. "Andy? Why are you...?"

Saladin could hear, very faintly but still distinctly enough, a breathless and panicked voice on the other side.

"Mal, they know. They know. I don't think I can..."

"Andy, listen to me. Don't wait for them to do anything that you can't... come down, and meet us, we're on our way, right now. We're just outside the place, we just have to get to the door. It will take us a minute. Less than that. Come down and get the door, *now*, and we're right here."

"Okay," the voice said, still breathless. "Okay."

"Come on," Mal said, slipping the phone back into his pocket and zipping up his jacket. "We need to go. Now."

"I have a bad feeling about this," Saladin said quietly.

Mal's eyes flicked sideways, slid away again. "I know."

He slipped out of the car, into the drifting snow, gesturing to the rest of his team in the second car – pack stalwarts like Wilfred Sand and Robin Foxworthy, and a young floater by the name of Joseph Redmayne who had been with Mal's pack for just under a year. They all gathered at the edge of the open area, five of them, measuring the distance which they would have to cross, an exposed white stretch where first they and then any tracks they might leave would be wildly visible to anyone who looked. That might not have been an issue, if they had had the element of surprise – but if their inside guy had made that phone call that meant that something had made the people inside the castle house wary. They would be watching.

"We could skirt around the edge of the trees, there," Robin said, pointing to what looked to be the boundary of the open driveway, a little less well lighted, with drifts piled against the tree trunks. "And then cut across from the side. Over from the shadows. They may not be looking in that direction."

"Or that might be the direction they would expect us to take, and watch it particularly closely," Saladin said.

"Have you got any better ideas?" Joe Redmayne snapped.

Wilfred glanced at him with both disapproval and curiosity – the boy was young, he clearly had no real idea just who Saladin was and what he was doing there, and that meant that his social stature had to be lower than his own because he was an outsider. The Omega Wolf of Mal's pack was trying to ensure that his wasn't, for once, the last place in the hierarchy.

But Saladin didn't appear to be in the frame of mind to take offense, or even snap at the bait. "Unfortunately, no," he said. "Mal, this was not exactly…"

"I know," Mal said grimly. "I had a different idea about how things were going to go down. Come on, then."

They bent over, keeping as low a profile as they could, scurrying in and out of the shadows, until they reached the side of the house. Only one window looked out in this direction – but it had a light behind it, and it was too high for them to know if someone was watching from that lighted room.

They had to take the risk, or abandon the enterprise altogether. Mal led the way across, with Saladin on his right, the others following in their wake. They had just made the safety of the wall, flattening themselves against it underneath the mullioned window in a place where they could not be observed from the house, and Mal stepped away to measure the distance between their position and the front door… at the precise moment that his phone buzzed again.

He looked back, meeting Saladin's eyes for a moment, before plunging his gloved hand into his pocket and retrieving the phone, turning a gimlet stare back at the door.

"Andy...?"

"I can't," the breathy voice came out. "I can't make it – they – "

"Andy, we need you to..."

Mal's earnest voice broke in mid-sentence as something fluttered behind him... *wings*... and then a shadow crossed the wall above him, a white owl winging over his head and angling out into the trees before turning towards the roof of the house. Mal whirled, dropping the hand that held the phone to his side, knowing before he fully turned just what he would see – a pile of clothing, still settling down into the snow. Clothing most recently seen on the back of Saladin van Schalkwyk.

"Ah, *damn it,*", Mal said.

"What just happened?" Joe asked, staring at the place where Saladin had just been. "Where did he...?"

"We need to get to that door. Now." Mal broke away from the group, began sidling along the building towards the entrance, keeping as close to the wall as he could. "Robin," he said, over his shoulder, "pick up those clothes. Bring them."

"This didn't happen," Wilfred said to Joe, reaching out to close a gloved hand around the boy's forearm. "You saw nothing."

"Who was that guy? How did he...?"

"We don't have time for this now," Wilfred said. "Just go. And keep this quiet."

"But how...?"

Robin had been with the pack long enough – had been married to one of the fiery Manion twins for long enough – to be part of the family, and privy to its secrets. He knew about Saladin, about his identity, about the lengths the pack went to in order to erase any knowledge of him or connection to him where other Lycans were concerned.

But he had just shown his hand, and Robin, obeying the instruction to gather up the discarded clothes on the snow, threw the confirmation over his shoulder to the bewildered youngster who had not been in the know.

"You heard about the shifter?" Robin said, efficiently scooping up most of the clothing with a broad sweep of one arm and picking up a pair of ankle boots with his free hand. "You just met him."

"Move," Wilfred said.

They made the door, single file, Mal at the front and Robin bringing up the rear with his armful of cargo. Mal tried the door, very gently; it was firmly locked.

"Crap," he said. "Dammit. Andy has bailed – and for all I know has already told the others all about the raid and we may already be too late – and I have no clue what Chalky is trying to..."

As though that name had been an Open Sesame spell, they heard the lock quietly click back, a bolt being drawn, and then the door – such a formidable barrier only a moment ago – eased open a crack.

"The lab is in the basement," a soft voice came from the shadows in the dimly lit hallway beyond. "Hurry."

Mal stepped through, paused as he saw Saladin, barefoot on the cold flagged stone floor of the hall and without a stitch of clothing on, holding onto the door he had just opened.

"Are you..." he began, but Saladin waved him on.

"Go. Now. Do what you came to do."

Robin had thrust the clothing he held into Joe's arms, and gave Saladin an apologetic half smile as he dropped the boots beside him and then hurried forward into the hallway and towards the back of the hallway stairs.

Joe stepped up, bewildered, his eyes wide as saucers. "I have your clothes," he said, staring, offering up his load. "Er, are you all right? Do you need help?"

"They need it more. Go. Mal, dammit, *go*."

Mal tore his eyes away from Saladin's face, and took a couple of paces towards the back of the hall where Wilfred and Robin had already gone.

"It's freezing in here," he said. "Put those clothes..."

"Go," Saladin said. "I've been dressing myself for years, I know what to do. I'll be along in a moment, just let me catch my breath."

Mal hesitated for another long moment, looking haunted, and then he and Joe both took off towards the basement stair with long strides.

Things got chaotic, for a while. There were more locked rooms than they expected, and some turned out to contain prisoners – two frightened children, released by Robin, unable to give a coherent account of their being there, but there had been folders in the lab with names on them, names the kids gave as theirs. Mal had taken a quick look inside and then passed them grimly on to Wilfred to be carefully packed away as evidence. The two of them stared at the rescued kids, trying to figure out what to do with them, where to take them.

Distracted by all the extracurricular activity Mal, failed to notice Saladin's continued absence until he turned at last, with a sense of triumph, to show him a folder with information which connected the dots, gave Saladin the shifter the hard proof for all those things he had only been able to get hints and educated guesses of during all the years he had spent searching for the truth behind his origins. But Saladin was not at his elbow, waiting for the information to be shared. He was not in the lab at all. Mal's eyes darted to the door, through it and up what he could see of the stairs, and all were empty of his friend.

With a stab of sudden fear, Mal raced up the basement stair, back up into the hallway.

The first thing that struck him was the stab of cold – the stone flags of the floor were cold, the air was icy, and a lick of arctic air touched his hands, his face. It was with a sense of inevitability that he realized that the front door was not shut – it had been pushed almost to, but not completely, and a crack a handspan wide was allowing the winter wind and a swirl of snowflakes to enter. The snow was starting to stick, to pile into a small drift against the far wall.

Behind the door, in the angle between the door itself and the equally cold stone wall, Mal saw a crumpled figure. It took his brain a moment to sort out what he was looking at – the long legs were clad in Saladin's trousers, one leg bent at the knee with the foot tucked under the other thigh, the other lying straight and stiff, the foot bare, with Saladin's warm honey-colored skin turned almost blue with cold. It looked like he was wearing his parka, but on closer examination Mal realized that the coat had merely been pulled over Saladin's front, like a makeshift blanket. The shoulder that showed underneath, where the jacket had slipped off, was also bare, underneath the trailing strands of Saladin's dark hair. Mal caught himself thinking, ridiculously, *when did he get so gray?* – the once black hair was now liberally streaked with silver, and Mal found himself fumbling with the idea that there were only two years between the two them. Two years. Not nearly long enough for Saladin to look as though those two years had turned to twenty overnight.

As though aware of the scrutiny, Saladin looked up. Dark shadows had spilled under his eyes and across his cheekbones, but other than that he was so drawn and pale that Mal sucked in his breath.

"I'm sorry," Saladin said faintly. "I seem to have... exhausted my capacity for being a grown up..."

Mal crossed the hall with three long strides, shoving the door closed with one hand in a futile attempt to restore warmth to the room, thumping down beside Saladin on one knee in the same motion.

"What the hell happened?" he said, reaching for the coat, discovering Saladin's shirt and his sweater crumpled in his clawed hands underneath as though he had tried to untangle them and attempt to put them on but it had all become too much for him.

"I haven't shifted for a while," Saladin said. "It may be that I had forgotten how. Or that doing this much this fast after a long break was just..."

"What did you do?" Mal demanded, tugging the shirt free and lifting one of Saladin's unresponsive arms to stuff into a sleeve in an attempt to drag it on around the naked torso. Saladin's skin felt cool, almost clammy, to the touch. "I saw the owl."

"There was an attic window," Saladin said, looking down at the stiff arm being forced into a shirtsleeve as though the limb did not belong to him at all and he was wondering just what Mal was doing with this foreign object which was somehow attached to his body. "I had to turn into something smaller, to get in, but that was easy enough – and then into something unobtrusive, to get down here without anyone noticing – and then into me, to open the door for you – and it all became a little too... did you get it? The thing you hoped to find?"

"Yes, dammit," Mal said, yanking the shirt straight, tugging at the buttons, trying to get Saladin's arms into the sleeves of the sweater and then his head and shoulders bent into a position where he could pull the sweater down over him. "Where are your shoes?"

Saladin nodded towards the wall beside him. "Couldn't reach them."

"Why didn't you tell me you were..." Mal stopped, screwed his eyes closed in pain and frustration, lost in the inability to ask a coherent question, appalled that he already knew the answer to the questions that he wanted to ask, even more appalled that he had not noticed the things he should have noticed, known the things he should have known, seeing a chasm of devastation open deep inside of him knowing that he might have pushed this moment forward too fast.

When he looked up, Saladin wore a faint smile. "Mal," he said, "if you had known, what would you have done differently?"

"I... I would have..."

He stopped as a shudder jackknifed Saladin's body, and an expression of pain crossed Saladin's narrow face.

"Can you try and get me home?" he asked quietly. "There are things... that Gray..."

Mal swore, softly but fiercely, and fumbled for the phone in his pocket.

Asia answered on the second ring.

"It's Chalky," Mal said, and then paused at Asia's swift intake of breath. "What, you knew?"

"Greta... found out... years ago," Asia said carefully.

"Found out *what*?" Mal said desperately. "Was it something I did...?"

"He was... his clock was ticking... He was just living *faster* than most of us. Wearing himself out."

"And every time he changed...?"

"It probably turned the screws," Asia said.

Mal closed his eyes briefly. "Ash... he shifted tonight. Here. It all went wrong, and our plans went... and if it hadn't been for him, we would never have... he's..." A flicker of his gaze caught Saladin sitting limply with his head leaning back against the wall. He looked sallow, almost waxen. "He's not good," Mal said into the phone. "He said – he wants me to get him home..."

"Do that," Asia said. "I'll send Greta."

Mal slowly thumbed the call off, and stood staring down at his friend. He was suddenly sure that Greta, Wilfred's wife, the pack's doctor, would find very little to do when she got there.

"Hold on," Mal said to Saladin, his voice low and intense. "Hold on just a little longer."

He took a few steps back towards the basement stairs and called out Wilfred's name. After a few seconds there was a swift patter of feet on the stairs and Wilfred poked his head around the doorway at the head of the stairs.

"Take over," Mal said. "You know what to do."

Wilfred took another step or two, to emerge fully from the staircase, his face suddenly changing. "Is it...?"

"We have to go," Mal said. "Now."

Wilfred looked past Mal, towards the door, and his lips tightened as he evaluated the situation at a glance.

"Right," he said. "The blizzard was getting worse. It'll take you a while. Go."

Mal turned away without another word, his expression bleak, and then stopped as he heard Wilfred say his name.

"What?" he said over his shoulder.

"I'm sorry," Wilfred said.

"Yeah," Mal said. "Me, too."

He crossed back over to Saladin and crouched down beside him. "The car's across the drive there. Can you manage?"

"I can manage all that's needful," Saladin said. "Help me up."

The wind drove a flurry of snow into their faces as Mal opened the door with one hand, his other arm around Saladin's waist, supporting him heavily as they stood there. It no longer mattered about tracks in the snow, and Mal took the shortest, most direct route across the snowy expanse towards the copse of trees which hid the cars. He managed to fold Saladin into the passenger seat, slipped into the driver's seat rubbing his cold hands together as he fumbled for his keys, felt his stomach clench as the car failed to catch the first time and then, as he tried to move forward, felt the wheels spin briefly in the snow. But then the tires bit, and snow crunched, and the car lurched forward. He had the wipers on but snow was coming down almost too fast for them to do anything more than smear it across the windshield; in the beams of his lights, the blizzard was a reflective white wall less than a foot from the car's front bumper. Mal gripped the wheel tightly.

"Hang on," he muttered. "God, it would be faster if you changed back into that owl and *flew* home."

"I'd never make it," Saladin said quietly.

"I thought you trusted me," Mal said, staring straight ahead into the blizzard, only partly because he had to in order to simply keep to the road; the other part of it was that he couldn't trust himself to look at Saladin right now.

"I do," Saladin said. "But you were going to feel the way you feel when this moment came... whenever it came. I merely... made it come... as late as possible."

"Stop talking," Mal said. "Rest."

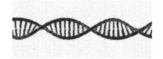

When the car finally pulled up outside Saladin's house, the building was dark, no lights showing. Mal helped Saladin out of the car and then supported him up the couple of steps onto a narrow porch. With his free hand he knocked urgently on the front door; after a moment, it opened a crack, and then wider as a gust of wind and Mal's own hand pushed it swiftly open all the way.

He met Gray's eyes across the threshold. There was no need for words, not of explanation, anyway.

"I tried," Mal said. "I tried to at least bring him home."

Gray stepped aside so that Mal could stumble into the house, bearing almost the full weight of Saladin who was leaning heavily against him, his face hollowed out, his eyes closed as though it was too much effort to hold them open. But his eyelids flickered up for just a moment as Mal spoke, and he tried to lift a hand.

"Gray," he said, but his voice seemed to come from very far away.

"Take him..." She was going to say the living room, instinctively, but she suddenly and painfully hesitated. The power had been off for hours, and the house had grown cold; she had bedded the children in the living room, wrapped in quilts, directly in front of the wood stove. Sehar and Gabriel. They were only eight years old. Were they old enough for goodbye...?

Saladin made the decision. "The study," he said softly. "Take me through into the study."

Mal glanced at Gray. She nodded. She closed the door against the winter night, shutting the wind out, and, pausing only to collect a single candle and the quilt from the bed in the master bedroom, followed.

There was an old armchair in the corner of the study, and Mal had helped Saladin subside down into it. Gray simply draped the quilt over him where he sat. His eyes were closed again, and his breathing had become a little harsher, a little shallower.

Gray straightened, faced Mal.

"What happened?"

"He should have told me," Mal said, his eyes bright in the flickering candlelight. "*You* should have, if he was stubborn enough not to."

Gray lifted her hands in a helpless gesture. "Told you what? Told you something that would have kept him from being at your side if you said you needed him? Do you really think it would have? Told you that another Turn might still work – but might be the last? It wasn't mine to tell. He didn't want to be wrapped up into a cocoon and left to wither slowly in his own time. You of all people know that. He and Asia..."

"Yes," Mal said. "*Asia* knew."

"They made an arrangement," Gray said. "Years ago."

Mal drew an unsteady hand down over his face. "My own mate – my own pack – and she didn't... "

"She did what he asked," Gray said. "He said – he told me – he asked Asia not to tell you anything. He didn't want you to know, to wait, to watch him. To mourn him before his time."

"And he thought this would be better?" Mal demanded. "This – this sudden avalanche – this planet-killing *asteroid* coming down on me from out of blue sky – "

Asteroid. Comet. Gray's mind suddenly swam with the memory. *I hitched my wagon to a shooting star...*

"You think it was easier, knowing every minute of every day, hoarding the time we had together like a beggar?" she said quietly. "He knew what you could handle... what you should handle. And he knew what he wanted you to have – those last years you and he had together, unmarred by the sound of the ticking clock in the background." She stopped, and then gathered herself up, drawing her breath in a huge sigh. "You'd better tell me what happened out there."

"We needed into a fortified place," Mal said faintly. "Tonight. Before they moved something irreplaceable... or destroyed it. And then it all went south, at the last minute – and we could have lost it all. And he..."

"He was the only one with a way in without a key or a stick of dynamite," Gray said. "The usual."

"I'm sorry," Mal began, and Gray lifted a hand to stop him, looking away from his face. She knew from his stricken expression that he was feeling this moment just as much as she was. But he reached out for that hand, took it, held it, made her turn towards him again.

"No. Listen. This is what happened out there. He Turned into what was necessary. He opened the door to us. We went in, and we retrieved what we came for... and there was something else, too. Something I hadn't even known about, going in. They were holding two children there, locked away in rooms down in the basement, next to the lab. One of them was younger than your two, the other only a year or so older. Kids. If we hadn't gone in..."

Gray glanced back towards the other room where her twins slept on. "Tell me," she whispered. "I want to know... I need to know..."

"I went in first," Mal said, "at the head of the team. I honestly didn't realize that he wasn't with us until I turned to look for him after we'd found those kids, and realized that he wasn't there, where he should have been, where he always was, right there beside me. And I left everything to the rest of the team and ran. And I found him. By the door he had opened for us. Lying there by the door, where I had left him as he'd let us in, with the door still half open, and he hadn't even had the strength to get fully dressed. He just... lay there... and he said... he just said I'd better get him home, and fast. I looked but he wasn't wounded – not physically – there was no blood – but I could see... I could see..."

After a moment Gray squeezed his hand. "I know," she said quietly. "I know."

Saladin's eyes flickered open. "Gray...?"

"I'm here," Gray said. "I'm just outside the door. I need... to check on the kids." She squeezed Mal's hand once more, hard, and then let go. "Don't take... too long," she said. "I need..." And then, not trusting her voice or her eyes further, she turned and fled.

It wasn't just the candle that was flickering in this room. And they all knew it.

Mal stepped across to the armchair and squatted down beside it. "Chalky," he said. "I never told you..."

"Like I didn't know," Saladin said.

"That was always your problem," Mal said. "You always knew everything. Long before anyone else did."

Saladin looked at him, and his eyes were clear, and full of an urgent passion. "There are things you should do," he said. "I promised Asia..."

"You told Asia," Mal said. "You told *Asia*. And you never said a word to me."

"I didn't tell Asia. Greta told Asia."

Mal let out a short sharp bark of a laugh. "The entire *pack* knew?"

"No, just them. Just the two of them. Greta... looked at me... and knew something was wrong... so we checked... and oh, was she right... and then she had to tell Asia. She had to, it was pack law. Don't blame Asia. Don't blame either of them."

"But you – you kept it quiet – why could you not have just said..."

"Because *this* scene would have played out the moment I said anything at all, and then every day from then until now," Saladin said. "I don't know about you but *I* couldn't have handled that. But as far as Asia is concerned – she and I had an agreement – she could have what was left of me... after I didn't need the shell any more. You make sure that happens. It would have been up to Gray to arrange it but you're here, and you can take it on. Not that it matters – not any more – not in the way that it used to – but I gave Asia my word, and it's up to you to make it happen. That, and to make sure that they don't know about Gray, and about the kids."

"I'll take care of the kids," Mal said.

"I can tell you this, about those two. It's like they split up whatever it is that I am, between them. Sehar has all the heart. Gabriel has all the anger. I don't know which of those is more dangerous, or more vulnerable. I wish I could have seen if one of them – I wish I could have been around, to help, if one of them – but you know as much as anyone. You, and Gray. You protect them. And if either of them – or both..."

"Chalky," Mal interrupted, "I'll take care of the next shifter as well as I know how." He swallowed. "I don't actually remember," he said, "a time before I knew you. Well, I do, but it seems unimportant. Everything that mattered in my life happened with you there to see it, to make it happen, to help me see it through. The Lycans... Asia... *Celia*... all of it..."

Saladin closed his eyes again. "I only," he said faintly, "ever had *one* brother."

Gray, pushing the door to the study open a fraction so that she could peer inside, paused as she saw Mal kneeling by the armchair, his head bowed, his face twisted into an expression of almost unbearable loss – but he was aware of her, looked up, folded Saladin's hand back into his lap and got to his feet.

"I have my instructions," he said faintly, trying for a wan smile. "Go to him. I'll watch the children."

He left the study without looking back. Gray stepped inside and then closed the door behind her, very slowly and deliberately.

Saladin was quiet in his chair, his eyes closed, but when Gray came to kneel beside him, he turned to look at her, and there was something in his face that made Gray's breath strangle in her throat.

"You didn't even know my name," he said, apparently at random, but it was the thing that had bound them, from the beginning – the moment when he had walked into the den of wild beasts who were all baying for his blood in order to spirt her out of there... just because he thought it was the right thing to do... and when she had followed him, a stranger whom she didn't know, purely on the strength of instinct and an immediate sense of having found the only possible place in the universe where she could possibly completely belong, without ever having asked him for his name.

"Your name didn't matter," she said softly. "I knew who you were. Who you've always been."

He reached out a hand and she took it, folding it against her cheek.

"I told you," he said faintly, "that I would leave you quickly..."

"We're given what we're given," Gray said. "I told you once, I hitched my wagon to a shooting star. I knew what I was doing."

But oh, I did not know it was going to hurt this much watching the light of that star go out...

Saladin's fingers curled briefly on her face, cupping her chin and her jaw. "I won't be here to help," he whispered. "If Sehar or Gabriel should turn into..."

"I will tell them about you," Gray said. "And if that happens... they will have to find their way... just as you had to, once... but I'll be there to help, in whatever way I can. And I'll never let them forget you."

"I'm sorry," he said, "I didn't plan this very well."

And then, just like that, he was done. His eyes closed, and his breath stopped.

Beside them, on the desk, the candle suddenly shivered, and went out.

Gray sat beside Saladin, in the darkness, feeling as though there were oceans of tears surging inside of her... and unable to cry. Not now. Not yet. It went too deep; it was too soon.

She had seen it unfold, at his side. Saladin had always been an asset, valued only for what practical use he might have been to the factions that were squabbling over the fate of the Were – for the secrets locked deep inside his blood and bone, inside his genes. Well, they would get that, now – all of those secrets. But only a few – a handful – those whom he had loved – would know just how much more their world had just lost.

It might have just been the wind of the winter storm, but Gray looked up at the window, through the gap in the curtains, trying to see out into the dark night... where she was sure beyond a shadow of a doubt that she had just heard a rush of dark wings take off for the sky through the veil of the falling snow.

ACKNOWLEDGMENTS

The usual ones apply – my thanks to all the people who had a hand in the birth of this book, the original editors and designers of the trilogy as it first appeared (Danielle, Jessica) – and to the BVC folk who helped with the omnibus edition (Maya, for her usual magic with the cover design...) – and, of course, to Deck, for helping create an omnibus edition out of three separate novels and make them into a new and very special whole in the form of this book you're holding in your hands.

Specific ones, for specific issues in the books, I reproduce here:

WOLF: Two specific things to single out here.

One is the contribution made to 'Wolf' by Fiona Tanzer, once-colleague in the halls of science and academe, now a fellow writer – but still a scientist with an inquiring and knowledgeable mind who consented to being the sounding board for my off-the-wall ideas about Were genetics. She was the one who gave me the marine viruses. There are, still, probably, infelicities of science in this book. Many of them I will simply have to chalk up to poetic licence, because if true and valid genetics for a Were person did exist then we'd have them among us for real and I would have had to make no invention at all – but for all those avoidable errors from which you saved me, Fiona, thank you.

The other is the 2013 Rainforest Writers Retreat, run by Patrick Swenson, where a large chunk of 'Wolf' was written and nutted out – despite the fact that I managed to forget the files I had wanted to load and bring with me to the retreat to work from. Perhaps it was just as well that I was unfettered by these files and what they contained, because I used my retreat time and the invaluable writing solitude to work on a literal blank canvas... and many good things came of that. So. To you, Rainforest, with gratitude, I raise a glass.

SHIFTER: one specific one, which may not sound like a lot but it is a great example of how a writer lives and exists and is part of a net that is always there to call on. I had a character in 'Shifter' who is a Japanese man – a VERY secondary character, to be sure, but an important one in the life of my protagonist, and I wanted to get this guy contextually and culturally right. So I reached out to a friend – a Japanese friend who knows more about the vocabulary and the etiquette which would need to be involved, and about the attitudes and the context in which this character could exist. And Kaichi Satake (a writer and artist himself) stepped up and helped me shape the character into what I needed. Arigato, Kaichi-san. My thanks, also, to James Longo for casting a pharmacist's eye on Adaptadyne's specifications when those became necessary to discuss.

And – last but by no means least, thank you to Dr Ralph Kirby, the man who guided me on the road to the achievement of my own MSc degree in Microbiology and Molecular Biology which in no small part informed this entire trilogy, for writing the foreword to the omnibus edition. When he told me, back when the original books were first published, that the science within was 'as good as it gets', that was a badge of honor for me. I am very grateful that he was willing to put that in writing, in the foreword that he wrote for me. He has been in turn a mentor and a colleague but he has become, in the fullness of time, a friend.

I might also add a word of thanks to those readers who have been in touch over the years with their responses to these books, and giving me the honor of sharing the effects these stories have had on their own lives. In particular, Melinda and Isabel. Here's hoping you continue to walk in light, and I am grateful beyond words that my tale might have held a torch for you to see by in your darker days.

Alma Alexander
2020

ABOUT THE AUTHOR

Alma Alexander's life so far has prepared her very well for her chosen career. She was born in a country which no longer exists on the maps, has lived and worked in seven countries on four continents (and in cyberspace!), has climbed mountains, dived in coral reefs, flown small planes, swum with dolphins, touched two-thousand-year-old tiles in a gate out of Babylon. She is a novelist, anthologist and short story writer who currently shares her life between the Pacific Northwest of the USA (where she lives with her husband and two cats) and the wonderful fantasy worlds of her own imagination. You can find out more about Alma

on Twitter (https://twitter.com/AlmaAlexander)

at her Patreon page (https://www.patreon.com/AlmaAlexander)

on her FB page
(https://www.facebook.com/AuthorAlmaAlexander/)

or at her website (http://www.AlmaAlexander.org)
(where you can sign up for her newsletter or find a contact form to let her know what you thought about the books you just read)